(To the tune of
"The Twelve Days of Christmas")

ON THIS DAY FOR CHRISTMAS,
SILHOUETTE BRINGS TO THEE...

four adorable kids,
(Marilyn Pappano's ROOM AT THE INN)

three sexy men
(all three heroes!)

two spectacular weddings (at least!)
(Elizabeth Bevarly's JAKE'S CHRISTMAS)

and a hero from another time!
(Joan Hohl's CHRISTMAS STRANGER)

Happy Holidays!

JOAN HOHL was born, raised and still lives in southeastern Pennsylvania. Writing on a personal computer in her third-floor office of the home she has lived in for nearly thirty years, Ms. Hohl has produced some forty-plus novels under both her own name and the pseudonym Amii Lorin. Winner of numerous awards, including the Romance Writers of America Golden Medallion Award and two *Romantic Times* Reviewer's Choice Awards, Ms. Hohl describes her books as "running the gamut from contemporary to historical to time travel, and even a historical ghost story." One of Silhouette's bestselling authors, she also writes mainstream historical romance.

ELIZABETH BEVARLY is an honors graduate of the University of Louisville and achieved her dream of writing full-time before she even turned thirty! At heart, she is also an avid voyager who once helped navigate a friend's thirty-five-foot sailboat across the Bermuda Triangle. "I really love to travel," says this self-avowed beach bum. "To me, it's the best education a person can give to herself." Her dream is to one day have her own sailboat, a beautifully renovated older model forty-two footer, and to enjoy the freedom and tranquillity seafaring can bring. Elizabeth likes to think she has a lot in common with the characters she creates, people who know love and life go hand in hand. And she's getting some firsthand experience with motherhood, as well—she and her husband welcomed their firstborn, a son, a few years ago.

MARILYN PAPPANO followed her career Navy husband around the country for sixteen years. Now they make their home high on a hill overlooking her hometown. With acreage, an orchard and the best view in the state, she's not planning on pulling out the moving boxes ever again. When not writing, she makes apple butter from their own apples (when the thieves don't get to them first), putts around the pond in a boat and tends a yard that she thinks would look better as a wildflower field, if the darn things would just grow there. You can write to Marilyn via snail mail at P.O. Box 643, Sapulpa, OK 74067-0643.

A Family CHRISTMAS

Joan Hohl
Elizabeth Bevarly
Marilyn Pappano

Silhouette Books

Published by Silhouette Books

America's Publisher of Contemporary Romance

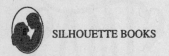 SILHOUETTE BOOKS

by Request

A FAMILY CHRISTMAS

Copyright © 1997 by Harlequin Books S.A.

ISBN 0-373-20142-7

The publisher acknowledges the copyright holders
of the individual works as follows:

CHRISTMAS STRANGER
Copyright © 1989 by Joan Hohl

JAKE'S CHRISTMAS
Copyright © 1992 by Elizabeth Bevarly

ROOM AT THE INN
Copyright © 1988 by Marilyn Pappano

Printed in U.S.A.

CONTENTS

Dear Reader,

Happy Holidays!

I love the holiday season—most especially Christmastime. There just seems to be something shimmering in the air, and inside me, and others, for people appear friendlier, warmer, during the holidays.

In the midst of all the frantic activity of preparations—shopping, wrapping, cooking, decorating—smiles and greetings seem to be more freely offered, and returned.

One finds it easier to believe in the possibility of miracles, to adopt a childlike quality, perhaps, of trusting and openness to a belief in goodness and love.

Which brings me, not unsurprisingly, to my own Christmas offering to you, in the form of a story about one, rather unusual, Christmas miracle.

I have always been fascinated by the concept of time travel, and I personally believe the concept lends itself to the spirit of this particular season.

Is it possible for a person to travel through time from one historical period to another? I don't know...but then, neither does anyone else.

Do you believe in miracles?

I do.

I hope you enjoy the miracle I fashioned for Matt Hawk and Virginia Greyson in "Christmas Stranger."

CHRISTMAS STRANGER

Joan Hohl

For
Parris Afton Bonds—

Who understands
that though we can never really know,
we can dream of all the wondrous possibilities

Prologue

Montana Christmas Eve, 1889

The snow fell soundlessly through the cold of the winter night. Drifting flakes shimmered in the light cast from the window of a small, isolated cabin near the edge of town. Inside the cabin, a man stood peering into a cracked, wavy mirror, muttering to himself as he raked his long fingers through his unruly, silver-sprinkled dark hair.

"Needs shearing." United States Marshal Matthew Hawk grimaced at his distorted reflection. "Needs washing, too." His thin lips twisted in distaste, Matt wiped the sheen of oil from his fingertips onto the threadbare towel he had moments before tossed onto the washstand.

Critically narrowing his eyes, he stepped back to get a partial view of his tall, rangy form. The sight was not one to ease the frown from his brow.

Not new to begin with, his jacket was deeply creased

from being rolled up inside a tarp and tied behind the saddle. His one decent pair of pants was in the same condition. Matt had tried to smooth the wrinkles from the material with a damp towel; the results were less than he'd hoped for.

Matt shrugged and turned away from the mirror. If nothing else, his shirt, though worn, was clean and neatly pressed. The white shirt, along with his black string tie, at least gave the impression of respectability that Matt was striving for.

What did it matter, anyway? The thought brought a grim smile to Matt's lips. He was a stranger in this small, barely surviving mining town in the Anaconda Mountains of Montana. Except for the local sheriff and a few concerned citizens, nobody knew him. All the same, for reasons that weighed upon Matt's mind and conscience, suddenly it mattered.

It was Christmas Eve, and it mattered because he was going to church. He, Matthew Hawk, a hunter of men, the loner-lawman known as The Hawk to friends and foes alike, the cool, withdrawn man who hadn't been to church for over twenty years, was getting spruced up to attend the Christmas Eve service at the town's solitary, rough-hewn little house of worship.

Dipping his fingertips into the tiny pocket at his waist, Matt withdrew a round silver railroad watch. With a flick of his thumb he flipped open the lid. As if in prayer, the black hands lay together on the six. It was six-thirty. Church services were scheduled for seven. It wouldn't take him more than ten minutes to climb the low hill from the cabin to the church. Sighing, he snapped the lid shut and slipped the watch back into its pocket.

What to do for twenty minutes? A new frown tugging his dark brows together, Matt glanced around the small room, searching for something to occupy the time. The room contained nothing of interest—just a rusted metal bed with sagging springs, a lumpy mattress and a threadbare blanket. Also a table and two chairs, none of them matching, all of them nearing collapse. Over there was the warped washstand, trembling beneath the weight of a chipped pitcher and washbowl. And on the rough wooden floor lay a handmade rag rug, which had probably been ugly even when it was new, way back when.

A sigh of acceptance whispering through his lips, Matt began pacing the floor and gave in to the unwelcome thoughts that were tapping at the back door of his mind.

He had killed a man less than twenty-four hours ago, and he had done it with cool, professional deliberation.

Matt shivered in response to the wave of revulsion that washed through him at the memory. The fact that he had committed the act in the line of duty didn't negate his reaction to it. The fact that the man had been a particularly vicious outlaw didn't alleviate Matt's sense of unease, either. His work as a peace officer had been causing him a mounting dissatisfaction for some months, and lately the dissatisfaction had bordered on despair.

Pivoting at the washstand, Matt retraced his steps across the room. Distracted by his thoughts, he no longer noticed the shabby furnishings or the ugly rug that was bunching beneath his boots.

He was tired, but his weariness was more of the spirit than the flesh. He was tired of assignments like this last one, which had sent him trailing an outlaw for close to a month from central Texas to the mountains of Montana. He was tired of sleeping with one eye open and forever watching his back. He was tired of the slaughter, of killing men who seemed more animal than human. The outlaw Matt had been forced to bring down the day before when the man refused to surrender had been such an animal.

Matt was thirty-five years old. He had spent ten of those years wearing a badge, tracking the lawless, protecting the law-abiding. He knew it wouldn't be too long before the passage of time began to work to his disadvantage. He knew that once he'd lost that fine sharp edge, his days on earth would very likely be numbered.

Matt was well acquainted with death. He had witnessed it countless times; more times than he cared to recollect. Death was never a pretty sight. Yet strangely, Matt felt no fear or anxiety about the very real possibility of his own demise. No, the driving force behind his growing despair was an awakening sense of the value of life…any and every life. And with each new assignment the knowledge was impressed upon him of how very precious the tenuous thread of life was…to every living creature.

For over a year now the feeling had been growing inside Matt, something that sickened him whenever he was faced with a situation ending with death by the gun.

But in a raw, untamed land, what other options were there other than six-gun law enforcement? Matt asked himself, raking a hand through his freshly smoothed hair. The law-abiding citizens had to be protected from the aberrants who chose to walk on the wild side. It always meant violence that—more often than not—resulted in death.

Matt was increasingly certain that there had to be a better way. But what that way might be eluded him. Maybe, in another time, another place…

"Damn," Matt muttered, breaking into his fruitless musing. He needed answers, and all he could come up with was more questions. Frustration was a weight that was becoming too heavy to bear.

Was the mental torment the reason he had decided to attend the Christmas Eve church service? A wry smile flickered over Matt's compressed lips. He had to admit to himself that he had a lot of gall to seek solace in God's house after all these years.

But he was more than a lawman, Matt defended himself. He was a human being, a man with needs and longings and dreams like other men. He was tired of living on the back of a horse. He wanted a home of his own, a woman of his own—and yes, God willing—a child of his own.

Maybe it was time to quit, to end the slaughter, at least his participation in it. What he needed was a second chance, a new beginning, a decent life.

Since Matt had saved a large portion of his earnings, all paid in solid American gold coin, the first part of his dream, owning a small ranch, was within his grasp. On second thought, there was no "maybe" about the situation; it was definitely time for him to quit.

Reminded of the time, Matt again checked his watch. It was growing late, five minutes shy of seven. If he was going, the time was now. Hesitating, he absently repocketed the timepiece. It had been so long since he'd set foot inside a church. Would he be welcomed? Not by the townsfolk for sure, though Matt didn't give a damn what they thought. But would he be welcomed by the ultimate Boss?

His answer came as he recalled a scene from his youth, when he had sat squirming beside his mother on a hard church pew. How had the words gone? He couldn't remember all of them, but the ones he did remember offered comfort and certainty.

Come unto me, ye who are heavy laden, and I will give you rest.

Deciding that rest was surely the first of his needs, Matt shrugged into his woolen coat, settled his weathered Stetson low on his brow with a brisk tug, walked out of the cabin and into the gently falling snow. There wasn't a soul in sight. Concluding that all the good folk of the town were already congregated, he glanced up at the beckoning light that was streaming through the church windows. After pausing to flip up the wide collar on his coat, he began trudging up the hill. He was halfway to his destination when the shouted sound of his name broke the silence of the night.

"Hawk!"

Alarm splintered through Matt. Conditioned reflexes took over. He was moving before the echo of his name faded on the crisp air. His leg muscles flexing as he spun, Matt dropped to one knee, and his hand streaked to the pistol that had become almost a part of his right thigh. Even as his pistol cleared the leather holster, a rifle shot rang out, shattering the illusion of a blessed and peaceful night.

Matt's body jerked from the force of the bullet that slammed into his chest. His eyes wide with shock and amazement, he felt his hand jam the pistol back into the holster. Darkness swirled through his mind. Then he was falling forward, his motion so slow that his hat remained firmly in place when he crashed, face first, into the cold cushion of snow.

The shock of cold brought a moment of lucidity. He was going to die! The realization shuddered through his ebbing consciousness as assiduously as his life's blood was seeping through the material of his shirt. His breathing ragged, his teeth gritted, he shifted around until he was lying on his back. Now he no longer felt the biting cold or the snow. The flakes no longer melted on his rapidly chilling skin.

He was going to die. There would be no second chance, no new, decent life. No home. No woman of his own. No child. There would be nothing, an eternity of nothing.

His lips twisted into a wry grimace. This was not exactly the kind of rest he'd had in mind.

As from a far distance, he heard the sound of church bells. No! No! Matt protested in silent anguish. He couldn't die. The thought was like a flicker of light in the encroaching darkness. Not tonight, of all nights.

It was Christmas Eve, for God's sake!

One

The snow began to fall late in the afternoon of Christmas Eve, delighting the children and dismaying their parents. At first it was a gentle sprinkle of light, delicate flakes, but by midevening the storm front had pushed its way over the Pocono Mountains to unleash its fury upon the small town of Conifer, Pennsylvania. And by the time the churches pealed their bells at midnight to announce the arrival of Christmas, over six inches of the glittering white stuff blanketed the town.

Driving through the swirling cloud of snow was tricky, hazardous for the most alert motorist. Dr. Virginia Greyson, however, was tired, which made negotiating the roads even more harrowing.

It had been a long day for Virginia, beginning at seven that morning with the first of three surgeries. She had seen patients in her offices until six that evening. After leaving the office complex, she'd had to rush home for a quick

shower and change of clothes, then had dashed out again
for a dinner engagement at seven-thirty.

When she rushed from her apartment, the snow was falling gently, creating a sparkling winter scene suitable to the
season. She'd had no difficulty in driving to the secluded
restaurant, which was the latest hot spot for the local professional group of doctors, lawyers and such. Though she
herself was something of a loner, Virginia's date was a
member in good standing of that select group.

At thirty-three, Richard Quinter was firmly entrenched
among the elite of Conifer. A direct descendant of one of
the town's founders, he was the only child and heir to the
Quinter family fortune, the product of innumerable insur-
ance and real estate sales. And, since he was a personable
and handsome bachelor, Richard was also firmly entrenched as the prime catch of not only the town of Conifer
but the county of Hunter.

By rights it should have been a pleasant, relaxing evening for Virginia. It was Christmas. Since she had scheduled a break for the holidays, she was free for ten days.
The only notation on her calendar was an invitation for
Christmas evening supper at the home of Richard's parents.

Virginia liked Richard. He was interesting and fun to be
with. But this had been different from their previous dates.
The tone of Richard's conversation had suddenly shifted
from casual to serious. She frowned with annoyance as she
recalled the most pointed of the remarks he had made during the course of the evening.

"I'm afraid driving conditions are going to get steadily
worse," he'd said immediately after greeting her on her
arrival at the restaurant. "I shouldn't have allowed you to
drive out here. It would have been no trouble at all for me
to run into your apartment to pick you up."

Virginia supposed that most, or at least many, women
would have felt pleased by his concern—but she never had
reacted to much of anything like most other women. She
hadn't been pleased; what she'd felt was anger at his words.

He shouldn't have allowed her to drive? Who was Richard to prevent her from doing anything?

But not wanting to start off the evening with an argument, Virginia hadn't bothered to correct him. As it turned out, her silence was a mistake. No sooner were they seated at their table when Richard further injured her sense of independence.

"I'll follow you home when we leave," he'd said, "to make sure you get there safely."

Virginia had bristled, but had managed to reply calmly enough. "That will not be necessary."

"But—" he had begun to protest.

She didn't allow him to finish. "Richard, I'm perfectly capable of driving myself home." He opened his mouth again to argue the point. Virginia distracted him by making a simple request. "Do you think I could have a glass of wine?"

Ever the gentleman, Richard hastened to grant her request by attracting the attention of their waiter. Afterward, Virginia had hoped that they might spend the evening discussing the usual trivialities that they had in common. But it quickly became obvious that Richard was set on a far different, even unsettling course.

His attitude had taken on a proprietary possessiveness that had set off warning bells inside her mind. Though Virginia liked Richard she was not in love with him. And by her choice they were not lovers. While she enjoyed his company, Virginia felt no inclination to deepen their relationship, either physically or emotionally.

She was thirty-one years old, used to her freedom and independence, and in no hurry at all to change the status quo. She was successful in her profession and financially secure, looking neither for love nor an affair. And right now she was anticipating a restful holiday, not an emotional game of hide-and-seek.

Now, at twelve twenty-seven on a snow-tossed Christmas morning, Virginia decided that the last thing she needed was involvement, with Richard or any other man.

Gripping the steering wheel, she gritted her teeth and drove her car at a crawl along the deserted streets. At an intersection she carefully eased the car into a right turn, and immediately revised her decision. Absolutely the last thing she needed on this particular Christmas morning was the disheartening sight of flashing blue and red lights atop two police cruisers that were diagonally parked midway along the street.

A fender bender or a serious accident? Virginia wondered, bringing the car to a stop a safe distance from the parked police vehicles. Either way, there was the definite possibility of someone having suffered an injury.

What to do? Should she back out to the intersection and continue home using a different route, stay where she was until a police officer waved her forward, or get out of her warm car, plough through the cold snow and offer medical assistance?

Her shoulders slumped as she contemplated her options. It took her all of ten seconds to reach a decision. Virginia was an excellent, very scrupulous physician. Unconscious of the habitual action, she raked slender fingers through the honey-blond waves that cascaded to her shoulders. Her own principles limited her options to one. She was a physician—end of inner struggle. Sighing, she pushed open her door and stepped into the biting wind. Flipping up the deep collar on her ankle-length coat, she sighed again, then began tramping through the snow.

With each step she took, visions of malpractice suits danced in Virginia's head.

Skirting the cruisers, she stepped into the glare of the car headlights. The harshly illuminated scene didn't fit the festive season at all. She recognized the four uniformed men standing in a semicircle. The smile of greeting that tilted her lips took on a downward curve as her glance settled upon the body of a man sprawled in the snow.

"Eve'n, Dr. Greyson." Patrolman Jeff Klein respectfully raised his gloved fingers to his cap.

Virginia gave a brief nod in response. "What have you got here, Jeff, hit-and-run?" she asked, noting the absence of another vehicle in the street as she moved toward the body.

"No." Jeff's frown and tone conveyed consternation. "We got a call about fifteen minutes ago from a couple of the residents." He jerked his head to indicate the lighted houses along the street. "They reported hearing rifle shots." He inclined his head. "When we got here, we found him." He grimaced. "He's got a bullet in his chest."

Virginia came to a halt beside the still form lying in the snow. "Who is he?"

"Lord knows." Jeff shrugged. "We searched him, but couldn't find a scrap of identification on him. All we found were a couple of things, a watch and a badge, all old looking, like antiques."

"Odd," Virginia murmured, shifting her gaze from the officer to the victim.

The man was dressed strangely, the garb Western, but in the style of an earlier time period. A dirty-gray Stetson cradled his head. The wide brim framed his face, throwing into relief the taut planes and sharp angles of his bone structure. He had a long, straight nose, high, slashing cheekbones and a firm jawline. His hair was as scruffy-looking as his hat, though the overlong, silver-streaked strands appeared healthy and vital, for all their obvious need of a good scrubbing with an industrial-strength shampoo.

A latter-day mountain man? she wondered, skimming a professional glance over his sprawled body. Her normally soft brown eyes widened slightly in shock as her gaze collided with the holstered pistol tied to the man's leanly muscled right thigh. A hunter of animals...and perhaps even men? Whichever, Virginia thought bleakly, it was a shame to see him lying there, so cold and still. The stranger had been a handsome and virile-looking man.

The observation was wiped from her mind when her gaze next collided with the large, dark red stain that was soaking the outdated attire covering his broad chest. An odd sensation—a confusing mixture of defeat and bereavement—settled in her heart at the sight of the gaping wound where the bullet had entered the right side of his chest, close to his broad shoulder. She did not know this man, yet Virginia felt a sudden, inexplicable need to weep for the senseless waste of his life.

He was cold, so cold. Pervasive tendrils of darkness clung to his consciousness as tenaciously as the chilling snowflakes clung to his skin and eyelashes. Was he dead? Matt asked himself, straining against the dark cloud that enveloped his mind. Was this frightening, cold-to-the-bone sensation death?

Matt experienced a deep, inner shiver. He felt no pain. Yet there was this creepy sense of anxiety and cold. For some reason, he had always felt that death was nothing more than a state of nothingness... warm nothingness. But he was cold, indeed more than cold....

The darkness dissipated slightly, dissolving into shades of gray. He was wet! And there was something else! At the outer edges of his consciousness he could hear voices!

Maybe he wasn't completely dead, Matt mused. Maybe he was hovering in some netherworld, some limbo between the sweetness of life and the nothingness of death.

The voices were coming nearer. He could hear different tones, several deep and masculine, one lighter, pleasant, female. There was a minute change in the grayness that numbed his mind, a partial clarity. Collecting his weak powers of concentration, Matt fought to discern the content and meaning in the blurred syllables spoken by those voices. The garbled sounds meshed, then separated. Slowly the words became distinct and penetrated his consciousness.

* * *

"He's got the coldest eyes I've ever seen," observed Patrolman Raymond Horsham.

Virginia shivered as she gazed down into the ice-blue eyes in question.

"Well, of course his eyes are cold," retorted Cal Singer, Raymond's partner. "He's dead."

Unable for some reason to wrench her gaze from the stranger's blank eyes, Virginia pulled off her gloves and sank to her knees in the snow beside his lifeless body. A confusing sense of hopelessness and weariness washed through her as she reached toward his throat to confirm the absence of a pulse.

"I'm not dead."

Blending with the impact of his oddly fascinating eyes, the whispery-rough sound of the stranger's voice induced a ripple of shock inside Virginia. Startled, she gasped and pulled back her hand. He was alive! She jumped to her feet even as her rattled senses assimilated the realization.

Without a thought for her own welfare, Virginia whipped off her full-length coat to cover him. She had no idea how long he had been lying there, exposed to the elements, but she knew he was in trauma and shock. Unmindful of the wet chill permeating her body, she dropped to her knees again to tuck the woolen garment around him, then once again raised a hand to his throat to take his pulse. His skin was cold to the touch, which made the sudden charge of heat that tingled up her arm to her shoulder all the more devastating.

Controlling an urge to pull back her hand again, Virginia forced herself to concentrate on the strong but erratic pulse at the base of his throat. Touching him, feeling his life throbbing against her fingers, gave Virginia the strangest sensation she'd ever experienced. Her mind went blank, and her mouth grew dry with the realization that her own hitherto regular pulse beat was modifying, merging with the rhythm of his.

What was this?

Momentarily frozen, Virginia stared down at the man. She didn't hear the ambulance come to a stop or the dying wail of its siren. Trembling, stunned by the power of her reaction to someone she'd never seen before, she watched as his eyelids slowly fell. When he opened them again an instant later, his eyes were clouded by confusion but focused. Now they were a riveting, vibrant diamond-bright blue.

"Then again, maybe I am." Matt wasn't aware of the faint, raspy sound of his own voice, or even of the fact that he'd spoken aloud. All his attention was centered on the face that seemed to be floating above him. He had to be dead, he decided in a removed-from-it-all haze. For surely that soft-eyed, beautiful face, illuminated by a golden aura, could only belong to an angel. "I'm dead and gone to heaven."

The sound of his voice pierced the odd bemusement that was clouding Virginia's senses and restored her good judgment. What in the world had possessed her? she chastised herself. This man was injured. He was bleeding. He needed immediate medical attention. Blinking to break the eerie allure of his stare, she turned her head at the sound of approaching footsteps. The arrival of the paramedics snapped back her professionalism.

"Ambulance chasing, Dr. Greyson?" one of the paramedics asked drolly. Both of the ambulance attendants knew her, of course. All the ambulance personnel knew her. Conifer General was a small hospital in a small mountain town; just about everybody knew everybody else.

Virginia didn't respond to the young man's wry question. Jolting upright, she stepped back, indicating the injured man with an impatient sweep of her arm. "Please hurry," she said in a brisk tone of authority. "This man has been shot in the chest, and he has lost a lot of blood."

Instantly the men were all business, proving the effectiveness of their training. Though she moved out of the way to give them space to do their work, Virginia observed the procedure with sharp-eyed intensity.

After immobilizing his head, the men carefully lifted the stranger onto the litter. When they moved him, he gave a deep grunt of pain, then lost consciousness.

His eyelashes were incredibly long.

The thought rocked Virginia like a physical blow, forcing her to clamp her lips to contain the gasp that leaped into her throat. Helpless against the welter of emotions that was whirling inside her, she stood staring down at the unconscious, defenseless man.

Even with the weapon tied to his thigh, he looked heartbreakingly vulnerable.

Compassion stirred. He couldn't die. She wouldn't let him die! Blinking to clear her suddenly blurred vision, Virginia glanced around, startled, when one of the men handed her her coat. Watching in silence as the attendants covered the injured man and strapped him securely to the litter, she sent out a fervent prayer for the stranger...and for guidance for her own operating skill.

Virginia shrugged into her coat as she walked beside the litter to the ambulance. A shiver trickled the length of her spine as she folded the garment around her. The sensation was one of enveloping warmth and safety, as if the coat retained not only the heat of the unknown man's body but the protective radiation of his strength. Yet she knew there had to be precious little warmth or strength remaining in that depleted body.

She didn't understand why something inside her was responding to this oddly dressed stranger; indeed, Virginia felt that she didn't want to know. In any case, there wasn't time to examine her feelings and reactions. She had work to do. Whether or not she was granted unseen guidance, that bullet had to come out of his chest.

"When you call in, tell the receptionist in Emergency to collect an OR crew for me," she said, turning to trudge through the snow to her car as the driver shut the ambulance's rear door. "I'll be right behind you."

The motion of the vehicle jolted Matt into a blurred state of semiconsciousness. Given a choice, he would have preferred to remain cocooned in the security of darkness. He wasn't quite as cold as before, but now he was aware of a burning pain in the vicinity of his chest and right shoulder. He'd have preferred the feeling of cold.

Matt was also aware of forward movement. The sensation confused him still further. The motion was too smooth, too even to be that of a wagon or buckboard. Yet he sensed that he was in some sort of conveyance.

But what form of conveyance could it be?

The question continued to tease him. He knew of no horse-drawn vehicle that afforded such a comfortable ride. Gathering his limited strength, Matt decided to open his eyes and investigate the situation. He swiftly discovered that deciding to open his eyes and actually doing so were two entirely different things.

His eyelids were heavy, as if lead-weighted. The most Matt could manage was a mere slitting of his eyelids. The effort was exhausting, and not worth the results. He could see very little. Either it was night, or he was partially blind. And the exercise was not only tiring, it was frustrating.

Where in hell was he?

Matt moved restlessly, painfully as the silent cry exploded inside his throbbing head.

"Hang on, buddy, we're almost there."

Matt grew still at the sound of the encouraging voice. Questions, all without discernible answers, tumbled through his mind.

They were almost where? And who were they? Who was speaking? Where in hell was he, anyway? And damn, why was his chest on fire? The final question sparked Matt's memory. For an instant he could feel again the bite of night air, experience the sensation of swirling snowflakes fluttering against his freshly shaved cheeks. Within that instant of clarity, Matt heard the resounding echo of a voice sharply calling his name.

"Hawk!"

Matt's body jerked. Once more he heard the church bells summoning the faithful, relived the shock of feeling the bullet slam into his chest, experienced anew the slow motion of his own body, sinking into the cushioning blanket of snow on the ground.

He had been shot...ambushed!

The realization shuddered through Matt's depleted body. And with that knowledge came a mind-numbing question.

Was he dead?

Blackness invaded Matt's consciousness, and the question remained unanswered.

Organized confusion. The phrase was the only way to describe the activity that ensued upon the arrival at the hospital of the ambulance and Virginia's car.

"What are his vital signs?" Virginia asked as she leaped from the car she'd brought to a jarring stop alongside the larger vehicle that had backed up to the Emergency entrance.

"He's hanging on," the young attendant replied without glancing away from the injured man. A note of wonder was in his brisk tone. "Don't ask me how, but he regained semiconsciousness for a moment. Looked to me as if he was trying to speak. The man must have the constitution of a war-horse."

Leaving her car door open, Virginia strode to the rear of the ambulance to oversee the patient's transferral from the vehicle to the hospital. "Outdoor type," she said, making a snap judgment on hearing the report of the man's obvious tenacity.

Her comment was accepted with a grunt of agreement; there were enough "outdoor types" in and around Conifer, every one of them tested, weathered and tough. That the breed died hard was not only a given but a point of pride with the area residents.

That exchange was the last bit of idle conversation Virginia was to engage in for some hours. She began issuing terse instructions the instant the automatic doors swept open, to reveal the hospital personnel waiting to move the injured man from the litter to a gurney. Bespeaking the esteem in which Virginia was held by her contemporaries, her instructions were followed immediately and efficiently, without question or doubt.

Unaware of the police car that had swept into the emergency area moments after her, Virginia spun around when a hand was laid on her shoulder, prepared to deliver a blistering admonition. She bit back her tirade on sight of the blue uniform, but her tone betrayed her impatience.

"Yes, Jeff, what is it?"

"I'll need some information for my report." Though the officer's tone was scrupulously polite, it held a note of adamancy.

"Information?" Virginia repeated in angry astonishment. "Jeff, the man is unconscious, barely alive."

"Well…I know, but…" His voice faltered as he met her direct, cool-eyed stare.

Relenting, she softened her forbidding expression and tone. "He's being prepped for surgery. If he lives, you'll get your information."

"And if he dies?"

Virginia felt sick at the very real possibility, but concealed her feelings behind a calm exterior. "Then I'm afraid you'll have a John Doe for your report."

"Right," Jeff agreed on a sigh.

Obeying her mounting sense of urgency, Virginia turned away. She had taken less than a half dozen steps when she was halted once again, this time by an anxious feminine voice.

"Dr. Greyson, wait!"

Suppressing an expletive, she whirled around. "Yes,

what is it?'' Virginia demanded of the harried-looking Emergency Room receptionist. The middle-aged woman came to an abrupt stop to keep from cannoning into her.

"Regulations. Admittance forms,'' the woman panted, rattling the papers she held clutched in one hand. "Your patient. I need some information.''

Virginia's patience snapped and her temper flared. "I can't give you any information on my patient, because I have no information about him.'' She drew a breath, then went on with more control. "The man is wounded, dying. I must get him into surgery.''

The woman looked flustered. "But, Doctor, the cost! Who will be responsible?''

"I will.'' Swinging away, Virginia strode down the corridor toward the elevators. Her set expression was all the warning necessary to discourage anyone else who might attempt to delay her progress.

Virginia arrived in the operating room to discover a crew scrubbed and waiting for her. A sense of satisfaction obliterated her irritation. Within minutes she had changed into sterile operating-room garb and was standing at the sink, scrubbing her hands and forearms.

"Where did you find your patient, Doctor,'' a drawling female voice asked from the doorway behind Virginia. "On a hoof dust and gunpowder Hollywood back lot?''

Startled, Virginia scraped the brush over her knuckles. Frowning, she glanced over her shoulder at the small woman standing in the doorway. "Are you trying to give me a heart attack, Sal?'' she demanded.

The woman grinned with the easy familiarity of a long-standing friendship. Sally Wentworth was the head nurse in the intensive care unit, and the closest thing Virginia had to a best friend. Her small, fragile appearance was deceptive. Sally was a veritable powerhouse of energy and as resilient as tempered steel. She was also the best nurse Virginia had ever worked with.

"Sorry," Sal said, grinning unrepentantly. "I didn't mean to startle you. Curiosity got the better of me."

Virginia drew a blank. "Curiosity?" She scowled. "And what are you talking about—hoof dust and gunpowder?"

"Your patient." Sally moved her head to indicate the double doors leading into the operating room. "He looks like he just stepped off the set of a Western film."

"Oh! Yeah." Virginia resumed scrubbing. "The police found him lying in the street with a bullet in his chest."

"Interesting." Sal's comment was indicative of the woman's unflappable character. "Who is he?"

"I don't know." Virginia shrugged. "The police didn't find any identification on him."

"Do they have any idea who shot him?"

Virginia sighed. "As far as I know, they haven't got a clue. They received calls from several residents of the neighborhood who reported hearing gunshots."

"More and more interesting," Sal mused. "In fact, it's darned intriguing."

"I could manage to live without this particular type of intrigue." Virginia retorted.

"Do you think you'll be able to save him?"

Virginia ran her hands and arms under the hot water for a final rinse. "I'm going to give it my best," she said with grim determination.

Sal's smile was slow and confident. "In that case, I'll get busy preparing a bed for the cowboy."

Holding up her wet hands, Virginia smiled her gratitude for her friend's confidence in her ability. "In that case," she said, turning toward the double doors, "I suppose I had better get to work."

It was exactly 1:45 a.m. Christmas morning when Virginia drew a deep, steadying breath and stepped to the side of the man on the operating table.

Two

The angel was back.

Peering through remnants of anesthetically induced fog, Matt stared into the composed, beautiful face once more floating above him.

Questions crowded into his hazy mind. Where was he? Was he dead? Was he in heaven or hell?

How did he feel? What *did* he feel? His eyelids were heavy. Closing his eyes, Matt brought his limited powers of concentration to bear on his present condition. He felt…comfortable. There was no sensation of pain. He was neither too cold nor too warm. The conclusion appeared obvious. He had to be dead.

Curiosity overcame the weight on his eyelids. When he opened his eyes, the woman hovering above him smiled.

Must be in heaven, he decided. That serene and lovely face could not be a product of hell. An angel, pure and simple. His own guardian angel? Matt fervently hoped so, because he never wanted to lose sight of her.

"How are you feeling?"

Shock jolted through him at the soft sound of her voice, the compassion evident in her tone. Did angels speak? Had she spoken aloud, or had he only heard her inside his mind? He thought he had heard her with his ears, but...Matt blinked. What had she asked? Oh, yeah. How he was feeling.

"Strange." Matt hardly recognized the croaking sound of his own voice.

The angel's smile held understanding. "It's the anesthetic," she said. "It'll wear off soon."

Anesthetic? Confusion deepened in Matt's mind. What in he...heaven was this "anesthetic"?

The soft voice continued. "I imagine you're thirsty," it said.

In that instant Matt realized that his mouth and throat were very dry. "Yes," he answered, wondering how he could feel physical discomfort if his body was dead. Once again, her soft voice interrupted his distracted thoughts.

"Here, this will help."

A shiver slithered the length of his body when Matt felt her slip one hand beneath his head. She was touching him! Matt thought in stunned wonder. An angel was touching him! And her hand was soft and warm...and amazingly strong! Then a secondary consideration hit him. His body! He still had a body! He still had feeling...something smooth and solid was being inserted between his lips!

"Slowly now, take just a sip or two."

Obeying her without conscious thought, Matt drew on the tubelike object. Cool water bathed his parched mouth and trickled down his throat. The moisture felt heavenly. Greedily he drew on the object again, and groaned in protest when it was gently removed from his pursed lips.

"Take it easy," the gentle voice cautioned. "That's enough for now. You may have more later."

Still thirsty, Matt longed to argue but didn't have the energy. Darkness began closing in on him. Feeling himself being drawn back into unconsciousness, he groped with one hand until he made contact with one of hers. Vaguely the thought occurred to him that she felt real, solid, physical. Exerting the last threads of consciousness, he murmured a raspy plea.

"Don't leave me."

"I won't," her answer whispered to him through the swirling darkness.

For over two hours, Virginia patiently sat on the uncomfortable chair placed alongside the stranger's bed. She had little choice in the matter; her hand was imprisoned within the steel-like grip of his rawboned fingers.

She was still sitting there, dozing fitfully, when Sal came to tell her that she was going off duty. Virginia came instantly alert with the feather-light touch on her shoulder. Her first thought was for her patient. Snapping up her head, she stared into his sleep-softened face.

"He's doing remarkably well."

A sigh eased from Virginia's throat at the hushed sound of Sal's voice. Glancing around, she gave her friend a wan smile. "I must have dropped off to sleep for a moment."

"Is it any wonder?" Sal observed, her tone understanding and compassionate. "How long has it been since you've been near your own apartment, let alone your bed?"

Virginia shrugged. "Somewhere around five yesterday morning...I think." She frowned. "That is, if it's now Christmas morning."

"It is." Concern as well as amusement tinged Sal's lowered voice.

"What time is it?" Virginia muttered through an unsuccessfully stifled yawn.

"Exactly 7:06:22."

Moving carefully so as not to disturb her patient, Virginia arched her spine to ease the cramped muscles in her back. "You on your way out?" she asked, raising her free hand to smother another yawn.

"Yes." Sal's smile held the warmth of friendship. "But I couldn't leave without wishing you a merry Christmas."

Virginia's drawn features softened. "Thanks, Sal. I wish you the same."

Sal laughed. "I don't believe I'm up to merry—I'm beat. I'll settle for peaceful." Her dark eyes probed Virginia's pale face. "And you look about ready to cave in. What you need is about ten hours of sleep."

"I'm okay," Virginia murmured. "I rested for an hour or so after the surgery on the cot in the doctor's lounge."

"Wonderful." Sal shook her head. "At any rate, Hopalong Skipspurs was doing pretty good when I made my rounds fifteen minutes ago."

Virginia's mouth curved into a wry smile at the realization that she had dozed through Sal's going-off-duty patient check. "Hopalong Skipspurs?"

"Yeah." Sal inclined her head toward the man in the bed. "His vital signs are good, and he is sleeping naturally. Why don't you leave him in the excellent care of the day crew and go home to bed?"

"Two reasons." Virginia displayed the first two fingers on her free hand. "Number one—" she wiggled her index finger "—I promised him I wouldn't leave." She wiggled her second finger. "And number two...he's got a death grip on my hand." She nodded her head to indicate the tanned, bony fingers tightly curled around her hand.

"So I see." Sal rolled her eyes. "Well, there's one consolation. I doubt that you'll be shackled much longer. I figure he'll be waking up soon."

"I sincerely hope so," Virginia drawled. "This chair is beginning to feel like a torture rack."

"Oh, I almost forgot!" Sal exclaimed. Making a half turn, she picked up a clipboard from the low cabinet beside the bed and thrust it into Virginia's hand. "Speaking about torture, I was asked to give you this."

It wasn't necessary for Virginia to look at the papers clipped to the board; she knew what they were. "Admittance forms," she muttered, heaving a tired-sounding sigh as she slid the board onto the foot of the bed.

"Regulations, Doctor."

Virginia grimaced. "You mean—a pain in the—"

"Here now," Sal interrupted, lips twitching with a grin. "Is that any way to talk?" She shook her head. "And on Christmas Day, too. Aren't you ashamed?"

"No," Virginia retorted. "Actually, I'm too tired to feel much of anything."

"I can relate to tired," Sal quipped, giving in to a yawn. "It's been a very long night, and I'm ready for bed." She leveled a stern look at Virginia. "And if you had any sense, you'd follow my example."

"I intend to," Virginia assured her, then qualified, "as soon as possible."

"Yeah, right." Sal looked unconvinced. "I hear the breakfast trays rattling down the hall, and if I know you, you'll probably still be here when the lunch trays are served, hovering over Ol' Smoking Guns there like a ministering angel."

Angel.

Like the annoying buzz of summer gnats, Matt had been hearing the indistinguishable murmur of voices for several seconds. The actual words being spoken hadn't registered in his mind, until the sound of that one word—angel.

Was she still there?

The question both tantalized and terrified Matt. He was almost afraid to open his eyes to see for himself if the beautiful blond angel was still with him…almost, but not altogether afraid.

He pried his eyelids open to a tentative slit. For a moment his sight was fuzzy, clouded. As his vision cleared, Matt saw a dark-haired woman dressed in white, murmuring a farewell and smiling as she turned and walked away.

Who was she? he wondered. Another angel? Confused, Matt kept his narrowed gaze fastened on the woman's back.

As she drew near to a portal or door, another figure in white caught his attention. This one, a much taller female with gray hair, was carrying what appeared to be a serving tray of some kind, and she was walking toward him.

An old angel? Matt mused, forgetting the first, dark-haired woman. Maybe this older one was in charge—somewhat like a mother superior in a convent?

The woman smiled kindly at him as she passed by. Matt was working his stiff, dry lips to reciprocate when she spoke, startling all thoughts of a smile from his mind.

"Your patient's awake."

Patient! Awake? In that instant, Matt realized he was lying in a bed…and not on a fluffy cloud.

Were these ladies nursing angels? he wondered. Were there such things as nursing angels? And if he was dead, why would he need a nurse? And if he wasn't dead and gone to heaven…

Where in hell was he?

Matt moved with restless agitation. Pain exploded in the upper right side of his body. Damn, he…

"Well, hello there."

The soft, familiar voice froze everything in Matt except his eyes; they darted in the direction of the soothing sound. She was there, the soft-voiced, gentle angel, *his* angel, and she was bending over him, smiling at him.

"How are you feeling now?"

"My shoulder hurts," Matt answered, shocked at the weak, unsteady sound of his voice.

"I'm afraid it will for a few days." Her smile was gentle with commiseration. She tugged against the grip he had on her hand. "Could I have my hand back, please?"

"No." Matt tightened his hold on her, afraid she'd escape if he let go.

"But I need it," she said in a tone of infinite patience. "Please let go."

"What do you need it for?" he demanded with belligerent suspicion.

The angel laughed softly. The beguiling sound of her laughter stole his breath and drained the resistance from him. With reluctance Matt opened his hand, releasing hers.

"Thank you."

"You're welcome." Matt had no idea of the depth of disappointment revealed in his eyes as he voiced his fear. "Are you going to fly away now?"

Surprise flickered across her lovely face. "No, of course I'm not going to fly away. I'm going to examine you."

"Examine me!" Matt exclaimed in a hoarse croak, experiencing a sense of embarrassment and anticipation. "What do you mean, you're—?" He broke off, eyes narrowing, as she raised her hands to a tubular device draped around her neck. "What is that thing?"

"This?" The angel frowned as she inserted the ends of the device into her ears. "It's a stethoscope," she explained. "Surely you've seen one before?" Her eyebrows arched, her face frowning in puzzlement.

"No," he admitted. "What does it do?"

"It allows me to monitor your heartbeat," she said, demonstrating by placing a metal, disc-shaped thing at the other end of the tubes to his chest.

Matt shivered. "It's cold," he excused himself. "What do you hear?" he asked curiously.

"A good strong beat," she responded, sliding the disc to another section of his chest. "And your lungs are clear." Straightening, she smiled at him as she removed the device called a stethoscope from her ears. "In fact, you're doing better than expected. Are you comfortable?"

"I'm thirsty." Matt was suddenly aware of a surprising sensation of emptiness that confused him. Maybe he wasn't dead, after all. A man didn't have physical needs after death...did he? Everything about his situation was more than passing strange, he reflected, and then mentioned the need gnawing in his stomach. "And I'm hungry."

The angel's expression brightened. "That's an excellent sign. I'll give you some water, but I'm afraid you'll have

to wait a little while for food. They'll be moving you
soon.''

"Moving me?'' Matt felt a twinge of panic. Was he being banished from heaven...from her? Deciding to clarify
his position, he went on, "Moving me to where, from
where?'' He frowned. "Where am I now?''

"Postop ICU.'' Though her response was prompt, it
merely increased his confusion.

Matt could feel his expression go blank. What in Sam
Hill was a postop ICU? "What is a postop ICU?'' he asked.

"Postoperative intensive care unit,'' she answered.
"You're in a hospital...where you underwent surgery five
hours ago to remove a bullet from your chest.''

The mention of the word "bullet'' brought memory
slamming into Matt's mind as forcefully as the actual slug
had slammed into his body.

Hawk!

The echo of a harsh voice calling his name ricocheted
inside his head. Matt suddenly recalled that it had been
Christmas Eve. It was snowing. The welcoming light of
hope and redemption was beaming from the long narrow
windows in the church at the crest of the hill. He had been
walking toward that light, that promise of hope, when the
call had shattered the night silence. A shot had rung out.

He'd been bushwhacked!

Reliving the incident, Matt slid his right hand to his
thigh, wincing as pain streaked up his arm and across his
chest. He ignored the pain when he realized his thigh was
naked. His gun was gone! Suspicion crawled through him.
Somebody had taken his weapon. Without the piece he was
vulnerable. He would be unable to defend himself. Eyelids
narrowing over eyes suddenly cold and deadly, he sliced a
look at the woman.

"Where is it?'' His voice had gained strength, and was
as cold and deadly as his eyes.

The woman appeared genuinely perplexed. "I don't understand. Where is...what?''

"My gun."

"Oh, that." She moved her shoulders in a delicate shudder. "It's with the rest of your things which, I assure you," she hastened to add, "will be returned to you."

Robbed of the question he was about to ask, Matt grunted in response. His mind was becoming clearer, sharper, as the lingering effects of the sedation dissipated. He was becoming aware of his surroundings, of himself. "What in hell is this thing?" His hand moved from his thigh to the tube fastened to the back of his left hand.

"Don't touch the IV!" The woman's hand grasped his to pull it away. "And don't strain your right arm. You could reopen that wound."

Matt's eyes narrowed even more. What was this woman talking about with all these initials? His voice was edged by his growing impatience. "IV?"

"Intravenous tube, of course." Her own tone betrayed a thinning patience.

Matt didn't understand, but that was nothing new at this point; he didn't understand much of anything he'd heard since awakening. But as the wispy clouds receded from his mind, the suspicion grew stronger that he wasn't dead, after all. His lips tightening with determination to get clarification, he asked a point-blank question.

"Are you a nursing angel?"

"Nursing angel?" For a moment she appeared astonished. Then she laughed, producing a light, beguiling sound that affected Matt with the power of a lethal body blow. "Believe me, I'm neither a nurse nor an angel."

"Then I'm not dead…and in heaven?"

Her laughter vanished, to be replaced by a soft smile of compassion. "No, you are decidedly not dead."

Matt suffered conflicting feelings of wild elation and vague disappointment. Shaking his head in an attempt to dispel confusion, he sighed and inquired, "Then…where am I, and who are you?"

"As I said earlier, you are in a hospital recovery room,"

she answered in a warm tone—which sent chills skipping the length of his spine. "And I am Dr. Virginia Greyson...the surgeon who removed the bullet from your chest."

The chills along his spine intensified, but for an altogether different reason. His eyes flew wide, then narrowed again. "You are a doctor...a surgeon?"

Her smile could only be described as wry. "Yes. I am a doctor—" her incredulous tone mimicked his "—a surgeon." Her eyebrows lifted and her voice held a chiding lilt. "Now, don't tell me you have never seen a woman physician before today."

Matt was about to tell her exactly that, when his attention was drawn to the two women and one man who were suddenly surrounding the bed.

"Time to head 'em up and move 'em out, cowboy," the beefy, white-coated man drawled.

Wondering what the man was talking about, Matt shot a helpless look at his "angel," who claimed to be, of all things, a doctor.

"They are going to transfer you to another room," she explained.

Not seeing the point of the exercise, Matt frowned. "Why? What's wrong with this room?"

"Nothing," she answered, leveling a stern look at the others when they laughed. The laughter ceased abruptly, and she continued. "But this room is for postoperative patients needing constant care." Her features relaxed into a smile. "And I've just downgraded your condition from critical to serious."

"What does that mean?" Matt grumbled, feeling stupid and hating the sensation.

"It means you're being moved." She nodded at the others. "At once."

"I don't want..." he began in protest. She stifled his argument with one coaxing sentence.

"If you cooperate, I'll have someone get you something to eat as soon as you're settled."

Matt decided to cooperate—but not before gaining a concession from her. "Will you go with me?" He didn't see the grins twitching on the lips of the other three; his full attention was riveted on her reluctant smile, the indulgent note in her voice.

"Yes."

The activity that immediately ensued was bewildering for Matt. He was carefully shifted onto what looked like a narrow bed, but which the beefy man referred to as a gurney. Metal sides, much like those on a child's bed, were raised, and then Matt, gurney and the apparatus taped to his hand were rolled from the room and along a wide, brightly lighted corridor.

Every muscle in Matt's body clenched when the conveyance was rolled into what appeared to be a box-sized room with gliding doors. His stomach seemed to drop when the compartment slowly began a smooth descent.

Thoroughly rattled by the amazing, moving room, Matt was too fascinated by everything to do anything but glance around, trying to look at every aspect of his surroundings at once. Though the trip from one floor to the floor directly below was not far in actual distance, it encompassed a giant leap in time and space for Matt. By the time he was comfortably ensconced in the bed in his new room, he was utterly exhausted.

But Matt liked his new quarters and said as much to Virginia, the moment the other three had left the room.

"It's nice," he admitted.

"I know." Barely concealed amusement tinged her tone.

"Bright."

"Yes."

Catching the underlying hint of laughter in her voice, Matt shot a narrowed look at her. "Do you think this is funny, Doctor?" he asked softly.

She shook her head and bit her lip. "I'm sorry."

She didn't look sorry, but Matt let it pass. "You promised me some grub," he reminded her.

"And I always keep my promises." Pivoting, she headed for the door. "I'll be back in a minute with your...grub."

He opened his mouth to object to her leaving, but it was too late; she was gone. Disgruntled, Matt glanced around him, confused wonder filling his mind at the clean, cheerful look of the place. He had never personally been inside a hospital before, but had heard about them, and nothing he had heard compared in any way with what he was seeing. Of course, the most startling thing of all was that this obviously large, new building was located in a dying town in the foothills of the Anaconda Mountains in Montana.

Frowning at his thoughts, his gaze moved on, then settled on a small, windowed box placed upon a shelf on the wall. Now what in hell was that? he asked himself, exhaling a tired sigh. What could it be used for? He scraped his mind for a possible function for the box but came up blank.

Suddenly his head felt weighted, and his shoulder hurt. Absently rubbing the dressing over the wound in his chest, Matt rested his head on the soft pillow and continued to stare at the strange box.

Damn, he mused sleepily, this sure was a strange place. Closing his eyes, he decided he'd have to ask his "lady doctor" about two dozen questions when she returned with his food. But in a smaller number of seconds Matt was sound asleep.

He was out like a light.

The food tray in her hands, Virginia stood beside the bed staring at her sleeping patient. As rugged-looking as he was, the stranger appeared helpless, vulnerable in slumber. His impossibly long eyelashes brushed the shadowed hollows of his eyes, relieving the hard lines of his cheekbones and clenched, chiseled jaw. The pallor of illness was visible beneath the taut sun-darkened skin.

A tender smile crept across her lips as Virginia absently

set aside the tray. The stranger was a tough-looking customer, and at the moment none too clean, and yet there was something about him that had touched her in an odd, inexplicable way. She didn't know him, but that didn't matter. From the instant she had first stared into his crystal-blue eyes, she had wanted him to live with every particle of her being, and with a sense of desperation that went way beyond anything she had ever felt for any other patient.

And now he was out, deep within the reaches of natural sleep, but he *was* going to survive the damage inflicted by the bullet wound in his chest.

The sense of relief Virginia experienced left her feeling drained and exhausted. She didn't understand any of the emotions she was feeling, and was too tired to examine them. For the moment it was enough to know that he would live, thanks to her skill as a surgeon—and perhaps to her fervent, if secret, prayers.

It was only then that Virginia realized that deep inside herself she'd been praying harder than ever before in her life. The realization startled her, for she was not as a rule what anyone would think of as a religious person.

Virginia shook her head, her smile tilting derisively. Praying…her? Incredible. Wasn't she the one, she chided herself, who had always believed it presumptuous to appeal to God in times of trouble—that is, if one believed in God to begin with?

Yep, that was she, Virginia acknowledged.

Yet, didn't she also know—from firsthand experience—of patients who had managed to defy reality by sudden cures? There was always the possibility of the unforeseen happening or—for want of another, logical explanation—the occasional miracle.

Now, bone weary, Virginia shrugged. When it came to the bottom line, who knew the answers? While it was true that there was no concrete proof to substantiate the existence of a Creator, in absolute truth, there existed no concrete proof against Him, either.

Wow! She really was tired! Virginia thought, dragging her gaze from the stranger's arresting face. When she started ruminating about the metaphysical, it was time to give the mind and body rest, she decided. She turned and strode from the room.

Less than five minutes were required for Virginia to divest herself of the unattractive operating-room greens she was still wearing, and pull on the dress she had slipped into for dinner.... Had it really only been last evening?

Shrugging into her coat, she headed for the double plate glass exit doors. She almost made it.

"Dr. Greyson, wait a minute!"

The call came from the front desk receptionist an instant after Virginia strode by. The woman had appeared swamped by questions from a group of holiday visitors, asking for room numbers and directions.

Smothering a sigh and raising her eyebrows, Virginia turned to face the other woman. "Yes?"

The receptionist nervously wet her lips at the note of impatience in Virginia's tone, but said bravely, "About the man who came in through Emergency last night..."

"Yes?" Virginia's tone now held a decided chill. "What about him?"

"I, umm..." The receptionist moistened her lips again. "I have no admittance forms on him."

Damn regulations, red tape and paperwork, Virginia railed inwardly. Tired to the point of barely managing to remain erect, she kept her temper by reminding herself that the receptionist was only doing her job. From somewhere she even found a smile for the hapless woman.

"I know." She shrugged. "He hasn't been conscious long enough for me to get the information from him." Her smile grew wry. "Are you getting flack?"

The woman returned the smile. "Of course."

Dumb question, Doctor, Virginia told herself, exhaling a sigh. You had better get home and get some sleep soon, she mused on, before the brain completely atrophies.

"Would you like me to send someone else for the information, after the patient wakes up?"

The receptionist's voice jarred Virginia out of her own meandering thoughts. "No," she said with a definite emphasis. "I'll be back later this afternoon. I'll get it for you then." Her mouth curved into a conspiratorial smile. "Do you think you can hold off Admissions until then?"

"I'll confuse them with overworked vagueness." The woman contrived a little-girl-helpless, wide-eyed look, which drew a burst of laughter from Virginia.

Still chuckling to herself, Virginia pushed against the plate glass door. As a blast of cold air hit her in the face, a parting call rang in her ears.

"Merry Christmas, Doctor."

Responding in kind, she stepped outside into the full bite of a frosty winter morning. After depositing upward of fourteen inches of snow on the ground, the storm had moved on. The sunlight reflecting off the mantle of white was a glaring assault on the eyes.

Squinting, Virginia burrowed into her coat and strode toward the hospital parking lot, confident that someone would have moved her car there from where she'd left it in the parking bay at the Emergency entrance. Her confidence wasn't misplaced; she found her car, cleared of snow, in the first slot marked Reserved for Doctors.

"Merry Christmas, Doctor," called the elderly gentleman stationed in the parking lot toll booth, as she waited for the gate to be lifted.

The greeting revolved inside Virginia's head, stirring the memory of her promise to have Christmas supper at the home of Richard's parents. Reminded of the commitment she had made, she groaned aloud.

Richard was to pick her up at her apartment at six that evening. On the other hand, *she* had moments ago promised to return to the hospital later that afternoon.

What to do?

Virginia worried the question like a dog with a bone

during the short but tricky drive to her apartment complex. Should she call Richard and ask him to pick her up at the hospital? Or excuse herself from the date, citing business before pleasure?

But which was business, and which was pleasure?

The taunting query plagued her while she rode the elevator to her floor and trudged along the corridor to her apartment door. As she unlocked the door, a vision, unbidden and unwelcome, rose in her mind of the stranger lying alone and vulnerable in a hospital bed. At the same time, an echo of the proprietary note in Richard's voice at dinner—was it only last night?—replayed in her memory.

Dropping her coat and handbag onto the nearest chair, Virginia began undressing as she walked to her bedroom. Her shoulders were slumped from weariness, her eyes felt gritty and her mind had gone numb. She needed sleep—in her professional opinion, about twelve hours of sleep. A glance at her bedside clock told her it was 10:00 a.m.; she'd have to make do with less than five hours of slumber.

Virginia had long since learned to accept things as they were, rather than as she wished they would be. With a shrug, she picked up her phone receiver.

The first call she made was to her answering service, requesting a wake-up call for four. The second call wasn't nearly as simple. Richard was not happy about her canceling their date. He was inclined to argue. She was inclined to hang up on him.

Virginia fought down the inclination, but she hastened the conversation to its inevitable end, simply by refusing to allow Richard to prevail.

"I'm sorry, Richard," she said with more sincerity than she was feeling. "But if you'll remember, I've always told you that my patients come first...and I mean Christmas or any other day."

He objected.

She said a polite goodbye.

Minutes later Virginia was as dead to the world in sleep as the stranger who was her patient.

Three

God!

Matt stared in stunned amazement at the blond woman walking toward his bed. He had experienced a number of baffling events since awaking an hour ago, but the appearance of this woman was the most puzzling and interesting of all.

Without doubt she was the same woman whom he had earlier believed to be an angel. The woman had introduced herself to him as Virginia Greyson, a doctor and surgeon. And yet her appearance both baffled and shocked him.

Her hair was loose, attractively tousled by the wind. Her enticing lips were painted crimson, and looked slick and shiny in the glare of the bright overhead ceiling light. Gold hoops were fastened to her earlobes. A glittery bronze shaded her eyelids.

In comparison to the decent women of his acquaintance, who were all paint-free, she looked like a wanton. His nostrils quivered; damned if he couldn't smell her scent clear across the room. Wanton looking or not, she was the most beautiful female he had ever seen...the cleanest, too.

Feeling his body tighten in response to her, Matt lowered his eyes to her body—and experienced an even greater shock.

When he had first seen her after awakening from surgery, her hair was pulled back off her pale face, and she was dressed in what had appeared to be a wrinkled, shapeless green sack.

Now the sacklike covering was gone; its replacement caused a delightfully painful reaction in every particle of Matt's suddenly taut body.

She was dressed in a two-piece red thing—a short coat worn over a snow-white blouse. The bright red color of the coat lent a rosy glow to her cheeks. It was the bottom of the two-piece thing that rattled Matt. It was a skirt—of course, he knew that. But what shocked him was that the scarlet skirt barely covered her knees.

Matt scored a scandalized, appreciative glance down her shapely calves and neatly trim ankles, eyes widening as his gaze came to rest on her black shoes, which had narrow heels he judged to be at least three inches high.

Speculation gleamed from the bright blue eyes he raised to hers. In contrast, her doe-soft brown eyes were dark with question.

"Is something troubling you?" she asked in a musically soft voice that sang an alluring siren song all the way down his spine.

"There's a whole hell of a lot of things troubling me," Matt replied in a dry drawl, not mentioning that her nearness was suddenly the most troubling of all.

"Well, perhaps I can help clear up some of those things for you," she offered, smiling as she drew a chair next to the bed and settled her trim bottom on it.

You could clear up the most urgent of them by climbing into this bed with me, Matt thought. Aloud, he responded with a terse, "Maybe."

She was quiet for a moment, waiting, then arched her brows in that attractive way that did funny things to Matt's equilibrium. "Well?"

Distracted, he simply stared at her. "Well, what?"

She laughed on a sigh. "Not very forthcoming, are you?" She didn't wait for him to respond, continuing, "The nurse told me you're progressing surprisingly well, and that you were out of bed for a while after you awoke."

"Yeah," he muttered, "on your orders."

Virginia had to smile at the disgruntled note in his voice. "That's correct. I did leave instructions for the staff to get you on your feet. How did it go?"

"They didn't tell you?" His smile chided her.

"Yes, of course," she chided back. "Now I want to hear how you thought it went."

He shrugged, but admitted, "I felt a little wobbly, a little weak. I didn't like the feeling."

"Nobody does," she said, intuitively positive that he'd hate it more than most. Her brows inched up again. "How are you feeling now?"

"Hungry."

She appeared startled by his growled response. "But I was told that you had been served a meal!"

Deep in his throat Matt made a rude noise. "Maybe the folks around here call a swallow of broth, weak tea and a spoonful of some squishy, jellylike stuff a meal, but I sure as hell don't," he snapped.

"But a soft diet is necessary following surgery," she explained.

"Why?"

"Because of the anesthetic." Her smile attempted to soothe; his expression told her that it didn't work. She moved her shoulders in a half shrug. "Some patients experience nausea and even vomiting from it."

"I didn't," he said pointedly. His smile was designed to induce, if not actual fear, than at least trepidation in its receiver. Its feral quality had always worked for him be-

fore—it still did. Matt had to admit that the lady doctor
had courage. He also had to admire the way she faced his
teeth-bared smile without flinching.

"What would you like?' she asked, rising from the chair
in one fluid move that intensified the chills still tingling at
the base of his spine.

You, Matt thought, yearning to appease a deeper hunger.
"Something I can sink my teeth into," he answered,
searching out the softest, most vulnerable morsels of her
body with a narrowed, raking glance.

The way her eyelashes flickered gave evidence that his
silent message had been received. "I...ah—" she took a
step back "—I'll see what I can do."

His low growl of satisfied laughter trailed after her as
she hurried from the room.

Well...damn!

Virginia stood in the corridor beside the wall next to the
stranger's room. She felt breathless and was trembling with
an inner excitement. What was it about this man that affected her so? she wondered in amazement, staring in disbelief at the trembling of her fingers.

He was just another male patient among many and with
his lank hair and dark bristled jaw a rather scruffy-looking
one, at that.

Unlike many of her female acquaintances, Virginia had
never felt an appreciation for a masculine five o'clock
shadow. She preferred a man clean-shaven, shampooed and
redolent of soap.

Nevertheless, this particular man had merely to look at
her with his lids narrowed over those incredible blue eyes,
and she had the distinct sense of something vital collapsing
inside her. And the reaction she'd just experienced from his
smile didn't bear thinking about.

Of course, while standing there, gulping in deep breaths,
Virginia was powerless to think of anything else but the
startling effects of his smile.

"Lost, Doctor?"

Virginia started at the question asked by a nurse she hadn't even seen approaching her. "Er, no." Virginia shook her head, contemplating the possibility of becoming "lost" to a stranger's uncanny attraction. "I was thinking."

"A problem with your patient?" The young woman indicated the stranger's room with a nod of her head.

"Actually, yes," Virginia said, her smile wry. "Not medical," she explained. "He's hungry."

The nurse frowned. "But he was served a late lunch a little while ago."

"He claims the meal left a lot to be desired."

"The first meal after surgery always does." The nurse laughed. "But the dinner trays will be served in less than a half hour."

Virginia glanced at her watch, then at the doorway to his room. She didn't relish the idea of telling him there'd be another half hour until dinner. "I'm afraid he's not going to be happy about the delay," she said with a sigh.

"We've got a fruit cake at the station," the nurse said. "I can give you a slice of it and a cup of coffee for him," she offered generously.

"Well, what are we standing here for?" Virginia said, flicking her hand in the direction of the nurses' station. "Let's get it."

Virginia reentered the stranger's room a few minutes later, a steaming cup of coffee in one hand and a small paper plate bearing a thick slice of fruit cake in the other.

"That's a meal?"

Suppressing an urge to dump the hot coffee over his straggly hair only by reminding herself of his weakened, postop condition, Virginia maintained her cool by gritting her teeth. "No, this is not a meal," she told him, grinding out the words, "but it will suffice until the dinner trays are served."

Virginia was expecting him to growl. Contrarily, his lips

twitched with a secret inner amusement. But the twitch
turned into a grimace when he tried to sit up unassisted.
The curse he muttered was unprintable, if inventive.

Virginia wasn't shocked by the expletive; she had heard
them all, or at least most of them. Patients, male and female, had a tendency to curse while under sedation.

"Lie still," she ordered, setting the cup and plate on the
tray attached to the bed. "I'll raise the bed." Finding the
control, she pressed the Up button, then found herself staring, fascinated by the amazed expression that filled his face
and eyes as the head end of the bed slowly rose.

"Damn!" he exclaimed, grasping the mattress. "What
kind of contraption is this thing?"

Thoroughly confused by his reaction, Virginia glanced
from him to the bed, then back to him. "I don't understand," she murmured. "It's a common hospital bed."

He glared at her, blue eyes flashing angry, suspicious
sparks. "There ain't a damn thing common about it."

"You've never seen an automatic hospital bed?" Virginia asked skeptically.

"I've never seen a whole helluva lot of the things I've
been seeing in this place," he retorted. Releasing his grip
on the mattress, he squirmed into a more comfortable position and reached for the piece of fruit cake.

"Like what—for instance?" Virginia asked, frowning as
she looked around at the familiar, ordinary room.

He finished chewing the large bite of cake he'd taken
into his mouth, and swallowed a gulp of coffee before answering. "Like that—for instance." He flicked his hand to
indicate the TV mounted on a shelf on the wall. "What in
Sam Hill is that thing, anyway?"

"The television?" Virginia frowned.

"Is that what it's called?" He peered warily at the set.
"What does it do?"

Virginia's frown gave way to tolerant acceptance. "Are
you having fun?"

Now he frowned. "What do you mean?"

"You're putting me on, right?"

"Putting you on?" he repeated, his frown deepening into a fierce scowl. "Putting you on what?"

"Playing head games," she said grittily. "Pulling my leg."

His scowl lifted at her last remark, to be replaced by an expression of utter confusion. "Why would I yank at your leg?" he demanded with such sincerity that Virginia was forced to believe him.

"You honestly don't know what a television is?" Her voice was soft, her tone one of awe. "What it does?"

His voice held an edge of panic. "Lady, I don't know what any of the things in this room are—or what it is they're supposed to do."

"Good grief!" Virginia stared at him in wonder. "You really were in the mountains a long time, weren't you?"

"Yeah," he agreed, but still looked skeptical. "But—"

"Never mind," she interrupted him. "Eat your cake, and drink your coffee before it gets cold. I'll do my best to answer all your questions after you've finished."

Her mind boggling at the task she'd set for herself, she returned to the chair beside his bed. As she settled onto the hard seat, her gaze fell on the clipboard lying atop the bedside cabinet. She sighed softly.

"Something wrong?" he demanded, eyes narrowing again.

"No, not wrong," she replied, picking up the clipboard. "I promised to fill out these forms and get them down to Admissions this afternoon."

"What forms?" he asked around the cup he was raising to his lips. "What are they for?"

"Admission forms," she told him. "And they're for the information on you that the hospital requires. They really should have been filled out before you were admitted."

His lips curled. "Paperwork."

Virginia smiled at the derision in his voice. "Exactly," she said in agreement. "Policy, regulations…and all that."

She rolled her eyes. "But, since there is no escaping it, we may as well get it over with." She lowered her eyes to the first line on the form. "Name?" she asked, looking up at him with more curiosity than she cared to admit to.

"Matthew Hawk."

Virginia liked his name; somehow it fitted him. "Middle initial?"

His lips twitched in an intriguing way. "M," he answered with a rigidly straight face.

She was forced to smile. "Is there something odd or unusual about your middle name?"

The intriguing twitch melted into a grin. "My mother was a devout woman, read the Bible every day." He raised his brows promptingly. "Can you guess?"

Virginia didn't have to guess, she knew. "Mark?"

"'Fraid so," he drawled. "Ain't it pitiful?"

Virginia's spontaneous burst of laughter eased the tension that was coiling along her nerves. "Oh, I don't know," she observed. "I think it's rather nice."

"Only another woman would," he observed in a dry-asdust tone, finishing off his coffee. He shot a glance at the door, then at her. "When did you say supper would be coming?"

"Soon," she assured him, smiling and shaking her head. "Meanwhile, can we get on with this?" She tapped her pen against the form.

He shrugged. "Shoot."

She complied. "Home address?"

"Fort Worth."

Virginia's head jerked up. "Texas?"

"There's another one?"

"But—" she began, frowning.

"Can we get this over with?" he cut her off irritably.

"Certainly," she snapped. "Occupation?"

"United States marshal," he responded at once.

"Really!" Virginia stared at him in stark astonishment.

The way his lips twitched sent a thrill of warning through her.

"Now, Doctor," he drawled. "Would I put you on?"

"Incredible," she retaliated. "I had no idea the United States Government hired idiot savants as marshals."

Matthew Hawk didn't appear insulted; he looked interested. "What's an idiot savant?"

Virginia literally threw her hands into the air. "Oh, never mind!" she cried. "Date of birth?"

"June 13, 1854."

That does it! Virginia decided with disgust. She would not be the brunt of his humor any longer. Raising her head, she glared, prepared to verbally blast away at him. The angry words dried on her lips as she met his clear-eyed stare.

He wasn't kidding!

The realization raised the hair on Virginia's scalp, and she had the weird sensation of having been plunked down smack in the middle of the Twilight Zone.

Telling herself to get a grip on herself, Virginia cleared her tight throat. "You do mean 1954...don't you?" she asked in a please-tell-me-I'm-right whisper.

"1954?" He exploded with laughter. "1954! Lady, are you loco?"

Virginia had an eerie feeling that she didn't want to think about, let alone investigate. He was joking, she assured herself, either joking or stark, staring mad. That was it, he was....

A chill shuddered through her body as her memory flashed scenes into her mind, scenes of the way he was dressed when she'd first seen him, scenes of the way he had been reacting to his surroundings since regaining consciousness. She saw again his cold eyes, the frightening expression on his face when he'd demanded to know what she had done with his pistol. Staring now into those eyes, which were staring back at her in question, she began to tremble.

But it wasn't possible! He had the appearance and the physiological structure of a man in his mid-thirties. Unless he had discovered the fabled fountain of youth, he couldn't possibly be...

"Are you telling me you are over a hundred years old?" she demanded irately.

His jaw dropped. "Over a hundred?" he repeated, eyeing her warily. "Lady, you're not loco, you're plain crazy!"

Virginia shook her head very slowly. "I don't understand any of this."

"Well, don't think you're riding point alone," he growled. "I haven't understood anything about this place ever since I woke up."

Virginia's heart was beating so rapidly that she could barely breathe, never mind speak. "O-okay," she said, between gasping breaths. "Let's see if we can clear up the mystery. Suppose we start at the beginning. I want you to tell me exactly how your accident happened."

"Accident, hell!" he exclaimed. "I was bushwhacked."

"In the middle of the street?" she cried.

"No!" Now he shook his head. "I was on the path, heading for the church at the top of the hill."

"What hill?" Virginia envisioned the street where the police had found him—the level street. "Where?"

"Here." He waved his arm, as if to indicate not only the room but the entire area. "Right here in the Anaconda Mountains in Montana."

Virginia could feel her eyes growing wide. "You were shot in Montana?"

"No, I was shot in the chest," he retorted with dry humor. "But I was here in Montana at the time."

His humor sparked her temper. "You can make jokes if you like, Mr. Hawk, but I feel I must tell you that you are not anywhere near Montana. You are in a hospital in the town of Conifer, Pennsylvania."

The humor disappeared from his eyes, leaving them hard and shrewd looking. "You are crazy."

"No, I am not," Virginia snapped. "And—for your information, we are in the last decade of the twentieth century."

"And—don't tell me," he said in an infuriatingly soothing voice. "You're Annie Oakley?"

"Of course not!"

"Belle Starr?"

Virginia had reached the absolute end of her patience. "I've had enough of this!" she said, jumping to her feet and slamming the clipboard onto the cabinet. "What kind of games are you playing?"

"Games? Is that it? This is a game to you?" His eyes narrowed on her face, while his hand tugged at the covers. "I'm wounded, and you want to play games. I see, but no thank you, ma'am." As he spoke, he pushed aside the covers.

Thinking that now even the Twilight Zone had begun to tilt, she cautiously said, "No, I don't want to play games. And where do you think you're going?"

He grimaced with pain as he slid to the edge of the bed. "I am getting out of this madhouse," he said with determination.

"No!" Virginia cried, reaching out to stop him. "You're in no condition to leave!" Her hand brushed his arm, and she was startled by the sudden heat she felt on her fingertips. Her palm grew moist, her throat went dry. There was a definite lack of substance to her voice, and no authority whatever. "You'll reopen that wound."

"Too bad," he retorted, grunting as he thrust one leg from beneath the covers. The short hospital gown he was wearing revealed his leg from his bare foot to his long, lightly haired, tautly muscled thigh. "Dammit! Where's my pants?" he growled, glancing around. "And where are the rest of my things...my clothes and my gun?"

Distracted, confused, Virginia dragged her gaze from his

naked thigh and her hands away from his arm to motion toward the dresser opposite the bed. "In there, I suppose." Blinking herself out of her bemusement, she argued, "But you can't leave now. You're not well!"

His lips curved again into that cold, feral smile. "Who's gonna stop me, lady?"

Who indeed? Virginia gave a brief thought to hospital security and even the police, but immediately dismissed the idea. Instead, she shivered...and backtracked. "Look, I'm sorry I upset you." She raised her hands in a placating gesture. "Please, Mr. Hawk, stay in bed. I'm positive we can work this through...somehow."

He hesitated, eyeing her warily. "I want my things." His voice was low, his tone adamant. "Will you bring them to me if I stay in bed?"

Considering it a small concession, she nodded. "Yes, if you insist on seeing them."

"I do." Moving slowly, teeth clenched against the jarring pain in his shoulder, he shifted toward the center of the bed, then hesitated once more. "There's something else."

Virginia stiffened, instantly on guard. "And that is?" she asked cautiously.

"I'm called Matt."

The pent-up breath she'd been unaware of holding eased from her constricted throat. Virginia hadn't known what form his request would take, but she had never expected him to ask her to use the diminutive of his given name. The sense of relief that washed through her left her feeling weak and produced a shaky smile. "All right...Matt."

"And I'll call you Ginnie."

Since she had never cared for that particular nickname, Virginia made a face. "I prefer Virginia." Her tone held a deliberate, I'm-in-charge-here, edge.

His grin left her in little doubt of who actually was in charge of the situation. "I prefer Ginnie." He waited, half in half out of the bed, for her reaction.

She shrugged. "Whatever."

Matt cocked one dark eyebrow. "Is that an okay?"

Virginia gave him a don't-push-your-luck stare. "Yes, Matt, that is…" Her voice trailed away as a nurse carrying a tray swung into the room.

"Sorry dinner is late," the nurse said in a cheerful voice. "But I don't think you'll be upset when you taste the special holiday meal you're getting." She slid the tray onto the narrow, tablelike attachment to the bed, then turned and smiled at Virginia. "Hi, Dr. Greyson."

"Hello, Marsha," Virginia said, returning the pleasant young nurse's greeting, while silently encouraging Matt's struggle to position himself closer to the food tray.

The nurse turned to leave, then paused at the doorway. "Oh, can I bring something for you, Doctor? Coffee, tea?"

Virginia was about to politely decline the offer when the aroma wafting from the tray caused a pang in her stomach, reminding her that she hadn't eaten since the previous evening. She had felt confident on leaving her apartment a short while ago that her business at the hospital—checking the progress of her patient and getting those dratted admittance forms completed—would take her less than an hour. After that her time would be her own, since she had canceled her engagement to join Richard and his parents for supper. She had even entertained the idea of returning home, fixing a light meal, making herself comfortable in front of the TV, and enjoying a ghostly Christmas movie.

So much for that plan, Virginia thought with a sigh. Besides, since she had as much as said she would pay the hospital costs, if necessary—and from the looks of things it would be—she might as well derive something from her generosity, even if it was only a meal.

"Yes, thank you," she finally replied. "I missed lunch, and I'd appreciate a dinner tray."

"Coming right up," Marsha called, swinging out of the room. She was back with the second tray moments after Virginia pulled the chair nearer to the bed.

Virginia sat, hands folded in her lap, until the nurse
swept from the room once more. She watched in fascination
as Matt studied the plastic-wrapped utensils next to his
plate, and she ached somewhere deep inside when he
looked at her in blank appeal. Feeling a rush of sympathy
for him, she remained silent, but made a detailed production
of tearing open the plastic and removing the knives, forks
and spoons.

A crooked, self-deprecating smile tilting his lips, Matt
followed her example—to the letter. When he had freed the
utensils, he carefully loosened the napkin wrapped around
them. Frowning at the white plastic cutlery, he laid the
pieces aside, then proceeded to tuck the napkin under the
material of the gown where it edged his throat.

Fully expecting him to tear into the food, Virginia was
nonplussed when he didn't as much as touch the domed
cover over the plate, but sat patiently, staring at her.

"Is there something wrong?" she asked, shifting her
puzzled eyes from his tray to his face.

"No, ma'am."

"Then why aren't you eating?"

Matt looked affronted. "My mother taught me manners
while I was still in britches." He inclined his head toward
her tray. "I'm waiting for you to begin."

Under the circumstances, his display of simple, old-
fashioned gallantry pierced Virginia to the core of her being. He was hurt and angry, and more than a little disoriented and confused. He was also very hungry. And yet this
strange and strangely attractive man sat still and quiet, waiting for her to begin the meal.

The ache deep inside Virginia spread. Her sympathy
crystallized into an overwhelming feeling of protectiveness.
She didn't know this man, but in that instant she didn't
care. Her mind was filled with questions about him, but
they could wait. Thoroughly disarmed, but completely
aware of what she was doing, she smiled and lifted the
cover from her plate.

Four

"**F**eeling better?" Virginia smiled and ran a casual glance over the two trays. The plates and side dishes were literally scraped clean of the contents, of which she had eaten less than half.

"Mmm." Matt nodded. Cradling his coffee cup in one broad hand, he relaxed against the pillow that supported his back. "This is good coffee." He took a sip and raised his dark brows into a teasing, nudging arch. His eyes gleamed at her over the rim of the cup.

"Would you like some more?" Virginia's low voice contained understanding laughter.

"Yes." He drained the cup and held it out in front of him. "Please."

She gave him a wry smile, but stood and walked from the room. Moments later, she returned with the half-full glass coffeepot from the nurses' lounge. "It's not good for you, you know," she informed him, refilling both his and her own cups with the steaming dark brew.

"No?" His eyebrows went up again. "Why not?"

"The caffeine, of course." Her smile chiding, she leaned forward to add milk and sugar to the liquid in his cup. "It rattles the nerves."

"I don't have any nerves," Matt said. His nostrils flared slightly as he inhaled. "Smells good."

Straightening, Virginia smiled and fussed with the dishes on the tray. "The nurses make good coffee."

"I wasn't talking about the coffee," he said, grinning at her as he took a tentative sip. "Although it smells good, too."

Virginia felt a fluttering sensation glide along her spine. "What...were you referring to?" she had to ask, even though she instinctively knew the answer.

Matt's bright eyes grew dark and heavy-lidded, and glittered with a blatant, sensual glow. "You, and the perfume or whatever it is that you're wearing," he murmured. "I can smell you clear down to my gut." His voice became low, raspy. "Makes me think of dark nights and darker bedrooms. I like it...the smell, and the hot-cold feeling it gives me inside."

The fluttery sensation along Virginia's spine intensified, causing a hot-cold feeling inside her, too. Determined not to think of dark nights and darker bedrooms, yet trembling in a reaction that was out of all proportion to his compliment, she moved to sit on the chair beside the bed. A startled gasp broke from her throat when he reached out and curled his fingers around her wrist.

"You feel it too, don't you?" His voice was still lower, even more raspy than before.

"No!" Virginia exclaimed, emphasizing her denial with a sharp shake of her head. "I don't know what you mean." Feeling vaguely alarmed, yet strangely excited, she pulled against his hold on her. His fingers tightened, not painfully, but in an oddly secure and sensual way.

"Don't you?" Matt persisted, continuing to smile at her. Draining the cup with a couple of deep swallows, he set it beside hers on the tray. His fingertips brushed against the tender skin on the inside of her wrist, and his voice grew still deeper, soft with a knowing sexiness. "Come into this bed with me and I'll show you."

Her pulse began to hammer and her mouth went dry. The awareness of him as a male, a dangerously attractive male, drowned her normal common sense. The urge to acquiesce to his invitation, however, clashed with her natural reserve and helped to restore her equilibrium.

Chastising herself for her juvenile reaction to him, Virginia brought her senses under control by exerting sheer willpower and advising herself to grow up. She'd had similar invitations from other male patients, and had always laughingly rebuffed their overeager postoperative amorous advances.

Telling herself that this man was no different from the others, and that in actual fact he was a lot less clean looking than all her previous male patients, Virginia did manage to conjure up a faint smile.

"I'll pass, thank you," she said, tugging once more against his encircling fingers.

Matt frowned. "Is that a no?"

"It is." Virginia gave him a reproachful look. "You're in no condition to perform, at any rate. So—" she arched her eyebrows "—could I have my arm back...please?"

Though Matt stared at her indignantly, he did release his grip on her wrist. "What do you mean, I'm in no condition?" he demanded. "Come closer, and I'll—"

"Probably reopen your wound," Virginia interrupted, carefully stepping back out of harm's way. Her wrist tingled, but she won an inner battle against the urge to rub her fingers over the spot he had imprisoned and brazenly stroked.

"I won't reopen the damn wound," he said, dismissing the idea with a shrug. "Being wounded never interfered with my...ah...performance."

Virginia gaped at him. "You've been shot before?"

"Twice." Matt nodded in affirmation. "Once in the leg, once in the side."

"But that's incredible!" she gasped.

"Not too," he drawled. "I'm a lawman."

His terminology struck a discordant note in her mind. Lawman? The last time she had heard the expression was in a Western film she'd half-heartedly watched on TV. "Hmm, that explains everything."

"Sure." He grinned at her. "Besides, I'm feeling better all the time. The grub did the trick."

Grub. Virginia shook her head, but asked, "Then you enjoyed your meal?"

"That was the best Christmas dinner I've had since I left home."

Virginia was suddenly alert. "When was that?"

"When I was seventeen, the summer of seventy-one." A challenging smile bared his hard-looking teeth. "Eighteen and seventy-one."

His words, his phrasing, instilled a tremor inside Virginia. Because the tension between them had dissipated during the conversation they had engaged in while eating dinner, the sensation was even more shocking than before. She gave him an imploring look.

"Please, Matt, don't start that again." Virginia was too rattled to notice that she sounded more like a concerned woman than a detached professional.

"Start what?" Though his voice remained free of inflection, his eyes revealed renewed wariness.

"This silliness about dates!" she cried.

"It's not silliness to me," Matt retorted. "I know what year I was born. I know what year I left home. I also know when and where I was ambushed. I was shot last night, Christmas Eve, eighteen hundred and eighty-nine."

Since Virginia was a surgeon, not a psychiatrist, she wasn't certain how to proceed in handling his apparent delusion. Yet she felt that she must break though to him, if only because in every other respect, Matt appeared stable and well balanced. Acting intuitively, she turned and again headed for the door.

"Where are you going now?" he demanded.

"For proof," she answered without breaking stride. "I'll be back in a moment."

As Virginia had expected, there was a folded, much-read newspaper at the nurses' station. After receiving permission to borrow it, she clutched the paper in one hand like a weapon and marched back down the corridor and into Matt's room.

"There," she said forcefully, slapping the paper, front page up, onto the bed. "This is the special holiday edition of today's paper," she went on, tapping the headline with one slim finger. "Please note the date."

After subjecting her to a hard, narrow-eyed stare, Matt lowered his eyes to the paper. A shudder, visible and intense, shook his body. The face he raised was pale, the brilliant blue of his eyes was dulled by confusion. His voice, so confident moments ago, held an uncertain tremor.

"I don't understand."

"That makes two of us," Virginia replied. "Taking everything you said at face value, I have no idea where you got the idea that it was 1889, and that you were in the mountains of Montana when you were shot." Again she tapped her finger against the paper. "As you can see, this paper not only has the correct date but the location, as well. The police found you lying in the middle of the street, and you are now in a hospital in Conifer, Pennsylvania."

Matt didn't return his puzzled gaze to the paper, but continued to stare at her as he slowly shook his head. "Police...in the street...Pennsylvania?" he muttered in disjointed spurts.

"Yes." Though quiet, Virginia's tone was firm, unequivocal, straightforward.

His broad shoulders drooped an instant before he sagged back against the pillow. He was quiet for long seconds, as if trying to assimilate her assertions. When he looked at her again, his gaze was sharp. "You think I'm crazy and need a head doctor," he said. "Don't you?"

"Not at all," Virginia denied, with what she hoped was reassuring promptness. "I believe your mind is probably suffering from shock due to the combination of your wound and exposure."

"But, you see, Doctor, I'm not confused about what happened or where and when it happened," Matt murmured. "The only things I'm confused about are the things that have happened since I woke up, clearheaded, a little while ago."

"But you do know it's Christmas Day?"

Matt shot her an impatient look. "Yes, I know it's Christmas Day. We just finished eating the holiday meal." His voice was strong and his features grew taut, vanquishing the expression of uncertainty and defeat. Sitting upright, he straightened his shoulders, as if infused with renewed purpose. "I also know that I was shot last night, Christmas Eve, nineteen hundred and eighty-nine." His lids narrowed over glittering eyes. "What I don't know is how I got from Montana to here...or why I'm not dead."

Virginia's sigh said volumes about her growing sense of frustration; the way she raked a hand through her hair underscored every line. For whatever reason, Matthew Hawk was certain he was from another place and century. And unless she could convince him to face reality, and soon, she knew she would be left with little option but to call upon the expertise of a psychiatrist.

Virginia generally held the field of psychiatry and her colleagues practicing in that field in the utmost esteem. At any other time, with any other patient, she would not hesitate in seeking their assistance. Yet now she felt justified in pausing to reflect.

She had noted the unvoiced trepidation in Matt, had correctly read his body language and facial expression when he'd asked her if she believed him to be crazy.

In Virginia's professional opinion, Matthew Hawk would

react to the presence of a "head doctor" in exactly the same manner as he would react to a coiled rattlesnake.

So that left it up to her. Virginia concluded that, at least temporarily, she'd play it by ear. But how and where to begin? Staring into his wary eyes, she decided the gentle route would be lost on him. Matt was obviously tough, and in her opinion, equal to a mild form of shock therapy.

Testing her theory, she reached for the TV remote control and pressed the On button. As the screen flickered to life, the voices of a choir, raised in exultation, blared from the speakers. Virginia was both amazed and fascinated by Matt's response.

His eyes growing wide with unmistakable shock, grimacing with pain, Matt scrambled backward, as if attempting to escape danger by pushing himself through the headboard of the bed and the wall behind it. His breathing was harsh, irregular. The pulse at the base of his throat fluttered wildly.

"What in hell!" he exclaimed, staring at the screen with an expression of stark disbelief. "How did they get all those little people in that box?"

In other circumstances, his reaction might have been funny. But the fear visible beneath Matt's incredulity left little room for humor. The fear and amazement on his strong-featured visage were not a laughing matter.

Intuitively and intellectually, Virginia knew he wasn't faking. She was convinced that Matt's response was a genuine reflection of what he was feeling. Simultaneously, deep inside, she felt a growing suspicion that everything he had said about himself and his origin was the absolute truth. In the name of sanity she denied it—but she felt it.

"There are no little people inside that box," she replied with calming reassurance.

He flashed a confused look at her. "Then how—?" He broke off, returning his gaze to the TV set. "Then how can I see them? How does it work?"

Good question. Exactly how did it work? Virginia was

flooded with a sense of inadequacy. Like most, her comprehension of the technology that had produced television was limited. She simply accepted it, along with all the other many wonders of modern science.

"I don't know how it works," she said, impatient with her own ignorance. "But that's not important now. The thing is—Are you listening to me?" she asked, in a tone sharpened to draw his fascinated attention away from the special Christmas production that was being presented on one of the network channels.

"Huh?" Matt turned his head and blinked at her. "Oh, yeah, you said you don't know how it works." He shrugged. "That's okay. I don't know how the steam engine automobiles work, either. But I know they do, because I saw one." He raised his eyebrows. "You ever see one?"

"An automobile?" Virginia asked, fighting against an inner sense of unreality.

Looking at her in a way that indicated *she* was acting strangely, Matt nodded in response.

"I own one."

He frowned. "I can't figure out why in hell anyone'd want one. They make one helluva noise."

An eerie chill permeated Virginia's body as she realized again that Matt wasn't acting or playing some sort of sick game with her. He was dead serious. Perhaps, she mused, feeling a crushing sense of failure, she'd be better advised to seek psychiatric counsel, after all.

"Why are you looking at me like that?" he asked, startling her from her reverie. "What are you cooking up inside that beautiful head of yours?"

At that, the first thought to flash into Virginia's head was: did he really think she was beautiful? The thought was immediately followed by another, this time a self-ridiculing condemnation. What difference did it make whether or not he thought her attractive? Her appearance had little to do with the matter.

Still, Virginia experienced a secret thrill of pleasure from his left-handed compliment.

Mentally shaking off the unusual effect she was feeling, she instilled a stern note into her tone. "I'm not cooking up anything, and if I'm looking at you in any strange way, it's simply because I'm trying to decide exactly what it is you're hoping to gain by claiming to have been shot in Montana in 1889."

Matt bolted upright to glare at her. "If I'm trying to gain anything," he said in a deadly hard voice, "it's to make some sense out of this whole crazy business."

Virginia felt the raw anger from his glittering eyes all the way to her toes. Suddenly fearful that she just might be dealing with a raving lunatic, she held out her hands in a pacifying gesture. "All right, calm down," she said, careful to keep her own voice soft and soothing.

He actually sneered at her. "I'm not an infant to be spoon-fed pap and crooned to," he snarled, his eyes shooting fiery sparks at her. "Get me my things."

The abrupt demand threw her off balance. "What?" she asked, and immediately added, "Why?"

"My own things," he answered, in an unpleasant tone. "Because I want them...now."

Virginia didn't even contemplate refusing him. In fact, she didn't pause as much as a moment to reflect. Jumping up, she moved to the built-in closet and dresser drawers in the wall opposite the bed. She found his clothes hanging in the closet, his hat and boots on the floor beneath them, and his personal effects in a large plastic bag in the top dresser drawer. Not stopping to examine them, she scooped them into her arms. The bag was bulky and heavy. Frowning at it, she turned and dumped the lot onto the bed.

"Thank you." Sarcasm laced Matt's voice.

"You're welcome." Virginia matched his tone. "Would you care to tell me what you intend to do with them?"

"Yeah, I'll tell you," he retorted. "I intend to get dressed and get the hell out of here."

"But you can't!" she cried in protest.

"No?" His lips thinned, twisting into a sardonic smile. "Watch me."

She didn't doubt him for an instant. Virginia instinctively knew that if he said he would do something, he would do it...come hell, high water or an anxious physician. She also knew she had to stop him.

"Your wound," she said, infusing authority into her voice. "You're in no condition to leave the hospital."

Matt flexed his shoulder, grimaced, then shrugged. "I've traveled with worse." His eyes became hooded as he raked her face and figure with a bright, hot glance. "Too bad. You're one tempting lady, and I'd've liked nothing more than getting to know you better...a whole lot better." He sighed, but shrugged again. "But I will be damned if I'll hang around and listen to you call me a liar."

"I didn't!" Virginia exclaimed in heated denial, while silently denying an inner melting sensation caused by the sensuous heat that was blazing from his eyes.

"You did!" Matt growled. "Oh, maybe you didn't say it outright, but I'm not stupid. I don't need the words spelled out for me." He laughed harshly. "You believe I'm either a bald-faced liar or crazy as a critter set loose in the loco weed...don't you?"

She shook her head. "No, as I said earlier, I think you're still suffering the effects of—" She was interrupted by the slicing motion of his hand.

"I'm not in shock," he said. "I told you, I'm clear-headed and thinking straight." He reached for the clothes she'd dropped in a heap at the foot of the bed. "And I'm getting out of here."

"To go where?" Her question was deliberate, designed to stop him. It succeeded.

His hand hovering above the pile of clothes, Matt raised consternation-filled eyes to hers. "You were telling the truth? This place really is in Pennsylvania?" His voice held a note of uncertainty that pierced directly to her heart.

Virginia sighed. She was no longer sure which one of them was unbalanced. What she was suddenly sure of was that she couldn't bear that uncertain note in his voice. The entire situation was insane, and yet she felt an overwhelming desire to reassure him, if only to bring back the angry fire into his eyes and the ring of confidence into his voice.

"I'm no more a liar than you are, Matt," she said softly. The expression darkening his eyes tore at her.

"How did this happen, Ginnie?"

At the pleading note, Virginia raised her hands, then let them drop in a helpless gesture. "How can I answer you?" she cried. "I'm as much in the dark as you are!" He opened his mouth to speak, but she silenced him with a quick shake of her head. "I'm not suggesting that you're a liar or confused or anything else." She smiled through a deep sigh. "Look, why don't you start at the beginning and tell me exactly what happened, and we'll work on it from there?" Her smile tilted coaxingly. "Okay?"

His sigh echoed hers. "Okay."

His story took the better part of two hours. In a tired-sounding tone devoid of inflection, Matt began his recitation with the day of his birth—in June 1854.

Biting her tongue to keep herself from interrupting him, Virginia listened in astonishment as Matt painted a sketchy but vibrant verbal picture of life and the frequently hazardous conditions of growing up in the freewheeling West of the latter half of the nineteenth century.

Against her will and common sense, Virginia found herself caught up in his story. She was there with him, feeling his sense of despair and helplessness as he witnessed his father's death beneath the slashing hooves of a maddened horse. She wept inwardly with the seven-year-old boy he had been, trying to take some of the burden from the shoulders of his overworked mother as she grew old too soon laboring to eke out a living from a small, unproductive ranch. And Virginia was by his side, wilting in the intense glare of the summer sunlight, as Matt the man, his taut, harshly set features concealing the agony clawing at his insides, stood beside a hole in the ground, watching his mother being lowered into her final resting place.

In expressionless tones stark with inner pain, Matt unwittingly revealed the frustration he still suffered from knowing that the relative ease he had been able to provide for his mother from the time he'd become a man—at the advanced age of fifteen—until her death before he'd reached his majority, was too little and had come too late.

She waited in breathless silence when he paused, absently reaching for her untouched coffee. Watching the tendons flex in his strong throat as he tossed back the now tepid liquid, a funny little ache stirred deep inside her. When he resumed speaking, she had the uncanny sensation of actually feeling the dry harshness that shadowed his voice.

Unwilling, yet powerless against the strength of his narrative, Virginia rode beside Matt, wearing the badge of a United States marshal, in the pursuit of outlaws. She knew he was nearing the end of his story when he told of his month-long assignment, trailing a particularly vicious killer into the Anaconda Mountains of Montana.

So vivid was his description of that Christmas Eve, so poignant the despair and revulsion he had felt at the necessity of killing the outlaw, that Virginia, too, shivered in the crisp night air and felt his sickness of spirit deep within her own body and soul.

Matt stared bleakly into her face. "I was…am…so damn tired of living on the trail and watching my back. I had decided to quit, to get as far away as I could from law enforcement. It's kinda funny how it turned out." An ironic smile curved his thin masculine lips. "I was on my way to the church at the crest of the hill for Christmas Eve services. Goin' begging to the Lord for a fresh start on a decent life." A new shudder rippled the length of his rangy body. "Instead, I got a bullet in the chest." His eyebrows lifted into a sardonic arch. "The Lord's callin' card, maybe?"

His last remark shattered the remaining shreds of Virginia's objectivity. "No!" she cried out in protest. "You're here, you're alive!"

"Yeah, I'm here and I'm alive," Matt retorted. "But why am I here, in this place?" He didn't allow her time to respond, but continued. "And dammit! Why am I alive? I was dying. I knew I was dying. So why ain't I dead?"

Virginia recalled him asking the same question earlier. On hearing it repeated, she had a flashing memory of the first time she had seen him, lying still and sprawled in the street, staring sightlessly into the falling snow. She recalled, too, the one policeman's reply to his partner's comment about the victim's eyes.

"Well, of course his eyes are cold. He's dead."

She herself had believed him to be dead, Virginia remembered, suddenly trembling...and she was a physician!

What did it mean? It didn't make sense. None of it made sense. Here he was, very much alive, and yet slightly out of sync...out of time. Virginia would have bet her professional reputation that Matt wasn't acting, lying or deluded.

That left...what?

Virginia was afraid to contemplate the answer to the riddle of Matthew Hawk. She was also afraid that she knew the—unacceptable—answer.

Out of time.

The phrase revolved in Virginia's head as she stared into the eyes of the man, the stranger, seated taut and expectant on the bed.

Was it possible? she asked herself, while the certainty of that possibility welled up inside her. But how? she demanded in silent desperation.

Even as her mind groped for explanations, she heard again Matt's whispered words. An answer?

"Goin' begging to the Lord for a fresh start on a decent life."

Virginia swallowed against a sudden tightness in her throat. Had the Lord granted alms of life to the beggar?

The rational, logical part of Virginia's brain immediately rejected the hypothesis. Things of that nature simply didn't happen, couldn't happen...not in the waning years of the twentieth century.

But couldn't they...didn't they? a tiny inner voice demanded. Think, remember. Earlier she herself had recalled instances she'd witnessed, and others she'd heard about from colleagues, of the unexplainable and seemingly miraculous recovery of terminally ill patients.

But time travel? Virginia was slowly shaking her head in repudiation of the very idea, the very way-out idea, when the sound of Matt's rough, impatient voice jolted her from her introspection.

"Well, say something, dammit!"

"What do you want me to say?" she cried.

"You heard my story." His body was quivering from tension. "Do you believe me?"

"Yes, I believe you."

He exhaled harshly, as if he'd been holding his breath for a long time. "You said that maybe we could figure out what happened. Do you have any ideas?"

Without pausing to consider, Virginia blurted aloud the speculation that had lodged in her mind. "Do you think it's possible that you were transposed from then to here through some sort of time warp?"

Five

"**W**hat in hell is a time warp?"

"No. Forget it." Virginia shook her head, as if to literally shake herself back into the world of reality. "Just forget it."

"Forget it?" Matt repeated in a baffled tone. "How can I forget it? I don't know what *it* is."

Virginia gave one final shake of her head. "It was too farfetched, a ridiculous idea."

"What was a ridiculous idea?" Matt raked a hand through his hair in frustration, then grimaced at the sheen of oil slicking his palm.

Virginia shifted her gaze from his shiny palm to his hair. It was long, lank and shaggy—looking exactly like one would expect on a man who had spent over a month on the trail of a criminal...and quite like every photograph she had ever seen of men in the old West of the late eighteen hundreds, over a century ago.

Ridiculous? Virginia repeated the conclusion to herself.

Yes, of course it was, but, then again... She jumped, startled, when Matt reached across the bed to grasp her hand. His long fingers quivered from the tension still gripping his body.

The weathered, sun-bronzed skin on his face was drawn tight over his strained features. "Dammit, Ginnie, tell me what you're thinking!" His voice held a raw, pleading note that went straight to her heart. "I'm lost—help me."

His cry was the deciding factor for Virginia. Irrational, illogical, inconceivable as her idea definitely was, it was still the only one that made sense.

"Okay." Virginia surrendered with a sigh. "I'll try to explain." She gave him a warning look. "I'm afraid it is going to sound more than a little crazy to you."

Matt shrugged. "Right now everything seems more than a little crazy to me." His lips tilted in a crooked smile, easing the tension that had formed grooves around his mouth. Visibly relaxing, he loosened his grip on her hand, then, instead of releasing her, he entwined his fingers with hers. "Even a crazy explanation is better than no explanation."

The warmth of the fingers curled around hers caused a shivery feeling inside Virginia and interfered with her breathing process. Though only their hands were touching, she experienced the uncanny sensation of feeling him with every particle of her body.

Talk about ridiculous, she thought, staring at the sprinkling of dark hairs on the backs of his fingers. At that moment, she would swear she could feel the texture of every one of those wispy hairs.

"Ginnie?" The puzzlement in Matt's tone shattered her reverie.

"What?" Virginia's head snapped up. "Oh, yes, my idea." She paused to draw a calming breath.

"Is something wrong?"

"No," she denied, shaking her head and collecting her

wits. "Ah...I was thinking." Along dangerous lines, she thought.

Matt's fingers tightened for an instant. Leaning toward her, he brought his face close to hers...his mouth close to hers. His voice grew low, seductive. "About me?"

His breath swept over her lips. From eyes wide with surprise, Virginia could see every masculine nuance of his chiseled features, every individual stalk of dark stubble on his squared jawline. And she could smell the slightly musky male scent of him. His unique fragrance went straight to her head, permeating her senses, defusing her defenses.

"Ginnie." Breathing her name, Matt advanced, moving his mouth nearer, ever closer to hers.

"Matt." His name little more than a yearning whisper, Virginia parted her lips to receive his.

The touch of his mouth was at first tentative, then, on a low growl, tenacious. She felt the gentle but commanding rake of his teeth along her lower lip an instant before his mouth forced her lips farther apart. The gentle savagery of his mouth against hers stole both her breath and her sense of propriety. Sighing, she returned his kiss with equal fervor. His response was immediate and devastating. His tongue swept into her mouth, deepening the kiss into an erotic play evocative of a more complete possession.

Virginia felt his kiss, the penetration of his tongue to the very depths of her femininity. With mindless abandon she clung to his mouth, drinking sensuous sustenance from him as greedily as he devoured the sweetness of her. When he withdrew, releasing her mouth with obvious reluctance, her breathing was as harsh and labored as his own.

"Why...why did you do that?"

Smiling, Matt raised his hand, drawing her fingers to his lips. "Because I wanted to," he said with simple directness. He kissed her fingertips, sending shards of sizzling awareness throughout her body. "I've had a hankering to kiss you ever since I opened my eyes and saw you this morning, there in that room you called the ICU unit."

"Really?" Virginia felt like an idiot for voicing the question, but she didn't care. In fact, at that moment she didn't care much about anything. On the fringes of her mind, she knew she was acting, reacting, in an uncharacteristic manner, but she didn't care about that, either. What she did care about was the sensations he was creating inside her by stroking his tongue over her fingers.

"Yes," Matt murmured, curling his tongue around one finger and drawing it into his mouth. "And since this morning, the hankering's grown into something fierce." Though his voice was raw, muffled, she heard every word.

"It...it has? In what way?" Virginia knew, yet a need that had been buried and suppressed, demanded she hear his answer.

His laughter was low, dark, exciting. "In every way imaginable," he replied, staring candidly into her wide eyes. "I've been itchin' to tear your beautiful, shocking clothes off and pull you into this bed. I want to feel you, warm and soft, beneath me."

Virginia was already soft, from deep inside to the surface of her skin, soft and warm and...astonished at herself. She also noted his use of the word *shocking*. Dragging her gaze from his hooded, sexy eyes, she glanced down at her clothing. She agreed with part of his remark. The suit and blouse were beautiful, but...

"Shocking?" She frowned and raised her eyes to his. "What's shocking about my clothes?"

Matt's gaze drifted to her legs, and lingered appreciatively on the exposed expanse of nylon-clad calves and ankles. "Not that I'm complaining, you understand," he said, a slow smile curving his lips as he returned his gaze to hers. "But you've only got half a skirt, and I never have seen heels that high on a lady's shoes."

The term "lady" was a tip-off. Comprehension dawned in Virginia's mind, clearing the fog of sensuality. It also underscored her belief in his credibility.

"You really are from the nineteenth century," she said in a tone of sheer awe. "Aren't you?"

Her question had an immediate, deflating effect on him. All the fire and passion visibly drained from him, leaving him looking exhausted and bereft. He heaved a deep sigh. "Yes, I am from the nineteenth century," Matt replied in weary tones that tore at her heart. "I swear that everything I've told you is true, Ginnie."

"I never doubted that you believed what you were telling me, Matt," Virginia said softly. "But I—" She broke off, startled by his sudden violent curse and movement.

"Dammit, Ginnie, I am not crazy!" he exploded. "Look at this!" Letting go her hand, he reached for his belongings at the foot of the bed. "I want you to look at this stuff, examine all of it, and then tell me I'm crazy."

Virginia was hurting for him, hurting so badly that her throat ached and felt raw and tight. "Matt, I never said that I thought you were—" But again he cut her off, this time with a sweeping gesture and a rough command.

"Look at it, damn you."

An odd sensation coiling in the pit of her stomach, Virginia moved to obey. With a sense of disbelief and amazement she identified the sensation as fear. Matt looked so fierce, sounded so angry that he actually frightened her. Speechless with incredulity, she reached out for an article of clothing. She was obviously too slow to satisfy him.

"Look at this," he ordered, scooping a heavy, thigh-length, dark-colored coat from the pile. "And these," he continued, holding aloft a jacket and pants, both obviously made from the same black, rough-textured material.

Having registered the fact that morning that his attire appeared to be from an earlier epoch, Virginia was nodding in mute agreement when he growled a low curse.

"Dammit, that was my best shirt." Clutched in his big hands was a white shirt with a small hole and a large blood-stain on the right front breast panel. "It's ruined," he muttered, reaching again for the coat and jacket. "And so are both of these.'' Shaking his head in disgust, he dipped his hand into the pocket of the coat and withdrew a mangled-looking small pouch and a packet of papers. ''The wet soaked through to my makin's,'' he murmured in a mournful tone.

''Makin's?'' Virginia repeated.

Matt gave her an impatient glare. ''My tobacco and papers,'' he said. ''They're soggy, useless. Wouldn't you know it? Just when I needed a smoke, too.''

Virginia's response was automatic. ''You shouldn't smoke, anyway. It's unhealthy.''

Matt stared at her for what seemed to stretch into a very long time. ''First coffee, now tobacco.'' His lip curled. ''Next you'll be telling me sex ain't healthy.''

No, she wouldn't be telling him that. Virginia kept her response to herself. To avoid a reply, she returned her attention to his belongings. The boots and hat were well-worn, similar to yet different from their modern counterparts. ''What's in the bag?'' she asked, raising her eyes to his.

''Not much.'' Matt shrugged. ''I travel light.'' Grabbing the bag, he pulled it to him, then proceeded to empty the contents onto the bed. There was underwear—a pair of long johns—all in one piece. There was a pair of thick, off-white socks. Next he produced an official-looking badge, with the words United States Marshal carved around the rim. After the badge, he withdrew a large silver pocket watch, the lid of which was beautifully chased with the outline of a locomotive. The final article was the largest and deadliest looking of the lot. In her opinion, a gun and holster were not a pretty sight.

''Ugly things,'' she said, giving way to the shiver of revulsion moving through her.

Matt frowned as he shifted his gaze from her to the holster, then back to her. ''Ugly?'' he echoed indignantly. ''I'll have you know that this here is a hand-tooled scabbard, made to my specifications for this Colt Peacemaker.'' As he spoke, he drew the long-barreled pistol from the leather holster, and held it out for her inspection.

Virginia recoiled as if he had offered her a ticking bomb. "I don't like guns!" she exclaimed.

Matt made a wry face, but shoved the revolver back into the holster. "The gun won't hurt you, you know," he drawled. "It can't do a damn thing all on its lonesome."

"I've heard that argument," she snapped. "I still don't like guns." She suppressed another shiver. "I'd appreciate it if you'd put it back in the bag."

"In a minute," Matt promised, smiling faintly. "The scabbard carries a few things other than artillery." Turning it over, he began poking at the inside of the broad belt.

Watching him, Virginia frowned and asked a question. "Why did you call it a scabbard?"

The glance he shot at her said reams about what he thought of her intelligence. "Because that's what it is."

Controlling her irritation, she retorted, "I know that casings for rifles are called scabbards, but I've never heard the term in reference to a pistol."

"That so?" he drawled. "Strange, but where I come from it's called a scabbard."

"Not a holster?" she persisted.

Matt shrugged. "By some, maybe. Mostly by greenhorns."

Studying him while he continued to poke his fingers along the inside of the belt, Virginia decided that Matthew Hawk could prove to be a living, breathing history lesson on the life and times of the old West. Intrigued by the possibilities he presented, she wasn't paying much attention to the objects he removed one by one from small slits in the belt. She jumped when he let out a muffled whoop of satisfaction.

"Aha! There you go," he announced, dropping a handful of shiny gold coins onto the bed in front of her. "I'd be obliged if you'd take some of those and buy me a new shirt."

Some of those? Systematically counting the coins, Virginia was jolted once again by shock. The gold coins appeared newly minted...all bore the date 1889. At face value, their total amounted to $275. She couldn't begin to as much as guess at the value of the coins to a numismatist.

"Where did you get these?" she asked without thinking, glancing at him in surprise.

"Well, I sure as hell didn't steal them," he shot back at her. "I was paid right before I left Texas, tracking that longrider."

"I didn't think that you stole them," Virginia protested. "And what is a longrider?"

"An outlaw," Matt said. "And what did you think, if not that I'd stolen the money?"

Virginia felt as though she had been plunged back into far-out land. "I didn't mean anything," she said in soothing tones. "I was just so surprised. Do you have any idea what these coins are probably worth?"

"Sure, $275," he replied, frowning.

"No." Virginia shook her head vigorously. "They were worth that in 1889," she said. "I couldn't begin to evaluate their worth to a numismatist on today's market."

"A new what?"

"Nu-mis-ma-tist," she enunciated. "An expert who collects rare coins."

"Well, fancy that," he murmured, smiling in a secret, contemplative way. "You really think these couple little coins are valuable, then?"

"Yes." Confused, and suspicious of his enigmatic smile and attitude, Virginia narrowed her eyes and demanded, "What are you thinking?"

"Right now, this minute?"

"Yes."

"I'm thinking that I've gotta go." He moved restlessly and glanced around the room. "If you would just point me in the right direction, I'd be much obliged." Favoring his shoulder, he began shifting to the edge of the bed.

"Wait!" Virginia flung out an arm to stop him. She missed. He slid off the bed and stood up...to a height she judged to be at least six foot three. "You don't have to get up. I'll call the nurse for the bedpan."

"No, thank you, ma'am." Matt gave a short, decisive shake of his shaggy head. "The nurse brought that pan in this morning." He shuddered. "I'm not going through that embarrassment again. Tell me where it's located. I'll go out."

Out? Virginia's mind went blank. When she realized what he meant, she went pink. "For heaven's sake, you don't have to go outside!" Jumping up, she strode to the closed bathroom door. Pushing the door open, she indicated the room beyond with a flick of her hand. "It's in here."

He gave her a dry look. "I should've known. Even back in my time I'd heard about them."

Virginia's eyebrows flew up. "Really."

"Yes, really," he drawled, moving toward her.

The regulation hospital gown he was wearing did little to conceal his long-muscled, rangy body. Feeling her avid interest in the width of his shoulders, the narrowness of his waist and hips and the powerful length of his legs unprofessional, Virginia drew her fascinated eyes away from him. Her gaze flew back to his when he laughed softly.

"Now don't tell me the sight of a nearly naked man embarrasses you," he murmured as he stopped beside her. "And you a doctor, ma'am."

What Virginia could have told him was that the sight of a man, nearly or fully naked, hadn't embarrassed her since her second year of medical school. It was only the sight of *his* nearly naked body that had this effect on her. Of course, she didn't tell him any of it. She didn't say a word. Managing to look superior she gave another, impatient flick of her hand toward the bathroom.

She followed him inside. He turned to scowl at her. She offered him a sweet smile. "Wouldn't you like the accommodations explained?"

"Make it quick."

She did. "I'll be right outside the door if you should need me," Virginia said, retreating.

Fighting persistent images of his too-attractive body, while denying the pull of attraction she was feeling for him, she stood outside the bathroom door, alternately hoping he'd need her help and praying that he wouldn't. She heard the loud rush of water from the flush, then a less forceful flow from the sink tap. She started when he suddenly pulled open the door.

"What is all this stuff?" Matt asked, frowning at the plastic case he was holding.

"This is a very up-to-the-minute hospital," Virginia informed him in smug tones. "That case contains the basic necessities a patient might need."

"Yeah?" He arched his dark brows. "But, like I said, what is it all...what's it for?"

With amused forbearance, Virginia named the articles and described their use as he removed them one by one from the case. "Toothbrush—to clean the teeth," she said when he extracted the plastic-handled brush.

"I knew that," he retorted. He pulled out one of several small tubes. "This?"

"Toothpaste." She grinned. "To clean the teeth."

Matt looked impressed. "I always used salt." He withdrew another tube.

"Bath and shower gel."

"Like soap?"

"Yes." She fought a smile.

"What's a shower?"

The smile won. "I'll show you in a minute. Next?"

Yet another tube was withdrawn. "This is the last of these little things."

"Shampoo." Virginia bit her tongue to keep herself from adding that he really had use for that particular product. "For cleaning the hair."

"What's wrong with soap?"

She shrugged. "Too harsh."

Matt snorted derisively. "And this?" He held up a small pump spray plastic bottle.

"Deodorant." She nearly choked on the word. Before he had a chance to ask, she explained. "After removing the cap, you hold it like this and depress the button," she said, demonstrating as she spoke.

"Perfume?" he said indignantly.

"No, it's antiperspirant." Virginia frowned. "Well, there is some scent added."

"Uh-huh." He returned the bottle to the case.

Virginia hid a smile. "I'm sure you recognize the pocket comb and brush. Any other questions?"

"What's a shower?"

She burst out laughing. "You're like a dog with a bone! Okay, pay attention." Walking past him, she drew back the curtains to reveal the tub and shower. Bending over, she turned the water taps. "You adjust the cold and hot flow until the water is the temperature you prefer. Then you flip this switch—" again she demonstrated "—and there's your shower," she finished as the water sprayed forth.

"Thank you," Matt said politely. "Now get out."

"What?" Virginia stood erect and turned to stare at him. "Why?"

"Because I'm going to test the shower."

"Oh, no you're not!"

"Oh, yes, I am." His smile dared her to argue further. "Would you like to test it with me?"

"No, thanks," Virginia retorted, thinking that men obviously never change. "You'll soak the dressing on your wound."

His grin widened. "That's okay. My doctor can apply a fresh dressing when I'm through."

After years of confrontations with patients, Virginia had learned when to stand and fight and when to cut her losses and withdraw; since Matt was yanking at the gown with supreme unconcern, she chose prudence and withdrew.

Matt was beneath the shower spray for a good half hour, during which Virginia put away his clothing and other belongings, got a clean gown and a robe out of the drawer for him, and then paced the small room. In the back of her mind, she registered the tinny announcement over the PA that it was eight o'clock and visiting hours were now over.

The wait was worth the agitation. When he walked out of the bathroom, Matt looked like a different man. His chiseled, angular face was shaved smooth. His towel-dried but still damp hair was gleaming clean. And he looked rawly masculine but almost presentable in the tightly belted cotton robe.

"You do a good job of work, lady," he said, raising his hand to his right upper chest. "That's the neatest I've ever been sewed up. The others are kinda rough and jagged."

Virginia winced at the description. "I'll be the judge of that. Come over to the bed and sit down, and I'll have a look at it," she instructed in her most professional tone.

"Yes, ma'am," he said smartly, padding barefooted to the rumpled bed.

Giving him a wry look, Virginia carefully moved aside the gown and robe. On viewing the wound, she was forced to agree with him. Her skill was apparent, and the wound was healing nicely. "I work neat," she drawled, reaching into the bedside cabinet drawer for a packaged sterile dressing.

"And I feel like a new man." Perched on the edge of the bed, Matt grinned at her as she tugged the robe into place over the fresh bandage she'd applied to his wound.

His innocuous remark triggered a memory that ricocheted through Virginia's mind. "Matt," she said in a small voice. "If the idea I had about your situation is correct, you *are* a new man…in a new place."

"What do you mean?" he asked, losing his grin to a frown. "Are you talking about that time warp thing?"

"Yes." Virginia sighed.

His eyes were cool, his voice was steady. "I think it's time you explained it to me."

"Yes, I think it is." Sliding onto the chair pulled up to the bed next to him, she began, "I don't know much about it, myself, but I'll explain as best I can." She paused to sort through her thoughts. He gave her a verbal nudge.

"Shoot, time's a'wastin'."

"Well, as I understand it, there have been some stories and reports of people who, caught in some manner of a warp or crack in time, have been transposed from one period of time to another, both backward and forward. It's commonly called time travel. These stories and reports are all undocumented and unsubstantiated, of course."

"Do you believe that this time travel is possible?" Matt's bright, shrewd eyes pierced hers.

"No." Virginia drew a deep breath before qualifying, "At least I didn't until today."

Matt was quiet for several minutes. When he did finally speak, his voice held a faraway, thoughtful softness. "Do you think that's what happened to me...that I was somehow picked up there and dropped here?"

"I don't know, Matt," she answered honestly. "But I can't think of any other explanation."

"Hmm," Matt murmured, nodding. Then, suddenly rigid, he asked, "Do you think it could happen again? I mean, that I'd be swept up here and dumped down there again?"

Virginia was developing a pounding headache. Massaging her throbbing temples, she gave him a helpless look. "I don't know. As I told you, I really know very little about it. Up until today I assumed the theory of time travel was pure fiction."

Matt looked as helpless as she felt. He nodded in agreement, but said, "Yet here I am."

"Yes." The single word held a wealth of emotion.

There ensued a long period of silence, during which both

were sunk in their own thoughts. Matt shattered the quiet with a soft, anguished cry.

"What am I gonna do, Ginnie? I can't go back over a hundred years…can I?"

"No." Answering him was difficult, but even more difficult was the terrible thought that suddenly occurred to her. The image of a woman, perhaps with her children around her, rose to torment Virginia. "Matt!" she exclaimed. "Are you…were you…married?"

He gave a quick but reassuring shake of his head. "Never stayed in one place long enough," he replied. He paused, frowning, then said slowly, "It's funny, but a woman, a wife, was one of the reasons why I was going to church last night—" He caught himself, then corrected, "that night."

"I don't understand." Virginia felt a stabbing twinge that she wasn't inclined to examine. "Do you mean you were going to the church to meet a woman?"

"No. I didn't know any of the women in that town." Matt shrugged. "But I had decided to quit, turn in my badge." Unconsciously he mixed his tenses. "I'm so tired of it…the hunt and the kill when nothing else works but killing. I was thinking that there had to be a better way to keep the peace, and a better way to live."

The brilliant blue of his eyes dimmed and grew opaque. "I was thinking of a decent life…starting with a horse ranch, nothing big, just a small outfit to begin." His smile was weary, and sympathy welled up within her. "I suppose what I was planning to do was ask the Boss for a second chance, with a place of my own, a child of my own, a woman of my own." He gave a short snort of laughter that held little humor. "Instead, I find myself in a strange place, in a strange time, with a box with little people in it, and a woman who believes I'm loco."

Near tears, Virginia impulsively reached out to grasp his hand. "Matt, no, I don't believe that, truly I don't." Until then she had only a vague idea of how disoriented and displaced he must be feeling. The enormity of the sensation he had to be experiencing hit her like an actual blow. "You're not alone, Matt. I'm here."

His eyes cleared and he smiled at her. "I appreciate that, but it's not being alone that bothers me. I've been alone a long time. I'm used to it." Moving his head slowly, he glanced around the room. His fingers tightened around hers when his gaze settled on the television set, still animated and blaring away on its shelf. "I don't understand half of what I've seen and heard since I woke up. I can't go back, and I don't know my way around your time and place." He turned to her, his expression stark. "Ginnie, when I leave your hospital, I'll have nowhere to go."

While he was still speaking, Virginia thought of a solution to his dilemma. She blurted it out before she had a chance to change her mind. "You're wrong, Matt. You do have someplace to go to when you leave here."

"Where?"

Virginia was already regretting her impetuousness. Nevertheless, she replied in a steady voice. "You can stay at my place."

Six

Now that she had him, what in the world was she going to do with him?

Wondering if she had lost her mind, Virginia shut the door and slumped back against it. Resting her head on the smooth panel, she stared at the man standing in the center of the living room.

What had possessed her to offer him the haven of her home? He was a stranger, not only to her but to everyone in the community. Virginia had regretted her impulsive invitation moments after making it, but she hadn't had the heart to retract it. He had looked so lost, so vulnerable.

While she was questioning herself and studying him, Matt was taking slow, comprehensive stock of her apartment. Her reaction to seeing him there, seeming to dwarf her private space, was as unnerving and thought-provoking as his appeared to be…if his expression was anything to go by.

Thirty-odd hours had passed since Virginia had made the

impulsive offer to Matt. During that period, every one of her waking hours had been crammed full with seventy minutes' worth of things to do. Through some innate wizardry she hadn't realized she possessed, she had managed to complete every one of those things...except provide him with "the makin's" he had asked her to pick up.

Matt's reaction to her offer was immediate and grateful—and followed at once by a demand to know when he could leave the hospital. He had seen his wound when she'd redressed it, and knew that it was well along in the healing process. Arguing that he was feeling, in his words, "Strong enough to lick my weight in wildcats," he pressed her to release him.

Since her professional opinion coincided with his argument, Virginia made a bargain with him, telling him she would allow him to leave if he behaved himself for one more day. Matt gave her his word, and she was left with little more but to follow through on her promise.

In retrospect, and under the circumstances, she decided that the sooner he was safely installed in her apartment, out of sight of curious eyes and questions, the better.

Virginia had encountered the first of those eyes and questions as she was leaving the hospital around nine o'clock Christmas night. Carrying the admission form, which she and Matt had reworked together—in her opinion a creative piece of fiction, indeed—she had run into Jeff Klein, the young patrolman who had been at the scene of Matt's advent into the twentieth century.

"I'm on my way in to see your patient," Jeff said. "I stopped by before I went off duty this morning, but the nurse told me he was asleep." His smile was tired. "I need some information for my report. I hope he's awake."

"Sorry, Jeff. I just left his room, and he's out for the night." Virginia uttered the untruth with a silent prayer for forgiveness. "Perhaps I can help you." She displayed the admission form. "I have all the pertinent information on him, but I must warn you that there isn't much."

"I'll say," he muttered, scanning the form. Producing a notebook from his inside pocket, Jeff jotted down the information. "Did he tell you anything about what happened?" he asked hopefully, returning the notebook to his pocket.

Because she and Matt had rehearsed the account to be given, Virginia was prepared to answer. "Yes, but again, there really isn't all that much."

"Some cops have all the luck." Jeff sighed. "Okay, I'm listening. Fire when ready."

Virginia registered in passing the realization that men seemed to have a penchant for identifying with guns. Matt had said "Shoot," and now Jeff said, "Fire when ready." She couldn't help but wonder if there were some psychological, quintessentially masculine reason for the association. Maybe she'd discuss the idea with the hospital's resident psychiatrist. Then again, maybe she wouldn't. The staff psychiatrist was a gun collector.

Shrugging off the odd thought, Virginia launched into the story that she and Matt had concocted.

"Well, from the sketchy information he's given me, I gather that Matthew Hawk is a drifter. Not a vagrant, a drifter," she hastened to clarify. "As you've seen from the admission form, he is originally from Texas...Fort Worth, and was drifting through Conifer when the accident occurred."

"Accident?" Jeff queried, raising his eyebrows into a skeptical arch.

"Hmm." Virginia nodded. "Mr. Hawk insists the shooting must have been accidental, since he doesn't know anybody in the area, and hasn't been here long enough to have made any enemies. He suggests that perhaps the accident was caused by a youngster, secretly fooling around with some adult's rifle." She held her breath when she finished, positive that Jeff would reject the theory. To her astonishment, he didn't.

"Possible," he said thoughtfully. "Around here, more

than possible." He sighed once more. "Was there any identification on him that I missed when I searched him? Driver's license? Social security number? Anything?"

"No, nothing. All we have is what he told me." Virginia swallowed and plunged. "Really, Jeff, I believe you can write this one off as an accident, caused by person or persons unknown, and forget it."

"He was wearing a gun, Doctor!" Jeff exclaimed. "And I've been kicking myself all day for not taking it off of him when I had the opportunity."

"Oh, come on, Jeff!" Virginia forced an easy-sounding laugh. "Every other male in this community owns a gun and either wears it or carries it at some time or other."

"Yeah." Jeff nodded. "Even so, I'm going to run a record check on him through Fort Worth and Washington, just in case he's wanted somewhere."

Lots of luck, Virginia thought wryly. Aloud, she agreed that the precaution was wise. "Let me know what you learn about him," she added, with more interest than Jeff could imagine, or than her casual tone implied.

Virginia slept badly Christmas night. She had arrived home to find three messages from Richard on her machine. She listened to his injured-sounding voice, then without a qualm erased the tape, reset the machine, and dropped into bed. Yet sleep eluded her. Her tired mind whirled with disjointed fragments of the day, the first day of her holiday break.

What a Christmas present! Virginia thought, muffling an incipient burst of hysterical laughter. Time travel! It was simply too much—too weird, too outlandish. Who would believe it? She was finding it nearly impossible to believe herself.

But Matt was real...Lord, was he real! His searing kiss attested to that. Virginia's lips still burned, her senses still vibrated in response to his sensuous brand of reality.

But time travel?

Impossible. There had to be another explanation. The concept of time travel was the stuff of fiction.

But...how to explain Matt's genuine bafflement?

Matt.

When Virginia finally did fall asleep, it was with unanswered questions teasing her mind and the taste of a nineteenth-century man on her lips.

It was early when she awoke, startled from slumber by a dream in which she was flying through space and time, with the sound of Richard's voice calling to her to come back.

Getting up and dragging her tired body from the rumpled bed, Virginia caught a glimpse of herself in the mirror and decided she looked like the leftovers from the holiday meal....

And now, watching in silence as Matt examined his new surroundings, Virginia smiled and ran an appreciative, self-congratulatory glance over his new attire.

Armed with her credit card and the measurements she had taken from his clothing, she had left the apartment early yesterday morning to do battle with the throng of shoppers, eager to take advantage of the traditional day after Christmas sales. The chore had been exhausting, but the results were definitely worth the effort expended.

The articles of clothing she had selected for him were identical to the winter apparel that the majority of male residents generally wore: jeans, plaid flannel shirts and an outer jacket, in this case a ski parka instead of the more usually seen hunting jacket. She had purchased socks and packages of underwear for him, as well. So Matt should have looked much the same as every other man in town.

He didn't, and the difference couldn't solely be attributed to the Western hat pulled down low on his forehead or the scuffed boots sticking out of the bottom of his jeans. No, the difference between Matt and every other man Virginia had ever met involved much more than mere appearance, even though the way he looked played a large part in it.

The soft material of the shirt delineated the width of his shoulders and the breadth of his flatly muscled chest. The jeans appeared to have been made expressly for his long, rangy body, riding low on his hips and smooth over his narrow, tight buttocks.

In summation, on Matt the clothes were not an affectation or a fashion statement, but a reflection of a man of his time. The clothes fitted—in more ways than one. The only item missing was his gun belt, and that was hidden inside one of the store bags he had set on the floor next to his booted feet.

Observing him as he absently removed the hat and parka, Virginia concluded that Matt looked even less like the more formally dressed businessmen in the community—a hundred years less like them.

An image of one such businessman came to mind. Frowning in concentration, she attempted to draw a comparison between Matt and Richard Quinter. It was an exercise in futility, because there *was* no comparison. Though Richard was without question handsome, urbane and up-to-the-minute in his choice of attire, he paled into insignificance beside the more simply clothed, magnificent presence of Matthew Hawk.

Odd. She had always considered Richard to be the epitome of maleness.... Virginia's thoughts scattered as Matt chose that moment to turn to look at her.

"It's all...all..." His voice faded, as if he couldn't find words to describe his feelings.

"All a bit much to take in?"

"Yeah." Matt gave her a wry smile. "I think I might still be in shock from the ride."

Recalling his expression at his first sight of her car when they left the hospital, Virginia laughed. "You didn't appear in the least shocked," she said. "As a matter of fact, I would have sworn you enjoyed the ride immensely."

Matt's eyes gleamed with amusement. "As a matter of fact, I did. It sure as hell beats freezing your butt on the back of a horse.'' He laughed. ''Come to that, it's a damn sight faster and more comfortable, too.''

The enticing sound of his laughter curled around her heart. In an effort to combat the growing familiarity of the warmth that was spreading through her, Virginia pulled her expression into stern lines of disapproval. ''You swear a lot,'' she said in a cool, chastising tone. ''Don't you?''

''Sure.'' Matt's teeth flashed dazzling white in a teasing grin, giving silent testimony to one of the three twentieth-century conveniences he had quickly become addicted to; Matt loved the taste of toothpaste. He also loved standing under the shower and staring at the television screen. ''Must've picked it up from the company I keep.''

''*Used* to keep,'' Virginia said, reminding him that he was no longer in the old West.

''Yeah.'' He sighed. ''Even with all I've seen in the last couple days, it's still hard to believe.''

''I know.''

''I suppose it's a lot for you to handle, too,'' he said, smiling faintly.

''Yes.''

His smile widened into a grin and he nodded toward a spot behind her. ''I can't help but wonder. Are you propping it up, or is it supporting you?''

''What?''

''The door.'' He arched an eyebrow. ''Are you too tired to move, or are you hanging there by the door to make a quick break, if I jump in the wrong direction?''

Reminded in turn of the kiss they'd shared Christmas night, Virginia was suddenly infused with a different kind of warmth. Both startled and made wary by the blatant sensuality of that warmth and her own responsive heat, she had avoided close contact with him since then. How she was going to manage now, with him installed in her apartment, was the question she had yet to answer.

''No, of course not,'' she denied, straightening as she

stepped briskly into the room. "I was giving you time to get accustomed to the apartment."

His eyes glittered, silently calling her a liar. "Is this the whole of it?" he asked, glancing around the room.

"No," Virginia replied, slipping out of her coat as she walked by him. "This is the living room. Let me hang your jacket and hat in the closet, then follow me. I'll give you the grand tour of the place and show you your room."

The apartment was spacious, and equivalent in size to an average house. Virginia didn't rent the place, she owned it. It contained a kitchen with a tiny dining area attached, the living room, three bedrooms, the smallest of which she had made into a den, a central bath and a half bath connected to the largest bedroom. It was tastefully furnished, yet homey and comfortable—the kind of place where a woman or man could relax after a rough day on the job.

Matt was noticeably impressed by the size of the place and its furnishings and appliances. "This is all yours?" he asked as they returned to the living room. "And you live here alone?"

"Yes." Virginia laughed. "This is my home."

His brows shot up in surprise. "It's yours?" Matt asked with undisguised incredulity. "You own it?"

"It's mine." Virginia felt a thrill of justifiable pleasure and pride in what she considered the fruits of her skill and dedication to her chosen profession. "I own it."

Matt responded true to form. "Damn," he murmured, skimming his gaze around the room. "The house I grew up in wasn't half this big or half again this pretty." He returned his gaze to her, stunning her with a blaze of undiluted admiration. "You are one impressive lady, Doctor."

Delighted by the compliment, warmed all over by the heat from his eyes, Virginia was reduced to a flustered stammer. "Why, tha-thank you! I...I'm..." Not sure herself what she wanted to say, she averted her gaze from his gleaming eyes and changed the topic. "Ah...I suppose we ought to get you settled," she improvised, catching sight of the bags containing his things. "If you'll grab those bags, I'll—" The sudden sharp ring of the phone interrupted her.

The trilling ring had an astonishing effect on Matt. His head snapped up and his eyes, narrowed and alert, searched out the source of potential danger. Although there had been a phone on the cabinet beside his bed, and Virginia had explained the functioning of the instrument to him, it had not rung once during Matt's short stay in the hospital.

The instrument might be something of a marvel, but not to the extent of transmitting a call from the Montana of the 1890's, Virginia thought, commiserating with his reaction.

"It's only the phone, Matt," she said in a calming voice. "If you'll excuse me, I'll be with you in a—"

"Go ahead," he interrupted her, his lips curving into a self-mocking smile. "I can find my way."

Tossing him a quick smile in return, Virginia took off at a run for the kitchen phone.

Gathering up the store bags, Matt headed for the room she had told him would be his. His long strides faltered at the breathless sound of Virginia's voice as he passed the archway into the kitchen.

"Oh, hello, Richard."

Irritation flickered inside Matt as he continued into the short hallway leading to the bedrooms.

Richard? he thought, swinging shut the door to his room with more force than necessary. Who in hell was Richard?

There was no way he could know the answer to his question. He knew practically nothing about Virginia in general, and nothing at all about her personal life in particular. A scowl drew Matt's dark brows together at the realization that he in fact knew nothing about much of anything in this strange new world in which he found himself.

Crossing the room, he dropped the bags onto the bed, then stood looking around at his temporary new home. Even though Virginia had apologized for what she called the room's sparse utilitarian furnishings—a plain single bed, dresser and nightstand—Matt liked the room. It was by far cleaner, brighter and better furnished than any other room he'd ever had. In truth, he liked the entire apartment, with all its intriguing gadgets and appliances yet to be investigated. But most of all Matt liked Virginia, and was looking forward to investigating her, even more than the gadgets and appliances.

Virginia.

Merely thinking her name set Matt's blood on fire and caused a sweet, painful tightness in his body. A vision of her as she'd entered his room on Christmas morning filled his mind. Tall, slender, breathtaking, with her shining blond hair flowing around her shoulders and her beautiful legs exposed to his hungry gaze. At his very first sight of her, he had thought he'd died and she was an angel, but when she'd come to his room later with her face painted and her legs revealed, he had equated her with the loose women of his acquaintance…not an angel at all, but a wanton.

Matt had never been slow to learn. And through that amazing box she called a television, he quickly realized that her attire, her enhanced coloring and her overall appearance were the style of the day. Virginia looked like every other female he saw on the TV, only better…a whole helluva lot better.

From the very beginning, she had created an ache inside him that gnawed and fiercely tortured his body. More than anything he'd ever wanted before in his life, Matt wanted Virginia. But all he had received so far was a large dose of frustration.

Because she had kept her distance from him since Christmas night, he had only kissed her that one time, yet one kiss had fanned the flames of his desire into an insatiable appetite for more of the same. A taste of Virginia was not nearly enough for Matt; he craved, nay ached, to devour her like a sumptuous banquet, beginning with her luscious mouth and ending…

Matt shuddered and longed for a cigarette. Damn, how

he wished Virginia had bought him the makin's he had asked her to get.

Virginia. To Matt she was richer, headier than the tobacco from the state that bore her name. And his need for her was infinitely stronger than his desire for a smoke.

In an attempt to suppress both, Matt absently stowed his few belongings in the deep dresser drawers. Although the bags were quickly emptied, he wasn't very successful in controlling either one of his clamoring desires.

The chore finished, Matt sat down on the bed and tried to ignore his appetites by contemplating his present situation.

How had he gotten here? he wondered, glancing around at the room that existed, in effect, over a hundred years after his own time. Even though Virginia had explained the theory of time travel to him, Matt was having difficulty in believing, let alone accepting her explanation. And yet everything he had seen since regaining consciousness confirmed that he was definitely not in the same time frame he'd been in when he was shot.

Recalling the events of that Christmas Eve, Matt frowned in concentration.

He had been tired, filled with despair, a sickness growing inside him against the kind of life he was living. He had been on his way to church. Seeking what? Solace? Redemption? Or simply to beg God for another chance, for a decent life, for a...

Matt's thoughts fragmented, then regrouped to focus on his thinking process during those final moments before he had lost consciousness. He had been thinking that there would be no second chance, no decent life, no *woman* of his own, and then...and then he had cried out, invoking God's name, silently screaming that he could not die. And when he had regained consciousness, he had opened his eyes and seen...

Virginia!

Stunned by the implication, Matt's mind went blank for

an instant. When it cranked up again, it spun off thoughts almost faster than he could assimilate them.

Feeling the lifeblood draining from him after he'd been shot, Matt had felt, known he was going to die. And yet here he was, not dead but very much alive. Had he been granted another chance by calling on the name of God? Had some spiritual hand plucked him up in the hills of Montana and set him down again in the mountains of Pennsylvania, right in the path of this one particular woman?

Matt shook his head like a greenhorn whose senses had been rattled by a toss from the back of a bronc.

The notion was crazy, he told himself. Even more crazy than Virginia's idea of a time warp. Why, he reasoned, would the Almighty fling him over a hundred years into the future? Then again, what was time to God?

In much the same manner as had happened that night, old, forgotten words whispered through his mind. He didn't know if the words were complete or in their proper order, but they settled the issue for him, just the same.

The Lord works in strange and mysterious ways.

Matt was still sitting on the bed, pondering strange and mysterious ways, when his introspection was interrupted by a light rap against the door, followed by the soft, beguiling sound of Virginia's voice.

"Matt, may I come in?"

"Sure," he replied, in a laconic tone that belied the excitement shimmering inside him. He was standing beside the bed when she entered, an inquisitive expression on his face and a feeling of possessiveness in his soul.

"Settled in?" Her smile tore a chunk out of his heart.

"Who's Richard?" Matt asked the question that had been simmering beneath his surface thoughts.

Virginia's smile dimmed, just a mite. "A friend."

Matt raised his brows. "A special friend?" His tone deliberately suggested intimacy.

"I beg your pardon?" Her smile vanished.

"You know what I mean," Matt chided softly.

The warmth drained from her beautiful eyes. "No," Virginia said in a cool, distant tone. "I'm afraid you'll have to spell it out for me."

Matt was suddenly positive his suspicions were correct, but he wasn't at all sure he wanted to hear them confirmed. Still, some inner, green-eyed demon had to know. "I mean," he said with soft emphasis, "have you been together?"

"In the biblical sense?" she asked in frigid tones.

Matt exploded. "Yes, dammit!"

Virginia raised her chin and looked him squarely in the eyes. "That, Mr. Hawk, is none of your damn business."

His steps slow, Matt advanced on her. "I'm making it my business." As he moved forward, she retreated, until her back made contact with the door. He caged her there by planting his hands against the panel on either side. "Now," he murmured when she was trapped, "have you been with him?"

Helpless but clearly undaunted, Virginia continued to hold his gaze and glared at him in apparent fearlessness. He'd respected her before and now the sense deepened. "You are a guest in my home," she said bitingly. "You have no right whatever to question me about my love life or anything else."

"Oh, but I do have that right, Virginia," Matt corrected her, lowering his head to brush his mouth over hers. The fact that her response was evidently against her will sent shards of candescent pleasure to every inch of his body, a pleasure deepened by the breathless quality of her voice.

"By what right?" she demanded.

"Oh, didn't you know?" Matt lifted his head to smile at her. "You are God's answer to my Christmas prayer."

Seven

"What did you say?" Virginia asked, positive she hadn't heard what she thought she'd heard.

"I said I have the right, because you are God's answer to my Christmas prayer," Matt repeated.

"That's what I thought you said," she muttered, thinking that perhaps she should have consulted the psychiatrist, after all. "But you don't really believe that," she went on hopefully. "Do you?"

"Sure," Matt drawled. "It's the only explanation that makes any sense."

"Well, it doesn't make sense to me!" she cried. "Why would you believe that?"

"You remember I told you I was on my way to church when I was shot?" He raised his head a few inches to look into her wary eyes.

"Yes, I remember, but—"

"But wait," Matt cut in. "I didn't tell you all of it." He paused, his eyes cloudy with recollection. "I thought I was a goner for sure.... No, I knew I was dying.'' He shook his head. ''And I knew I wasn't going to get another chance, a chance for a decent life, a place of my own, a woman of my own.'' His eyes cleared, glittering with inner conviction. ''Right before I passed out, I called out to God, telling him I couldn't die.'' He stared into her widened eyes with a drilling intensity. ''When I came to, you were the first thing I saw.'' He smiled. ''At first I thought you were an angel. Now I believe that you were God's answer to my dying prayer.''

A spasm of unease flickered in Virginia's stomach as the precariousness of her position hit her. She was trapped in a bedroom with a man who believed she had been given to him in answer to his prayers. The added realization that the merest brush of his mouth over her own sent desire racing through her certainly didn't improve her lot. What if he decided to claim her—here and now?

The thought had an unnerving effect on Virginia. The uneasy feeling in her stomach flared into a blaze of excited anticipation. Her senses went wild, demanding...all kinds of tempting but forbidden pleasures. The very intensity of her involuntary response alerted her more rational, controlling common sense.

Pull it together, Doctor, Virginia advised herself, infusing strength into her weakened spine. Retain professional distance. You cannot afford to become emotionally involved in a situation that's already too bizarre to be believed. He's lost. Don't get lost with him. And the first order of business is to get yourself out of the bedroom!

Acting on her own excellent advice, she assumed her best bedside manner. ''What makes you so certain that I'm the answer to your prayer?''

''I told you,'' he said. ''It's the only thing that makes any sense.''

Virginia bit back an impatient retort in favor of a more reasonable reply. ''But you see, it doesn't make sense to me. I don't understand. I want you to explain it to me.''

"I want to kiss you."

"I don't think that would be wise," she said, talking to herself as well as to him. She was the only one listening; he was staring intently at her mouth.

"Ginnie, I need to kiss you." His breath whispered over her lips as he brought his mouth closer.

Virginia's blood raced in time with her heartbeat. Her pulse leaped and her throat went dry. Pressing the back of her head against the door, she shook it slowly, denying him, denying herself. "Matt, listen to me." Her voice was reedy, almost nonexistent. "I think we must talk about—"

"I think you talk too much," he murmured, silencing her with his mouth.

Virginia resisted the temptation of his hungry kiss for all of three seconds. Then her inner resources dissolved. Giving in to her own need, she surrendered to the irresistible allure of the hard mouth and body pressing against her. Raising her arms, she curled them around his waist. Trembling from the riot of sensations that were racing through her, she clung to him, absorbing his heat and hard strength, drowning in his taste.

His broad hands clasped her hips, aligning them to his own. Virginia gasped when he arched his body, making her aware of the need and passion she had aroused in him. She moaned low in her throat, when he thrust his tongue into her mouth, simulating a more complete possession.

She was on fire, and so was he. Virginia could feel his heated skin through the soft material of his shirt. She couldn't breathe, she couldn't think...and she didn't care. She didn't want to think, didn't even want to breathe; she wanted his kiss to go on for ever. He began to move; she moved with him. It was then that Virginia realized that he was trembling, too. She blinked and murmured a soft protest when he broke the kiss.

"Ginnie, come to bed with me." Matt's voice was raspy and his forehead was beaded with moisture. But it was the pallor beneath his sun-weathered skin that brought Virginia to her senses.

"Matt, are you in pain?" Snapping back into her role of physician, Virginia raised her palm to his face.

"I'm all right," he said, pulling away from her hand. "Or at least I will be, if you come to bed with me."

Even with only that brief touch, she had felt the fever in him sear her palm. "No, Matt. You're going to bed, but you're going alone," Virginia said decisively. "You've been under great strain, and your wound is not completely hea—" she broke off in alarm when he winced. "What is it? Are you in—? Matt!" she exclaimed as his arms suddenly dropped to his sides.

He tried to smile, but it came off as a grimace. "Shoulder hurts like hell." He took several quick, deep breaths. "I don't know," he said, shaking his head. "I feel kinda funny."

Slipping one arm around his waist, Virginia guided him to the side of the bed. "There's nothing funny about it," she said, yanking back the spread and covers with her free hand. "I think you'd better lie down before you fall down."

Running true to character, Matt resisted her efforts to help him onto the bed. "I'll be all right in a minute. I just need to catch my breath."

The emotional upheaval he had put her through, immediately followed by anxiety, took their toll on Virginia's nerves and patience. "Dammit, Matt, get into that bed!" she ordered, giving him a gentle shove.

Matt rocked on his feet but remained standing. "I will, if you'll lay down with me." He clenched his teeth and set his jaw at a determined angle.

Virginia's already frayed nerves were beginning to unravel. Silently railing against his obstinancy, yet reluctantly admiring his strength of purpose, she glared at him in mounting frustration. "Matt, listen to me," she said with soft entreaty. "You need to rest."

"I need you with me, beside me."

She could have withstood defiance or even belligerence, but against the forlorn note woven through his low voice she was defenseless. Virginia surrendered with a sigh. "All right, but it's time for your medication," she said, referring to the antibiotic she had prescribed to ward off infection. "You get undressed and get into bed, while I get it for you."

Matt caught her hand as she turned away. "You promise you'll come back?" His palm was hot and dry.

"Yes, of course I'll be back." She tugged against his hold, discovering how weak he really was when her fingers slipped free of his limp hand. "Do you need help undressing?"

He shook his head. "No, I need you," he muttered.

"I'll hurry," she promised, concern charging her with energy. Striding from the room, she went in search of her handbag, in which she had stashed his medication before they'd left the hospital. She found it exactly where she had set it down, on the kitchen table.

Moments later, carrying a glass of water, the antibiotic and two aspirin to combat his fever, Virginia reentered the room. She found Matt, clad now in cotton undershirt and shorts, seated on the side of the bed, his face strained from the effort of removing his boots. Crossing to him, she thrust the water glass in front of him with one hand and pushed him upright with the other.

"Here, you take these," she instructed, opening her hand to show him the capsule and aspirin. "I'll take care of those." She inclined her head to indicate the boots.

Virginia found the chore easier said than done...for more reasons than the simple fact that his boots resisted the tug of her hands. There was an element of distraction, and that element made her feel as feverish as he was.

Matt's jeans were bunched around the tops of his boots. His long legs were bare. His briefs were...brief...and molded to his manhood. While yanking ineffectually on his boots, Virginia trailed a glance up the length of his pale-skinned, dark-haired legs. She noted the tremors of fatigue rippling the long, solid muscles of his thighs, then stared in arrested fascination at the narrow scrap of navy blue cotton swathing his hips. She had no idea how long she had been staring, or how much longer she would have continued to do so, when her trancelike state was broken by the movement of his arm as he raised the glass to his lips to swallow the pills. Heat rushing to her head, Virginia pulled her gaze back to his boots.

What in heaven's name was wrong with her? she chastised herself scathingly, yanking at the footgear with renewed force. She had seen all manner of men stark naked, young, old, stout, slender, without batting an eyelash. She was a physician, a professional, and the last time she had flushed or felt uncomfortable about viewing the unadorned human form was in her second year of medical school. Yet now, with this one man, this obstreperous, demanding man, she fell apart, becoming all hot and squishy inside.

Ridiculous! An angry yank and the first boot pulled free.

Ludicrous! Another yank and the second boot joined its partner on the floor.

But true. Exhausted, Virginia flopped back onto the floor next to the boots.

"Thanks." Matt heaved a tired sigh and offered her a weak smile. "I was beginning to think I'd have to sleep with the damn things on."

"It plays hell with the sheets," Virginia retorted, smiling back at him.

"You're picking up my bad habit, Doc," he chided her, slowly raising a hand to rake his fingers through his long, shaggy hair. "But that's okay, I still like you." His eyelids drooping, he fell back and stretched his length on the bed. A blissful-sounding sigh escaped his slightly parted lips. "Get out of your clothes and come to bed, Ginnie. I need you beside me." Still suffering embarrassment over her unaccustomed reaction to his nearly nude body, she was on the point of refusing, when he demolished her will by appealing to her sympathy. "I'm cold and lonely."

Virginia was a qualified diagnostician. Judging by his symptoms, she was fairly certain that Matt would be physically unable to present a problem to her if she crawled into bed with him. But Virginia was wary, as well, and there was no way she was about to undress before getting into bed beside him—whether or not he was weak and running a fever.

She hesitated for a moment, then cast a rueful glance at her skirt and crisp, shirt-style blouse. Without a doubt the material would be crushed. Lifting her shoulders in a tired shrug, she scrambled up off the floor and onto the bed. Rather the skirt and blouse than herself.

Matt slung his good arm around her an instant after she slid onto the mattress next to him. Virginia went as stiff as a board. Mumbling her name, he drew her close, and tightening his hold, anchored her there. His body radiated a dry, burning heat. Compassion and another, more intimidating, emotion drained the resistance from her.

"Go to sleep, Matthew Hawk, United States marshal from the nineteenth century," she murmured, brushing the tousled curls from his face with a gentle touch. "Virginia Greyson, liberated woman physician of the twentieth century will watch over you."

Smiling at her unusual whimsy, Virginia cradled Matt's shivering body in her arms and pressed her soft lips to his moist brow. Within minutes, their bodies entwined, both Matt and Virginia were sound asleep.

It was late afternoon when the screech of tires on the parking lot beneath the bedroom window woke Virginia. Darkness had already settled in. For a moment, disoriented and feeling somewhat smothered, she didn't know where she was. A gentle snore near the top of her head brought memory rushing back.

Her first thought was for Matt. He appeared to be in a

deep, restful sleep. The heat of high fever no longer radiated from his relaxed body. Virginia felt the skin on his face and neck with a feather-light touch of her hand. It was cool. Holding her breath, she slipped free of the lax, heavy weight of the arm he had draped around her waist and the leg he had flung across her thigh. Matt grunted, but slept on. Sighing with relief, she tiptoed from the room.

Though her skirt and blouse indeed looked dead, a shower brought Virginia's mind and body back to life. Revived, she pulled on a cherry-red cotton knit sweater and black straight-legged jeans, then stepped into fur-lined house moccasins. Leaving her skin to breathe without makeup, she gave her hair a vigorous brushing, tossed the crackling mane off her shoulders, and left her bedroom in search of something to appease her complaining stomach.

Canned soup was heating on the stove, and Virginia was slicing cold chicken for sandwiches, when the unexpected sound of Matt's voice jolted her. She gasped and jumped. The sharp knife missed her finger by a hair.

"You're wearing men's pants!" he exclaimed in a sleepy voice.

Dropping the knife to the countertop, Virginia whirled to confront him. "For heaven's sake, Matt, you startled me so badly, I nearly amputated my finger!"

"Dammit, Ginnie, you're wearing men's pants," he repeated, as if her attire held priority over her person.

Virginia rolled her eyes, then swept her gaze down the front of her body. "Well, darned if I'm not," she muttered in exaggerated astonishment. She raised her eyes to give him a wry look, and felt her senses swim from the impact of the way *he* looked. He was fresh from the shower, his hair still wet, long strands curling down the back of his neck and over the collar of his shirt. The taut skin of his face wore the sheen of health and a smooth shave. Coincidentally, he too was wearing black jeans but with a red and black plaid shirt. The overall effect his appearance had on her equilibrium didn't bear thinking about—so she dragged her thoughts back to the conversation.

"This is the twentieth century, Matt. Women wear pants all the time." Virginia's throat went dry, and her voice grew uneven before she'd finished speaking. For while she was studying him, he had obviously been inspecting her, and his hooded eyes were plainly measuring the circumference of her breasts.

"You look good in red." His voice was low, sexy, suggesting the thoughts multiplying in his mind. His long fingers flexed, as if in readiness to confirm his mental calculations.

Virginia's legs trembled and seemed on the point of quitting their job of supporting her body. Her breathing appeared ready to go on strike. "Ah...thank you." She drew a quick breath and uttered a silent moan at the revealing huskiness of her voice.

"Ginnie." Murmuring her name, Matt took a step toward her, then stopped dead, his head snapping up alertly when the phone rang. He stood watching her as she walked to the instrument, mounted on the opposite wall. "More than likely that Richard person again," he muttered.

Virginia hoped he was wrong. She didn't want to speak to Richard, not after the argument he had initiated with her during his earlier call. He had insisted on stopping by to talk to her, and she had had a hard time convincing him that she was too busy to see him. There was a confrontation brewing, and Virginia knew it. She also knew she wasn't up to it at the moment.

Fortunately it wasn't Richard. When she lifted the receiver, Jeff Klein responded to her cautious greeting.

"Oh, hello, Jeff," she said on a sigh of relief. Matt scowled. She ignored him. "Have you learned anything?"

"Not much," Jeff replied. "He's not wanted anywhere. In fact, the only information either Washington or Fort Worth could come up with on a Matthew Hawk was an old record on a U.S. marshal by that name. But that record dates back to 1889, the year the marshal disappeared, presumed murdered in Montana by the outlaw he was after." Jeff sounded baffled. "As for this Matthew Hawk, who may or may not be a descendant of the marshal, they can't come up with a thing, no social security number, no service record, nothing, zilch. As far as the authorities are concerned, he doesn't even exist."

It was true! Virginia thought. Every word Matt had said about himself was true. Shaken by the realization, she had to exert every ounce of willpower she possessed to maintain her composure long enough to ask one final question.

"And as far as you're concerned?"

"He doesn't exist."

Virginia held herself together until she had thanked Jeff and hung up the receiver. Then, trembling with reaction, she closed her eyes. She didn't hear Matt move on his stockinged feet, but an instant later felt the support of the arm he slid around her waist.

"Ginnie, what's wrong?" he demanded in a tone laced with anger and concern. "What did that man say to you?"

She drew in a deep breath to restore her sense of balance, and immediately wished she hadn't. The clean male scent of him went straight to her head. Needing distance from him, room to breathe, Virginia stepped away from his protective hold and walked to the stove.

"That man was Jeff Klein, one of the patrolmen at the scene the night you were…found," she told him. "He called to tell me the results of the record check he requested on you from Washington and Fort Worth."

"And?" Matt's very stillness betrayed his sudden tension.

Virginia relayed the information Jeff had given to her. When she finished, she stared at him as if he were a ghost. "It's true, Matt. You were shot in Montana in 1889, and somehow wound up here, in Pennsylvania, in the twentieth century."

Matt was silent for a moment, then he started moving

toward her, a slow, satisfied smile curving his lips. "I told you that you were God's answer to my prayer—didn't I?" He arched his brows over eyes gleaming with purpose.

His remark reverberating in her mind, she watched him closing the space between them. The full meaning of his words registered as he drew within reaching distance. Matt actually believed she was his by divine decree!

"Ah...supper!" Coming to her senses, she spun around, grabbed a spoon and gave the bubbling soup a frantic stir. "I don't know about you, but I'm starving."

"Yes, I'm hungry."

Something, some sly, sensuous something about his low tone drew her around to face him again. Passion glittered in his eyes. A faint but blatantly wicked smiled teased the corners of his mouth. Virginia didn't need to have his meaning explained—he took care of that.

"I could eat something, too."

The man was impossible! Virginia thought wildly. And she was a wreck. When did she lose control of this situation? she asked herself, stirring the soup for all it was worth. When did you ever have control of the situation? her inner self responded—and why are you beating the innocent soup?

Shaking away the thoughts, she glanced down just in time to see the hot liquid slosh over the rim of the saucepan. As she listened to the broth sizzle on the electric coil, her lips set into a straight line. She switched off the burner, and determination rang in her voice when she turned to confront her tormentor.

"I can offer you canned soup and cold chicken sandwiches," she said firmly.

Matt wasn't slow on the uptake. His expression revealed perfect understanding. Still, he gave it another shot. "No dessert?"

Virginia expelled a harsh, impatient sigh. "Butter pound cake."

"That's it?"

"That's it," she repeated with a note of finality. "Take it or leave it."

Matt shrugged. "I'll take it." Then he grinned. "There's always tomorrow."

"Not if you want a roof over your head," Virginia said through gritted teeth.

His eyebrows shot up. "What do you mean?"

"I'll give you the house rules over supper."

While she sipped her soup and toyed with a sandwich, Virginia enumerated the rules. Making them up as she went along, she instructed him in the proper behavior of a guest—at least a guest in *her* home. Of course, since she was beginning to fear that she couldn't trust herself, she dumped the responsibility onto his shoulders. The bottom line was, naturally, that Matt was to make no further suggestive remarks or overt moves directed at her person.

"In other words, keep your hands to yourself," she concluded. "Or you will find yourself out on the street, on your own in a world, I might remind you, that you know nothing about." Finished, she met his disconcerted stare. "Agreed?"

"Why, Ginnie?" Matt frowned in confusion. "You couldn't get enough of me, my mouth, before. If I hadn't had that weak spell we'd have been all over each other in that bed, and you know it. What's changed since then?"

Being reminded of her eager responses to his kiss brought a flush of heat to her face, but Virginia managed to keep her tone detached and cool. "My professional opinion is that my response to you earlier was simply a reaction to the stress incurred by the unusual circumstances surrounding your sudden appearance in my life." Even to herself, the explanation sounded like a load of intellectual gibberish. Nevertheless, she babbled on. "And now that the stress valve has been released, the buildup of excess emotions has dissipated."

"Which means exactly what?" he asked tersely.

"I lost my head for a moment," she admitted.

Matt looked confounded. "But you enjoyed it every bit as much as I did. Why not—?"

She didn't let him finish. "I don't have time in my life for emotional involvement, Matt." Before he had a chance to question her, she rushed into an explanation. "Ever since I can remember, all I wanted was to be a doctor, a surgeon, to help people, hopefully to cure them. My schedule is tight. My life is full and satisfying. I neither need nor want a man cluttering up my life and messing with my concentration."

"What about that man you were talking to before?" he retorted. "That Richard somebody?"

"Richard is a friend, nothing more." The thought flashed into her head that she needed to make that clear to Richard, also. "And his last name is Quinter."

"Can't I be your friend, too?"

Matt's wistfully muttered request not only surprised Virginia, it almost undermined her resolve. Matt was so utterly alone. She fully understood his desire to attach himself to someone. But she couldn't be that someone; she couldn't afford to allow herself to become involved with him. Her reaction to him was too strong, too intense. She had to keep her distance, keep him at arm's length. Her independence depended on it.

Denying an urge to reach across the table and grasp his hand, she offered him a smile instead. "Of course we can be friends," she said, but added quickly, "as long as you remember that friends don't pressure one another."

Matt obviously wasn't satisfied with her reply, but he nodded his agreement. "I don't have much choice, do I?"

"No, you don't."

Though he had agreed to play by her rules, his eyes had a cloudy, stormy look. He finished eating his meal, and then the storm broke. Exhaling harshly, he exclaimed, "Dammit, Ginnie, what am I going to do all day while you're away from the place, keeping your tight schedule?"

"Do you read?"

"I'm not uneducated! I went to school!" Matt exploded. "Of course I can read."

Virginia sighed. "I didn't ask you if you *can* read, Matt," she said. "I asked you if you *do* read." She gave him a tolerant smile. "There's a difference, you know."

Matt had the grace to at least appear chastised. "Oh, yeah," he muttered. "I do like to read, although I never had the time or the books to do much of it. Why?"

"Why?" Virginia repeated. "Why, because, in case you hadn't noticed, there are all kinds of books in my den," she pointed out in a dry tone. "And since you have over a hundred years of history to catch up on, I'd say you have plenty to do while I'm working."

His latest ploy thwarted, Matt slumped against the back of his chair. "Well, from where I'm sitting," he grumbled, "I'd say it looks like it's going to be a long, cold winter."

Eight

Though the snowfall from a late-winter storm the week before still covered the ground, the scent and feel of spring was in the air. The sunshine was warm, the breeze balmy, lifting the spirits of the winter-weary residents.

His shoulder completely healed, Matt loped along the sidewalk, his step light in his latest acquisition. Virginia called them jogging shoes. He called them comfortable...and expensive. He had become aware of current prices the first time he had gone shopping with Virginia. Fortunately, due to the mind-boggling amount of cash Virginia had received from a collector for his gold coins, Matt could now pay for his own purchases. The cost of jogging shoes had come as a shock to him; the shock had still not completely worn off, but he did enjoy walking in the comfortable footgear.

The low-cut shoes, so different from the heeled boots that made extended walking difficult, were a minor revelation in comparison to the startling information he had absorbed over the past three months.

Early in the New Year Matt had begun walking, exploring the town of Conifer and its environs, after Virginia had returned to work when her ten-day holiday was over. He had learned a lot during the intervening weeks, about life and history as well as about the small town in the mountains of Pennsylvania.

"Afternoon, ma'am." Matt smiled, raised his hand to give a respectful tug to the wide brim of his hat, and stepped aside, close to the snow banked at the curb. The middle-aged woman who was passing him looked startled for an instant, then tentatively returned both smile and greeting.

His smile turned wry as he continued on his way. He had grown accustomed to the initial hesitation of most folks to respond to a stranger. And, though Christmas was long past, Matt was still a stranger, not only to the town and its residents, but to the twentieth century.

But he was making definite progress. He no longer stiffened at the sudden, shrill ring of the telephone or the unexpected blare of a car horn. He didn't duck reflexively at the sound of a plane overhead. On the contrary, he now spoke on the phone with Virginia as though he'd been doing so all his life, and was eagerly looking forward to getting behind the wheel of a car and to his first flight in a plane…preferably in one of the big jets he had read about.

He had solved the intriguing mysteries of working the automatic washer and dryer, the dishwasher, the microwave and the VCR, and was learning the intricacies of the personal computer. Most days when he walked, it was with the earphones to Virginia's tiny cassette player clamped to his head—beneath the restored Stetson that Virginia had had cleaned and blocked, when he'd refused even to consider wearing any other hat. And he had had his long shaggy hair trimmed—not lopped off, he wouldn't even consider anything above the ears—by a stylist, no less. In addition to all the other radical changes in his life, he had quit smoking, thanks in part to Virginia's opinion on the habit, but due mostly to his dissatisfaction with both pre-made cigarettes and the tasteless version of the modern makin's.

To Virginia's surprise, Matt favored rock music over country and western—even though he liked C and W. But his real favorites were her tapes of classical music, and he was hooked on TV and history books, both factual and fictional.

The events that had occurred since 1889 astounded Matt, most particularly the happenings and inventions of the latter half of the twentieth century. He found it incredible that from the beginning of recorded history, including his own time, most men had never set foot in an automobile, and yet within the short span of less than a hundred years, man had gone soaring through space to set foot upon the moon.

In Matt's opinion, people, by and large, had not changed all that much. He believed as he had before that the majority of people were basically decent. But, as before, there were the aberrants, those who chose for whatever reason to walk on the wild side, living outside the accepted boundaries of the law. His greatest disappointment was in the discovery that, to all intents and purposes, law enforcement had not changed very much.... It was still the good guys against the bad, the shoot-out at the OK corral, except that the weapons were far more sophisticated.

To Matt it was all rather overwhelming and confusing, while at the same time exciting and stimulating. There was also one other great disappointment. He and Virginia had read everything on the theory of time travel that she had been able to unearth at the lending library and in bookstores. There had been relatively little concrete information to garner, for the books available on the subject were primarily from the romance genre, interesting and imaginative, but hardly scientific in approach. So, although Virginia continued to search for other material on the subject, they had both resigned themselves to the prospect of never finding anything really enlightening.

To a certain extent, the days never seemed quite long enough, packed full as they were with new things to do and learn about. In addition to his pursuit of knowledge, he had acquired skills in activities he had never before dreamed of attempting.

Determined to "earn his keep," as he termed it to Virginia, Matt had taken over the housework. He had become proficient at doing the laundry and keeping the place tidy, and was even a fair-to-middlin' cook. He did not feel in the least demeaned by performing the chores—possibly because no one had told him the work was beneath him. Virginia was pleased with the arrangement, and that in itself was incentive enough for Matt.

But, as he had predicted the day Virginia brought him from the hospital to her apartment, it had still been a long, cold winter.

Matt was oblivious to the display of pastel-hued spring merchandise in shop windows as he strode along the town's main street. Inside his mind visions rose, replaying fragments of incidents that had occurred during the previous weeks.

"Now watch carefully," Virginia had instructed him. "When the apple gets to the base of the pole, the crowd will go a little crazy."

They were seated side by side on the sofa, watching a TV special event. Virginia had purchased a bottle of champagne for the occasion. Sipping the wine—a new and delicious experience for him—Matt kept his gaze trained on the screen. When the apple reached the base of the pole and a sign reading Happy New Year flashed on, his interest sharpened. It wasn't the noise and revelry that riveted his attention as much as the fact that everybody was kissing everybody else.

"Why are they doing that?" he'd asked, switching his gaze from the TV to the woman beside him.

Virginia had looked a trifle flustered, but had replied, "Kissing has become the traditional way of welcoming in the New Year."

"I think I like it." Smiling, he had set his glass aside and reached for her.

"Matt, remember what I said about keeping your hands to yourself." Frowning, she had shaken her head and tried to avoid his arms.

He was faster than she. He caught her by the shoulders as she started to bolt from the sofa. "Can't afford to break with tradition," he'd murmured, ignoring the twinge of pain in his shoulder as he drew her into his arms. "Might bring a whole year of bad luck."

After her initial resistance, the kiss they shared had been long, deep and hot to the point of sizzling. Aching for her with every cell in his being, he had glided one hand around her midriff and up to the enticing fullness of one breast. The feel of her warmed his palm and set his body on fire. Needing, wanting, he'd deepened the kiss by thrusting his tongue into the honeyed depths of her mouth. Aroused and bemused by the sweet wonders of her mouth and body, Matt had dropped his guard—and Virginia had seized the moment to make good her escape.

The memory of that searing, blatantly sensuous kiss, more intoxicating than the wine, had tormented Matt throughout every cold, empty night since then. There had been no repeat performance. While his body burned with desire to be a part of her, Virginia had kept her distance.

Matt's lips tightened as another vision sprang into his mind, a memory of the unpleasant scene that had taken place the evening Richard Quinter had appeared, uninvited and unexpected, at her door.

"Why, Richard! What are you doing here?"

Matt had heard Virginia's surprised response to the visitor from the den, where he was puzzling over a computer program instruction book, which was written in the foreign language she called "computerese." At the sound of the visitor's name, he'd set the book aside.

"I should think the answer would be obvious," Richard had replied in a superior tone of voice that Matt immediately took exception to. His eyes narrowed as the man continued. "I came to see you, of course. And to find out why you've been avoiding me for over a month."

"Richard, please, I don't want to discuss this now. I'm—" That was as far as he'd allowed her to go.

"I thought we had an understanding," Richard said, cutting her off in an overbearing way.

"Richard, I never—" Virginia had begun again, only to be rudely interrupted once more.

"You never dated any other man. I, my parents, all our friends considered us a couple." His voice had taken on a definite note of ownership—and Matt had felt his anger begin to rise.

"We were never a couple," Virginia had corrected the unexpected visitor, sighing in exasperation. "I tried to explain this to you when we spoke on the phone at Christmas."

"You said your patient came first," Richard had retorted. "I assumed your patient was either cured or dead by now," he'd added nastily.

Matt had heard enough. His movements noiseless, he ambled out of the den and into the living room. "Trouble, honey?" he'd drawled. While Richard stared at him in astonished disbelief, Matt strolled to Virginia and slipped an arm around her waist in a manner both familiar and possessive.

Taking her cue like a trained actress, Virginia had smiled, moved closer to him and murmured, "Not at all, darling. Richard just stopped by to say hello."

"Then I suggest he say goodbye," Matt had replied, treating the other man to a cold smile and an even colder, lethal stare. "It's time for bed."

Richard had fallen for the performance. Looking insulted

and offended, he'd swept a look of disgust over Virginia, then turned and stormed away.

Virginia had slipped out of Matt's encircling arm the minute the door closed behind the other man. Her color high, her voice dangerously low, she had then proceeded to give Matt royal hell for his interference. He had listened for a moment, then interrupted her.

"He's a shadow rider."

Angrier than he had ever seen her, Virginia had glared at him and demanded, "What in hell is a shadow rider?"

Amused by her growing tendency to swear when she was riled, Matt had hidden his smile and explained. "A shadow rider is the term used to describe a vain cowboy, a man so impressed with himself, he might find his own shadow attractive." He'd arched his brows. "The term fits Richard like his expensive suit...doesn't it?"

Virginia had held her stern expression for several seconds, then burst out laughing. "Yes," she'd admitted. "The term fits him to perfection."

The memory brought a smile to Matt's lips and lightened his loping stride. There were moments when he missed the creak of saddle leather and the feel of a horse beneath him, but those moments were growing fewer and farther between. All things considered, he knew he was adjusting well to the shock of finding himself in this sometimes incomprehensible, yet exciting new environment.

Given the choice between returning to his own time or remaining in the twentieth century, Matt knew without doubt that he'd choose to stay where he was. Even with pollution, the fear of the greenhouse effect, international tensions and the specter of nuclear devastation, he much preferred the convenience and comfort of the present. Because, most important of all his considerations, Virginia resided in the present.

Virginia.

Matt was suffused with a warmth unrelated to the bright sunshine. Thinking about her never failed to warm him.

Being around her never failed to set his mind and body on fire. He was in love with her. Matt accepted his love for Virginia without question or doubt.

By the grace of God or not, Matt now knew, intellectually and emotionally, that Virginia belonged to him. He knew as well that he belonged to her. To his way of thinking, his mystical slip through time had had to happen, for they were surely destined to be together.

The long winter of confinement within her apartment had proven their compatibility to him. They were both strong, determined, and basically loners, and yet they had coped, not only well but smoothly with the necessity of sharing their space. At times they had clashed, as would be expected of two strong-willed individuals, but those incidents were few in number compared to the times they had laughed together, as they had on the night Richard had stormed off in a huff.

Turning a corner at an intersection, Matt quickened his pace. After three months, he now knew the route by heart. He was headed home. And to Matt, home meant Virginia...in any century.

Letting himself into the apartment with the key she'd had made for him, Matt shrugged out of the parka, then went directly to the kitchen. Even though Virginia spent little time in it, the place always felt empty when she wasn't there. After switching on the radio to dispel the silence, he began gathering the ingredients needed for a casserole for dinner. With his thoughts his only company, he prepared the dish, slid it into the oven, then glanced around, looking for something else to do to occupy his time. There was nothing; everything was neat and orderly. He looked at the clock and sighed. Virginia wouldn't be home for at least another hour.

Restless, he ambled into the living room and to the wide window overlooking the foothills at the rear of the apartment complex. In his opinion, Virginia worked too hard and relaxed too seldom. Scanning the snow-covered scene beyond the window, Matt's gaze came to rest on the clearing in a stand of pines. A smile relieved the tightness of his lips as he studied the results of one of her too few periods of relaxation.

The snowman certainly wasn't a work of art, but he and Virginia had laughed a lot together while building it after the storm earlier that week.

Together. The word revolving in his mind, Matt pulled on his jacket and left the apartment. Moments later he was in the clearing, scooping up snow to shore up the drooping snowman…Virginia's snowman.

Virginia and he belonged together, were fated to be together. He knew it. His problem was in convincing her of it. Matt worked on the problem while he worked on the snowman.

Virginia parked her car in her designated slot in the parking lot at the apartment complex. It was still light! The realization struck her as she walked toward the entrance of her building. Spring had arrived, the daylight hours were growing longer, and she hadn't noticed until that minute. Of course, she was earlier than usual. By some stroke of luck, her last two scheduled patients had both called to cancel their appointments.

Closing her eyes, Virginia inhaled deeply. Yes, the unmistakable scent of spring was in the cooling afternoon air. The scent permeated her being, inducing a heady feeling. The scent? she chided herself. Or the man waiting for her inside the building?

Matt. His name teased her senses, causing a much more potent headiness than any scent of spring. Matt was waiting for her. Anticipation shimmering through her, she entered the building and hurried to the elevator. After a scant three months of having him at the apartment, Virginia couldn't imagine him not being there, waiting for her.

She was in love with him, of course. After a fierce inner battle, Virginia had finally admitted to herself the reality of the love she felt for him. It scared her witless. Falling in love wasn't in her life plan. She loved her work, her independence, her freedom. She didn't want to be in love with any man, most especially not with a man from another, earlier century.

And Matt had proved himself a man of his time. He was tough, rugged, and not above turning a situation to his own advantage, as he had on New Year's Eve and again on the night Richard had suddenly appeared at her door.

The thought of the latter incident brought a smile to Virginia's lips. The memory of the former occasion sent a shiver skipping down her spine. Nearly three months had passed, during which she had carefully avoided any form of physical contact with him, yet she could still taste him, still feel the heat and urgency of his mouth and hands.

It was enough to make a strong-minded woman weep. She didn't want to be in love with Matthew Hawk. She didn't want to feel the quickening of her pulse whenever she thought about him or he drew within scenting distance of her. Still, while Virginia's mind resisted, her emotions sent her rushing from the elevator and into the apartment.

The tantalizing aroma of simmering food enveloped Virginia the moment she stepped over the threshold. Smiling in appreciation of Matt's growing culinary skill, she followed the scent to its source in the kitchen. Expecting to find the creator of the meal, she frowned when all she found was an empty room. In fact, the entire apartment was empty. Matt wasn't there.

Wondering where he could have gone, Virginia went to her bedroom to change out of her attractive but subdued suit and into her more comfortable jeans and pullover sweater. There was still no sign of him when she left her room fifteen minutes later.

Thinking that perhaps he had decided to take a short nap, she went to his room. The door was open. His room was as empty as all the others. Strangely uneasy, Virginia drifted aimlessly from one room to another. Where was he?

she asked herself, becoming anxious. He was always there when she got home. It wasn't like Matt to disappear this late in the afternoon, not even to run out to the sto—

Virginia's thoughts shattered. *Disappear.* The word echoed in her mind. A flashing memory left her feeling as cold and empty as her apartment. The memory was of one of the time travel novels she and Matt had read. In the story, the heroine, from another time period, had in the end, without warning, suddenly disappeared.

It was fiction, Virginia reminded herself, clasping her arms around her trembling body. But what if?... *Stop this at once,* she ordered herself. Attempting to escape her own churning thoughts, she retraced her steps, pacing from room to room. At the open doorway to Matt's bedroom she came to a halt. A wrenching pain of loss tore a cry from her throat. She loved him, and if he was gone, lost to her, he would never know.

"Matt." Virginia was unaware of calling his name aloud. Frantic, frightened, she turned away. What would she do if he had just disappeared, like a puff of smoke in a stiff breeze? she asked herself. How could she bear the emptiness of whatever remained of her life?

At that moment, Virginia would have given everything she valued—her work, her independence, her freedom—for the sound of his voice, his laughter.

Feeling lost, bereft, she wandered into the living room. The delicious aroma of the meal he had prepared wafted to her once more from the kitchen. Tears filled her eyes, blurring her vision. Chafing her shivering arms, she walked to the window. The day was losing the light. It would soon be as dark outside as she felt inside. Remembering their snowman, she wiped the tears from her eyes and raised her head to look at the clearing.

"Matt!" This time his name exploded from her throat. As real as life and twice as beautiful, Matt was in the clearing, shoring up their melting snowman.

Virginia was absolutely still for an instant, devouring the

sight of him. Relief and sheer joy washed over her, bringing a smile to her lips and wings to her feet. Spinning around, she ran to the closet. Grabbing her ski parka, she pulled it on as she dashed from the apartment.

"Matt," Virginia called to him as she raced from the complex to the clearing. He turned and waved.

"Hi," he responded, smiling with evident pleasure. "You're early, aren't you?"

"Yes," she replied, coming to a halt in front of him. "Two appointments canceled." Flushed and breathless, she gazed into his eyes and blurted out her fears. "I couldn't find you. I was worried."

The crease lines at the corners of his eyes crinkled when he laughed. "Afraid I'd skipped with the silver?"

"No." Virginia was powerless against the emotions roiling inside her and the tears that rushed to her eyes. "I was afraid you were...gone," she whispered.

Matt frowned. His brilliant eyes searched her face. "Gone? Gone where?"

"Back." Virginia sniffed, and didn't even care. Matt obviously did care.

"Ginnie, you're crying!" he exclaimed, pulling her into his arms. "What is it? What's wrong?" he demanded. "And what do you mean by 'back'?"

Sobbing, she flung her arms around his neck and held him fast. She didn't care that they were in view of the other residents of the complex. She didn't care that she was revealing her feeling to him. All she cared about was holding on to him, feeling the solid reality of him. "Hold me," she pleaded. "Please hold me. Oh, Matt, I was so scared."

Matt's arms tightened, crushing her soft body against the hard strength of his own. "Ginnie, were you afraid I'd gone back in time again?"

"Yes." Virginia muffled a sob in his jacket. "When you weren't there, and I couldn't find you, I thought...I was afraid...." She shuddered.

"I'm here." The muscles in his arms flexed. "Ginnie, don't cry, honey, I'm here."

Neither of them knew how long they stood there, clinging to each other like lost and frightened children. Matt was only alerted to the chill evening air by the shiver that rippled through Virginia's body.

"You're cold," he said, drawing back to look at her. A smile tilted his lips. "Matter of fact, so am I. What are we standing out here for, when it's warm inside?"

Virginia sniffled and returned his smile. "It smells good inside, too."

"Oh, hell!" Matt exclaimed. "I forgot all about the casserole in the oven." Grasping her hand, he took off at a loping gait for the complex. Virginia was forced to run to keep up with him.

The meal was not ruined. But then, it wouldn't have mattered much if it had been. Though they picked at the food, neither Virginia nor Matt really tasted it. Their gazes were locked, and in the depths of their eyes burned the desire to appease a far greater hunger. Before his meal was half-finished, Matt pushed his plate away and stood up. Without saying a word, he held out his hand to her. Letting her fork drop to the table unnoticed, Virginia rose and placed her hand in his. Then, in silent agreement, they walked to her bedroom.

Murmuring of his need for her, Matt stopped beside her double bed and drew her into his arms. Answering his plea, Virginia offered her mouth and herself to him.

His kiss began with slow reverence but swiftly escalated to a hard, driving demand. She returned his kiss with an eagerness born of awakening passion. His hands skimmed over her with restless intent until they found and claimed her breasts. Her hands slid down the length of his arms to cover his in silent approval of his possession.

"Ginnie, Ginnie." Matt's voice was rough with desire. The trembling hands that removed her clothes were gentle.

"You are so very beautiful," he whispered when the last wisp of silky material lay in a shimmering pool on the floor.

"And you are incredibly handsome," Virginia whispered back, staring with unabashed admiration at the magnificence of his naked masculinity.

She went into his arms as if it was the most natural thing in the world. They sank to the bed as one. Murmuring delicious enticements, Matt set Virginia on fire with his hands and lips and tongue. Glowing like a flame, burning only for him, she drove him on by exploring his muscled, hard body.

When he could endure no more of the sweet torture, Matt slid between the silken lure of her trembling thighs. Her soft, strong hands grasped his taut hips. Moving slowly, savoring the moment, he entered her. He frowned when he met with resistance and, arching, he thrust forward, then froze when Virginia went stiff and cried out in pain.

"Ginnie?" Matt's voice betrayed his utter astonishment. "You're a virgin?"

Virginia drew a slow breath before answering. "Yes. Is that a sin?" A hint of laughter tinged her voice.

Matt shook his head, as if in disbelief. "I hurt you—and you're making jokes?"

She smoothed her palm over the muscles contracting in his buttocks. "I'm a physician, Matt—remember? I knew what to expect." She pressed against him with her hands, drawing him deeper within her. "The pain is gone now, and the tension is easing."

Matt could feel the truth of her words. The stiffness was draining from her body, being replaced by a different, exciting tension. Passion flared anew, and again he began to move, stroking into her with gentle thrusts.

"Yes, yes!" Virginia cried, sinking her nails into his flesh as she arched to meet his advance. "Love me, Matt. Show me how very real you are!"

"I'm real, love," he said in a voice tight with strain. "You'll see." Bending to her, he pressed his open mouth to hers and matched the measured thrusts of his tongue to the increasing rhythm of his body.

Virginia felt drenched in sensation. Her body was on fire, every nerve ending burning, screaming for release from the sensual tension. She had never dreamed it could be like this...that anything could feel like this. She cried out in wonder when the tension snapped, flinging her into the depths of the shudders that were cascading through her body.

A moment later she heard Matt's muffled cry of satisfaction, and felt the rippling tremors that shook his long, muscular form. Locked together, they rode the storm wave to the tranquil shore.

"God!" Matt groaned as he levered himself onto the mattress beside her. "I've never experienced anything like that in my life." He drew several deep breaths. "That was wonderful. You're wonderful." Reaching for her, he gathered her into his arms, close to his flushed body. "I'm sorry for hurting you," he murmured, kissing her with tender concern.

"Don't be," she whispered, teasing his lower lip with the tip of her tongue. "After the initial shock, I loved every tension-filled minute of it."

Matt's roar of joyous laughter danced in the dark room. "I was wrong," he said after his laughter subsided. "You aren't wonderful, you're damned fantastic."

"I might say the same about you," Virginia responded, loving the afterglow of teasing banter. "But I don't want to risk inflating your male ego."

"My ego?" Propping himself on his forearm, Matt loomed over her. "What would you say if I told you that you were in real danger of inflating something other than my ego?"

"So soon?" Virginia stared at him in amazement. "I mean really?"

"Really," he repeated, his lips twitching with amusement. "I wasn't merely hungry for you, Ginnie. I was starved."

"Has it been such a long, dry spell for you?" she asked, innocently falling into his trap. Her eyes narrowed in suspicion when he grinned with wicked intent.

"Over a hundred years."

Nine

"You devil!"

Virginia slapped her palm against his shoulder, laughed, then curled her fingers into his long hair and drew his mouth to hers.

"You angel," Matt murmured, teasing her with nibbling little kisses. "I knew you were an angel from the first moment I saw you, standing there above me, with the light shining on your hair, making a halo around your beautiful face."

"Oh, Matt." Tears rushed to her eyes, and she cradled his lean cheeks with her palms.

"I don't want to terrify you, Ginnie," he murmured, brushing his mouth back and forth over hers. "But I love you, you know, and now that I have you, I'll never let you go."

His teasing mouth was driving her crazy. Feeling herself losing control, Virginia pressed against his face, holding him still. "Matt, wait," she said when he strained forward to reach her lips. "I must tell you."

"Make it quick," he growled. "I can't wait much longer. I want to kiss you, love you."

"That's what I wanted to tell you." She was getting breathless, because his mouth was getting closer. "I love you, too. I didn't want to, but I do."

"I know you didn't want to." Breaking her hold, he gave her a quick but proper kiss. "But I thank God that you do."

His mouth claimed hers in a hungry kiss hot with renewed passion. Virginia was lost, but she didn't mind, didn't care, because she was lost inside Matt's arms, his gentle, urgent possession, his encompassing love.

Deliciously drained, they slept, Virginia's head nestled on his broad chest, Matt's arms holding her close.

Virginia woke to Matt's hand stroking her back. "What time is it?" she asked, sensuously arching into his touch.

"Who knows?" Matt replied, massaging the base of her spine. "Who cares."

Opening one eye, she peered at the digital clock on the nightstand and read the numbers aloud. "It's 7:46." She arched again, rubbing her breasts against him. "Mmm... that feels good," she murmured, nuzzling through the dark whorls of chest hair to press her mouth to his warm skin.

"So does that," he said on a sharp, indrawn breath. His big hands grasped her hips to shift her body onto his, making her aware of her effect on him. "That feels even better."

"Greedy devil, aren't you?" Virginia gasped, and moved her hips into alignment with his.

"Sure." Matt groaned his appreciation and ran one hand down the backs of her thighs. "Like I told you, it's been..."

"Over a hundred years," she finished for him, muffling her laughter against the silken mat on his chest.

Matt's laughter blended with hers, setting the tone for their lovemaking. Laughing, teasing, tickling, tormenting each other, they played an ancient male-female game. They were all over the bed—as well as one another—and at one point even rolled to the floor. Landing on the soft mound of covers, which had preceded them by some minutes, neither one felt the fall. Their laughter ceased when at last, panting from exertion and heightened passion, they joined again, two individuals fused, body, mind and soul into one.

"I'm hungry," Matt said much later. Sprawled beside her on the bed, he raised his arms and stretched like a huge, satisfied cat.

Pushing her wildly tangled hair from her face, Virginia looked at him in blank astonishment. "Already?"

"For food, woman." Matt grinned at her.

"Oh." Virginia grinned back at him.

"So what are you going to do about it?"

"Not a thing." She yawned behind her hand. "You're in charge of the kitchen, remember?"

Matt groaned. "Yeah, and it's a mess."

"Uh-huh." Virginia nodded in solemn agreement. "You could always warm up the casserole."

"Ugh," he grunted. "Aren't you hungry?"

Virginia's smile was sweet. "Not if I have to make the food myself."

"I've got you spoiled."

"And I love it."

"What about me?"

Virginia's voice went soft. "I love you, too."

"You win." Matt rolled from the bed. "I'll get a shower, then fix us something." He strode to her bathroom, then paused in the doorway to glance at her. "But you can fix the bed." Her laughter followed him into the shower.

* * *

"When did you first realize that you were falling in love with me?" Coming from Matt, the age-old lover's question sounded brand-new.

They were seated at the kitchen table. After Matt had finished in the bathroom, Virginia had showered, then stripped and remade the bed, while he cleared away the dinner remnants and cooked scrambled eggs and bacon.

"Oh, not long after I brought you here from the hospital, I guess," she replied on a sigh.

"That long?" Matt gaped at her, egg-laden fork poised near his open mouth. His movement slow, absent, he lowered the fork to his plate. "Dammit, Ginnie, I've been going crazy for three months, trying to think of a way to make you love me! Why didn't you tell me?"

"Because I didn't want to be in love with you," she answered with simple honesty.

"Because of who I am? Where I come from? The time I come from?"

"No, of course not," Virginia said in quick denial. "I didn't mean just you," she explained. "I didn't want to fall in love with any man."

"But…why?" Matt looked baffled.

"I tried to explain all this to you before, Matt," she said, breaking pieces off the slice of toast she was holding. "I keep a tight schedule. I never had the time or desire to rearrange my life to suit a man."

"Bull," Matt snorted rudely, startling her. He shoved back his chair and stood up. "You've kept to your schedule ever since I've been here," he pointed out. Lifting his coffee cup, he drained it, then carried it and his empty plate to the sink. When he turned to face her again, his expression was bland…too bland. "And I don't expect things to change all that much now…except that we'll be sleeping together, instead of apart."

"We will?" Virginia challenged him, arching her brows.

"You know we will." Matt smiled. "And don't try to change the subject."

"What was the subject?"

"You, and the reason you were still a virgin."

Virginia pushed away her unfinished meal for the second time that evening. "I don't know what the big deal is about my being a virgin!" she exclaimed, tossing the mangled toast onto her plate with a show of temper.

"It's about you," he said. "Finished?" He inclined his head to indicate her plate. When she nodded, he cleared her things away, and continued as if there'd been no break. "And your fear of men."

Virginia stared at him in amazement. "I'm not afraid of men. Did I act like I was afraid of you?"

"Yes, now that I think about it," Matt replied, bringing the dishcloth to wipe the table. "The first day I was here, when you told me the 'house rules,' you weren't angry, you were scared silly. Why?"

"Matt, really..." she began.

"Why, Ginnie?" he persisted, flinging the dishcloth into the sink. "Tell me."

Virginia glared at him. He smiled with gentle patience. His smile defeated her. She sighed and moved her shoulders in an I-give-up shrug. "I don't actually fear men, Matt," she said in a soft, tired voice. "In fact, as friends, they're fine. It's simply that, ever since I was old enough to notice such things, I've seen what usually happens to women when they make the mistake of falling in love."

Matt frowned. "What does happen?"

She shrugged again. "Because his own self-image is fragile, he bolsters his ego by undermining hers. You know—Mr. Machismo and his mate. She may even earn as much money as he does, but don't forget, he is the man of the house—never mind that when the man of the house has an illness as minor as a little cold, he is more of a child than the youngest infant in the family. And so, if only to keep peace, the woman suppresses her own individuality. Over time he exerts his will until she has precious little of her own, becoming, not the full potential of her own self, but *his* wife, the mother of *his* children, *his* echo and shadow.'' A faint smile played at the edges of her lips. ''I decided before I was fifteen that I would never allow the same thing to happen to me. I knew what I wanted to do, what I wanted to be. And I was determined that no man would ever get the opportunity to play out his fantasy of lord and master over me.''

Matt looked pensive for a moment, then grinned and said, ''Lord and master, huh? The idea has appeal. I can see it all now,'' he went on, enlarging on the theme. ''Me lounging by a roaring fire, and you, naked of course, pampering my ego, bolstering my self-image, stroking my—''

''Stuff it, Hawk,'' she drawled.

His laughter reverberated in the small room. ''Honey, I must admit that I'm glad you were so determined to resist other men.'' Matt's eyes gleamed with inner amusement. ''But I gotta tell you, I can't see you knuckling under to any mere male.'' His smile became a grin. ''Hell, if I thought it might work, I'd give it a shot myself.''

Virginia's smile was wry. ''It wouldn't work.''

''Well, isn't that what I just said?''

She nodded.

''Knew I heard it somewhere.''

Virginia laughed. ''Matthew Hawk, you're crazy.''

''No, honey.'' The amused gleam vanished from his eyes, overshadowed by serious intent. ''I'm just happy to be alive, and to be here…with you.''

''Oh, Matt.'' She reached for him. He pulled her out of her chair and into his arms.

''You know, the first time I got a clear look at you, when you walked into my room Christmas afternoon, I kinda got the idea that you were…well, sorta like a lady of the line.''

They were back in bed. Matt was propped against the headboard, one hand wrapped around a steaming cup of coffee, the other wrapped around Virginia.

''A what?'' She lifted her head from his chest to stare at him in bewilderment.

Matt shrugged, then winced as the coffee sloshed over the rim of the cup and splashed his hand. "A lady of the line is…eh, well…something like a loose woman."

"*Something* like a loose woman?"

Matt grinned. "Okay, more like a prostitute."

"A pros—Matthew Hawk!" Virginia exclaimed. "Whatever made you think a thing like that? I…I…"

"Calm down, honey." Risking being scalded by the sloshing coffee, Matt silenced her with a kiss. It was only after his mouth claimed hers that he realized she was shaking with laughter, not fury. The kiss ended when the hot liquid seared his skin again. "Damn!" he muttered, setting the cup on the nightstand. "Now look what you made me do."

Virginia laughed into his face. "Serves you right. A lady of the line, indeed. What an expression. I love it!"

"Well, it doesn't fit you, anyway," Matt grumbled.

"Why did you ever think it did?" she asked.

He shrugged. "You were wearing paint on your face, and your legs were exposed, and I'd never in my life seen heels that high on a lady's shoes."

"Paint? Legs? Heels?" Virginia almost choked on the words, again convulsed with laughter. "Oh, Matt, that's a riot!"

"You gotta remember, I didn't know where I was." But Matt's indignant expression was ruined by the twitch at the corners of his mouth.

"And then I told you you could stay at my place!" she gasped around a fresh bout of laughter. "You must have really believed you'd died and gone to heaven!" She gave him a sparkling look. "No wonder you were so shocked at finding that I was still a virgin."

Matt's expression changed, becoming sober and concerned. "Are you hurting, Ginnie? I mean, was it too much?"

Virginia raised her hand to smooth the frown lines from his face. "I'm fine…a little tender, that's all."

"But…"

She slid her fingers over his lips. "Matt, I'm a doctor, and I've made my diagnosis. The patient will live."

"Good," Matt muttered against her fingers. "I'm glad."

That night set the precedent for the following weeks. Their days continued as they had before, with Virginia working and Matt learning and walking. But their nights had changed. Instead of sitting in front of the TV or with their noses buried in their respective books, Virginia and Matt spent the majority of their time in bed, her bed, making love and conversation—not necessarily at the same time.

The very next night conversation came first and concerned protection…Virginia's.

"Of course, I'm willing to go on the pill, but I can't start taking it until next month," she said, after explaining the various methods of birth control that were available. "So, until then…" Her voice faded as she dropped a foil-wrapped packet into his hand. "You don't mind?"

"No, I don't mind," Matt replied. He looked at the packet, then at her. His eyes were warm, glowing with love for her. "But then again, I wouldn't mind seeing my baby growing inside of you, either."

Melting, Virginia threw her arms around his neck and admitted, "Oh, Matt, I love you so much, and I'd love to feel your baby growing inside of me!"

The packet was tossed into the nightstand drawer, and the prescription for the pill remained in Virginia's purse. As was soon evident, it was already too late for either.

"I've told you most of my life story," Matt said one night the following week. "But you haven't said much at all about yourself."

Virginia almost never spoke about her past. But, snuggled against his warm body, replete and relaxed from his special brand of lovemaking, Virginia was amenable to being forthcoming, if not expansive.

"There's not much to tell," she said. "I was born and raised right here in Conifer, went to a university in Philadelphia, then came back here to finish my internship at Conifer General."

"Family?" Matt nudged, wanting more.

"I had one."

"Ginnie."

She shrugged, and heard him catch his breath as her body rubbed against his. "My parents endured a long, unhappy marriage. She was repressed. He was bored," she said in a monotone. "They finally divorced a couple of years ago. They have since both remarried. My mother now lives in California. Her husband's in real estate development. And my father lives in upper New York State. His new wife is exactly what he always wanted...an adoring doormat."

"You're bitter?"

"No," Virginia denied. "Realistic."

Matt shifted to his side to look at her. "Our marriage won't be like that, honey."

She arched her brows. "We're getting married?"

His eyes held hers. "Aren't we?"

"Yes."

"Yes," he echoed softly. He smiled, then scowled in consternation. "That is, if we can. I have no identification of any kind. How—?" he began.

Virginia interrupted him. "There are ways," she assured him. "I met all types of people while I was doing residency in Emergency. I remember one man had identification in three different names." She smiled at the memory. "He told me that if I ever needed anything, a birth certificate, whatever, I shouldn't hesitate to call him." Her smile turned rueful. "Oh, yes, there are ways... None of them legal, of course, but..." She allowed her voice to trail away.

"But we'll do what we have to do," Matt finished for her.

And they did. A week and a half later, Matt had all the identification he required, and all in his own name.

After a cold snap, spring arrived in full force. The sunshine was bright and warm. The grass turned from brown to a lush green. Buds appeared on tree limbs. Flowers burst into bloom...and so did Virginia. In late April she visited the hospital's staff obstetrician. She confirmed Virginia's self-diagnosis.

Virginia held her news close to her heart until later that night, when Matt lay beside her, exhausted and content.

"Matt?"

"Mmm?" Yawning, he pulled her into his arms.

"Do you remember the discussion we had last month about birth control?" she asked softly.

"Uh-huh." He yawned again. "Why?"

"Do you remember what you said at the time?"

Matt was quiet for a moment, thoughtful. "Yeah. I said that I didn't mind using something," he said slowly, "but that I also wouldn't mind seeing you grow—" He stopped speaking abruptly, his questioning gaze probing her eyes. "Ginnie, are you trying to tell me that you're pregnant?"

Virginia's smile was tremulous, uncertain. Her voice was little more than a whisper. "Yes."

His arms tightened, crushing her to him. "Honey, that's wonderful!" He kissed her hard, then drew back, his expression hopeful, his voice hesitant. "Isn't it?"

Virginia laughed and cried at the same time. "Yes, Matt, I think it is wonderful."

"We've got to get married," he said, suddenly wide-awake and exuberant. "The sooner the better."

"Tonight yet?" Virginia teased, smiling mistily.

"No," he answered seriously. "I've got other plans for tonight."

"Really? Like what?" she asked, certain she already knew. She was wrong.

"Like the future," Matt replied, surprising her. "I've been meaning to discuss it with you."

Virginia squirmed, working her soft curves into a comfortable position around his angles. "Okay," she said, after she'd succeeded in drawing a protesting groan from him. "I'm all ears. Discuss."

"Oh, honey," Matt muttered, gliding his hand down her back and over her hip. "Believe me, you are definitely not all ears. You're all soft, and silky, and warm, and—"

"Matthew," she cut in on him in a warning tone. "Stop feeling and start talking. Discuss."

"Nag," he groused, gliding his palm to her waist. "Anyway, I've been thinking about what I'm going to do with myself, how I'm going to support my—" he shot her a happy grin "—my growing family."

Virginia refrained from pointing out to him that she earned an excellent income and had a tidy sum saved. She knew better. Matt was a proud man. He paid his way...as he had taken great pains to inform her, when he had insisted that she keep the lion's share of the money she had gotten from the collector for his gold coins. Recalling that scene and his obstinacy, she asked with genuine interest, "Have you decided on something?"

"Yes."

She sighed with impatience. "Were you planning to tell me? Or must I guess?"

Matt laughed. "Well, first of all, I'll need some money."

"Okay," she agreed. "I have some savings. How much do you think you'll need?"

He looked astonished. "I don't want your money."

"But you just said you needed some," she reminded him in exasperation. "Why won't you take mine?"

"Because I have my own."

Ten

"**Y**our own money?" Virginia frowned. "I don't understand. I thought all you had were those gold coins."

"All I had on me at the time I was shot," Matt agreed. "But I have more."

"Gold coins?" She felt as confused as he sounded confident.

"Of course," he said. "I was always paid in gold, and I always set some of it aside."

Virginia smiled. She remembered him telling her that the coins in his belt were his pay. Assuming he was paid monthly, as was usually the case at the time, Matt had earned $275 a month. How much could he have set aside? And what had the marshal been saving for...a rainy day? Or, more likely, a wild time with the ladies of the line when he got back to town? Curious, and maybe a trifle jealous, she twined a finger into the curly mat of hair on his chest and casually asked, "Were you saving for anything in particular?"

There was nothing casual about Matt's response...to her query or to what her finger play was doing to his libido. "Sure," he said on a sharp breath. "But if you want to know, you'd better corral that maverick finger of yours."

She released the dark swirl at once and curled her fingers into her palm. "Sorry."

"I'm not," Matt chuckled. "But anyway, I was saving it to buy a place of my own someday in the future, after I was past it." His voice took on a dry drawl. "Of course, I never dreamed it would be this far into the future."

His answer, his odd phrasing, confused her. "What kind of place of your own? And what do you mean by 'after you were past it'? Past what?"

"Past being a mite faster than the hombre I was after," he said, splaying his hand against her ribs when she shuddered as she recalled the bullet wound in his chest. "Easy, honey. It's over, I'm alive." His voice grew lower and held a note of wonder. "Hell, being shot was the best thing that ever happened to me! It gave me you."

Virginia shuddered again. "I hate guns," she said with passion. "And I hate the thought of that gun you have hidden away in your dresser. I wish you'd get rid of it."

"Forget it." Matt's tone was flat, hard, final. "You never know when I might need it."

"Matt, this is the twentieth century!" Virginia cried. "Men no longer need to carry guns for protection."

"Yeah, I noticed that," he retorted dryly. "I can tell how protected decent folks are by all the reports in the papers and on TV about killings and muggings and rape. Forget it, honey. I'm keeping the Colt."

Virginia longed to argue further but, since he'd made a valid point, she backed away from the subject. "Tell me what kind of place you were hoping to buy."

His fingers flexed gently into her ribs in a silent gesture of appreciation of her retreat. "A small spread," Matt replied. "A place to raise horses...and babies," he added softly, sliding his hand to her still flat tummy.

"Thank you," she whispered, reciprocating by placing her palm over the back of his hand. Virginia had no idea how much a small spread would cost, but she had a depressing notion that his meager savings wouldn't be enough. "How much had you saved?" she asked, determined that Matt would have his "place," even if she had to wipe out her bank balance.

"The last time I checked, it came to a little over three thousand dollars."

Virginia jolted back, knocking his arm away from her body. "Over three thousand dollars!" she repeated in shock. "In the same kind of gold coins?"

"Exactly the same." Matt smiled.

"If you could sell them for the same amount that you got for those other coins, you could see a return of..." She broke off to do some rapid mental calculations, but was too excited to think straight, let alone count. "A bundle!"

His smile grew into a wicked grin. "Yeah, honey, that's the way I figured it."

"Matt, that's wonderful for you. I'm deligh—Oh!" she cried as she was struck by a deflating thought. "Matt, it's been over a hundred years. You don't know if your account is still on record, or even if the bank still exists."

"Bank?" Matt snorted. "Honey, you ever hear of bank robbers? I never trusted my money to a bank."

"Then where *did* you keep it?"

"Don't worry, honey," he soothed. "It's in a safe place."

Virginia sighed. "Where, Matt?"

"I stashed it in the well on that scraggly piece of land that came to me when my mother died."

"Oh, Matt." Virginia's shoulders drooped.

Coiling his arm around her, he drew her down to him again. "What's wrong, Ginnie?"

"You keep forgetting that it's been over a hundred years," she replied sadly.

"I haven't forgotten anything, honey," he murmured,

brushing his mouth over her temple. "Don't worry, the money's safe. That well was built to last a lot longer than a hundred years."

"Unless someone built a high rise on top of it," she said morosely. "Or a whole town."

"Oh, hell," he muttered.

"My sentiments exactly," she concurred.

"Well, there's only one way to find out," Matt said. "I'll have to go back and see for myself."

"How are you going to do that?" Virginia asked.

"By jet?" Matt's tone held a boyish-sounding note of hope.

The 727 rolled into position on the runway. Buckled into the window seat beside Virginia, Matt's body was taut, his eyes bright with expectation.

Over two weeks had passed since the night he had stated his decision to return to Texas. Matt had wanted to leave at once but, as Virginia was adamant about going with him, they had been forced to wait until she could arrange her schedule to allow her to take time off.

The jet engines revved and the plane moved forward, gathering speed as it dashed down the runway. The long fingers clasped around Virginia's tightened with heightened tension when the plane left the ground, seeming to rise straight up into the cloudless sky.

"Damn," Matt breathed. "This is great."

Sharing the experience with Matt made the flight as adventurous and exciting for Virginia as her first air trip had been. Observing him, loving him, she suddenly realized that she had been reexperiencing many aspects of life during the previous months. She was seeing everything through his eyes, and finding it all new and exciting.

When the plane reached altitude and leveled off, Virginia settled back to relax for the remainder of what she knew would be a relatively boring flight.

Matt wasn't bored, he was interested in everything. He

plied Virginia with questions and he even enjoyed the in-flight meal, eating every bit of his own and half of hers. Fortunately, the descent and landing were made smoothly, although Virginia doubted that Matt would have noticed if they hadn't been, since his nose was pressed against the window.

Matt was amazed by the crowds of travelers and the hustle and bustle of Dallas-Fort Worth airport, and stunned by his first close look at a city. Seated beside Virginia in the rental car that she had arranged to have waiting for them, his head swiveled from side to side as she drove the beltway around Dallas, before heading for Fort Worth.

Despite the obvious changes, Matt recognized Fort Worth, if only because the famous stockyards were still there. Like any other tourist, he admired the bronze statue of Texas longhorns and a cattleman sculpted by T. D. Kelsey. But he was quiet and withdrawn as they strolled along Exchange Avenue.

"It must all seem rather strange to you now," Virginia murmured, indicating the shops lining the street with a wave of her hand.

"Yeah, it looks a lot different from my old stomping grounds." He nodded, then he grinned at her. "It's a whole lot cleaner, too." With a final glance around, he grasped her hand and strode off in the direction of the parking area. "I've seen enough," he said. "Let's go get my money."

Finding the small ranch proved easier than Virginia had feared it would be. After he studied a detailed map he'd purchased in one of the tourist shops, Matt pinpointed the section, located some distance southwest of Dallas. He told her when to turn off the highway onto a secondary road, and when to turn off that onto a back road. Then, with the instincts of a natural tracker, he told her to turn onto a narrow dirt road that was barely visible.

"You just drive nice and slow along here for a mile or so," Matt said, narrowly studying the terrain. "I'll tell you when to stop."

When he gave the word, Virginia braked the car, then sat staring at the barren bleakness of the landscape. This scrap of nothing was his heritage? she thought, aching with love and compassion for him.

"It's a real mess, isn't it?" Matt observed, correctly reading her expression. "And that mess killed my father and mother." Sighing, he pushed open the car door. "The sight of it churns my gut. Let's find my money and get out of here."

Virginia had to step lively to keep up with Matt's determined stride. At a near trot, she followed in his wake as he skirted the remnants of a collapsed building, then jumped, startled when he let out a sudden loud shout.

"Eu-re-ka! What'd I tell ya, honey?" he yelled. "Hurry over here and look. The well's still here."

And there it was. Panting, Virginia stared at the round, foot-wide stone wall. Parts of the wall were crumbling, but it was still there. Fascinated, she watched as Matt moved unerringly to a spot in the wall that looked to her like any other. She caught her breath when he sank to his haunches, and gnawed her lower lip as he worked one large rock, jiggling it back and forth until he could pull it free.

"Now pray," Matt said, slanting a grin at her over his shoulder as he inserted his hand into the hollow.

Excitement and hope making her feel slightly sick, Virginia kept her gaze riveted to the wall. She gasped aloud when Matt withdrew his hand. His fingers were wrapped around the top of a bulging, soft buckskin pouch. He repeated the process three times; she gasped each time he did it. By the time he had examined the pouches, she felt exhausted.

"It's all here," he informed her, exhaling deeply. "Just as I left it over a hundred years ago."

"Now you can have that place you wanted," Virginia said, blinking against a surge of hot tears.

"Yes." Walking to her, Matt drew her into his arms. "Now I can raise horses...and babies."

Virginia went absolutely still, for in that instant the moment of truth, her moment of truth was upon her. From the time she was old enough to make her own decisions, she had known that the one thing she didn't want was a commitment to a man, any man. When Matt had talked about his own place before, the idea was nebulous, contingent upon the reality of the gold he had stashed away. Now the gold was real, she had seen it, and Matt was no longer talking about a nebulous hope but about a definite place, somewhere to raise horses and babies.... Matt was talking commitment.

Could she handle it? The thought flashed through Virginia's mind as she gazed into his shining blue eyes. She was carrying his child, but her pregnancy alone did not imply commitment; Virginia was confident of her ability to cope with the rigors of single parenthood. No, the fact of the child growing inside her body had little bearing on her deliberations. The single aspect she had to deal with was whether or not she could agree to a commitment with this man.

A shadow of uncertainty flickered in Matt's eyes, dimming the bright light of expectancy. A line of consternation drew his dark brows together. A pang tugged at Virginia's emotions. No one she had ever met frowned quite like Matt. Come to that, she suddenly realized, no one, no man she had ever met did anything or was anything quite like Matt.

Matt was definitely a man of his own time—a confusing, exasperating, delightful mixture of hidden tenderness and obvious toughness. He had adapted extraordinarily well to his strange new environment, yet had retained a certain quality that set him apart from other men. Virginia knew without a shred of doubt that Matt would always be the man he had been over a hundred years before. He would grow—she had already seen the beginning of that growth. He would deepen in emotional understanding—the process had already begun. But basically she knew that Matt would always be Matt, a man confident in his identity and comfortable with his own masculinity, a man secure within himself.

And in that instant, Virginia intuitively knew that this man was perhaps the only one she could ever make a commitment with. She was head over heels in love with him, but in addition to that she felt instinctively that they were soul mates, destined to be together. Matthew Hawk had traveled through time and space to be with her. She was as exclusively his as he was obviously hers.

Her fears resolved, Virginia was almost afraid to ask the only question left in her mind, afraid of hearing his answer, but she had to know. "Where? I mean, did you have any place special in mind."

"Well, I had kinda taken a fancy to the foothills near the Anaconda Mountains of Montana."

Virginia's spirits nose-dived. But he wasn't finished. Lifting her chin with one finger, Matt smiled at her in tender understanding.

"But foothills are foothills," he murmured. "And the foothills surrounding Conifer, Pennsylvania suit me just fine." He arched his brows. "How about you?"

Tears of relief and happiness rolling down her cheeks, Virginia whispered, "They suit me just fine, too."

"Good." Lowering his head, Matt kissed her tear-wet eyes, her damp cheeks and trembling lips. When he raised his head, his eyes were once again smiling, bright with purpose, alive. "Let's go home."

Virginia and Matt were married the Saturday after they returned to Conifer from Texas. With no fuss, no fanfare, but a wealth of love, they exchanged their vows in a civil ceremony. Holed up in Virginia's bedroom they had a one-day honeymoon, and then she went back to work.

Matt's gold coins were sold before spring gave way to summer, portioned out to a dozen eager and rich private collectors. His profit was, as Virginia had aptly predicted, "A bundle."

They spent almost all of Virginia's free time driving around the foothills, looking at property offered for sale. Most of the prospects were either too large or too run-down. There were two that Virginia considered workable, but shaking his head, Matt held firm in his belief that he'd know the place when he found it.

Late in August, becoming discouraged, they made a Sunday appointment to look at a small farm. The location was perfect for Virginia, since it was fifteen minutes from her office and the hospital. In fact, from the realtor's description, the property sounded entirely too good to be true. To her surprise, the farm was everything the realtor claimed it to be and more. Set in a valley nestled at the base of the foothills, the farm was a beautiful piece of real estate.

Virginia fell in love with it at once. Her eyes shining, she looked at Matt, and saw the emotion she was feeling gleaming in his blue eyes.

"It'll need some fixing up," he said laconically.

"Well, if you'd rather not bother..." Virginia let her voice trail away, as if she really didn't care.

Laughing, Matt swept her into his arms. "It's ours, and you know it." Planting a hard kiss upon her smiling mouth, he promised, "I'll have it ready by the time the baby comes."

Virginia had never really believed it was possible to be so happy. She had an ardent, caring husband who, from all indications, had no problem whatever with his self-image—Matt was all male in the best definition of the word. She was healthy and enjoying her pregnancy. She was working, and since the baby wasn't due until after Christmas, she planned to keep working until Thanksgiving. She was content.

By the time summer surrendered to fall with a blaze of color, Matt had completed all the renovations in the farmhouse except for the natural stone fireplace he was installing in the living room. The glorious leaves withered and drifted to the ground as the wide stone chimney climbed up the living-room wall to the ceiling.

After Thanksgiving, Virginia went on maternity leave... and on a shopping spree. While Matt worked around the house, she shopped for things to make it feel like a home.

It was during one such shopping expedition, this one for Christmas presents for Matt, that Virginia stopped by a used bookstore on her way back to the apartment. Throughout the eleven months that had passed since Matt had appeared, Virginia had continued to search for books on the subject of time travel. She had visited the shop before, and so went directly to the section where the books dealing with all forms of paranormal material were kept.

Virginia examined several paperback books before noticing a slim hardcover volume stuck between two hefty tomes. The title—*Here and Gone*—was scripted in faded gilt on the spine. Intrigued, she removed the book and opened it at the preface. She began to tremble as her eyes skimmed the three paragraphs of information. The book was a compilation of ten separate instances of what could only be explained as actual accounts of travel through time. Excitement curling through her, Virginia paid for the book, then rushed home to read it.

Several hours later, when Virginia closed the book, her happiness was shattered and her contentment gone. Though she tried to reject the conclusions drawn by the journalist who had compiled the accounts, uncertainty had been instilled into her mind.

Though each of the ten instances covered in the book had taken place at different times and in a variety of places, there were similarities in every one of them. The journalist had garnered the information in ten states along the eastern seaboard. The accounts concerned the sudden and unexplained appearance of ten different people, some male, some female, all of whom were reportedly disoriented and confused, insisting that they were not where they should be. In eight of the cases, the people claimed to be from a former time period. In the other two, they maintained they were from the future. The journalist stated that in every case the people were tested by experts in the proper fields and declared healthy and fit in mind and body. Further, the author maintained that in every instance, the person involved disappeared again—exactly one year later.

Matt came home late in the afternoon to find Virginia sitting in a corner of the sofa, pale and trembling.

"Ginnie?" Dropping to his knees on the floor beside her, Matt stared into her frightened eyes. "Honey, what's wrong? Is it the baby? Are you in pain?"

"No, no." Virginia shook her head. "I'm…it's this book, Matt." She thrust the slim volume into his hands. "Read it, Matt. Then, please, please, tell me it's all a fake, that it's not true."

"A book?" Matt frowned. "Honey, what is this?"

"Just read it, Matt, and then we'll talk."

But they didn't talk after he had finished reading, not really. They denied, derided and rationalized, but didn't really talk, not verbally. But they communicated with their eyes, and in those depths was revealed the uncertainty and terror that lurked in their hearts.

By mutual agreement, Virginia and Matt decided not to move into their new home until after the baby was born. The reason they gave each other for the delay was the closeness of her apartment to the hospital. But they both knew the real reason.

It began snowing around dawn the day before Christmas. Virginia went into labor late in the afternoon. The apparent coincidence in the time frame terrified her, though Matt was by her side every minute, coaching, encouraging, soothing, even joking with her. Only his eyes betrayed the fear he refused to let show or give voice to.

At 10:25 p.m. their daughter came into the world, squalling loudly against the indignity of it all. Exhausted, eyelids drooping, Virginia clung to Matt's hand.

"I love you so much," she whispered in a cry from the heart. "Don't leave. Please, don't leave me."

"I won't." Matt's voice was hoarse from strain. "You know I could never leave you. You're my life."

Virginia was half-asleep when she heard him begin to murmur. "I love you, Ginnie. Thank you for my daughter. She's beautiful, like her mother. Take care of her for me, if I..."

Matt's voice trailed away. Virginia was asleep.

Feeling the need to be alone, just in case he should do a disappearing act, Matt walked beside the litter that transported Virginia to her room, saw her settled into bed, then turned and walked to the visitors' lounge.

The room was empty. A partially finished puzzle was set out on a card table. Matt stared at the scattered pieces and sighed. It all looked so normal, so permanent. He was tired, and he was scared. Dropping into a chair by the window, he folded his arms on the wide windowsill and stared at the shimmering snowflakes dancing in the air.

In memory, Matt relived the events of his year in the twentieth century. Within that one short year he had seen and done things never dreamed of in his own time. And yet the most important event of all was something that had been happening through all time.

He had found love.

Leaning forward, Matt rested his head upon his folded arms and closed his eyes. It was Christmas Eve, almost Christmas morning. Within one short year, everything he had wanted had come to him. He had a decent life. He had a beautiful new daugher. He had Virginia's love.

A woman of his own.

Had he found it all, only to lose it again? Praying for Virginia, for their child and for himself, Matt fell asleep.

He wakened to the sound of church bells celebrating the arrival of Christmas. They sounded exactly like the ones he'd heard ringing from the crest of a hill in Montana. For an instant Matt was afraid to open his eyes. He flexed his fingers. They scraped against a hard surface, not cold snow. Drawing a deep breath, he raised his head and opened his eyes.

He was not lying on the ground in a pool of his own blood. It was Christmas morning. He was in the hospital's visitors' lounge. The year was up. He was alive. *He was no longer a stranger.*

Virginia.

Springing from the chair, Matt strode along the quiet hospital corridor to her room. He entered cautiously, so as not to disturb her. She was awake, and she was crying.

"Ginnie!" Crossing the room at a run, Matt sat down on the edge of the bed and lifted her into his arms.

"Matt! Oh, Matt!" Clinging to him, she sobbed against his chest. "I was so frightened. I thought you were gone... that you had disappeared, gone back."

"I know." Tears trailing down his cheeks, Matt held her close and murmured a silent prayer of thanks. "But I'm here, and I'm going to stay. Merry Christmas, honey. I'm home."

Epilogue

Virginia paused in the archway, a smile curving her lips as she skimmed a glance around the living room. It presented an attractive picture, not unlike those found on Christmas cards. A cheery fire crackled in the huge stone fireplace in the wall opposite her. The mantelpiece was festooned with garlands of deep green holly. Standing before the large window in the front wall was the enormous tree that Matt had dragged into the house earlier that week. The tree's decorations glistened and shimmered with dozens of white lights. Beyond the window, drifting snowflakes sparkled in the glow from the tree lights.

Dressed in tight jeans and bronzed male skin, Matt was sitting on the floor near the tree, the fingers of one hand toying with the gold bow on the small, gift-wrapped package he held in the palm of his other hand. As if sensing her presence, he looked up and smiled.

"All quiet?"

"Yes, finally," Virginia said, moving into the room.

"But for a minute there, I was beginning to think Amanda would never settle for the night."

"Give the kid a break, it's her birthday." Matt grinned, and ran a slow, appreciative glance over the filmy red negligee Virginia was wearing. It was a gift from him. "On second thought," he murmured, "come down here and give me a break. You look sexy as hell in that thing."

"Talk about sexy," Virginia retorted softly, sinking to the braided carpet beside him, "you forgot to wear your shirt."

Matt's grin grew wicked. "I didn't forget it."

"That's what I thought."

"I have a present for you."

Virginia smiled. "That's what I thought."

Laughing, Matt leaned forward to give her a quick kiss. "That present comes later," he murmured. "This one comes first." He placed the small package in her palm.

"But Matt," she protested. "You've already given me this gown, and it's only Christmas Eve."

"This one's special, in honor of the occasion," he said mysteriously. "Go on, open it."

Her curiosity aroused, Virginia carefully removed the bow and wrapping paper, then raised the lid of the black velvet jeweler's case. "Oh, Matt!" she whispered, tears filling her eyes as she stared at the gleaming piece of gold that nestled in the white satin lining the case. With trembling fingers she lifted the coin from its bed, murmuring again when she saw that the coin, bearing the date 1889, had been rimmed with gold and hung on a gold chain. "Oh, darling, thank you. It's beautiful. I love it. And I love you."

Drawing her into his arms, Matt kissed the tears from her cheeks. "You're welcome," he whispered. "And now we can get to the best present of all." Laughing, he lowered her to the floor. "Just in case I haven't told you often enough, let me show you how much I love you."

From the far corner of the room, the grandfather clock

struck the hour of midnight, announcing Christmas with its bell-like chimes.

Matt's mouth claimed Virginia's, and the last thing she saw before her eyes drifted shut was the solitary decoration on the wide stone chimney above the mantelpiece.

Hanging from a hook painted gold was a worn leather gun belt, complete with a Colt Peacemaker.

* * * * *

Dear Reader,

Christmastime at our house is a Very Big Deal. My husband, David, and I always host my entire family, and with the recent additions of my son and three nieces, we now have the laughter of children to bring even more cheer.

Naturally, food and spirits are a traditional part of our celebration, and because of my family's Southern and rural roots, the Christmas goose is actually a country ham with red-eye gravy. My mother's cheese grits are the perfect complement, but somehow our traditional dessert has become a rather *un*traditional chocolate cheesecake created by my brother Danny. David always makes wassail and his Killer Eggnog, and my aunt Sissy's Tom and Jerries are the best you've ever tasted.

But what makes the holiday extra special is that we live in the house that belonged to my grandmother until she passed away. When she was alive, we always came to this house to enjoy Christmas dinner as a family—much like the Bellamy family does in "Jake's Christmas." And in many ways, I feel like my grandmother is still with us on that day, joining in the celebration, uniting the family.

Wishing you the happiest of holidays this season,

Elizabeth Bevarly

JAKE'S CHRISTMAS

Elizabeth Bevarly

For my two sisters-in-law, Maritza and Laura,
who took on the toughest jobs of all.
Much love, and good luck.

One

"The wedding was wonderful, Rebecca, even lovelier than your last one."

"Yes, dear, they just keep getting better and better. How many have there been now?"

Rebecca Bellamy listened to the praise of the two elderly women seated at her table and smiled modestly. She gazed out at the collection of people dancing and laughing in the cavernous white greatroom of the Peterson-Dumesnil House—her favorite place to hold her receptions—and sighed contentedly. Fluffing her long, dark curls discreetly and smoothing a hand over the lapel of her shell pink suit jacket, she replied proudly, "Twenty-two. And would you believe I'm already in the planning stages for number twenty-three?"

The other women exchanged meaningful looks and nodded their approval.

"Keep up the good work, dear," one of them said as she patted Rebecca's hand.

Murmuring her thanks, Rebecca excused herself from the table with the explanation that she needed to check on how the food was holding out at the buffet. Her weddings were indeed some of the most talked-about events in virtually every Louisville social circle, and she couldn't help but feel a tremendous sense of pride and accomplishment. She had come a long way in five years.

Planning weddings for other people almost made up for never having been able to plan one of her own. Still, Rebecca knew deep down that she was saving all of her best ideas for the nuptial celebration she hoped to enjoy herself someday. Just because her first hastily executed marriage had ended up in a shambles didn't mean she had to remain alone for the rest of her life. All she had to do now was find the perfect mate. Unfortunately, she was beginning to wonder if that particular aspect of her wedding plans might take some time.

The new Mrs. Daphne Duryea-Prescott, Rebecca's most recent employer, swooped in on her then, looking like a white, poofy cloud with her platinum blond hair and elaborately decorated wedding gown topped by an eight-foot-long veil. It was an ensemble that probably cost more than a number of Rebecca's clients spent on their entire wedding budget. At twenty-three, Daphne was only seven years Rebecca's junior, but the look of complete innocence and excitement that lit her eyes indicated a youthfulness that Rebecca could scarcely recall experiencing herself.

"Rebecca, come quick," Daphne said anxiously.

Rebecca snapped to attention. "What is it? What's wrong?" She knew things seldom ran entirely smoothly at weddings, and Daphne's should certainly be no different. But whatever was amiss could surely be corrected. She hoped.

Daphne clutched a fold in her white lace gown in one hand and lifted a battered bunch of flowers with the other. "I'm getting ready to throw the bouquet."

Rebecca smiled indulgently. "That's more a matter for

the photographer, Daphne. I'm sure you'll do fine without me.''

''But you're a single woman,'' Daphne protested. ''You have to be there. I kind of wanted you to be the one to catch it.''

Rebecca's heart kicked up a funny rhythm at hearing Daphne's declaration. The last time she'd caught a bridal bouquet, she'd wound up with a husband before the year was through. Five years after that, she'd found herself divorced. Another five years had passed since then, and Rebecca was just starting to reap the benefits of all the hard work she'd put into building her business. Despite the fact that she certainly had no aversion to marriage, she still wasn't sure she was ready to risk an investment like that again just yet.

''Oh, I don't think so, Daphne,'' she hedged, ''but thanks, anyway. Grappling with bridesmaids for the bouquet isn't exactly in my job description.''

''Oh, come on,'' Daphne pleaded. ''You said you'd do anything for me where my wedding was concerned.''

''And your parents are paying dearly for it,'' Rebecca pointed out. ''I'm here as your wedding planner. And as much as I've enjoyed doing it, it is, after all, my job.'' Her expression softened as she smiled and took Daphne's hand in hers. ''Throw your bouquet to someone who will cherish it. Now, I really must go and check on the buffet.''

''Rebecca...''

''It is what you hired me for, Daphne.''

''I know, but I want to do something nice for you, because you've made my wedding day so memorable.''

Rebecca, ever the astute businesswoman, replied with a wide grin, ''Then recommend me to your friends.''

Daphne's shoulders drooped in defeat. ''I already have,'' she told Rebecca petulantly. ''You know, for someone who plans weddings for a living, you sure aren't every romantic.''

Rebecca's grin grew broader. "On the contrary, I'm all for romance. It keeps me working."

"You know, you're as bad as my Uncle Jake," Daphne muttered. "You guys would get along just swell." Her eyes widened then, full of speculation, as she added, "Hey, by the way, have you met my Uncle Jake yet?"

It was perhaps one of the most dreaded questions a single or divorced woman in her thirties wanted to hear, rivaled only by the one about someone's nephew. Or cousin. Or brother. Or barber. "Oh, gee, Daphne, I really do have to check on the buffet," Rebecca assured the other woman as she began to back away in fear for her personal safety. "Maybe some other time, okay?"

"But—"

"I'm sure we're starting to run low on crab puffs and stuffed mushrooms. Gotta go."

As she threaded her way through the crowd of well-wishers attending the Duryea-Prescott affair, Rebecca's panic at being cornered by a paunchy, balding uncle who probably worked as an undertaker or door-to-door salesman began to ebb, and she began to feel festive once again.

There was simply something magical about weddings, Rebecca thought. Her own had been prepared on the spur of the moment and had claimed none of the flourish for which she had become famous in Louisville. As college students, she and her ex-husband had found themselves spending spring break in Bermuda during her junior year. One night, in a fit of romantic nonsense resulting from too many piña coladas, they had rounded up the first clergyman they could find, and had gotten married on the beach at sunrise.

Her parents had been extremely upset by the revelation when Rebecca had announced the deed, a reaction for which she had been fully prepared. Ruth and Dan Bellamy had never approved of Eliot, had worried from the start that he was only interested in Rebecca because of the Bellamy wealth. Upon learning of the marriage, they had offered an equally upsetting revelation of their own—their daughter and her new husband would be completely cut off from them financially.

Thinking back now, Rebecca supposed the action had been her parents' way of making sure Eliot's affections were genuine. Had the two of them remained married and been able to prove to the world that love was indeed what had kept them together, her parents would have no doubt reinstated Rebecca's ample allowance. But Eliot had proved instead that his affections were anything but genuine. And thankfully, when the marriage did fall apart, her parents had lovingly welcomed her back into the family circle, and to their credit had never issued a single word of reproach.

But that was in the past now, she reminded herself. Eliot was living with his wife in California, where he had set up a law practice, and was about as far removed from Rebecca's life as he could possibly be. Why, she scarcely even thought about him anymore. Except occasionally, late at night sometimes, when she was watching TV and saw all those commercials for sleazy, unethical, ambulance-chasing attorneys. Only then did Eliot's impression brave even the tiniest entry into her brain.

Rebecca was so preoccupied by thoughts of the past that several moments went by before she realized she had been halted on her journey to the buffet by a group of women who were casually chatting in the middle of the greatroom. At first, she didn't understand exactly what they were all doing there, just standing around. Then, when she heard someone cry out her name, she glanced up quickly, startled to find a large collection of gardenias, white roses, calla lilies and sweetheart ivy descending rapidly in her direction. Instinctively, she threw up her hands to ward off the projectile…and discovered much to her dismay that she had just caught the bridal bouquet.

"Gotcha!" Daphne called out with a chuckle.

Rebecca had the decency to look caught, then graciously

lifted the flowers to her nose. They smelled sweet and fresh and alive, exactly how a marriage between two people should be. For just a moment, Rebecca allowed herself to believe such a state of wedded bliss was in store for her someday.

"I'll get you for this, Daphne, if it's the last thing I do," she assured the blushing bride quietly, only half joking.

"Invite me to your wedding," Daphne replied, clapping her hands in delight.

Rebecca shook her head hopelessly, lifted the bouquet to inhale its sweet aroma one final time, then settled it against her shoulder as if it was a burden to be borne. She promised herself she would put the flowers in water as soon as she got home. But in the back of Rebecca's mind, all she could think was that before the week was through, the tender, fragile blossoms would surely all wither and die.

On the other side of the room, Jake Raglan sat at the bar savoring his Scotch and water and watching the byplay on the greatroom floor with much disgust. God, now there was another one out there—another woman looking to land a husband she could drain dry and suck the life out of. He should probably finish his drink and get the hell out of there before she set her sights on him. There was no way he was going to get caught in another mantrap like the one his ex-wife had set for him. He'd chew his own foot off first if he had to.

"Would you care for another drink, sir?"

Jake looked up at the bartender's question and told himself he should say no, that he had to get going before something terrible happened. Instead, he nodded, reasoning that since he was Daphne's favorite uncle, his niece would certainly notice his early departure, and then he'd never hear the end of it from the mouthy kid.

Involuntarily, his gaze traveled back to settle on the woman who had just caught Daphne's bouquet, lingering as he took in the tantalizing curves her suit did little to conceal. She was some piece of work, he'd grant that. He watched as she silently saluted the bride and spun on her heel, carrying the fragile white flowers as if they would dissolve before she took two steps.

He wondered how she knew Daphne. The woman looked to be several years older than his niece, so therefore probably hadn't been a classmate or sorority sister. And because Daphne had majored in landing a husband in college rather than focusing on career training, the recipient of the bouquet couldn't be a co-worker. Daphne didn't have a job. The two of them probably enjoyed some social tie, Jake decided, showed up at all the same parties or did the same charity work. The other woman looked like she came from a moneyed background.

When he realized the object of his appraisal was approaching the bar, Jake's earlier apprehension returned, and he suddenly felt like a deer on the highway, caught in the headlights of an oncoming semi. He chuckled quietly at his analogy. No, he would be a *stag* on the highway of life, he corrected himself with masculine pride, and from the slight build of the woman coming his way, he would be caught in the headlights of a sputtering moped. He'd probably do considerably more damage to her than she could ever do to him.

Frowning, he wondered where in the hell that idea had come from and took another swallow of his drink. Still, he continued to study the woman as she neared, because she was without question someone worth studying. Small but slender, she gave the impression of height, regardless of the fact that she was probably no more than five-three in her stocking feet. Her hair was a tousled mane of near-black curls that spilled down her back in a tangle. As she came nearer—and was that incredible smile meant for him?—he realized that her eyes were a magnificent color he'd never seen on another human being, a dark olive green that hinted at a deep-seated passion.

He watched while she exchanged pleasantries with the

bartender, then turned on his stool to face her fully. As soon as she had been close enough to do so, she had set the bouquet of flowers on the bar and now avoided looking at them. Jake thought such a response intriguing. Wasn't catching the bouquet supposed to be the ultimate feminine achievement? Wasn't that matrimonial trophy what every single woman strove to win at wedding receptions?

As the bartender placed a glass of club soda before the woman, Jake couldn't help the devilishly playful thoughts that bounced around in his head. Before he realized what he was doing, he had risen from his place at the bar to move closer to the woman.

"Run while there's still time," he said quietly as he took his seat on the bar stool beside her.

She glanced over with an expression of genuine surprise and stammered, "I...I beg your pardon?"

Jake noted then that her eyes weren't completely green. The part of the iris around each pupil was stained with brown, looking like a scattering of winter leaves. The color made her seem more...unattainable, somehow. He suddenly wanted nothing more than to pull her as close as he possibly could without getting himself arrested.

Pointing to the neglected bouquet, he grinned as he repeated, "Run. While there's still time." Only at this point, Jake wasn't sure if he was talking to her or to himself.

The woman smiled back at him, a little uncertainly at first, then with what Jake for some reason suspected was a rarely displayed shyness. He was ridiculously pleased that he seemed to have scored a point with her.

"Is it that obvious?" she asked.

The smile that punctuated her question threw him off guard for a moment. It was a disconcerting realization. No woman had caught Jake Raglan off guard since his ex-wife. And look how that had turned out.

"Is what that obvious?" he finally asked, still reeling from the odd sensations burning up the air between them.

Rebecca considered the man who had made himself at

home beside her, trying to conjure a polite reason to excuse herself from this conversation before it could get started. Not because she didn't want to talk to the man—he was, after all, rather breathtakingly handsome—but because she had only come over to the bar to check the wine situation on her way to the buffet and didn't have time to dawdle.

"Never mind," she replied absently to the question she couldn't remember now.

She had seen him earlier, of course, at Daphne's wedding ceremony, the moment he'd entered the cathedral. He was the kind of man a woman couldn't help but notice. At roughly six feet in height, he would tower over her, she knew, if he were standing beside her instead of sitting. As it was now, she stood eye to eye with him, even in heels. And what eyes they were—as dark blue as an early nightfall, and full of any number of suggestive ideas. His hair was dark, too, claiming more hints of nighttime color— black threaded with bits of silver. Even his suit was dark, complemented by a discreet dove gray necktie. He looked to be in his late thirties, and was, to put it mildly, a very attractive man.

"I'm sorry, Mr...."

"Raglan. Jake Raglan."

He *would* have a name like that, Rebecca thought absently. "Mr. Raglan," she repeated a little breathlessly. Then his first name registered, too, and her eyes widened in surprise. "You can't be Daphne's Uncle Jake?"

Jake, too, was surprised by the question, but smiled indulgently as he rejoined, "Why can't I be?"

"Well, because you're supposed to be paunchy and balding," she blurted out before she realized what she was saying. "You're not supposed to be so..."

Now Jake's smile became dangerous. "Not so what?"

Rebecca felt herself blushing, and bit her lip to prevent any more blathering that would cause her to further embarrass herself. Feeling more and more flustered with each passing second, she said hastily, "I really do have to run, Mr. Raglan. I'm on my way to the buffet."

"You're that hungry?"

Why, all of a sudden, did everything he said sound like a sexually charged come-on? Rebecca wondered wildly. "No, I..." What was it she had to do, again? "I have to check on the, uh, crab puffs and...and the stuffed mushrooms."

"Delicious," Jake told her in a very smooth, very seductive voice.

Rebecca didn't pause to ponder what exactly Jake Raglan might be thinking was delicious. She only knew she had to be going, and the sooner the better. "I, ah... Excuse me, will you?"

Without waiting for a reply, Rebecca spun around and headed for the buffet, completely forgetting that she had left her club soda and the bridal bouquet on the bar.

Jake chuckled to himself as he watched her leave, enjoying the fact that he could still fluster a beautiful woman, in spite of his much despised and all-too-quickly-approaching fortieth birthday. As he turned to pick up his drink once again, Jake saw his niece's bouquet lying on the bar and realized the woman had forgotten to take it with her. It was a good sign. It meant the ultimate symbol of impending matrimony meant very little, if anything at all, to her. She might be just the kind of woman he was looking for. And he didn't even know her name.

Jake was about to get up and make a little trip to the buffet himself when he saw the woman in question penetrate the crowd on the dance floor to begin an unsteady journey toward the bar once more. He told himself he had *not* breathed a sigh of relief at her reappearance, but merely wanted to clear his lungs in preparation for that tantalizing scent that had clung to her when she'd stood so close to him before.

She approached him slowly, uncertainly, casting her gaze everywhere except on him, as if she was trying to sneak past without alerting his attention. Fat chance, Jake thought. Gingerly, she extended her left hand toward the white flowers that lay in a heap on the bar. The moment she touched the delicate leaves, Jake gently circled her wrist with long fingers and lifted her hand for his inspection. Only then did she meet his gaze, and only then did he realize the mistake he'd made in touching her.

She was soft. Her skin was warm and smooth, and the bones in her wrist and hand felt as small and fragile as a child's. Below his thumb, he could feel her pulse quicken and dance at his touch. But her eyes were what held his interest most of all. They were dark and full of longing, and as panic nearly overcame him, Jake realized the desire he saw flickering to life in her eyes must only reflect his own. Oh, boy, was he in trouble.

"No ring," he said softly, trying to quell his own pulse rate as it threatened to run wild at the realization that she responded to him so quickly, so completely.

Rebecca's heart felt as if it were about to burst behind her rib cage. Somewhere deep within her soul, a flame that had smoldered to life when she first beheld Jake Raglan exploded into a raging wildfire. She took a deep, unsteady breath, but told herself she wouldn't succumb to him so easily this time.

"No, no ring," she replied levelly.

"So that means you're single?" Jake assured himself he had no further interest in her answer beyond casual curiosity, but for some reason, the thought that this woman might be joined to another man made his heart do funny things.

"Divorced, actually," Rebecca confided reluctantly.

He nodded in silent understanding, then laced her fingers through his. "You don't have a ring, but you must have a name."

"Yes…"

The silent pause between them seemed to grow until it was a dangerous, limitless chasm. Jake didn't quite seem certain he wanted to know her name, and Rebecca wasn't quite certain she wanted to offer it.

Finally, he put an end to their silent queries by commanding simply, "Tell me."

"Rebecca," she replied without hesitation. "Rebecca Bellamy."

For one long moment, they looked at each other as if neither could understand what was happening between them. Rebecca felt herself falling into the dark blue depths of his eyes and spinning out of control as if caught in a hot, raging whirlpool. The fingers wrapped around her wrist were warm and rough in texture, but gentle in their embrace.

"So, Mr. Raglan—"

"Jake."

Her heartbeat quickened again at the thought of being more familiar with this man than she already felt she was. "Jake," she repeated quietly in an effort to break the spell that seemed to have settled over them. "What...what kind of man are you that you can make people reveal things about themselves they weren't necessarily willing to surrender?"

His lips curled into a smile at her surprisingly accurate observation. "I'm an attorney."

Jake felt Rebecca's skin temperature drop about twenty degrees at his statement, watched as her entire posture changed. Her eyes darkened dangerously, and her body became rigid. Slowly, effortlessly, she withdrew her hand from his loose grasp to grip the bar tightly, and for some bizarre reason, Jake got the impression that she clung to the bar because to let go would cause her to wrap her fingers firmly around his throat. Suddenly his tie felt extremely constrictive, and almost as an involuntary reaction, he fumbled to loosen it.

"An attorney. How nice," Rebecca said blandly. "Well, it was very nice meeting you, Mr. Raglan. Now, if you'll excuse me, I really must be going."

"Hey, wait a minute," Jake protested, taking her wrist in his hand once more. This time he was less willing to release it when she made the move to do so. He studied her intently, but she refused to meet his gaze. "Rebecca, what's wrong?"

Rebecca's shoulders slumped in surrender. It had happened again. Every time she met a man who identified himself as a lawyer, she set her interior temperature to frostbite and walked away. As much as she might try to deny it, Eliot Madison still influenced her life, even after being absent from it for five years.

"I'm sorry, Mr. Raglan," Rebecca apologized. "I didn't mean to be rude. I'm…" She waved her hand at nothing. "You just took me by surprise, that's all."

"Yeah, well, I'm not the only one who came as a surprise here. You don't exactly seem like the type of woman who would scorn weddings. Of course, now that I realize you're divorced—"

"Who says I scorn weddings?" Rebecca asked, drawing her eyebrows down in confusion. "I don't understand."

Jake was also puzzled. "I… No one. No one *said* you did. I just meant… Well, you walked off and left Daphne's bouquet sitting here after going to all the trouble to catch it. I just figured that meant you weren't real keen on the topic of matrimony."

Rebecca stared at him thoughtfully for a moment before replying. "In the first place, I didn't go to all the trouble to catch it. Daphne threw it at me. In the second place, I didn't leave it here because I don't want it, I left it here because I forgot to take it with me." She neglected to add that the reason she forgot was because she had been so addled by Jake's imposing presence. "And as for the topic of matrimony, Mr. Raglan, no one could be more supportive than I am of the institution of marriage. I plan weddings for a living. I planned this one. Someday, I even hope to plan one for myself."

Jake tamped down the desire to make a cross out of his

two index fingers and back away from Rebecca, but instead wondered at the vehemence with which she delivered her words. "But you said you were divorced," he mumbled lamely, not knowing what else to say.

"Yes, I am that," Rebecca agreed. "I worked three jobs for five years to put my husband through school, only to have him dump me the day after he earned his degree. Despite that, I still believe it's worth celebrating when two people find each other and want to spend the rest of their lives together."

Jake had stepped on more than a few toes in his time. In his profession, it was impossible not to. But he had never once felt guilt or remorse for hurting someone else's feelings or for putting them on the defensive. Yet as he looked at Rebecca Bellamy, saw her attempt an aggressive stance despite the pain in her eyes she couldn't hide, Jake suddenly felt like the worst kind of creep. And then he got angry, too. Because he didn't like it when someone else had control over his emotions.

"Yeah, well, I'm beginning to understand why hubby took a powder," he shot at Rebecca in retaliation, damning himself for feeling even worse when the pain in her eyes made them appear even larger. "If the poor sap had to listen to tirades like that one all the time, I can sympathize with the guy."

Rebecca chuckled humorlessly before snatching the bridal bouquet viciously from the bar. "That doesn't surprise me for a moment, Mr. Raglan. Because the school I put my husband through was *law* school, and his degree was a *law* degree. *He* was trained to be a coldhearted bastard, too."

Before Jake could say another word, Rebecca turned her back on him and disappeared into the gradually thinning crowd. What had begun as a day meant to celebrate the lifelong union of his niece and her new husband had ended up bringing Jake together with someone only long enough to thoroughly drive them apart. He told himself he was better off, that women like Rebecca Bellamy were nothing but trouble. Unfortunately, all he could think about instead was the way she'd looked at him when he'd told her he sympathized with her husband.

It had been a lie, of course. Jake couldn't begin to imagine any man having Rebecca Bellamy and then letting her go. Only an idiot would do something like that. An idiot or a bastard whose heart was indeed cold. As he drained the last of his drink from the glass, Jake had to admit grimly that maybe Rebecca Bellamy's assessment of him hadn't been so far off the mark, after all.

And that, more than anything else she had said to him, made Jake Raglan feel like a fool.

TWO

"**Y**ou're going to do *what?*"

"Alison and I are getting married. And keep your voice down, will you, Jake? She's over in my office right now."

Jake glared at his partner, Stephen Flannery, then down at the array of paperwork scattered across his desk. He'd been working all morning on the Sinclair divorce case—one that was making headlines throughout Louisville thanks to the local businessman's wealth and prominence—and he had come to the conclusion that any man with even half a brain would never, ever, allow himself to get roped into marriage unless he was the worst kind of masochist. Now his partner and best friend was admitting that he was in fact just such a madman.

"How could you possibly let that woman talk you into something like this?" he demanded caustically. "You, above all people, should know better."

"Jake..." Stephen began, his voice edged with warning.

"Just think of Gordon Sinclair," Jake continued, jabbing

a finger pointedly at the clutter on his desk as he rose to move in front of it. "The poor sap gets tangled up with some bimbo half his age, and the next thing you know, she's got him down on his knees proposing to her. Less than two years after that, his lovely wife is leaving him, tearing every strip of flesh from his bones as she goes."

"Knock it off, Jake," Stephen cautioned. "For one thing, Alison is nothing like Elaine Sinclair. If you'd ever taken the time to meet her, you would have realized that by now. And as for Gordon Sinclair, the guy robbed a cradle, begged the kid to be his wife, then spent the next two years sleeping around on her. If I were Elaine, I'd want a piece of his hide, too."

"You're missing the point," Jake objected.

"No, *you're* the one missing the point. Just because you suffered a messy divorce at the hands of your ex-wife— whose brother, incidentally, happened to be as brilliant a divorce attorney as you are and went for the jugular on an already-wounded man—it doesn't mean every woman in America is suspect."

"I never said every woman in America is suspect," Jake corrected him. "I said every woman in the *world* is."

Stephen shook his head hopelessly. "Look, will you just come out and meet Alison? She's really nervous about making a good impression."

"Yeah, I'll bet she is," Jake muttered. To himself, he added, She's probably afraid I'll be able to see her for what she really is, and not with the muddled, foggy outlook of a man besotted by what he thinks is true love.

"I'm busy right now," Jake hedged. "I promised Gordon I'd have this financial statement prepared by this afternoon."

"You're going to have to have to meet her eventually," Stephen said wearily. "And it would be especially convenient if the introductions took place before the nineteenth."

"Why then?"

"Because that's the date of the wedding—"

"In three weeks?"

"—and I want you to be my best man."

Any other objection Jake might have voiced was cut off by his partner's request. Best man? In a ceremony he could never condone? Uh-uh. No way.

"Forget it, Stephen," he said simply. "You want to wreck your life, that's up to you. But don't expect me to be there facilitating it."

"I'm not wrecking my life."

"Yes, you are," Jake told him. "You're not even thinking this through. Three weeks isn't long enough to consider all the implications that come with marriage."

"Alison and I have been talking about getting married for over two months," Stephen informed him. "Last week, we finally set the date."

Jake could tell by the expression on his partner's face that there was no way he would be able to talk him out of the horrible mistake he was about to make. In a last-ditch effort, however, he stressed, "Three weeks isn't long enough to plan a wedding. You need more time."

Sensing his friend was weakening, Stephen braved a smile as he replied, "The wedding planner Alison hired said she could organize a very nice celebration in only three weeks."

The words "wedding planner" caught and held Jake's attention more than any others his partner had uttered. Immediately, his brain filled with images of a dark-haired, green-eyed beauty in a soft pink suit, a woman who had possessed his dreams for more than three months now, ever since Daphne's wedding in June.

Jake had never been plagued by such an experience before—meeting a woman once, and very briefly at that, only to have her totally bewitch him until he could scarcely think of anything else. Even after three months, he could picture Rebecca Bellamy very well, only instead of seeing her in the simple pink suit she'd worn that day, Jake usually conjured her up in something dark and lacy and thoroughly arousing. It had caused him to suffer more than one sleepless night.

"Wedding planner?" he heard himself repeating out loud, his voice sounding tinny and hollow, as if it were coming from someplace far away.

Stephen nodded, his smile broadening suggestively. "A real knockout, too. Now *she* might be able to change your mind about being in the wedding. Come on out and meet her. She's with Alison in my office."

"Is she...?" Jake caught himself before he said anything further. No, it couldn't be. A city this size must have a number of women who did what Rebecca Bellamy did for a living. Just because Stephen had said she was a knockout... "Oh, all right," he finally relented, hating himself when he realized he was unconsciously straightening his tie and fingering his hair back into place.

"I knew it," Stephen said with a triumphant chuckle. "All it takes is the mention of a beautiful woman, and you're hooked."

Jake grumbled something unintelligible under his breath, but followed his partner out of his own office and across the reception area to Stephen's. Their secretary had left to run an errand, and an eerie silence hung over the room, foreshadowing, Jake was sure somehow, what would be an equally eerie situation.

"It's okay, Alison," Stephen said as he opened the door. "Jake promised to be on his best behavior."

Jake was about to state emphatically that he had made no such vow, but was silenced when he saw the two women who stood to greet him. His eyes skimmed briefly over the one he knew must be Alison, taking in her short blond hair and tailored dark suit. She was...cute, he mused. Really...very cute. Somehow, he had expected a loud, overbearing, fire-breathing vixen with long red fingernails perfectly honed into hooks that could seize a man by the loins and never let go. Instead, Stephen's fiancée looked like a well-educated, even-tempered, normal, everyday kind of woman.

On the other hand, her companion did indeed turn on the heat, no less intense now than it had been three months ago. Rebecca Bellamy was still an exceptionally beautiful woman, Jake reflected, and she still touched a part of him deep down inside that he hadn't known existed—a raw nerve that shuddered and burned simply because she was present in the same room.

Today she wore loose-fitting brown wool trousers and a man's-style tweed jacket over an ivory blouse. Her hair was bound loosely at her nape with a gold clip, cascading over one shoulder like a wild, night-drenched river. But her eyes were what held Jake's attention most, fascinating him with the play of emotion that she was clearly unable to hide. He couldn't mistake the fact that she was surprised by his appearance, nor could he deny that she was obviously none too pleased as a result of it. Before he could comment on what either of them might be thinking or feeling, however, Stephen launched quickly into introductions.

"Alison, this is Jake Raglan. See? I told you he wasn't a monster. Not around women, anyway." Hastily, he qualified, "Except, of course, for those women who are married to his clients. And Jake, this is my fiancée, Alison Mitchell. Just for the record, she's not a monster, either. Except around the month of April. CPAs are like that sometimes. Taxes…you know what I mean."

"Alison," Jake managed impatiently by way of a greeting. Somewhat reluctantly, he extended his hand, prepared to leap on whatever faults he could find in Stephen's fiancée. He was surprised to discover that Alison had a very firm, self-assured grip, one that mirrored his own.

"Jake," she replied in a tone of voice similar to the one he'd used with her. That surprised him, too.

"And this," Stephen continued, indicating his fiancée's companion, "is—"

"Rebecca," Jake interrupted, his voice softening involuntarily when he turned his attention to her. He extended his hand to Rebecca as well, and couldn't help but smile when she unconsciously swiped her palm across the leg of her trousers before settling her hand in his. Her skin was every bit as soft as he remembered it being, but her grasp on his hand wasn't nearly as confident as the attitude she tried to project. Again, Jake was delighted that he was able to set her off kilter.

"Mr. Raglan," she replied coolly.

"Jake," he corrected her.

"You've met," Stephen said quietly, clearly aware that he was intruding on something.

"Mr. Raglan," Rebecca repeated meaningfully, avoiding the use of Jake's first name.

Stephen raised his eyebrows in speculation. "She knows you well, then," he mumbled to his friend.

"Not as well as she's going to," Jake responded just loudly enough for everyone in the room to hear. After a pregnant pause during which no one said a word, he added, "Since I'm going to be in the wedding, I mean."

The others nodded quickly, mumbling agreement.

"Of course," Rebecca repeated after swallowing with some difficulty. She hurriedly explained for the others' benefit, "I planned Mr. Raglan's niece's wedding some months ago. That's where he and I met."

"It was a terrific bash," Jake said enthusiastically. "Especially the, uh, little set-to that ensued after the bride threw her bouquet."

"How is Daphne?" Rebecca asked before Jake could say any more.

"She and Robby are doing fine. She's putting on weight, though." He grinned wickedly as he added, "My sister is terrified that her daughter might be in a family way. At forty-five, Ellen is less than willing to become a grandmother."

"And that would make you a great-uncle, wouldn't it?" Rebecca asked conversationally.

Jake wasn't sure, but he could almost swear her eyes sparkled when she posed her question. He hadn't thought about that when he'd made the teasing remark about his sister. However, the suggestion—and realization—that he himself was old enough to be of the "great" generation was less than grand.

"Yeah, I guess it would," he replied thoughtfully.

"Hey, Alison, do you feel like we've intruded into a conversation that started a long time ago?" Stephen asked suddenly.

Both Jake and Rebecca started visibly, as if each had forgotten that the other two people were in the room.

"Kind of," Alison agreed with a grin. "Look, since Jake and Rebecca know each other, why don't you guys join us for lunch? We were just going to walk down the street to Charley's."

Jake noted that Rebecca was shaking her head as vigorously as he was when he said, "No, I don't think so."

"Oh, come on," Alison cajoled. "We'll be talking about plans for the wedding, and you'll both need to be briefed on them, anyway. We'll be killing two birds."

Somehow Alison's choice of cliché seemed very appropriate to Jake. Whenever he was around Rebecca Bellamy, he did indeed feel as if someone had dashed a stone against his head. He only hoped the dizziness and nausea he was experiencing now wouldn't wind up being a permanent condition. He knew he should decline the offer, knew it was foolish to spend any more time with Rebecca than he absolutely had to. Then he imagined what she might be wearing under her man's-style clothes and smiled dangerously.

"Lunch sounds good," he finally said quietly, throwing Rebecca the hungriest look he could manage. He only wished it would be Rebecca Bellamy, and not something as bland as a club sandwich, that he would be sinking his teeth into.

* * *

For Rebecca, lunch was only the prelude to what she was fast becoming to think of as the wedding from hell. She had thought it would be a wonderful challenge, planning an elaborate celebration for fifty people in less than four weeks. She had thought it would be fun. Alison Mitchell and Stephen Flannery had seemed like such nice people, she thought, as she gazed over her spinach salad at the two of them seated on the other side of the booth. How could they be doing this to her now?

"What do you mean, you want to have the ceremony at Jake's house?" she heard herself asking in disbelief, shocked by her own rudeness, but helpless to disguise her distress.

Ever since she had stood up in Stephen Flannery's office to find Jake Raglan entering her life again, Rebecca had been unsteady on her feet and ready to bolt at any moment. Wasn't it bad enough that she had remembered him looking so incredibly handsome in a dark suit? Now she had to see how gorgeous and sexy he was in a light-colored one, as well? For three months the man had haunted her thoughts and dreams, and for three months, Rebecca had been telling herself it was only a matter of time until she would weed him out of her system.

But her preoccupation with him hadn't ebbed at all. In fact, the more she had tried to deny how attractive she'd found him, the deeper her thoughts of him seemed to take root in her mind. She had told herself she was blowing his physical attributes out of proportion, that no man could possibly be as handsome as she was remembering him. And now she had to admit uncomfortably that her recollections of Jake Raglan didn't even begin to do the man justice.

The blue eyes she had found so compelling then were now lit with easy humor and fun as he witnessed her obvious anxiety, and the dark hair sprinkled with bits of silver called to her traitorous hands like a siren's song, urging her to bury her fingers there and pull him close until they could lose themselves in each other.

Almost as if he sensed the avenue her thoughts had taken, Jake shifted his position on the seat beside her in the booth, and his thigh brushed briefly against hers. Immediately, Rebecca wondered what the same action would feel like if they were both undressed, then felt her cheeks flame in horror that she was entertaining such uncharacteristic thoughts. Oh, no, Rebecca hadn't forgotten Jake Raglan at all. And now she would have to start trying all over again.

She wasn't sure if he was doing it on purpose when he changed positions again and this time let his leg linger against hers, but his smile was suspicious when she glanced over at him. For some reason, though, she did nothing to put a little distance between them.

"I think it's a great idea," Jake said in reference to his earlier offer. He still wasn't sure why he'd made it, but now that it was done, it seemed appropriate. "I've been living in that house for six months now, and I have yet to entertain anyone. There will be plenty of room, and weather-wise, late October is generally a beautiful time of year around here. There will still be flowers in the backyard." And that, he told himself, was the only reason he was doing this. It had nothing to do with the fact that now Rebecca would be forced to spend a good deal of time at his house and, consequently, with him. Nothing whatsoever.

"But..." she began to object.

"Rebecca, you have to see this guy's house to appreciate it," Stephen told her. "It really is a showplace since he had the decorators in. You'll love it."

Rebecca's smile was hollow as she tried to calm her frantic thoughts. This was not going at all as planned. When she and Alison had spoken on the phone last week, the bride-to-be had described a dream she had embraced since childhood, to have her wedding occur outdoors, against a well-manicured, parklike backdrop.

Immediately, Rebecca had thought of Gardencourt at the Presbyterian Seminary, a beautifully landscaped and recently renovated location. It would have been magnificent. Mid-autumn weather, chrysanthemums of yellow, gold and amber springing up amid leaves of red, ocher, copper and plum, a color scheme for the wedding of scarlet and ivory and black.... She sighed inaudibly at the memory. It would have been so lovely.

But now... *Now* Stephen was suggesting mutiny, and Alison was going along with him. Had the words "Jake Raglan's house" come up during their conversation last week, Rebecca would have slammed the telephone receiver down into its cradle and bolted every door and window in her office, then would have placed the Out to Lunch sign in the window indefinitely and caught the next flight to Tierra del Fuego.

"Of course, Alison will want to have a look at the house before deciding," Stephen was saying when Rebecca finally pulled herself back into the conversation. "But it was awfully generous of you to offer, Jake. I must say, you're taking a more active role in this wedding than I thought you would."

Jake waved a hand negligently and replied magnanimously, "Well, that was before I realized what a wonderful woman you were marrying."

However, it wasn't Alison who claimed his attention as he spoke, Rebecca noted uncomfortably. It was she herself. "I'll need to approve the house, as well," she spoke up softly, turning away from his lingering gaze to address her clients. "It may not be appropriate for fifty people. The size of the yard—"

"Over an acre," Jake told her. "No problem."

"We'll also need to consider the size of the kitchen—"

"It's big enough."

"Whether there's one room large enough to seat all the guests, just in case it rains—"

"I have a huge dining room. We can just move the furniture out."

"If Mr. Raglan has pets, there are guests who might be allergic—"

"No pets. Don't worry."

"And, of course, we must make sure no one will be... ah...inconvenienced," Rebecca concluded a little awkwardly.

Unwillingly, she turned to face Jake once again, and found him staring back at her with obvious confusion. She cleared her throat delicately before explaining. "I...I know you aren't married," she stammered, "but there may be someone who is a...a frequent, um...*visitor* to your home and who may be, as I said, inconvenienced by fifty people invading the premises."

Jake laughed outright. "Are you trying to find out whether I have a girlfriend, Rebecca?"

She could feel heat seep up from her breasts to her cheeks, and cursed herself for being so easily embarrassed. "Why, no, I, uh...I just want to make sure all the bases are covered, that's all."

His smile turned smug as he replied, "There's no one in particular who spends weekends with me, and I don't have a girlfriend, if that's what you want to know." He leaned toward Rebecca until their shoulders touched and whispered further, "But you never know who might turn up."

Then with a wicked grin, he straightened in his seat again, and Rebecca had to stifle a strangled groan when she felt his thigh rubbing slowly and deliberately against hers once more. Now she knew he was doing it on purpose. But strangely, she kind of liked it.

"When would you like to see the house?" he asked the other couple, still smiling cryptically.

"As soon as possible," Alison said, her words laced with excitement. "Tonight?"

"That's fine with me," Stephen agreed.

"I can't," Rebecca told them. "I'm sorry, I have another engagement. It's business...another wedding."

She told herself she added the explanation for the benefit

of her clients—who were entitled to know why she was unable to be present—and not because Jake threw her a look that was rife with suspicion. Damn him, it's none of his business, she told herself. So why did she feel as if she owed him an explanation, more than she did the others?

"Stephen, you and Alison can come over this evening, and Rebecca can come when her schedule permits," Jake suggested. "Tomorrow night?" he asked her casually.

Rebecca wanted more than anything to be able to tell him no, but that was impossible. She would definitely need to see Jake's house if that was where Alison decided she wanted to have her wedding. In a fit of futile optimism, Rebecca told herself, Maybe Alison wouldn't like Jake's house. Maybe the bride-to-be would decide to go with Gardencourt, after all. Maybe she herself was worrying in vain. Tomorrow morning, her clients could very well call to say that they had decided not to have the wedding at the best man's home. Maybe this time, Rebecca concluded her pep talk hopefully, the gods would smile on her instead of laughing at her, and pull her out of harm's way. Harm in this case, of course, being Jake Raglan.

"I think tomorrow evening will be fine," Rebecca finally replied, telling herself in the meantime that their rendezvous might never take place. "Say, six-thirty?"

"Better make it seven o'clock," Jake said. "I seldom leave the office before six-thirty."

He gave her directions to his house, and Rebecca was surprised to discover it wasn't far from her own. But Jake's address in Bonnycastle, near Cherokee Park, indicated his home was probably worth five times what her modest Crescent Hill tollhouse had cost her. Still, his was a beautiful neighborhood full of old houses, huge trees and lush yards boasting colorful gardens. A wedding at Jake's house might indeed be a splendid celebration. So why didn't Rebecca feel more festive?

Jake's *was* a beautiful house, Rebecca decided immediately upon pulling up in front of it the following evening.

A sprawling structure of yellow creek stone with a pale gray tiled roof, Jake's house looked warm and inviting in the dying rays of the setting sun. She was surprised to see a yard full of flowers and a porch populated by pots of flowering plants, normally an indication of feminine influence, then decided quickly that she shouldn't be. Naturally a man like Jake Raglan was going to know lots of women, and she suspected one of them probably claimed a hand in teaching him to care for the place.

Rebecca felt depression settle over her as she realized that Jake must share an intimate tie with at least one other woman. Then she chastised herself for considering herself in the running to begin with. There was absolutely no reason that would warrant getting involved with the man whose home she would be invading for the next three weeks. Jake had made it more than clear how he felt about the topic of matrimony, and it was completely at odds with the intentions Rebecca herself embraced.

Now all she had to do was keep repeating that over and over in her head so that no other thought of Jake Raglan would dare brave entry. Unfortunately, at that moment, the front door to the big house before her opened, and the man she swore she would be able to ignore stood framed in the arched doorway that offered entry into his home. For a single, crazy moment, Rebecca was overcome by the feeling that she belonged exactly where she was, that this scenario was one that should be played out every day. Coming home to a man like Jake, to a house like this, just seemed right somehow. Taking a deep breath, Rebecca closed her eyes and, with no small amount of effort, willed the feeling to go away.

How had she allowed herself to get roped into this? Rebecca asked herself as she began what felt like an endless journey up the walkway toward the front door. A few days ago, she had been looking forward to a couple of weeks off. Her most recent clients had canceled at the last minute the wedding ceremony she was planning for them, opting instead to elope in an effort to escape the parental meddling that was threatening their relationship. As a result, Rebecca had planned to use her sudden break from work and the couple's nonrefundable deposit to do a little skiing and unwind.

Then Alison Mitchell had called, hoping against hope that Rebecca Bellamy was free to plan a wedding in three weeks, because she wanted more than anything in the world to be married in October, outdoors, before the chilly weather set in. Rebecca had thought, Why not? Skiing would be around all season, and she really did love doing autumn weddings—the colors, the sounds, the smells, the onset of the holiday season. It would be fun, she had thought then. It would be a good time for a celebration.

Now, as she approached an awaiting Jake Raglan, she felt strangely detached from the real world, as if she was no longer in control of anything that was happening to her. When he pushed the storm door outward, she saw that he was wearing clothes like none she had ever seen him wear—faded, form-hugging jeans and a slouchy navy blue sweatshirt. The fingers of one hand were curled around the stem of a glass half-full of ruby-colored wine, and as she drew nearer, Rebecca could smell the bouquet of the burgundy mingled with something rawly masculine and potently intoxicating.

Crazily, the only thought that went through her head was that she was overdressed in her forest green suit. But instead of wanting to be dressed as casually as he, Rebecca had the wild, uncontrollable desire to simply step out of her clothes and into his arms.

"I halfway thought you wouldn't show," he murmured when she was close enough to hear him.

His voice was low, deep, smoothly intimate, as if he knew exactly what she was thinking and couldn't wait to help her carry out her intentions.

"That wouldn't be very fair to my clients, now, would

it?'' she countered a little breathlessly, trying to still the ragged thumping of her pulse.

"Ah, yes. You're only here because of business, right? No pleasure allowed."

Normally, Rebecca would have denied that such was the case at all, because she took great pleasure in her work. If she was honest with herself, she would even admit to a few thrills of excitement and anticipation in planning *this* wedding. But she knew Jake would choose to misinterpret any enthusiasm she might show for this project—after all, there was pleasure, and then there was *pleasure*—so she only smiled at him and said, "No, no pleasure allowed. Not tonight."

"Then I guess there's no point in asking you if you'd like to take your coat off and stay awhile, maybe have a glass of wine?"

Again, Rebecca found herself wanting to answer differently than she actually did. "No, I guess there wouldn't be."

He sighed in resignation and invited her to come in, closing the door behind them when she was safely inside. Rebecca stared in amazement at the room in which she found herself, trying to align the inside of Jake's house with the outside. The living room was large and spacious, and the furnishings were dark, expensive and beautiful, but something was missing, something very important—warmth.

Where the flowers outside attested to loving care and domestic tranquillity, the arrangement of Jake's things inside were in no way evocative of such tenderness and affection for one's surroundings. Although the room looked like something from the pages of a glossy magazine, it wasn't…real. There was no soul here, no feeling. It didn't appear as if any living went on in the living room, and Rebecca wondered if maybe it was because he just never used it.

"The dining room is this way," Jake said, jumping right to the point of her visit. "And then I'll take you out back."

Through each room they passed, Rebecca noted curiously that Jake's house simply did not exhibit any kind of personal touches. There were no photographs, no mementos, no souvenirs, no awards. Her own house was very small, but was crowded with the tokens she had earned to commemorate her rites of passage through life—from the Raggedy Ann doll and homecoming mum in her bedroom, to her Best of Louisville award in her living room. And on her hallway walls were photographs of just about every relative she had, right down to her four-week-old niece.

Rebecca's house reflected everything in Rebecca's character, everything in her very soul. Jake's house was like the backdrop for a stage play—paint and fabric and wood, and not much else.

Upon entering the dining room, Rebecca saw that it would indeed be commodious enough for fifty people with the removal of the table, chairs and china cabinet. With further exploration, she also decided that the kitchen—a sprawling white room full of high-tech appliances—would be ample enough for the caterer. And when they stepped through the back door and wandered out into the yard, Rebecca confirmed that it, too, would be large enough to hold both the ceremony and reception outside if the weather was agreeable. She also couldn't help but note that it was as lovingly planted and painfully tended as the front, as lush and full of warmth as the house was lacking in it. Jake's home was, to say the least, an enigma.

"It's beautiful out here," she said softly, genuinely. The sun had nearly dropped completely from the sky, and in the pink-and-amber twilight of another gorgeous Kentucky sunset, Jake's backyard was awash with red and gold. "You must have some green thumb to keep everything in such good shape. Me, I've never had much luck with anything except house plants."

"Oh, I don't take care of the yard," Jake told her. "I have someone come in to do that. I bought the house from an elderly couple who were moving to Georgia to be closer to their kids. Mrs. Eddleston was the real gardener. She's the one who put all the flowers out and everything. It all looked so nice, I hated it that everything would choke and die at my hands. So I have a gardener come in once a week to take care of everything. As you can see, he works wonders around here.''

That explains a lot, Rebecca thought with a silent nod. Obviously, Jake was a very busy man, and it would be crazy to think of him out tending to his roses in the manner of a gentleman-gardener on a warm Sunday afternoon. Still, despite his assurances to the contrary—which he offered frequently—Rebecca sensed something about Jake Raglan that was indeed nurturing and domestic. She wasn't sure why she should think such a thing—certainly he had never shown any indication of hearth-and-home tendencies—but Rebecca couldn't shake the feeling that there was some secret place in his soul that wanted very badly to be part of a family. Before she could ponder the suspicion further, though, his voice distracted her, posing a question she didn't quite hear.

"Hmm? What?" she replied absently, still gazing with unseeing eyes out at the yard.

"I...I asked if you wanted to go back inside."

Jake was watching Rebecca closely, wondering what it was that kept her thoughts so faraway. There was a dreamy, thoughtful expression on her face, and for the first time, he knew he was seeing her without her guard up. In the quickly fading light, her skin was almost translucent, rosy with warmth and as fragile-looking as porcelain. The breeze kicked up then, nudging a stray lock of hair across her face, and before he realized what he was doing, Jake lifted his hand to push it back over her shoulder. When he did, she turned to look at him, her expression still hazy and distant, her defenses still dropped.

Cupping her cheek gently in his palm, Jake thumbed another curl back from her face, unconsciously parting his lips as if to speak...or to kiss her, which was what he really wanted to do. Before he could commit to either, however, Rebecca's eyes focused on his again, and he was surprised when she didn't push him away. Instead, she placed her own hand softly over his, smiling sadly, sympathetically, as if she felt exactly what it was that tore him up inside. Then she slowly moved his hand away, and turned to go back into the house.

"I think Alison and Stephen will have a lovely wedding here," she told him without looking back. "I'll get together with the florist and the caterers this week, and I'll arrange for the photographer. They may or may not want to see the premises before the wedding day, so I'll be in touch to let you know. If it will be inconvenient for you—"

"Why don't I just give you a key to the house?"

His question stopped Rebecca in her tracks, and she pivoted to face him with an expression that indicated his offer couldn't have shocked her more.

"That isn't really customary—" she began.

"That's okay," he stammered with a shrug. "I trust you. And I know you're probably going to need access to the house on a number of occasions over the next three weeks. I'm in and out of my office all the time, and I usually work well past normal business hours, so you might not be able to reach me, and I might not be available every time you need to get in."

"Jake, I don't think it's a good idea."

It was the first time she had called him by his first name since Daphne's wedding, and Jake decided he had missed hearing it from her lips. Just why had he suggested that she take a key to his house? *No one* had ever been offered a key to Jake's house, not even members of his family. But then, he had never been particularly trusting of anyone in his family, and no one in his family except Daphne had ever really expressed an interest in seeing his home to begin with. Yet here was a woman he'd met on only three occasions, and he was ready to allow her access to everything he owned. For some reason, it seemed perfectly acceptable for Rebecca to have a key. More than that, it just seemed...right.

"I don't know," she hedged. "I'm not sure I'm comfortable with an arrangement like that."

Fearing that Rebecca would make an excellent argument, Jake quickly approached her, placed his hand gently in the small of her back and propelled her back into his house. Setting his wine on the kitchen table, he strode purposefully toward a corner hutch and lifted the lid on a canister marked Tea.

"I never drink the stuff," he explained as he withdrew the one spare key he possessed. Until now, he had always assumed that if he ever needed to give the key to anyone, the recipient would be Stephen, on some occasion when Jake had to be out of town for a protracted length of time. Never in his wildest dreams had he thought he would be surrendering his spare key to a woman.

"Really, Jake, I—"

Taking her hand in his, Jake turned it up to drop the key into her palm, closing her fingers gently over it after he did so. "Don't worry about it," he told her. "I'm not going to."

And surprisingly, he wasn't, Jake realized as a strange kind of serenity settled over him.

"Call first, if you can," he concluded. "But even if I'm not home, you're welcome in my house anytime, Rebecca."

With a slight lifting of her shoulders, Rebecca smiled shyly and said, "Thanks, Jake. That's nice of you. I promise not to take advantage of the situation."

Which, of course, was more than he was willing to do. In the back of his brain, Jake wondered if maybe he hadn't simply orchestrated this entire escapade so that he could take advantage of Rebecca Bellamy. All he knew was that he looked forward to finding her in his house. The sooner the better.

Three

It wound up being sooner than Jake thought. Three evenings after telling Rebecca Bellamy goodbye at his front door without so much as a handshake, Jake came home to find her in his dining room, crouched on the floor with tape measure in hand, scribbling in a notebook. Apparently she hadn't heard him come in, so he took advantage of the opportunity to study her unobserved.

Instead of her usual working uniform of tailored suit, tonight Rebecca was dressed casually in a deep scarlet sweater and faded blue jeans, and her dark hair was woven into a thick braid that swung over her shoulder like a length of rope. As Jake leaned silently in the doorway, she turned on her knees away from him, placed one end of the tape measure against the wall opposite his position, and began to crawl backward, unwinding the measure as she did so. Her movements provided him with an intriguing picture, to say the least. Jake bit his lip to keep from speaking out loud the suggestive comment he wanted to utter as he beheld the exquisite curves and motions of Rebecca's back-side coming toward him. Instead, he focused on trying to stem the rush of heat that invaded and overtook some very dangerous parts of his body.

Only when Rebecca backed into his shin did she finally realize she wasn't alone. As if jabbed by a cattle prod, she leapt forward awkwardly, trying to turn around and identify what had obstructed her progress as she did so. The result of her action was to send her sprawling onto her bottom, hands outstretched behind her to break her fall, legs spread wide. When she looked up to find Jake Raglan laughing at her, Rebecca's relief that he wasn't a burglar quickly turned to annoyance that he found so much humor in something that had scared the living daylights out of her.

"What are you doing here?" she demanded, still shaken by his appearance and sounding, she realized belatedly, very proprietary.

Jake smiled down at her as he continued to lean lazily in the doorway. "Gee, how quickly they take possession," he said mildly. "In case you've forgotten, Rebecca, I live here."

"Sorry," she apologized sheepishly. "I didn't mean to snap. I just wasn't expecting to see anyone. I called your office before I came over, but Stephen said you were having dinner with a client and couldn't be reached, and that you'd probably be tied up for most of the evening. If I'd known you'd be home, I would have waited until you were here."

It had felt very strange to come over to Jake's house and use his key to gain entry. An unsettling, lonely silence had greeted her when she'd opened the door, and Rebecca had been uneasy the moment she set foot inside. When she came home from work to her own house, her two cats, Bogart and Bacall, immediately raced to the front door and loudly demanded her attention, each rolling around on the rug and vying to see whose tummy would get rubbed first. There was always some interesting dialogue or commentary sounding from the radio, because Rebecca left it tuned to

National Public Radio during the day so that the cats would have human voices to listen to. Between that and the wind chimes on her front porch, and the Benny Carter tapes she listened to when she was home at night, Rebecca's house was never, ever, quiet.

But Jake's was. Even now that he was home, except for the sounds of their voices, a silence still hung over the house that was anything but comforting.

"My client was called away between cocktails and ordering so I came on home to eat," Jake told her. He didn't bother to add how much he detested eating in restaurants alone.

Although he rather liked the position into which Rebecca had fallen, he reluctantly extended his hand to offer her assistance in getting up. "Imagine my surprise to find a vintage roadster parked in my driveway," he added as he pulled her toward him. "That's some car you've got there, Rebecca."

The pressure Jake exerted in helping her up was a little more than was actually necessary to successfully complete the task. As a result, Rebecca found herself nestled quite perfectly against his chest, her hand still captured by his, his palm settled intimately against her hip in an effort to steady her. She had sought balance by splaying her hand over the front of his shirt, and she marveled at the hardness and warmth of the flesh she felt beneath her fingertips. Suddenly, the air around her, which she'd considered so empty before, was filled with a tension and electricity like nothing she'd ever experienced. Suddenly, Jake's house was warm indeed.

For a moment, neither of them moved or spoke, but their gazes met and held as if magnetically drawn. Then gradually, hesitantly, Jake pressed his fingers more firmly into Rebecca's jeans-clad flesh, and raked them down her thigh with maddening slowness. Rebecca gasped softly, her eyes widening in surprise, but she did nothing to stop his motions. Without thinking, she bunched a fistful of his shirt

and tie in her hand, as if willing him closer. Jake responded
with a quiet groan, dragging his fingers up the back of her
thigh until his hand cupped over her derriere. With gentle
pressure, he urged her hips forward until they were settled
against his own, then he bent his head down toward hers.

Instinctively, Rebecca lifted her face to receive Jake's
kiss, senseless to everything around her except him. At first,
he only brushed his lips softly against hers, nipping, teasing, leisurely tasting, as if asking her permission to go further. Rebecca's eyelids fluttered downward at the tantalizing sensations that went zinging through her body with
every brief, feathery caress. And when she felt the tip of
his tongue tracing a slow circle around her mouth, Rebecca
nearly collapsed in his arms, issuing a single, soft sigh of
surrender.

That quietly uttered sound was Jake's undoing. It was as
if a dam of emotion split open inside him then, and all the
pent-up frustration of wanting Rebecca for three months
without having her finally gushed forth without control. His
kiss deepened perilously, became a sensual foray that challenged Rebecca, dared her to go as far as her desires would
carry her. In the back of her mind, she knew that things
were going way too fast, that nothing could have prepared
her for the position she was in now, and that nothing good
would come of it. Still, she was as active a participant as
Jake was, and his passion only mirrored her own.

Then, without warning, the kiss ended. And Rebecca was
chagrined to realize she hadn't been the one to end it. Jake
seemed to tower over her when she looked up to meet his
gaze, his chest rising and falling raggedly and rapidly. For
just an instant, Rebecca was shocked to see fear—real
fear—glinting in the depths of his blue eyes, but as quickly
as she had detected it, the frightened expression was gone,
replaced by the easy humor that seemed to be such an in-
tegral part of his character.

"Hi, honey, I'm home," he mumbled softly, his words
punctuated by quiet, unsteady laughter.

Rebecca didn't know what to say. Her heart was pounding like a jackhammer, her blood racing like a roller coaster, her nerves as jagged and jumpy as a chain saw. "I...that..." She took a deep breath and tried again. "That shouldn't have happened," she finally stated shakily. Then to her horror, she realized she was still grasping the front of Jake's shirt as if he were her most prized possession, and she released him as if he were something poisonous. "I'm...I'm sorry," she whispered quickly, nervously smoothing her fingers over the soft fabric. "I have to get home."

She jerked away from him then, scrambling to pick up her coat and portfolio from the dining room table, stuffing her notepad and tape measure unceremoniously into her purse. As she tried to push past Jake, he reached out calmly and wrapped his fingers gently around her wrist, halting her attempt to flee.

"Don't go."

Those two little words stuck in Rebecca's heart like nothing she'd ever experienced before. So much pleading, so much sorrow, so much...loneliness...permeated them, that she couldn't help but look up into his face.

He wasn't gazing down at her, but instead focused his attention on the empty wall opposite them. His jaw was rigidly set, and he swallowed with some difficulty. All the while, his thumb stroked over the rapid pulse in Rebecca's wrist, his loose grip telling her she was more than free to go if she insisted.

"I'm sorry, too," Jake said, still not looking at her. "You're right. It shouldn't have happened." Then he did turn to observe her with quiet scrutiny. "Not yet, anyway. But I'm not going to promise that it won't happen again."

She really should go, Rebecca thought. She'd only come because she wanted to get the dimensions of the dining room and kitchen for the florist and the caterer, who would need to know how much space they had to work with, should the ceremony and reception wind up being held inside. Now that she had the information, there was no reason to stay. None except for the fact that she simply didn't want to leave. None except for the fact that she honestly wanted to spend more time with Jake Raglan.

"That's okay," she finally told him. In an effort to dispel the uncomfortable tension that still stained the air so heavily, she added playfully, "Who says you're going to get another opportunity, anyway?"

Jake smiled, but he was feeling anything but happy. Just what the hell had come over him, anyway? Good God, he hadn't come on to a woman as quickly and uncontrollably as he had with Rebecca in his entire life. What was it about her that tied his libido in knots? Why couldn't he keep his hands to himself where she was concerned? And why, dammit, did it feel so good to come home from work and find her here?

"I bet I do," he rejoined, as relieved as she that the uneasy moment had passed.

Rebecca shook her head slowly, but knew deep down that hers was an empty promise. She was going to be spending the next three weeks planning a wedding that was to take place in his home, and for which he was to be best man. Certainly a number of opportunities would arise between now and the nineteenth. She just had to decide once and for all what she was going to make of them.

"Have you eaten dinner?" Jake asked her.

He still hadn't released her wrist, so Rebecca glanced down at it meaningfully. Reluctantly, Jake let go and lifted his hands in surrender, then crossed his arms over his chest to await her reply.

Rebecca adjusted the strap of her purse on her shoulder, as if such an act would help her insist that she had to leave. "No, I ate a late lunch today, then spent the rest of the afternoon sampling wedding cakes and treats at a new bakery that opened in the Highlands, so I haven't been hungry for a while."

That's funny, Jake wanted to reply. I've been starving

for something ever since I met you. He wondered idly how she managed to stay so slim when she must attend dozens of functions where rich, high-calorie foods were served. Oh, how he'd love to help her burn a few of those calories off now and then.

"So, are you hungry now? We could go out for something," he suggested. "Or order in."

Rebecca hesitated before responding, telling herself she was making a big mistake as she asked, "What would you have done if I hadn't been here when you came home?"

Besides be utterly disappointed and thoroughly lonely? he wondered. Pushing the thought away, he replied, "I'd have called China Joe's for Hunan shrimp and a couple of egg rolls."

Rebecca grinned. "That's closer to my house in Crescent Hill. I didn't think they delivered out this far."

"I'm one of their best customers."

She nodded as her smile grew wider. "Make it three egg rolls, and throw in an order of cashew chicken, and I'll stay."

Jake grinned back. "Evidently I have competition in the 'best customer' category."

"I work a lot of evenings," Rebecca explained. "It's easier than cooking."

Actually, she just hated cooking when it was only for herself. Invariably, whatever she whipped up in the kitchen went bad before she had a chance to enjoy the leftovers, and grocery shopping for one was often a futile expedition. Everything seemed to be family-size these days—side dishes, main dishes…even canned soup provided two servings. She couldn't get fresh produce in quantities suitable for one, unless she waited until the store clerks turned their backs and provided her with an opportunity to break up bunches of bananas or divide the rubber-banded stalks of asparagus. She had come to feel like a criminal whenever she went to the grocery store, so she had simply opted to eat out or order in most of the time.

While they awaited the arrival of their dinner, Jake and Rebecca retired to the living room. Jake had changed clothes after making the call, and now crouched in front of the fireplace in jeans and a Berea College sweatshirt. Rebecca observed him intently as he tended to the tiny flames flickering to life amid the kindling, pondering what few things she knew about him, curious to discover more. He had opened a bottle of chardonnay to enjoy with their simple carry-out dinner, and now as he sat back against the hearth, he twirled his glass thoughtfully at the base, gazing unseeingly into its transparent depths.

"You went to Berea?" Rebecca asked conversationally, indicating the word stretched across his chest.

"For my undergraduate degree, yes," he told her. "My law degree is from Vanderbilt."

"But you wear your Berea sweatshirt," she pointed out. It was a remarkably good school, but one that was little known outside collegiate circles. Berea was noted not only for its academic excellence, but because it provided an opportunity to underprivileged students who wouldn't otherwise be able to pay for college. Virtually everyone enrolled at Berea was required to work in some capacity to oversee the cost of tuition, most opting for the arts and crafts that generated a good portion of the university's income. Others worked in Boone Tavern, a hotel and restaurant well-known for its local fare. She was surprised that Jake Raglan had attended such a university. The vast majority of the students at Berea were from rural, economically depressed areas, particularly Appalachia.

"I liked Berea a lot," Jake said as he sipped his wine. "It's a wonderful school. Ellen and I both went there."

"Are you from Louisville originally?" she asked curiously.

Jake shook his head. "Nope. Hazard County. A little smudge on the map called Acorn Ridge."

"No kidding?"

"No kidding." His voice was flat as he spoke, indicating

quite clearly that Jake harbored absolutely no affection for his hometown. When he'd voiced the name of the community, he had almost spat it out.

"You, uh, you don't have a rural accent at all," she said softly.

"No, I followed Ellen's example and worked hard all through college to get rid of it."

Rebecca was puzzled. "But why? Some of those accents are lovely."

Jake shifted uncomfortably in his position on the floor, threading the fingers of one hand restlessly through his hair. He didn't look at her when he spoke, and his thoughts seemed to be far, far away. "Because, Rebecca, nobody takes you seriously when you talk like a hick. And for a lawyer who wants to make it big outside his hometown, a Southern accent is nothing but a hindrance."

"Do you go home very often?"

"Home is here now."

"But what about your parents?"

"Dead."

His voice was low, and Rebecca had to strain to hear it. She wasn't sure exactly when it had happened, but Jake had almost completely withdrawn from her. Not that he had been especially generous with himself before, but this side of Jake Raglan was one even she wouldn't have anticipated. It was as if he had placed himself on automatic pilot and was replying to her questions without considering the import of his answers. He displayed no emotion whatever in relation to the images of his past that must be vivid in his memory.

"I'm sorry," she said quietly.

Jake waved a hand airily in her direction, but still didn't look at her. "It was a long time ago. Life in the mountains wasn't the easiest in the world. My old man contracted black lung long before he was my age and died about fifteen years ago. My mother held on for a couple more years, but she finally gave up, too."

Rebecca was at a loss. She'd never met anyone who had seen the passing of both parents at such a young age. Except for the death of her grandmother when she was seventeen, she'd never experienced the loss of a family member herself. She couldn't imagine how she would react to such a tragedy. It would be devastating. Yet here was Jake Raglan talking about the deaths of the two people who had given him life as if he hadn't even known them.

"Well, at least you still have your sister, Ellen, and her family."

Jake drained the ample amount of wine left in his glass before responding. "Yeah, thank God for Ellen," he ground out bitterly. "At least she did one thing right when she decided to keep Daphne."

"Jake, what are you talking about?"

"Look," he muttered impatiently, "would it be too much to ask that we change the subject?"

"No, of course not." Rebecca remained silent for some moments, confused about everything Jake had just revealed, and intrigued by all the things he hadn't. She posed the first question that came to mind, one that seemed perfectly harmless and conducive to less volatile discussion. "So, what's your undergraduate degree in?" She still wanted to discover as much about this man as she possibly could, despite the fact that he didn't seem overly inclined to conversation.

"English."

"Really?" She couldn't hide her astonishment. She might have expected anything else, but this came as a surprise.

"I know you like to think that all lawyers are an insensitive bunch, Rebecca," he said bitingly, "but one or two of us actually do have an appreciation for the finer things in life."

Her back went up automatically, defensively. He could see immediately that he had hit a nerve. "Oh, you'll get no argument from me there. The finer the better, I'd say.

Louisville wasn't good enough for Eliot's practice, so he took off for San Francisco. I wasn't good enough to be Eliot's wife—ironically enough, because I wasn't a college graduate—so he became involved with a graduate student in sociology who was more intellectually stimulating.''

"Rebecca…''

"And coincidentally, she was from a wealthy family, too,'' Rebecca went on relentlessly, nearly choking on her words. "I'm sure that was a big bonus as far as Eliot was concerned. Her folks probably didn't pull the plug on her finances, either, the way mine did.''

"Rebecca…''

He rose from his position on the floor as if he intended to approach her, but the doorbell rang then and startled them both back to reality. When Jake had paid the deliveryman and closed the door behind him, he stared at Rebecca for a moment in the soft amber glow of the fire.

"I'm sorry I overreacted,'' he finally said quietly. "You just touched on a sensitive issue.''

Rebecca lifted her chin defensively. "So did you.''

"Truce?''

She nodded, braving a small smile. "Truce.''

"Then let's eat.''

They passed the remainder of the evening in companionable conversation, skirting questions and topics that might lead to unwelcome probing, sticking to the small talk that people pursue when they don't know each other very well. It was awkward, Rebecca thought, because she at least didn't feel as if Jake was a stranger to her. The kiss they had shared only a short time ago still lingered on her lips like a warm, familiar caress, and she continued to marvel that she could have reacted so quickly, so heatedly, to a man she barely knew. What she experienced with Jake Raglan was truly puzzling.

The awkwardness became an almost-palpable discomfort when it came time for Rebecca to leave. Having already kissed once, it seemed perfectly realistic to expect the evening to end with another one. Yet at the same time, both had agreed that their earlier embrace shouldn't have happened. Because she wasn't sure how she should act, Rebecca wound up staying later at Jake's house than she would normally have done, simply because she was uncertain, and not a little fearful, about what would occur. When the grandfather clock in Jake's hall tolled eleven times, however, she knew she couldn't put it off any longer.

"It's late," she said softly after the last chime had faded away. "And we both have to work tomorrow."

Jake nodded, but remained silent, rising from his position on the floor. It wasn't that he had nothing to say to Rebecca—just the opposite, in fact. He wanted to tell her how wonderful it had been to come home from work and have someone to talk to for a change. He wanted to plead with her not to leave just yet, that there was so much they had left to discuss. He wanted to describe the strange stirring of desire her presence in his home aroused in him. He wanted to laugh with her some more, to be with her a little longer. He wanted... He wanted so much. Perhaps too much.

So Jake said nothing. He was afraid that if he opened his mouth, one thing would lead to another, and he would wind up telling Rebecca things he wasn't sure he was ready to acknowledge to himself. Instead, he moved silently to the front door, opened it while Rebecca gathered her things together, then waited restlessly for her to say goodbye.

But Rebecca didn't say goodbye. She paused before stepping outside, turned to Jake and asked uncertainly, "How about dinner at my house Friday night?"

It probably wasn't a good idea, Jake thought. His odd thoughts and feelings tonight aside, there were other things to consider. Rebecca Bellamy simply wasn't the kind of woman to have a brief affair with a man. She had made it quite clear on their initial meeting that she was indeed the marrying kind—more specifically the kind who was looking forward to it ASAP. If she was inviting him over to her house for dinner, it was no doubt because she wanted to get to know him better—better in the sense that she wanted to discover his husband potential. He owed it to both of them to stress that he had absolutely no potential in that department at all.

"Friday," he repeated, trying to come up with a good excuse why he was unavailable. "Friday, let's see…"

Rebecca felt her heart drop. She'd been single long enough to know when a man was stalling. Come to think of it, she'd been married long enough to know when a man was stalling, too.

"That's okay, never mind," she said quickly, throwing up a hand to affect an indifferent goodbye. "It was a bad idea. I know you must be very busy." In an awkward rush, she started to push past him, adding hastily, "I probably won't have to bother you again for a couple of weeks, so you won't have to worry about me invading your house again. I'll be in touch, Jake. Goodbye."

Jake blocked her retreat by stretching a muscular arm across the doorframe, at a height that coincidentally fell right below Rebecca's breasts. She was able to stop herself just before she would have barreled right into him. When she looked up at him, his expression was bland, offering her no insight into what he might be thinking or feeling. His eyes were dark and assessing, however, and Rebecca began to feel like an insect trapped beneath a microscope.

"Friday sounds great," he said finally. "But there's something you have to remember about me, Rebecca, something I have to make perfectly clear. I enjoy spending time with you. You're attractive, intelligent and fun to be with. But I'm not looking for anything long-term. I'm not looking for a relationship. I can't stress it enough—I'm not going to marry anyone, ever again."

Rebecca studied his features long and hard. Hadn't he already told her that once? Hadn't he reemphasized by his words and actions on numerous occasions since then that those were his precise feelings? It should matter to her, she told herself. She wanted to find a man with whom she could settle down for the rest of her life. But suddenly she didn't want any man but Jake Raglan.

"I didn't ask you to marry me, Jake," she heard herself say playfully, scarcely recognizing the flirtatious fluffiness her voice carried with the statement. Even Jake seemed surprised by her lighthearted response. "I just asked you if you wanted to have dinner with me."

"What time?"

Rebecca shrugged. "Seven?"

"Seven it is, then."

Before he dropped his arm so that she could pass, Jake leaned toward Rebecca with a predatory smile. All he could think about was how much fun it would be to unwind her braid and bury his hands in her hair, then wondered if the opportunity to do so would arise again on Friday. And because he was so overcome by the anticipation of making advances toward Rebecca, instead of taking her mouth hungrily with his, as his desire demanded he do, he only pressed his warm lips against her cheek and murmured his good-night.

Maybe he'd been wrong about Rebecca, he thought, watching the easy sway of her hips as she strode down the walkway toward her car. Maybe she was no more ready to settle down just yet than he was. So she wanted to get married. So what? She hadn't put a time frame on her intentions, had she? She hadn't said she insisted on being married by a specific month of a specific year. Maybe she just wanted to have a good time until the right guy came along. And maybe, Jake concluded as warmth filtered to every part of his body, he was just the guy to help her.

Four

Rebecca couldn't remember the last time she had cooked a meal for a man. Even when she and Eliot had been married, they'd usually cooked together. It was the one memory of her marriage that she carried fondly. She scarcely knew how to go about performing the task now. Briefly, she had entertained the thought of calling China Joe's for delivery, but had quickly dismissed the idea. No, she was determined to do this right. Jake Raglan was an interesting man, one she definitely wanted to get to know better. It had been too long since she'd met someone she even wanted to go out with, let alone see more than once. Jake just might turn out to be a man she could see a lot of. He might even turn out to be a man that she could love.

Don't do it, Rebecca ordered herself, as she sliced the ends from asparagus stalks. Don't even allow yourself to hope that something substantial might result from your time with Jake. He's already told you he has no intention of ever marrying again. Don't expect much from him in the way of reciprocity.

Although Rebecca's head assured her such was the case—Jake had, after all, spelled it out for her in no uncertain terms at his house earlier this week—in her heart she sensed that there was another part of him, a deeper, stronger part, that would assert just the contrary.

As if conjured up by her musings, a series of rapid knocks at the front door announced his arrival. Rebecca shouted out that she was coming, finished the last of her preparations, tossed aside her chef's apron and smoothed a hand over her hair to tuck a few errant strands back into her braid. After a quick glance in the mirror, she opened her front door to find Jake Raglan looking polished and handsome in dark corduroy trousers and a creamy fisherman-knit sweater, a bottle of wine in one hand, and a huge bunch of amber spider mums in the other.

"The last ones in the garden," he told her.

Rebecca's pulse rate skittered erratically at the sight of him. *Might* turn out to be a man that she could love? she asked herself again. That was a laugh. She was already three-fourths of the way there.

"Thank you," she murmured a little nervously as she took the bouquet from him. She tried not to think about the other bunch of flowers that had come between them three months ago—Daphne's bridal bouquet. Instead, she invited Jake inside, belatedly remarking, "I hope you don't mind cats."

Jake gazed mildly down at the two felines—one black and one white—twisting and curling between his legs, moaning and purring for attention. "What if I do?" he asked mischievously.

Rebecca grinned. "Then I'll have to ask you to leave."

He lifted his eyebrows in surprise. "One of those, are you?"

Rebecca shrugged. "Hey, love me, love my cats."

"You'd choose your cats over the city's most eligible bachelor?"

She feigned surprise. "Oh, so *you're* Louisville's most eligible bachelor. I've been wondering who was."

"Planning on making a play for me?"

"Why? You planning on resisting?"

"Not a chance."

Laughing, she replied, "Well, let's just put it this way—my cats have seen me in the morning before I have my coffee and they're still around. I can't say that about many men."

Jake pushed the door closed behind him, disengaged himself from her cats, and strode into Rebecca's house with a proprietary air. "Just how many men *have* seen you in the morning, Ms. Bellamy?" he asked with a playful wiggle of his eyebrows.

Rebecca felt herself color. "No, I meant... I mean, I *didn't* mean..." She sighed in exasperation, surrendering to her inability to be eloquent when someone's presence was making her extremely nervous. "Eliot, okay? Eliot's the only one besides Bogart. Bacall is a female cat."

Jake thought about that, wondering if it was true. Was her husband the only man Rebecca Bellamy had slept with? If so, then coming here tonight had been a big mistake, and it could make things between them complicated. He himself had been anything but discriminating in girlfriends before he was married. And although he had enjoyed a number of relationships with women since his divorce, none had been anywhere near serious enough to call exclusive, nor had they been particularly fulfilling.

As a result, Jake had adopted an attitude that simply prohibited him from attaching too much significance to any romantic dealings he might have with women. Sex was nice. Sex with someone he liked was even better. But even to suggest that something permanent might result from such a liaison was ridiculous. If Rebecca had been with only one other man in her life, she was liable to place far too much emphasis on emotional entanglements, and far too little on physical satisfaction.

However, that wasn't something he really needed to be thinking about right now, he told himself. Instead, he should be focusing on how delectable she looked in her full, shin-skimming skirt of sage green beneath a loose, belted shirt of pale yellow. Her hair was plaited again, hanging between her shoulder blades to the center of her back, and all Jake could do was rejoice in the fact that he would indeed have another chance to tug it free and untangle the mass of curls over Rebecca's ivory, naked skin. He took a step toward her, uncertain of his intentions, but was held up by the fat, furry presence of two cats rolling around on the floor in front of him.

Rebecca chuckled when she noted his dilemma. "Sorry, but no one gets past that front door until the cats have been amply satisfied."

Jake bent to give each a perfunctory rub on the stomach, then stepped over them until he was face-to-face with Rebecca. "And what about their mistress?" he asked in a dangerously soft voice. "When do I get to satisfy her?"

His eyes were so blue, Rebecca thought absently, suddenly feeling as if she were dangling precariously in the most fragile of webs. A dark, midnight blue like none she'd ever seen before. But instead of being cool and detached, the way they had been the first time she'd seen him, now his eyes were filled with a heat and intensity that seemed to underscore his desire for the most intimate kind of bonding. Before she could stop herself, Rebecca lifted a hand to trace the lines that fanned out from his eyes, letting her fingertips glide into the silver-touched hair above his ear. All she could think about was how much she wanted Jake to kiss her, and instinctively, she turned her face up toward his.

Jake set the bottle of wine down onto an end table by the couch, then he, too, raised his hand to cup Rebecca's cheek gently in his palm. Slowly, he skimmed his fingers down her jaw to the back of her neck, and pulled her braid forward over one shoulder. Rebecca trembled at the caress of his fingertips on her heated, sensitive flesh, but told herself it was only because his skin was cool from the temperature outside.

As Jake ran his thumb down the length of her braid, his knuckles casually brushed the fabric of her shirt and paused at the scrap of yellow satin that bound her hair. He lifted the braid slightly away from her body, his hand hovering just above her breast, and although it seemed a harmless-enough gesture, Rebecca felt a shiver rush from her scalp to the tips of her toes. It was as if his touch sent a part of his spirit spiraling through her body, stealing a little bit of her soul for himself in the process.

For long moments, Jake gently fingered her dark hair, his eyes never leaving hers as he studied the face that had haunted him all week. If she were any other woman, he could free her hair as he had in his fantasies and they could both be writhing naked on the couch in no time. But Rebecca Bellamy wasn't any other woman. And Jake was more than a little astounded to discover that, deep down inside, he didn't want to treat her like one.

Rebecca never replied to the question he posed, so Jake didn't press his luck. Instead, he jumped track and took off in an entirely new direction when he asked, "What's for dinner?"

Rebecca blinked in confusion several times, as if he had just spoken to her in a foreign language. "What? Oh. Oh, yes. Dinner." She stepped away from him resolutely, tossing her braid back over her shoulder when it fell from his fingers. She took a very deep breath and expelled it before she continued. "Lamb chops, new potatoes, asparagus, baby carrots and corn bread. If you'd like to open the wine, I'll just get everything going. Shouldn't take long."

As Rebecca arranged the flowers in a vase and placed them in the center of the table, Jake hastened to do as she instructed. When he had poured glasses of merlot for them both, he added, "What else can I do?"

Rebecca shook her head. "Nothing. You're my guest, so relax. Have a seat and talk to me."

Jake did talk to her, but instead of sitting down, began to prowl around Rebecca's living room. Her Crescent Hill neighborhood was one of the many in Louisville in which the very wealthy mingled with the not-so-very-wealthy, in which the socially and artistically advantaged took up residence right alongside those whose day-to-day existence consisted of simply earning enough to stay alive. When Rebecca had first told Jake where she lived, he had assumed she must be of the former group. But when he had pulled up in her driveway, it had struck him that perhaps she wasn't very successful in her business, after all. Otherwise, why would she be living in such a tiny, tiny house, something that was little more than a cottage, complete with gingerbread trim and a wraparound porch?

However, now he was beginning to change his mind again. Although it was true Rebecca's house was considerably smaller than his own, comprised perhaps of a third of the rooms he himself could claim to wander around in, it was by no means indicative that she was unsuccessful. The interior—like the exterior—was immaculate, her furnishings immediately identifiable as genuine, quality antiques, even to an unpracticed eye like Jake's. The living room dimensions couldn't possibly have exceeded ten feet by twelve feet, but she had made use of every bit of space available. The walls were covered with paintings and awards—another indication that she was indeed successful—and the bookshelves and end tables were stacked with every variety of reading material. There were knickknacks and mementos everywhere Jake looked, and he realized that simply by standing in her living room, he was learning more about Rebecca Bellamy than she had ever told him.

The living room abutted the kitchen, the two rooms separated simply by a counter. The kitchen itself was a mere corridor with cabinets and appliances on one side. Beyond it was a door opening onto a small hallway that must lead to a bedroom and a bathroom, but from the size of the exterior building, Jake speculated that there could be space for little else inside. Despite the close quarters, though, he was surprisingly comfortable in Rebecca's house.

Jake had always sworn that once he was out of school, he would never be satisfied until he bought a house that was huge. Growing up in Acorn Ridge, he and Ellen had actually been forced to share a bedroom, because his parents' house hadn't been much larger than Rebecca's. It was probably one of the reasons he and Ellen hardly spoke to each other, even today. As teenagers, they had come to resent each other because neither had ever enjoyed any privacy. Ellen had grown up with the same intentions Jake claimed. When she had married Leonard Duryea twenty-four years ago, it was only because the guy had money, and more important, could provide her with a big house.

Ellen hadn't even wanted to share it with children. The first Christmas she and Leo had spent as husband and wife, she had invited Jake up from Acorn Ridge to show off her big new house to him. Over the holidays, she had discovered she was pregnant with Daphne, and one night, because she was feeling frightened and insecure, she had desperately confided her condition to her brother, voicing her reluctance at the prospect of becoming a mother. Jake had experienced a number of mixed emotions. He could sympathize with Ellen, because he didn't want to have children, either. But the thought that his sister might provide him with a niece or nephew had done funny things to his insides, even as a teenager. He'd told Ellen the decision was hers to make. Then he'd been very relieved when she'd informed Leo and the two of them had worked through it together.

And when Daphne was born, Jake had made himself available whenever necessary to baby-sit, telling himself it was because his sister needed a break now and then, and not because he simply enjoyed doing it. Once a month, he would drive to Louisville from Berea for the weekend to visit his niece. Babies, he quickly discovered as a college student, defied any preparation university studies or life experience could offer. His niece's antics had made him view the universe from an entirely new perspective, and offered him a much-needed diversion from his studies. He'd loved baby-sitting for Daphne.

But he'd hated doing it in Ellen's house. He wasn't sure why. Maybe because he and Ellen never got along as kids, or maybe because she, like he, was very territorial in relation to her home. Perhaps it was a combination of the two. But for some reason, Jake had simply never felt welcome in his sister's home.

And it was a feeling he continued to experience to this day. He could count on one hand the number of times he'd entered Ellen's house in the past ten years. Despite the fact that she issued an invitation to Jake to spend his holidays there every year, he knew it was only because she felt it was her obligation to do so, as Daphne doted on him. But Jake had always avoided the tension that inevitably ensued when he visited his sister and her husband by beginning a tradition of taking Daphne out to dinner every Christmas Eve—even during the years that he was married.

Now that *she* was married, would she continue their tradition? he wondered. Probably not, because Daphne was married to someone who cared as much for her as she cared for him. Unlike Jake, who had married someone more concerned about her own entertainment than about the comings and goings of her spouse. Daphne would doubtless spend the holidays with Robby. So where did that leave Jake for Christmas?

The thought hadn't even occurred to him until this moment. Now that his niece was married and had begun her own family, Jake's ties to his sister were effectively cut. Ellen probably wouldn't even issue him an invitation this year. Not that he would accept it, anyway, but still… It was

odd to think about being alone over the holidays and beyond. Of course, Jake had in effect been alone since his
divorce, but in the back of his mind, he had still claimed a
family tie to Daphne. Now she claimed a tie to someone
else's family. Which left Jake well-and-truly alone.

When his brain formed the startling realization, for some
reason, Jake instinctively glanced up at Rebecca. She had
her back to him as she stirred something on the stove, and
didn't seem to realize she was singing along to a jazzy
instrumental rendition of "Sweet Georgia Brown." As the
music grew more lively, she began a little dance of her
own creation, and Jake felt himself drawn to her as if she
were winding an invisible thread attached to his heart. Before he knew what was happening, he was standing beside
her at the stove, and she looked up quickly, seeming as
surprised as he was by his appearance.

"I want to help," he said simply.

To Rebecca, Jake seemed to stumble over his words,
until it almost sounded as if he'd said, "I want help."

"It...it's done," she replied, speaking as hesitantly as
he. "I'm just getting ready to bring it in. You can help me
carry these things to the table."

He nodded and extended his hands to take whatever Rebecca might offer him. Her cheeks were flushed from the
heat of the stove, the hair around her face curling from the
humidity. The kitchen was filled with the most delectable
aromas that could only result from food that wasn't pre-
packaged, and the jazzy, danceable music had faded into a
slow, bluesy number that spoke to some dark part of Jake's
soul. Outside, the wind whipped against the house suddenly, savagely, and all he could think was that he was so
damned grateful to be exactly where he was.

Home.

For some reason that word jumped instantly into his
head. Despite the fact that this house was even smaller than
the one he'd so detested growing up in, despite the fact that
nothing, absolutely nothing he owned could be found under

this roof, in this tiny room with Rebecca, Jake felt more at home than he'd ever felt in his life.

The realization frightened him. And then, he acknowledged reluctantly, it comforted him. After admitting that, Jake refused to speculate further. He carried the plates full of food to the table, lit the candles, topped off their wine, and sat in the chair opposite Rebecca.

Rebecca wasn't sure what was going on, but she could swear that things had suddenly, drastically changed between her and Jake. Gone was the casual banter and sly innuendo in which he loved to indulge, and gone was the easygoing humor in his blue eyes. Jake suddenly seemed so serious, so anxious, and she wasn't sure what she had done to make him change.

They ate in rather stilted silence, but all through dinner, neither could stop looking at the other. When they did chat, it was amiable, though a little stiff, covering a variety of topics before finally lighting on Rebecca's job.

"How did you get started doing this?" Jake asked. "It's kind of an unusual occupation. And, no offense, but you seem to harbor a few negative feelings about your divorce. The fact that you take so much pleasure in planning weddings seems a little contradictory."

"No offense taken, and incidentally, I do plan other things besides weddings—I can organize *anything*, any kind of celebration you might conjure up." Rebecca thought for a moment before continuing. "As far as my divorce is concerned, I simply married the wrong person. It wasn't so much that my marriage was bad, as it was that my *husband* was bad."

Jake began to object, as she'd known he would, so she put up a hand to stop the flow of words. "No, wait, let me finish. Eliot was a jerk—that's all there is to it—and I was too young, too naive, and too ignorant to notice or accept it."

"Why do they always blame the men?" Jake posed the question in exasperation to no one in particular.

"I'm not blaming men," Rebecca stated adamantly. "If I'm blaming anyone, it's myself for putting up with Eliot for as long as I did." She'd never told anyone else about everything that had gone on between her and Eliot, only that her husband had married her for her money, and when it had run out, he'd left her. She wondered if maybe that's all she should tell Jake. Then she decided, hey, he was a big boy. He took pride in taking off the gloves, so why couldn't she?

"Eliot married me because I came from a wealthy family," she began. "And he stayed with me when my parents cut us off only because I offered to quit school and find a job that could support us both while he went to school full-time. I wound up taking three jobs to do that, Jake. I worked more than eighty hours a week most weeks for the entire time I was married. I hardly ever saw Eliot. But a lot of my friends did see him. Mostly at parties and bars, and nearly always with other women.

"But when my friends told me that, did I listen?" Rebecca shook her head. "No way. I was so sure there was some reason for it. I even made up excuses for it. Oh, Eliot has a tough time of it in law school. Those tests are so hard, he has to study all the time. He deserves a little R & R, he deserves to go out and party sometimes. I never once thought that maybe I deserved a little of that, too."

Jake said nothing, only looked at her from across the table. Rebecca reached for the nearly empty bottle of wine and divided the rest between their two glasses.

"You know, I think back on it now, and I'm amazed at how surprised I was when Eliot said he was leaving me. I can't believe how stupidly I behaved for five years. Five years," she repeated for emphasis. After a moment, she added, "And now you think I'm going to try to rope you into marriage, don't you?"

Jake decided that honesty was the best way to go here. "The thought had crossed my mind, yes."

Rebecca smiled sadly, then lifted her wine to inspect it

in the candlelight. "I've learned the hard way that it's better to be alone than to be with someone who's wrong for you." She paused for a moment, then seemed to recall that she had set out to tell him something completely different. "But then, you were asking how I got involved in my job, weren't you? Not whether you'd be getting out of my house alive and unattached, right?"

That *was* what he had been asking her about, wasn't it? Jake tried to remember. He couldn't recall further than thinking about how much he'd wanted to pull Rebecca into his arms to console her as she'd described what had gone on in her marriage. He didn't dwell on how many things Eliot seemed to have in common with his own ex-wife, nor did Jake think about how much he'd like to deck the son of a bitch if he ever met up with the man.

"I only brought up my marriage because my job is a direct result of it," Rebecca went on after a thoughtful sip of her wine. "Because I hadn't graduated from college, I wasn't really skilled in anything. I wound up working in a local department store, in the china department of the bridal registry. I also got on part-time with a bakery and a florist. As a result, I was surrounded by all things matrimonial whenever I went to work. I learned a lot about the different businesses and gained a lot of insight into what people were doing for their weddings these days. Suddenly I realized I had some pretty good ideas of my own, too.

"My parents were more than willing to lend me enough money to get my business off the ground. I think maybe they still felt guilty for cutting me off while I was married to Eliot. Since then, I've repaid that loan with interest, and the business has really taken off."

"And I bet your folks are extremely proud of you," Jake guessed.

Rebecca smiled a little sadly, as if she was remembering something long past. "Yes, they are. They're wonderful people. We had some tough times while I was married, but it was only because they saw Eliot for what he was when

I couldn't. When he took off, they never uttered an 'I told you so' or 'It's about time.' They only told me I was welcome if I wanted to come home."

"Do you have brothers and sisters?" Jake asked, telling himself he was only making idle conversation, that Rebecca's family couldn't have mattered less to him.

"An older sister and brother."

"Do you get along with them?"

What a question! Rebecca wanted to shout. Then she remembered how he had described his own upbringing and the tension he and his sister shared, and instead she only smiled. "Yes, we get along very well. We've always been very close in my family. My sister and brother are both married with children, and I baby-sit frequently for them. They have great kids," she added parenthetically, forcing herself to refrain from stating that they were just like the children she hoped to have for herself someday.

But Jake seemed to know what she was thinking, anyway. "I don't want kids myself," he stated in a matter-of-fact tone.

It didn't surprise Rebecca at all, but still she asked, "Why not? I think you'd make a terrific father."

He couldn't hide his astonishment at her assessment of his character. "You have got to be kidding."

"No, I'm not."

"What could you possibly find paternal about me?"

She shrugged, as if she was about to voice the obvious. "You're strong in your convictions. You seem to have a solid grasp on what's right and what's wrong. You're intelligent and relatively open-minded—"

"What do you mean 'relatively?'"

"—And, well, look at you—you obviously come from a terrific gene pool," she finished with a laugh.

That got Jake's attention. "Oh? And just what makes you say that?"

Rebecca realized suddenly that she had somehow managed to sink herself in far too deeply this time. Jake was gazing at her across the candlelight as if she was to be his dessert, his expression suggesting any number of intimate prospects. She tried to squash down the part of her that wanted to explore more fully whatever he might have in mind, but try as she might, the fires stirring inside her grew incandescent. "You...you have nice eyes," she finally whispered in response to his question.

Jake rose from his chair and slowly circled the table until he stood behind her. Rebecca's stomach exploded into a swirling fireball at having him so close, and her heart began a ferocious tattoo behind her rib cage.

It was going to happen, she thought feverishly. And nothing she might say or do could stop it, even if she'd wanted to. Which, of course, she did not. Making love with Jake simply seemed like the most obvious course of nature, like the first law of the jungle. Deep down inside, part of her knew they were meant to be together. And deep down inside, part of her knew it wouldn't be for long.

"I want to make love to you, Rebecca," Jake rasped out above her. He cupped her shoulders with his hands and gave them a gentle squeeze. "I haven't been able to stop thinking about you since the moment I first saw you."

Rebecca closed her eyes against the fiery sensations his words and his touch sent blazing through her body. "It's nice to know I'm not the only one who's been afflicted with that particular obsession," she whispered roughly.

The hands on her shoulders raked slowly down Rebecca's arms, the subtle friction starting little fires all along the way. At the juncture of her elbows, which she had rested on the arms of her chair, Jake pushed back her sleeves and formed soft circles on the tender flesh with his thumbs. Then, flattening his palms over her forearms, he continued his intimate journey farther, until his hands were covering the ones she had settled limply in her lap. As Rebecca marveled at how warm his skin was, Jake curled his fingers around hers and lifted her hands, crossing her arms over her chest and urging her to stand, kicking away her chair as she did so.

For long moments, he only held her against him in a warm embrace, luxuriating in the feel of having her so close, rejoicing that they would finally be together. Then, with a final squeeze and the gentlest of tugs, Jake lifted her arms above her head, and spun her slowly around like a ballerina until they were face-to-face.

Rebecca almost felt as if they were moving in slow motion, as if what they were doing was indeed a dance of sorts. Without releasing her wrists, Jake lowered her arms again, behind her back, until she was willingly held prisoner in his embrace. Tangling his fingers with hers at the small of her back, Jake urged Rebecca forward until nothing separated them but the thin barrier of their clothing. He dipped his head and brushed his lips softly, ever so softly against hers, then pulled back to gaze at her expression before he continued.

When he saw that she was every bit as lost as he was, Jake smiled and leaned forward again. At first, he barely touched Rebecca's lips with his, rubbing gently, tugging softly, only tasting her until their breaths mingled as one. When he could stand it no longer, he pressed his mouth to hers more insistently, urging her lips to open with his, exploring her deeply, kissing her to the depth of her soul.

Rebecca reacted with equal fire and passion, feeling more alive, more enraptured, than she had ever felt in her life. It was as if this embrace with Jake was her initiation into the realm of the senses, as if she'd never truly *felt* anything before now. His lips pulled persistently at hers, demanding a response, and Rebecca gave him whatever he wanted, taking for herself what she desired in return.

For long moments, they remained entwined, releasing all the pent-up passion, desire and emotion they had been forced to hold in check since meeting three months before. But instead of satisfying their needs, their actions only intensified them. As their quiet kisses turned to heated demands, as their tender explorations became insistent needs, each began to forget anything that had come before. All that mattered now was quenching their thirst for each other, extinguishing the flames that had turned so quickly into raging wildfire.

Before Rebecca realized what was happening, Jake had lifted her into his arms and was carrying her through her house. Vaguely she wondered if he knew where he was going, but she couldn't make herself stop kissing him long enough to offer him directions. However, it didn't seem to matter, because all too quickly he was releasing her, laying her on her back in the center of her bed. It was only when he stood towering over her, gasping for breath and gazing at her hungrily, that Rebecca finally began to regain some semblance of coherent thought.

"What's happening?" she asked herself more than Jake. "Where did all that come from?" More important, she wondered, where was it going to lead them?

Jake took a moment to steady his breathing before he replied. "I think we both know the answer to that. What's happening is that we're about to make love. And where all this came from is one of those mysteries of life I don't think anyone will ever be able to solve."

Rebecca didn't know what to say. Rationally, she realized what they were about to do was probably a big mistake. She hadn't been with anyone since her divorce, was almost uncertain how to go about all this man-woman business now. What was it about Jake that made her throw caution so utterly to the wind? Why did he shake her so profoundly where other men had left her completely cold? There had been others who had expressed an interest in Rebecca beyond the sexual, a number of men who had made it clear to her that they were available for a lifetime commitment. But none of them had seemed exactly appropriate for one reason or another. None had seemed quite…right.

But Jake Raglan did. God knows why, because he had

done absolutely nothing but discourage her, but after only a few meetings, Rebecca felt better with Jake than she had with any man, even with Eliot. Especially with Eliot. When she was with Jake, bits of the puzzle of her life just seemed to slip right into place. Things fit with him. Things felt good. So why did he have to be so completely wrong for her?

"What do you want, Rebecca?" he asked her suddenly. "You call the shots here. What do you want?"

I want a life with you, she thought immediately. I want a house full of children and warm feelings and holidays, I want the white picket fence and flowers, I want cats and dogs and canaries. I want everything, Jake, I want it all.

"You," she replied simply. "Oh, Jake, I just want you."

It was all he needed to hear. With one savage tug, Jake yanked his sweater over his head, then pulled Rebecca up off the bed and into his arms once again. As she tangled her fingers in his hair, he unfastened her belt and tossed it to the floor, then undid all the buttons on her shirt. Beneath it she wore a breezy confection of champagne-colored lace, something that clung lovingly to her body and only hinted at what was to come. Jake groaned in delight that she had turned his fantasies about her into reality, then pushed the soft fabric of her shirt over her shoulders until it, too, was pooled on the floor.

Rebecca gasped when he slid his hand down her warm back and spanned her derriere, then her eyes grew wide as he stroked his hand over her skirt and the back of her thigh, cupping his hand behind her knee to lift her leg. Pulling her toward him, Jake raked his fingers down her calf and around her ankle, then pushed her shoe from her foot. Grinning the predatory smile that sent Rebecca's temperature skyrocketing, Jake let her foot go, then performed the exact same service for her other leg.

This time, however, when her shoe hit the floor with a delicate thump, Jake continued to hold Rebecca's foot for a moment. Ever so slowly, his hand skimmed up to circle her ankle, then his fingers raked back up over her calf, under her skirt, to curve at the bend in her knee once again. Rebecca's eyes widened in shock when Jake tugged on her leg to jerk her body forward against his, moaning out loud as her torso came into contact with his.

He was already ready for her, she realized, as heat coursed through every part of her body. All ready. But apparently he still wasn't willing, because instead of hurrying them into bed, Jake only rubbed his open palm up the length of Rebecca's thigh and over her hip, curving and pressing his fingers into the soft flesh above.

"Oh, Jake" was all Rebecca could manage in response, but her fingers flexed in his hair, then dropped to squeeze his shoulders. When Jake wrapped her leg around his waist, Rebecca instinctively tightened her hold on him, until she wasn't sure where her body ended and his began. However, as his fingers crept back up her thigh to explore her further, initiating a gentle, insistent, intimate caress, she realized all too well, and she could only gasp for breath as she shuddered with exquisite delight.

Jake continued with his ministrations as he unfastened Rebecca's skirt, pausing just long enough to push it and her thigh-high stockings down her legs until she stood before him in only her brief, ivory teddy, shaken and delirious at what had just happened and what was to come.

"You are so beautiful," he whispered when he could trust his voice not to quiver.

Rebecca smiled a little shakily. "You're not so bad yourself."

That was an understatement, she thought feverishly. Jake Raglan was, in a word, glorious. His broad chest was a collection of the most wonderfully placed muscles she had ever seen, corded and hard and covered with a dusting of black curls that spiraled across his abdomen and down to his trousers. Almost involuntarily, Rebecca reached out and unfastened the button resting below his navel, noting triumphantly that he sucked in an unsteady breath as she did so. Ever so slowly, she tugged on his zipper until it would open no farther, and feeling more reckless than she ever had in her life, tucked her hands deep inside his waistband.

Jake didn't resist when Rebecca curled her hands around his waist to cover his hips and pull him close. Instead, he leaned forward until they both lost their footing and fell onto the bed. He propped himself up on his elbows to gaze down at her, stunned to see fear lurking in her green eyes.

"What is it?" he asked her softly, laying his palm flat against her cheek and stroking her hair back from her face. "Why do you look so frightened?"

Rebecca swallowed hard before answering him. "Because I *am* frightened. Jake, I..."

He kissed her temple gently, then brushed his hand down to cup her jaw. "You what?" he asked her softly.

"I haven't been with a man since my divorce," she confessed quickly. "It's been five years..."

He stopped the flow of nervous words by placing a finger over her lips. "Shh. I know that."

"You do?"

He nodded. "I suspected, anyway. A woman like you..."

When he said no more, Rebecca prodded, "A woman like me...?"

Jake just shook his head, looking a little melancholy as he clarified, "A woman like you wouldn't sleep around. You need something more than a physical attraction."

"Yes."

"You need a little emotion."

"Yes."

"You need a lot of emotion."

"Yes."

Hearing her confirm his suspicions so honestly, Jake knew he should stop what he was doing and be honest with her, too. But the fact of the matter was, he wasn't sure what the truth was anymore. Before Rebecca, he would have sworn he couldn't offer a woman anything more than sex,

that emotion would never play into the game. But now...
Ever since meeting her, he had reacted to things in ways
he never would have thought possible. He had experienced
emotions unlike anything otherwise within his grasp. Why
shouldn't he make love with Rebecca? he thought selfishly.
Why shouldn't he explore this further?

He didn't say anything in response to her admission, but
gazed down at the pearl buttons that kept her teddy together. He lingered for a long time over the first one, as if
making the most important decision of his life, then he
slowly slipped it through its hole. One by one, he undid
each of the tiny buttons until the lacy fabric gaped open
between her breasts. When he leaned down to place a warm
kiss over her heart, Rebecca sighed in contentment and buried her fingers in his hair once again.

"Don't stop," she pleaded softly. "Please, Jake. Don't
ever stop."

Ignoring the little voice at the back of his brain demanding that he consider the repercussions of what they were
about to do, Jake pushed aside the fabric covering her
breast and kissed Rebecca's ribs one by one. Gradually he
moved upward until he found her breast, then, cupping her
warm flesh in his hand, he circled the dusky peak with his
tongue before drawing her more fully into his mouth.

Rebecca's breathing grew rapid and uneven as he tasted
her, and she cried out loud when he cupped her other breast
and gave it a gentle squeeze. Instinctively, deliriously, she
scored her fingernails down his back until she found the
waistband of his trousers, and she pushed insistently until
he finally understood her demand.

Lifting himself away from her long enough to shed the
rest of his clothing and help her out of her teddy, Jake took
a moment to gaze at her once more. The only illumination
in the room came from the yellow rectangle of light spilling
through the bedroom door, and in it, Jake could see how
rosy Rebecca's skin had become, how fragile she seemed
to be. Vaguely, he realized he had never even thought to

free her hair from her braid, but her dark tresses had somehow come loose anyway and lay spread across the pillow
like dark fire. He knew he shouldn't do this, knew he was
going to wind up hurting Rebecca. Then she lifted her arms
to him, inviting him in, and he knew he would only hurt
himself more if he didn't have her.

Jake was as helpless to stop himself as the doomed sail-
ors of lore had been upon hearing the sirens' song. It was
no longer a matter of wanting Rebecca. Now it was a matter
of needing her.

Like a man possessed, he came to her then, taking Rebecca with all the passion, all the fire, all the intensity his
body commanded. Deeper and deeper he drove himself,
until every fiber of his body melted with hers, until each
was consumed in a burst of white-hot combustion.

And as incoherence turned to rational thought once
again, Jake knew he had done the wrong thing. It wasn't
just that he had heard Rebecca cry out that she loved him.
It was that he had heard himself cry out that he loved her,
too.

Five

It was dark when Rebecca awoke, feeling fuzzy and unsure of her surroundings. She was in her own bed, she realized vaguely, in her own house with all of her own things surrounding her. But somehow they didn't seem like her home and her possessions any longer. Everything felt…different than it had before. And the silence surrounding her—that was new, too. Too many nights during her marriage, she had lain awake in tension-filled silence waiting for Eliot to come home. After her divorce, the silence every night had become intolerable, and Rebecca had taken to sleeping with the radio on, tuned to a nerve-soothing classical-music station. So why was her house so quiet and lonely now?

All at once, Rebecca recalled what had happened. She had made love with Jake Raglan, had experienced the heights and depths of a passion she had never known she was capable of enjoying. As memory after memory washed over her, she smiled at the heated sensations seeping into every cell in her body. Instinctively, she reached across the bed to touch him, finding the space empty, yet still warm from his presence. Pulling his pillow sleepily into her arms, Rebecca squeezed it to her breast and inhaled deeply the aroma of Jake Raglan that still clung to it. He had been so loving, so tender, so sweet. And she had fallen madly, desperately, hopelessly in love with him.

Surprisingly, Rebecca wasn't alarmed by the recognition of her feelings. It was as if a part of her had known from the moment they'd met that things would develop between them as they had. Somehow, making love with Jake just seemed like the natural conclusion to an association that had begun a long time ago, and now had come full circle. To her, such a realization brought with it comfort, and an almost serene outlook. She was sure, however, that Jake would react a bit differently. How was she going to make him understand that they were meant to be together? And what was she going to do if she couldn't?

Rebecca rolled onto her back, still clutching Jake's pillow to her heart, and stared unseeingly at the ceiling. Where was he now? she wondered. Was he out in her kitchen, carelessly opening another bottle of wine for them to enjoy, to share in their newfound romantic intimacy? Or was he out in her living room, pacing nervously, pondering all that had passed between them and puzzling over his feelings as she was? Her heart sank as the next thought entered her brain. Or was he perhaps already on his way home, driving along with the stereo turned up, dismissing what they'd just shared together as another night's adventure, worrying over what awaited him at work Monday morning?

Only one way to find out, Rebecca told herself reluctantly.

She rose from bed and went to her closet to wrap herself in a blue chenille bathrobe. Not the most revealing piece of clothing in her wardrobe, she reflected, but the room had grown cold without Jake's presence there to warm her, and at the moment, for some reason, she wasn't feeling particularly sexy, anyway.

Padding from the bedroom in bare feet, Rebecca made her way silently down the short, narrow hallway and peeked through the door leading to her kitchen. The light above the stove was on, as it usually was at night, but the radio was off. That accounted for why the house was so eerily quiet. The reason it felt so coldly empty was even more obvious.

Rebecca's gaze wandered around her living room, slowly, deliberately, so that she wouldn't miss a thing. She took in the remnants of her meal with Jake that lay cold and unappealing on the table, the odd shadows cast by the tree-obscured light from a streetlamp outside, and the silent forms of Bogart and Bacall sleeping serenely on the back of the sofa, oblivious to her turmoil. Pulling the collar of her robe more snugly around her throat, Rebecca lowered her eyes to her bare feet rooted nervously against the chilly wood floor, willing the tears she felt welling to subside. No, there was no question why her house was so cold tonight.

Jake Raglan was gone.

How could I have been so stupid? she berated herself viciously. *How could I have thought he would be different? How could I have told him that I loved him?* And as she shuffled slowly into her kitchen, Rebecca asked herself the final, most persistent question. *How could I have felt that I loved him?* The evening that had caused her to feel hopeful for the first time in five years had left her with nothing more than a table full of dirty dishes and an arctic cold that surrounded her heart. Rebecca shivered involuntarily and swiped at a trickle of water that tumbled down over her cheek.

"Damn lawyers."

Moving automatically, she turned her radio on to drown out the silence that had begun to deafen her, then went to run water in the sink. There was nothing worse than waking up to dirty dishes that should have been done the night before, she thought.

Nothing except waking up cold and alone.

* * *

It was only because she'd been sleeping so soundly and he hadn't wanted to wake her, Jake thought rationally, emphatically, and not because he'd scared the hell out of himself. As he lay awake in his own bed, scarcely aware of the approaching sunrise, he repeated to himself yet again the reason he had left Rebecca without saying goodbye some hours ago. So he had cried something out in a moment of passion that he shouldn't have, he told himself. So what? Every day people said things they didn't mean. Every day men told women they loved them when they really didn't. Lots of men did that.

But Jake didn't.

At least, he hadn't before. Maybe he was just imagining things, he tried to reassure himself. Maybe he only thought he'd told Rebecca that he loved her. They'd both been so consumed by feverish ecstasy, neither one of them could have been too coherent about the things they were saying. Hell, she probably hadn't even meant it when she'd said it to him. She'd told him over dinner that she knew better than to get involved with a man who was wrong for her, hadn't she? And who could possibly be more wrong for a marrying kind like Rebecca Bellamy than a forever-unattached bachelor like himself?

Because forever unattached was precisely how Jake intended to remain. Attachments led to entanglements, then entanglements led to involvements, then involvements... well, involvements invariably led to relationships. And everyone knew where relationships led—straight into marriages. Jake had already been down that crooked path once. There was no way he would ever be stupid enough to follow it again.

Jake tossed restlessly onto his side and stared blindly out at the gray light of dawn creeping into his bedroom. He recalled another morning similar to this one, the morning after a night when he had lain awake alone in bed thinking, worrying, wondering. Only it hadn't been Rebecca Bellamy who had inspired his troubled thoughts. It had been his wife, Marie. They had argued when he'd arrived home from work late and had missed a dinner party Marie had thrown for her mother's birthday. Jake had truly forgotten all about it, had been so caught up in a case, that he had worked until nearly nine o'clock before realizing what time it was.

He'd come home to find Marie seated alone in her cocktail dress, elbows on the dining room table still heaped with the remains of dinner. Everyone else had gone home. Marie only stared at him for a moment, then blew out the candles and rose from her seat in silence. She went to the hall closet and collected her coat and purse, then turned to speak to Jake one final time.

"This was your last chance, Jake," she'd said in a quiet, even tone of voice he'd never heard her use before. He recalled thinking that she'd sounded almost...defeated in some way. "I'm going to spend the night at David's. I'll collect the rest of my things later."

Jake had suspected that Marie had been having an affair, but he hadn't known with whom. To hear her state it unequivocally, to hear her offer the man's name with such casual familiarity, tore like a dull knife at something inside him. David. David what? Jake had never bothered to find out. To this day he had no idea who the man was or where Marie might have met him. And a part of him still couldn't believe that his wife had betrayed him so thoroughly. It had hurt him, hurt him badly. And Jake had sworn to God that it would never, ever, happen to him again. He would go to great pains to see to it that no woman ever touched him that deeply again, that no woman ever reached the secret part of him that Marie had once warmed and then so brutally chilled. No woman. Not even Rebecca Bellamy. Especially not her.

She'd have to be crazy to get involved with a guy like him, thinking it would lead to something substantial, Jake reminded himself viciously. Hey, he'd made it clear where he stood with her, hadn't he? He hadn't led her on, encouraged her to believe he was anything other than what he said he was. Jake Raglan was *not* going to marry, ever again. And Rebecca knew that unequivocally. If she had consented to carry their little attraction to each other further, then she had no one but herself to blame.

So why did Jake feel so damned guilty? Why did he feel like he should crawl over to her house and promise on bended knee to make an honest woman of her? Why, dammit, did he want nothing more than to call her on the phone this instant and apologize for running out on her the way he had? To call her and murmur silly, romantic bits of nonsense to make up for hurting her?

Because Jake was absolutely certain that he had hurt Rebecca. And that knowledge only made him feel even worse about what they had done. He tried to convince himself that he wasn't behaving like a coward when he decided it would be best not to see her again. Then he remembered that his closest friend was to be married in his house two weeks from today, and that the woman he sought to avoid would be orchestrating the entire event. There was no way Jake could refrain from running into Rebecca. He had no choice but to see her again. However, that didn't mean he couldn't put it off as long as possible.

And put it off he did. Jake didn't see Rebecca for nearly two weeks. Once, only once, did she leave a message on his answering machine. It was three days after they had made love, a Monday when Jake came home from work feeling detached, defeated and depressed. The red light on the machine in his kitchen flickered at him once, twice, three times, before he looked away from it. Cautiously, he pushed the replay button as he shed his coat and loosened his tie. After a moment, Rebecca's quiet, steady voice filled the room, and suddenly the day didn't seem quite as gloomy as it had before. Her tone was light, breezy, just the way he remembered it, as if nothing in the world had changed between them. She simply told Jake that she was thinking about him, and would he please give her a call when he got the chance.

He didn't return her call. But he did come home from work one evening and knew immediately that Rebecca had been in his house while he was at work. The moment he opened his front door, he picked up the scent of her perfume, something sweet and delicate and reminiscent of a Victorian garden. Foolishly, he hurried through the house looking for her, certain she was still there measuring a room or laying out decorations for the wedding. But she was gone. Without a note, without a trace. And Jake couldn't get over how cheated he felt at the realization. He assured himself his own reaction couldn't have been anything like what Rebecca must have felt at finding him gone that Saturday morning.

Even when Jake settled into bed that evening, it somehow seemed as if her fragrance was there, too. He knew he must be imagining things, but his dreams that night had been filled with images of Rebecca and those exquisite moments when they had hit the heights of passion together. And he hadn't been able to stop thinking about her since.

It wasn't until the evening before the wedding, when Stephen and Alison hosted their rehearsal dinner at a local restaurant known for its good food and avant-garde ambience, that Jake saw Rebecca again. The first thing he noticed when he saw her enter the restaurant was that she looked more beautiful than he had ever seen her, and the second thing he noticed was that she wasn't alone. She had come with a date. A man. A man who was young, good-looking and exceptionally well dressed. A man Jake was sure he knew from somewhere.

"Oh, there's Rebecca," Alison said, rising slightly from her seat between Jake and Stephen to beckon to the other woman. "Over here, Rebecca! You and Marcus can sit across from me and Stephen."

Marcus, Jake muttered to himself. What kind of man allowed himself to be called by a name like that? And then it hit him. Marcus Tate, a divorce attorney who worked in town and was well known for two reasons: he was utterly amoral, and he went through women faster than most men went through underwear. Why he was with Rebecca—a woman who professed to despise lawyers—was anyone's guess.

Rebecca had promised herself not to lose her composure at seeing Jake again. She tried to remain calm and unruffled, tried to forget about the fact that this was a man who had made love to her and left under cover of darkness, and who hadn't even bothered to call since doing so. But it was very difficult to remain cool in the face of someone so handsome and intimidating. Someone to whom she had bared a part of her soul no one else had ever seen. Someone she loved who didn't love her back.

The past two weeks had been perhaps the dreariest and the loneliest Rebecca had ever experienced. Even the days following Eliot's rejection hadn't left her feeling as empty and achy inside as Jake's abandonment had. How could she have been so wrong about him? she asked herself for perhaps the hundredth time. Why were her feelings for him clearly so much stronger than his were for her?

Rebecca thought back to the afternoon when she had left a message for him on his answering machine. She had felt like an adolescent with her first crush, her stomach balled up into a painful knot as she listened to his phone ring at home. She had chosen a time when she'd known he would be at work, because she simply hadn't been sure she could react rationally if he had actually answered the phone. So, like a frightened, insecure teenager, she had pretended his night flight meant no more to her than a stubbed toe, had airily, coyly mentioned that she was thinking about him, and had left the simple request, "Call me when you get a chance."

And thus she had thrust the responsibility for their relationship onto Jake's shoulders. And he, evidently, had simply let it drop into the dust. So much for being so certain he was the right man for her. So much for hoping what he'd told her at the peak of their lovemaking was true.

Apparently Jake was one of those men who could tell a woman anything without regretting it later. He probably wasn't even aware that he'd said it, probably told all of his partners that he loved them. The word "partner" bothered Rebecca terribly. To think that she was Jake's partner only in sex and nothing else made her feel sullied and cheap, just one more in a string of affairs.

And now to take her seat across from him, at a table full of people who had met to celebrate the union of a couple so much in love they had decided to marry... Well, it was something of a blow to Rebecca's already-battered ego. It helped little to realize that Jake had come alone. It helped even less to realize he had yet to look at her. It only served to reinforce the misgivings she still harbored about having invited Marcus to come with her this evening.

Normally, Rebecca wasn't the kind of woman to orchestrate elaborate setups as she had done tonight. And really, it hadn't been her idea. Not entirely, anyway. Although she had asked Marcus to come with her strictly because she knew what kind of man he was and hoped it might rattle Jake, this wasn't the first time he had been her escort to some function. He and Eliot had been good friends in college, so Rebecca had known him for years. She was well aware of the fact that Marcus was considered a womanizer in social circles, and a coldhearted snake in legal circles.

But he was also a damned effective attorney who succeeded in doing exactly what he'd been hired to do. And, although most people would shake their heads in disbelief, Marcus was Rebecca's friend. He was the only one of her acquaintances in college who hadn't treated her like a pariah after her divorce. Instead, he had turned his back on Eliot, deeming the man a fool.

Rebecca was perhaps the only person in the world Marcus felt tenderly toward. And she was probably the only person in the world who felt tenderly toward Marcus. It

was why she had been able to confide in him about Jake.
And why Marcus had been able to hatch a plan to make
the other man feel jealous.

Now she felt as if her behavior tonight was as childish
and ridiculous as it had been when she'd left the message
on Jake's machine. No good would come of trying to ma-
nipulate a situation, Rebecca thought. She probably should
have simply declined Alison's invitation to attend the rehearsal dinner and stayed at home with a good book. But
Alison Mitchell was a very persuasive woman, and when
she'd told Rebecca she was welcome to bring a date, Rebecca had thought, Why not? Obviously Jake Raglan had
no intention of seeing her again. And although she knew it
would be a very long time before she had worked through
her feelings and was over him, Rebecca thought perhaps
she could take some consolation in knowing she had left
him with the impression that he meant as little to her as
she evidently did to him.

And the evidence was in. He hadn't even noticed that
she had taken her seat directly opposite him. Beside her,
Marcus smiled encouragingly and pushed back a pale blond
lock of hair, his gray eyes twinkling merrily.

"You look beautiful tonight, Rebecca," he murmured
just loudly enough for Jake to hear.

His comment provoked the desired response from the
man across the table. Out of the corner of her eye, Rebecca
saw Jake's attention wander from Alison to Marcus, then
to herself. His gaze was indifferent, however, his expression revealing nothing about what he might be feeling.

"Hello, Rebecca," he finally greeted her amiably, as if
they were the most casual of acquaintances. "Marcus. Long
time no see."

At first, Rebecca thought Jake had offered his offhand
greeting to her, and she wanted to slap him unconscious
for being so cavalier and uncaring. But when Marcus responded with a less-than-enthusiastic chuckle, she realized
the two men must be sharing some private joke.

"Not long ago, I beat the pants off Jake in court," Marcus told Rebecca, leaning toward her much closer than was necessary.

Jake's hand clenched involuntarily around the old-fashioned glass in his hand when he observed the other man's proprietary gesture, nearly shattering the delicate crystal. So that was what Marcus and Rebecca had in common, he thought idly. They'd both had him out of his pants lately, one figuratively, the other literally.

"My client," Marcus continued, adopting a pathetic tone of voice, "was a poor, downtrodden, helpless woman whose husband was a total sleazoid. I won a settlement that proved to the world women wouldn't tolerate being victimized by such scum any longer."

Jake rolled his eyes toward the ceiling. "Oh, please. Your client was a scheming, conniving ex-*hooker*, for God's sake, who panicked when her husband found out about her past. You won that case by the skin of your teeth and you know it, Marcus," he concluded evenly, successfully disguising the effect the other man had on him.

Marcus grinned, shook his head knowingly and pointed a finger at Jake. "You know, if you wouldn't focus so heavily on clients who are tired, bitter old men who feel like they've been shafted by the very women they drove away to begin with, you might enjoy your work a little more. But then, I guess, birds of a feather... Right, Jake?"

Rebecca saw Jake flinch as if he had indeed been slapped, saw a nerve in his jaw twitch once, then go rigid. He downed his drink, mumbled, "Excuse me," and pushed himself away from the table without offering any indication that he would return. All eyes followed as he threaded his way through the maze of tables and up the steps toward the bar, but no one uttered a word. The members of the wedding party simply looked at one another, then went back to the various conversations they'd been enjoying when the interruption occurred. Only Rebecca turned to Marcus and silently demanded an explanation.

"Trust me," Marcus said softly. "Guys like Jake Raglan don't take kindly to hearing the truth. Give him a few minutes. He'll be back."

But when ten minutes passed without bringing Jake's return, Rebecca began to worry. "Just what were you trying to imply by your comments to Jake?" she asked Marcus insistently.

Her companion swirled his drink casually in the glass and replied, "There's something you should know about your friend, Mr. Raglan."

"Oh?" Rebecca asked mildly. "And what might that be?"

"He went through a *very* nasty divorce about three years ago."

"That's not exactly a secret, Marcus."

Marcus eyed her skeptically. "Are you telling me Jake told you about his divorce?"

"Well, no. But it doesn't take a genius to figure out it must not have been pleasant. He's more soured on the institution of marriage than anyone I've ever met."

Marcus said nothing for a moment, then posed a question to which he already knew the answer. "Your own divorce was pretty awful, wasn't it, Rebecca?"

She sighed. "You know how awful it was, Marcus. You represented me, remember?"

"Yeah, I remember," he muttered distastefully. "And I could have won you a bundle, too, if you hadn't been so damned softhearted where that bastard, Eliot, was concerned. I still can't believe you declined alimony and any kind of settlement after the way he treated you. It's incredible how you—"

"Marcus, it doesn't matter," Rebecca interrupted, her voice edged with the finality she felt toward her own disastrous marriage. "It's over now. There's no need to rehash it. We were talking about Jake's divorce, not mine."

"My point is that you both suffered at the hands of your

spouses, yet you've gone on to bear no grudge, to harbor no ill feelings at all."

"Oh, I have ill feelings toward Eliot," she began to confirm.

"But they don't cloud your perception of life," Marcus pointed out. "You don't live every day colored by your experiences with your ex-husband."

"I thought we decided not to talk about my marriage, Marcus."

Reluctantly, Marcus let the subject drop and explained, "But Jake Raglan's everyday life *is* colored by his feelings toward his ex-wife, and what he sees as his mistreatment at her hands."

"What do you mean, 'what he *sees* as his mistreatment?'"

Marcus thought for a moment before he began to describe the gossip that had burned up the legal grapevine a few years back. "Jake's wife left him for another man three years ago," he told Rebecca. "But not because she was the screeching siren he tries to make her out to be. Marie Raglan was just a lonely woman. Jake worked constantly, put his job before everything else, including his wife, and Marie went to bed alone too many nights, waiting for her husband to come home from work. Then one day, she met a nice man who put her first in his life, and she began to see what a farce her marriage was. So she left.

"Her older brother represented her, and, as big brothers are wont to do, he set out to protect his sister in any way he could. That meant airing the whole dirty business for the entire legal community, painting Jake as a complete ogre, and exploiting his pain and guilt to win a very hefty settlement."

Marcus paused for a moment before continuing. "It was a lousy experience for everyone involved. No one's fault, really, just one of those things. Happens every day. But Jake Raglan took it to heart. Marie hurt him, and he's been a bitter, vengeful man ever since." After a moment, Marcus concluded, "But I'll tell you something else—the episode turned him into one hell of a divorce lawyer. Obviously, he prefers clients who have been through what he sees as experiences similar to his own."

Rebecca shook her head in disbelief. "And true to form, you went for the throat, too, just to make him squirm."

"Rebecca, I was only trying to make him see how unfair he's been to you and to himself."

"Oh, Marcus, how could you? I'm going to look for him," she said suddenly, rising from her chair before Marcus had a chance to stop her.

Rebecca followed the route she had seen Jake take, stopping at the entrance to the bar. It was dark and hazy with blue smoke, filled to capacity on a Friday night. Despite that, she had little trouble making him out, seated at the bar with one hand wrapped around a drink, the other bunching a fistful of hair over his forehead. Silently, she made her way through the crowd until she stood behind him, then she placed her hand gently on his shoulder.

The moment she touched him, Rebecca felt Jake relax. Muscles that had been bunched beneath her fingers eased and rolled, as if bands of steel melted into fluid mercury. For a long moment, he didn't turn around, but the fingers in his hair smoothed the dark locks back and settled calmly on the bar. Only then did Jake turn in his seat, and for the first time in two weeks, he looked Rebecca squarely in the eye.

"Trying to make me jealous?" he asked softly, almost wearily, the ghost of a smile playing around his lips.

Rebecca smiled back, feeling the ice that had encircled her heart for two weeks begin to trickle away like a warm stream. "Why? *Are* you feeling jealous?"

Instead of answering her truthfully, Jake glanced down at the floor, and evaded her question by replying, "I never made any promises to you, Rebecca."

She shook her head almost imperceptibly and lifted her

shoulders in a slight shrug. "I don't recall ever saying that you did."

"You knew where you stood with me."

Rebecca said nothing for a moment, then told him, "You made it clear as crystal."

"What's that supposed to mean?"

"Nothing, Jake. It's not supposed to mean anything." She sighed impatiently, wishing they could go back to the first moment they'd seen each other at Daphne's wedding. "I...I don't guess there's any chance we could start all over again, is there?"

Jake had found himself wishing the exact same thing a number of times over the past two weeks. "No, I don't guess there is."

Rebecca nodded in resignation. "So I guess we just chalk it up to one of those things?"

Jake studied her face for a long time before responding. "I guess we do."

The minutes dragged into an awkward silence, and Rebecca knew there was nothing she could say that would change the way things were between them. "I'm sorry about Marcus," she finally said quietly.

Jake didn't know if she was sorry she had brought the other man, or if she was apologizing for what Marcus had said. Either way, it didn't really matter. Ultimately, it all boiled down to one thing: he and Rebecca wouldn't be seeing each other socially any more. The realization brought him none of the relief or serenity he had thought it would. Instead of feeling as if he could close a chapter of his life and move on, he somehow felt as if there were loose threads dangling everywhere.

It didn't feel good to Jake. It didn't feel right.

Six

The Mitchell-Flannery wedding went off without a hitch the next day. Rebecca had never felt more drained or more relieved to be through with an affair than she did by Saturday night. Long after Alison and Stephen had left Jake's house to pursue their marital bliss, Rebecca was still working, corralling the most festive guests who were unwilling to end their revels, thanking and paying the musicians and the clergyman, and double-checking to be sure that the cleanup crew she had scheduled would arrive early Sunday to work on the house. As per her own suggestion and with Alison's blessing, Rebecca made sure that what was left of the catered food went to a downtown shelter that night, and the flowers were delivered to a local hospital.

By 1:00 a.m., everything was again peaceful and quiet in Jake's house. Rebecca stretched like a cat and sank down onto the overstuffed burgundy-and-hunter-green striped couch in his living room, kicked off her shoes, and rubbed her eyes. She had removed her cinnamon-colored suit jacket earlier, and at some point in the evening had untied the lace collar and unfastened the top two buttons of her ivory silk blouse. Now she sat with her elbows on her knees, her face in her hands, hovering at the edge of consciousness because she was so exhausted.

It wasn't that this wedding had been a particularly difficult one to arrange, she reflected wearily. On the contrary, Alison had been a remarkably easygoing bride, and Rebecca had planned a number of other weddings infinitely more difficult. Nor was it that the day had been an especially long one. Alison and Stephen's ceremony and reception had been no more time-consuming than those for any other couple of Rebecca's acquaintance.

No, the reason Rebecca felt so beaten and weary was that she had been forced to spend the day in continuous contact with Jake Raglan. At every turn she had found herself confronting him for one reason or another, and there were times when she almost felt he had even orchestrated situations, simply because he wanted to talk to her. Of course, she told herself that such suspicions were ridiculous—after all, *he* had been the one to run out on her—but she still couldn't shake the uneasy feeling that, despite their conversation of the evening before, there were too many important things that had remained unsaid between them.

All in all, Rebecca had been left feeling as if every cell in her body had been drawn out, trampled over and replaced in the most painful manner possible. She hurt everywhere, in every possible way—physically, emotionally, psychologically and spiritually. And deep down inside, she wasn't certain she would ever feel good—honestly *good*—again.

Because her hands were doubled into loose fists over her eyes, Rebecca heard more than saw Jake come into the room. She remained motionless and silent, however, willing him to go away and leave her alone. But when she heard the sound of something being set on the coffee table before her, she reluctantly removed her hands and opened her eyes. Before her, a long-stemmed crystal flute sparkled with

ale gold champagne, looking at once harmless and invit-
ng, and very, very dangerous. It was champagne meant to
elebrate a new beginning, a new life for two people very
uch in love. Rebecca was torn between wanting to drain
he glass dry with thirsty sips and wanting to dash it vio-
ntly against the wall.

"Last of the champagne," Jake said softly as he took a
eat much too close beside her on the sofa. "Cheers."

Rebecca stopped herself from laughing derisively out
oud. Cheerful was perhaps the last word she would use to
escribe the way she felt. Nonetheless, she curled her fin-
ers around the stem of the glass and lifted it to her lips.

"Cheers," she rejoined in a hollow voice when she had
wallowed.

"You look beat," Jake told her. He slid one hand across
er back, wrapping his fingers over her upper arm, turned
er to face slightly away from him, and began massaging
er shoulders lightly in a gesture that was at once strange
nd familiar.

"That's because I feel beat," Rebecca murmured on a
ired sigh, loving the feel of Jake's hands so gentle and
varm on her aching body.

She should tell him to stop, she thought, as his fingers
neaded the taut flesh stretched over her shoulder blades.
But what he was doing felt so good. Rebecca sighed again
s he circled his thumb at the base of her nape, closing her
yes to enjoy his touch more fully. Little by little, she felt
erself growing sleepier, until she wasn't quite sure if she
vas conscious or dreaming. When her head rolled forward,
ake skimmed his fingers up her neck and into her hair,
nd before Rebecca realized what was happening, he was
oosening the pins that held her chignon in place, tangling
is fingers playfully in her dark curls.

"Jake, don't," she protested halfheartedly as her scalp
egan to tingle everywhere his fingers touched.

"Shh" was all he offered in reply.

When her hair cascaded to the center of her back in an

unruly mass, Jake bunched a fistful in his hand and swept it aside, pushing it over her shoulder. Rebecca groaned softly when he began to rub his hands over her neck and back once again, moaning quietly in contentment at the vibrations tingling throughout her body as a result.

This is nice, she thought, as a warm, fuzzy fog surrounded her brain. She'd never had someone to come home to after work, someone who would pamper her and speak softly to her and put her needs before his own. Eliot had usually been in bed by the time Rebecca got home from work, or else he'd been at the library studying until well past her own bedtime. At least, back then she'd thought he was at the library. Now, of course, she realized he had probably been out trying to impress some sweet young coed with his extensive legal knowledge.

But Jake was nice to come home to....

For long moments Rebecca only allowed herself to feel, to become caught up in the sweet sensations wrought by Jake's soft caress. And when his lips joined his fingers in wreaking tender havoc on her senses, she could only smile in dazed satisfaction. Still caught up in the hazy sensation that she was lost in the most exquisite kind of dream, she unwittingly murmured Jake's name in an intimate whisper uncertain whether she had asked him to please cease his assault or to never, ever, end it.

"Rebecca," Jake ground out on a ragged breath.

He wasn't sure what had possessed him to touch her in the familiar way he had been for the last several moments, but suddenly all he wanted to do was become lost in her warmth and softness as he had two weeks ago. With quiet, deft maneuvering, he tugged gently on Rebecca's shoulders, dragging her across his lap until he could gaze down at the face that had haunted him for months, dreamy looking and glowing in the pale amber light from the fireplace. Her hair fell back over his arm like a black waterfall, and her eyes glistened like expertly cut gems. She was so beautiful, so desirable. And with no small amount of panic, Jake realized he wanted her more than he'd ever wanted a woman, any woman.

Cupping her jaw with his hand, he smoothed her hair back from her face and leaned down to kiss her. He expected her to push him away, expected her to bolt, but Rebecca did neither. She reached up and threaded her fingers insistently in his own hair, and pulled him down to receive her kiss instead. Jake complied willingly, eagerly, rejoicing in the knowledge that they would make love once more, completely forgetting that he had sworn it wouldn't happen again.

As their kiss deepened, Jake leaned forward until Rebecca lay beneath him on the sofa. His hands began a subtle exploration of curves and valleys he remembered well, starting at her hip, then fingering each rib as if counting them, only to curve below the swell of her breast. Rebecca arched upward then, positioning herself until Jake was cupping his fingers snugly over her breast, then flexed them open and closed them again. When he thumbed the rigid peak to even riper fullness, Rebecca moaned, placing her hand over his and urging him to venture downward.

Jake's smile was full of promise when he gazed down at Rebecca again. There would be time enough for that later. They had the rest of the night together, and he wanted to go slow. He wanted to make sure nothing was overlooked, wanted to be sure that ultimately they were both completely satisfied.

As Rebecca stared back at him silently, heatedly, her chest rising and falling in ragged gasps for breath, Jake rose enough to pull her blouse from her skirt and began to unbutton it. One by one he slipped the fabric-covered buttons through their holes, then he pulled Rebecca's blouse open and discovered to his joy the front closure clasp of her lacy brassiere. Immediately he hooked his finger beneath it and unfastened it, then flattened his palms against her warm skin and pushed his hands up over her breasts, shucking the linen and lace as he did so.

Rebecca's fingers were still tangled in his hair, and when Jake lowered his head to leave a chaste kiss over her heart, her hands fell down to his neck and rubbed uneven circles across his back. Gradually, Rebecca let her fingers dip lower, and the more intimate her caresses became, the more insistently Jake tasted her. When she curved her palms over his taut hips, he opened his mouth wide and drew as much of her breast inside as he could, flattening his tongue against her. Rebecca cried out softly and squeezed her hands into fists, pulling his hips against the cradle of her thighs with anxious insistence, entwining her legs with his.

The feel of her softness so close, yet so unattainable, nearly drove Jake into an uncontrollable frenzy. Instinctively, he pushed himself more intimately against her, and instinctively Rebecca arched her body upward, crying out his name as she did so. It was only then that Jake realized how close they were to making love again, and it was only then that he began to think coherently about what they were about to do.

"Rebecca," he gasped out, his breath hot and damp against her skin. "I'll make love to you again, but you have to know that I don't—I can't love you."

His words were like a bucket of icy water on Rebecca's inflamed emotions. She looked dazedly down at their partially undressed and intimately entwined bodies, observed in shock the carnally possessive manner in which she cradled him against her, and nearly choked on her horror. Oh, no, how had she let this happen to her again? How could she have allowed things to progress this rapidly, to this extreme, between them? Her brain was inundated with questions to which she could provide no answers. But louder and more insistent than any of the others was the one that had bothered her subconscious for weeks. Why couldn't Jake love her?

For a moment Rebecca remained helplessly silent. Then, without thinking, she uttered the first thing that launched itself into her brain. "But...but you told me you loved me," she said in a very small voice.

It was the last thing Jake wanted to hear, the last thing he wanted to be reminded of. Slowly releasing a breath he had scarcely been aware of holding, Jake dropped his head forward in defeat. The action simply served to offer him a view of Rebecca's delectable, pink flesh, reddened now by his relentless mauling. Reluctantly, he disengaged himself from her long enough to push her clothing back into place, and then he sat up straight on the couch. Dangling his hands between his knees and dropping his gaze to the floor, he looked every bit as weary and defeated as Rebecca had only a short time ago.

"Rebecca," he began quietly, uncertain exactly what he had planned to say. He felt the sofa shift beside him and knew that she, too, had risen to remove herself from the dangerous position into which they had put themselves.

"Don't, Jake," he heard her say softly. "Don't say anything. I understand. Just let it go."

God, what had she been thinking? Rebecca asked herself caustically as she buttoned up her blouse too quickly, noting when she reached the neck that she had skipped a buttonhole somewhere along the line. Dropping her arms to her sides in frustration, she doubled her hands into fists and quickly released them, then began to stuff her shirttail furiously back into her skirt.

Jake was nice to come home to. That was what she'd been thinking about when she'd allowed things to go too far.

But this wasn't her home, she reminded herself viciously. And Jake wasn't hers to come home to. She would have been smart to remember that, would have been smart to remind herself what had happened the last time she'd felt so comfortable, so cozy with Jake Raglan. She'd gotten hurt. Badly hurt. And it wasn't going to happen again.

"Rebecca, don't... Don't do that," Jake said when she

circled the coffee table until it lay as a barrier between them. "We need to talk."

She chuckled without humor, trying to fight back the tears she felt threatening. No, she would not cry. Not now. Not yet. "Talk," she repeated coolly, her voice edged with something akin to cynicism. "No way, Jake. You've said more than enough."

"Rebecca…"

"It's late," she stated brusquely, yanking her jacket from a chair near the fireplace and thrusting her arms into its sleeves. "I think I'm pretty well finished here. If there's anything I've forgotten, let me know and I'll take care of it in the morning."

"Rebecca—"

"It was nice of you to let Alison and Stephen use your house for the wedding," she added in an effort to keep him from saying anything further about their situation. "It's a beautiful house, Jake. I know you'll be very happy here." She wished she had the nerve to add the word *alone* in a meaningful way, but at the moment all Rebecca wanted was to be gone.

Reaching into her coat pocket, she closed her fingers over the key he had given her two weeks ago. Without a word, she placed it on the coffee table, picked up her purse from the chair where her coat had been, then turned and headed for the front door.

Jake made a halfhearted effort to go after her, wondering why he was even bothering. "But—"

"'Night."

And with that, Rebecca hurried out the front door, jarring the entire house as she slammed it behind her, and leaving Jake silent and dumbfounded in the middle of his living room. After a moment he heard the sound of her sports car roar to life in his driveway, and the squeal of tires as she rushed away from his house. And then, Rebecca was well-and-truly gone, effectively removed from Jake's life forever. All that remained was the scent of her perfume, a scattering of hairpins lying on his coffee table, and a head full of memories that wouldn't even begin to keep him warm at night.

"Dammit," he bit out angrily.

Everything had been moving along nicely between him and Rebecca all day, and Jake had begun to think that maybe, just maybe, they would be able to salvage something—God knows what—from their time together. So what the hell had he done wrong?

Everything, he answered himself immediately. He'd done everything wrong. Slumping back onto the couch in the spot Rebecca had just vacated, Jake sighed wearily, just as she had. He felt as if he'd lived a lifetime in the past three weeks. Rebecca Bellamy had careered into his life from out of nowhere four months ago, had invaded his thoughts and his libido until he could think of little else, then had exploded onto the scene again in all her glory. Then as quickly and thoroughly as she had gotten under his skin, she had retreated, and this time he was sure she wouldn't be coming back.

But that was good, wasn't it? Jake asked himself. That meant he didn't have to worry about being roped into a wedding by a woman who was determined to get married, right? No more having to defend himself and his position on the topic of matrimony. No more feeling guilty about wanting to stay single every time she looked at him with those huge green eyes of hers. No more catching himself wondering what it would be like to wake up next to Rebecca every morning and see her looking soft and vulnerable as she had that night two weeks ago. As she had again tonight. He could continue to wake up every morning completely, blissfully alone. Wasn't that exactly what he wanted?

Jake wove his fingers viciously through his hair, then slammed his fist down hard onto the coffee table. Yeah, that was what he wanted, all right. To be alone.

Leaning forward from his position on the sofa, he lifted

the glass that was still filled with softly bubbling champagne. There was a pale scarlet, crescent-shaped stain on one side, and Jake turned the glass until that side faced him. Placing his lips exactly over the spot where Rebecca's had tasted the wine, he drank deeply and scowled. It tasted a little flat to him. Slowly, he walked to his kitchen and approached the sink, then tipped the glass and watched with much disinterest as the champagne cascaded downward into the drain.

It had been a nice wedding, Jake reflected morosely, as he turned out the kitchen light and headed off to bed. Too bad such celebrations always had to end in marriage.

Rebecca was having trouble concentrating. In fact, she'd been having trouble concentrating for nearly a month now, ever since severing any ties that might remain to Jake Raglan. As she sat at her desk in her Frankfort Avenue office, chin in hand, staring out the window, she realized absently that she was daydreaming again. Normally Rebecca didn't have time for daydreams. Usually November was a very hectic month for her because of the upcoming holiday season. But more and more often this month, she had found herself turning down clients who requested her services to plan both weddings and holiday gatherings, citing a busy agenda and full schedule instead of the physical fatigue and spiritual weariness that actually caused her to decline.

What was it with her lately? she wondered. Gone was the enthusiasm she had once felt for her profession, and gone was the happy zeal with which she had undertaken every project. Ever since the Mitchell-Flannery affair, Rebecca had taken little interest in any prospective nuptial celebration she might be asked to plan, thinking instead that she had grown tired of organizing weddings. What was so great about two people declaring their lifelong devotion, anyway? Statistically speaking, half of them were going to wind up alone again in the long run, so really, what was the point?

Rebecca sighed and toyed with a pencil on her desk blotter, noting vaguely as she continued to stare out the window that it had started to rain. Might as well call it a day, she thought. She couldn't focus on anything, anyway.

As she rose to collect her black greatcoat from the hook behind her door, she heard someone enter the outer office, heard her assistant, Claire, say that, yes, Ms. Bellamy was in her office and able to accept a client. Rebecca sighed again and went back to her desk, smoothing the wrinkles out of her plum-colored wool suit and assuming a posture she hoped made her look terribly busy. But when her office door opened and she glanced up to find Jake Raglan entering, Rebecca knew any facade she tried to erect around herself would fail miserably. So she only stared at him silently, and wished he were nothing more than a hallucination.

"Hello, Rebecca," he said quietly, as he closed the door behind him. Instead of walking toward her desk, he leaned back against the door, clinging to the knob as if to prevent her escape.

"Hello, Jake," she replied cautiously, amazed that she was able to keep her voice level and indifferent.

"Aren't you going to ask me what I'm doing here?"

Rebecca shook her head. "I figure you'll get around to telling me eventually. You've never been one to beat around the bush. You'll make your intentions clear right off."

Jake wasn't sure how he had expected Rebecca to react upon seeing him again, but "cool, calm and collected" hadn't been in his top five choices. He had hoped she would react differently. Evidently, however, his hopes had been in vain. Apparently, Rebecca Bellamy had already put him behind her, and now what he'd come to do wouldn't be as easy as he'd thought. But he was here and it was too late to turn back, so he might as well get to the point.

"I want to hire you."

Rebecca's heart nearly stopped beating at the announcement. "You're getting married?" she asked in a shallow voice, her breath having left her lungs in a steady rush.

"Married?" Jake asked incredulously. "God, no, I'm not getting married."

Inhaling deeply, Rebecca discovered she could only nod silently in response.

"No, I want you to plan a Christmas party for me," Jake clarified. "In fact, I want you to plan my entire Christmas. That is, if you're not already booked up for the season."

Rebecca gazed at him thoughtfully for a long time before replying. Just what was he up to? she wondered. Why would he hire her to perform such a service when a number of other people in town could do it for him? He had made it clear that there was no reason to pursue their relationship any further, had been more than open in his assertion that they wouldn't be seeing each other anymore after Stephen and Alison's wedding. Why her? Why now? Why ever?

"I've got a pretty full calendar, Jake," she lied reluctantly. "Corporate parties, social soirees, even a couple of weddings."

Jake tried not to let her see how deeply her rebuff unsettled him. Although he told himself he should simply accept things for what they were between them—over—and go along on his merry way, instead he heard himself asking, "You couldn't grant me a few weekends? An extra weekday here and there?"

"I won't be *granting* you anything, Jake," Rebecca reminded him. "You'll have to pay me for my time."

"So you'll do it?"

It was only then that Rebecca realized her words had indicated she was willing to accept him as a client. She tried to tell herself her acquiescence had resulted from nothing more than a slip of the tongue. But if she was brutally honest with herself, she knew that deep down inside, nothing would have pleased her more than seeing Jake Raglan again.

She drummed her fingers restlessly against the surface of

her desk before voicing her assent. "What exactly did you have in mind?"

Jake had given much thought to his wishes, surprising himself immensely when he first came up with the idea to have a big Christmas celebration at his house. The night following Stephen's wedding had been full of introspection for Jake. He had lain awake in bed for hours, marveling at what a good time he'd had during the wedding and reception, and at how much it had pleased him to see his house full of people having a wonderful time. And at how good it had felt to know Rebecca was responsible for it.

When he'd first bought his house seven months ago, Jake had never once entertained the thought of ever having anyone over. He had simply liked the size of the massive creek-stone structure—especially the fact that it was even larger than the house Ellen shared with her family—and he had liked knowing he would be living in one of Louisville's most prestigious neighborhoods. It would impress his clients, he'd thought then. And it would get under Ellen's skin. That was all. Those were the only reasons for buying that particular house. Not because of any entertainment potential, and certainly not because it would provide enough room for a big family.

But oddly enough, both of those ideas had careered into his mind the night after Stephen's wedding. For the first time since Jake had moved in, his house had been full of people. And even though those people were friends and relatives of someone else, Jake had realized another first—his house felt like a home. The place had simply felt warm, comfortable and full, reinforcing how thoroughly empty it was when he was home by himself. And somehow it had also occurred to Jake then that only Rebecca Bellamy would be able to make it feel that way again. It had taken him almost a month to actually admit it.

"I want you to do everything," he told her.

Rebecca raised her eyebrows in speculation. "Come again?"

Jake finally released the doorknob and moved across the room to take a seat in the chair opposite hers. "You once told me that the 'Plus' in 'Weddings Plus, Inc.' could be anything. You told me that you had even organized a Christmas once, everything from the shopping to the decorating to the wrapping to the cooking. I want to hire you to do that for me."

"Why?" Rebecca thought it was a fair-enough question. Jake was a grown man who had come far in life. Surely this wasn't the first Christmas he had celebrated. Surely he knew how to go about performing the usual tasks. But his answer proved she was mistaken.

"Because I've never really celebrated Christmas before, that's why."

Rebecca eyed him doubtfully, but said nothing.

"It's true. When Ellen and I were growing up in Acorn Ridge, my family couldn't afford to have Christmas. Oh, we went to church, and chopped down some sorry excuse for a tree, but there were no gifts, no parties, no eggnog or Santa Claus. Then when we got older, Ellen...well, Ellen wanted to spend Christmas with her new family, not with me. I carried too many reminders of what she'd left behind. When Daphne was old enough, she and I would go to dinner every Christmas Eve, but that was the extent of my holiday revels." He paused for a moment, fixing Rebecca with an almost desperate expression. "I've never had a Christmas before, Rebecca. Not the way most people do."

He looked so forlorn seated across from her that Rebecca wanted to reach over and take his hand in hers. Here was a man, one of the most successful attorneys in town, wealthy beyond his dreams and completely unable to enjoy a holiday. How could she turn him down? she asked herself. She, who knew better than anyone in the world how to celebrate, she who found celebration in *everything* life had to offer...how could she say no to such a simple request as his?

"Okay, I'll do it," she said with a smile.

Jake hadn't been aware he was holding his breath until he let it out on a long sigh. He smiled back at Rebecca with genuine relief. "When do we start?"

"Right now," she told him as she went to a file cabinet and pulled open the top drawer. "Let's see now," she said to herself as she began to thumb through manila folders. "Anniversaries, babies, birthdays, bridal...ah, here it is. Christmas."

She held the folder aloft as if it were a trophy, returned to her desk and spread it open before her, then glanced up at Jake again. "You sure you want me to do it all?"

"Absolutely positive," he assured her with a firm nod.

"Then I'll need you to supply a few things for me."

"Such as?"

"A list of people for whom you'd like to buy gifts and how much you'd like to spend on each. If you can supply me with a few ideas, it would be an enormous help. If you want to entertain, I'll also need a guest list, and I'll have to go over menus with you. You'll need to tell me about any food allergies or dislikes you or your guests might have, any specific dietary needs that might have to be met—vegetarian, low-salt, diabetic, that sort of thing...." Her words trailed off as she sifted through more papers. "I'll need price ceilings, dates of availability—"

"Rebecca?"

It was the voice Jake had used when he'd made love to her, and it almost made Rebecca want to cry at hearing it once again. Slowly, she lifted her gaze from the papers on her desk to the man who sat before her, and slowly, her senses began to go berserk. He was looking at her as if he cared for her, gazing at her as if all he wanted to do was hold her close and never let her go. Oh, how she wished he would. Oh, how she wished Jake Raglan was a man who could love her until her dying day. But that was a futile wish, an empty dream. Jake would devote himself to no woman. Jake Raglan would never marry again.

"Yes?" Rebecca asked faintly.

For long moments he said nothing, only continued to stare at her with that maddeningly tender expression. "Thanks," he finally uttered quietly.

Rebecca's heart hammered hard in her chest. "For what?"

Jake's smile became softer then, and his voice was so low when he answered her that she almost didn't hear. "For everything."

For a moment, Rebecca didn't—couldn't—respond. Her mind was too muddled, her thoughts too confused. Gradually she calmed herself down, took a deep breath, and spoke in a voice that surprised her with its evenness and composure. "There's something we need to get straight, though, Jake."

His expression indicated nothing as to what he might be feeling or thinking. "What's that?"

"What happened between us before…it won't happen again."

She waited for him to respond, but his posture remained unchanged, and he only gazed at her, unfazed, as if demanding that she clarify her intentions.

"I'm serious, Jake. If I take you on as a client, there's to be no flirting, no innuendo, no longing looks…in short, no hanky-panky."

She could tell he was biting his lip in an effort to prevent his laughter from erupting. "Hanky-panky? Now there's a phrase I haven't heard in a couple of decades. Hanky-panky… Golly gee whillikers, is that still around after all this time?"

Rebecca ignored his sarcasm and explained, "I'm going to be spending a lot of time at your house, Jake, and I want you to promise me that you won't try anything funny."

Jake rose from his chair and leaned over her desk, so close that she could smell familiar scents that evoked dangerous memories. His eyes were dark, stormy and very, very serious when he told her, "Rebecca, I can safely say that you won't find anything I try funny. Erotic, maybe, arousing, certainly, but…funny? No way.''

"Jake…''

"Okay,'' he finally conceded. "No funny stuff. No hanky-panky, whatever the hell that is. I'll be your client, and you'll be my holiday organizer. Nothing more. Is that what you want?''

"Yes." She tried to sound assertive and strong, but Rebecca's voice was breathless and ragged when she replied.

"Are you sure?''

Not trusting her voice to comply with her demands, Rebecca simply nodded silently.

"Okay, then. We've got the record straight.'' Jake returned to his seat, and assumed once again the pose of a successful man who wanted to employ her expertise for his holiday entertaining. Gone was the heated gaze, the promise of pursuit. In its place, Jake had inserted a bland expression of neutrality.

Rebecca thought back to how he had looked and sounded when he'd told her thanks only moments ago, then cautioned herself not to overreact. He had simply been thanking her for taking him on as a client, nothing more. Still, deep down inside, she couldn't prevent the little flame of hope that flickered to life in her heart. No matter how often she tried to squelch it with the waters of reason, the spark sputtered back to life again. Rebecca called herself foolish and naive. She called herself a dupe. But she couldn't help feeling excited that she'd be there to plan Jake's Christmas.

And, despite the warning she had given him only moments earlier, in the most secret chamber of her heart, Rebecca couldn't help but hope that she might be there to enjoy it with him, too.

Seven

By the middle of the third week of December, Rebecca had completely transformed Jake's house. He had told her he wanted to have a cocktail party and open house for his neighbors and a number of his associates that evening, and she was well ahead of schedule in her planning of the night's festivities.

The color scheme in Jake's living and dining rooms was perfect for the season—deep crimson and forest green—so Rebecca had simply added accessories to enhance the rooms. Over the fireplace she had hung an enormous wreath made of grapevines interwoven and sprayed with holly and greenery and a huge golden bow. A garland of twisted pine and spruce boughs touched with the same golden ribbon adorned the mantel and bannister leading to the upstairs. Opposite the fireplace and tucked into a corner created by the stairway and wall, she had placed an eight-foot-high Scotch pine decorated completely in gold—glittery gold trim, twinkling gold lights, shiny gold balls and glistening gold tinsel. Beneath it lay the gifts Rebecca had purchased as Jake had indicated—every one of them for clients, save the one he'd ordered for Daphne, Rebecca recalled dryly—all wrapped in foil paper of green, red and gold. Rebecca had always loved shiny things. She supposed that in her next life she would probably come back as a magpie.

Now as she stood in the center of Jake's living room studying her handiwork, she smiled to herself in satisfaction at what she had accomplished in such a short time. Jake had been more than generous in his price ceiling. For the most part, he had told Rebecca that money wasn't a concern, that he simply wanted to make up for all the Christmases he had ever missed, and that she should do whatever necessary to make such a celebration memorable.

She had taken him at his word and organized a holiday celebration that would surpass even her own family's revels. Christmas for the Bellamys had always been, to put it mildly, a very big deal. And the only celebrations Rebecca threw herself into with the zeal she embraced for weddings were her Christmas festivities. She found great joy in bringing to other people's homes many of the traditions and holiday treats she had enjoyed herself as a child. And for some reason, sharing these things with Jake, in his house, caused Rebecca to feel even more joyful than usual.

Lifting her nose to inhale the spicy aromas coming from the kitchen, she remembered that she needed to see how her holiday libations were coming along and went to check on them. Simmering on the stove were two large stockpots—one filled with dark beer, cloves, orange peel and cinnamon for wassail, and another with apple juice and similar spices for a non-alcoholic hot cider. In the refrigerator were three one-gallon jugs filled with Rebecca's own recipe for eggnog that she had perfected over the years—two of them containing enough liquor to qualify as "Rebecca's Killer Eggnog," as her father liked to call it. She had also made arrangements for a caterer to provide the requisite holiday foods and preparations—ham, turkey, mincemeat, pumpkin pie, fruitcake, jellies, candies and the like—and she had personally undertaken and nearly exhausted herself with the annual baking of a dozen varieties of Christmas cookies from recipes handed down by her great-grandmother.

As she stood at the stove, tasting the wassail one last time before straining it off into the huge crystal punch bowl that had been in her family for years, Rebecca felt oddly at home. Because she had found Jake's kitchen and china cabinet to be sadly lacking in many of the pieces necessary for large-scale entertaining, and since she was reluctant to spend what would amount to a small fortune to buy him things he might never use again, Rebecca had opted to bring many of her own special belongings to Jake's house for use at his party. Rented china was always so boring looking. Hence her great-grandmother's crystal punch bowl and cups. Hence her grandmother's fine china and crystal stemware. Hence her own silver flatware.

Rebecca told herself that her actions were not unusual in any way. She had often used her own things when she herself catered small parties, because people almost never had enough of their own to entertain in numbers larger than those in their family, or else they were often unwilling to risk the breakage and loss of their fine china, crystal and silver to casual acquaintances. However, Rebecca had never, ever, used her older and more-valuable pieces—the heirlooms that had belonged to generations before her. Only with Jake had she felt it acceptable, indeed even desirable, to use her most beautiful crystal, china and silver. And now, seeing her things mingled so comfortably with his own, a feeling of strange serenity settled over her like a soothing hand.

You're doing it again, a little voice in the back of her head piped up unbidden. You're beginning to feel at home in Jake's house.

Rebecca couldn't honestly deny it. Because Jake was the only client she had agreed to take on this holiday season,

and because Jake's Christmas was the only project she had
to organize until almost February, she had thrown herself
into the planning of this celebration with all the fervor she
normally saved for her own holiday. With no small amount
of chagrin, Rebecca had to admit that she had probably
spent more time in Jake's house this week than she had her
own. In fact, she realized uncomfortably, here it was only
one week before Christmas, and she hadn't even put up a
tree at her home.

But of course, that was because she had been so busy
lately, getting things organized at Jake's house, trying to
make sure everything ran smoothly here. Her lapses in getting her own home decorated went no further than that,
Rebecca assured herself. And if it felt different now going
home at night alone, if her house had suddenly begun to
feel like a strange place to her, well, that was simply because she'd been under a lot of stress lately. It was perfectly
understandable. Any woman would react the same way under the circumstances—planning a holiday celebration for
a man who had made love to her only to turn his back on
her romantically. Thinking about it now, Rebecca realized
she must have been mad ever to accept Jake as a client to
begin with.

It wasn't the first time the thought had occurred to her.
But Rebecca was beginning to understand exactly why she
had agreed to take on Jake's Christmas. There was still a
part of her deep down inside that thought—hoped—that
Jake might change his mind about marriage. And although
she had lain awake at night wondering if she would ever
have a second chance with him, wishing that he would take
her in his arms just one more time, she knew it was ridiculous to dream. She should be delighted that Jake had stuck
to their agreement and hadn't so much as touched her since
she'd entered his house again, Rebecca reflected morosely.
It had kept her from making a complete fool of herself.

Glancing up at the clock on the wall, Rebecca realized
she had been lost in thought longer than she could afford

to be, and would be cutting her time too close if she went home to change her clothes. Fortunately, she had brought her entertaining outfit with her in anticipation of just such an emergency. The party didn't start until eight, and it wasn't yet five, and Rebecca had discovered that Jake made it a habit never to leave his Main Street office before six-thirty. Therefore, if she started now, she knew she could be more than ready by the time he got home. Dusting her hands off absently on her pants, Rebecca grabbed her garment bag from its hook on the inside of the kitchen door and headed upstairs.

To say it was unusual for Jake to leave the office early in order to go home would be a gross understatement. Although it wasn't customary for him to leave the office at all before the end of the workday, if he did, it was to perform some function that directly pertained to business— dinners with clients, depositions, case-related appointments, that sort of thing. But today for some reason, Jake had been feeling restless and edgy, had been nearly overcome by the desire—almost a *need*—to get home as soon as possible.

It had begun around midmorning, when Jake discovered that he was scarcely listening to the verbal meanderings of a newly acquired client. Mr. Landrow was an older gentleman who suspected that his wife—a woman from one of the city's most prominent families, a woman who was noted throughout the community for her selfless charity work—had been cheating on him for some time with the strapping young teenager who delivered the groceries, despite her assurances that such allegations were ridiculous. Normally Jake would pounce on the potential a case like Landrow's seemed to have, but today, he simply wasn't interested.

Instead of paying attention to the less-than-convincing reasons the other man had for his feelings, Jake found himself lost in thoughts of his own, all of them centering around Rebecca Bellamy and what she was doing in his house at that very moment. Every night this week he had come home to find her there, either on her way out or putting the finishing touches on her day's work and preparing to leave. Every night he had asked her to stay for a little while, maybe have some dinner with him. And every night she had said no.

What had he expected? Jake asked himself. She had made it clear from the beginning that she wouldn't tolerate any *hanky-panky,* as she'd so archaically put it. And she had made it clear that what had happened between them before would *not* happen again. In other words, Jake thought, angry with himself, Rebecca wouldn't allow herself to be hurt again. Not by Jake Raglan, anyway.

When he came home at night to find her there, his house seemed fuller and more inviting than he ever would have imagined it could feel. And as soon as she left, the warmth and welcome vanished with her. Then Jake's house became lonelier and more silent than he'd ever noticed it being before. Then Jake's house became empty.

What was she up to right now? he wondered, still sitting idle at his desk hours after Landrow had left him. For the life of him, Jake couldn't even remember what the other man's beef about his marriage had been. Poor old guy simply couldn't believe that his wife still loved him, even after forty-two years of marriage.

The thought caught Jake off guard for a moment, then he pushed it away, suddenly remembering quite clearly what the other man's problem had been. An unfaithful wife. Yet another woman who couldn't be true to the man who loved her. Why shouldn't Mrs. Landrow dump her husband for some young stud? Jake asked himself with all-too-characteristic suspicion. Women did that every day. She had money and connections and was reasonably attractive. And face it, he himself knew Landrow left a lot to be desired in the conversation department. There was every reason in the world to believe that Mrs. Landrow was a wandering wife. And if Mr. Landrow wanted to divorce her because of it, that was his business. All Jake had to do was provide the best legal counsel he could for his client.

But he would have to do it tomorrow.

Because today, Jake wanted to leave the office early and go home. Home to his house, home to the holidays, home to Rebecca. He refused to contemplate how much his feelings had changed over the past two months, refused to consider how important she had become to him, refused to accept that he might honestly be falling hard for this particular woman. He only knew he wanted to go home. And in his mind, that meant being wherever Rebecca was.

Rebecca paused in her preparations when she heard the front door open and close downstairs, followed by the sound of heavy footsteps crossing the living room floor. It couldn't possibly be Jake, she thought. It was barely past five o'clock. She'd scarcely had enough time to step out of her cooking-and-baking clothes and stuff them into a duffel bag heaped in the corner of the bathroom, and now stood barefoot, dressed in only a lacy slip. Her cosmetics lay scattered about on the pedestal sink, her dress hung on the shower-curtain rod still enclosed in its garment bag, and some intruder was downstairs.

With a sudden sense of relief, she realized it must be Donnie, who drove the truck for his father's catering company, and who was supposed to be stopping by with some canapés he'd forgotten to bring with the other food earlier that day. Rebecca had told him she'd leave the front door open in case she was out of hearing range. Opting to simply call downstairs to the teenager that he should put the items into the fridge and tell his father she'd telephone him later to settle up, Rebecca looked around for something to throw quickly over her slip and saw Jake's bathrobe hanging on the back of the door. Oh, what the heck, she thought. It would only be for a minute.

Thrusting her arms into dark blue velour sleeves that hung down well past her fingertips, Rebecca threw the bathroom door open and rushed toward the stairs, all set to bellow out her instructions to the caterer. But the moment she came around the corner and saw Jake topping the highest step, she skidded to a halt and stood rooted to the spot, feeling like a naughty child with her hand in the cookie jar.

At a quiet, oddly strangled sound, Jake glanced up from scanning over the day's mail in his hand and saw what he told himself must surely be a figment of his extremely overactive imagination. There in his upstairs hallway, bundled up in and swallowed by his bathrobe, her toes digging nervously into the lush, dark gold pile carpet, stood Rebecca Bellamy. She looked vulnerable, panicked, uncertain and adorable. And, Jake thought, taking a few reluctant steps toward her, she also looked very desirable.

"Jake," she said, drawing his name out on a long, breathless sigh. "What are you doing home so early?"

"Hi," he said quietly, willing his feet to stop before he got close enough to take her in his arms and scare the hell out of both of them. "I'm sorry. I didn't mean to surprise you like this. I just... I had a light load today, and since the party was tonight, I thought I'd leave early and see if there was anything I could do to help you."

Rebecca seemed to realize then that she was wearing his bathrobe, and fumbled with the sleeves until her hands appeared, so that she could tug the collar up more snugly around her neck. After clearing her throat delicately, she said softly, "I...uh...I was expecting the caterer."

Jake knew full well that her announcement didn't imply what it in fact suggested, but he couldn't help but smile when he replied, "So this is how you greet the caterer. I was wondering how these professional deals worked. I hope he gives you some substantial discounts for this."

Rebecca's eyes widened when she realized how her statement must have sounded, and she fumbled over her words as she tried to explain. "No, wait.... That...that came out wrong. What I meant to say was that I was expecting the caterer's son—"

Jake's eyebrows rose in speculation.

"No, I didn't mean that, either." Rebecca sighed in exasperation, tangling a hand in her hair to push it back off her forehead. "I wasn't expecting to run into anyone. I was planning on just calling out to him down the stairs to leave the stuff in the fridge."

"I see." He gazed at her for a long time in silence, until he finally seemed to remember where they were and what they were doing. "The house smells wonderful," he told her softly.

"Thanks," she responded a little breathlessly.

"And you look wonderful."

Rebecca laced her fingers together nervously, then unlaced them, then began to twist them up restlessly in the sash of the robe. Her heart beat in irregular rhythms beneath her breastbone, and her stomach knotted into an anxious fist. "I'm…I'm sorry I have on your bathrobe. I…it was handy."

Jake's grin broadened. "You wear it well. I don't think I'll ever be able to look at it in quite the same way again."

Rebecca felt heat seep into every fiber of her being, and little sparks of fire flashed like tiny explosions throughout her body. Jake was gazing at her the way a starving man studies a sumptuous banquet, the way a parched wolf eyes a sparkling mountain stream. More alarming than that, though, Rebecca thought, was her realization that her own feelings of hunger and thirst at the moment were even more demanding.

"I'll…I'll just go change," she said quietly.

Jake followed her as far as the bathroom and let his gaze rove past the door to where she had scattered her feminine weapons all over his sink. Marking her territory? he wondered. For some reason, the thought that she might be doing just that did little to raise his hackles. In fact, he reflected, as she closed the door and he headed farther down the hall to his bedroom, it occurred to him that Rebecca Bellamy had probably marked his house the moment she had entered it, and he honestly didn't mind at all.

He should, Jake tried to remind himself viciously. He should mind a lot. Before he'd bought his house, when he'd been renting apartments, he had hated it when he'd discovered a stray lipstick or hair clip or earring tucked discreetly into his medicine cabinet, or between his couch cushions, or under the pillow opposite his in bed. It had meant the owners of the items were leaving a message for any other woman who might happen along, stating that the premises were already covered. It was why he had never invited a woman into his house for a romantic evening and had instead insisted on either going out or going to her place. Jake hadn't wanted his house to be marked the way his apartments had been.

But now it was. Rebecca Bellamy was there in every nook and cranny, and had been for months. Ever since that first night that she had come to inspect the suitability of Jake's house for the Mitchell-Flannery wedding. Ever since she had told him his house was beautiful. Because when Rebecca was there, it was indeed a beautiful house. When Rebecca was there, it was a home.

Just as it was now. For Jake, it had been wonderful to come home every night this week and find Rebecca performing her job downstairs in the most public rooms of his house. But coming home tonight to find her upstairs, in the more private domain of his home, enveloped in a garment as personal and intimate as his bathrobe…it stirred flames so deeply buried inside him that he had nearly forgotten a fire could still burn there. Oddly enough, he realized, as he closed his bedroom door to change clothes, at the moment, there was one burning brighter than it ever had before.

Eight

"Uncle Jake! Uncle Jake! I have the most wonderful news!"

Jake had been speaking at length with one of his neighbors when he heard Daphne's voice coming breathlessly from behind him, and he turned to find her approaching him with eyes as shiny as the Christmas tree behind her and cheeks as red as the velvet cocktail dress she had on. He recalled the first Christmas Eve that he had taken her out to dinner. She had worn a red velvet dress then, too, but as a five-year-old had opted for a much more modest style than the off-the-shoulder number she had on now.

Five years old, Jake thought, with an almost indiscernible shake of his head. That had been nineteen years ago. In an effort to impress his only niece, he had taken her to one of the most expensive restaurants in town. Daphne had deemed the Caesar salad and coq au vin yucky, but had found the raspberry torte to be very much to her liking. Last year when he'd taken her out, she had behaved like nearly every other date Jake had ever escorted to dinner—she'd chosen the garden salad and poached salmon, cooing enthusiastically over both, then had skipped dessert because they were all so fattening. If he hadn't been feeling so strange at the moment, Jake might have laughed at the changes. But all he could do was wonder when Daphne had grown up to become such a beautiful woman.

"Hi, Daphne." He greeted her with a smile, noting that the warm feelings he felt whenever his niece was around were still as strong as ever. "How's married life treating you?"

Daphne's grin couldn't have been broader if she'd put her fingers in her mouth and stretched it. "It's fantastic," she told him. "I never thought I could have this much fun with another person."

"How's Robby?"

Daphne's smile became almost coquettish, and she blushed a little more deeply. "He's fine. He just got a promotion at work. He's regional sales manager now. Takes care of the entire southeast."

"Where is he?" Jake asked, glancing around to inspect the guests. "I'll congratulate him."

"No, wait!" Daphne objected, tugging on Jake's sleeve as he caught sight of his nephew-in-law and began to head in that direction.

Her insistence surprised Jake, and his voice reflected his feelings when he turned back to face her. "Why? What's wrong?"

For a moment, Daphne only stared at her uncle, biting her lip nervously. Finally she blurted out, "You'll have two reasons to congratulate him, Uncle Jake. I'm...I'm going to have a baby."

His expression probably would have been the same if she had just told him she was migrating to Antarctica. "You're *what?*"

Daphne was suddenly overcome by a wave of shyness, and she shrugged a little nervously as she clarified, "I'm going to be a mother, Uncle Jake. And you're going to be a great-uncle.''

Whoa, whoa, whoa, Jake wanted to say. He was only... he was only...oh, dammit, go ahead and say it, he told himself. He was only forty years old. That was way too young to be a great-anything. Unless, of course, it was a great lover.

"A baby?'' he asked softly. "You and Robby are going to have a baby?''

Daphne nodded vigorously. "If it's a girl, we're naming her Carmen, after Robby's mother. But if it's a boy...if it's a boy, we'd like to name him Jacob. That is, if that's all right with you.''

Jake didn't know what to say. A baby boy named after him running around in the world? It was something to which he'd never given thought. After his debacle with Marie, he had simply assumed he would never have children of his own, obviously because he would never marry again. Certainly he would have liked to have children of his own. In fact, if he had ever allowed himself to think about it, Jake would probably have felt great remorse that he would never hear the word "Daddy" used for him. But he had consciously forced himself *not* to think about it. At least, he had until now.

"I'm flattered, Daphne. Of course I don't mind if you name your son after me. How could you think that I would?''

"I just figured that when you have a son of your own, you might want to name him Jake, Jr. or something. I didn't want there to be any confusion when my little Jake and your little Jake play together.''

His little Jake? he thought wildly. *His* little Jake? "I don't think you have to worry about that ever happening, Daphne.''

"You're not one of those guys who insists his name be carried on, is that it?''

Jake shook his head. "I'm not one of those guys who will ever have children."

Daphne smiled at him knowingly. "Don't count on it, Uncle Jake. It might take you longer than most, but you'll be up to your elbows in diapers and strained carrots. Just you wait."

Before he could contradict her again, Daphne spun on her heel and went to find others of her acquaintance to whom she could deliver the good news. Jake watched her leave, feeling oddly happy, though for the life of him he couldn't put his finger on exactly why. Telling himself it was simply because Daphne always brought out a gentler side of him, he sipped his drink and tried not to smile like an idiot.

When Daphne's husband, Robby, strode past, Jake caught his eye and congratulated him on both his promotion and his impending state of fatherhood.

"Thanks," the other man said with a huge smile. Like Daphne, he was blond and blue eyed, and Jake couldn't help but think that their child was probably going to look like an angel from a Renaissance painting. "We haven't told my parents yet," he continued. "We're going to spring it on them on Christmas Eve."

The announcement took Jake by surprise. "Christmas Eve?" he asked, puzzled. His reaction must have been obvious, because suddenly Robby seemed to become very nervous.

"Uh, yeah, Christmas Eve. Oops. Didn't Daphne mention it? She wanted to be the one to tell you, Jake, because I know the two of you always spent Christmas Eve together. But my folks want us to celebrate with my family at their house. Dinner, drinks, holiday reveling, the usual. Boy, Daphne's going to kill me when she finds out you heard about this from me." Robby paused for a moment, clearly reluctant to dig himself in any deeper than he already had. In what Jake supposed was an effort to change the subject, he added, "My mother's going to go bananas when she hears the news."

"Christmas Eve," Jake repeated absently.

Robby nodded, prepared to apologize further, when someone called his name. "Oh, excuse me, Jake. There's someone here I really have to talk to."

And with that, Daphne's husband vanished, along with Jake's plans for the holidays. Certainly he shouldn't be surprised that his niece would want to spend Christmas Eve with her new husband and his family, and certainly he didn't condemn her for wanting to. It was just that now he was going to be alone during the entirety of the holidays. And the idea simply didn't sit well with him.

Lifting his drink for an idle sip, Jake glanced over the edge of his glass and saw Rebecca on the other side of the room, speaking to one of the guests, and paused. Her dark green, long-sleeved dress was cut low in the back, and when he'd first seen her wearing it, he'd realized the color made her eyes seem even deeper than usual. Her hair was bunched atop her head in a careless sweep, a few short ringlets tumbling down her neck and over her forehead. She was indeed a perfect hostess, Jake thought. She had mingled quite successfully and seemed to have a warm smile and a nice word for everyone who had come. Everyone, that was, except for him.

Each time he had tried to draw Rebecca away from the crowd to attempt a moment of privacy, she had suddenly remembered something that needed attending to. First it had been the dip, then the cheese ball, then the wassail, then the eggnog. When she'd run out of edible items, she'd begun to get more creative, first citing the capacity of the hall closet for the guests' coats, then the size of the centerpiece, then a lost earring. Before long she would be losing the guests themselves, Jake thought dryly. Anything to keep her from having to talk to him.

Well, Rebecca Bellamy was about to learn that there were some things in life she simply couldn't avoid. And

while she was in his house, at his party, she was going to
have to realize that he himself was one of those things.
Setting his glass down on a cocktail table near the fireplace,
Jake began to take deliberate strides in her direction.

"You know, I've been wondering all this time about the
people who moved into the Eddlestons' house." Jake's
across-the-street neighbor, Mrs. Dorset, eagerly popped a
stuffed mushroom into her mouth and took her time to suck
the remainder from her fingers before she continued. "It
was so nice of you and your husband to have a holiday
open house for the neighborhood, Mrs. Raglan. Although
it would have been nice to meet you both sooner."

"Mrs. Dorset, as I told you twice earlier, I'm not
Mrs.—"

"Do the two of you have any children, dear? My two
grandchildren, Eddie and Sophia—my son's little boy and
girl—are ages seven and five, respectively, and they always
seem to be lacking in playmates whenever they come to
visit."

Rebecca finally surrendered to the other woman's insistence, and simply sighed. "No, Mrs. Dorset, we don't have
any children."

Mrs. Dorset reached for one of the nut nibbles heaped
on her plate, put it to her mouth, then withdrew it again as
another thought struck her. "Well, you don't want to wait
too long, you know. No offense, dear, but you realize of
course that the two of you are no spring chickens anymore.
You don't want to wind up at the last minute with a full
heart and an empty bassinet, do you?"

Rebecca closed her eyes and rubbed her forehead in an
effort to dispel the migraine she felt threatening. "No…"

"My Alicia did just that thing. Wanted to get settled in
her career first, then have a family. Well, of course you
know what happened."

Rebecca was about to say that no, of course she did not,

having never met Mrs. Dorset's Alicia, but Mrs. Dorset saved her the trouble.

"My Alicia discovered too late that she was...well, that she had put all her eggs in one basket, so to speak—no pun intended—and then had dropped the basket on her way to market."

Rebecca gazed at Mrs. Dorset through eyes narrowed in confusion, wondering if she had just spent the last fifteen minutes conversing with a recently released mental patient. The other woman seemed like a sane-enough person. Still, one could never tell these days....

"Ah, there you are."

It was the first time this evening Rebecca had been relieved to hear Jake's voice. As she had watched him weave in and out of his guests, looking so incredible in an exquisitely cut dark suit, her heart had hammered like rain on an empty drum, bouncing around behind her rib cage as if it were about to shatter. She simply didn't trust herself around him. Ever since running into him while wearing his bathrobe, she had felt as if she'd become oddly intimate with him all over again. Now she feared that if he said just the right thing, or looked at her in just the right way, she would damn the consequences and follow him straight to bed.

It was just that he was so handsome, Rebecca thought, feeling her mouth grow dry as she looked at him. When she had ordered the table arrangements from the florist, she had been struck by a fit of whimsy and had ordered a boutonniere for him to wear, a trio of red berries nestled in a sprig of holly. Now he looked festive and happy and at home, more satisfied than Rebecca could ever recall seeing him. It was all she could do not to sigh dramatically, throw an arm to her forehead and swoon into his arms.

"Excuse me, won't you, Mrs. Dorset?" Rebecca asked her companion, trying to make a quick break before the other woman said something bizarre.

"Mr. Raglan!" Mrs. Dorset exclaimed, when she realized the identity of the man who had joined them. "I was just telling your wife how nice it is to finally meet the two of you and be able to welcome you to the neighborhood. You could have done something like this earlier, you know."

Jake looked first at Mrs. Dorset, then at Rebecca, then back at Mrs. Dorset again. "I'm sorry?" he said softly, clearly in the dark about what the other woman was talking about.

Rebecca closed her eyes and drew in a deep breath, then linked her arm fondly with Jake's. "Excuse us, Mrs. Dorset," she repeated patiently. "Jake? May I have a word with you?"

Before he could decline, she gently eased him away, glancing over her shoulder only once to see if Mrs. Dorset was following them. Jake's neighbor had already latched on to someone else, and Rebecca couldn't help but smile when she realized it was Daphne. The two of them should have plenty to talk about, Daphne's condition being what it was.

"Congratulations on becoming a great-uncle," she told Jake as they ventured out of the living room and into the hall. She wasn't sure where they were going, but only knew it was well away from Mrs. Dorset.

"You heard," Jake said, his voice flat and emotionless.

"Are you kidding? Daphne corralled everyone she could with the news. I don't think she even had her coat off before she blurted it out to me."

Jake nodded but said nothing.

"Jake? Is something wrong?"

They were at the end of the hall now, in a part of Jake's house into which Rebecca had never before journeyed. The sounds of voices and Christmas music and clinking glasses raised in holiday cheer were muted and distant behind them; here the lighting was somewhat dark and recessed. Rebecca halted in her steps when she realized how alone she was with Jake, and involuntarily began to take a few steps backward. Before she was able to complete even two, Jake tugged gently on her arm and pulled her into a room that appeared to be a library, closed the door behind them, and then settled Rebecca against the door and himself against Rebecca.

"Jake, what are you—?"

He kissed her then, long and hard and deep, and the last thing Rebecca remembered thinking was that it felt so good to be this close to him again. Instinctively, she circled her arms around his waist and pulled him toward her, spreading her hands open against his back, skimming her flattened palms upward until she could cup one at his neck.

At her encouragement, Jake crowded his big body even closer to hers, arching one arm above her head, as if daring anyone to try to open the door, cupping his other hand possessively over her hip. Rebecca moaned softly from deep inside her soul, bunching a fistful of his jacket in her hand.

"Mrs. Dorset thought we were married," he murmured raggedly when he finally tore his lips away from hers.

Rebecca didn't trust her voice, so she only gazed at the floor and nodded mutely.

"Where would she get an idea like that?" Jake wondered aloud further.

He didn't sound angry the way she would have thought he would, so Rebecca braved a glance up at his expression and discovered much to her surprise that he didn't look angry, either. "Jake, I swear I never told her we were. In fact, I denied it three times. She's just one of those people who has her own view of the world and refuses to see it otherwise."

"You don't have to get defensive, Rebecca. I know you wouldn't do something like that. I thought maybe Daphne had put some weird notion into her head, that's all."

Now Rebecca was confused, too. "Why would Daphne do something like that?"

Because she's just dying to see me married with children,

Jake wanted to say. And dammit, ever since she'd brought it up, he hadn't been able to completely push the thought away. Now, as he looked down at Rebecca leaning against the doorway, her fingers still playing with the hair at his nape, her breathing still as ragged and edgy as his own, some window opened up in the back of his mind, filling it with sunlight and fresh air. Immediately, Jake slammed it shut again, and in the darkness that ensued, told himself his next question was only idle curiosity.

"Are you doing anything Christmas Eve?" he asked suddenly.

Rebecca couldn't prevent the rapid-fire beating of her heart, couldn't prevent the flicker of hope that sprang to life inside her. She wasn't sure what Jake was doing or why, but she couldn't help thinking he might be presenting her with precisely the chance she'd been wishing for.

"I'm spending it with my family," she told him. "I always do."

His hand on her hip slipped lower then, down to her thigh, then back up to her waist. Leaning forward again, he gently, lightly kissed her lips, then her jaw, then her forehead. Rebecca's eyes fluttered closed as she tipped her head back against the door. Jake took advantage by rubbing his lips softly against her neck, tasting her collarbone where it peeked out from the neckline of her dress.

"Oh…oh, Jake."

"Could I maybe make you change your mind about that?" he asked in a rough whisper.

Heat seeped into Rebecca's body everywhere he touched her, and she brought her hand around from his back to splay across his chest and toy with his necktie. "No can do," she told him regretfully. "I'm catering it."

He pulled away from her then, studying her intently to see if she was serious. "You're making that up," he finally said with a doubtful smile.

Rebecca shook her head. "Nope. Sorry. It's where I try out new stuff. New recipes, new activities, new music, new floral arrangements, new color schemes, you name it. I use my family for guinea pigs, and what they like I incorporate into my work.''

Jake sighed in resignation. Oh, well. He was going to have to get used to spending his holidays alone sooner or later. Why not sooner? There must be something good on TV that night. Didn't they usually save up the Grinch or Charlie Brown or something for Christmas Eve?

"You could come over, if you want," Rebecca offered experimentally, uncertain how he would react to her invitation. "My parents' house will be loaded down with relatives. There will probably be more than thirty people there. No one's going to notice one more." Except me, she added to herself. You'll probably drive me to distraction.

Jake told himself he should turn her down, that he had been crazy to even ask her what she was doing Christmas Eve in the first place. Instead, he thought once again how quiet the house would be without her. There would be no luscious smells coming from the kitchen, no platters piled high with festive food, no punch bowls full of wine and garnishes of oranges studded with cloves, no Rebecca wandering around his upstairs in his bathrobe. It would be a lousy holiday.

"You sure no one would mind?" he asked hesitantly, still feeling for some reason that he was doing the wrong thing in accepting her invitation.

Rebecca tugged on his necktie until his face was near hers again. Feeling inordinately playful, she smiled and kissed him quickly, then cupped his jaw in her hand. "My family will love you," she told him honestly. Probably almost as much as I do. Then, as an afterthought, she added to herself, I only hope they don't pull a Mrs. Dorset on you.

Nine

Jake wasn't sure what he was expecting where meeting Rebecca's family was concerned. Hell, he still wasn't altogether sure what had made him agree to meet Rebecca's family in the first place. Yet he had come willingly, had taken pains to make himself look presentable in dark trousers and a forest green sweater over an ivory shirt and discreet necktie, and had even dug into his limited wine cache to find a bottle that might impress Mr. Bellamy, who, Rebecca had told him, had rather a fondness for expensive Pinot noirs. Now, as Jake stood beside Rebecca at the front door of a house in Shelby County that was more than twice the size of his own, he was finally beginning to wonder what he had gotten himself into.

He couldn't remember the last time he had been taken to a woman's home to meet her family. Oh, wait. Yes, he could. It had been Marie's family on their sprawling Thoroughbred farm outside Lexington nearly ten years ago. Jake had been forced to spend the evening dodging blunt ques-

tions about his financial status and plans for his newly
formed partnership with Stephen, and for two hours had
been trapped by Marie's father in his study, trying not to
gag as he sampled some of the old man's expensive cigars.
To top the evening off, Marie's parents had gotten into one
of their usual arguments about God-knows-what and had
called each other names Jake never would have uttered to
his worst enemy.

Ah, yes, he remembered it all now. All too well. Just
when he was wondering if he had enough time to cut and
make a run for his car, the front door before him opened
to reveal a woman in her early sixties, with silver hair,
laughing green eyes exactly like Rebecca's, and a huge
smile on her face.

"Sweetie!" the woman cried as she pulled Rebecca into
her arms for a ferocious hug. "Welcome home!"

Rebecca's smile was contented, unresisting and full of
love as she hugged her mother back and replied, "Oh,
come on, Mom. I was here just yesterday. You're going to
make Jake think I'm a horrible daughter, never coming to
see you and Dad."

Mrs. Bellamy circled her arm around Rebecca's waist as
she turned to Jake and extended her hand. "And of course,
you must be Rebecca's friend, Jake. Welcome to our
home."

Hearing himself referred to as Rebecca's friend came as
a surprise to Jake. He'd been prepared for interested looks
as he was less-than-jokingly referred to as her "boyfriend,"
or her "young man," or some other parental term to indicate that Mrs. Bellamy wanted to know his intentions
toward her daughter. But to be labeled something as innocuous and vague as "friend" simply threw Jake for a
loop. He was going to have to readjust his perspective on
things a little now. He'd been ready to feel defensive while
he was visiting Rebecca's family, fielding questions about
any future they might have together. Instead, Rebecca's

mother made him feel like nothing more than a guest who was welcome in her home.

"Mrs. Bellamy," Jake said, nodding in greeting as he shook her hand.

"Oh, please, call me Ruth."

"Ruth," he repeated obediently as her smile grew broader.

"Come in, come in," Ruth instructed them further, stepping back into the house to allow them entry. "It's so cold outside today. Your father thinks we'll get snow tonight. Wouldn't that be wonderful? I can't remember the last time we had a white Christmas around here."

"Dad and his snow," Rebecca said as if it was an old joke, chuckling with her mother. "He's probably already got the sled out and waxed and sitting at the top of Edgar Hill, ready for the kids."

"Well, of course he does," Ruth replied in a tone of voice that suggested Rebecca's was a silly speculation to begin with. "Everyone is back in the solarium sampling Rebecca's new treats," she continued. "Give me your coats and go on back and say hello. I'll be right there."

Jake and Rebecca shrugged out of their coats and handed them to Ruth as she requested, then wandered into the living room off the foyer. Jake tried to be discreet as he gazed at everything, still unable to get over the size of the Bellamy homestead. He had received the impression from Rebecca some time ago that she came from a moneyed background, but he'd had no idea it was something like this. For a man who judged a person's success by the size of the house he lived in, Jake assumed the Bellamys were indeed more successful than most.

Yet there was something else about this house that struck him as he followed Rebecca through it. For a building so large and roomy, there didn't seem to be any empty spaces. Jake's house was only half this size, yet felt almost vacant, even when he was there. But the Bellamy home was a huge house that felt utterly full, despite the fact that he and Rebecca still hadn't stumbled upon any other people who might be visiting. There were photographs on every wall and every table, plants that had obviously been growing for years tumbling from every nook and cranny, books on every subject crammed in bookcases in every position imaginable, knickknacks, magazines, games, toys....

The house looked like someone was not only in residence there, but actually *lived* there—enjoyed life, celebrated life, squeezed every ounce of pleasure possible out of life. And that, Jake realized with no small amount of panic, was precisely why his own house felt so empty all the time. No one who resided there really lived life to the utmost. No one had ever brought that to his house except Rebecca. Only under her influence had his house come alive.

"When you said you were catering this thing, I was afraid I might only see you in passing today," he told her as they strode down a hallway toward the back of the house.

"No way," Rebecca assured him, turning back to face him fully. She looked festive and beautiful in a red sweatshirt that was painted and bejeweled with a Christmas-tree design, her hair caught up in a tousled ponytail, shiny red and green bells dangling from her ears. "I never, ever, miss out on a Christmas celebration. I prepare everything in advance and put it in Mom's fridge. Then she gets it all out in the morning, and for the rest of the day we all take turns refilling the bowls and platters. So far, it's a tradition that's worked out well."

"Your family seems to have a lot of those," Jake said thoughtfully.

"A lot of what?"

"Traditions."

Rebecca smiled at him, a smile that was warm and affectionate and full of fond remembering. "Yeah, we do. And it's never too late to start new ones."

Before he had a chance to ask what she meant by that,

Jake and Rebecca entered a room full of laughing, chattering people. Everything that could be decorated was, from the enormous fireplace behind them to the floor-to-ceiling windows boasting fragrant evergreen wreaths that must have been three feet in diameter. Even the people were decorated, all dressed in red and green, some sporting Santa hats, some wearing bells, others with sprays of holly tucked in headbands and lapels and behind their ears. The Bellamy clan, it appeared, consisted of more than a few party animals.

Jake and Rebecca were met by cries of "Merry Christmas" and "Welcome" and "It's about time you arrived," then were plied with punch, eggnog and wassail. Jake found himself being introduced to people whose names he would never be able to remember, shaking hands, receiving brief kisses, being slapped on the back. Never did any of Rebecca's numerous relatives refer to him as anything other than Rebecca's friend, and never did he feel uncomfortable.

"Uh-oh, here comes my father," he heard Rebecca say beside him as the last of her relations wandered away, leaving Jake feeling dizzy and maladjusted, having had all of his expectations of feeling matrimonial pressure thoroughly shot to hell.

"What?" he mumbled. Then her words registered, and he thought, Ah-ha, here it comes. The official meeting of the father. Now he would begin to feel the pressure, Jake thought. Now he would be getting the treatment. He was really going to get worked over...but good.

"Dad, over here!" Rebecca called out to a distinguished but festive-looking man in his late sixties.

Mr. Bellamy was tall and slim, and carried himself like one who was supremely at home in his surroundings. In a single glance, Jake could tell everything about Rebecca's father that he needed to know. He was a powerful, successful man who in no way lacked confidence, a man who would speak his own mind and be able to read those belonging to other people. He was the kind of man who would insist that his daughter be treated right. And he would stop a suitor dead in his tracks if he came up lacking in any way.

"Rebecca, dear." Rebecca's father swept her into a hug and kissed her warmly on the cheek. "So you've finally arrived. This must be Jake."

For the first time since arriving, Jake wondered what Rebecca had told her parents about him. Had she intimated that they were romantically involved? Had she led them to believe their relationship might turn into something substantial? Had she gone so far as to tell them there might be wedding bells in the future? Nothing in anyone's behavior so far had indicated she might have said anything other than that he was her friend, but Jake couldn't help wondering if there was something everyone else knew that he himself did not.

Trying not to gulp audibly, Jake extended his hand to Rebecca's father and shook it firmly. He felt an inexplicable need to let the man know he would not be overrun, wanted to be sure Mr. Bellamy knew Jake Raglan wasn't a man to be taken lightly. He wanted him to know that although he had feelings for the youngest Bellamy daughter, they were feelings of Jake's own, feelings over which *he* had control, and they concerned no one else but Rebecca. Then he proceeded to offer the other man a bribe.

"Mr. Bellamy," Jake greeted Rebecca's father staunchly, pressing the bottle of wine into his hand after shaking it. "This is for you and your wife to enjoy later. Rebecca told me you favor Pinot noirs."

Mr. Bellamy studied the label closely, arching his eyebrows in obvious admiration for Jake's choice. "Yes, I do. This is a wonderful vintage. Thank you very much. And please, it's Dan. All that 'Mr. Bellamy' business is completely out of place in this house."

"Dan," Jake replied, thinking the other man's observation about formality a very astute one. This house did indeed inspire one to relax and take it easy.

"Rebecca tells me you're a lawyer," Dan continued.

What else had she told him? Jake wondered. "Yes, I am. A partner in Raglan-Flannery Associates."

"Do you specialize?"

"Divorce," Jake replied simply.

Dan Bellamy seemed to be honestly surprised by his vocation, and Jake was puzzled. Perhaps, like Rebecca, they didn't much cotton to the profession because of her experiences with her ex-husband, he mused. Or perhaps Rebecca truly hadn't told her family much about him, after all. Maybe she hadn't thought him important enough to go on about at length. Hadn't considered him a part of her life worth mentioning. Jake couldn't understand why the realization bothered him so much.

"Well, we certainly could have used your services around here about five years ago, let me tell you," Dan said frankly.

"Daddy, don't you dare bring up Eliot...." Rebecca began.

"I was talking more about Marcus and the crummy way he represented you, Rebecca."

"Marcus represented me exactly the way I wanted to be represented. Now let's—"

"Becca, he didn't even win a financial settlement for you. The least that jerk you married could have done was—"

"Daddy, I didn't *want* a financial settlement from Eliot. I didn't want anything from Eliot. At that point, I just wanted to be rid of him. Now let's drop it."

Dan Bellamy treated his daughter to a stern look, then his face softened and he smiled. Draping an arm over Rebecca's shoulders, he pulled her close and turned to Jake. "She's an independent cuss. Simply drives her mother and me into a frenzy sometimes. But she's such a wonderful cook, we can't possibly turn our backs on her."

Rebecca smiled, too, rolling her eyes heavenward. "Gosh, thanks, Daddy. It's so nice to be wanted."

Jake watched the byplay between Rebecca and her family with much interest. This was a side of her he'd never witnessed before, a side that was fully contented to the point of playful. He couldn't imagine what it must be like to be this close to one's family. But, Jake admitted reluctantly, it looked like it might be kind of nice.

Then his thoughts rewound, and he was struck by what Rebecca's father had just revealed. She had turned down the opportunity to receive a financial settlement from her ex-husband. And with what was probably a good deal of evidence that Eliot had indeed been unfaithful to her, and considering the amount of financial support Rebecca had offered him during their marriage—not to mention having a shark like Marcus Tate as her attorney—her settlement could have been a hefty sum indeed.

But Rebecca had instead chosen to return to her family for help and support, and had simply put aside any feelings of vengefulness or vindictiveness she might have entertained about her lousy marriage. It was a realization that told Jake he should think hard about a lot of things.

What's he thinking about? Rebecca wondered. Jake had been thoughtful and not a little distant ever since entering her parents' house, and for the life of her, she couldn't even begin to guess what might be causing his preoccupation. She hoped he wasn't as attuned as she was to her family's intense curiosity about him. She had told her mother yesterday that she would be bringing a friend with her today, that her friend just so happened to be male, and, too, just so happened to be single.

But she had cautioned both of her parents sternly about snooping. Jake Raglan was a man who had hired her to plan his holiday, Rebecca told them, and when she had discovered that he would be spending Christmas Eve alone, she had invited him to share it with the Bellamys instead. That was the extent of their tie to each other, she had stated emphatically. There was absolutely no need for her parents to think there might be anything more to it.

However, she'd seen the expression on her mother's face when she'd opened the door, Rebecca recalled now. The moment Ruth Bellamy had seen what Jake Raglan looked like, it was as if a little light had switched on in each eye. Her father also appeared to be more than a little speculative right now, and was obviously impressed by Jake's gesture with the wine. Oh, great, Rebecca thought miserably. Now she would never hear the end of it from either of her parents.

"Jake, will you give me a hand in the kitchen for a minute?" Rebecca asked suddenly, feeling for some reason that she had to get Jake out of there right away before her father asked some probing question like, "So, when will the two of you be tying the ol' knot?"

Jake glanced over at her, a curious expression on his face, but didn't immediately respond, as if he was still lost in thought somewhere.

Rebecca looped her arm through his and urged further, "I want to check to be sure that I didn't put too much dark rum in the eggnog."

Jake, like every other guest at his party, had fallen madly in love with Rebecca's eggnog. She hoped by mentioning it now, it would serve to bribe him into accompanying her as she requested. As further incentive, she added, "I also want to make sure the alterations I made to the recipe haven't ruined it."

That got his attention. Jake turned to her with an expression that was almost crushed. "You changed the recipe?"

Rebecca smiled at him. "Only a little. Come on."

The remainder of the day passed just as every other Christmas Eve at the Bellamy homestead had. The Bellamys made much merriment, opening gifts and playing games, passing the wassail and joining in song.

And just before dinner it started to snow. And snow. And snow. And snow...

The children in particular seemed to enjoy themselves

most, running in and out of the house, indecisive about whether they wanted to play with their new toys or out in the snow. Some carried their new toys out into the snow, but most remained inside, content to drink hot chocolate and enjoy the warmth of family ties.

Rebecca found herself continuously trapped by one toddler or another on her lap. Her big brother, Michael, and his wife had three children, and her older sister, Catherine, and her husband had two. Also present were the children of a number of Rebecca's cousins. None was older than eleven, but all were equally demanding of her attention.

"Aunt Becca, Aunt Becca, will you come and play dolls with us?" was the constant cry of her nieces, while her nephews and second cousins of the masculine persuasion insisted more on video games. But Rebecca secretly favored the company of her newest niece, three-month-old Grace, who was, as far as the Bellamy clan was concerned, the most beautiful baby on earth. Every chance she had, Rebecca cuddled the baby on her lap, cooing and gurgling and making silly noises in an effort to arouse the contented little smile that Grace offered so frequently for her Auntie Becca.

It was in such a position that Jake found Rebecca some hours after a dinner of enough food to feed a small sovereign nation, and enough wine to make Bacchus sleepy. He had looked out the window and discovered to his surprise a countryside covered in sparkling white, and snow still plummeting to earth in fat, festive flakes. A white Christmas, he had thought whimsically. Who would have thought? Somehow it topped the day off perfectly. However, he had realized reluctantly, if he and Rebecca wanted to make it back to the city in one piece, they probably should be leaving right away.

Jake was feeling mellow and contented and very much at ease among Rebecca's family when he stumbled upon her in her parents' library, sitting by the fireplace and humming quietly to her infant niece. She hadn't seen him arrive, so he took a moment to observe the scene, wondering why it tugged so insistently at some dark, unnamed part of him.

He should turn right around and pretend he hadn't found her, Jake told himself. Should run screaming in fear for his life and much-cherished bachelorhood. Instead, he found himself taking slow, careful, silent strides forward, though he wasn't sure if it was a sign of his unwillingness to disturb the baby or Rebecca or himself. Only when he stood beside the big, overstuffed club chair did Rebecca look up to meet his gaze, and only then did Jake realize what a mistake he'd made in approaching her.

Her eyes were full of a shining emotion that was without question love at its purest and most powerful. Baby Grace lay motionless and slumbering in the cradle of Rebecca's arms, blissfully oblivious to everything that made the world so unbearably confusing. Before he realized what he was doing, Jake dropped a finger to stroke softly over the baby's cheek, smiling when she turned her face in the direction of his hand and pursed her lips with a sigh. He was suddenly reminded of all those weekends baby-sitting Daphne when she was just a baby, and he was suddenly reminded of something else he hadn't allowed himself to recall for years.

Suddenly Jake remembered how desperately he had once wanted to have children of his own. And now, because of his determination to stay single, it would never happen.

"She's beautiful," he murmured. "How old is she?"

"Three months," Rebecca told him.

"She's Michael's daughter?"

Rebecca nodded.

"He must be very proud of her."

Rebecca chuckled softly. "You can't imagine. After two boys who scuffle all the time, he nearly busted his buttons when Diana told him amniocentesis revealed they were expecting a girl the third time around." She snuggled the baby on her lap a little closer and added, "You're going to be such a daddy's girl, aren't you?"

The words tore at Jake's heart more than anything else Rebecca could have uttered. It occurred to him then that perhaps his devotion to Daphne was as much from his realization that he would remain childless as from his love for his niece.

"Can I hold her?" he heard himself asking, as surprised by the question as Rebecca seemed to be.

Without replying, she rose from her chair and silently bid Jake to take it instead. When he had situated himself comfortably, Rebecca placed the baby gently in his arms, showing him how to support Grace's head and balance her miniature body. Immediately after Rebecca let go, Jake wished he had never given voice to his desire to hold the baby. Grace was tiny and fragile and soft, and having her enfolded in his arms took him back more than twenty years, to all those evenings marveling at Daphne as she slept.

"God, she doesn't weigh anything," he said quietly, still amazed by the size of the infant in his embrace.

In response to his voice, Grace opened her eyes and gazed up at him, and Jake wondered what she was thinking about, waking up in the arms of a total stranger. He was prepared for a bout of very loud crying, but instead, Grace smiled softly and closed her eyes again, perfectly at ease in the big man's keeping. The understanding of her complete trust touched Jake in a part of his soul he'd never known existed.

"She likes you," Rebecca stated unnecessarily, easing down onto the arm of the chair beside him, settling her hand casually along the back of the chair. "But then, that's not surprising, is it? Every woman here today has fallen for you, Jake. Even my mother has a crush on you."

Jake didn't know what kind of madness was coming over him to make him pose his next question, but he was as helpless to prevent it from coming as he was to keep his heart from beating. "And what about you, Rebecca? Does 'every woman here today' include you, too?"

Why couldn't she simply ask him? Rebecca wondered.

Why couldn't she just look him straight in the eye and demand to know what his feelings toward her were? *Jake, I love you, and I need to know if you love me, too*. Why couldn't she just say that? Why was a short string of monosyllabic words so difficult to utter?

Immediately, Rebecca answered her own question. Because she was afraid to hear his answer. She was afraid of what he would tell her. *No, Rebecca, I don't love you. I'll never love you. I can't love you.*

"Have you looked outside lately?" she asked instead, her words sounding rushed and overanxious. "Dad said snow, and he got snow, didn't he? I heard Michael say something about pouring the rest of the hot wassail and cider into a couple of thermoses and heading for an all-night sledding session at Edgar Hill. What do you say?"

When she finally turned to look at Jake, he had dropped his head back down to study the baby, so she was unable to gauge his reaction to her evasive maneuvering. However, when he replied, his voice was quiet and even, touched with just a trace of disappointment.

"I can't. I have to work tomorrow."

"On Christmas Day?"

He nodded, his attention still focused on the baby.

"But no one works on Christmas Day," Rebecca objected. "Everyone sits around feeling fat and reading the paper and eating more food than they normally would in a week."

"The movie theater and restaurant workers of the world, not to mention a host of others, would loudly disagree with your statement, I'm afraid."

"But you're not a movie theater or restaurant worker. You're an attorney who owns his own partnership and who can easily give himself a day like Christmas off. Have you ever gone sledding in the middle of the night?"

Finally Jake looked up at Rebecca, just the trace of a smile playing about his lips. "No, Rebecca, I've never gone sledding in the middle of the night."

"Not even on Acorn Ridge?"

He shook his head. "My parents kept a pretty tight rein on Ellen and me when we were kids. Nine o'clock curfew, even in high school."

Rebecca grinned at Jake, helpless to stop herself when she pushed back a lock of dark hair that had fallen over his forehead when he'd had his head bent. "Well, then, Mr. Raglan, you're in for a treat."

Ten

"**W**hy is this called 'Edgar Hill?'" Jake asked as he stood at the top of a snow-blanketed bump on the earth, staring down into what would have been a black abyss if not for the bright full moon overhead. "Does this have anything to do with your Uncle Edgar? More specifically with the fact that your Uncle Edgar's arm is in a cast?"

Rebecca laughed at Jake's reference to her mother's brother, who had come to the Bellamy Christmas celebration straight from having his arm encased in plaster from shoulder to fingertip. "Yes, this hill is named after my Uncle Edgar, and, yes, he has wiped out here on a number of occasions over the past sixty years. However, today's incident stemmed from his waking up thinking it was Christmas morning and moving a tad too quickly to get downstairs to see what Santa Claus had left him. He slipped, and...well, let's just say that everyone at Mercer General Hospital is on a first-name basis with Uncle Edgar."

Jake shook his head doubtfully. "I don't know about this

midnight-sledding thing, Rebecca. It's awfully dark to be racing at breakneck speed over an icy surface and into the black beyond, isn't it?''

Rebecca sighed in mock disgust. "Oh, come on, Jake, don't be such a coward. My mother and her brothers and sisters grew up in that house and have sledded this hill for decades. Michael, Catherine and I have carried on the tradition for the past three ourselves. Only minor injuries, I swear. No lives lost at all.'' After a moment's thought, she added, "None that have been recorded, anyway.''

"Terrific.''

Rebecca gazed around at the group of people who had gathered at the top of the hill and then slowly began to smile devilishly. "Come on,'' she instructed Jake in a soft whisper. "Grab your snow saucer and follow me. It's going to be too crowded to really get good speed up here. I know a better spot.''

"Good speed?'' Jake repeated skeptically, reluctantly allowing himself to be led as Rebecca tugged insistently at the sleeve of the down-filled jacket he had removed from the trunk of his car before they'd departed on their hike. "Frankly, a crowd sounds like an excellent idea to me. I'm not so sure I want 'good speed' to begin with.'' Lifting the fluorescent orange plastic disk he held in his gloved hand, he further demanded, "And what's this 'snow saucer' you shoved into my hands out in your parents' garage? Is this thing actually supposed to transport a human body? I mean, am I expected to believe that this flimsy little piece of plastic is actually supposed to be considered *safe?*''

"Oh, Jake, will you quit complaining?'' Rebecca said, halting in her tracks and spinning around to face him fully. "You're the one who wanted to experience Christmas to its fullest, remember? And in the Bellamy tradition, to top off the holiday right, you have to do something really fun. In my opinion, sledding at Edgar Hill is about as fun as it gets.''

"But we're not at Edgar Hill anymore," Jake pointed out unnecessarily. "We're out in the middle of nowhere."

True enough, they had managed to thoroughly distance themselves from the other late-night revelers and now stood at the top of what seemed to Jake an even bigger hill than the first. All around him, the earth was at peace, no movement, no sound, nothing stirring at all. Even the silence seemed more quiet than usual, muffled, he supposed, because of the way the ground was blanketed by several inches of snow. The night was surprisingly bright with the moonlight reflecting off the white hills, and hundreds of stars winked at him from billions of miles away. If he had been a whimsical man, Jake would have bent an ear and listened for the sound of sleigh bells and eight tiny reindeer. But, of course, he wasn't a whimsical man, he reminded himself. Besides, those reindeer had flown at midnight, and by now it was well past one.

"It's beautiful, isn't it?" he heard Rebecca say softly, almost reverently, her voice easing through the still night like a warm wind.

Jake nodded. "It reminds me of..." He cut himself off when he realized he had almost said the word "home." "Of Acorn Ridge," he finished softly. "We didn't get a lot of snow there, but when we did, it looked like this. Clean, untouched, almost mystical in its beauty...and full of possibilities." Still staring out at the countryside, he added so quietly he wasn't sure Rebecca would even hear him, "Too bad life isn't like that."

"Oh, life is very much like that, Jake," she replied immediately, confidently, and he knew he must have spoken more loudly than he had thought. "You just have to know how to approach it."

He turned to her then, loving the way her dark curls framed her face beneath the red knit cap she wore. Her cheeks and nose were pink from the brisk air, and her eyes shone with a light to rival that reflecting off the hillsides. Bundled up in a navy blue ski parka with a thick red scarf wound around her neck what appeared to be a half-dozen times, her hands swallowed by two monstrous red mittens, Jake thought she looked more wonderful than he'd ever seen her before. And he'd seen Rebecca looking pretty wonderful in the past few months.

"And just how should I approach it?" he asked finally.

Instead of replying, Rebecca grinned broadly and lifted the fluorescent yellow snow saucer she had been carting for the entire half-mile trek from the house. Tossing it casually onto the snow just where the hill they stood upon began to curve downward, she plopped herself unceremoniously onto the disk, fanny first. The action was orchestrated in just such a way that the force of the movement propelled the saucer forward, and before Jake realized what was happening, Rebecca was skimming quickly and easily along the top of the snow, maneuvering her mount with expert dexterity, whooping loudly with delight.

"Hey!" he shouted after her. "Hey, wait for me!"

Jake tried to mimic precisely the same execution of movement Rebecca had so elegantly performed, but wound up somehow with one leg tucked beneath the other, one arm flailing wildly in the air while the other gripped the suddenly very tiny disk for dear life, rushing backward down the hill at a speed much greater than any he would have thought a snow saucer could achieve. As a result he landed some distance away from Rebecca, in a position that reaffirmed all too well the fact that he had never been snow saucering in his life: facedown in the snow, beneath a brambly thicket, behind a huge hickory tree that he was certain had almost ended his life.

"I call it the Rebecca Bellamy approach to life," Jake heard a familiar, feminine voice say from behind him as he licked at the dusting of snow on his upper lip. "Just throw yourself into it with all the force you can muster and hope for a safe landing."

Turning awkwardly onto his back, Jake stared up at Rebecca for a long time without speaking, wondering how she could be so damnably annoying and adorable at the same time. Then he lifted his hand toward her as if soliciting help, and when she took it to pull him forward, yanked her down on top of him instead.

"You know, I think it's about time somebody put snow down your pants," he told her meaningfully.

Rebecca's eyes widened in surprise, and he suspected it wasn't so much because of what he was suggesting as it was that he was so blatantly teasing her.

"Now, Jake..." she began to protest.

"No, really, Rebecca," he continued, unobtrusively digging his fingers into the snowdrift pushed up around them by the weight of their bodies. "I'm of the opinion that there's simply no better way to humble someone who's behaving smugly than to put a big handful of cold..."

"Jake..."

"Wet..."

"Jake..."

"Icy..."

"Jake..."

Without further ado, and with as much dexterity as he had lacked controlling the snow saucer, Jake grabbed a fistful of snow, pushed aside Rebecca's open parka, and carried out his threat quite capably. Rebecca shrieked with laughter and surprise, then grabbed a mittenful of snow and plunged it down the front of Jake's shirt, thankful that he had removed his necktie some time ago. For a moment, he lay stock-still, as if he couldn't believe what she had just done. Then, with a burst of energy and laughter, he shoveled more snow into one hand, tore off Rebecca's ski cap with the other, and unloaded a pile of snow onto her head.

"Okay, that does it, buster," Rebecca warned him playfully. "No more Ms. Nice Gal. Now it's time to take off the gloves and get rough."

As if to illustrate, Rebecca pushed herself awkwardly up on her elbows—settling them on Jake's chest because there was nowhere else to settle them—and put forth a great deal of effort to remove her mittens. Jake watched in amusement, thinking he was having more fun with Rebecca now than he'd ever had in his life. But when one of her elbows slipped off his chest and brought her upper body down hard on top of his, Jake's amusement quickly fled, to be replaced by a very demanding need. Without thinking, without planning, he wrapped both arms around her, rolling their bodies in the snow until they had reversed positions.

Rebecca wasn't sure exactly when things had taken a turn from playful to sexual. She only knew that one minute she and Jake had been participating in the harmless, silly kind of teasing couples sometimes enjoy, and the next minute they were gazing into each other's eyes with the most desperate kind of longing. Where once there had been nothing but cold night air, now there was heat, and Rebecca thought vaguely that the snow around them would surely be turning straight into steam at any moment. Before she had a chance to utter a protest she didn't want to voice, Jake lowered his lips to hers for a kiss that left no part of her chilled.

After that, everything ceased to exist for Rebecca except for the night, the snow, the thicket behind the hickory tree, and Jake. Together, they combined to form a kind of haven for her, a sanctuary to which she could escape from everything that had ever caused her harm. With Jake she felt truly alive and happy and safe for the first time. She had always considered herself a woman who enjoyed life to its fullest, yet with Jake Raglan she had found something else to celebrate, the most important thing of all—love, true love in its purest, most perfect form.

Circling her arms around his neck, she pulled him closer, then was disappointed when she realized they were still separated by the barrier of their clothing. Mindless of the cold and snow, Rebecca pushed at Jake's sweater until her hands were beneath it, unbuttoning his shirt enough to feel the warm skin stretched across his taut muscles beneath.

At the feel of her cool fingers on his hot skin, Jake

groaned aloud, intensifying his kiss until neither of them was sure where one body began and the other ended. Then, mimicking Rebecca's actions, Jake, too, began to let his hands go wandering, first up under Rebecca's sweater, until he could cup his palm over the lacy brassiere beneath. She, too, sighed with pleasure at the contact, arching her body upward as she pulled him even closer.

When he first touched her skin, Jake's fingers were cold, but Rebecca soon realized he was a man who warmed up quickly. Flexing his fingers over her softness, he kneaded her tender flesh with the persistence of a man who has gone a lifetime without any human closeness. Spanning his hand over her breasts, he captured one peak with his thumb, the other with his ring finger, and with maddening circles drove Rebecca into a near frenzy. Then, wedging his thigh between hers, he urged her legs apart and settled himself intimately against her.

This time it was Rebecca who groaned aloud, loving the feel of having Jake so close and full, so heavy against her. Pushing her hands around over his back to cup his buttocks, she pulled him toward her, pressing herself against him as she did so. She remembered how exquisite it had felt to make love with Jake Raglan, and all she wanted now was to feel that way again, damning the consequences, whatever they might be.

Jake let his body drop fully onto Rebecca, rubbing himself sinuously against her over and over again, until they were both crying out in frustration at being unable to consummate their passion. Knowing only that she wanted to be joined with Jake in the most intimate union two souls can share, Rebecca tugged at his belt and unbuttoned his trousers, exploring him with gentle fingers as she freed him, marveling at his strength and softness, remembering his tenderness the first time he had made love to her. She touched him gently at first, then with more insistence, until he pulled away from her with a ragged gasp.

"Not yet," he muttered with something akin to exhaustion. "Not just yet."

Jake took Rebecca's wrists in one hand, and held them over her head, cradling them in his palm so that it was his skin buried in snow instead of hers. Then, his eyes never leaving hers, he unfastened and unzipped her blue jeans, and flattened his palm against her belly. Slowly, he moved his hand downward to the waistband of her panties, dipping his fingers quickly inside to the depth of his knuckles.

"No snow this time," he promised softly. "Only heat."

And with that vow, he plunged farther, stroking over Rebecca's hot skin like a penetrating balm. With long fingers he explored her, touching her more deeply, more intimately than any man had ever done. Rebecca could only feel, could only luxuriate in what he was doing to her. Gone was the winter night, gone was the snow and cool breeze. Instead, she was plunged into an incinerator, consumed by a fire that burned white hot.

"Oh, Jake," she whispered when she felt herself close to the edge, turning her face to the snow in an effort to cool herself off, slow herself down.

Suddenly she felt herself being lifted, and somehow realized that it wasn't into a heated swirling vortex of sensual desire, but into Jake's arms. Unaware of how it had happened, Rebecca realized that Jake had removed his jacket and spread it open on the snow, and was now bending to place her back on it. As he did so, he tugged her jeans down from her hips until they tangled above her boots around her ankles. When Rebecca understood that they were about to make love still fully clothed, out in the middle of a snow-drenched landscape, she nearly cried out in celebration at the wild recklessness of it. It was the act of two people thoroughly consumed with passion, she thought dizzily. Two people who embraced a lust for life and each other.

Jake bent one more time to place what he intended to be a chaste kiss over Rebecca's heart before plunging into her warm, welcoming depths, but when he realized once again how soft her skin was, he had to linger for a taste. Closing his mouth over her breast, he circled the dusky peak with his tongue slowly, leisurely, thoroughly, then drew it more deeply into his mouth. Rebecca sighed in contentment, cradling his head in her palm as if willing him never to stop. Reaching lower to touch her in intimate promise one last time, he positioned himself atop her and plunged himself deep inside.

Rebecca gasped at being so filled by him again, but before she could wrap her arms around him and pull him closer, he withdrew, then plummeted deep inside her again. She curled her arms up over his back to keep him from going too far away, but again Jake withdrew completely before hammering into her again. Finally he seemed to have propelled himself deeply enough, and he initiated a slow, methodical rhythm that began to drive Rebecca slowly, deliciously mad.

"I love you, Jake," she heard herself whisper amid gasps for breath. "I love you."

Jake said nothing in reply, but continued his assault on Rebecca's senses until they were both delirious and dazed. Higher and higher they climbed, until there was nowhere else to go but down. Their culmination came amid an explosion more incandescent than any the heavens had ever seen, and like fireworks that dissolved against a night sky, so, too, did Jake and Rebecca slowly descend to earth, feeling as if they were part of a fiery cascade.

When they lay entwined on Jake's coat, panting for breath and groping for thought, Rebecca found to her surprise that she wasn't disappointed Jake hadn't cried out that he returned her feelings when she had voiced her love for him. She realized then that she didn't need to hear him say the words, because she had felt his love in the way he had kissed her and held her, in the way he had shown such gentleness and care in making her his. Jake Raglan loved her. Rebecca knew it as well as she knew her own name.

She recalled the time when he had indeed cried out in a moment of passion that he loved her, then had stolen away without so much as a simple goodbye. This time, he had kept his words in check. But somehow Rebecca knew that his emotions had been as wildly uncontrolled as her own, knew that the feelings of love and passion coursing through her were rampaging through Jake's system, as well. He loved her. The knowledge filled her with contentment, and for the first time in years, Rebecca felt honestly good about the course her life had taken.

"Are you all right?"

She heard Jake's voice coming to her from a very great distance away, sounding warm and soft and filled with a quiet tenderness. It made Rebecca smile. Gazing up at his handsome face, angular and strong against the star-spattered sky, she lifted a hand to push back a lock of dark, damp hair that had fallen over his forehead.

"I'm fine," she whispered with a soft chuckle, unable to quell the happy feelings bubbling up inside her. "I'd be hard-pressed to think of a moment when I've felt better than I do right now."

Jake smiled, too, cupping his hand along Rebecca's cheek, pushing her hair back from her face. "It won't last if we don't get up and get ourselves dressed. The heat of the moment wears off fast when you're lying in snow."

"What snow?" Rebecca asked languidly, letting her eyelids droop and her body relax. "We just survived a forest fire. There couldn't possibly be any snow around here."

"Tell that to the others when they happen across our cold, frozen bodies, fused together in a very unlikely survival pose."

That brought Rebecca's attention around. She had completely forgotten that they had left her parents' house with a dozen of her relatives who were still wandering around the countryside. Immediately, she disengaged herself from Jake and rearranged her clothing, trying not to blush when she remembered how incredibly erotic it had been to make love in the great outdoors, the way it was meant to be. The cold winter wind danced across parts of her body never exposed to the elements, and Rebecca shivered with chilly delight.

Jake saw the action and dropped his arm over her shoulders, pulling her close to wrap his coat around both of them. He couldn't believe what they had just done. He had never, ever, submitted to such a spontaneous desire in his life. Making love in the great outdoors was unlikely enough for him, but in the snow? It was completely unlike him. However, Jake had to admit that what he and Rebecca had just shared together also surpassed any other life experience he had ever enjoyed.

What could possibly exalt the act of living and enjoying life more than succumbing to one's most primitive instincts in the most primeval of surroundings? As he stood with his arms wound around Rebecca's shoulders, drawing from her heat and offering his in return, it occurred to Jake that he had just completely veered from the path he'd chosen for his life.

It also occurred to him that he'd never enjoyed another Christmas more than this one. And it wasn't simply because of Rebecca's presence, although obviously it all led back to that. It was a combination of everything—the holiday itself, the festive atmosphere at the Bellamy home, the decorations, the food, the children, and the close, loving kinship of her family.

But mostly, it *was* Rebecca who was responsible for the warm feelings wandering through Jake's body at such a leisurely, comfortable pace. It was Rebecca who had made him fall in love when he had sworn for years that it would never happen again. However, there was still one tiny problem. Jake had absolutely no idea what he was going to do about those feelings.

"Warming up any?" he asked her, his quiet voice seeming to boom like thunder across the silent hills.

When Rebecca met his gaze, Jake saw that her expression was one full of love and contentment. To see her looking at him that way—with such unadulterated emotion, such complete and uncompromising trust—twisted a dull knife deep into his gut. He wanted to order her to stop looking at him that way, wanted to command that she stop loving him, because he wouldn't love her back. The trouble was, Jake knew he would be lying if he said that. The trouble was, he wasn't honestly sure he wanted her to stop.

"They've built a fire at Edgar Hill," Rebecca said quietly, her words muffled against Jake's thick cotton sweater. "I can smell it. Hickory branches."

Looking over her head, Jake discerned a faint, distant amber glow warming a section of the night sky and nodded. "There seem to be a lot of fires burning tonight," he murmured against her hair, kissing the crown of her head soundly. "Bonfires, fires of passion..."

"Home fires," Rebecca finished for him. "Those tend to burn brightest and hottest, you know."

Jake wanted to reply that, no, he didn't know, couldn't possibly know, because he'd never felt their warmth. But tonight he had. Tonight, Jake realized, he had experienced everything he'd been missing out on in life, everything he had hoped to achieve with his marriage to Marie and hadn't come close to winning. A month ago, he had told Rebecca to make his Christmas one that would include everything he had never enjoyed with Christmases in the past. And like a Dickensian ghost, she had complied with more than ample provisions.

But could it last? he asked himself. Was it enough? December was a month full of holidays notorious for making people do things and act in ways they wouldn't even consider during the other eleven months out of the year. Christmas was a magical time, a special time. What he was feeling now was also magical and special. But could it last? Jake asked himself again. Or, like Christmas, would it be temporary and finite, ending with the melancholy that always follows a holiday?

"Come on, we'd better go rejoin the others," Rebecca said with obvious reluctance, interrupting his troubled thoughts. "They're probably wondering if we're lying sprawled at the bottom of a hill with every bone in our bodies broken."

However, when they had wandered back to the group of nighttime revelers, Jake and Rebecca discovered that they had scarcely been missed. Between the continuous up- and downhill movement of sledders and the freely flowing wassail, no one seemed to have noticed that two of their number had snuck off to enjoy a more intimate diversion. Instead, Jake and Rebecca were welcomed back as if they had just returned from a trip to the foot of Edgar Hill, with cries of congratulations that they had survived their ordeal.

It was nearly daybreak by the time the Bellamy clan returned to the house. Ruth and Dan had long since gone to bed along with the younger members of the family, but a pot of coffee was still hot and fragrant on the back of the stove. Most of the group ignored it, and with wide yawns and extravagant stretching made their way toward the stairs. Only Jake and Rebecca remained in the kitchen to sip their coffee and exchange longing glances, both fully comfortable with the silence that enveloped the house, both thoroughly uneasy about the way things were between them.

"I hate to leave when everyone else is sleeping," Jake finally said after draining the last of his coffee from its mug. "But we really should get back to the city this morning."

Rebecca set her own mug on the table, feeling an inexplicable sense of dread slinking over her. "You weren't kidding when you said you had to work, were you?"

Jake shook his head but said nothing.

"You're entirely too dedicated," Rebecca told him as she stood up. "Anybody ever tell you that you work too much, Mr. Raglan? It'll ruin your life someday."

Rebecca hadn't meant anything by her carelessly offered comment, had intended it to be nothing more than a simple, nonjudgmental observation that anyone else would have taken with a grain of salt. Instead, she recalled too late what Marcus had told her about Jake's ex-wife, about how Marie had left her husband for another man because she felt neglected when Jake spent more time at the office than at home. More than anything, Rebecca wished she could take her words back, mentally kicking herself because she hadn't thought before she'd spoken.

But when she looked up to gauge Jake's reaction, she could tell by his expression that nothing she might say would make amends for those words. Nor was there any way she could apologize without revealing that she knew more about Jake's past than he had told her himself. Caught in a dilemma she had no idea how to escape, Rebecca simply remained silent, hoping in vain that he would just ignore her comment and say something to alleviate the tension straining the air between them.

Jake stood, too, but instead of treating Rebecca to some sharp retort, he pulled her into his arms and pressed her against the doorjamb of the entryway leading from the kitchen to the dining room. Before she could voice her puzzlement, he leaned down and kissed her, a kiss that was bone-crunching, soul-searching, and seemingly without end.

With one hand on each wall behind her, Jake's arms formed an effective trap, one Rebecca was unwilling to escape. She wrapped her arms tightly around his waist to bring him closer, helpless to stop the little cry of surrender she uttered when he rubbed himself insistently against her. Instinctively, she thrust her hips forward in response to his gesture, and when she did so, Jake deepened his kiss, mimicking the act of lovemaking with his tongue because he was unable to fulfill their desire any other way without rousing the entire household.

It was as if he was trying to brand her in some way, Rebecca thought dazedly. As if he was trying to leave his mark on her so blatantly that she would never be able to think about another man for the rest of her life. No problem, she wanted to assure him. As if there could possibly be another man for her besides Jake Raglan.

When she gradually began to remember that they were standing in her parents' kitchen and could be interrupted at any moment, Rebecca pulled her lips away from Jake's and dipped her head into the hollow created beneath his chin. Trying to still the rapid beating of her pulse and steady her ragged breathing, she spread her palm open over his heart, smiling when she realized it was racing as unevenly as her own.

Hugging herself to him, she closed her eyes and murmured softly, "What was that all about?"

"Mistletoe," Jake whispered in reply.

He felt her place a warm, chaste kiss on his neck, and knew that she was smiling. "What?" she asked in a voice that was almost a purr.

Curling his index finger below her chin, he tipped her head back and pointed up at the bunch of greenery dangling from a hook on the doorjamb above them.

"Mistletoe," he repeated.

"Mmm. Potent stuff."

"I'll say."

Jake had no idea what had come over him to kiss Rebecca so insistently, so demandingly. But when he'd heard her accuse him of working too much, it had brought back all the painful memories of losing his wife that he thought he'd buried forever. Only this time there was a slight difference in his reaction. This time the pain wasn't caused by his loss of Marie. This time Jake realized it was Rebecca he'd be losing, and that had made the pain all the more unbearable. He'd realized then that he and Rebecca had no future together, because he realized what Rebecca had said was true. He did work too much, and it had ruined his life once. He simply couldn't risk it happening again.

He had never noticed until that moment how much Rebecca and Marie had in common. Like Marie, Rebecca liked to socialize. Hell, that's how she made her living. She was a woman who celebrated everything life had to offer, and Jake was a man who had never had the chance to learn how to do the same, a man whose entire identity was wrapped up in his job. Like Marie, Rebecca would surely tire of his long hours and all the time he spent away from home. Eventually she would probably wind up in the arms of another man, one who could treat her the way she deserved to be treated.

That's when Jake realized he was going to lose Rebecca someday. And he decided it would be better if it happened now instead of later. That way it wouldn't be quite so painful, he told himself. Although what could be more painful than the gut-wrenching sensations tearing up his insides right now, he didn't know. He had promised himself he would never allow himself to be hurt by another woman again. But he should have known he couldn't trust his own promises. That one about never falling in love again had been nothing but a lie, too.

Eleven

"**O**h, ho, look who's been caught under the mistletoe."

Rebecca and Jake both started at the sound of another voice in the long-silent kitchen. Tearing their gazes away from each other to look in the direction from which the noise had come, they found Ruth and Dan Bellamy standing in the opposite doorway, wearing matching robes and pajamas of burgundy silk, grinning slyly and suggestively from ear to ear.

"I knew that 'friend' business was just a red herring you threw us so that we wouldn't put Jake on the spot," Dan said, shaking his finger playfully at his daughter. "Now, how long has this been going on, and when can we expect the nuptials to take place?"

Rebecca cringed inwardly, trying to stifle the groan she wanted to utter. Don't overreact, she told herself firmly. She knew her parents had good intentions, knew they wanted nothing more than for their little girl to be happy. They had assumed—and correctly at that, she reminded herself—that things between her and Jake must have progressed well beyond the casual acquaintance stage. As the heat of embarrassment crept up from her breasts to her neck, it also occurred to Rebecca that, depending on how long her parents had been standing in the doorway, they probably had very good reason to suspect that she and Jake were even intimately involved.

"Dad, don't—"

"Now, Dan," Rebecca's mother intercepted for her.

Good ol' Mom, Rebecca thought. Ruth Bellamy was the most tactful, soothing person she knew. If anyone could smooth ruffled feathers and ease a tense situation, it was Rebecca's mother. With a few simple words, Ruth would be able to call off Dan and reassure Jake that the elder Bellamys were in no way suggesting that he marry their daughter.

"You know better than to put the kids on the spot that way," she said softly. As her smile broadened, she added, "When they set a date, they'll let us know."

Rebecca rolled her eyes heavenward. Thanks a lot, Mom, she said to herself. Nothing like putting the poor guy completely on the spot. This was just great. Now Jake would really feel uncomfortable around her family.

"Who's getting married? Rebecca and Jake?"

Now it was Rebecca's brother Michael and his wife, Stephanie, who entered the room with baby Grace in tow.

"Jake and Rebecca are getting married?" Stephanie asked, delight obvious in her tone. "How wonderful! Congratulations!" Holding up the baby in her arms, she continued, "I could tell by the way you are around Grace that it wouldn't be long before you'd be scouting out a man who was good father material. I must say, though, Rebecca," she went on with a sly wink at Jake, "that you certainly outdid yourself with this one."

"No, you guys, wait—" Rebecca tried to interject.

"Welcome to the family," Michael said, extending his hand to Jake with a brotherly smile.

Rebecca closed her eyes and willed the scene to go away, wishing this were nothing more than a bad dream, and wondering when such a magical evening had gone so utterly, completely awry. She waited for Jake's reaction with her breath held, half of her wondering if maybe, just maybe, he would laugh and take her brother's hand, then thank her parents for inviting him into the family so readily. But the other half of her knew better, and she tried to tell herself that's why she didn't fall apart when she heard Jake's reply.

"Uh, listen," he began, his words drawn out as if he was trying to be very careful in choosing them. "I'm not sure what Rebecca has told you about us, but...we haven't even talked about getting married, let alone starting a family."

"Well, then maybe it's about time you did," Dan Bellamy told him with characteristic frankness.

"Dan..." Jake took a step away from Rebecca as if putting physical distance between them might make what he had to say easier. "You have a wonderful daughter.... She's terrific.... But...but we're *not* getting married."

"Why not?" the elderly Bellamy asked pointedly.

"Daddy, please," Rebecca whispered with some difficulty, having grown more and more miserable with every word Jake had voiced, dismally aware of how very final he made them sound. "It really isn't any of your business. Don't blame Jake, he... I mean, he and I aren't...we aren't...um..."

We aren't what? she asked herself. We aren't in love? That wasn't true; she was more in love than she'd ever been in her life, and she was certain Jake loved her, too. We aren't ready for a commitment? she posed further. For Rebecca, that wasn't true, either—she would gladly jump in with both feet. For Jake, however, perhaps commitment was precisely the problem. Maybe he just needed to get used to the idea of including a woman seriously in his life again, she told herself optimistically. Maybe it would just take a little time for him. But maybe he would come around. Maybe...

Rebecca braved a glance in his direction and what she saw told her everything she needed to know. His jaw was set with anger and annoyance, his eyes were stormy blue and dangerously dark. It was the expression of a man who resented being put on the spot, and a man who was determined not to be moved in his conviction. She knew then without question that Jake would never come around.

He'd been hurt badly by his ex-wife and simply would not risk being hurt again by marrying. He had told Rebecca that flat out at the beginning of their relationship and had never led her to believe he would change his mind. Jake Raglan had been completely honest with her from the start in attesting to the fact that he intended to stay single. But Rebecca, ever-optimistic and overcome by her love for the man, had tried to tell herself there might be a chance that she could change his mind.

Obviously she'd been terribly mistaken. And now she and Jake were embroiled in a very awkward situation, one she wasn't entirely sure they'd be able to escape unscathed. The Bellamy family were fiercely protective of their own. If they sensed that Jake Raglan was about to hurt the youngest and perhaps most vulnerable of their number, they would circle and pounce and do everything they could to prevent it.

"What I'm trying to say, Daddy," Rebecca tried again after screwing up enough courage to make her sound convincing, "is that Jake and I haven't discussed marriage because I've decided I don't want to marry again."

"What?"

All four members of Rebecca's family who were present stared at her in utter disbelief.

"Rebecca..." she heard Jake caution her. "You don't have to—"

"The fact of the matter is," she went on, trying to sound indeed matter-of-fact, "I realized recently that of the more than twenty weddings I've planned over the past five years, nine of the marriages have already ended in divorce."

"So what does that have to do with you?" her mother asked skeptically.

Rebecca lifted her chin defensively. "It's made me re-evaluate my opinions on the subject of matrimony."

"And?"

"It's made me reconsider my desire to plunge into something that could wind up being a worse situation than my first marriage was. Statistically speaking, second marriages often end more quickly than the first."

Her mother gazed at her through narrowed eyes, then at Jake, then back to Rebecca again. "Kids today," she muttered softly under her breath. "What crazy notions."

The quiet that ensued stretched to an uncomfortable silence, until Rebecca mercifully ended it by announcing that she and Jake had to get back to the city by mid-morning. She felt like she was tiptoeing on the thinnest of ice as she gathered their things and bade goodbye to her relations. Certainly her revelation about her intentions to stay single must have come as a terrific surprise to them. They all considered Rebecca to be the most family-oriented member of the clan, the one who insisted the others get together on a regular basis. She was sure they were suspicious of what she had told them, but at least she and Jake had escaped with minimal fuss. She tried to reassure herself that such a victory was what was most important.

They made the drive back to town in complete silence. Jake seemed to be thoroughly wrapped up in his thoughts, and Rebecca wanted to draw as little attention to herself as possible. She seemed to do a very good job of it, because Jake didn't look at her once during the forty-five-minute period. It wasn't until he pulled up into the driveway of her little tollhouse that he finally seemed to remember she was there.

For several minutes he studied the house that looked like something from a fairy tale, all dusted with silver-white snow, before he finally turned to look at Rebecca. She would have expected him to say a number of things, but the question he posed was not included on the list.

"Why did you buy this house?"

He couldn't have caught her more off guard had he asked her to name the capital of Assyria.

"Because I liked it," she answered simply.

"What did you like about it?"

"It has an interesting history. It was built in the middle 1800s and used to be the tollhouse for the railroad that runs alongside Frankfort Avenue. About twenty years ago, the previous owners bought it and moved it back to this lot before renovating it. I kind of liked the idea of all the people who must have passed through it over the years and maybe left a little of themselves behind."

"What else did you like about it?"

Rebecca shrugged. "I don't know. I liked the size of it. It's cozy, perfectly sized for one. And I figured when I got married and moved out of it, I could still hold on to it for a rental property or maybe use it for my office if I could get it zoned for business use."

Jake nodded. "So even when you bought your house, you were thinking about getting married someday."

"Yes," she told him honestly. She wasn't about to lie to him, and she certainly wasn't going to let him make her feel as if she should defend her actions.

He nodded once more, gazing at her with an expression in his eyes she was helpless to understand. "I'll call you this weekend," he said softly, finally.

The words tore at Rebecca's heart as if it were nothing but paper, and she expelled a single breath of air that might have been a chuckle had there been something funny in her situation. "Sure you will," she replied coolly, hopelessly.

Before he could say anything more, Rebecca shoved open the car door with the ferocity of a Trojan, leapt out and rushed to her front door. She didn't look back, didn't want to see Jake driving out of her life forever. Instead, she went quickly inside, slamming the door behind her, gathering up her cats, and gazed solemnly at the cold, empty house she called her home.

She might as well get used to it, she told herself. What she had said to Jake was the truth. When she had purchased the house, it was with the intention that it would only be a temporary place of residence, that eventually she would marry and move out. Now, of course, she was sure she would be living here forever. Because the man she wanted to marry was a man who was determined not to. And he had spoiled any chance she might have for a life with someone else, because he had branded her his own. Jake Raglan had locked himself into the deepest part of Rebecca's heart, and she knew she would never meet another man who would rouse him from there.

Old Lady Bellamy, that's what she was destined to be. Just a little old spinster living with her cats in her cottage in Crescent Hill. Despite the whimsical overtones, it wasn't a life-style Rebecca looked forward to pursuing.

All in all, she thought morosely, this hadn't been one of her better Christmas celebrations.

It's just another New Year's Eve, Jake told himself as he stared out his living room window at the last scattering of flakes left over from the afternoon's snowfall. The sky above was slate gray and thick with clouds promising more snow later, the dying rays of sunlight were dim and chalky and harsh. The day outside reflected the way Jake was feeling inside. Cold and empty and barren.

It's just another New Year's Eve, he repeated silently, this time with a bit more fortitude. Then a little voice in the back of his head piped up unbidden, Another New Year's Eve spent alone. Jake tried to assure the little voice that he was alone because he wanted to be. Unfortunately, he wasn't quite sure of that at all. Because more and more lately, Jake had begun to think that the reason he led such a solitary existence wasn't because he chose to be alone, but because he was afraid not to be.

Tonight was a night when other people would go out to have a wonderful time, reflecting on the changes the past twelve months had brought to their lives, and making plans for the year to come. It was a night to put old hurts and differences behind and look forward to new beginnings. A night to forget about the pain and focus on the pleasure.

Ever since his divorce, Jake had made it a point not to go out on New Year's Eve. He hadn't wanted to bear witness to people who were able to pick themselves up and begin again, hadn't wanted to risk becoming part of such potential renewal himself. Because he'd been afraid if he did, he would ultimately, if inadvertently, open himself up to other things. Other things like chances—specifically the chance to love someone again. And in opening himself up to the chance to love someone again, he knew he would also be setting himself up to take another fall. A fall that might just leave him too broken up to pull himself back together again.

So Jake had always stayed home on New Year's Eve, and was sure he hadn't missed out on a thing. Certainly he hadn't felt as if his life was lacking anything. At least, not until lately he hadn't. But Rebecca Bellamy had changed all that. She had not only provided him with the best Christmas he'd ever enjoyed, she had also afforded him, if only temporarily, the chance to see what a truly full life was like.

Rebecca. Jake hadn't been lying when he'd told her he would call her last weekend. He truly had intended to call her. But for some unknown reason, he'd never picked up the phone. No, that wasn't true, he thought now. He did know the reason. It all came back to the same thing—his fear of not being alone.

For most people, loneliness was the worst thing life could bring, something to be avoided at all cost. They often resorted to drastic and dangerous measures to make sure they were never alone. For Jake Raglan, just the opposite was true. He went out of his way to make certain no one entered his life beyond a superficial, temporary presence. No attachments, no strings. That way he didn't have to worry if the other person had ulterior motives, didn't have to wonder how long it would be before he wound up alone and desolate again. Instead, he was the one who called the shots and kept the status quo. He was in charge of who came and went, and made sure people went before they became important. It was a system that had always served him well.

Until he met Rebecca.

Somehow, when she had entered his life, Jake had lost the upper hand. True, it was her job to organize things and take charge, but it was only his Christmas she was supposed to have taken control of, not his entire life. Yet she had done just that. Now there were reminders of her presence all over his home—in the holiday decorations that still adorned the rooms, in the piles of food left over from his party that she had wrapped up and put into his freezer for him to feast upon throughout the winter. Rebecca Bellamy was everywhere—in his house, in his head, in his heart. And Jake was beginning to think she would remain there forever, no matter what he did to try and chase her away.

She'd never spent more than a few hours at a time in his home, but it was as if she belonged here more than he did. Jake's house had been nothing but a collection of stones and tile and mortar filled with bits of wood and cloth before Rebecca had entered it. Now it looked warm and welcoming. It could *feel* warm and welcoming, too; he knew it could. But only if Rebecca were in it with him. Permanently.

Maybe it was about time he stopped being afraid, Jake thought. Maybe it was about time he took a chance. He was forty years old, soon to become a great-uncle. If he worked this out right, maybe he still had time to be a great father, too. But first he had to prove he could be a great husband. And for that, he was going to need a wife. Good thing there was someone he was already in love with.

He only hoped Rebecca didn't already have a date for New Year's Eve.

"Okay, so what's the big emergency?"

Rebecca still wasn't sure why she had agreed to come over to Jake's house. It had been surprising indeed to be interrupted during a leisurely bath and snatch up the phone on the sixth ring—having halfway decided not to bother—only to hear Jake's deeply intoned greeting at the other end of the line. He'd sounded almost as if he could actually see her standing in the middle of her living room wrapped in nothing but a damp towel, and his words had fairly dripped with the promise of pleasures never before experienced by any woman.

Reminding herself Jake had said he would call *last* weekend and hadn't, Rebecca had managed to collect her wits enough not to sound like a complete imbecile as she'd coolly responded to his numerous questions. No, she wasn't busy at the moment, but, yes, she *did* have a date for New Year's Eve. However, she had hastened to add, kicking herself mentally for doing so, they weren't plans that were etched in stone. In fact—although she didn't tell Jake, of course—she was sure Marcus Tate had only asked her to join him in attending a string of parties that night out of pity for her, having heard through the legal grapevine that Jake had given the brush-off to the woman everyone had thought would surely snag him.

When Jake had asked her if she would come over to his house that evening, Rebecca had been skeptical, wanting to know why. He had then cited that he had a slight emergency for which she was responsible, and could she please come over and help him deal with it? Thinking it must be something to do with the remnants of the party she had planned for him—although thoroughly puzzled by what could possibly be causing an emergency two weeks after the fact—she had reluctantly agreed to come.

But not before making herself look presentable in an

oversize amber sweater and brown wool trousers. Now she stood at Jake's front door damning herself for going to any trouble for this man who had turned her world upside down and tied her heart in knots, this man who clearly had no regard for his own appearance where she was concerned— although he did look rather...rather roguish and some-what...sexy in his faded jeans and rumpled denim work shirt with the tails untucked. After all, she reminded herself, there was an emergency somewhere—whatever it might be—and she couldn't expect him to be as pressed and pol-ished as a West Point cadet, could she?

"It's upstairs," Jake said simply, still leaning in the doorway as if weighing some very serious consideration, like whether or not he should allow her into his home.

"Upstairs?" she asked, now more confused than ever. "But I never did anything upstairs."

"Yes, you did."

"Well, I changed my clothes that one day, but that's all."

"Believe me, that was enough."

Rebecca sighed impatiently, doubling her fists and press-ing them against her hips in challenge. "Look, Jake, I drove all the way over here because you said I caused some kind of emergency, and now you won't even tell me what I did. I have better things to occupy my time than to stand here trying to outguess you. Now, what's the problem?"

Instead of answering, he crooked his index finger up-ward, slowly curling and uncurling it in the "come hither" gesture men have perfected over the centuries. Rebecca was no more immune than any other woman who had fallen prey to it in the past, and quickly found herself following Jake up the stairs and down the hallway of his big house. She felt just as strange being in his private domain now as she had the first time she had invaded it, but for some reason, this part of the house was still every bit as inviting as the rooms where she had spent so much of her time over the past few months. Jake's house was a nice house. It would be the perfect place to raise a large family.

Don't start, she warned herself. Just don't start again.

"In here."

Jake stood beside the door to a room Rebecca had never entered, a room she had never even braved a peep into, despite her constant curiosity about it—his bedroom. She had stopped walking when he had and now stood two feet beside him, well to the right of his bedroom door. Instead of taking the two steps necessary to bring her fully in front of it, Rebecca, still very confused, bent forward from the waist until she could peek around the corner of the door.

"It's your bedroom."

"Yes."

Biting her lip nervously, she straightened and met his gaze. For long moments neither of them spoke, until the silence became too much for Rebecca to bear.

"Although I wouldn't doubt that there have been a variety of…um…emergencies that may have taken place in this room over the several months you've lived here," she began, "I fail to detect the presence of one at the moment, particularly one for which I am responsible."

Jake smiled at her for the first time then, a wonderfully crooked, deliciously seductive smile that served to reveal a slash of a dimple in his left cheek that Rebecca had never noticed before. She was so intrigued by it that she was unaware she had raised her hand to trace a finger over it until it was too late. By then, Jake had captured her hand in his, and was placing a warm kiss at the center of her palm. Tiny shocks of electricity exploded throughout Rebecca's body, leaving tingling vibrations that shook her from head to toe.

"You don't see the emergency?" Jake asked her softly. "You don't *feel* it?"

He pushed the sleeve of her sweater up toward her elbow, trailing soft kisses behind it—first on the back of her hand, then on her wrist—then traced the tip of his tongue along the sensitive flesh of her inner arm until he reached the inside of her elbow, where he placed another tender kiss. Rebecca was helpless to stop the tremble of excitement that wound through her body like a mountain road, and couldn't prevent the little gasp of arousal that escaped past her lips.

"Well," she murmured quietly, drawing the word out as she fully considered the sensations heating every cell, every fiber of her being. "There is a certain…ah… insistence…but I don't know if I would call it an emergency…just yet."

With a gentle tug on her wrist, Jake pulled Rebecca into his arms, and all she could think about was how nice it felt to be there again. When he bent his head and took her lips with his, rubbing his mouth over hers in a kiss that was tender but still demanded response, she gladly obliged him. Circling her arms around his neck to pull him closer, she rose up on tiptoe to receive his kiss more fully.

Deeper and deeper Jake explored her mouth, tasting every inch of her he could reach. His hands on her back made reassuring up-and-down motions, moving lower and lower until he could spread his fingers open wide over her derriere. Only when he curled his fingers deep into her soft flesh and urged her hips forward to rub his hard length against her did Rebecca realize how intimately they had entwined themselves together, and only then did she force herself to put an end to what he had begun.

"Jake, stop it," she whispered raggedly when she finally tore her mouth away from his. "I didn't come over here for this." Doubling her fists against his chest, Rebecca pushed herself away from him, touching her fingers lightly to her lips in an attempt to dispel the lingering heat of his kiss. "I'm not the kind of woman who's going to come running every time you get the urge, only to have you discard me when you're satisfied."

Jake stared at her for a long time before replying to her suggestion that he only wanted her for sex and would tell her to go home as soon as he was through with her. With no small amount of guilt, he realized she had little reason to feel differently, because he had done just that both times they'd made love. Only then he had been running away because he was afraid to admit that he wanted to be with her. Now he wanted nothing else than to lose himself in Rebecca forever.

"I missed you," he told her softly, honestly.

Rebecca almost crumpled into a quivering heap on the floor at the sound of his voice—so full of emptiness and desolation and loneliness. "I missed you, too," she managed to whisper in reply.

"Rebecca, I..." His gaze was locked with hers, guileless, unflinching, and completely candid. "I love you. And I want you to come home."

"Home?" she asked in a very quiet voice, still not allowing herself to believe he was saying what she so much wanted to hear.

"My home," he clarified. "Our home. I want us to be together...here...forever. When I'm here alone, this house is just a building. But when you're here with me, it's...it's a home. I know that sounds corny, but there you have it. The minute you set foot in this place, you possessed it somehow. Just like you possessed me." He shrugged nervously, shoving his hands into his pockets, suddenly realizing how desperate he sounded, how desperate he felt. "I think we should make it official," he finally concluded. "I think we should get married."

It was as if a two-ton weight she'd been unaware of carrying was suddenly lifted from her back. Rebecca felt all the air leave her lungs in a rush, to be replaced by a flood of warm laughter. Jake Raglan loved her. And he was finally admitting it, not only to her, but to himself.

"Well, it's about time," she said as she threw her arms around him once again. "It's about damned time."

His laughter joined hers as he scooped her into his arms and carried her over the threshold and into his bedroom.

Gently, Jake set Rebecca down on her back at the center of his bed, leaning over her to gaze down into her eyes, amazed that he'd even tried to convince himself he could live without her. He'd been so blind for so long that he'd almost lost sight of the one thing that kept life bright—the love of another human being. He had been willing to deny himself the pinnacle of joy, because he had been afraid of being hurt again. Now Jake had found Rebecca. And now he feared nothing.

"I love you," he told her again, trying to make up for all the times he'd felt it and hadn't said it aloud. "I love you."

Rebecca threaded her fingers through his hair, pulling him close for a soft, chaste kiss. "I love you, too, Jake. And I won't hurt you. Just like I know you'll never hurt me."

He nodded silently, and each knew those would be the final words spoken on the subjects of their past marriages. Now they had the future to look forward to, a future that was brighter than either would have ever anticipated. Rebecca kissed Jake again, this time on his neck, then lowered her head and murmured something unintelligible against his chest.

"What?" he asked, smiling at what seemed to be a sudden, uncharacteristic bout of shyness on her part.

"I said this is an awfully big house for two people."

Jake's smile broadened at her less-than-subtle hint. "Well, your house is too small for two people."

Her eyes met his briefly, then Rebecca dropped her gaze again. "I wasn't suggesting that we live there instead of here. I love this house."

Jake kissed the crown of her head, and laced his fingers with hers. "Then what were you suggesting?"

When Rebecca lifted her head to face him boldly, her cheeks were tinged with pink. "I was thinking maybe we'd be better off filling it with the pitter-patter of tiny feet."

Jake feigned consternation. "You want to bring your cats with you? Ohh, I don't know, Rebecca...."

"Jake!"

"Well, all right. I guess I can handle a couple of cats."

"Jake!"

"But only if we can have a couple of kids, too."

Rebecca smiled at him in smug satisfaction. "There are those cat lovers who would argue that they are one and the same."

He grinned at her indulgently. "Nonetheless, I think I'm going to have to insist that at least some of our children bear some resemblance to us. And that means no whiskers until they've survived puberty, and even then, only on the boys."

"That sounds reasonable," Rebecca agreed. "But, Jake."

"Yes?"

"We're never going to have any children if we just sit here yammering all night."

With an expression that almost mimicked shock, he replied, "Aren't you planning on wearing white at our wedding?"

She shook her head resolutely. "Nope. Ivory silk. I've already decided. Besides, it's too late to worry about my purity, anyway. You soiled me for life months ago. Or have you already forgotten?"

Jake's grin became lascivious as he purred, "Remind me."

This time Rebecca grinned, too. "With pleasure."

The pleasure began for Jake when Rebecca worked free the buttons of his shirt and pushed the softly worn fabric from his shoulders. She was fascinated by the warm ridges and hard planes she discovered beneath her fingertips as she skimmed them across the scattering of dark hair that spiraled across his chest and down his flat abdomen. Jake's body was truly a work of art, she mused, more perfect than anything found in a museum.

As she explored further, Jake went on a little expedition of his own, tugging Rebecca's sweater over her head to discover she was wearing a very revealing brassiere of the most transparent fabric he'd ever seen, in a color reminiscent of a desert sunset. Her full breasts strained against the garment as if begging to be set free, but instead of unfastening the clasp, Jake leaned his head down to taste her through the sheer voile.

Rebecca groaned when he drew her into his mouth and tongued the peak of her breast to life despite the barrier of her brassiere, then removed it herself to facilitate his ministrations. So focused was she on the mind-scrambling sensations his mouth wreaked on her body, that she never noticed when he removed the rest of her clothing. She only knew that suddenly Jake cupped his hand over the most feminine part of her, and was delving into her softness with one long finger as he continued to stroke his tongue over her breast.

Finally he ended the twin onslaught long enough to fully disrobe himself, and Rebecca wanted to cry out in joy at seeing his hard, sculpted form in its purest sense. He was without question the most beautiful man she could imagine, certainly the most beautiful she had ever seen. And he was hers. The knowledge warmed Rebecca to the depths of her soul, and made her want to give herself completely to him in return. Opening her arms wide, she welcomed him to her, sighing when she felt his strength against the soft core of her, crying out in triumph when he joined his body to hers with one mighty thrust.

Slowly he plunged deeper, until their bodies were virtually fused by the heat they created together. Up and up they went, scaling every sensual peak, falling ecstatically into every sweet chasm only to rise higher than before. Again and again Jake thrust into Rebecca, until each was branded by the other's love. Finally they reached the point where they were made utterly certain that things would remain this intense, this incandescent, for them forever, and their releases came in a fury of emotion. Gradually the fires that had leapt out of control were banked to a comfortable, tender warmth, and then Jake and Rebecca held each other, murmuring words of love and hope and promise.

Rebecca recalled then that it was New Year's Eve, a time to reflect on the past and plan for the future, to forget old wounds and sow for new growth. She smiled in contentment as she cuddled closer to Jake, who pulled the blanket up over both of them. Outside the window, she saw that it had begun to snow once again.

"Happy New Year, Jake," she whispered softly.

"Happy New Year, Rebecca," he replied in a quiet voice. "And happy new life."

"Yeah," she agreed with a peaceful sigh. "Isn't it just?"

Epilogue

"**G**ather 'round, everybody, Rebecca's going to throw her bouquet!"

Rebecca gazed over and smiled at a round-bellied Daphne, looking pert and very pregnant in her peach organdy dress. Along with Rebecca's sister, Catherine, she had been a bridal attendant, and had somehow taken it upon herself to completely run the wedding. Now she was corralling the other fifty people in attendance for the throwing of the bouquet, and Rebecca couldn't help but recall that a little less than a year ago, she herself had caught Daphne's.

What goes around comes around, Rebecca thought affectionately. With any luck at all, before the year was out, she'd follow her newly acquired niece down the road to maternity, too.

Rebecca glanced up to find Jake staring at her as he had been all day, with an expression of pride, joy and promise. She knew exactly how he felt, embraced similar emotions for her new husband. She could scarcely wait until they left the reception and headed off for their honeymoon. They'd told everyone they were going to loll away the following week in the Caribbean. However, they were actually planning to spend the week at home alone with the phone unplugged.

Home alone, she thought. Now alone meant just the two of them, and now home meant the big yellow creek-stone house in Bonnycastle, filled with furniture and mementos that belonged to them both. Together, they would start a family, and together, they would establish traditions to be carried on by generations that followed them. Although it was still six months away, Rebecca couldn't wait for Christmas. Oh, the things she had planned for them. And as they filled their house with children, the holidays would only become more festive.

"Is everyone ready?" Rebecca called out from the top step overlooking her parents' living room.

All the single women present set their plates and glasses on whatever surfaces were convenient and assured Rebecca that, yes, they were. Turning her back, Rebecca silently counted to three, then tossed the collection of white flowers and holly bound with an ivory ribbon over one shoulder. In the living room below her, chaos resulted, and amid cheering and laughter and moaning, Rebecca turned to discern who would be the next bride.

"Who caught the bouquet?" she called out to Daphne.

"Oh, Rebecca, you'll never guess!" her niece replied with a laugh.

"Come on, who?"

But Daphne became so doubled up with laughter that all she could do was shake her head and brush the tears from her eyes.

"Jake?" Rebecca asked when she caught her husband's eye.

Jake, too, was smiling broadly, but he pointed his finger toward the opposite corner. When Rebecca allowed her gaze to follow, she saw that there beside her cousin, Denise—with whom he was no doubt trying to make time, she thought dryly—stood Marcus Tate with her bouquet cradled in his hands as if it were a newborn baby.

"Marcus, congratulations!" Rebecca cried with a chuckle as she hurried down the stairs. Then she added playfully for her cousin's benefit, "Run, Denise! Run while there's still time!"

Coming to a halt beside Jake, Rebecca looped her arm through his and pulled him close. "Remember when you offered me the same advice?"

Jake nodded, gazing down at his wife with unmistakable love and devotion. "Yeah, that was back when I was a coldhearted bastard. Good thing you warmed me up."

Giving his arm an affectionate squeeze, Rebecca eagerly agreed. "Gosh, I think this celebration has just about run its course, don't you?"

Jake looked around at the large group of people he now called his family. It felt nice to belong to such a gathering. It felt nice to know he was in this too deeply to get out. But what felt best was knowing he would be going home soon. Home with Rebecca.

"Yeah, I think you've got a point," he replied softly.

"What say we get home and start working on our next celebration?"

"And what might that be?" Jake wanted to know.

Rebecca smiled privately and said simply, "A baby shower."

Jake looked down quickly and whispered, "You're not...?"

"No," Rebecca told him regretfully. "Not yet. But you can never start planning these things too early, you know."

Jake nodded vigorously. "I see what you mean." As he wrapped his arm around his wife's waist and urged her toward the door, he said quietly, "You know, I suppose we could spend the rest of our lives planning celebrations and then celebrating. It's a good thing you do this for a living. You can get us all kinds of discounts."

Rebecca smiled as she cupped her palm under his chin. "Forget about the discounts, mister, and let's just focus on the celebrations themselves."

"Baby shower first," Jake agreed.

Rebecca's smile grew broader. "And maybe second and third."

And as their family and friends continued to revel well into the night, Jake and Rebecca went home to enjoy a little celebration of their own.

*   *   *   *   *

Dear Reader,

Who doesn't love Christmas? "Chestnuts roasting on an open fire…"

Frankly, I've never had a chestnut, roasted or otherwise, and I'd prefer that Jack Frost leave my nose alone. Still, Christmas is my favorite holiday. For us it starts on the first weekend of December. The tree goes up on Saturday, and the ornaments come down from the attic. Sunday is spent decorating the tree and reminiscing. Virtually every ornament has a special meaning—the faded glass balls that adorned our tree the first year of our marriage nearly twenty years ago, the brass baby in a cradle that celebrated our son's birth, the punched-tin heart from the Blue Ridge Mountains where we visited old friends, the tiny Gullah basket from Charleston where twice we lived.

The best moment comes that night, when the empty boxes are packed away and the tree is sparkling in the night. The house is warm and the night is cold. Harry Connick Jr. is singing "Ave Maria" on the CD player, and the scent of mulled cider on the stove mingles with fresh pine and mulberry. Everything is beautiful and peaceful and bright.

With a scene like that, who *wouldn't* love Christmas?

Marilyn Pappano

ROOM AT THE INN

Marilyn Pappano

Chapter 1

The rocking chairs evenly spaced on the long porch were dusty from more than a month of disuse, but Leah Cameron didn't mind. With her coat zipped and buttoned up snugly, and her hands hidden inside warm ski gloves, she sat down, rocked back and forth, and watched the snow fall.

It was going to be a busy weekend at Cameron Inn, and she wanted to spend the last peaceful hour outside, alone with the snow and her thoughts. She supposed she ought to be grateful that business was so good—every one of the twelve rooms was booked for the weekend—but it meant she would have little quiet, and very little private time. This weekend there would be even less time for herself than usual when the inn was full; her mother- and father-in-law, who normally helped run the place, had left this morning for Atlanta. Tomorrow would be Peter and Martha's forty-third wedding anniversary, and they were celebrating it in style in the city. She didn't expect them back until Sunday evening, after most of the guests had gone home.

Forty-three years. She gave a soft sigh. That was a long

time to stay married. Her own marriage had lasted only twelve years—unhappy years, mercifully ended by Terence's death in an auto accident six years ago.

A car turning off the highway caught and held her attention. The weekend's first arrival. That meant time to smile and be friendly. She took a deep breath to prepare herself.

A man got out of the car, glancing around without noticing her as he pulled on a pair of dark gloves. Maybe he wasn't a guest, she thought as he started toward the house. He had no luggage, and there were no skis strapped to the top of his car. He looked more like a businessman, with his heavy overcoat and neatly creased trousers. A salesman, perhaps, wanting to do business with the inn.

Smiling faintly, she watched him cross the snow-covered yard. Her oldest son, Douglas, had shoveled the sidewalk this morning before school, but it was buried again, marked only by a miniature snowdrift on each side.

As the man drew closer, she grew still, her rocking chair motionless. She had never seen this man before, but she *knew* him. There was something familiar in the way he moved—with such purpose; in the way he held his head up instead of ducking it against the heavy, wet snow; in the color of his hair and the stubborn line of his jaw. When she saw his face, she would know for sure. His eyes would be brown—a dark, warm, chocolaty brown—and she would know who he was.

He climbed the steps and stopped in front of the door to stomp the snow from his feet. For a long moment he just stood there, as unmoving as Leah, unaware of her at the end of the porch.

His eyes were riveted on the brass plaque that hung next to the door. Welcome, it proclaimed, the letters forming a graceful arch over a pineapple, the traditional symbol of hospitality. Then, slowly, as if feeling the intensity of her stare, he turned and moved toward her.

Leah waited until he was standing only a few yards in

front of her. Carefully she began to rock again, pretending an easiness that she was far from feeling. "Hello."

He didn't return the greeting right away. Instead he looked at her, as intensely as she had watched him, with eyes that were indeed brown. "Hello."

He sounded stiff, uncomfortable. She suspected that he would have preferred to ignore her greeting, but his manners, as deeply ingrained as her own, had won out. Did he know who she was? She decided that he must. There was probably very little that escaped his attention, and for the past month, they—Peter and Martha, Leah and the house—had received a great deal of that. "I wondered when you would come," she finally said.

How had she known, after talking to him twice on the phone, that he would come? Bryce Cameron wondered skeptically. Had she planned what she would say to him when he came—what strategy she would use to stand in his way?

He looked from her to the other chairs, but found them too dusty. Brushing snow from the railing, he leaned back against it, pushing his hands deep into his coat pockets. "So you were expecting me."

"Yes. Not today, of course, but soon."

Of course. Tilting his head to one side, he asked bluntly, "Why?" He hadn't even known it himself until just this week. After a month's worth of phone calls and letters had accomplished nothing, he had decided only three days ago to fly unannounced to Angel's Peak, to surprise his Uncle Peter and Aunt Martha and the lady with the lovely Southern drawl. And the lady had expected him. "How did you know?"

She lifted her hands, palms up, and shrugged. "You're a Cameron."

That simple answer could cover a multitude of sins, he thought with a grin. Camerons were stubborn; they liked to get their own way. They were fighters who hated to admit defeat. They were also too thickheaded to know when they

were whipped, or to realize when they weren't welcome.
He suspected that she was referring to the latter. "The
black sheep always returns to the fold, doesn't he?"

"Are you?"

"Returning to the fold?" The smile grew cynical and,
at the same time, more attractive.

"The black sheep."

He mimicked her shrug. "That's what Peter says, isn't
it?"

"Actually, Peter says very little about you or your father.
I thought you might tell me."

He pushed himself away from the railing and started toward the door with an easy, comfortable grace that Leah
envied. "Sorry, sweetheart," he said over his shoulder. "I
didn't come more than six hundred miles to give you my
version of the family history."

She watched him take four steps, then five, then six,
before she spoke. "I'm afraid you'll have to settle for me."

He turned, looked at her again and smiled, as if amused
by the thought of "settling" for her. "Would you like to
explain that?"

She told him about Peter's trip to Atlanta as she walked
toward him. She held the door open, followed him inside,
then closed it with a quiet click. "So," she finished, un-
zipping her coat, "do you want to have a cup of coffee and
talk to me, or do you want to waste a six-hundred-mile
trip?"

It took Bryce only a moment to choose his course of
action. A few minutes later they were seated in her office,
a tray holding a pot of coffee, mugs, cream and sugar on
the desk between them. While she fixed his coffee, he
glanced around the room. It wasn't much bigger than the
closet down the hall where she had hung their coats, with
barely enough space for a desk and chair, a set of shelves,
a filing cabinet and a straight-backed chair for visitors. But
it was charming, with its rose-colored wallpaper and match-

ing curtains, its handwoven rugs and potted plants and photographs.

He looked at *her*, too, all soft and pretty and feminine. She was of average height, but slender, which gave her that delicate, fragile appearance that Southern women wore so well. In her case, he would bet, appearances were deceiving. He knew that she was a widow, raising four children and running the inn; she was probably stronger than he was.

"Have you eaten lunch?" she asked in that soft drawl of hers as she handed him a cup of steaming coffee.

He nodded. Not expecting much of a welcome in Angel's Peak, he had stopped at a fast-food restaurant in Asheville before starting the trip up the mountain.

She sat back comfortably in her chair, her fingers laced loosely around her cup. "I suppose it's time for formal introductions. I'm Leah Cameron."

"You're going to feel very silly if I'm not who you think I am," he warned.

She smiled—not the hesitant, uncomfortable grimace that he expected, but a full-blown, sunlight-bright smile that warmed him all the way to his toes. "I *know* who you are."

Taking in the glow of her smile, he revised his earlier opinion. She wasn't pretty—she was beautiful. Undeniably, achingly beautiful. For a moment he envied his dead cousin for having been able to claim this woman as his wife.

She was waiting—calmly, patiently silent. "All right," he said at last, tearing his gaze from her face. "I'm Bryce Cameron."

She gave a shrug to indicate that she'd known all along, then sobered. "I'm sorry you missed Peter."

"Are you?"

She didn't object to his skepticism. He had tried for weeks to talk to Peter, and she certainly hadn't helped him. He was justified in doubting her. "Yes, I am. I think it's unfortunate that this feud between your father and Peter has gone on for so long. I'm surprised they can even remember what it was about."

His eyes, so dark and warm, narrowed. "Oh, they remember," he said coolly. "Believe me, we all remember." He took a sip of his coffee, then set it on the desk. "What are the chances that you might tell me where Peter and Martha are staying in Atlanta?"

She chided him with her gaze. "Even if I knew, which I don't, I wouldn't tell you. They're celebrating their anniversary. I wouldn't do anything to ruin it for them."

"And you think I would." He said it flatly, knowing her answer before she gave it. Just what had she been told about him? he wondered. Enough to judge him?

"Yes." She had been tactless, but she wouldn't lie to make up for it. "Peter has made it pretty clear that he doesn't want to talk to you. He said a few years ago that he never wanted to see you or your father again."

"That was a few years ago." Six, to be exact. Bryce remembered the occasion well. He imagined Leah did, too. "Maybe he's changed his mind."

"I doubt it." She sat quietly for a moment. There were a hundred questions she wanted to ask him—about his father Frank, about the feud that had split the Cameron family in two, about himself. Especially about himself. Was he married? Did he have any children? What kind of man was he? They were questions whose answers were none of her business, because this man was none of her business.

Her thoughts were wandering, Bryce realized. Selfishly, he wanted to call them back to himself. "How did you know who I was out there?"

She focused on him once again. From the half dozen photographs on the file cabinet behind her, she selected one, handing it across the desk to him. "That's my son, Douglas."

He set down his coffee, took the frame and studied the picture for a long time. Although he didn't know the boy, he knew the face—it was his own about twenty-five years ago. He stared at the picture and envied Leah this big handsome son. He would have liked to have children—in fact, he had insisted on it until the desire had threatened to tear his marriage apart. Then, giving up the dream of being a father, he had held on to the marriage and to Kay. Ten years later, *she* had let go.

At last he handed back the photo. "Gran said we all looked alike—but only the men, fortunately. The Cameron women are prettier."

"I don't think the Cameron men are too shabby," Leah disagreed absently as she set the picture back in its place.

He grinned. "Is that supposed to be a compliment—not too shabby?"

"You don't need my compliments." Smoothly she changed the subject. "Do you have a place to stay tonight? With all this snow, you'll never find a room in town."

"I was planning to finish my business with Peter, drive back to Asheville and fly home tomorrow." He picked up the mug again, just for something to do with his hands. "Are you offering me a room here?"

What could it hurt? she questioned. Peter was about two hundred miles away in Atlanta; by the time he returned, Bryce would be back in Philadelphia, his home since he'd left Angel's Peak so many years ago. "Yes," she replied evenly. "I am."

"Then I'll take it."

"It's not one of the guest rooms," she cautioned. "Those are completely booked for every weekend from now until spring. But I do have an empty room in the family wing. It may not be as quiet as you'd like—I have three other children besides Douglas."

"Matthew, Megan and Laurel. Ages six, eleven and thirteen. Douglas is seventeen." He was pleased with himself for keeping the names and ages straight.

Leah looked dismayed. "You've been checking up on us."

"Not me—Dad. He wanted me to know what I was up against."

"What else did he tell you?"

Bryce shrugged. "Not much. Does that mean I lose the room you just offered?"

The idea of a complete stranger snooping into her life made her distinctly uncomfortable. There were too many things in the past that she wanted to remain there—not deep, dark secrets, just...private things. The place where she had grown up, the circumstances of her marriage to Terence, the details of that marriage. How much did Bryce Cameron know?

But her manners wouldn't allow her to take back her offer. "No," she said slowly. "If you're finished, I'll show it to you."

She led him through a maze of hallways to the family's private quarters. They walked through a small, cluttered living room, with a smaller dining room and kitchen just beyond, and down the hall to an open door. "You can use this room," she said, her voice a bit cooler than before.

Bryce walked into the middle of the room and looked around. This had been his grandmother's bedroom, a place he had been allowed to visit only when he'd been very, very good—which hadn't been very often, he ruefully recalled. Leah had changed nothing. The mismatched furniture was just as Gran had left it—the big brass bed with its incredibly soft feather mattress; the solid pine armoire that was taller than he was at six feet; the hexagonal marble-topped tables that served as nightstands on each side of the bed, holding the antique brass lamps; the oak-framed cheval mirror; and the pine rocker, draped with a wedding ring quilt that had been made by his great-grandmother. Even the old family Bible still stood on one of the marble tables.

Leah stopped just inside the room. "The bathroom is next door. Dinner will be served at six-thirty in the old ballroom. Do you remember where it is?"

He turned to look at her, his smile reaching his eyes now. "I grew up in this house, Leah," he gently chided. "I remember."

She nodded. "There's a phone in the little room under

the front stairs, and television in our living room down the
hall and in the sitting room. If you need anything, the clerk
should be at the front desk, there's always someone in the
kitchen, and I'll be around somewhere."

Bryce watched her leave, then closed the door and sat
down on the bed, running his hand over the quilted cover.
He had planned such a simple trip—talk to Peter, settle the
past, return to Philadelphia—but nothing was working out
simply. He hadn't considered the possibility that his uncle
might be out of town, or that he might feel such a sense of
homecoming. He hadn't given any thought at all to meeting
his cousin's widow, and he certainly hadn't entertained any
idea that he might *like* her—might even be attracted to her.

He removed his suit coat and tie, tossing them across the
arm of the rocker, then kicked off his shoes and stretched
out on the bed. He was here on business, he reminded himself as he closed his eyes. Strictly business.

He awoke several hours later to the ringing of chimes.
For a long moment he remained still, his eyes closed, trying
to remember where he was. The bed was softer than his
bed at home, and the room smelled of wood and polish and
spices, and just the faintest hint of perfume.

The inn. He was in Gran's old room at the estate, in
Angel's Peak, North Carolina, and the chimes had to mean
dinner, since his stomach was rumbling and the sky outside
the lace curtains was dark.

He felt for the lamp, finally finding the key that switched
on the light. His shirt was rumpled, but with his jacket on,
it wouldn't be too noticeable. Standing in front of the mirror, he knotted his tie and tugged at his jacket. His suitcase
was still in the car, so he combed his hair with his fingers
before he left the room.

He had gone only a short distance when he met Leah in
the main hall. "I was just coming to get you," she said,
stopping before she bumped into him. "I couldn't remem-

ber if I told you that the chimes meant dinner was being served.''

"No, you didn't." For a moment he stood still, letting his gaze sweep over her. She was wearing the same clothes she'd had on that afternoon: jeans and a sweater—casual, easy, comfortable. But she looked good. Very good. The sweater was gray and fitted snugly enough to reveal the soft curves of her breasts and hips without being too tight. Her jeans clung close to long slender legs before disappearing into soft leather boots. Her hair, brown with just a hint of red, curled loosely down to her shoulders. Her mouth was full, her nose small and straight, and her eyes... Her eyes were like the sky—cool, clear and blue. Icy blue.

His expression, faraway and troubled, puzzled her. "Is something wrong?"

Grimly he shook his head. "You're a lovely woman, Leah." And *that* was wrong. She wasn't supposed to be pretty, wasn't supposed to have eyes the color of the sky, wasn't supposed to gift him with rare, fragile, beautiful smiles. And he sure as hell wasn't supposed to like her. Or want her.

Instantly wary, she took a step back. She had no illusions about her appearance. She was passably attractive, but, as Terence had occasionally affirmed, she would never be beautiful. She would never make men stand still in their tracks, or overwhelm them with her loveliness.

That meant Bryce was lying. An odd sense of disappointment shot through her. She had hoped they could be friends—she had precious few relatives, and she would love to welcome a new one into the family—but how could they be friends when he started off by lying to her?

"We'd better go. Colleen, our cook, doesn't like it when we're late," she said. But she made no effort to move; she just watched him with eyes filled with suspicion and doubt.

Bryce grew wary, too. Considering the circumstances, she had been unexpectedly friendly, until he had said she was lovely. His compliment had, for some reason, offended her, but why? Did she expect him to make a pass at her now? If so, she would be disappointed. In spite of the fact that he'd been single—he liked that word better than divorced—for six years, he didn't make passes at women; Kay had taught him that such passes weren't often well received. And he had lacked skill, she'd claimed. Finesse.

The tension between them reminded Leah uncomfortably of Terence; too much of the time spent with her husband had been tense. When the chimes rang again, she gratefully used them as an excuse to turn away. "We'd better go."

He walked silently alongside her, matching his longer stride to hers. When she stopped in the doorway of the ballroom, so did he.

The original dining room had been too small to accommodate the guests, so the ballroom down the hall, which filled half of the first floor, had been converted. The teal-blue walls were stenciled near the top with a floral pattern in deep peach. The same pattern had been enlarged and painted in the center of the high ceiling, where it was shadowed by the lights below. In front of the tall, wide windows, a mahogany table, seating fourteen, gleamed in the light of twin chandeliers. Smaller tables, seating four each, were grouped at each end of the room, covered with dark peach linen cloths and lit with tall, slender tapers in silver and pewter candlesticks. Against the inside wall a fire crackled in the fireplace, filling the air with the sweet scent of pine.

Leah's gaze traveled swiftly around the room, automatically lighting with pleasure at the simple beauty of the room. The large table, along with half the smaller ones, was filled with hungry guests. Her children were waiting at two tables pushed together in the corner, and visitors from town, who made dinner at the inn a Friday night event, filled the others.

As if on cue, the wide doors to the kitchen swung open, and Colleen's staff began serving the dinner. It was roast beef with all the trimmings; Leah knew without looking or even sniffing. The kitchen was Colleen's domain, but planning the menus was Leah's chore.

She wished she could seat Bryce with the guests—there were empty seats at several tables—but that would be rude when there were also empty seats at the family's table. Without looking up at him, she said quietly, "You can sit wherever you like—with the kids and me, or with the guests."

That last phrase sounded hopeful, so he deliberately disappointed her. If she didn't want him around, she would have to say so, though he doubted she could be that ill-mannered. "I'd like to meet my cousins."

She accepted his response with a nod. Greeting the guests as she went, she made her way to the family table, leaving him to follow. There were three empty chairs at the table—two at the closer end and one at the other. She went to the far end, putting the length of the table and one child between them. "We have a guest tonight, kids," she said softly, sliding the chair out. "This is Bryce Cameron. He's your grandfather's nephew."

His brow wrinkled at the odd phrasing. Wouldn't it have been simpler to introduce him as their father's cousin? It started him wondering about her relationship with her husband. During the brief time they had talked, she had never mentioned Terence, not even when she'd explained how she had recognized Bryce. As closely as he and Douglas resembled each other, he and Terence must have looked almost like twins, but she had avoided comparing him to Terence. Because he couldn't compare? he thought with a hint of bitterness. Or because she'd loved her husband too much to bring up his name?

Her soft drawl and the four steady, curious gazes directed his way brought his attention back. She recited the names he already knew, giving each child a gentle smile in turn.

All four children looked alike, with dark brown hair and darker brown eyes. Douglas—who was tall and, judging from the size of his feet, promised to be taller—was at the opposite end of the table. He stood up, circled around and politely shook hands. Laurel and Megan sat on Bryce's right, young and giggling and pretty. On his left, the barrier between Leah and himself, was Matthew. Mimicking his brother, he stood up and gravely extended his hand. "I'm pleased to meet you," he said in a childishly serious voice. "Do I call you Mr. Cameron, Mr. Bryce, or Cousin Bryce?"

When was the last time he'd seen a six-year-old concerned about the proper way to address an unknown relative old enough to be his father? he wondered as he solemnly accepted the small hand. "How about just plain Bryce?"

Matthew shook his head. "We're not allowed to call grown-ups by their first names, are we, Mom?"

She was about to give him permission, as long as Bryce didn't object, when he spoke again. "How about uncle?"

"You can't call him that," eleven-year-old Megan said sarcastically.

"Why not?"

"Because he's *not* your uncle, silly," Laurel replied, sounding bored.

"You can figure it out later." Leah sent a warning look at her daughters as she slid into her seat. "Eat your dinner now, before it gets cold."

The four children monopolized the dinner conversation, relating the events of their day to their mother. Bryce was, for the most part, silent, answering an occasional question from one of the children, observing the way Leah responded to each of them, giving her full attention to each speaker. She was a good mother, he thought with respect. A loving mother. That was the one thing that Kay, in their fourteen years together, had never wanted to be.

As soon as they'd finished eating, the kids left the dining room, leaving Bryce and Leah alone at the table. As he moved with easy confidence into the seat Megan had vacated, Leah wished she had skipped the last cup of coffee so that she could leave, too.

"Your children are very nice. You must be very proud of them."

"Yes, I am." She finished her coffee and set the cup on its saucer.

He glanced out the window at the snow. It was coming down harder, weighing down the shrubs that circled the house. He wanted to talk, to say something that would keep her from leaving the table, but his mind was blank. All he could think of was that he wanted to keep her with him a while longer. "Business must be good."

She shrugged. "We can't complain."

"Is it this crowded during the week?"

"No. We get some guests for a week or two, especially over Thanksgiving and Christmas, but most of our winter business is on weekends."

The silence that settled over them was uncomfortable. He glanced around and saw that more than half the guests were gone. His uneasy gaze also took note of the near-perfect condition of the room. "The house looks good."

"Yes, it does." She scooted her chair back. "If you'll excuse me..."

His mouth thinned into a narrow line. "Why are you so eager to run away from me, Leah?"

Laying her napkin on the table, she stood up and slid the chair back into place. "I have things to do."

And at the top of that list was getting away from him. That was okay, he decided grimly. He could use some time alone.

Leah wanted to flee both the room and the house, but she couldn't just walk away and leave him sitting there alone. She stood stiffly, her hands gripping the back of the chair. "Is there anything you need?" she asked haltingly.

"Nothing that you can give me." He stood up, too, knocking a napkin to the floor, and walked away. All the way across the room he felt her eyes on him, but he didn't slow or turn back. In the hallway he retrieved his coat from the closet and left the house.

He had to brush the snow off the trunk of his rental car before he could open it. The suitcase inside was small and cold against his bare hand. Quickly he slammed the trunk and started back toward the house, bag in hand.

"I would have gotten that for you," came a husky voice from the porch.

Bryce looked up at Douglas. "That's okay."

"It's part of my job. Since you got here this afternoon, I just assumed that you'd already taken your luggage in." The boy watched as Bryce brushed the snow from his hair, then his shoes and trouser legs. "You aren't exactly dressed for this weather, are you?"

Bryce found a smile somewhere inside for his cousin. "No," he agreed ruefully. "I'm not." He noticed that Douglas was bundled up. "Are you going somewhere?"

"Yeah, we have a basketball game tonight. Mark's supposed to pick me up in a few minutes."

"It won't be canceled because of the snow?"

Douglas's grin was engaging. "If they canceled everything every time it snowed, we would have to hibernate all winter. Angel's Peak is the highest mountain in North Carolina, and the town is the highest town. But I suppose you know that, being born here and all."

Bryce put the suitcase down and stuck his hand inside his pocket. "I suppose I must have, but I forgot. I really wasn't expecting this kind of weather."

Douglas leaned back against the wall, seemingly unaware of the cold. "Yeah, the snow's coming early this year. They say we're going to have a hard winter. Of course, a hard winter is great for a town that depends on skiing for its living." He grinned again. "How long are you planning to stay, Mr. Cameron?"

Bryce blinked. "Don't you think there are a few too many of us around here with that last name to be calling me mister? You're almost an adult. Aren't you allowed to call grown-ups by their first names?"

"Only if they say it's all right."

"Well, it's all right with me. As far as how long I'll be here…I don't know. I need to see your grandfather."

"You haven't seen him in a long time, have you?"

Bryce shook his head.

"Why not?"

He liked the boy's straightforward approach. He knew Leah would have liked to ask that, too, but propriety had stopped her from snooping. Still, he had no intention of answering the question. His business with Peter was private.

A car slowed to a stop near the side of the house, and three short honks broke the silence of the night. Douglas pushed himself away from the wall and bounded down the steps. "See you tomorrow, Bryce," he called on his way.

Picking up the suitcase again, Bryce went inside and down the long halls to his room. Unpacking the few clothes he'd brought took only a few minutes; then he sat alone with nothing to do. Most of the guests were in the sitting room—he'd heard their laughter and conversation when he had passed by—but he didn't want to join them. He usually made friends among strangers easily, but tonight the effort seemed too great.

He picked up the heavy family Bible and carried it to the rocker with him. The wooden slats creaked when he sat down and opened the book to the record pages in the middle. Most of the entries, the spidery ones in faded ink, had been made by Gran, the final one dated thirty-nine years ago on the page marked "Deaths": Katherine Johnson Cameron. His mother. Gran's own death had been recorded next, followed by an entry for Terence, only six years ago.

Curious, he turned to the "Births" page and compared dates. Terence had died three months before Matthew's birth. It must have been difficult for Leah, losing her husband in the middle of her pregnancy.

He had told her the truth in the office that afternoon when he'd said that he knew very little about her, other than her name and the names and ages of her children. Now he couldn't resist the urge to find out more, and the family records were a good place to start.

Brief but complete histories of every person who had married into the Cameron family in the last hundred years were listed in the Bible—histories of everyone but Leah. The lines under her name were blank—mother's and father's names, grandparents' names, place of birth, all of them. Her birth date was listed as Christmas Eve; her maiden name was Douglas; she had been seventeen when she married Terence; and less than three months later her son Douglas had been born. That was the extent of the information on her.

Bryce closed the Bible and returned it to the table. He shut off the lights and walked to the lace-curtained window, then stared out at the snow. Leah Cameron meant nothing to him. He was only here to settle his business with Peter, and she wasn't part of that business.

Then he impatiently shook his head. He had never lied to himself before, not even when Kay had left him, and he wasn't going to start now. Leah was a beautiful woman, the kind he should have married—gentle, considerate, kind and loving. It was only natural that he would be attracted to her. There was nothing wrong with that attraction.

As long as he did nothing about it.

Leah stayed busy on Saturday, seeing to the dozens of little details that running the inn required: replacing the fresh flowers in each guest room; helping the staff launder the loads of table and bed linen; making sure the steps and a path to the parking lot were kept clear; overseeing breakfast, lunch and preparations for dinner; checking the firewood supplies, and so on. She saw little of her children and nothing of Bryce.

She told herself that she should be grateful he wasn't around. The man disturbed her more than anyone she'd ever known; at least he was making it easy for her to do her work by avoiding her. No, she corrected herself, it was possible for her to work, not easy. Even though he'd stayed out of her sight all day, he hadn't left her mind. With an awareness far more acute than she would have believed possible, she could *feel* him—a strange, unfamiliar and somehow compelling presence in the house she knew so well.

She told herself it was silly to pay so much attention to him, even if it was only in her thoughts. She had male guests at the inn on a regular basis—men who were more handsome and more charming than Bryce Cameron—and she had never let any of them affect her this way.

But she wasn't *letting* Bryce affect her. It just happened—the way the sun came up each morning and went down each evening. She had no power to control it, and trying just made her tense with frustration.

Taking a break from the piles of mail in front of her, she swiveled her chair around to face the window. The snow had stopped earlier, after depositing more than eighteen inches. The yard and the woods beyond wore a heavy coat of white, presenting a romantic picture from the warmth of her office.

What did she know about Bryce Cameron? Not very much, she admitted with a rueful smile. Peter had done little more than confirm his nephew's existence, something he could hardly deny, since it had been documented in the family Bible. The only child of Frank and Katherine Cameron, Bryce was in his early forties and lived in Philadelphia. He was obviously a businessman of some sort and, judging from the expensive quality of the suit he'd worn yesterday, a successful one. That was all she had learned about him.

A slow smile lighted her face. No, that wasn't all, honesty compelled her to admit. She knew that he was handsome—better looking than Terence, but perhaps not as attractive as Douglas showed the promise of becoming. She knew that he had the warmest, kindest, darkest eyes she'd ever seen. She knew from the captivating smile that came so easily to his lips that he was good-natured and charming. And she knew, from the brief time they'd spent together, that something in him could reach through her defenses and touch her in ways, in places that she'd never before been touched.

The problem was that she didn't want to be touched—not by Bryce or any other man. She had spent more than one third of her life married, relying on a man to meet her physical and emotional needs. Although Terence had met the physical needs—with food and shelter—emotionally, she would have died a slow death, had it not been for the children. She liked her life the way it was now, with no need and no desire for a man—any man.

"And that," she said to herself softly, "most definitely includes Bryce Cameron."

All this worrying was probably for nothing. She felt a strong pull toward the man, but he'd given no indication that he felt the same tug. He was here on business—business that didn't include her—and probably had no interest whatsoever in his cousin's widow. Philadelphia was a big city; if he wanted a relationship, he could easily find plenty of willing women right there at home. He wouldn't bother with one who lived six hundred miles away.

She turned back to the mail on her desk. It was divided into three piles—bills, reservation requests and deposits. The junk mail went directly into the trash, and there were no personal letters. She couldn't remember the last time she'd gotten one of those; her life revolved around her business.

The chimes, faint and distant, interrupted her sometime later. She straightened her desk, stood up and stretched, found a suitable smile and headed for the dining room.

She spent a few minutes talking to the guests, asking the skiers about their hours on the slopes and the nonskiers how they had spent their day. By the time she reached her table in the corner, she was wishing Peter and Martha would return soon. They interacted with the guests so much more naturally than she was able to; after less than two days of playing hostess, she was all out of small talk.

She got her first glimpse of Bryce as she approached the table. He was sitting near the end again—the end where Douglas usually sat. The end where Leah *always* sat. His dark head was bent as he listened intently to something Matthew was saying.

Whatever problem she personally had with Bryce's presence at the inn, she couldn't fault his behavior with the children. So few adults took the time to really listen to kids, and often they were patronizing. Bryce seemed to offer her six-year-old son the same respect that he would give an adult, and she admired that.

She didn't need to look for things to admire about the man, she scolded herself. What she really should do was concentrate on becoming oblivious to his presence.

Strengthening her smile with a deep breath, she slid into the chair on his right and greeted everyone with a soft hello. Matthew paused to return the greeting, then picked up his thought in midsentence.

"...Diplodocus wasn't so bad, because he only ate plants and not other dinosaurs. But Triceratops—he was tough. He had three horns and could even kill Tyrannosaurus, and Tyrannosaurus was the king of the meat eaters," he finished, wide-eyed and breathless.

Bryce's smile was warm. "Maybe you could show me your dinosaur collection after dinner."

"Okay, sure."

Bryce turned his head to include Leah in his smile. "Have you noticed that he can rattle off names just like that—" he snapped his fingers "—that you and I probably couldn't pronounce with a guide?"

"Speak for yourself," she responded. "I've read too many bedtime stories about dinosaurs. I can tell you anything you want to know about Archaeopteryx or Ichthyosaurus or Pteranodon."

His smile deepened, bringing a gleaming light to his dark eyes. "You like being a mother, don't you?"

She raised her hand to indicate the children. "If I didn't, I would be in serious trouble, wouldn't I?" In spite of her light tone, her thoughts were serious. Was there anything she wouldn't do to receive smiles like that on a daily basis? There was such warmth, such genuine goodness in his smiles, and they made her feel good, too.

"I asked Douglas to trade seats with me tonight. Do you mind?"

"No. Why should I mind?" She spread her napkin as Colleen began serving them. "This looks wonderful, as usual," she told the older woman.

"Don't you know by now that everything I make looks *and* tastes wonderful?" Colleen set a plate in front of Bryce, then stood back, hands on her hips, and studied him. "You must be Frank's boy," she said bluntly.

"Yes, I am." He turned his attention from Leah to the other woman. "Do you know my father?"

"I used to, years ago—and your mother, too. They were good people, Frank and Katherine. When did you get back?"

"Yesterday."

Colleen directed a mock glare at Leah. "And you didn't tell me?"

"I didn't know you knew his parents," she said, defending herself, unable to hide the smile that said she knew Colleen wasn't really angry.

The cook picked up two plates from the tray behind her and set them down in front of the girls. "Peter will certainly be surprised to see you when he gets back."

He noticed that she said surprised—not pleased or happy. Just surprised. "I'm sure he will be," he agreed. A quick look at Leah showed that she concurred.

"I was sort of hoping you would leave before Peter and Martha get home," she said hesitantly when Colleen had gone. She was trying to be tactful, but how could she tactfully tell someone that his welcome was about to run out?

"Why are you so anxious to get rid of me? You don't even know why I'm here."

He spoke in a good-natured tone, but Leah sensed that his question was serious, and that he would like a serious answer. "You're right, I don't know," she said after a glance confirmed that the children were involved in their own conversation. "But I *do* know that Peter doesn't want to talk to you. I know that he doesn't want to see you."

He sighed as he picked up his fork. "Do you think I came here because I wanted to? If my reasons weren't important, I wouldn't care if I never saw Peter or Angel's Peak again."

She stared at him, her mouth hanging open. "You don't mean that. He's your family."

"And do you know what family means to the Camerons? Nothing. Not a damn thing. You look out for yourself, and everybody else can go to hell."

She was still staring at him, her expression both troubled and dismayed. He had disappointed her, Bryce thought, regretting his harsh words. Obviously his opinion of Peter as an uncle differed greatly from her opinion of him as a father-in-law and grandfather.

"Look," he said quietly, wearily, "you worship your family, but don't expect me to do the same."

Leah dropped her gaze to her plate. Growing up without a family, she had dreamed and hoped and prayed for one. When she had gotten one through marriage to Terence, she'd made them the most important thing in her life, and now Bryce was telling her that they didn't mean a damn thing. What had happened between him, his father and Peter to make him feel that way?

Bryce laid his fork down again and touched her hand where it rested on the edge of the table. She jerked her eyes upward to meet his. "I'm sorry," he said. Sorry he had offended her. Sorry he had disappointed her. Sorry he had even opened his mouth in the first place. And sorry he couldn't do as she wanted—as *he* wanted: go back to Philadelphia and never see her, or Peter, or Angel's Peak again.

"It's all right," she murmured, but he could tell by her downcast eyes and troubled expression that it wasn't.

She remained quiet through the rest of the meal, grateful when it ended and she could make her escape. A quiet walk in the woods soothed her nerves, but not her worries about Bryce and the effects his presence might have on her family. On *her*. Putting her troubling thoughts aside, she returned to the house in time to read Matthew a story and tuck him into his bed.

"I like our cousin, Mom. He's awful nice." The words were interrupted with a yawn. "Do you think he'll be here very long?"

Disturbed by her son's simple sentiments, she gave a casual response that hid her concern. "I don't know, honey. I don't think so." She smoothed the covers over him, then laid his favorite stuffed dinosaur on the pillow next to him.

Matthew tucked the dinosaur under the blankets and snuggled him close. "He treats me like I'm all growed up. I hope he stays a long time. I hope he lives here with us forever. I love you, Mom. G'night."

Leah turned off the lamp on the bedside table, then watched her son. Within minutes he was deep in sleep, a soft, innocent smile touching his lips.

She loved all her children, but Matthew was her baby. He needed her caring and protection more than the older kids did. And protect him she would, she vowed. Bryce Cameron wasn't going to come here and destroy her family. He wasn't going to break her son's heart. She would make sure of that.

Chapter 2

Bryce lay in bed Sunday morning, staring at the ceiling. He had heard Leah leave her room more than an hour earlier, but he remained where he was, warm and comfortable and troubled.

If he had any sense, he would get dressed, make the reservation for his return flight and leave Angel's Peak once and for all. But each time he decided to do just that, he remembered the sorrow in his father's eyes, his voice, his entire manner. The old man was going to die, and he wanted to make peace with his brother first; he wanted to live out the rest of his life at home. Was that so much to ask?

And was it so much to ask of Bryce that he make the arrangements with Peter? He had come here prepared to cajole, beg, bribe or threaten his uncle—to do whatever it took to get permission to bring his father home again. Now, after only a few hours' exposure to Leah, he was ready to give up and go back home, without even setting eyes on Peter.

Twenty-four hours more. That was all he needed. Peter would be home this evening, Bryce would work out an agreement with him tonight, and he would leave for Philadelphia in the morning. It was another simple plan—one that he was determined to carry out.

Outside the window he heard laughing voices, the slamming of car doors, the revving of engines. The guests were heading out for the day, to the slopes or to do some snowy sight-seeing, he supposed.

There was a knock at the door, sharp and heavy—one that couldn't be ignored. Bryce rolled onto his side and called out an invitation.

Douglas stuck his head in. "Last call for breakfast," he said cheerfully. "The food's on the stove in the kitchen. Everyone else has already eaten. We're all going to church. Want to come?"

Bryce politely declined, and the boy's grin grew wider. "I didn't think so. That's why I brought these—in case you want to go outside." He opened the door wide enough to slip through a pair of waterproof boots. "My feet are probably bigger than yours, but at least you'll stay dry. See you at dinner."

In a few minutes the house was quiet. Bryce got up, showered and shaved, and dressed in his last set of clean clothes. He tugged on Douglas's boots, which were at least a size too big, then went to the kitchen to see what was left over from breakfast.

The silence in the house was eerie. He couldn't remember any place other than his own house in Philadelphia that was so still. Uncomfortable, he drank a cup of coffee and made a sandwich from a biscuit and a slice of ham, then got his coat and gloves from the closet. This was as good a time as any to go outside, as Douglas had suggested.

By the time he'd reached the edge of the yard, he had chosen his destination. Back in the woods, far away from the inn and the two guest houses, was the family cemetery, where his mother had been buried almost forty years ago, and where Gran had been laid to rest fourteen years later. He hadn't been there since he was fifteen, but he easily found the path that led into the woods. There was a road farther back, barely wide enough for a car, but he chose the winding path that circled and snaked through the densely growing trees. It was quiet here, too, but this was a natural quiet, the only noises the tramping of his footsteps and the occasional crackle of a twig.

Suddenly he emerged into a clearing. Surrounded by an iron and stone fence, the cemetery was large and filled with crosses and headstones. The oldest grave was that of old Abraham, the man who had built the house in 1787, then died three years later. The ones Bryce was looking for were side by side near the back. He had to brush the snow away to read the names.

Katherine Johnson Cameron, wife of Francis Patrick Cameron. She had died when Bryce was barely two. His only memories of her came from old photographs in his father's albums. She had been a rather plain woman, fragile and unsubstantial-looking. He didn't know her, but she had been his mother.

Next to her was Anna Dawson Cameron, his grandmother. She was the one he remembered—the one who had raised him, comforted him, punished him and loved him. She had taught him about life, about joy and satisfaction and peace. She had prepared him for the day when all this—the house and the land—would be his. Then she had died; and Peter, not Frank, had inherited the estate, and the family had been torn apart. Was it too late to put it back together? he wondered.

He realized that he was cold and that he was being watched at the same time. But when he first turned, he saw no one, and he put the feeling down to his location. Even on sunny, bright winter Sundays, a cemetery wasn't the most pleasant place to be. Then he heard a crackle and found the slender figure that was trying to slip away, unnoticed, into the woods.

"Always running away," he said softly, shaking his head.

Leah stopped and approached the gate. "I wasn't running away. I didn't know you were here until I saw you, and I thought you might like to be alone."

"Why? It's a cemetery. These people aren't here—they're gone forever."

She pushed her hands into her pockets. "This is the last place I would expect to find a man whose family doesn't mean a damn thing to him."

His face flushed a dark bronze. "You're not going to forgive me for saying that, are you?" Without waiting for an answer, he continued. "My father is the only family I have, and I love him. Peter, Martha—they can go to hell."

"Does that include your cousins?"

"My—" He realized that she meant her children. He hadn't quite gotten used to the idea of having cousins. "I like your kids, but it's not as if we're really family. I didn't even know they existed until a month ago."

Leah gestured to Anna's tombstone. "Your grandmother was proud of being a Cameron—proud of her house and her land, of her sons and her grandsons. It would break her heart to hear you talk this way."

He opened his mouth to argue, to ask where she got off telling him anything about Gran, then shut it again. She was right. If Gran knew what had happened to her family after her death, she would be ashamed to claim any of them.

Walking through the gate, Leah followed his footsteps in the snow to stand beside him. "How is your father?"

The sun glinted off her hair, setting the auburn tints afire. Resisting the urge to touch it, to see if the curls were as soft as they looked, Bryce turned his gaze away. "My father?" he echoed.

"Yes—Frank. How is he?"

"He's all right," he answered cautiously. There was enough truth in the statement to keep it from being a lie, but not enough to be called honest. "Why do you ask?"

She bent to wipe more snow from the front of Katherine's marker. "Your father's an old man—in his seventies now, isn't he? And after spending more than half your life elsewhere, you suddenly come home, determined to see Peter." She waited silently, hoping that he would tell her something, anything, about the reasons for his return. It was more than curiosity that prompted her—she wanted trust. She wanted him to trust her enough to confide in her. She wanted honesty.

Bryce looked at her for a long, long time, his dark eyes solemn and unrevealing. He weighed the merits of telling her the truth, knowing that she might take Peter's side and use it against him, versus lying, knowing that she would probably guess it was a lie and look at him with the same disappointment that still haunted him from last night. Or he could say nothing at all. Still holding her gaze, he chose the latter course and kept silent.

She nodded and took a step back, breaking his hold on her.

To stop her from turning away, he asked, "Why aren't you at church with the kids?"

"Someone has to stay at the inn."

"But you aren't at the inn."

She smiled. "I will be in ten minutes."

"Can I walk back with you?"

She wanted to say no, but she couldn't. Giving him a tight little smile, she started away, leaving him to follow.

"So what do you do when you're alone at the inn on Sunday mornings?" he asked, catching up with her.

"Paperwork...check on Colleen's dinner...enjoy the quiet."

"Too much quiet can drive you nuts." He knew that from experience. There were times when he hated to go home to his empty house. It had taught him the meaning of the term "deathly silence."

She gave him a chastening look. "I have four children, two in-laws, between three and thirty guests, and ten to fifteen people on staff. There's no such thing as too much quiet around here.'' When they crossed the driveway Leah turned on impulse and walked to the front of the house. Bryce unquestioningly followed.

She walked at a leisurely pace, scuffing her feet in the snow, enjoying the clean, fresh wintry scent in the air and pretending to ignore the man at her side. She loved winter—the weather was cold and the snow was plentiful. More importantly, it brought the holiday season. Every holiday was celebrated at Cameron Inn, but the winter holidays were special. Thanksgiving, Christmas and New Year, added together with Douglas's, Megan's and Leah's own birthdays, made November and December a joyous season at the inn.

Her birthday. She gave a soft sigh that brought Bryce's chocolate-dark eyes to her. This year she was going to be thirty-six years old, give or take a few months. No one at the home had known when she'd been born—they had taken her word for her age, and the day had been chosen at random. Long ago she had quit questioning it, had quit longing for a real birthday, a day to celebrate that was her own. She was content to call herself a Christmas baby.

''Something wrong?''

She stopped walking to look up at Bryce. With a faint smile she shook her head. She didn't mind growing older—she didn't feel old, anyway, until she realized that, a few days after her birthday, her oldest child would turn eighteen. Could she possibly be the mother of a newly matured adult?

Bryce wanted to bring her attention back to him. He wanted her to look at him, to talk to him in that soft, sensuous drawl he found so enchanting. His gaze settling on the house in front of them, he fixed on a subject. ''Whose idea was it to turn Gran's house into an inn?''

Together they studied the house. It was two stories tall and painted a pure, brilliant white. A veranda completely encircled it, its roof was supported by slender round pillars.

Sets of black wooden shutters flanked every window, and the wide ornate door was also painted black. Wide stone steps led to the veranda, and at the top sat a basket spilling over with pumpkins left over from Halloween and the multicolored gourds and ears of Indian corn that had been gathered for Thanksgiving.

"It was my idea," she admitted softly. She had spent many long hours fixing up the house that had been her inheritance when Terence died. Seeing what she had accomplished filled her with pride. Old Abraham would be pleased to know that the house he'd built with his own hands had survived two hundred years in such a lovingly cared-for state. He might not like the fact that it was now an inn, Leah acknowledged with a wry grin—she had definitely detected a note of hostility in Bryce's voice—but at least it was cared for.

When Terence died, opening an inn had seemed logical. The huge old house was far too big for Leah and the children, and Peter and Martha had insisted that they were happy living in the guest house. It had been a big gamble, but Leah had seen no other choice. She hadn't worked outside the home during her marriage, so her only marketable skills had been her ability to run a household efficiently and her willingness to work hard. She had wanted a job that would allow her to spend time with the children, and she had needed one that would let her keep the house she loved so much. Opening an inn had been the perfect answer.

She tilted her head back to meet his eyes. "You don't approve, do you?"

He didn't try to deny it; instead he smiled sheepishly. "I have to admit, when I first heard about it, I didn't like the idea. The only thing worse than an inn would be making it a museum."

"The Camerons do whatever it takes to keep what's theirs," she said with forced lightness.

And to take what they wanted, he grimly added. His

uncle Peter had taught them that lesson well twenty-six years ago. "What about you, Leah? Are you a Cameron in name only, or would you do whatever it takes, too?"

She gave him a long, cool look. "I suppose that depends on what's at stake."

"The inn? Your children? Your comfortable little life?"

He saw the flash of emotion before she succeeded in hiding it—annoyance, anger, defensiveness. She was fiercely protective of the things that were important to her—the inn, the children, Peter and Martha. Would she love a man as fiercely? he wondered. Had she loved Terence that way? He wanted to know—needed to know—but knew she would freeze up and walk away if he asked.

"I need to get to work," she said quietly, warily. "Excuse me."

He wanted to keep her with him, so, perversely, he let her go. When she left him standing alone in the center of the yard, some of the warmth went with her, making him shiver.

He had a couple of hours to kill before the kids returned from church. Inside, he changed from Douglas's boots into his own shoes, then set off to explore the house, to see what changes Leah and her inn had made.

The living room was at the front of the house, across the broad hallway from the ballroom. It was a large room, with pale yellow walls. Graceful moss-green leaves curving around tiny dark gold flowers were stenciled at the tops of the walls, and the dark yellow was repeated in the fireplace, the window trim and the moldings over the doors. Elegant draperies in white striped with gold hung at each window, framing the winter views outside. Portraits of long-dead Camerons hung on the walls, keeping watch over their home. The furniture was old, some of it faded or scratched, but all of superior quality. The rug in front of the fireplace was old, too, its rich reds, blues and greens faded after more than a hundred years of use.

The next room was the sitting room. Here the color

scheme was reversed, with dark gold walls and pale yellow accents. The furniture was sturdier, not so ancient, and most of it was grouped around the single piece that spoke of the twentieth century: the television set.

There were other rooms—the ballroom, the original dining room, the library, the study, another smaller sitting room—and they were all the same: polished and dusted and waxed, lovingly kept in perfect condition. The only concessions to the present were electric light and television.

He chose not to climb the stairs. All the rooms up there were bedrooms, and all were occupied by guests this weekend. He would have to ask Leah to show them to him when the guests were gone.

He sank down into a wing chair in the second sitting room, tilted back his head and closed his eyes. He liked what she had done with the house—or rather, what she *hadn't* done. It was still beautiful—still home. He had almost hoped to find terrible changes, reasons to dislike her, but she had given the house the same respect Abraham had had when he built it, and the same love Gran had shown when she lived in it.

There was a timid knock at the door, one that he ignored in the hope that whoever it was would go away. But the door swung silently open, then shut again; and a soft little voice inquired, "Are you asleep or just resting your eyes?"

He opened them to see Matthew standing beside his chair. "Just resting them," he replied. "You have to do that when you get old."

"You're not old, not really. Grandpa is, but you're only about as old as my dad. Were you and my dad friends?"

"Sort of—we were cousins."

"Can't you be friends with cousins? 'Cause that's what we are."

Bryce easily lifted the boy over the high arm of the chair into his lap. "Yeah, we can be friends."

Matthew relaxed easily against Bryce's chest. "But you didn't like my dad," he continued.

How could he tell a six-year-old boy who had never known his father that he was right—that Bryce had never liked Terence? "You know how sometimes Laurel and Megan tease you and don't want you hanging around because you're too young?" he asked, hoping that the girls were like all the girls he'd known when he was a kid.

Matthew rubbed his nose. "Yeah, I know."

"Well, you still love them when they're mean to you, because they're your sisters, but you don't really like them. That's how it is for cousins sometimes. Sometimes your father and I just didn't get along." Like ninety-nine percent of the time, he finished silently.

"You look a lot like my dad. I seen a picture of him at Grandma's house."

The innocent remark raised several questions in Bryce's mind. Why didn't Peter and Martha live in the main house along with Leah and their grandchildren? And why did Matthew have to go to his grandmother's house to see pictures of his father? Why didn't Leah have pictures of her husband in their living quarters, for the kids, if not for herself? That brought him back to his earlier unasked question: had Leah loved Terence deeply? Did she still love him? Or had their love died, the way his and Kay's had?

"His name was Terence, and he died 'fore I was born," Matthew said solemnly. "I don't know much about him—Mom never likes to talk about him." He gave a heavy sigh. "I wish he was still here. I'm the only kid in my whole first-grade class that don't have a dad."

Bryce didn't know what to say. Even though his mother had died when he was small, he didn't really know how the boy felt. He'd had Gran to replace his mother, so he had rarely missed Katherine. "Do you like being in the first grade?"

The boy raised his head and gave Bryce a knowing look. "You're changing the subject. That's what Mom says Douglas does when he does something wrong and doesn't want to get in trouble for it." He rubbed his nose again.

"Yeah, school's okay. But I don't like homework, and I don't like going when I could be outside playing in the snow." His stomach growled, and he looked down at it, his eyes lighting. "I knew I was supposed to tell you something. Mom says dinner is ready and for you to come on. She says someone always has to find you when it's time to eat."

Bryce could practically hear Leah saying it. "Well, come on," he said, getting to his feet, holding Matthew in his arms. "Let's not keep people waiting."

"Oh, they won't wait. Miss Colleen says that if us kids aren't at the table on time, then our food can just get cold, because she isn't gonna keep it warm for us." He wriggled to the floor when they reached the dining-room door and led the way to their table.

"I was beginning to wonder if you'd gotten lost," Leah said as Matthew sat down next to her.

"*Mom.*" He spread his napkin over his lap, then said with a strong dose of self-importance, "I was talking to my cousin."

The girls snickered, but were silenced by a stern look from Douglas. Leah frowned at all three of them before glancing at her youngest son. Matthew still hadn't decided what to call the older man—his sisters had vetoed "Uncle"; he didn't like "Cousin Bryce"; and he didn't want to use the first name alone. It amused his sisters, but Leah was worried about the importance Matthew had placed on the title and, through that, the man. Once Bryce completed his business with Peter, he would return to Philadelphia, and they would probably never see him again. How would Matthew feel then?

She looked at Bryce, who was cutting the roast chicken on his plate. "Peter called about an hour ago."

He met her gaze, surprised, but hiding it behind an expressionless mask. He waited patiently for her to continue.

"He and Martha will be home around five o'clock."

"Did you tell him that I'm here?"

She flushed. "No."

She was hoping he wouldn't be. She was hoping he would be polite enough, well-mannered enough, to leave before then, without causing trouble. He wasn't. "I guess he'll find out soon enough, then."

There was another flare of disappointment in her eyes, which set off a responding flare of anger in his own—anger, not surprise. He wasn't measuring up to the standards she had set. Well, according to Kay, he rarely measured up. His failures with his ex-wife had been many and painful. Why should Leah be any different?

He didn't speak to her during the rest of the meal, although he took part in the children's conversation. Leah was torn between relief and regret. The last thing she needed was Bryce's attention. The last thing she wanted was his anger.

When dinner was over, she sent the kids off to play, then headed for the front desk. Vicky, the clerk, wouldn't be in until four o'clock, so Leah was filling in for her. She began checking through the records, preparing bills for the guests who were scheduled to leave that evening.

"Can I talk to you?"

The sound of Bryce's voice made her stiffen, and the little hairs on her neck stood on end. Slowly she raised her head to see him leaning his elbows on the polished mahogany counter. "What do you want?" she asked cautiously.

Now that she was listening, he wasn't sure what to say. He wanted to talk to her about Matthew, but the boy was really none of his business. If Leah perceived his concern as meddling or criticism, she would be offended or, worse, hurt. But he felt that what he had to say was important— out of line, maybe, but important.

She waited quietly. Four children and occasionally demanding guests had taught her patience.

He chose to overcome reluctance by leaping in—possibly over his head. "It's about Matthew. We were late for dinner because we were talking. About his lack of a father.'' He watched her closely and saw the dismay pass through her eyes. He had been right: she was offended.

She rose slowly from the high stool. Standing in front of him, she could see directly into his eyes. ''If you have any questions about Terence, I would prefer that you ask them of me and not of my children.''

He was definitely in over his head—way too deep. Her eyes were angry and bright, as frigid as the sky outside. He broke contact with them and took a step back. ''I didn't ask him anything!'' he snapped in self-defense. ''He mentioned that I looked like the picture of his father that he'd seen at Martha's. Why don't you have any pictures of Terence here? Why don't you ever talk to Matthew about his father?''

''This is none of your business.'' She spoke in a calm, flat, unemotional voice, then turned away with a dismissive gesture.

But Bryce wasn't going to be dismissed so easily. He circled the counter, blocking her only escape. ''Whatever your feelings for Terence, he was Matthew's father. The kid has a right to know about him.''

''‘The kid’ is *my* son, and I will decide—'' She stopped suddenly, forgetting what she'd been about to say. He was too close. Her pink sweater came within a breath of touching his green one, and she could feel the heat from his body. She could sense his eyes on her, willing her to look at him, and at last she did.

His eyes were just like Terence's—dark and mesmerizing. His nose was a little too big, his mouth too hard, his jaw too square, but he was more handsome than any man she'd known.

Bryce, too, had forgotten their conversation. He breathed slowly. He couldn't name her fragrance, couldn't even think of words to describe it. It was simply…wonderful.

He drew in a deep breath so his voice would be steady when he spoke. Instead the increased intensity of her scent made his mind go blank. The only word he spoke was her name, and it was merely a whisper.

Leah trembled. She wanted to move away, to run as fast as she could and hide, but she couldn't take a step without touching him, and she knew that would be a mistake. She had to stand there, had to wait until he let her go.

Without thought he lifted his hand. Briefly, hesitantly, gently he laid it on her hair. A coppery mix of brown and red, it was soft and sweetly scented.

Would one kiss cost either of them too much? he wondered, gliding his fingers over her curls before dropping his hand to his side. He was leaving tomorrow; would it be too risky to kiss her, just once, before he left?

Before he'd found the answer to that, he'd already taken action—by tentatively brushing his mouth against hers. He felt her stiffen, might even have heard her gasp over the pounding of his heart. But she didn't push him or run away or demand that he leave her alone, so he did it again.

Her lips were soft, bare of color, and her mouth tasted warm and sweet. He resisted the urge to pull her to him; instinct told him that she wouldn't accept his embrace so easily. He had to satisfy himself with her mouth, with its moist softness and the shy touch of her tongue.

The telephone on the desk beside them jangled, startling them apart. Leah gasped, and Bryce swore silently. He took a step back as she answered the phone with a welcoming, "Cameron Inn." After a moment she extended the receiver to Bryce.

He took it, wrapping his fingers around the warmth left behind by hers. His heart rate, which had been slowing after the kiss, was increasing again. Only two people knew to call him here—his secretary and his father's doctor—and neither would call unless it was an emergency.

"Mr. Cameron, this is Dr. Upton." The cardiologist's voice, for all its feminine softness, was businesslike.

"What's wrong?"

"Your father has had a little setback today. He seems to

be all right, but this morning, and again this afternoon, he's had a series of transient ischemic attacks. These attacks are associated with hypertension and atherosclerosis, both of which he has. The first attacks lasted only a few seconds, but the last ones have been between five and ten minutes each.''

Bryce stared at Leah but didn't see her. His voice was quiet and hoarse when he asked, ''Is this serious?''

Leah busied herself sorting the registration cards with fingers that trembled, but she couldn't stop herself listening to his end of the conversation. She wished she could leave, to give him privacy for the call—to give *herself* privacy to deal with what had just happened—but he was still blocking the only way out and showed no interest in moving.

''It can be,'' the doctor answered. ''T.I.A.'s are often the precursors of strokes. Now, I've made arrangements for your father to be examined right away by a neurologist. There don't seem to be any problems at this time. In the periods between attacks he's lucid and understands what's going on, but to be on the safe side, I think you should cut your trip short and return to Philadelphia today, if at all possible. I've talked to Frank about it, and he would like to have you here.''

''All right. I'll be there as soon as I can.'' There were thin, tight lines around his mouth when he hung up the phone. His hand remained on the receiver. ''Do you have the airline numbers handy?''

Wordless, she found them for him. Bryce dialed the first number while speaking to her. ''Well, you were hoping I'd leave before Peter got home. You're getting your wish. Can you get my bill ready?''

He couldn't make it to Asheville to catch the next flight, so he booked a seat on the following one. When he hung up, he looked expectantly at Leah.

''There's no bill,'' she said with a shrug. ''You were our guest.'' She wanted to say more, to offer him some sort of reassurance. The news he'd received had obviously been bad; he suddenly looked tired and ten years older. She wished she could offer him comfort or just a shoulder to lean on, but she couldn't.

He looked at her for a moment. There were things he should say—things he should do—but he had waited too long. After a moment, she looked away. Turning sharply, he went to his room and quickly packed his bag, then went to find Matthew. In his search he found each of the other three children and said goodbye, but Matthew, the most important and the most elusive, wasn't around.

Leah was still at the front desk when he was ready to leave. "We'll continue our conversation at a later time," he warned her.

She looked up with a calmness she didn't feel. "Will we?" Would he be back? Would he care to see her when he came back?

"We will." He studied her for a moment, his gaze on her mouth, full and soft and set in a very faint smile. She was thinking about the kiss. He smiled, too. "I'll be back, Leah, and we'll finish that, too," he promised. He took a few steps toward the door, then turned back. "I couldn't find Matthew. Tell him I'll call—"

"No." Concern for her son overrode her concern for Bryce. "I'll tell him that you had to leave unexpectedly. I'll tell him that you said goodbye, but I won't tell him that you're going to call."

His eyes narrowed suspiciously. "Are you forbidding me to call him?"

"No." Clasping her hands together to hide her uneasiness, she continued softly. "Matthew is a cute kid—he's polite, friendly, bright, and he likes you. He's pleasant company while you're here, but when you get home...? How long will it take you to forget a nice six-year-old kid?"

He was angry—blindingly angry. Only the realization that she was trying to protect her son from disappointment stopped him from unleashing his temper on her. "I like Matthew—better than I like anyone else around here. I'm not going to string him along, then let him down. I don't take my pleasure in life from hurting kids.''

. Leah took a deep breath. She was shaking—both from her own emotions and from the intensity of Bryce's. ''I didn't mean to imply that you did. But he's a little boy— a little boy who never knew his father, who's always wanted a dad, who's finally met you. You not only look like his father, but you like *him* as much as he likes you. Don't you see what that means to him?''

He did. Matthew was looking for a father, and he thought he'd found a good candidate in Bryce. It was something he would worry about later. ''I'll call him,'' he said flatly. ''Goodbye, Leah.''

He closed the door behind him and walked quickly to his car. He was almost there when Matthew came racing up. His little brown eyes took one look at the suitcase, then met Bryce's gaze. ''Where're you going?''

Bryce put the suitcase into the trunk, then lifted Matthew. ''I was looking for you inside. I have to go back to Philadelphia. Something's happened, so I have to leave today.''

Matthew clasped his hands behind Bryce's neck. His gloves were cold and damp from the snow. ''Something bad?''

Bryce thought of his father, so thin and frail in his hospital bed, and nodded gravely. Yes, something bad.

''When will you be back?''

Not ''*will* you be back?'' Bryce noticed, but *when*. He was beginning to understand the saying, ''the faith of a child.'' It hadn't occurred to Matthew that he might not return, that he might not care enough about the family home or his new cousins to come back again. ''I don't know,'' he said softly, honestly. ''First I have to take care of the problems at home.''

''Okay.'' Matthew hugged him, then slid to the ground. ''Be careful.''

Sometimes the boy was so serious that he reminded Bryce of a three-and-a-half-foot-tall adult. ''You, too. I'll see you soon." As soon as he said the words, he knew that Leah wouldn't approve. Well, that was too bad. He *would* see Matthew again soon, and he couldn't care less what Leah thought about that.

Early Sunday evenings were busy at the inn. Most of the guests, who were scheduled to be back at work the next day, waited until the last possible moment to check out, so Leah and Vicky had their hands full.

It was during a brief break that Peter and Martha arrived home. Leah left the desk to hug her mother-in-law. "Did you have a good time in Atlanta?"

"It was wonderful." Martha looked at her husband and actually blushed. "It was just wonderful. Did you have a good weekend? You weren't too busy, were you?"

"We got along fine—but I'm glad you're back." She rose onto her toes to kiss Peter's cheek. "I'm glad you're back, too," she teased.

"Did anything interesting happen while we were gone?" he asked gruffly as he helped Martha remove her coat.

"Just had the same old stuff," Vicky said.

Not quite the same old stuff, Leah silently corrected. She would have to tell her father-in-law about Bryce's visit—but not yet, not when he and Martha hadn't even settled in. Maybe after one of Colleen's delicious dinners, when the kids were tucked into bed and everyone was satisfied and relaxed...

But the choice of when to tell them was taken from her by the arrival of Megan and Matthew. Peter swung his grandson into his arms and gave him a bear hug, then demanded, "Did you miss me?"

Matthew was grinning. "Sure did. But guess what, Grandpa? I met my cousin—we all did—and he's really nice, and I liked him, and he told me—"

Leah didn't hear what Bryce had told Matthew, because her troubled blue gaze was locked with Peter's. The old man's smile was fading, and his eyes were dark with that stubborn look that she was beginning to associate with the Cameron men. Martha was looking worriedly from her husband to her daughter-in-law, and Vicky seemed puzzled. Even Megan felt the tension between the adults in the room.

Sensing that he'd lost his grandfather's attention, Matthew laid his hand on Peter's cheek. "Grandpa, are you listening to me?" he asked impatiently. At least his cousin always listened, even when other grown-ups were around.

"What cousin, Leah?"

If she hadn't known Peter so well, the coldness in his voice would have frightened her. Linking her hands together, she came forward, brushing her hand over her son's hair. "Bryce Cameron."

The sound Peter bit off was a curse, swiftly stopped when he recalled that the children were present. "He was here?"

"Yes."

"In this house?"

"Yes. I don't think this is the time or the place to talk about it, Peter."

He looked from her to the children, then nodded. "After dinner?"

She silently agreed.

"Well, where are Laurel and Douglas?" Martha asked, reaching for a bag she'd set down when she greeted Leah. "I believe I have some small gifts here for my grandchildren, if someone could find the missing two." Her cheer sounded false, but the kids didn't notice.

"I'll find them, Grandma," Megan offered.

"And I'll help," Matthew chimed in.

Finally tearing his eyes from Leah, Peter said quietly, "I think I will, too." He took Martha with him when he left.

Alone once more with Vicky, Leah sat down behind the counter. The clerk pretended to be busy for a few moments, then gave up and faced her boss and friend. "This Bryce—who is he?"

Leah knew that Vicky had seen him over the weekend;

she was asking for specifics. "Bryce's father Frank is Peter's older brother."

"I didn't know Peter had any family besides you and the kids. Where has this brother been hiding?"

Leah's smile was strained. "Frank and Bryce left Angel's Peak before you were born. They live in Philadelphia." When the younger woman would have asked another question, Leah quickly and transparently changed the subject. "Do we have any more brochures on the inn around here? I think we're running low. Could you check and make a note to order more if we need them? I'm going to see if Colleen needs any help with dinner."

Only a handful of guests remained for dinner that night. As soon as the meal was finished, Leah asked Douglas to put Matthew to bed while she, Peter and Martha went to the small sitting room down the hall for a private talk.

Peter barely gave her a chance to sit down before he demanded, "Tell me about Bryce. What did he want? What did he say?"

Leah clasped her coffee cup in her hands, feeling the warmth seep into her fingers. Outside the narrow windows snow was coming down again, a light, fluffy white powder. An unusually harsh winter had been predicted for the Blue Ridge Mountains, and these early heavy snows seemed to bear out those predictions. She didn't mind. She liked snow.

"Well?"

"He wanted to see you, Peter. I don't know why—just that it's important to him." She remembered their conversation in the cemetery that morning and added, "I think it might be about his father."

Peter's eyes shifted away from hers—almost guiltily, she thought. "What about Frank?"

"I don't know. I think you should see him, Peter. He's your nephew, and Frank is your brother. Except for us—" she indicated herself and Martha with a nod "—and the kids, they're the only family you've got left in the world."

"You think family is so important, don't you?" He smiled at her with a touch of pity. "Just because someone is family doesn't make them worthwhile. Families aren't perfect, wondrous, magical creatures, Leah. They're human beings—people just like you and me. They've got flaws."

Family *was* important to her. It came from all those years of growing up, of wishing more than anything in the world to be part of a family—anyone's family. "What flaws could Frank and Bryce possibly have to make you act this way? You've spent a third of your lives separated by some old argument. How can you refuse to even talk to Bryce, just to find out what he wants?"

Peter's scowl was fierce. "The last person in this world I want to talk to is Bryce Cameron! You want to know about his flaws? He is a selfish, deceitful, lying son of a—" Once again he bit off the word. Lifting one trembling hand to his face, he rubbed his temples for a moment.

A selfish, deceitful, lying son of a bitch. Leah tried to reconcile those words with the man who had spent the weekend with them. The man who had treated her six-year-old son with more respect than most adults afforded other adults. The man who had kissed her, who had made her feel things she'd never felt, who had made her long for things she'd given up hope of having.

"The man who came here was polite and friendly," she said carefully. "The children liked him." And so had *she.*

Peter's smile was sardonic. "He fooled you, didn't he? You looked at him with those damn naive and innocent eyes, and he knew exactly how to make you believe what he wanted you to believe."

Leah didn't like what he was implying, but she couldn't argue. For a woman who had been married twelve years, she *was* naive. She *was* innocent. Had it been that obvious to Bryce? Was that the reason behind his warm, friendly gestures, his compliments, his faultless behavior with her children—to get all five of them on his side? Had he strung them along to achieve his purposes?

"He's coming back, Peter," she said, ignoring her punctured ego. "He's not going to give up until he gets what he wants."

"What he wants is to destroy me!" His voice thundered in the quiet elegance of the room, making Martha jump.

"You don't know that!" Martha exclaimed, unable to remain silent any longer. "Bryce is not a vindictive man—"

"How do you know? How do you know what kind of man he is?"

Martha sank back in her chair. "No, you're right," she agreed sadly. "Thanks to you, I haven't seen him since he was a boy. I *don't* know what kind of man he's become."

"Well, *I* do! Remember when I called him, when I tried to talk to him? Remember what he told me?" Peter was enraged, his face white, his breathing ragged.

"Yes." Martha's answer whispered in the air. She laid her hand on her husband's arm. "I remember. But that was six years ago—*six years*. How long does it have to go on? Bryce is no more stubborn, no more difficult than you. Why can't you forgive him for being a Cameron and meet with him? See what he wants?"

He shrugged off her hand and surged to his feet. "He can rot in hell for all I care!" he shouted. "Do you understand me? In hell!"

The room was eerily, heavily silent following his departure. Martha's shoulders sagged; Leah was uncomfortably still. At last she spoke. "He's going to come back, Martha." She was more sure of that than anything else in her life. "What do you want me to do?"

Her mother-in-law shook her head. "I don't know." Bowing her head, she gathered herself, then looked up. Now, she seemed stronger, younger, more vital. "Do what you feel is right, Leah."

"Even if that means welcoming him to the inn again?" She knew that was a good possibility, in spite of Peter's reaction. "He makes Peter so angry."

"It's not Bryce," Martha said. "Peter is angry with himself, I think, more than anyone else. What he said—about not being worthwhile just because you're family—I think he was talking about himself. I don't think he feels he deserves to be on good terms with Frank again."

Leah wanted to ask what had happened so many years ago between the two men, but she kept the question to herself. As much as she wanted to know, the details would have to come from Peter himself. She wouldn't pump her mother-in-law for information.

"Well, dear, I guess I'll go home." Martha laid her hand on Leah's shoulder.

"Let me get my coat and I'll walk with you." Leah got her jacket and a knitted scarf and gloves from the closet, then stopped in her room long enough to change her moccasins for knee-high waterproof boots.

"We really did have a lovely time in Atlanta," Martha remarked as they strolled across the back lawn.

"I'm sorry this had to spoil the weekend for you."

"Did it spoil *your* weekend, Leah?"

Giving the older woman a sidelong glance, Leah saw the smile touching her face. What would Martha like to hear? she wondered. That Bryce had been an unwelcome burden? That the family had liked him? That Leah had been attracted to him? "No. For the most part he was pleasant company."

"For the most part?"

"He seemed a little bitter, especially about the family. He said...that the Camerons look out for themselves and everybody else can go to hell." She repeated the sentiment hesitantly, not wanting to upset Martha. The other woman's laugh surprised her.

"Well said, Bryce." Then she tempered her words. "In a sense he's right. The family as he knew it *was* selfish. Peter wanted what was best for himself, Terence and me, and Frank wanted the same for himself and Bryce."

"That's called love, Martha, not selfishness."

"A wrong committed in the name of love is still wrong." Martha climbed the steps to the porch of the guest house, then turned back to Leah. "Are you going to take a walk?"

"Yes."

"Be careful." She sighed softly. "I can't tell you what to do about Bryce, Leah. Trust your own judgment. Do what you think you should."

As far as advice went, Leah thought as she wandered into the quiet woods, Martha's was worthless. She wanted her mother-in-law to tell her what to do, what to say, what to feel. She didn't want to trust herself; when it came to men, she wasn't a very good judge of character. She only had to look at the mistake she'd made with Terence to know that.

If only Bryce hadn't touched her, hadn't smiled at her—Lord, if only he hadn't kissed her. When was the last time she had received such tenderness from anyone, let alone a man? When he'd laid his fingers against her hair, he had been so gentle that she had barely felt it. When he had kissed her...

Her cheeks burned with the memory. If a mere kiss could have such an effect on her, she was even more naive and innocent than Peter suspected. But Terence had never shown her gentleness—not before their marriage, and certainly not after. She had always believed that someday he would change, but she had finally accepted that he wasn't a gentle man.

Since his death, she had kept herself neatly divided into compartments. There was the mother, the daughter-in-law, the friend, the innkeeper—and, buried down deep, there was the woman. No one had been allowed to touch that part of her; no one was allowed to make her feel the things a woman felt—the wants, the needs, the desires.

Until now. Bryce Cameron made her wonder. How would it feel to be loved by a man? To be held and touched so gently, to be liked as well as loved, respected as well as desired? How would it feel to be loved by Bryce?

Some tiny bit of romance that had survived Terence was curious, but clearheaded common sense prevailed. She didn't need a man. She didn't need Bryce. She had her children and her in-laws. She loved them, and they loved her. It was enough. She would make it enough.

Chapter 3

Bryce stood next to his father's bed. The old man was asleep and had been since he'd arrived more than half an hour ago. On the opposite side of the bed stood Dr. Upton, one of the best cardiologists in the state. She definitely had to be one of the prettiest, too, Bryce thought with quiet detachment.

"The symptoms of transient ischemic attacks vary a great deal," she was saying. "As do the effects. But the neurologist was with him earlier, and it's his opinion that at this time there's been no permanent damage."

Edging forward, Bryce picked up his father's hand. It was bony, covered with papery-thin skin. "Why?" he asked. "Why him?"

"As I told you, they're associated with both hardening of the arteries and hypertension, and they're more common in men. Your father was at high risk."

"His heart attack had nothing to do with it?"

"No. T.I.A.'s are a disease of the brain, not the heart."

"You said these usually mean the patient's going to have a stroke."

"Well...generally. But that doesn't mean he *will* have one. It just means that he's a strong candidate." Dr. Upton looked at her patient for a moment, then turned her attention to Bryce. "Why don't you go home and get some rest? Chances are good that he'll sleep through the night."

Chances were also good that he could have another attack, or a stroke. Chances were looking really good that he could die. Bryce shook his head. "I'll leave in a little while."

She shrugged. "All right. But don't wear yourself out."

When she left, the room was still. All the lights but the one above the bed were off, casting dark shadows in the corners. Bryce sat down in one of those corners and watched his father, simply watched him.

After Katherine's death, Bryce had been raised by his grandmother. When she died, too, Frank had completed the job, giving his son every bit of love he possessed. Now it was time for Bryce to give it back. Whether his father had a few more weeks, a few more months, or—please, God—a few more years, Bryce was going to see that he was happy. He was going to take Frank back to Angel's Peak. He was going to do whatever it took—*anything*—to see his father living once again in the Cameron family home, in the house that was rightfully his. No one could stop him this time— not Peter, not Martha and the kids, not even Leah.

The memory of Leah, so soft and sweet when he'd kissed her, made him smile, but only briefly. In the six hours since he'd left her and Angel's Peak behind, he had been trying to convince himself that an involvement with Leah Cameron was the last thing he wanted.

He couldn't deny that she was pretty—outright lying was out of the question—but there were thousands of prettier women right here in Philadelphia, starting with Dr. Upton. He wouldn't deny, either, that she had touched him in ways no woman but Kay ever had. But look where it had gotten him with her: he'd had fourteen years of a marriage that had ended in pain and heartache.

There could be no future with Leah for him. As much as he liked children, he wanted his own, not another man's. Her home, her life, her friends, all were in Angel's Peak; his were in Philadelphia. He knew instinctively that she wasn't the type of woman to indulge in meaningless affairs; any relationship she established with a man would be a serious one. There was no way she would settle for the only thing he could give—the only thing he was *willing* to give: occasional weekends, and nothing more.

He had less than a week to make himself believe all his well-meaning excuses. Friday, if Frank was all right, Bryce was going back to Angel's Peak. He would see Leah again, and this time he would see Peter. This time he would fulfill the only request his father had ever made of him.

Leah's steps slowed when she heard a childish giggle from behind the closed door of the telephone room under the front stairs. There were only four guests at the inn this week, and all of them were out for the day. That giggle had to come from Matthew, home with a cold. Just who would he be talking to on the phone when all his friends were in school?

She knocked at the door and waited until he invited her inside. He was curled up in an armchair, the phone braced between his ear and shoulder, looking as if he was thoroughly enjoying himself. Leah took a seat in the other armchair and waited until he said, "Just a minute. My mom's here."

"Who is that?"

Matthew didn't think to cover the receiver. "My cousin."

She stared at him, bemused. So Bryce *had* called. Although she hadn't mentioned the possibility to Matthew, she was both surprised and grateful. It was nice to know that he'd kept his word. Honorable men weren't that easy to find.

Matthew listened for a moment, then held out the phone. "He wants to talk to you."

To say, "I told you so"? Leah wondered. She accepted the receiver and raised it to her face. It smelled of lemons, like Matthew's cough drops. "Go ask Miss Colleen to give you some orange juice, sweetheart," she suggested. When he was gone, she said a cautious hello.

"You were wrong about me, weren't you?" Without giving her a chance to reply, Bryce continued. "I told you I would call him. This is the first chance I've had."

"What do you want? Congratulations? An apology?" She sounded testy. "One phone call is easy. What if he expects more?"

The good humor left over from his conversation with Matthew fled, leaving annoyance in its wake. "You are damn hard to please, lady."

"I'm not asking you to please me. I'm asking you to leave my son alone, not to let him expect more than you're going to give. When do you get bored? When does someone else catch your interest? When will you call him again? When will he ever see you again? There's a lot of responsibility to the kind of relationship you're starting here—"

"Don't preach to me about responsibility or relationships," he interrupted sharply. "I don't get bored with people, Leah, and I'm perfectly capable of showing interest in more than one person at a time. I don't know when I'll call him again, but as for seeing him…I'll be there Friday."

She was silent for a long time. What was she thinking? he wondered. Would she welcome him…or throw him out the door?

She had known that this time was coming. Since her talk with Martha Sunday evening, she had known that Bryce would return and that she would have to decide how to deal with him. In the three days since then she had done a lot of thinking about him, but she hadn't yet reached a decision.

"Leah?"

Loyalty pulled her in different directions—loyalty to the family, and loyalty to Peter. Family was so important to her, and she hated to see Peter pretend his brother and nephew didn't exist. She wished she could make him appreciate that side of his family, too—could make him at least talk to them. For that reason, she wanted to tell Bryce that he was welcome.

But Peter was also very important to her. It was only his influence that had persuaded Terence to accept his responsibility when she was seventeen, alone and pregnant. Had it not been for Peter and Martha, her twelve-year marriage would have been as bleak and cold as the home where she'd grown up. If he didn't want to see his nephew, what right did she have to interfere?

"Leah, I'm not trying to cause trouble." Unless trouble was what it took to gain Peter's cooperation. "I just want to see my uncle. I want to settle some things. No one's going to get hurt, believe me."

"You don't know how angry he was when he found out that you'd been here."

His chuckle was soft and intimate. "I can imagine. He and Dad were always too much alike for their own good. They're both hotheaded and more stubborn than mules. Leah…"

Why did her name sound so soft and sensuous coming from him? It was only two little syllables that took about a second to say, yet it brought to mind images and emotions that she knew were better left forgotten.

Trust your own judgment. Do what you think you should.
Martha's admonition echoed in her mind, and it prompted her to answer his unasked question. "All right."

Now it was Bryce's turn to sit in silence. What was she agreeing to? Just a visit? Or a return to the house? "Then…you don't mind if I come."

"No." She closed her eyes and hoped she wasn't making a grave mistake. "You're welcome to stay here, if you'd like."

He could think of nothing he would like better. "Thank you. Then I'll see you Friday."

"Have you made your reservations yet?"

He hesitated. Admitting that he had seemed rather arrogant, but he couldn't lie to her. "Yes, I have. I'll get into Asheville about five."

"I have to pick up some guests at the airport at five-thirty. If you don't mind waiting, you can ride back with us...unless you prefer to rent a car." She squeezed her eyes shut. She was digging herself in deeper and couldn't seem to stop. Why had she offered him a room and a ride? Why couldn't she let him take care of his business with Peter himself, with no help from her?

Because he was family. Not hers—she couldn't think of him as one of her relatives; that persistent romantic in her refused—but her children's, and Peter's.

"I'd like that," he was saying. "I'll be waiting. Could I speak to Matthew again?" Quickly he qualified that. "Just to say goodbye, okay?"

She sighed softly. "Okay. Hold on."

Matthew was waiting outside the door, his eyes bright and shining. This phone call from Bryce had been better than all the cold medicine in the world, Leah reflected as she left her son alone. She just hoped that Bryce knew what he was doing.

Bryce didn't expect Leah to meet him at the airport; when it was time for her guests to arrive, he supposed, she would show up. Until then he could pass the time thinking. Planning. Scheming. In spite of the transient ischemic attacks, Dr. Upton had pronounced Frank ready to leave the hospital in a few days, and this was where Bryce would bring him. To North Carolina. Home. He just had to make Peter see it his way.

Even without expecting Leah, he picked her out of the crowd the moment he saw her. He stood motionless, quiet, watching her approach. In the time it took her to reach him, he'd made a complete inspection—and found everything to his liking. She was wearing a hip-length silver coat with a rose-colored scarf wrapped around her neck. The sweater underneath the open coat was blue, and her jeans, tucked into a pair of dark brown boots, were relatively new and unfaded. Her hair was a bit tamer than it had been last week, the curls more orderly. The memory of how silky they had been against his fingers made him want to touch them again. The memory of her softness, her scent, her warmth, made him want to do a lot of other things—things he couldn't allow himself to think about. Not here.

Leah tried to ignore the increased tempo of her heart. It was just because she had hurried inside, out of the bitter cold, she insisted. Nothing else.

"Hi."

She echoed his soft greeting, then said, "The others will be here in about half an hour. Would you like to get some coffee while we wait?"

Bryce nodded. He would like anything that meant time alone with her, time to look at her, to talk and to have her undivided attention.

She shrugged out of her coat, then led the way to the coffee shop, taking a seat at the first empty table she came to. She ordered two cups of coffee from the waitress, then folded her hands together on the tabletop, suddenly tongue-tied. What could she say to this man, this stranger who had entered her life such a short time ago and taken such a strong hold that she couldn't wrench herself away? She had decided only five days ago, on a snowy, late-night walk, that she didn't want or need a man in her life, not Bryce Cameron or anyone else. She wasn't going to be charmed by him, she had thought, or kissed by him, or touched—physically or spiritually—by him. And now here she was, sitting across from him, her good intentions shot to hell.

She was unable to remember *why* she didn't want a man; all she could think of was why she wanted *this* man, the kiss he'd given her, the longing he had awakened in her.

Bryce broke the silence after the waitress poured their coffee. "Aren't you glad to see me?" he asked, but Leah didn't answer. She was too well-bred to tell the truth and too polite to lie, he thought. "You know, you *did* tell me that I would be welcome," he good-naturedly reminded her.

She inclined her head. "Yes, to stay at the inn."

But not to get too close to the innkeeper. He didn't mind her distance. He would deal with that later. "How is Matthew's cold?"

"Fine."

"And how are you?"

She smiled faintly. "I'm fine, too."

If it had been left up to her, that would have been the extent of their conversation, but Bryce wasn't inclined to sit in silence. That made it too easy to look at her, to appreciate her loveliness, to think about her softness, to hunger for her tenderness. "Do you always play chauffeur to your guests?"

"No, only to the special ones." She flushed slightly as she realized what her reply implied—that Bryce was special.

It made him smile. She didn't give easily...but when she did, she would give everything. Everything that he'd told himself he didn't want and couldn't have.

"Providing transportation isn't a regular service of the inn," she went on awkwardly. "But these three people were our very first guests, and they've come back ever since on a regular basis, every few months. They deserve a little special treatment."

He let the ensuing silence lengthen while they drank their coffee. Finally, twining his fingers together around the warm cup, he raised his eyes to hers. "I'll give you two topics of conversation to choose from: Matthew, or Peter. Which would you like to discuss?''

Talk of Peter might very well lead to an argument, which she didn't want. But talk of Matthew would *definitely* lead in that direction. She chose her father-in-law.

''Does he know that I'm here?''

She shook her head. She still hadn't resolved her guilt over keeping Bryce's visit secret from Peter, but, as Martha had told her, she had to do what *she* thought was right.

''Why didn't you tell him?''

She traced a neatly rounded fingernail over the pattern in the tabletop. ''He was very angry when he found out that you were here last weekend. I thought it would be best not to tell him that I had invited you back.''

He laid his hand over hers, stilling its motion. ''Wait a minute. *You* didn't invite me—I invited myself. Keep that straight, all right?'' After a pause he asked, ''What did he say?''

His hand was big and warm, lightly clasping hers. Leah concentrated on that warmth, that slight connection, so she wouldn't have to look at him. ''He said you can rot in hell for all he cares.''

Bryce absently rubbed his thumb over the back of her hand. The skin there was soft, fragile—like the woman. With an effort he forced his mind back to the conversation. So Peter wanted him to rot in hell. Was that the reason for the distance Leah had placed between them? Had Peter told her about his past attempts to be reconciled with Frank, when Bryce had stood in the way, adamantly refusing to allow brother to speak to brother? If he had, Leah, so loving and loyal to her family, probably would have condemned him and his actions to hell herself.

But she had agreed to let him return. She had offered to pick him up at the airport, and she was letting him touch her. He thought it more likely that his uncle had simply given Leah his opinion of Bryce's character, rather than any specific details about the past; otherwise she wouldn't be here with him.

"What else did he say?" His eyes were grim, his mouth a thin, taut line.

"That you're a selfish, deceitful, lying son of a bitch." And that you used my children and me. That you knew I was naive enough to fall for whatever line you wanted to feed me. But she couldn't say the last aloud. If it wasn't true, his actions would bear it out. If it was, she would be ashamed to see it in his eyes.

"Do you believe it?"

She allowed herself to look at him. The expression in his eyes was somber, almost bleak, as if her answer truly mattered to him. She searched her mind for the answer but found it in her heart. "No."

Maybe she was being foolish. She had warned herself only last weekend that she wasn't a very good judge of character—especially male character. But her reply was honest. She didn't want to believe that Bryce was the kind of man who could callously use her and the kids, especially Matthew, for his own purposes. She didn't want to believe that she could be attracted to a man like that.

He smiled then, that full, bright, warm smile that made her forget her troubles. Raising her hand to his lips, he pressed a soft kiss on it. "Thank you." Then he quickly released her hand before he could think about keeping it forever and stood up. "It's almost five-thirty," he said in an almost-normal voice as he pulled some money from his pocket to pay for the coffee. "We'd better meet your guests."

As soon as she found her passengers, Leah introduced them to Bryce, then suggested that they get their luggage so they wouldn't miss Colleen's dinner.

The guests, a husband and wife and their teenage son from Charleston, insisted that Bryce sit in the front seat of the station wagon with Leah. Familiar with every member of the Cameron family, they questioned Bryce with friendly curiosity most of the way to Angel's Peak, making private conversation impossible. Very much aware of him at her side, Leah was grateful for the respite. Once at the inn, though, she was left alone with him again, while Vicky checked in the guests.

"You'll have the same room," she said as she walked along the broad hallway, Bryce at her side. "Dinner will be served in about five minutes, so don't be late."

He went into the room, setting his suitcase down next to the bed. One lamp was already on, the covers had been turned down, and a dish of spicy-scented potpourri was sitting on the marble table. The room was almost as welcoming as the woman behind him.

Bryce returned to the doorway and leaned against the frame. Leah had continued past his room to the sole door on the opposite side of the hall. "Is that your room?" He hadn't asked last weekend—not because he hadn't wanted to know, but precisely because he had. Now he couldn't stop the question.

She looked over her shoulder. "Yes."

He caught a glimpse of the bed right inside the door. She would be sleeping less than twenty feet from him. He liked that idea. "Who else has rooms around here?"

Leah felt the color warming her cheeks. "The children's rooms are upstairs."

His smile became a grin. "So it's just you and me on this floor."

She nodded.

Interesting. He crossed his arms over his chest and watched her enter the room and close the door. He remained there for a moment, alone in the hall. If he could keep his mind on business, this trip could end quickly, and he could return to Philadelphia, to his father. But as he turned back into his room, he caught a faint whiff of Leah's fragrance, and he knew he didn't want any of those things—didn't want to keep his mind on business, didn't want to end the trip quickly or to return to Philadelphia.

He wanted to stay here a while in Gran's old room, and he wanted to watch Leah—to look at her, listen to her, smell her scent. He wanted to see her smile, maybe even hear her laugh. He wanted to touch her, to hold her and kiss her.

He wanted to make her his.

Damn it, he wanted too much. He'd always been satisfied with what he had; even as a child, he had never fallen into the trap of wishing for things he couldn't have. And Leah fitted both categories: she was too much, and he couldn't have her. He told himself that sternly—how many times had he repeated the warning in the last week?—but he was beginning to resign himself to the fact that he was still going to want. He was still going to wish.

Leah was on her way to the dining room a few minutes after the chimes sounded when Douglas stopped her in the hallway. "How do I look?" he asked, running his fingers through his hair.

She took a step back to study him. He wore a crewneck sweater in a creamy beige with neatly pressed jeans. She looked wistfully at him for a long moment. He was almost eighteen—all grown-up. For so many years he had been her little boy, but now she could see the man in him. When had he gotten so big, so old?

"Mom?"

She smiled almost sadly. "You look fine, honey. Where are you going?"

"Tonight's the dance at school. I told you about it, remember?"

Her thoughts had been so full of Bryce that she had forgotten. Now she nodded ruefully. "Yes, I remember. Are you taking Tiffany?"

Blushing faintly, he nodded, and Leah smiled. Tiffany Wells was the dream girl in this year's senior class—very pretty, head cheerleader, homecoming queen, class president, talented actress, honor student, and a nice girl, as well. All the girls were jealous, and all the boys were in love with her. And my son's dating her, Leah thought with vicarious satisfaction. How things had changed from her own high school days in Angel's Peak, when no one had even known that she existed.

"You won't wait up, will you?"

She raised her hands palm outward. "If I'm up, it won't be because of you, I promise." More likely because the guest across the hall from her wouldn't leave her thoughts long enough for something as unimportant as sleep. Rising onto her toes, she kissed his cheek. "Be careful, please."

He returned the kiss quickly, then shrugged into his coat. "See you tomorrow."

When the door closed behind him, she continued her trip to the dining room. As usual on Friday nights, it was full.

"Does Douglas have a date?"

She looked over her shoulder to see Bryce standing there. "Yes," she murmured in answer.

"Doesn't that worry you? How old is he—seventeen?"

Her eyes narrowed and chilled by ten degrees. He knew—somehow he knew the circumstances of Douglas's birth. And those of her marriage? Had he found out from his father's sources, or his own? "Douglas is a good kid, and his girlfriend is very nice," she replied stiffly.

Belatedly he remembered the dates he'd found in the family Bible last weekend—dates that had shown that Leah, seventeen at the time of her marriage, had given birth to Douglas less than three months later. He had spoken carelessly, but he hadn't meant to offend or criticize her. Lifting his hand to rest it lightly on her shoulder against the silkiness of her hair, he said softly, "Even nice girls sometimes get trapped."

Trapped. Leah moved away from his touch, suddenly, sharply. How many times had she heard that word from Terence—that she had trapped him in a marriage he didn't want, with a woman he couldn't love and children he didn't need?

"We'd better sit down," she said stiffly, gesturing to the

corner table where the younger three children sat. "They're waiting."

"Douglas has a date tonight," Megan said as soon as her mother sat down. "With Tiffany Wells."

"I know, hon, I just saw him." Leah spread the dark peach linen napkin over her lap, then glanced at Bryce as he took the seat next to her.

Laurel and Megan gave him the warm greeting reserved for family members, while Matthew left his seat, solemnly shook Bryce's hand, then suddenly reached up for a hug. The scene tugged at Leah's heart. Earlier she had refused Bryce the opportunity to discuss his friendship with Matthew, hoping to avoid the confrontation, but now she knew that she couldn't put it off much longer. Matthew was a friendly boy, but he rarely offered physical contact to anyone outside the family; now here he was, giving Bryce his heart. She had to assure herself that the man knew what to do with it.

"Where are Peter and Martha?" Bryce asked. "I assumed they had their meals here, with you."

"Grandma and Grandpa went to eat in town," Laurel informed him. "There's a new restaurant, and Grandma asked Grandpa to take her there."

"A French restaurant," Megan added with a scowl. "I bet their food isn't as good as Miss Colleen's."

"No, honey, I'm sure it isn't." Leah smiled at her younger daughter, then turned her head to include the other two. The warmth stopped just short of Bryce. Resentment of the three children flared to life inside him, then died just as quickly. She would smile at him—*for* him—soon. He promised himself that.

When dinner was over, Bryce went with Matthew to the boy's second-floor room, and Laurel and Megan went to the sitting room to watch television. After making sure that everything was in order for the night, Leah followed a routine she had started many years ago: she gathered her coat, scarf and gloves from the closet and went outside for a quiet, moonlight walk.

The idea of walking for pleasure was one Terence had never quite grasped. Walking was something you did when you had no other choice. So Leah's nightly walk had been a solitary one, even then. At times it was the only peaceful hour she found.

The woods surrounding the inn and the guest houses were quiet, the snow knee-deep in places. She made her own trail to the cemetery, still and peaceful in the glow of the moon. The tombstones were odd-shaped humps of stone covered with snow. Only two inscriptions were visible, those that Bryce had cleared last weekend, marking the graves of Katherine and Anna Cameron.

"You actually hang around graveyards in the middle of the night?"

She hid both the brief spark of fear and the following stronger spark of pleasure that his voice had brought. By the time she turned to face him, her face was calmly, serenely blank. "It's not even eight-thirty."

Bryce checked his wristwatch in the bright moonlight. "It's eight forty-nine. Why are you here?"

"Why did you follow me?"

"To see where you were going."

"Why?"

He answered simply, honestly. "I wanted to be with you." It was that easy to explain. One moment he'd been in Matthew's room discussing dinosaurs and had seen Leah through the window; the next, after changing into the boots he'd brought with him, he'd been following her tracks in the snow. "Do you often come out here alone at night?"

She tilted her head to one side, and the end of her scarf swung free. Bryce resisted the urge to tuck it back into place. "There's nothing to be afraid of in a cemetery. Dead people can't hurt you. It's the ones who are still alive who do that."

Amen to that, he silently whispered. He moved closer to her, until only two feet of snow separated them.

His next question came out of the blue, softly, gently, and totally unexpected by either of them, but once it was asked, he realized that he wanted to know. He needed to know. "Did Terence hurt you?"

Leah stared at him for a long time, sensations racing through her—shock, surprise, fear, pain. She rewound her scarf, giving him a gleaming glimpse of her hair before the dusky rose fabric covered it again. "I'm going back to the house."

He laid his hand over her wrist. "Wait." He wanted an answer. He wanted to hear her say no, her husband hadn't hurt her. He wanted to hear that she had loved Terence, and that he had loved her. He wanted to hear that their marriage had been long and happy, because he had to believe that, sometime in her life, Leah had been happy.

Her eyes, as cool as his were warm, dropped to his hand. He wore gloves, and the thickness of her coat sleeve and her own glove protected her from his touch, but she felt it anyway. She wished that he would remove his glove and her scarf and touch her hair. She wished that he would touch *her*, in those ways that made her feel.

Dangerous wishes. Dangerous man. Pulling her wrist free, she took a step back, then another, until she'd reached one of several small paths that cut across the cemetery. "I'm going back to the house," she repeated numbly.

Bryce walked alongside her, not bothering to talk. He knew she wouldn't answer him, and he didn't like the sound of his own voice enough to break the night's stillness.

When they reached the house, Leah started up the back steps. Bryce took her arm once more. The tension that held her captive was strong enough for him to feel it through her sleeve. He released her and linked his hands together behind his back. "You don't have to run away from me, Leah."

"I'm not running away."

"Are you afraid of all men...or just me?"

She stood two steps above him, looking evenly into his eyes. "Are you so sure of yourself with all women...or just me?"

He leaned back against the railing and stared up at the sky. What would she think if he told her that the confident air was just that—an air? What would she think if he told her about Kay and the words she had used to describe him? Selfish. Boring. Unsatisfying.

Sometimes he forgot Kay's insults, like when he'd kissed Leah at the desk last Sunday. Other times he didn't care. Tonight he did. Would Leah find him an unsatisfying lover? Would he ever have a chance to find out?

He climbed one step, bent his head, brushed a kiss across her lips and murmured, "Good night, Leah."

After the door closed behind him, she pulled one glove off and touched her fingers to her mouth. Just a kiss—that was all it had been. A brief, insignificant little kiss. It wasn't enough to satisfy, yet it was more than she could handle.

"Please," she whispered, her fingers still covering her lips. "Let him go home soon...before it's too late."

With a shiver she went inside the house to her office, hanging her coat on the back of the chair. She heard the laughter from the sitting room down the hall before she closed the door, but wasn't tempted to join in. The family and the staff took turns playing host to the guests. Usually Leah enjoyed their company, but tonight she was grateful that it was someone else's turn—anyone else but herself. Tonight she preferred working alone to gaiety and cheer.

She turned her attention to the schedule for the holiday season's parties. The first would be next Saturday, the weekend before Thanksgiving; she and Martha had completed the arrangements for it several weeks earlier. It would be followed by nine more celebrations, including holidays and birthdays, in the next seven weeks. She would be exhausted by the end of the year, but pleasantly, comfortably so.

When the knock came at the door, she knew without asking that it was Laurel; only her older daughter could manage to sound so timid. "Come in."

"We're ready for bed, Mom," Laurel said, tugging her robe around her. "Do you want to read to Matthew, or should I?"

Leah pushed her papers into a file and rose from the desk. "Why don't you read to Matthew *and* me?"

"Okay." Laurel slipped her arm around her mother's waist as they left the office. "Grandma says you work too much."

She chuckled softly. "Someone's got to do it, honey."

"When I'm a little older, I can help with your paperwork. That'll be more fun than doing dishes or making beds." She made a face as she spoke to indicate her dislike of housework.

"When you're a little older, honey, you'll have too many other things on your mind to worry about paperwork."

"You mean like boys." Laurel gave a shake of her head, sending her long brown hair swinging. "Not me. I'm not ever going to like any boys."

"She's only saying that 'cause Travis is going steady with Darla Wells." Megan was sitting on the back stairs, her feet hidden in fuzzy pink slippers with huge rabbit ears flopping to each side. When they passed, she jumped to her feet and followed.

Laurel's only response to her younger sister's teasing was to stick out her tongue. When they reached the private living room, Matthew was waiting on the sofa. He handed his book to Laurel, then climbed into Leah's lap to hear the story.

It was a cozy little family scene, Bryce thought from his position in the dark kitchen, with Laurel in the center, Megan on one side, and Leah and Matthew on the other. All that was missing was a father.

How many times, early in his marriage, had he envisioned just such a scene—Kay and himself and their children? It had taken four years of Kay's unyielding insistence that she didn't want children to chase such thoughts from his mind. He had loved his wife and had accepted her decision. Now he was forty-one, almost too old to have children, and Kay was gone. If he had known, back when she was refusing to have a baby, that eventually their love would die and their marriage end, maybe he would have gotten a divorce then and found a woman who wanted kids—a woman like Leah.

But Leah had already been taken.

He cut off that train of thought and stepped farther back into the shadows. He should have made his presence known when Matthew skipped into the room a moment ago. Now he couldn't leave without being seen by the family in the living room. He felt ridiculously guilty, as if he were spying on them—and wasn't he?

Laurel read in a low, quiet voice that sounded so much like her mother's. Lamps at each end of the sofa cast bright circles of light over its occupants, but the rest of the room was deep in shadow. It was warm, snug and peaceful.

When the story was over, each of the children gave Leah a hug and a kiss, then trooped down the hall. The second floor of their wing could be reached only by the back stairs near the kitchen. Bryce listened until the scuffling sounds of their feet were gone, then waited for Leah to leave the living room so he could go to his own room.

She reached across to turn off one lamp, then stood up. But instead of leaving, she turned toward the kitchen. When she flipped on the light switch and saw Bryce standing there, she stopped short, folded her arms across her chest and waited.

His expression was a cross between embarrassment and guilt. "Only a mother could look so disapproving."

She moved past him to take a glass from the cabinet. After filling it from a pitcher of water in the refrigerator, she gestured toward his glass. He held it out for a refill and murmured his thanks.

"Do you do that every night?"

"Usually." She took a long, cold drink.

"That's nice."

"Yes," she agreed quietly. "It *is* nice. It's one of the few private times we have as a family."

She was too polite to say it more bluntly, but he received her message, anyway: he had intruded on their privacy. He changed positions uncomfortably. "I didn't mean to eavesdrop. You were all there before I had a chance to leave."

"You could have passed through at any time."

"Correct me if I'm wrong, but I got the impression after our walk that you'd really rather not see any more of me tonight."

It wasn't "our" walk, she silently protested—it was *hers*. She didn't want to think in terms of "our" with Bryce. She didn't want to share anything with him. It was too pleasant, too warm, too lovely a thought, and it would be too painful. After pouring the remaining water into the sink, she set her glass on the counter and turned to leave. At the bar that separated the kitchen and dining room, she looked back. "You're right," she said quietly. "I'd rather not see you again." She walked away.

Bryce set his glass next to hers. If she had said the words as an insult, he wouldn't have minded. But she hadn't spoken in anger; she had simply told the truth: she would be happier if she never had to see him again.

He was amazed at how much the truth could hurt.

Leah awoke early Saturday morning. For a few minutes she took the luxury of doing nothing, simply lying in bed and listening to the stillness. It was barely six-thirty; the younger children would sleep until at least eight, and Douglas, who had sneaked up the stairs shortly before one-thirty, would probably sleep even later. She doubted that many of the guests were up yet, and those who were, were considerate enough to be quiet.

With a sigh, she rolled from the bed, her feet making contact first with a braided, heart-shaped rug, then the cold wooden planking. Tugging on her robe, she hurried down the hall to the bathroom, closing the door quietly behind her. She adjusted the water temperature in the shower, tugged a brush through her hair, then shed the robe and stepped into the tub, drawing the plastic curtain shut.

Minutes later she stepped out again, drying herself quickly with a pale green bath sheet that reached to her knees. She towel-dried her hair while the steam cleared from the mirror. For a moment she studied her reflection.

Last weekend Bryce had called her lovely. Now she looked at herself and saw what he had seen and wondered again at his lie. She wasn't lovely, wasn't pretty, not even attractive. Her hair lay in wet curls more suitable to Laurel or Megan than to an almost thirty-six-year-old woman and was touched at the temples with a few silvery-gray strands. Her nose was crooked, her mouth was too thin, and her eyes were such an odd shade of blue.

Turning on the hair dryer, she began running her fingers through her hair while the warm air moved over it. Every woman deserved one man who thought she was beautiful, she mused. For a time she had thought Terence was that one man for her. It hadn't taken long for him to shatter her illusions. He hadn't thought she was beautiful. In the last years of their marriage, except for his occasional visits to her bed, he hadn't thought of her at all.

Working quickly and efficiently, she used the blow dryer to relax her curls, then changed them into soft waves with a curling iron. She spritzed the waves with hair spray, letting that dry while she dusted her body with her favorite powder, sprayed her wrists and throat with perfume and switched the towel for her robe.

After styling her hair so that it curled gently away from

her face, she tidied the bathroom and returned to her room to dress. The steel-gray crewneck sweater that she tugged over her head barely disturbed her hair; she brushed it back into place with her fingers. She added her favorite pair of snug-fitting, button-fly jeans and a pair of white leather high-top tennis shoes, then left the room.

She looked more like a kid than a mother and business-woman, Bryce thought, waiting for her in the hallway. It was only when he reached those ice-blue eyes that he could see her age. There was something somber in their depths that came from years of learning and growing. Some of her lessons, he realized, hadn't been easy.

He pushed himself away from the wall. Before he'd taken two steps toward her, he could smell her fragrance—faint, sweet, enticing, sexy—and it tied his stomach in knots. It was too early in the morning to be feeling this way, he protested silently. After the encounter in the kitchen last night, he hadn't slept well; then he had awakened to the sound of the shower next door and known that it was Leah. Now he had to look at her, to smell her sweetness, to hear her voice. Did she know she was causing him this torment? He didn't think so—not yet, at least. He was going to have to tell her, though, because they were going to have to do something about it—together. And soon.

Leah closed her bedroom door, then waited for Bryce to speak. He looked so comfortable, so at ease with himself and his world, as if nothing ever bothered him. Seeing her had no effect whatsoever on him, while seeing *him* sent her whole system haywire. He was so handsome in khaki slacks and a navy-blue sweater that she couldn't even think of the proper words to say in greeting.

"I want to see Peter this morning."

She tried to ignore the faint disappointment that suddenly curled in her stomach. Hadn't she expected as much? Peter was his reason for being here—certainly not her.

"I'll call him and see if—"

He interrupted. "I just want to go over there, to his house. Let me talk to him." He realized that he was asking for her permission, even though he didn't need it. Since he knew she wouldn't give him her approval, he at least wanted her permission.

She nodded once. "All right. They live in the guest house across the driveway."

He nodded, too. He was familiar with the house; his aunt and uncle had lived there long ago, too, when his grandmother had lived in the main house. Stepping forward, he laid his hand on her shoulder. "Leah…" The tip of his finger slid underneath the knit ribbing and rubbed slowly back and forth. Her skin was soft, powdery and warm. Was she that soft all over? he wondered, adding another finger and letting them glide farther until the sweater covered them to the joint.

"Don't do that." She sounded husky but very certain.

He drew back his hand. "Where will you be when I finish with Peter?"

"Around the house."

Once again he nodded; then he turned and walked away. Wearing a heavy leather jacket, he left by the back door.

It was cold outside. Every breath he took seemed to freeze a little more of his insides. It had to be that, he insisted to himself. It couldn't be nervousness at finally seeing his uncle again.

The two guest cottages stood behind the main house, separated by the driveway. He passed the one he and his father had shared and carefully climbed the snow- and ice-covered steps to the second one.

Martha answered his knock with a warm smile that slowly faded when she recognized him. Bryce was preparing himself for a less than welcoming greeting when she took a step forward, wrapped her arms around him and hugged him close. "Welcome home, Bryce," she whispered.

Chapter 4

Martha led him through the living room to the eat-in kitchen, where Peter was seated at the table, the remains of his breakfast in front of him. He was pouring cream into his coffee when he saw his nephew, and the thick white liquid dribbled onto the lace tablecloth. Forcefully setting down the pitcher, he stood up and faced Bryce. "What the hell are you doing here?"

Pretending that he hadn't given the reason at least a half dozen times already, Bryce patiently repeated it. "I need to talk to you."

"If it's about your father, I don't want to hear it."

"You know it's about my father, and you *are* going to hear it." He paused for a moment while he looked at his uncle. Tall, thin, gray-haired, he was proof that the family resemblance never faded away; Peter looked as much like Frank now as he had thirty years ago—just a little bit younger and a whole lot healthier.

Realizing that his uncle was staring back at him, and that Martha was staring, too, Bryce said what he'd come to say, quietly, forcefully. "I'm bringing my father back to Angel's Peak. He's coming home."

Peter was angry, and as stubborn as an old mule. "I won't have him here! Not in this house!" he declared once Bryce's meaning sank in.

"No," the younger man mildly agreed. "In that house." He gestured through the bay window to the inn. "He's going to stay at the inn. He's going to die in the house he was born in." He paused. "In the house that should have been his."

Martha was in the process of pouring a cup of coffee for Bryce. Her hand shook, splashing the dark liquid. "Is Frank sick?" she asked, her eyes wide with concern.

"He's been in the hospital in Philadelphia for more than a month now. He's had two serious heart attacks in the last year and a half." Bryce spoke dispassionately, but his aunt could see his emotion.

"Is he dying?"

"He could live another twenty years, or he could die next month. He wants to come home. He's been away too long." His voice hardened when he looked at his uncle. "And I promised him that I would arrange it."

"I don't want him here," Peter said with a scowl.

"He's your brother, Peter," Martha chided. "Apart from us, he's the only relative you have left in this world."

"I *don't* want him here!"

Bryce gripped the back of the chair in front of him. "Damn it, Uncle Peter, I don't care what you want. He's an old man, and he's sick and he's scared. I'm bringing him back."

"Hmm. He's just looking for a way to get us out of here. He swore he'd never forgive or forget what happened then."

Bryce rolled his eyes upward and sighed. "He's an old man," he repeated. "He doesn't have the strength to try to get the house back. He doesn't care about it anymore."

Peter walked to the window to stare at the inn. "Do you

expect me to believe that? That this place means nothing to you or your father anymore?''

''Of course it means something. It was our home for a long time.''

''You plan to take it back, don't you? That's why you've been using Leah and the kids—getting close to them so you can turn them against me.''

Bryce reached the end of his patience with a jolt. ''My friendship with Leah and her children has absolutely nothing to do with you. Don't ever, ever suggest that to her.'' There was both a warning and a threat in his voice. If Peter did anything to hurt Leah...

Taking a calming breath, he dragged his fingers through his hair and sighed. ''Look, my life is in Philadelphia. I don't want to live in Angel's Peak again. I'm here for Dad, no other reason. He wants to see his home, and you. He wants to set the past aside and enjoy what's left of the future, and he thinks he can't do that without you. He needs you, Peter.''

His uncle's laugh was ugly. ''He needs me?'' he echoed. ''Remember when *I* needed *him*? Remember when my son died, and I needed to talk to Frank, to see him? Remember what you told me?''

Bryce lowered his head, a flush of shame burning his face. His response to Peter's request six years ago had been cruel and brutal. It didn't matter that Bryce had been going through the worst period of his life, arranging his divorce from Kay; that for weeks he'd been unable to deal with anything except on the most basic level, without emotion, without feeling; that he had been bitter and angry and willing to strike out at anyone to lessen the pain that was eating away at him. Nothing changed the fact that he had been cruel, and wrong.

Finally he looked up, his eyes troubled. ''I'm sorry about that. I'm sorry about Terence. You can hate me for that for the rest of your life...but don't punish Dad for it. Please, Peter...''

Peter looked ready to say no until Martha added her own, soft, "Please?"

He sank into his chair, bowed his head in his hands and closed his eyes. He wanted to say no, but he knew it would be wrong. He would be punishing his brother for something that Bryce had done. There had already been so much punishment, so much anger and hatred and sorrow. How could he be responsible for any more? "I'll see him," he said grudgingly. Before Bryce or Martha could show too much joy, though, he quickly added, "But I'm not promising anything. And I can't give him a place to stay. There's no room for him here."

Simply getting Peter to agree to being in the same state with Frank was a major victory in Bryce's view. Even so, he decided to press for more. "Why not?"

"Winter is a busy season—the inn is full."

"What about the other guest house, where we used to live?"

"Leah uses that for a workshop."

"What kind of workshop?"

It was Martha who answered. "She makes things—ornaments, decorations, crafts. She mostly uses them at the inn, but there's a shop in Asheville that sells whatever she can send them."

Bryce made a gesture of annoyance. "Leah can use the damn basement for a workshop. I'm asking for two rooms, and I'll pay your rates, Peter. You won't be out any money."

Martha looked up curiously. "Two rooms?"

"I plan to stay for a while, to get him settled in, to be with him."

"How long is a while?"

Bryce shrugged. "A month, maybe six weeks. That's about all the time I can spare from my job."

She nodded thoughtfully. "Until after Christmas. That will be a nice visit." Then she looked at her husband. "Tell him the real reason you can't give Frank a room, Peter. He's family. He has a right to know.''

Bryce looked from his uncle to his aunt, then back again. "A right to know what?"

Peter's shoulders sagged as he stared down at his hands. "I don't own the estate anymore."

Shock was written on Bryce's face. In two hundred years the house and land had never passed out of Cameron hands. He had never expected it to happen, certainly not in his lifetime. "After what you did to get ownership of this place, you sold it?" he asked, his voice sharp with disbelief.

"No, I didn't sell it," Peter snapped defensively; then he suddenly looked very old. "I gave it to Terence. When he died, it passed to his widow."

"To Leah." Bryce was dismayed by the news. She wasn't even a Cameron, yet she owned his family home—cool, calm, lovely Leah. "Why the hell did you give it to Terence? Why couldn't you have waited until you died, like everyone else, to pass it on?"

"He was a young, stubborn man, and Leah—"

Peter broke off when Martha laid her hand on his arm. "Your reasons concern several people," she gently reminded him. "Terence is dead, but the others are still living, and you have no right to discuss this with a stranger without their permission."

Bryce turned his frown on his aunt. Not five minutes ago, she had reminded her husband that Bryce was family; now she was calling him a stranger. "What it boils down to is that I have to get *her* permission before I can bring Dad here. Right?"

Both Peter and Martha nodded.

Bryce stared grimly at the tabletop. What had happened to his simple plans to come here and settle this business once and for all? Why was everything in his life suddenly getting complicated with Leah?

He would ask this favor of her, and she would grant it,

because she was gracious and generous, and because she understood the powerful ties of family that were drawing Frank back. And to the long list of attributes that connected him to her—attraction, affection, wanting, longing, needing—and now Bryce felt indebted, far beyond the simple price of the rooms.

And what payment would she extract in return for this favor? In his mind he could hear her soft drawl, enticing in spite of her words: "I'd rather not see you again." Would she welcome his father on the condition that Bryce fulfill that one little wish for her?

"I'll talk to her." He cleared his throat. "Thank you, Uncle Peter, Aunt Martha."

Following breakfast, Leah took refuge in the attic. Checking their Christmas decorations was a tedious task that no one but herself enjoyed, so doing it practically guaranteed privacy.

The cartons were stacked in the center of the room, next to a hand-hewn table made more than a hundred and fifty years ago by an earlier Cameron. Leah carefully pulled the clear packing tape from the top of the first box and began removing its contents.

There were ceramic scent pots painted with merry Christmas scenes, ready to be filled with potpourri, and candle holders in wood, glass, silver and pewter. Music boxes in the shapes of reindeer, angels, Santas and snowmen, and bows made of red velvet and green calico. Miniature sleighs for centerpieces and tiny woven baskets to be filled with a few pieces of candy and hung on the trees. Tablecloths and napkins in bright red and green for formal dinners, and place mats in cheery Christmas prints for casual use. Miniature wreaths no bigger than a silver dollar and others as much as three feet in diameter, with every size in between, fashioned out of a variety of materials from pine cones and braided strips of fabric to wheat and Spanish moss. Ornaments in every shape and variety, from expensive delicate china to finger-painted bells made from cardboard egg cartons, and lights—literally thousands of lights. Tiny multicolored bulbs for the trees, fat round white bulbs to outline the house. Last year, Leah remembered, they had used more than five thousand lights at Christmas. She gave a little sigh. Untangling and checking all those strings of lights was part of her job.

She was unwrapping the broken pieces of what had once been a round green ball when the door opened. Looking over her shoulder, she recognized the dark brown hair immediately. She wished he would disappear before he climbed the final three steps into the room, and yet at the same time she was pleased that he had sought her company.

"Are you busy?"

She continued to sort through the box in front of her. Rather than give the obvious answer to his question, she ignored it and asked one of her own. "How did your meeting with Peter go?"

He crossed to the table, leaned against it and watched her. "It was okay."

"Did you finish your business with him?" She was dying to know what had been so important, and she suspected that Bryce knew it. But if he wouldn't offer an explanation, she certainly wouldn't ask for one, she promised herself as she moved around the table.

"What's wrong, Leah?"

Startled blue eyes met his. "I—I don't understand...."

"Every time I get near you, you try to put distance between us, either physically or emotionally. What's wrong? What have I done?"

She unwrapped a ceramic boy angel, his head bowed to reveal his halo. When filled with sand the angel sat on the mantel, a stocking looped over his upturned foot. There were seven altogether, one for each of them: three boys and four girls, their robes painted in soft Christmas colors—pale pinks and muted golds and mossy greens. Usually Leah admired the workmanship each time she looked at one of the angels, but this morning her hands were shaking too badly. With hardly a glance, she set it on the table.

He asked the question so sincerely; how was she supposed to answer? How could she tell him, "It's not you, it's *me*"? She gave him only half the answer. "It's not you," she murmured.

"Are you afraid of me?"

Afraid of what she felt when he was around, she acknowledged silently. Afraid of what she felt when he *wasn't* around. Afraid because she was helpless against those emotions. But afraid of *him*? "No, I'm not."

He took note of the heightened color in her cheeks and of her trembling hands, and decided that it was a good time to change the subject. "We never did finish our talk about Matthew," he reminded her.

"M—Matthew?"

He picked up a music box, gave the knob on the bottom a twist and set it down again. Santa turned in a slow circle to the tune of "Santa Claus Is Watching You." After a few notes he reached for a heavy glass angel standing next to it. "Matthew," he repeated. "You think I'm a bad influence on him. I think you're cheating him by not telling him about his father."

Leah took the angel from his hands and carefully set it down again. "How much experience have you had with children?"

He gave her a grin. "Almost none. That's why they like me. I don't know how to treat kids, so I treat them like people." While the first music box still played, he set another turning, this one a reindeer twirling to "Rudolph the Red-Nosed Reindeer."

When he reached for a third music box, Leah frowned at him. "Would you stop that?"

He walked to a dusty old rocker in the corner and sat down, folding his hands over his stomach. "Do you want to start the argument, or should I?"

Leah opened yet another box, looked inside and set it

aside. "I don't think you're a bad influence," she said slowly, "but you *are* influencing him. I don't think you understand just how much."

"I do understand. Matthew is lonely, and he feels a little cheated, because he's the only kid in his entire first-grade class who doesn't have a father. He's looking for someone to fill in, and he's decided that I'll do nicely." He watched her, gauging the effect of his summary on her. She acknowledged its correctness with a simple nod.

He understood her concern, and that made it difficult to argue, especially when he couldn't explain his feelings to her. He had felt an immediate bond with Matthew—the ties of family, the attraction between a boy who wanted a father and a man who wanted a son. He would never do anything to hurt Matthew, but Leah couldn't know that.

"That's great while you're here, but what about when you leave? Your business with Peter is finished, and you'll be returning to Philadelphia soon. What happens to my son then?"

Nothing, he wanted to say. He wasn't the sort of man who took commitments lightly. He wouldn't get involved with Matthew, then forget all about him when he left Angel's Peak. "You don't think long-distance relationships can work? You know—letters, phone calls, visits?" Even as he asked it, he knew what her answer would be. It sounded implausible to him, too.

"Not when a six-year-old boy is involved." As the strains of music from the Santa slowed and distorted, Leah laid a gentle hand on it to stop it.

What about when a thirty-five-year-old woman is involved? he wanted to ask. Did age improve the odds? "Okay. So why don't you give him a father?"

She stared at him with a hint of derision for his suggestion. "That's a very simple solution for a very complex problem," she said, bringing a low stool from the corner and brushing it off before sitting down.

"Even a one-horse town like Angel's Peak has to have

at least a few single men to choose from." He rocked the chair with the toe of his booted foot until he realized he was sending showers of dust into the air. "Terence has been dead for six years. That's long enough to grieve. That's more than long enough to be single and celibate. Why don't you get married again?"

Leah's surprise changed to bewilderment. How on earth had she gotten onto the subject of marriage with him? "It isn't that easy," she protested. "Why aren't you married?"

"How do you know I'm not?"

Her mouth opened, but no words came out. She had assumed, because he had touched her and kissed her, that he was single. She should have known better than that. Not all men felt bound by their marriage vows; she had sometimes suspected that Terence was one of those who didn't. Her face grew warm. She had indulged in all sorts of fantasies about this man without even bothering to find out if he was married.

"I'm not," he said, feeling a warm rush inside because it mattered to her. "But I was—for fourteen years. We've been divorced for six years."

"I'm sorry," Leah murmured, but only because it seemed appropriate. She wasn't sorry—she was relieved. She didn't want to care at all about him, but she couldn't deny the relief.

"So was I." Bryce leaned his head back to study the dusty ceiling beams. He had been very sorry. The end of his marriage had been the most painful time of his life— even worse than Gran's death. It had come as a total surprise to him when Kay had told him about her affair with Derek Wilson, but he had been willing to forgive her, to continue loving her and mend their shattered relationship. But Kay hadn't felt she'd done anything that required his forgiveness, and she certainly hadn't wanted his love. All she had asked for was a divorce, so she could marry Derek. Maybe if he had paid more attention he would have seen what was happening, but his job had demanded so much of his time, and Kay had never complained.

Until the end. He had been stubborn about the divorce, insisting that they could work out their problems; they simply couldn't throw away fourteen years of marriage. *Then* Kay had complained—about the time he'd devoted to his job. About the energy and emotion he'd given it, leaving little or nothing for her. About the dissatisfaction and the emptiness in her life that he couldn't fill anymore. About *his* emptiness, his selfishness, his inability to give or care or feel or satisfy. By the time she'd finished with him, his heart and his ego had been in shreds, and he had given her the divorce—sadly, painfully, but willingly.

Leah watched the expressions that crossed his face as he remembered—sorrow, pain, despair—and wanted to offer him comfort. Painful memories were something she understood very well; she had more than a few of her own. But fear held her back—fear of being rejected, and fear of being accepted. She couldn't let him get too close.

He lowered his head again to look at her. "So...we were talking about finding you a husband." What he had approached in a lighthearted manner had suddenly become a serious subject. He didn't want to think in terms of other men with Leah. He hadn't yet accepted his own attraction to her; how could he tease her about attracting another man?

"No," she corrected firmly. "We were talking about your friendship with Matthew." She reached into the big box in front of her and withdrew a handful of cotton batting. As soon as she began unwrapping it, she could feel the broken pieces inside. For a house filled with people and at least four kids for the holidays, they had very little breakage at Christmas, but she would give anything to know how in the world the few items that did break managed to do so in the packing cartons.

"Do you feel threatened by it?"

She glanced at him as she carefully emptied the contents

of the batting into the wastebasket. This ball had been glittery gold. "Why should I?"

"Because you've had Matthew all to yourself. He was born after Terence died, so you never even had to share him with his father. Are you afraid that he'll love you less if he finds a substitute father to love?" Simply saying it gave him a warm feeling. The love of parents and friends was nice; the love of a woman was wonderful; but the love of a child was special. Children loved unconditionally, accepting your flaws in ways that few adults could.

"No," Leah said honestly, her blue eyes making contact with his. "I'm afraid that he'll love you too much. I don't want to see him hurt. He's such a little boy, and he has so much faith. If you disappoint him..."

"I won't."

"How can you be so sure of that?"

"Because I know myself."

Exasperation was woven through her sigh. How had Matthew chosen such a stubborn, single-minded man for a father figure? She had no doubt that Bryce could be a good father—but to his own children, not hers. He had already displayed a degree of patience that Terence had never possessed, and he'd been kind and affectionate and respectful with the children. But they were *her* children, and she would be the one who had to comfort Matthew when the novelty wore off for Bryce.

Her voice sharp with frustration, she said, "He may as well accept the idea that he'll never have a father."

His voice came quietly in the stillness. "Do you hate men so much?"

Her hands were trembling too much for her to be handling the fragile glass ornaments. She pushed the box away, turned her back on him and folded her hands together. "No, of course not."

"Then how can you say you'll never marry again?"

"I didn't."

"You said Matthew will never have a father."

Her knuckles turned white when she squeezed her hands tighter. Risking a glance over her shoulder, she asked, "Do you know many men who want to raise someone else's kids? Four of them?"

The answer, if he chose to give it, was no. Hell, as much as he wanted children himself, he wouldn't choose to take on such a burden—but who could choose when it came to love? If a man fell in love with a woman who had four children, he accepted the children, too, and did his best for them.

"If *you* want to get married again, it's simple: you find a woman you can love, one who loves you. If *I* want to get married, I have to find a man I can love, one who not only loves me but all four of my children, one who they can love in return. What are the odds of six people falling in love with each other?"

"Any man who loves you has to love the kids. You're a package deal."

The frustration flared again. He saw things so simply, in such idealistic terms, while Leah knew from experience that life was complex, full of problems, and that idealism had little or nothing to do with reality.

"I annoy you, don't I?" he asked, sounding both curious and amused.

"You don't understand. You simplify things. You make them sound so much easier than they really are."

"Maybe you make them more difficult than they really are. You had problems in the past, and you expect problems in the future. Life doesn't have to be so hard, Leah."

She shook her head in dismay. "I live my life the only way I know how."

"Carefully. Cautiously. Without taking chances. Without risks." The floorboards creaked when Bryce left the rocker. He took a few steps, then crouched directly behind her. The tall, narrow windows were covered with dust, and the sunlight that came through them was weak, but there was enough to play up the coppery tints in her hair. He touched it with just his fingertips, drawing them lightly over it.

Last week the curls had been wild, tangling together. Yesterday she had combed them into something approaching order. Today they were gone altogether, transformed into soft, feminine waves. His fingertips gently skimmed over them until they brushed her ear.

Leah couldn't control her shiver. She didn't try to move away or tell him to stop, because she didn't want him to. She wanted him to go on touching her this way—gently, lightly, barely there—forever.

Slowly he turned her to face him. Now his fingers moved over her throat and curved upward to her chin. His index finger hesitantly touched her mouth, drew back, then moved to it again. Her lips were soft and smooth, drawing him to test them with his own. He skimmed the very tips of his fingers from one corner of her mouth to the other; then, with great care, he parted her lips with one finger, feeling the moist warmth enclose it.

"Take a risk, Leah," he encouraged, his voice barely above a whisper. "Take a chance with me."

She recognized the first faint stirrings of arousal that swirled in the pit of her stomach. Lord, how long had it been since she'd felt that need? When his mouth touched hers, the need exploded, robbing her of her ability to breathe, to think, to protest. All she felt was desire—hot, liquid, unfamiliar in its intensity.

Bryce laid his hands on her shoulders. He felt the tension in her muscles, but it wasn't because she didn't want his kiss. Maybe it was because she wanted it too much? Her mouth opened to his, welcoming the tentative, easy explorations of his tongue. She tasted dark...sweet...innocent.

He changed positions, shifting his weight to his knees. The taste, the feel, the scent of her were weakening him, sending shivers of delight through his body and creating a sudden, erotically uncomfortable swelling of need. One kiss wasn't supposed to be this good, this...devastating to his senses.

He slid one hand from her shoulder, over her sweater, until his palm was molded to her breast. Her nipple was hard, easy to find beneath the bulky fabric. But he had barely touched it before she pushed his hand—then him—away.

Her face was flushed, she was breathing hard, and her eyes, for the brief moment that they met his, were uneasy. Hugging her arms protectively across her chest, she dropped her gaze and saw the desire that he made no effort to hide. Her blush deepened. "I—I—" She rose from the stool, shrinking back to avoid contact with him, then circled the table for safety.

Bryce rose slowly, his gaze intent on her face. "What's wrong?"

"N-nothing. Just...don't do that again, okay?"

"Do what again? Kiss you? Touch your breast? Arouse you? Make you feel something?"

She didn't know how to answer. Her sensible side wanted to scream, "Yes, all those things!" She didn't want him to do any of them again. The romantic side, though, simply wanted. She sought safety in giving no answer at all.

Bryce watched her ignore him. She was a frustrating woman, he decided—probably as frustrating to him as he was to her. She needed time. Time to get to know him, to learn to trust him, to let herself want him. He could give her that.

Letting her arms fall to her sides, Leah busied herself with rearranging the table. When everything had been neatly shuffled into a new position, she said abruptly, "I'm going downstairs now. Please turn off the light and close the door when you leave."

Bryce was only a few steps behind her. "Will you have lunch with me?" he asked when they reached the second-floor landing.

"You're welcome to sit at the family table—"

He shook his head impatiently. "In town. You don't have to stay here, do you?"

He wasn't the first man to ask for her company in the years since Terence had died, but he *was* the first she'd ever wanted to say yes to—yes to lunch, and a whole lot more. After a moment's hesitation, that was what she said. She might be making a mistake spending more time with him than was absolutely necessary, but she had made a lifetime of mistakes, and she had survived every one of them. Even Terence. "All right. Let me tell Vicky."

Bryce recognized the clerk's swiftly hidden expression at the news that Leah was having lunch in town with him as surprise. So Leah didn't spend much time with men, other than customers. He found that very interesting—and very encouraging. Though he knew that it would probably embarrass her, he chose to comment on it when she returned with their coats. "I take it you don't go out often," he said as they descended the broad front steps.

She didn't look at him. "There's no reason to. Everything I need is right here."

"Everything?" There was her family, of course, and her job, but what about her social life? Didn't she ever need friends, laughter and fun? Didn't she ever need a man?

"This *is* my life," Leah replied, her words a not too subtle warning. "I don't want anything else." Pushing her gloved hand into her pocket, she pulled out a set of keys and offered them to Bryce. He accepted them silently, just as he accepted her warning.

Their drive into town was quiet. He pulled into the parking lot of the first restaurant they came to and followed Leah inside.

"How long have you lived in Angel's Peak?"

She looked up from the menu. "Since I was five."

"Where did you live before that?"

She dropped her eyes evasively. "I don't know." All the important facts about her early life were missing—things like her mother's and father's names, her exact age, her real birth date. When she had been abandoned by her parents thirty years ago, she had been clutching a piece of paper with the name Leah on it. She had supplied the last name and the age herself, but no one had been able to judge the reliability of a hysterical little girl. No one had been able to prove if she was right.

"You've never lived in a city, have you?"

She shook her head. "I've never even seen a city larger than Asheville. I like Angel's Peak. I can't imagine living anywhere else."

After they ordered their meal, Bryce settled back comfortably in his seat. "I can't imagine living anywhere but Philadelphia. I never wanted to see Angel's Peak again."

"Why did you come back?"

He studied her for a moment. Her eyes were cool again, and her emotions were under strict control. Yet he hesitated. He didn't want to tell her about Frank and Peter. He didn't want to spoil this time together by asking for favors. "We'll discuss that later. Right now I want to talk about you."

She sat back, too, folding her hands together in her lap. She was studying him so calmly that Bryce was certain she was going to refuse his request. But after a moment she tilted her head to one side. "Why?"

He searched through a list of possible answers and discarded each one: because I like you; because you interest me; because I want to make love to you. That last one had slipped in unexpectedly, making him remember the kiss in the attic, the feel of her breast, the heaviness in his body, and it made him flush just slightly.

None of those answers were acceptable, but he had one that was. "Because we're family, Leah." She valued her family above all else, and he was going to persuade her to include him in that family one way or another. If she would accept him only as her children's cousin, he would settle for that. For the time being.

She sighed softly. "What do you want to know?"

Bryce restrained himself from saying, "Everything," and offered a nonthreatening question instead. "How long have you been running the inn?"

"Since it opened three years ago."

"Do you enjoy it?"

"Yes. I like meeting people from other places, people who appreciate old houses as much as I do. And I like the responsibility—it's the first job I've ever had."

"The first *paying* job," Bryce corrected. "Being a wife and mother of four is a job, even if it doesn't pay a salary."

She smiled then, shyly. "Yes," she agreed in a soft voice. "It is."

He watched until her smile faded, then closed his eyes. The desire to kiss her again and again was becoming a need, and she wasn't even aware of it. She didn't know that her smile could spread such heat through him that he burned for her. He smiled just a little mockingly. And Kay had called him unfeeling. She would be surprised at just how much he could feel.

Leah was watching him, waiting for his next question. He reached for his coffee cup as he asked it. "Do you like dealing with people?"

She wondered why that surprised him so much. "Of course. I like people."

"You seem so..."

"Snobbish?" she supplied. "Snooty? Stuck-up?"

Those were words that had been applied to her, Bryce suspected, and she hadn't liked them one bit. He chose his own carefully. "No, not any of those. Aloof, maybe. Cautious." As if letting anyone get close to her would be a mistake that she might not survive.

"Cautious." Even the tone of her voice was careful as she repeated the word. "That sounds better. I guess I am cautious. I have to be."

"Why?"

She studied him for a moment. His manner was relaxed,

his curiosity friendly, his interest appealing. At this moment, *he* was the best reason in the world for caution on her part. Did he have any idea how strongly he attracted her? Would it matter to him if he did know? "Don't you know any easy questions?" she asked in her smile-softened drawl.

"All questions are easy. Only the answers are hard." He gave the waitress time to serve them before continuing. "So you like people. Is that why you have four kids?"

"I wanted a large family."

"Are you an only child?"

"I don't know." She sprinkled cheese on her fettuccine before meeting his gaze. "I grew up in the home on the north side of town."

He looked down quickly. He remembered the home. The kids who lived there were outcasts in school and in town, sticking together because they had no one else. They lived a tightly controlled, regimented life, with little fun and less affection. Most of them were orphans, but there were always a few whose parents couldn't—or wouldn't—take care of them. Which was Leah? he wondered.

She moved restlessly, her appetite gone. She had made it a rule to rarely offer information about her childhood—reactions like Bryce's had taught her better. Knowing changed the way people looked at her, as if they were trying to figure out what kind of horrible child she'd been, that her parents hadn't wanted her. She waited for him to change the subject awkwardly, as people always did, and wished she had said nothing.

"Are your parents dead, or did they abandon you?"

He spoke in a matter-of-fact tone, as if they were discussing the weather outside. Leah's first reaction was surprise, followed by gratitude that he was still being friendly. "They left me there. I don't know who they were, and I've never seen them since."

What kind of people could walk away from the child that Leah had been—from their own daughter? he wondered. Deep inside he ached for her—for the girl, and for the woman—but he kept it hidden. She would see his sympathy as pity, and she wouldn't appreciate it. "So you lived at the home until you met Terence."

Mention of her husband brought a wariness to her eyes. "Yes. Do you ski?"

He frowned at her graceless change of subject. "If you don't want to talk about Terence, Leah, you only have to say so," he chided.

She gave an accepting nod. "Now it's your turn to answer some questions."

"In spite of your attempts to discourage me, you're interested in me after all, aren't you?" Moving his dinner plate away, he reached for his coffee. "What do you want to know?"

"Did you talk to Peter this morning?"

"Yes."

She waited expectantly.

"We took care of part of my business."

"And the rest?"

He wouldn't get a better chance to tell his father's story and to ask his favor, but, stubbornly, he refused the opportunity. Once he asked her, he would have no reason to stay any longer; he would have to return to Philadelphia to make arrangements for his father's move and his own leave of absence. Even though he would be back soon, he wanted to put off leaving a little longer, wanted to enjoy her company a little longer. "I'll take care of the rest later. Do you want dessert?"

She considered it, then shook her head. "I should get back to the inn."

"You have a perfectly competent staff. I'm sure they can get along for a few hours without you."

She led the way across the dining room, Bryce close behind. "I'm sure they can get along for a few years without me, but I can't get along without them."

He paid the bill, then held her coat while she slipped it

on. Facing her, he lifted her hair from beneath the collar, then traced a finger over the rose-colored scarf. "I like this color. It makes you look...soft."

Leah solemnly returned his gaze. How easy it would be to grow used to him, she thought with regret—to his simple outlook and pretty words and easy smiles and gentle touches. How easily she could make him a part of her life. But his presence here was only temporary, while her life was here forever. Forever and ever. Soon he would be gone, and if she let him get much closer, he would take a vital part of her with him.

"I'm not soft," she said in response to his remark. "I'm very strong."

His smile was faint. "You can be both, you know." Taking her arm, he led her outside, where he stopped on the cleared sidewalk, looking at the park across the street. "Let's take a walk in the park."

She looked at the park, too. There were small children in brightly colored jackets playing there, and creations of snow—men, angels, forts, unidentifiable creatures. She was tempted, but there were so many things she needed to do at home. Regretfully she shook her head.

"How about going for a drive?"

Another shake. "I need to get back to the inn," she said a second time, more forcefully.

Bryce's irritation succeeded in overcoming his smile. He dropped her arm and turned toward the car. Of course she needed to get back. At the inn she could busy herself with any number of tasks; she could lock herself in her room or her office; she could surround herself with her employees and her family and her friendly guests. At the inn she could keep him at a distance.

Which was exactly where he belonged. He didn't bother to enumerate the reasons why he should stay away from Leah, although he knew them by heart now. It would just be so much easier if he didn't *want* to be with her, if he didn't find so much pleasure in looking at her, listening to her, touching her and kissing her. Especially in kissing her.

He shoved his hands into his pockets and walked silently at her side, with more than enough distance between them to satisfy her. They reached the station wagon, drove home and entered the house, all without saying a word.

Puzzled by his coldness, Leah hung her coat in the closet beneath the front stairs, then wordlessly extended her hand for his heavier jacket. He gave it to her, then turned away.

"Bryce?"

He paused.

Her hands were cold; she rubbed them together until she realized that they were also trembling. "I take a walk every night after dinner." It was as close to an invitation as she could come.

His smile returned, not dazzling, but gentle. Without a word, he nodded and walked away.

They couldn't squeeze in one more person at the family table that night at dinner, so the two tables were separated to make room for Bryce. After supervising the rearrangement, Leah sat down at one table with Peter and Martha. There was an empty chair on her left, which she fully expected Bryce to claim. She was disappointed when he chose to sit with Megan and the boys instead, leaving the chair next to Leah for Laurel. Leah stared at the back of his head for a moment, then looked away—into Martha's sharp, curious eyes. Blushing, she shifted so that she could no longer see Bryce and turned her attention to her meal.

Was he angry because she had refused his invitations that afternoon? Or had he simply tired of her company? Terence had often gotten tired of her. He had never been cruel; he had simply been incapable of feigning a love—even an affection—that he didn't feel. Was Bryce more like Terence than she'd expected?

She'd made the best offer she could when she had told him about her evening walk. She didn't expect to see him, though, as she left the dining room to get her coat, scarf and gloves. By the time they had gotten back to the house that afternoon, he'd seemed to have lost all interest in spending time with her. But that wouldn't change her routine. She would take her walk alone, and she would enjoy it. She wouldn't let him steal that simple pleasure from her.

She held on to the rail as she descended the porch steps in back, making a mental note to ask Douglas to clean them again; then, breathing in the cold, frosty air, she set off across the yard.

Bryce saw her the moment she stepped outside. Leaning motionless against the tree trunk, he watched her as she moved down the steps, cautious but confident. She knew where the slick spots were. He wished, for her sake and his, that that confidence might be extended into the rest of her life.

As she neared him, he moved out of the dark shadow of the tree and stopped in front of her. "What took you so long?"

Suddenly the prospect of a long, snowy walk seemed much more cheerful. Leah was resentful that he could make such a difference, but resentment wouldn't stop her from enjoying his presence. "I didn't think you were coming."

"You think I'd pass up the only invitation you've given me?" He shook his head. "Not likely." He fell in step alongside her, letting her lead the way across the driveway and into the woods. The walk, like the drive back from town, was silent, but this time there was no annoyance, no irritation—just a simple, warm satisfaction at being with her.

Leah's soft voice broke the stillness. "You never did answer me today when I asked if you like to ski."

"You didn't really want to know, did you?" he asked with a grin, reminding her that the question had been a ploy to shift the subject away from Terence.

"Yes. I do want to know." She wanted to know everything about him—this man who so strongly affected her.

Gratified by the answer, he shrugged. "I learned how when I was a kid, of course. Everyone who lives in or on Angel's Peak learns how. But I was never very good at it, or very fond of it. What about you?"

"Skiing is a luxury, and luxuries had no place at the home." She answered plainly, without a hint of self-pity or bitterness.

Bryce stopped and touched her shoulder, urging her to look at him. The moonlight shone on her face, touching the wisps of hair that had escaped her scarf. "Was love a luxury, too, Leah?"

He spoke so gently and touched her so tenderly. Did he know that she craved a tender touch—that she was beginning to crave *his* touch? She wanted to run away; she was afraid of revealing her need to him, but she couldn't back away from the hand that was resting lightly on her shoulder. And she couldn't pull her eyes from his.

Bending slightly, he touched his lips to hers. With no more contact between them than his hand and his mouth, he could feel the pleasure that stole through her. Slowly but deliberately, he deepened the kiss, moistening her lips with his tongue. He slid one arm around her, raised his free hand to cup her cheek and closed the distance between them with one gentle tug.

Leah was lost. Warmth spread through her with his kiss, flowing with the heated blood through her veins. With a silent cry of despair at her helplessness, she raised her hands to his shoulders, then wrapped her arms around his neck.

His groan was a soft vibration in her mouth. When his tongue parted her teeth to seek hers, to explore the vulnerable softness of her mouth, he tasted of coffee, rich and hot.

He tugged off one glove, and it fell to the ground, a dark shadow on the moonlit snow. The other glove followed, and he slid his hands into her hair, pushing back her scarf and gliding his fingers through the strands of cold silk.

Holding her, kissing her—God, it felt good! He wished it could go on forever and at the same time wished for more. He wanted to undress her, to caress her, to bring her pleasure beyond belief. He wanted to make love to her. He had needed her for what seemed like ages, and tonight, with hungry kisses and gentle caresses, he knew that he could have her.

But where? The house was filled with people, including her children, and the empty guest house was too close to—

His mind commanded him to end the kiss as common sense took a grip on desire. Sure, he could seduce her— between his desire and her innocence, he had no doubt of that. But this was *Leah*, not some woman he could take to bed and forget tomorrow morning, and Leah wasn't ready to accept him as a lover. If he seduced her now, she would hate him when it was over, and he would lose her. That was a risk he couldn't take.

Abruptly he ended the kiss and pressed her face against the cool leather of his jacket. Although there was warmth in the shelter of his arms, she was shivering; he could feel it through the thickness of their coats. But that was all right, he thought with a rueful sigh—he was shaky, too, inside and out.

Eyes closed, face against his chest, Leah listened to the pounding of a heartbeat, not sure if it was Bryce's or her own, or just the rushing of the blood in her ears. She was unsteady, depending on him for support. Never, not in thirty-five years of living, had she experienced anything like his kisses.

At last he put her away from him. With hands that trembled the tiniest bit, he raised the scarf to cover her hair again, letting his fingers linger there for a moment. When he drew his hand back, he asked, "You're not afraid of me, are you, Leah?" He knew the answer; he just wanted to make sure that she did, too.

She had to try several times to get her voice to work. "I don't think you would hurt me."

"I won't—not ever." He continued to study her face, seeking answers, truths. He wanted to know it all. "Terence hurt you, didn't he?"

Suddenly she swung away, walking briskly through the snow. Bryce ducked to grab his gloves before following her. "Leah, you can't keep running from me!"

She didn't look at him or slow her steps to make it easy for him to catch up. Tucking her chin into the turned-up collar of her coat, she hunched her shoulders against the cold and walked even faster.

They had reached the clearing of the cemetery when Bryce grabbed her hand. "Leah!" When she didn't struggle or speak, he softened both his voice and his touch. "He hurt you, didn't he?"

"Does it matter?"

"Yes."

"Why?" she challenged him, meeting his gaze at last. The softness was in his eyes, too.

Bryce raised his shoulders in a helpless shrug. "Because *you* matter."

She repeated the single word, but this time the challenge was gone. "Why?"

"I don't know, but you do." He pulled back his hand, fighting the desire to take her into his arms again, to kiss her again. "Every time I touch you, every time I try to get close to you, Leah, you pull away. Is it because you still love Terence? Or because he hurt you? Did he teach you to distrust all men?"

"You said today that I don't have to talk to you about him."

He acknowledged that with a nod. "But you've got to talk sometime. Leah, I've got to know."

She walked over to the fence and wrapped one hand around a wrought iron spike. "What difference does it make? It's all in the past—you can't change any of it." Her voice sounded cool and distant and unnaturally calm.

He couldn't change the past, but he could heal the lingering wounds. Once again he followed, stopping behind her. He rested his hands lightly on her shoulders and spoke softly, his mouth only inches from her ear. "What did he do to you, Leah?"

She turned slowly, dislodging his hands, but made no effort to move away from him. Instead she raised her hands to his chest, gripping handfuls of his jacket, and pulled him toward her. "Kiss me again," she commanded. "The way you just did."

Sheer willpower held him back. Gently he unclasped her fingers from his coat, then held her hands together between his. "No, Leah. I won't let you use me that way. Tell me about Terence."

She leaned back against the fence. "Terence was my husband. We were married for twelve years, and we had four children, but he died, and I lived. End of story."

She made it sound so simple. He could make a similar statement about his marriage to Kay. It would be accurate, but it would say nothing about the love and the happiness, or the pain—the incredible pain. How much was Leah leaving out?

Sensing that her simplified answer annoyed him, she uttered a soft sigh. It would be easier to give him an honest response if she knew why he was so intent on getting it. Did it truly make a difference to him, or was he just curious?

"Terence didn't do anything to me. Nothing. He didn't love me…didn't want me…didn't need me. Marrying me was the price he paid to get ownership of the estate."

"What do you mean?" he asked, although he'd already picked up enough information to make a fairly good guess.

"I was seventeen, pregnant and alone. Peter and Martha used the estate as a bargaining chip to convince Terence to accept responsibility and marry me."

Bryce tried to imagine how she must have felt, frightened and alone, but he couldn't. He had always had the loving support of his father, had always been able to take care of himself. "Did you want to marry him? Even knowing that he was doing it only so he could have the house?"

She heard the disbelief he tried to hide and smiled faintly. "Yes, I wanted to marry him. I loved him, and I thought that he loved me. And I was carrying his child. I thought that eventually everything would work out all right."

"Did it?"

She shrugged. "He was the best husband and the best father that he could be. He gave me a home and a family, but he couldn't give himself."

Bryce reached for her to offer comfort, but she didn't want it. Moving swiftly, she avoided his hands and slipped away.

"Finish your business here, Bryce," she requested, speaking once more in her soft, angelic drawl, "and go home. Go back to Philadelphia where you belong."

"My business here is with you," he called after her. And that was where he belonged, too—with her. He smiled faintly. If he told her that, she would accuse him of simplifying things again, of making them seem easy when they weren't.

Slowly she turned. "I thought it was Peter you had to see."

"I thought so, too, but it turns out my business concerns you as much as him. More, even." He would have preferred to have this discussion in the morning, in the businesslike atmosphere of her office, but he wanted to stretch out this private time with her. "It's about my father."

"Frank?"

"Yes. He's in the hospital in Philadelphia. He had a heart attack."

"Is he all right?"

He shrugged. "As all right as a seventy-three-year-old man with a history of heart disease can be. He's old, Leah, and he wants to come home. He wants to reconcile with Peter, to see Martha again, to meet you and your children—besides me, you're the only family he's got. He wants to live the rest of his life here, in the Cameron house."

He was playing on her emotions, she knew. He was aware of how important family was to her, and to the kids. He had to know that he was making a request she could never turn down. "All right."

He couldn't believe it was that easy. "All right?"

"Your father is welcome to live here." With a slightly mischievous smile, she added, "You're even welcome to visit him while he's here...occasionally."

Should he tell her that his first "visit" would start the day he brought Frank to the estate and last at least six weeks? The answer, of course, was yes, but he said nothing. If he gave her advance warning, she would tell him that there was no room at the inn for *him*—that there was no room in her *life* for him. No, it would be better to surprise her, put her in a situation where she simply had no choice but to accept his presence. She was going to *have* to accept him.

"I realize that this is how you support your family, and I'll pay whatever it costs—"

She raised her hand to stop him. "I don't want your money. This is your father's home."

"But—" He broke off. He'd gotten what he wanted; he wouldn't push her to accept more. They would take up the matter of payment when he and Frank returned. Walking across the snow-covered ground to her, he bent and gently kissed her. "Thank you."

When he offered his hand, she hesitantly took it. His fingers closed firmly around hers, holding on to her, but giving her the freedom to pull away if she chose to. She liked the feeling that he wanted her close but wouldn't use force to hold her there. As with practically everything else about him, she liked it very much.

Chapter 5

Bryce looked out the airplane window at the snow-covered mountains below him. Slowly he smiled. He couldn't pick out Angel's Peak, but it was there. Soon *he* would be there, too. With Leah.

"How much longer until we land?"

He turned to his father. "A few more minutes. How are you feeling?"

"If you ask me that one more time, you'll find out," the old man grumbled. "Will anyone be meeting us?"

"No." Leah had offered to pick them up, but Bryce preferred to rent a car and drive up the mountain. He wanted his father's return to Angel's Peak to be a private one. He also wanted to get settled at the inn before he told Leah how long he was planning to stay. It would be harder for her to throw him out then.

"What are you grinning about?" Frank's faded brown eyes narrowed on his son's face. "For someone who put up such a fuss about coming back here only a month ago, you sure have changed your tune. I suppose this has something to do with Terence's wife.''

"Terence's widow," Bryce corrected. "Her name is Leah, Dad, and she's the one who's letting you stay at the house, so be nice."

Frank made a grimace of disgust. "Letting me stay in our own house. That house has never belonged to anyone but a Cameron, until her."

Bryce reined in his impatience with his father. That had been his first reaction to hearing that Leah owned the house, too. "What about Gran?"

"Well, that's different. She was a—"

"She was a Dawson."

"But...well, it was different, anyway. We always knew that she would keep the house in the family."

"Leah has four children who are as much Camerons as you are. She'll keep the house in the family, too." Bryce tensed slightly as the plane began descending. Five days had passed since he'd left the inn to prepare for Frank's move. He had said goodbye to the entire family after dinner before Douglas had driven him to Asheville. He hadn't been given a chance to say a private farewell to Leah, and he suspected she had planned it that way. He didn't know whom she distrusted more—him or herself. All he knew was that he had missed her.

"She must be pretty."

He glanced at Frank. "Yes, she is," he quietly agreed.

The rental car was waiting for them by the time Bryce had collected their luggage, and they set out for their final destination. Frank sat quietly in the seat beside Bryce, looking out the side window.

"It's beautiful."

Frank's first words came as Bryce turned into the long driveway that approached the house. Silently Bryce echoed them. He parked in the lot, then helped his father out of the small car.

Leah was waiting on the porch when they reached the

steps, Martha at her side. There was no sign of Peter. She stole a glance at Bryce before stepping forward to greet his father. "Mr. Cameron, I'm Leah." Rising onto her toes, she kissed him, first on one cheek, then the other. "Welcome home."

He took a good look at her before responding. "My son was right. You *are* pretty."

But he spoke in such an unfriendly tone that Leah was sure it wasn't meant as a compliment. She looked at Bryce, who merely shrugged.

"Come on inside, Frank, and leave the girl alone," Martha said, ushering him into the house. "You must be tired after that trip. You'll be staying in Anna's old room. Bryce will bring in your luggage...." Her words faded as the door swung shut behind her.

Leah, wearing a mint-green sweater, shivered and crossed her arms over her chest. "I take it your father doesn't like the idea of anyone but a Cameron owning the house."

Bryce shrugged again. "He's tired, Leah. It's been a long trip, and he's excited about coming home. He's just worn out." He considered moving closer to take her into his arms, then decided that, for a few minutes, he wanted the pure pleasure of looking at her. "Did you miss me?"

A rosy blush tinted her cheeks. "You've been gone less than a week," she reminded him.

"I missed you. I thought about you a lot while I was gone. Didn't you think of me at all?"

Unwillingly, she smiled. "Maybe once." One long, continuous thought, never leaving her mind since his departure Sunday.

"I'll take what I can get." He had looked long enough, he decided. It was time for a proper greeting. Moving across the porch, he wrapped his arms around her and brushed his lips against hers. "I'll take anything you can give me, Leah." Then he kissed her. His mouth was both hard and soft, gentle but demanding, taking yet giving, and instantly the need that had become manageable while he was gone sprang out of control. When he raised his mouth from hers to take a deep breath, he felt as unsteady as she looked. "What are we going to do, Leah?" he murmured, rubbing a finger back and forth over her jaw.

"About what?"

"This. You and me."

Instantly she looked wary. "We're not going to do anything."

He smiled gently. "Oh, yes, we are. Don't fool yourself, honey. When two people kiss, it isn't usually like that. This is special."

She leaned back against his supporting arm to protest. "It was just a kiss."

"Just a kiss?" He grinned at her transparent effort to deny what was happening between them. "Well, I've kissed a lot of women in my life, Leah, and you're the only one whose 'just a kiss' knocked the world out from under me. Do all men affect you this way?"

Reluctantly, she shook her head.

"Then I'll ask you again: what are we going to do?"

She gave the same response, just worded differently. "Nothing. *You're* only here for a few days. *I* live here. My life is here, my kids are here. We can't do anything, Bryce."

He kissed her forehead, then released her, opened the door and waited for her to go inside. "You're being negative about this, Leah. Try looking on the positive side for once, will you?"

She gave him a frown as she turned down the hall toward the family quarters. As far as she could see, there *was* no positive side to their situation. She was falling fast for a man who lived six hundred miles away, whom she would rarely see—a man who couldn't possibly be seriously interested in a widow with four children.

But Bryce *had* found the positive aspects in the five days he'd been gone. All along he had concentrated on the reasons why a relationship between him and Leah couldn't possibly work out. Lying awake late one night, unable to get her out of his mind, it had occurred to him that maybe there were ways around the obstacles. Every problem had a solution; it was simply a matter of finding the solutions to *their* problems.

So Leah was shy, innocent, unsure. He had his own share of insecurities; they could learn to trust together. So she had four children. He had always wanted children, but they didn't have to be his own flesh and blood. He had been surprised to find that he could love another man's children, but it was true. And Leah's kids were good kids—intelligent, well mannered, polite and likable. So her life was in Angel's Peak, and his was in Philadelphia. He wasn't irrevocably bound to the city; with his MBA and twenty years' management experience, he could find a job almost anywhere. Leah could certainly provide him with the proper incentive to relocate, even to a little place like Angel's Peak.

The key was compromise. If he wanted her badly enough, he would compromise for the rest of his life if it meant spending it with her. Now he had to convince *her* of that.

Leah was on her way to her room when she saw that the door to Frank's room was open and he was standing at the window. Tapping on the door, she stepped inside. "Mr. Cameron?"

Slowly, he turned. "My name is Frank."

She smiled faintly. "Frank. I hope you'll be comfortable here. If there's anything you need…"

He turned away again to stare out. "I never thought I'd be a guest in my own family home. Do you know how many years this house has been in our family?"

"Since it was built," she said evenly. "And it's still in the family, Frank. When I die, it will go to my children—and they're Camerons, too."

He made a derisive noise. "Why did you have to turn it into a hotel where anybody can stay for a price? Couldn't you get a regular job?"

Leah's smile broadened. "When Bryce called to say you were being released from the hospital, I assumed it was because you were much better. I'm betting now that it was because the nurses couldn't stand you any longer."

He faced her again, leaning one bony shoulder against the wall. "Bryce tells me you have four children—two boys who look like us and two pretty little girls who look like you."

She gave him a chiding look. She knew for a fact that it was Frank who'd told Bryce about the kids first. "He was being kind. The girls look like you, too."

"How old are they?"

"Six, eleven, thirteen and seventeen."

"You were mighty young when you got pregnant with that first one."

"Yes, I was." She admitted it openly, making no excuses, offering no apologies.

"I always wanted grandchildren, but Kay—that's Bryce's ex-wife—wouldn't hear of it. After she was gone, I'd hoped that he would marry again and have a baby or two." His eyes, narrowed and alert, fastened on her. "But he hasn't shown much interest in women until lately. How old are you?"

"Thirty-five."

"They used to say a woman shouldn't get pregnant after she turned thirty, but nowadays they claim it's her health more than her age that matters. You look pretty healthy to me."

Leah choked back a gasp, covering it with a cough. "I—I...uh...need to get back to work. If you need anything, there will be someone at the desk or in the kitchen." She backed out of the room and hurried down the hall. She wasn't fast enough, though, to escape the hearty, satisfied laugh that was coming from Frank's room.

* * *

Once his brother had arrived at the estate, Peter turned stubborn and refused to come to the house to see him. He even skipped dinner that evening, although Frank hardly seemed to notice. He sat at the middle of a long table, surrounded by the children, rarely taking time to even notice Bryce, Leah and Martha sitting together at one end.

Whatever Frank's objections were to her, Leah was relieved that he showed no animosity to her children. For a man who'd had little contact with kids, he got along marvelously with them, from Douglas down to Matthew, and they seemed to be good for him. Even in the few hours since his arrival he looked better—rested and more energetic. Being home with the family was going to be good medicine for him, she predicted.

She was rising from her chair when Bryce leaned over. "Meet me out back in half an hour," he whispered.

Aware that Martha had heard his invitation, Leah hesitated before nodding. Half an hour would give her time to change from the dress she'd worn to dinner in Frank's honor into jeans and boots. She slid her chair under the table, then stopped behind Douglas. "Frank, we're having a party tomorrow night for the guests and a few friends from town. We'd be pleased if you would come."

He looked from her to Martha. "Will Peter be there?"

The older woman shrugged. "Possibly. You know your brother, Frank."

"Stubborn as a mule," he accused.

"Just like you," she shot back. "You know, it's not impossible for you to walk a few feet across the road to our house to see him."

"I'm the invalid here. I need my rest."

Rolling his eyes, Bryce helped his father to his feet. "Then how about going to bed, where all invalids should be?"

Frank pulled his arm free. "All right, I'm going. You don't have to drag me." He addressed Martha with a steely stare. "You tell that husband of yours that I'll expect to see him soon."

"Stubborn old coot," she said, just loudly enough for him to hear as he walked away. She was smiling when she turned to Leah. "Why don't I put Matthew to bed tonight? I can read his story as well as you can."

"But Mom always does it, Grandma," Matthew interrupted.

"Yes, but tonight Mom's going to take a long, quiet, private walk in the snow. Won't you let me do it just this once?"

He considered it seriously, then nodded. "All right. Just this once."

Leah gave him a kiss before going to change clothes. When she was done, she left the house and sat down on a bench on the back porch to wait for Bryce.

He joined her a few minutes later. Silently they followed the path they had taken on their last walk. After a few minutes, though, he gave a sigh and said, "I should have warned you about Dad. He isn't intentionally rude.... Well, yeah, he is. It's just...he doesn't mean anything by it. That's the way he is with everyone."

"It's all right."

He gave her a sidelong look. "I'm not apologizing for him, Leah," he warned. "I'm just explaining that you shouldn't take anything he says seriously. He's just gruff and cantankerous by nature."

"I don't need an apology or an explanation. I like your father."

"I think he likes you, too—even if he doesn't approve of you having the house, or of what you've done with it."

She smiled then, bright and happy and teasing, and he thought she was absolutely gorgeous. "He may not think much of me as a homeowner and innkeeper, but he seems to think I'd be all right as the mother of his grandchildren."

He had been reaching out to touch her, to capture that smile, when her meaning penetrated the fog that was clouding his mind. It struck him around his midsection—in the region of his heart, he thought numbly. Leah as the mother of his children—it was a powerfully erotic idea.

"Would you have another baby?" he asked huskily.

"I went through most of one pregnancy and part of another by myself," she reminded him. "I couldn't do it again."

"We're talking about me. You know I wouldn't leave you alone."

He was still speaking in that husky, emotional voice that held Leah mesmerized. She shook her head to break the spell and answered him honestly. "No, Bryce, I don't know that. I really don't know very much about you." Except that he was handsome and charming. That thinking of him made her heart beat faster, that looking at him turned her bones to jelly, that simply being with him somehow made everything brighter and better than it had ever been before. Except that if any man could ever make her want and need, if any man could ever teach her to love and to trust, it was him.

She smiled crookedly. Those were the important things, weren't they?

When he moved toward her, she met him halfway, lacing her fingers through his hair as their mouths touched. They kissed hungrily, urgently. When he maneuvered his hands between their bodies to unzip her coat, she made no objection. A moment later she heard his gloves hit the snow with a soft thud; then she felt his hands, still warm, slide beneath her sweater, over her skin to her breasts. He didn't fumble with the thin, soft bra she wore, just stroked and caressed her breasts.

Except for that very brief incident in the attic, no man had touched her so intimately for longer than she could remember. Her husband had never been overly concerned with her enjoyment, had never cared if he gave her pleasure when they were together. She couldn't remember ever feeling so good, so tingly and alive, so needy.

His fingers found her nipples, hard and aching, and gently tormented them until she freed her mouth from his to drag in deep, gasping breaths of frigid air. He turned his kisses to her ear, moistly outlining it with his tongue. "Touch me, Leah," he whispered. "Feel what you do to me...how you make me need.... Give me your hand."

Slowly she offered her hand, and he removed his from her sweater to accept it. He pressed her palm to his chest, inside the warmth of his jacket, then patiently, slowly but deliberately, slid it over the waistband of his jeans, across his flat abdomen, to the painfully hard evidence of his arousal.

The contact lasted only seconds, then Leah jerked back her hand as if burned and pulled out of his arms, turning her back on him.

"Leah?" There was no anger in his voice, only bewilderment.

"I can't. I can't do this."

Her head was down, her voice muffled, but he heard the quiver of tears. His concern instantly overrode his desire. "You can't...what, Leah?"

"I don't want to do this...don't want you touching me. I—I don't want to touch you." The halting words were lies, every one of them, but they were better than the truth. She didn't want to tell him that she was afraid, that she knew nothing about touching, about giving pleasure and making love. She didn't want to tell him that sex with Terence had been unpleasant, sometimes painfully so, that she didn't want to go through it again.

He knew she was afraid—hadn't he known all along that she needed sweet, gentle coaxing?—but her words still hurt. He needed her touch the way his body needed oxygen to live, but her response had been one of disgust. "Leah, I'm sorry. I shouldn't have done that. I'm not going to hurt you. I won't make you do anything you don't want to do. Don't you know that?"

She took a deep breath, a cleansing, calming breath, then

turned to look at him. There was shame in her eyes—shame and fear. "I'm sorry."

He pulled her to him with gentle hands and held her against the hard strength of his body. He stroked her hair, the way he might stroke a tearful child, and murmured to her in soft, soothing tones. "It's all right, Leah. Just don't run away from me. Let me hold you. Let me help you." *Let me love you.*

He would give anything, he thought with a grim sigh, to know all the details of Leah's marriage. The little that she had told him had helped, but there was still so much he needed to know. What had those twelve years with Terence been like? What had she needed and wanted? What had she gotten?

She had needed love in all its forms—affection, physical intimacy, respect, gentleness, consideration, tolerance. Bryce knew that much. Had Terence given her any of those things? Sadly, he suspected that the answer was no. His cousin had taken, and had given little in return beyond the children.

In control again, Leah pushed lightly against his chest, and he immediately released her. "I need to go back and find a room for you tonight."

The cool, untouchable tone of her voice no longer annoyed him, now that he knew the depths of the passion inside her. He retrieved his gloves, then walked alongside her. "For quite a few nights, Leah. I want to stay."

She twisted her head to look at him. "To get your father settled."

Her hopefulness brought him a wry smile. "No. I want to stay until New Year's."

That was—she counted quickly—seven weeks! Her hopes sank to her toes at the same time that her heart sent up shivers of joy. But self-preservation conquered pleasure. "You can't do that. There isn't any room. We're all booked."

He gestured to the house ahead of them as they strolled

across the yard. "Look at that house, Leah—look how big it is. Are you telling me there isn't one single room somewhere in there that I could use as a bedroom for the next few weeks?"

"You can't just move in," she protested. "Why? Why do you want to stay?"

"I was with Dad when he had his last heart attack, and it scared the hell out of me. You're not the only one with strong feelings about family, Leah. I'm not going to leave him here and come back for occasional visits. I want to spend some time with him—and with you. We *need* time, Leah, time for you to get to know me, to learn to trust me."

Shaken by the intensity in his eyes and his voice as he spoke, she could only manage a soft hoarseness when she responded. "And time for you to get to know me?"

He smiled confidently. "I need to learn more about your past, but...I already know *you*, Leah." He knew that she was going to let him stay. He knew that soon she was going to give him her trust. He knew that he was going to make love with her, and he had a strong suspicion that they were going to spend the rest of their lives together. It would just take time.

She felt helpless—not against him, but against herself. She knew already that she was going to agree to let him stay—not because he wanted it, but because she did. Because, now she had gotten over her initial shock, she liked the idea of having him nearby, of being able to see him every day, of continuing to share her walks with him every night. She knew it wasn't wise—there was a good chance that she would pay for this foolishness in heartache—but it didn't change her mind. The last time she had acted foolishly had been with Terence, but she had survived that. If Bryce turned out to be another mistake, she would survive him, too.

"Well?"

She realized that they had stopped walking and were

standing at the back steps. With a slight shrug, she started to climb them. "The only space I have is a storage room on the other side of the downstairs bathroom." And down the hall from her own room.

"That's fine."

"It's very small," she warned. "Years ago my bedroom was the nursery, and this room was used by the servant who took care of the babies."

"That's fine."

"We'll have to clean it tomorrow. For tonight you can sleep in Douglas's room, and he can put his sleeping bag in Matthew's."

"I'll take the sleeping bag." Still more than a little aroused, he knew he wasn't going to sleep well, whether in a soft bed or on a hardwood floor. He closed the door behind them, then brushed a quick kiss across her forehead. "Good night, Leah." Quickly he climbed the stairs that led to the boys' rooms and disappeared.

Leah watched until he was gone, then slowly turned down the hall to her own room. Was she making a mistake in letting him stay? Probably, she admitted. Terence had sorely strained her faith in men. Was the pleasure she found in Bryce's company worth the risk?

She closed the door behind her and began undressing in the dark. As she tugged her sweater over her head, the fabric rubbed against her breasts, reminding her of the feel of his hands there, the taste of his kisses, of the strength in his body and the gentleness in his manner. Was he worth the risk?

Absolutely.

They spent the next afternoon cleaning. Leah, Laurel and Megan scrubbed the windows, floors and even the walls of the small room, while Bryce, Douglas and Matthew carried the room's contents to the empty guest house. On their return trips they brought back a bedstead with a mattress and springs, a single chest and a small table that could serve as nightstand. One of the advantages of running an inn, Leah thought as she and Laurel fitted clean cotton sheets over the bed, was that they always had plenty of furniture. There were other pieces in the guest house and the attic that she could offer, but the room was so small that it was already filled.

"Thanks, guys," she said to the four children lined up in the hall. "Now you need to get cleaned up for the party tonight. Douglas, make sure that Matthew washes his hair—with shampoo this time."

Bryce was leaning against the wall, his head tilted to one side. "What does he normally use to wash his hair?"

"Nothing, if he can get away with it. To Matthew, if it's wet, it's washed." She smoothed a wrinkle from the crocheted cotton coverlet that hung over the bed. "The party starts around six-thirty."

"What should I wear?"

He would look good in anything, she thought, sneaking a speculative glance at him. A suit, a tux, jeans, or nothing at all. That thought made her feel warm all over. She gave a little cough to clear the hoarseness from her throat. "Did you bring a suit?"

"The well-dressed executive never goes anywhere without at least one."

"What do you do?" she asked, realizing that he'd never mentioned his job, and that she had never asked.

"I'm in management with a company that does aerospace research."

She found his response depressing. The job sounded important and exciting and as far removed as possible from anything Angel's Peak—or even Asheville—could offer. "Do you enjoy it?"

"It's a job." And it was responsible for the first serious interest she'd shown in him when she wasn't in his arms.

"How can you take so much time off?"

"The head of the company is a good friend, and I haven't had a vacation in six years."

Since his divorce. Leah was getting more depressed by the minute. Giving the coverlet one last pat, she turned to leave the room.

"Leah? Thanks...for everything."

The guests from town began arriving a few minutes before six-thirty, and soon the living, dining and sitting rooms were full, but Bryce had no trouble finding Leah when he joined the party. He exchanged a few words with a couple from Georgia before taking a place near the door where he could watch her.

"Want a drink?"

He pulled his gaze from Leah to look at her son. "No, thanks."

Douglas mimicked his position, leaning one shoulder against the wall. "There are a lot of people here."

"Your mother must have a lot of friends." He recognized a few of the guests, and the family, of course, but everyone else was a stranger to him.

He felt uncomfortable as he watched Leah circulate through the room, speaking to this guest, listening to that one, smiling briefly at them all. Everyone, male and female alike, lighted up when her attention was directed at them, and he knew the same change came over himself whenever she was near. Still, he resented the little bit of herself that she was giving the others; he wanted all of her.

"You like my mom, don't you?"

Once again he forced his gaze back to Douglas. "She's a beautiful woman."

"And you like her."

"Yes," he admitted honestly. "Very much." He waited, curious about—and a little fearful of—the boy's response to that.

Douglas didn't keep him in suspense long. "Good. We talked it over—the kids and me—and we like you. Just be careful with her, okay?"

"Okay." Bryce watched Douglas leave for the dining

room and the food across the hall. When he turned back, he was grinning. He had just been given the stamp of approval by the four most important people in Leah's life—her children. With them on his side, how could he lose?

Leah approached him silently. "You look pleased with yourself."

He looked her over admiringly. Tonight she was dressed to match her cool, elegant voice in a sweater and skirt of cool, wintry white. The simple lines of the V-necked cardigan were softened by a wide lace collar that fell in narrow points over her breasts, and the slim skirt fitted closely, without clinging to her slender hips. His fingers itched to undo the row of round white buttons that fastened the sweater, but through sheer will he kept them at his sides. "No, I look pleased with you," he disputed her statement. "You're lovely, Leah."

The first time he had told her that, she had known that he was lying. She knew she still wasn't lovely—she was just plain Leah—and he was still lying, but hearing him say it made her *feel* lovely, and that was almost as good. "Is your father going to join us?"

"I saw him just a moment ago in the dining room with Matthew and Megan."

"Matthew thinks he's gotten another grandfather."

"The next best thing to a father." He said the words without thought, naturally, simply. The only way Frank could really be Matthew's grandfather was if Bryce became the boy's father, and that, he had already decided, wasn't a bad idea at all.

"And sometimes better." Leah changed the subject. "Have you met anyone?"

"No."

"Would you like me to introduce you to some of the townspeople?"

"No." He didn't try to be polite. "I came here tonight to look at you."

Her blush was automatic. "Why do you say things like that?"

"Because I mean them. Let's go someplace private."

"I can't."

"I'll be on my best behavior, I promise. I won't try to molest you, or anything."

Their gazes met and held, icy blue and warm brown; then Leah quietly, solemnly, said, "I know you wouldn't. But I'm the hostess tonight, and I can't leave."

Bryce accepted her refusal with a wry smile that said he couldn't be blamed for trying; then, with one hand, he gestured to her guests. "How do you do it, Leah? You give them your smiles, your attention, your hospitality, your time, but they don't really touch you, do they? Do you ever let anybody close enough to care?"

You. You've gotten that close. Too close.

When she turned to walk away from him, he was afraid that he had offended her. Then she stopped and beckoned him to follow.

Most of the guests were filtering into the dining room, where the long mahogany table was filled with treats from Colleen's kitchen. Leah led Bryce in the opposite direction, to a small, private corner of the sitting room. "When I was eight, my best friend was named Barbara. When I was nine, it was Katie, and when I was ten, it was Valerie. When I was eleven, I quit having friends, best or otherwise."

"What happened to Barbara, Katie and Valerie?"

"They were adopted, and I wasn't. When I was younger, none of the prospective parents wanted me, and when I was older, I didn't want them. At least I pretended not to want them. I learned not to count on people, not even best friends who promised to be your friend forever and ever."

And not him. Bryce didn't know if she was aware of her message, but he heard it clearly. She was afraid to trust him, afraid that—like her parents, like Barbara, Katie and Valerie—he would abandon her and leave her alone, forever and ever.

He laid his hand over hers, squeezing her cold fingers together. "Leah, no one can promise forever. Circumstances change. People change."

What was he trying to tell her? That he would offer no promises of a future, of a life together? That now he wanted her, but maybe next week, or next month, he wouldn't? "Some people need promises."

He had been talking about her parents and her friends, but now he realized that she was talking about *them*. He lifted her hand to his mouth, placing a moist kiss in her palm. "I can give you this much: I'll never do anything that might hurt you, and I will try like hell to never disappoint you, or disillusion you, or make you unhappy."

She nodded once. Demanding vows and assurances without offering any of her own was hardly evidence of the trust that Bryce hoped she would learn, but she had to do things her way; it was the only way she knew. Maybe one day she *could* repay him with her trust.

From the hallway a strident voice interrupted their quiet moment. "It's about time you came out of hiding, you old goat. I wondered when you'd find the courage to see me."

Leah and Bryce exchanged glances, then rose together and went in search of the voice's owner. In the broad hallway they found Frank facing his brother for the first time in twenty-six years. They had an audience of grandchildren and party guests to witness their dark scowls and less than affectionate greetings.

"Are you calling me a coward?" Peter demanded, and Bryce started to go to his father's side to stop the affirmative reply Frank was sure to make.

Leah laid her hand on his arm. "Let them argue. Have you eaten yet?"

"They're going to ruin your party."

"No, they're not. Come on. Colleen outdoes herself on her party food." Smiling serenely, she led him by the hand into the dining room, greeting Martha on the way.

His aunt, too, seemed unperturbed by the angry exchange

that was taking place in the hallway. "I told you they would argue," she said as she picked up a china plate that had been in the family for a hundred years. "Oh, doesn't all this food look wonderful?"

Leah handed a plate to Bryce, then took one for herself. "She may fuss about it, but Colleen loves cooking for parties. It gives her a chance to make the sugary desserts that we all love."

Bryce was puzzled by the women's lack of concern over Frank and Peter. A great deal of preparation had gone into this party: the house was immaculate and decorated with fresh and silk flower arrangements; the children were scrubbed and dressed in their Sunday best; and the elaborate buffet had taken hours to prepare and was being eaten from antique china at tables covered with antique linens. Meanwhile, two old men were in the hallway, calling each other names, and the hostesses couldn't have cared less.

As she slid gracefully into a seat at an empty table, Leah smiled at Bryce, seeing his confusion. "There's nothing wrong with arguing. It's a means of letting off steam, of easing the pressure. Frank and Peter haven't seen each other in years, and they parted under less than amicable circumstances. After all this time, they're not going to suddenly be best friends again. Give them a chance."

"How did you get to be so wise at such a young age?" he teased.

"Personal experience."

His smile faded. Yes, she probably knew all about unfriendly circumstances, about letting off steam and easing pressure. That unflappable control that he had often wished to see her lose was her way of dealing with pressure. He wondered if she ever got mad and yelled the way his father so often did. It was hard to imagine an outraged Leah, but any show of intense emotion—be it anger, joy or passion—would make her beauty come to life.

Passion. The gleaming silver fork trembled in his unsteady hand. He had been given a brief glimpse of her passion, and it had been almost more than he could bear. It would take time, he knew, before she gave herself entirely to him—time he could use to prepare himself for it. Loving Leah wasn't going to be easy—but it *was* going to be magnificent.

The party lasted several hours after the entertainment initially provided by Frank and Peter. Following a heated and loud argument in the hall, Peter had retreated to the sitting room, accompanied by Douglas and Laurel. Megan and Matthew had followed Frank into the dining room, and the two men had remained separated the rest of the evening.

After saying good-night to the last guest, Leah took a seat on the sofa, kicked off her high heels, stretched out her legs till her feet reached the coffee table and tilted her head back. She liked parties—a good thing, since she had to have so many—but she loved being alone in the quiet house when they ended.

"You look tired."

At least, she had once loved being alone. She could very easily grow used to Bryce's company when everyone else was gone or in bed. She smiled without opening her eyes when she felt the cushions give as he sat down next to her.

"Actually I lied. You look tired *and* beautiful."

She opened one eye. "Do you always give compliments so freely?"

"Only when they're deserved." He was sitting sideways so he could study her. Tonight was only the second time he'd seen her in a skirt. As nice as she looked in slim-fitting jeans, he realized what he'd been missing when his gaze reached her legs. Encased in sheer, creamy-tinted stockings, they were long, slender and shapely. They were the perfect length to make their bodies a perfect fit together.

He lifted one hand to touch her hair. It was full and bouncy and unbelievably soft.

"Not tonight, Bryce," she whispered, raising her head to look at him.

"Not tonight what?"

"Don't touch me. Don't kiss me."

"Why not?"

"Because...tonight I feel very...vulnerable. Don't make me want you, because I couldn't say no, and it would be wrong."

The surge of emotion that rushed through him made his smile sweet and very tender. She was the most complex woman he'd ever known—the mother of four children, yet still more innocent than most teenagers; cool and reserved outside, but filled with warmth and passion inside; wounded by love, by a man, but—he hoped—willing to try again with both. She had grown up deprived of the love and caring that most people took for granted, yet she hadn't lost her own great capacity for love. He wanted to take that love, every bit of it, and give back ten times more.

"All evening I've been fantasizing about kissing you... about undoing every button on this sweater so I could see you...." He knew from its smooth, unbroken lines that she was naked beneath it, that only eight buttons separated him from seeing, touching and kissing her breasts—eight buttons, a lifetime of fear and his hopes for their future.

Taking a deep breath, he leaned over her. "One kiss," he promised when he saw the faint alarm in her eyes. "Just one kiss, then I'll go."

Like everything else about him, the kiss was gentle. She could taste the heat, the hunger, the need—all tightly controlled. She wanted more—wanted it all—but when he raised his head, she let him go.

"Good night, Leah."

"Good night, Bryce," she whispered as he left her alone in the quiet, lonely room.

Business at the inn was slower over the next few weeks. A warm spell melted much of the snow, sending the skiers to slopes farther north for their holidays. Thanksgiving was a rather small affair, with only a handful of guests seated around the family table.

Knowing that the snow would come again, Leah was relieved by the slack period. She divided her time between her office, the workshop and the attic. She was inordinately pleased when, more often than not, Bryce joined her in the latter two places. He watched her work on the exquisite Christmas ornaments that she made by the dozen, and helped her by packing the ones for sale in tissue paper and boxes, and stacking the ones for the inn separately. He worked alongside her in the attic, patiently untangling string after string of lights, checking and replacing bulbs from the supply she kept and making suggestions for storage that would avoid the mess next year.

And they talked. He asked her dozens of questions, probing into every area of her life, curious about everything that had ever happened to her, everything she had ever wanted. No man had ever paid so much attention to her, not even Terence, not even in the beginning when, like many young men, he'd been more interested in Leah's body than her mind or her heart. It made her feel…special.

It also scared her. Wanting to feel special had led her to make a commitment to Terence—a commitment she hadn't been ready for and one he hadn't wanted. It had led to a long, unhappy period in her life, yet here she was, close to doing it again. She tried telling herself that things were different this time—she was thirty-five now, a mother and a successful businesswoman, not a frightened, lonely seventeen-year-old. And the commitment this time would be to Bryce, who, even on a bad day, was at least twice the man Terence had been. But the fear was still there.

Every time he kissed her, she panicked. She wanted so much more, and knew that he was offering it, but she was afraid to accept. Afraid of disappointing him, of being inadequate. Afraid of making a mistake that would cost her her heart. But she enjoyed him—his kisses, his company, his smiles. It was almost sinful to find so much pleasure in one person.

Bryce's voice interrupted her dreamy smile. "This is beautiful. Did you make it?"

She crossed the living room of the cottage that served as her workroom to join him as he lifted a small house from its protective box. When he set it on the low coffee table that stood in front of the fireplace, he knelt to admire the detailing on it.

"Peter cut out the pieces, Douglas put them together, and I painted and decorated it." Kneeling beside him, she reached out to carefully remove a piece of cotton.

The house stood eighteen inches high and was a perfect replica of the inn, from the snow on the roof down to the brass plaque beside the door. It was decorated for Christmas, with tiny green wreaths and tinier red bows on each window, and miniature white bulbs strung along the top of the veranda and the railing.

He reached out to give her a hug, pulling her off balance, and they both fell to the floor. "You're a talented lady," he said, wrapping his arms around her and lifting her on top of him.

"I'm good with my hands," she replied innocently.

"Anytime you want to show me just how good, I'm yours for the taking."

She raised herself with both hands on his chest to keep from getting too close, but that was a mistake, since the position merely pressed the lower half of her body more snugly against the lower half of his.

Bryce knew the instant she became aware of his arousal, because her face turned the color of the Christmas red around them. When she tried to move, he slid his hands to her bottom, holding her firmly against him. "This is something you need to get used to, honey," he said softly. "There's nothing shameful about it. Every time I get near you or look at you—practically every time I think about you—I get hard because I want you."

Leah dropped her head to his chest, where she could hear the erratic beat of his heart. How could she tell him that she knew nothing about desire, about rousing it or satisfying it? That she knew even less about men and the mysteries of their bodies? It was her naïveté that flooded her face with heat—but she knew her innocence wasn't responsible for the heat that flooded her body.

Carefully she moved away from him, scrambled to her feet and dusted off her clothes. Bryce got up, too.

She busied her hands with some of the more delicate decorations for several minutes before starting to speak. Her eyes were cast down, her voice low and strangely remote. "Sex with Terence was infrequent and sometimes painful and...unfulfilling. I knew nothing when I met him, and I had learned very little when he died."

Bryce was torn between anger for his cousin, sympathy for Leah and joy for himself. She was learning to trust him, learning to give him parts of herself that she'd kept hidden deep inside.

Sensing that she wouldn't welcome any words from him, he instead carefully considered hers. Infrequent, painful and unfulfilling. He had already suspected that the Terence he'd known as a boy hadn't deserved a woman as gentle and loving as Leah. He had apparently been a selfish and ungiving lov—partner, Bryce substituted. He wouldn't apply the word lover to Terence.

She set down the crocheted ornament she was holding and walked to the window. "If you want someone to sleep with, Bryce, you'd be better off finding someone in town. Someone who knows what she's doing. Someone who's... normal."

"Leah, Leah." Bryce put his arms around her from behind and pressed a kiss to her hair. "I quit looking for someone to 'sleep with' when I was twenty. I don't want someone else, Leah, I want *you*. Honey, there's nothing abnormal about being afraid. I haven't lived the kind of life you have, but do you think I'm not scared?" He paused, but she gave no reply. "I'm scared as hell that you'll be disappointed in me. I'm scared that I'm not good enough, handsome enough, smart enough, skilled enough, to make you forget the past.''

She slowly turned in his arms. "Really?"

"Does that surprise you?"

"Yes. You seem so confident all the time."

He grinned. "Believe it or not, so do you, a lot of the time." Then he sobered. "I'm not going to seduce you, Leah. When we make love—*if* we make love—it will be your choice. It will be because you want me, because you need me...because you trust me." He kissed her once, gently, then released her and began gathering the strings of big white light bulbs he'd brought with him from the attic. "Douglas, Matthew and I are going to start putting these up after school today, all right?"

That was usually a job she shared with the boys, but she was more than willing to give it up to Bryce. With every day, she thought dryly, there were more and more things she was willing to turn over to him—her home, her job, her kids, her heart. If only he would accept them for forever.

"Leah, where's the ladder?"

She surfaced from her thoughts. "In the storage shed out back. Want me to carry the lights while you get it?"

He chuckled. "I've spent the better part of a week getting your tangles out of these lights. You're not touching them again. I think I can handle it alone."

She watched him leave, the long heavy strings looped over his shoulder, before she returned to her worktable. The top was scattered with an afternoon's work—delicate hearts and wreaths shaped from wire, covered with ecru or white lace and colored glass beads in Christmas red, green and gold, and lavender, pink and light blue—ice blue, Bryce had called it. "The color of the winter sky...the color of your eyes." She smiled shyly, fingering one of the pretty blue beads.

With a sigh she took a book from the tall cabinet behind her. Written by North Carolina's best-known quilter, the book had provided Leah with the patterns for her newest project. Small pieces of wood, only two inches square, were stacked at one end of the table, next to small bottles of red, green, gold and white paint. She had already transferred the patterns to the thin wooden squares; today, with no distractions—particularly handsome, sexy, dark-haired, chocolate-eyed distractions—she was ready to try her hand at painting them.

Her first attempt was a disaster. The patterns, meant to create twelve-inch squares, were reduced to little more than a square inch on the tiny plaque, leaving an unfinished border on each side. Tossing the first one into the wastebasket, she reached for another piece of wood and chose a much smaller brush.

With practice, patience and a steady hand, the results gradually grew better. When she finished the last one, her jaw ached from clenching her teeth together and her right hand was tired from the tight control she'd needed, but the squares were almost perfect. When the paint was dry, she would insert colorful ribbons through the tiny holes she had drilled in each piece and tie neat little bows for hangers, and one more project would be finished.

She cleaned her brushes, resealed the bottles of paint and grabbed her coat from the old sofa. The children were home from school now, which meant that Bryce and the boys would be at work with the lights. If she hurried, she could watch them complete her least favorite job.

She entered the house from the back, intending to pass straight through to the front door, but the sight of Frank in the sitting room, with the television set tuned to his favorite soap opera, detoured her. He wouldn't openly admit to watching the soaps, but it was a habit he'd picked up in the hospital.

"Can I get you anything, Frank?" she asked, stepping inside the room.

"You could change channels for me, so I don't have to watch this drivel."

"Why, Frank, then you'd just have to get up and turn it back when I leave." She perched on the arm of the sofa and gazed at the screen for a minute before turning to the old man. He looked like Bryce would look in another thirty years or so, she decided. He was thin and stooped, but she attributed that to his illness. He had already gained about five pounds on the diet Colleen fixed for him and was looking stronger every day. "You know, if you really don't like these shows, you could do something else."

"Like what?"

"Like get some exercise. The doctor told you to start walking, didn't she?"

He pointed out the window with a bony hand. "That's snow out there, girl. An old man like me can't go wandering around in the snow. I've got a bad heart, you know."

"Your disposition is none too good, either. I take a walk every day. You can go with me. I'll make sure nothing happens to you."

"Hmm. You take a walk every *night*—so you can be alone with Bryce. Where *is* my son, anyway? About the only time I see him is with you. He follows you around like a bull in—"

"Frank," she interrupted gently, "Bryce is outside with the boys, hanging the Christmas lights. Have you seen Peter lately?"

He grimaced at the mention of his brother. "Him? Now why would I want to waste my time with him when there are so many more interesting things to do? I could sit and watch myself grow older, or watch the snow melt, or..."

Leah tuned him out with a fond smile. She had finally reached the conclusion that Frank's greatest pleasure in being here at the estate was bickering with his brother. They groused and griped, but nothing made their day like a good, rousing argument.

"You know, you're a pretty girl—a little bit too prim and proper for my tastes, but pretty all the same. When are you going to quit making Bryce dance around for you and give him what he wants?''

''When are you going to quit minding other people's business?'' she countered.

He laughed at that. ''I was afraid when I first came here that you were going to be too timid to speak up. If you could have seen the look on your face when we first met—the way you turned to Bryce, as if he could protect you.''

''But I don't need protection, do I? You're a harmless old man, Frank Cameron.'' She stood up, bent down to kiss his forehead, then left the room.

Chapter 6

When Leah stepped onto the porch, she nearly bumped into Douglas, who was perched above her head on the ladder. She swerved to avoid hitting him, calling up a greeting as she did so.

"Hey, Mom," Matthew called. "I'm helping hang the lights." He was up high, too, sitting on Bryce's shoulders, strands of wire and fat white bulbs wrapped around his neck and cascading over his arms. He was feeding the wire to Douglas, who, armed with a staple gun, was attaching it to the porch ceiling. "Don't it look neat?"

"Real neat," she agreed, sliding past them to reach the decorations Bryce had gathered earlier. There were wreaths with big red velvet bows to hang on each of the front windows—both upstairs and down—stacks of fresh pine boughs to form looping garlands along the porch railing and the wreath for the front door.

She leaned her shoulder against a post and watched them until they moved her out of their way once, then again. At last Bryce said, "As long as you're out here, you could help, you know."

"What do you want me to do?"

What a loaded question—and he couldn't even comment on it with both Douglas and Matthew so close. Lifting one hand from Matthew's leg, he pointed to the neat loops of tiny white lights. "You could start putting those in the bushes."

With a salute she picked up the first string and went to work. She had completed the shrubs on one side of the steps when one of their few guests returned. The woman stopped on the sidewalk next to Leah. "The house is going to look so beautiful, all decorated for Christmas," she said with a warm smile. "It's almost enough to make me skip Christmas at home and come here."

Leah murmured a polite response, but her gaze was on Bryce, watching him laugh and talk with the kids.

"Your husband seems to have a wonderful relationship with your sons. So many men these days just don't take the time to enjoy their children—they're busy with jobs and a million other things. Too often we put our children last, and that's such a shame."

Leah colored deeply. She opened her mouth to correct the woman's mistake, then closed it again. It would be easier to let her believe that Bryce was Leah's husband than to explain. Besides, she had to admit, there was a part of her that liked the assumption. She had decided long ago that Bryce would be a good father; now she was beginning to believe that he would be an even better husband. She was falling deeper and harder and faster than she'd dreamed possible. Falling in love.

The guest went inside, and Leah went back to work, putting her thoughts on hold. She concentrated on looping the wires over and through the fragile branches without breaking or damaging them, and on keeping thoughts of love and marriage and Bryce out of her mind.

"When you finish, Mom, come on up and supervise the hanging of the wreaths," Douglas suggested.

She slipped the last cord into the last bush, then hurried up the steps. Even in her boots her feet were numb from being buried in the snow for so long.

They hung a fragrant circle of pine on each of the downstairs windows, straightening the bright red bows; then Bryce and Douglas placed the last one on the door. The wreath was almost as wide as the door, about four feet across, and was simply decorated with two red tin doves. Narrow lengths of red ribbon extended from their beaks to a red tin heart that hung in the center.

"Are we finished?" Bryce asked, joining Leah at the top of the stairs.

Leah was staring at the wreath, seeing the heart and thinking about the serious condition of her own. "No," she replied softly, thoughtfully. "We've just begun."

He looked down at her, gauging the faraway look in her eyes. She wasn't thinking about decorations right now any more than he was. Although he had pretended not to, he had heard the woman's comment about him and the boys. What was more important, he *hadn't* heard Leah correct the mistake.

"Oh, Mom," Douglas groaned. "It's cold out here. Can't the upstairs wreaths and the garlands wait until tomorrow?"

Startled, she looked up, but met Bryce's eyes instead of her son's. "Yes, of course they can. Go on in and get started on your homework."

Both boys hesitated at the door. Leah looked from Bryce to them, then followed their glances upward, way up above her head. There they had hung not just a sprig, but an entire branch of mistletoe, with its thick green leaves and waxy white berries. She laughed softly. "Whose idea was that?"

"I confess." Bryce casually laid his arm around her shoulders. He was mentally holding his breath, awaiting her reaction. Leah disliked any demonstration of affection from him in front of the kids or the guests, an irritant that he'd willingly tolerated until now. But how could their relationship develop any further without some concessions on her part? It wasn't as if it were a secret; everyone, from the kids to Peter, Martha and Frank, as well as a large number of the guests, knew that they were involved.

Laughing again, she reached up to brush a pine needle from his hair. "Why doesn't that surprise me? Well, who am I to argue with tradition?" Locking gazes with him, she laid her hands on his shoulders for balance, rose onto her toes and brushed her lips slowly, teasingly, over his.

Matthew giggled, then clamped his hand over his mouth when Douglas shushed him. Without looking away, Bryce suggested softly, "Why don't you guys give your mother and me a little privacy? I want to show her a new tradition."

"What is it?" Matthew asked.

Douglas opened the door. "He's going to kiss her—a *real* kiss. Come on, you don't want to watch."

"What's your new tradition?" Leah asked, tilting back her head to smile at him.

He caught his breath. "I suppose making love under the mistletoe is out?"

She raised one brow. "On the front porch? In twenty-degree weather? I'm afraid so. Do you have another suggestion?"

Clasping his hands behind her back, he pulled her closer at the same time that he lowered his head. "I suppose we could try a real kiss, like Douglas said." But he sampled her lips, cold and soft and giving, only briefly before pulling back. "Leah...how long do we have to wait?"

She knew immediately what he meant. They were both adults. He wanted to make love to her, and she...Lord, how she wanted it, too. So why didn't she just say, "Come to my room tonight"?

Because she couldn't. It had to be more than just sex for her, and Bryce had said nothing about more. She knew that he liked her—he was so patient, so concerned, so sweet, so caring—but did he love her the way she loved him? *Could* he love her? Or was he merely enjoying her company while he was here? Would he forget her when he returned to Philadelphia?

A few weeks ago she had been asking the same frustrating questions about Bryce and Matthew. Now she was concerned about herself. How could she stand it if they became lovers, and then he went home at the beginning of January and she never saw him again?

"There's more going on in that mind of yours at one time than in anyone's I've ever known," Bryce said softly. He had been watching her—had almost seen her struggle as she sought an answer that would satisfy him without compromising herself. She was a complicated woman. "Have you ever done anything on impulse, Leah, without thinking about it, without considering the consequences?"

"Yes. Do you want to know what the consequences were?"

He had made a bad choice of question. Instead of showing her that not every situation required detailed analysis, he had given her the perfect opportunity to demonstrate why she shouldn't accept him as a lover yet. "I think I already know," he said grimly. "You found yourself pregnant, without a husband, without a family, without any means of support."

"I was a senior in high school. When I first found out I was pregnant, I was happy. I was naive, I guess. I thought that surely Terence would be thrilled, too, and he would marry me, and we'd be the perfect American family, with Terence going off to work every day, and me staying home to take care of the house and the baby. When he told me that he not only didn't want the baby but didn't want me either…"

He cradled her closer to his chest. When he spoke, his jaw rubbed against her silky hair. "But you're not seventeen, Leah, and I'm not Terence."

"No," she whispered in agreement. His simple argument meant everything—and nothing. She was thirty-five years old now, fully capable of risking an affair with a man who might or might not love her. But she was still so much like that seventeen-year-old girl. She still had the same needs, the same desires. The same doubts and the same fears.

Bryce raised her chin, kissed her hard and let her go. "Whenever you're ready…"

He had to know that if he tried to seduce her, he would succeed. That tinged Leah's smile with gratitude. "You'll be the first to know…. Thank you, Bryce."

Leah saw little of Bryce over the next few days. He wasn't exactly avoiding her—they still shared their meals and their evening walks—but he spent more time away from her, giving her time, she supposed, to think about their relationship. She found that she missed him a lot, even though he was living in the same house. If it was this bad now, how would she manage when he returned to Philadelphia?

When he came to her office Friday afternoon, she was pleased to see him, in spite of the work she had piled in front of her. She brushed a strand of hair from her eyes, making a mental note that she needed a trim before the round of Christmas parties began in earnest. "Hi," she greeted him with a warm, almost shy smile. "I haven't seen much of you lately."

He didn't comment on the fact that they'd had lunch together less than two hours ago. It had been an interesting meal, with Frank at one end of the table and Peter at the other, trading insults so fast and so loudly that Bryce hadn't had a chance to say more than a few words to Leah. "What are you doing?" Circling the desk, he looked over her shoulder at the monthly accounts. "Why are you working on these now? Why not wait until the end of the month when you have all your figures together?"

"Because it'll take me until then to get *these* figures

straightened out. I hate paperwork." She bent her head forward to stretch her neck. While it was exposed, Bryce bent to kiss it.

"You need somebody to handle this stuff for you so you can spend all your time doing the important things, like running the inn." Somebody like himself, who enjoyed keeping track of accounts, figures, payroll, correspondence and all the minor details of a business.

"I know, but every time I think of the salary I'd have to pay someone to do it, I decide I can tolerate it a little while longer."

He walked around the desk again, then sat down in the straight-backed chair. "I'm here, and I'm free. Why don't you let me handle it for you?"

Leah wanted to accept his offer immediately, but how could she? They were already into December, and he was planning to return to Philadelphia at the beginning of the year. She had already come to rely so much on him; if she gave him this job, it would be even harder when he left.

Whom was she trying to kid? she asked herself as she leaned back in her comfortable leather chair. Even if he never lifted a finger to help her out, it would be impossible to accept his departure. She had warned herself against getting involved with a man who lived so far away, then had gone and done it anyway. She had fallen in love with Bryce Cameron.

"Where do you go when you wander off like that?" he asked, calling her attention back to him. "Sometimes it's as if we're not even in the same universe."

She attempted to smile. "I was just thinking about something."

"Want to talk about it?"

"No thanks."

"Do you care if I talk about what's on my mind?"

"Of course not. Go ahead."

He stretched his legs out, crossed his ankles and folded his hands over his stomach. In faded jeans and a dark purple sweater, he looked incredibly handsome. "I'm thinking about selling my house."

She stared at him. "I didn't know you had one," she said stupidly.

"I had to have someplace to live in Philadelphia when I was there," he joked. "When Kay left me, I got to keep the house—Derek already had one that was much nicer, according to her. Anyway, I'm thinking about putting it on the market."

"But…where will you live?"

He lifted his arms in a wide embrace. "Here. Not necessarily *right* here, but Angel's Peak."

She swallowed hard. "But…"

"But?" He gently encouraged her to ask whatever she wanted.

"What about your job?"

"I would quit. Six hundred miles is a bit too far to commute, don't you think?" He was acting casual and unconcerned, but his insides were churning. In the last few weeks he had made incredible progress with Leah, but she was still hesitant about committing herself to their relationship. Finally his father had suggested the reason: the fact that Bryce was scheduled to return to Philadelphia at the beginning of the year could be holding her back. So he had found a solution to the problem: he would quit his job, sell his house and move back to Angel's Peak, North Carolina.

He hadn't made the decision lightly. Philadelphia had been his home for most of his life, and he knew the city the way Leah knew tiny Angel's Peak. He had worked for the same company for twenty years; he made a good salary, held a position of authority and knew the personal lives of all his co-workers. He owned a beautiful home there, and his friends were there.

He had asked himself repeatedly over the last few days if he was certain he wanted to make such a permanent move. Angel's Peak offered little to compete with a city like Philadelphia. The services in town were geared toward skiers—ski shops, motels and restaurants—but little else was available. Shopping for anything more complicated than groceries required a trip down the mountain to Asheville. If he got a job, it would have to be in Asheville, too, leaving him with a two-hour commute each day in less than ideal weather. For entertainment Angel's Peak offered a movie theater with one screen and a good high school basketball team, but nothing as sophisticated as a symphony orchestra or theater. There was one bank, one doctor and one dentist. Was he really considering giving up everything familiar in Philadelphia and spending the rest of his life here?

Yes. Because Angel's Peak had something that Philadelphia could never have: Leah.

"Can you afford to do that?" The questions coming out of her mouth were totally stupid, Leah realized, but she couldn't seem to make her brain work. She was too dazed by the possibility of Bryce remaining in Angel's Peak— with her—forever.

He chuckled. "I have some money from investments and the pension plan at work, but eventually I would probably have to get a job."

"But there aren't any aerospace companies around here."

"Honey, I'm in management," he reminded her gently. "I can work in almost any kind of business. It doesn't have to be aerospace."

"But..."

"Leah, are you saying that you don't want me living here?"

"No! I think—I think it would be wonderful." Her eyes were practically glowing. "You actually want to live here...with us?"

"With you."

"For how long?"

"Oh, not too long. Just the next fifty years or so."

A sobering thought struck her, and the light disappeared

from her eyes. Nervously she picked up a pencil, replaced it, then reached for a pen and put it back, too. "Bryce, you aren't doing this just because of me, are you?"

"Sort of." He sat up straighter. "When I first met you, Leah, I told myself all the reasons why I couldn't get involved with you—probably the same reasons you told yourself. One of those reasons was the distance between us. My life, my job, my friends—they're all in Philadelphia. But you couldn't live there. You couldn't give up this house, or Peter and Martha, and uproot your kids and move so far away. But it's a simple matter for me to sell my house and quit my job."

Simple! There he went again, making things seem so easy. He was talking about a change that would scare her senseless and calling it simple. "But your friends..."

"All of them together aren't as important to me as you and your family are."

She still looked faintly troubled. "But...what if things between us don't work out?"

He left his chair and knelt beside her. "That's a risk I have to take—just like trusting me is a risk that someday you're going to have to take."

Hesitantly she slid her fingers through his hair. It was still hard for her to return the little touches and caresses that came so naturally to him. "I'm not sure I'm worth that risk."

"I am."

Tears were building inside her, and she tried to stop them with a little humor. "You have a lot of faith in yourself, Bryce Cameron."

"No," he disagreed softly. "I have faith in you."

He left her then with a kiss and a hug, before she could argue, before she could think of more worries. She sat motionless for a long, long time, no longer dazed but considering the possibility of Bryce living in Angel's Peak. The excitement built inside her. They could see each other every day, not for the next few weeks, but for the rest of their lives. She would have unlimited time with him, to get to know him, to learn to trust him, to love him.

Maybe he did love her, after all, even though he'd never said it. She hadn't told him that she loved him, either, but she did. Besides, merely having an affair wouldn't require this kind of major upheaval in his life; only something more permanent would. Like marriage.

That was what she wanted, she admitted—the happy, love-filled, enduring, forever and ever kind of marriage that only Bryce could give her. She wanted to be his wife. Remembering his response the night she'd told him that she had received Frank's approval to bear his grandchildren, she smiled bittersweetly. She even wanted to be the mother of his children.

Ignoring the files in front of her, she left her desk and got her coat and gloves from the closet. If she was going to think about something as important as marriage, she needed to be alone, where no one could disturb her. She needed to take a walk.

As a kid growing up in the home, marriage had been her goal in life; in spite of women's lib, she had wanted nothing more than to be a wife and mother. But marriage to Terence had shown her that there was a great deal of difference between her dreams and reality. After his death, she had decided that she would never again marry and give that sort of control over her life—over her happiness—to someone else.

But Bryce wasn't like Terence. Bryce cared for her, and he was fond of her children. Terence had married her to gain ownership of the estate, but Bryce would gain nothing from the marriage but a wife and a family. He would treat her with the same respect and affection and gentleness that she received now.

She laughed derisively. What grand dreams she had! Here she was thinking about marriage when their relationship had gone no further than kisses and occasional stolen caresses. They hadn't even made love yet. She didn't know when she would be ready for that, but she was already making marriage plans.

Her wandering path had brought her to the family plot, but she wasn't alone there. She stopped short when she saw Frank's familiar figure, heavily bundled against the cold. He was standing in front of Katherine's grave, his head bowed. Even from a distance she could see the emotion that lined his face, and, feeling guilty at intruding, she began backing away. She had taken only a few steps when he heard her and turned.

"Don't go, Leah."

Hesitantly, she walked through the gate and to his side. "I didn't mean to disturb you."

"It's all right." He gestured to the marker. "This is my Katherine. She's been dead a long time."

Thirty-nine years; Leah knew without checking the dates inscribed on the stone. Practically a lifetime, yet Frank had never married again.

"I miss her. All those years in Philadelphia I pretended not to, because I couldn't come back here and visit her. But, Lord, I wish she was still here with me." He wiped one hand across his eyes, then looked at Leah. "Do you believe in life after death?"

"Heaven?" She nodded. "I guess I do."

"Heaven." He nodded, too, solemnly. "That's what it'll be like, seeing her again. She was younger than me by eight years...a bit shy...and not very pretty to other people. But I thought she was beautiful."

Leah smiled a little. She had seen pictures of Katherine. The other woman had been plain, colorless and unassuming—a lot like Leah herself. It said something about Frank's love that he'd found her beautiful.

And what did it say about Bryce that he found *her* lovely? a sneaky little voice inside her asked.

"When she died...if it hadn't been for Bryce, I would have given up. But he was just a baby, and my mother was too old to raise him alone. He needed me."

"And you never married again."

"I never found a woman who could compare with Katherine." With a gloved hand, he brushed a thin layer of snow from the top of the stone. "Sometimes love is like that. You meet someone, and you know right away that she's the only woman you'll ever love or want, even if you lose her. You know that you'll never stop loving her, right up until the day you die. And if someone loves you that way, Leah, and you love him back, you can have a happiness that most people only dream about." He raised imploring brown eyes to her face. "Don't be a fool, Leah. Don't throw it away."

She shivered uncomfortably. "I don't know what you mean...."

He waved his hand impatiently. "You do know."

"Bryce has never said—"

"Sometimes the words don't come easily, but there are ways to show love without saying them."

Such as giving up his job and the city that had been his home for twenty-six years? Such as moving six hundred miles to be close? "He was married for fourteen years. How do you know that his love for Kay wasn't the kind you described—the kind that doesn't stop, that goes on forever?"

"Because if it was, he could never look at you the way he does." He laid his hand on her arm. "My son is a good man, Leah. For growing up without a mother and only a crotchety old man for a father, he's a damn good man. You couldn't ask for a better husband or father for your kids." He gave a sigh of exasperation. "What are you so afraid of, girl? Why does being loved scare you so?"

She tried to respond teasingly. "Why do you spend so much time nosing around in things that don't concern you?" But there was no light in her eyes, and her voice sounded heavy.

With a forlorn sigh, she looped her arm through his. "Come on, Frank. Walk back to the house with me."

He wasn't ready to leave yet, but if Bryce found out that he'd walked alone through the snow to the cemetery there would be hell to pay. With one last look at Katherine's grave, he let Leah lead him through the gate and into the woods.

The weekend brought more parties—one for Megan's birthday on Friday night and the annual tree-decorating celebration Saturday. Small evergreens, only two to three feet tall, were placed in each of the twelve guest rooms, the dining room, the sitting room and the family's private living room. A larger one, more than fourteen feet tall, stood in the place of honor in the living room, having been wrestled into place by Bryce and Douglas. All the guests took part in the decorating, shared the lavish buffet prepared by Colleen and her staff, and joined in singing carols when the big tree was finished. It was a thoroughly enjoyable way to spend an evening, Bryce decided when it was over. Having to go to bed by himself afterward, would be the only part of it that he would change. Sleeping alone in a bed for two, while Leah was just a few steps down the hall, was growing more difficult and less restful with each night.

He heard her soft sigh behind him, but didn't turn. It was after midnight, and the guests had all wandered off to bed. The children were tucked in, the house was quiet, and the lights, except those shining on the tree before him, were out.

Leah slipped her arms around him from behind. It was the first private moment they'd had together all evening. "The tree is beautiful, isn't it?"

"Hmm."

"I love Christmas. There was never much money for gifts at the home, but...there was always such peace. A feeling that for a while, at least, nothing could go wrong." Then she smiled, pressing her cheek against the soft knit of his gray-striped sweater. "It doesn't make much sense, really—my parents left me there on Christmas Eve—but I still feel...safe.''

Bryce laid his hands over hers, clasped lightly at his waist. He could imagine her as a frightened, bewildered child, wondering where her parents were and when they were coming back, and his heart ached for her. And Christmas was supposed to be a season of love. He was surprised that she was able to celebrate the holiday at all. "Do you still wonder about them—who they were, where they are... why they left you?"

"Occasionally."

"Have you ever tried to find the answers?"

"The state tried for a while, but there was so little to go on. They didn't even know if Douglas was my real name."

"And you've never tried on your own?"

"No." She hugged him a little tighter. "They didn't want me. They must have had their reasons, and maybe they were good ones, but it doesn't change the fact that *they didn't want me*. I'm not going to show up in their lives now."

"But don't you want to know?" He turned, staying within her embrace, and wrapped his arms around her.

"No. I have everything I need right here—my children, Peter and Martha, the inn...."

He spoke hoarsely. "What about me, Leah?"

With a tremulous smile, she brushed her fingers through his hair. "Yes, I need you, too." Rising onto her toes, she pressed her lips to his, briefly at first, hesitantly, then surely and hungrily. "Stay with me tonight, Bryce," she invited, sliding her hands down to cup his face. "Please."

Clasping her hands between his, he pulled them away, then took a step back. "Are you sure, Leah?"

She nodded.

"Why?"

If he didn't seem anxious to take advantage of her invitation, she wasn't offended. He had waited a long time, willingly, patiently. She didn't blame him for wanting a few answers first. "Because you're a good, gentle man. Because you have faith in me. Because you've cared enough to let me make the decision myself." *And because I love you.* She looked at their hands, locked together, then at his face. She wanted to be with him, to be a part of him. She wanted to share her body, her life, her heart and her soul with him. Forever.

"Are you going to regret it tomorrow?" He couldn't bear it if he saw regret for their lovemaking in her icy-blue eyes.

"I will never regret anything about you, Bryce."

He raised her hands to his mouth for a kiss, then gestured for her to lead the way. He followed her to her room, where she paused, considering the proximity of Frank's room. Taking her hand once more, Bryce led her farther down the hall to his own room.

Laurel had donated a pair of pewter candlesticks from her bedroom to set atop the tall chest of drawers. Releasing Leah's hand at the door, Bryce picked up the box of matches that lay between the candles, struck a flame and held it to each wick.

Leah closed the door behind her. The candlelight gave a soft, warm glow to the small room, providing enough light to see by, but leaving enough darkness to shelter in. She took a few steps into the room, stopping near the foot of the bed, and waited. She had never taken part in a seduction before, and she didn't know what to do. Even her hands seemed to dangle uselessly.

Bryce moved slowly. From the corner of his eye he could see Leah's shadow falling across the crocheted spread, but he didn't look at her. She was nervous...but so was he. Kay's insults echoed in his brain, making his fingers tremble as he removed his watch and laid it on the nightstand. He had sworn to never disappoint Leah, but what if he did? What if she, like Kay, found him unsatisfying?

Slowly he turned to look at her. He loved her. That had to make a difference, didn't it? He didn't know when his love for Kay had died, but toward the end, their lovemaking had stemmed from habit, not passion. Not need. Not love. But what he felt for Leah was all those things—passion, need, love—and so much more. They would give him the skill, the patience, the gentleness, all that he needed to love her.

He bent to take off his shoes and socks. He kicked them under the bed, tugged his sweater over his head, dropped it onto the rug, then finally went to her. "Do you know how much I need you?" He followed her gaze to the bed and shook his head. "Not just like this—in my bed—but in my *life*. I want to spend the rest of my life with you, Leah. Every day and every night."

She raised one trembling hand to touch his lips. "Show me what to do. Teach me how to make love with you...how to touch you...how to please you."

He kissed her palm, then laid it on his bare chest. "Everything about you pleases me, Leah. The way you look at me, the way you smile. The way you walk, the way you talk, even the way you avoid looking at me when others are around."

She gave a soft, nervous laugh. "You're easily pleased."

His shoulders rose and fell in a shrug. "What can I say?"

She dropped her gaze to her hand, pressed flat beneath his against his chest. She could feel his heartbeat, strong and steady. Hers was racing at about a million beats a minute. "Can I...touch you?"

Moved by her timid request, he nodded silently, not trusting his voice to work, and lifted his hand from hers.

His chest was broad and smooth, soft warm skin stretched taut over hard muscles. She glided her hand across, then down to the barrier of his trousers. Bringing her other hand to him, she slid them back up to his shoulders.

The male body was something of a mystery to her. She had rarely touched Terence—cool and withdrawn, he hadn't invited that kind of casual intimacy—and in the twelve years of marriage, she could count on her fingers the number of times that she had seen him without clothing. Now Bryce was standing before her, welcoming her touch and, if the sudden change in his breathing was anything to judge by, enjoying it.

Her hands resting once more at the waistband of his slacks, she raised her eyes to him. Asking permission? Bryce thought, catching his breath. He couldn't stop her now if his life depended on it. He nodded in response.

She easily unbuckled his belt and pulled it free, dropping it to the floor. The button slid open; then, with agonizing slowness, she pulled the zipper to its end and touched a finger to the exposed skin above his briefs.

Bryce closed his eyes, assuring himself that she wasn't deliberately punishing him. She was unsure, innocent, inexperienced. She didn't realize the effect her questing, learning fingertips were having on him. His heart was pounding now, echoing like thunder in his ears, and his blood was heated and rushing to every part of his body, including the hardness that was swelling just below her hand.

Leah touched her tongue to her upper lip, pulled her hands back, folded them together and looked up at Bryce. He opened his eyes in time to see the anxiety in hers. "I—I don't know…"

Her misery was reflected in her flushed face, and her fingers were twisted so tightly that the nails were white. He remembered the night he had kissed her outside, when he had pressed her hand to him and she had pulled away as if shocked. His own fears forgotten, he lifted his hands to her warm cheeks and brushed his lips over hers. "Let me show you, honey," he whispered. "Let me love you."

He kissed her until her breathing was ragged and her entire body was as flushed and warm as her face. Her legs had grown weak, and she clung to him when his hands slid beneath her sweater to her breasts. He removed the jade-green sweater, then her bra, and laid her back on the cro-

cheted coverlet. The mattress gave way under his weight
when he joined her there.

Her breasts were small, firm, and aching for his touch.
He stroked them tenderly before lowering his head for a
kiss. Her hands tangled in his hair when his teeth nipped
at her, then gently held her dusky rose nipple while his
tongue simultaneously soothed and aroused.

Her cries were soft and helpless, erotically wrapping
around him, intensifying his need and his restraint at the
same time. He reminded himself that she was counting on
him to be gentle, to teach her, to love her. She had never
known the love of a man, had never known the pleasure
and the ecstasy of making love—only the pain of unfulfilling sex. His needs had to wait; hers came first. Hers were
more important.

Her eyes were shut, her breath coming in soft gasps. He
was teaching her a new meaning for the word "want." His
mouth and hands were unleashing a lifetime of wants until
she thought that desire would swallow her up. The intensity
of the emotions surging inside her brought her to tears,
made her cry out softly, to plead for…more. She wasn't
quite sure what she wanted, what she needed, other than to
feel Bryce inside her. She only knew she wanted *more*, but
she didn't fret over not knowing what she wanted more of.
Bryce knew. He would take care of her.

He slid her slacks down her long legs, then removed her
panties with one carefully controlled move. She was beautiful—incredibly, heart-achingly beautiful. Just looking at
her made his heart swell with love.

She opened her eyes the tiniest bit and watched him remove the rest of his clothes. He was handsome and strong,
she thought—her gaze drifting lower—and just a little bit
frightening. Then he lay down with her again, and her fear
faded away. He wouldn't hurt her. He was too gentle, too
caring. Too loving.

"Look at me."

She obeyed his command. He was leaning over her, supported by his upper arms. His hips were fitted intimately against the cradle of hers, his arousal warm and hard against her.

"Trust me, Leah."

She smiled, her ice-blue eyes a little teary. "I do."

Coming from her, he decided, that was almost as good as a declaration of love. His eyes intensely serious, he slowly lowered his body to cover hers, gently probing and finding his place within her.

She had never known such tenderness. He took control of her body, her feelings, her mind, and moved her gently and steadily upward, making her need, making her feel, and finally letting her shatter in an explosion of... She searched her lazy, foggy mind for the right word. Of love. Yes, definitely love.

Bryce's breathing was heavy in her ear, and his heart was pounding so loudly that he was sure she must hear it. He knew he should move off her, but he couldn't; when he had filled her, he had given everything—his seed, his strength, his energy, his love. He wanted to lie with her, inside her, just a little bit longer.

He nuzzled her neck, gently nibbling the sensitive skin there. He realized that he had used nothing to protect her against pregnancy, but he couldn't find it in himself to worry about it. If she got pregnant—God, what a gift! He had given up hope of ever having children of his own—had accepted that he would have to be satisfied with playing stepfather to Leah's kids—but the possibility of creating a child from their love was stunning.

He finally moved to lie beside her, his arms cradling her close. "Are you all right?"

Eyes closed, she raised her hand to his face. His skin was damp, his breathing still irregular. She slid her fingers from his forehead to his nose, then his mouth, where he parted his teeth to capture one fingertip. All right? she echoed silently. She had never felt so good, so special, so loved in her entire life.

The sight of a single tear on her cheek distressed him, and he hugged her tight. "Don't cry, Leah, please. Did I hurt you, honey? Talk to me."

"No, you didn't hurt me," she reassured him, finally looking at him. She was both laughing and crying when she kissed him fiercely. "I never knew.... In all my life, I never knew what making love was like."

He stroked his hand soothingly up and down her arm. He had never known, either—not with Kay or any of the few other women in his past—and for the first time in six years he was at peace, past hurts healed. When Kay had told him that his lovemaking was unsatisfying, he had accepted full blame for it, but now he knew he'd been wrong. No one was to blame. Somewhere in the fourteen years of their marriage their love had deserted them, and without it they had simply been going through the motions.

It had balanced out in the end. Kay had turned to Derek, and Bryce had found Leah. With a sudden swell of emotion, he held her even closer. Now that he had found her, there was no way on this earth that he was going to let her go.

Leah rolled over, expecting to snuggle closer to Bryce's warmth, but the bed was empty. She opened her eyes to a room gray with the first light of dawn, sat up, stretched her arms above her head, then propped both pillows behind her.

When she became aware of Bryce standing at the window, wearing jeans and nothing else, she smiled, her morning suddenly brighter and happier. It was frightening how the mere sight of him could make her life seem so much richer, so much more vital. But this morning there was no room for fear or anything else—just love.

He returned to the bed and sat down facing her. When she started to speak, he shook his head and touched his fingers to her mouth.

She watched, wide-eyed, as he stood up again. Moving quickly, gracefully, he removed his jeans. He was blatantly aroused, heavy with need. He stood beside the bed, awaiting invitation or rejection, welcome or rebuff. Leah didn't say a word—simply lifted the covers for him.

He settled between her thighs, his arousal searing her belly. Ducking his head, he placed a gentle kiss on her breast; then, very slowly, he found his way inside her, luxuriating in the snug, heated feel of her. "This…" He shuddered, closing his eyes until the need racing through his body had ebbed. Then he looked at her and finished the thought. "…is heaven."

He didn't know if he spoke aloud—he thought he did, but with every nerve quivering, with every heartbeat echoing, he couldn't be sure. It didn't matter; she understood.

His eyes were dark and alive with emotions—tenderness, desire, need, caring—and in that moment, Leah knew that Frank was right, that *she* was right: Bryce loved her. Maybe he had trouble saying it—a lot of men did—but there *were* other ways to show love than by saying the words, and he had shown her, in the most tender, most lovely way possible.

She smiled so sweetly that his heart melted, and reached up to cup her hands against his beard-roughened cheeks. "Yes," she agreed before bringing his mouth to hers. "Absolute heaven."

Her gentle kiss quickly grew fierce, then hungry, then desperate. She had never known this kind of passion, passion that flamed to life so quickly and so violently, that threatened to destroy her with its intensity. Unlike the tender, sweet loving of last night, this time it was quick and explosive—no lazy, controlled explorations, no gentle kisses, no gradual, nerve-racking buildup—and it left them shattered, clinging to each other, gasping for breath, whispering sweet, soft, meaningless sounds.

Heaven, she thought once more. Absolute heaven.

Bryce watched Leah dress from his position at the head of the bed, the pillows soft behind his back. He was wearing his jeans again, and though he held a shirt in his hands he made no move to put it on yet. He wanted her to stay a little longer, to prolong the intimacy just a little longer, but she had insisted on getting up, dressed and out of his room now, before someone found her. And so he watched her, enjoying the sight. She zipped her light green slacks, pulled on her sweater, lifted her hair free and pushed the sleeves to her elbows. "How do I look?"

Grinning, he left the bed to grasp her at the waist and pulled her close. "Like you've spent the night making wild, passionate love."

She laughed softly, then admitted a little awkwardly, "I feel...wicked."

"Why should you feel wicked?" he teased. "Because we made love all night in a house with thirty other people, including my father and your children?" Then gentleness softened his voice. "Don't, Leah. Don't feel ashamed or sorry or guilty, or any of those other things. What we did last night was good and right and—"

"Perfect," she supplied.

He kissed her forehead and repeated the word. "Perfect."

She pulled herself out of his arms and walked to the door. There she hesitated, then turned back. "Bryce...the kids..."

"What about them?"

She shrugged. "I tell them that making love is something very special, that they shouldn't do it just because they want to, or they're curious, or they get carried away."

He pulled his shirt over his head and tugged it down, then straightened the collar. "Did you want to make love to me, Leah?"

"Of course I did."

"Were you curious?"

"Well...yes."

"Did I carry you away?"

"You swept me right off my feet," she said with a faint smile.

"Are you a kid?"

"Of course not, but—"

He laid his fingers over her mouth once more. "Making love *is* very special, but you're right: kids shouldn't do it just because they want to, or are curious, or get carried away. But we're not kids, Leah, and we don't live by the same rules. What goes on between you and me is none of your kids' business. We can make our own decisions, Leah, because we have the age, the maturity and the experience to make good ones. You're not maintaining a double standard, or failing to practice what you preach."

She kissed his fingers before removing them from her mouth. "I just don't want them to be disappointed in me."

"Don't you know how much they love you? Do you think they're going to be disappointed in you because you're human, because you care for someone besides them?" His voice grew softer with his smile. "Don't you know how much I..." He started to say "love," but he wasn't sure she was ready to hear that. He wasn't even sure he was ready to say it. Abruptly he changed it. "...care for you?"

"Yes," she said softly. "I think I do." For once his knack for simplification didn't annoy her. Her children *did* love her, and that wasn't going to change when they found out that she loved Bryce, too. "Your father was right—you're a good man, Bryce Cameron." Leaning forward, she kissed his cheek, then was gone.

Chapter 7

When Bryce saw Leah again in the dining room after breakfast, she had changed from the green sweater and slacks that made her so lovely into a cheery red and white print shirt and jeans. She still looked lovely, he decided. But not as lovely as she had looked in his bed, wearing nothing at all.

They were alone in the house except for Frank, who was in the sitting room watching television. Martha had taken the children to church, and the guests had all gone skiing. He leaned against the door frame and watched Leah spread starched linens of rich red and bright green over the tables. "Can I help?" he offered at last, drawing her attention to him.

She looked at him and smiled. It was as dazzling as the morning sunlight that was streaming through the windows. "Yes, you can." When he started toward her, she raised her hand to stop him. "But not in here. Why don't you go sit with your father? I think he's feeling a little lonely."

"All right." Reluctantly, he left her and went to the sitting room. As soon as he saw his father in front of the television set, a warm sweater around his shoulders and a lap quilt covering his legs, the reluctance changed to guilt. He had taken time off work so he could spend it with Frank, but it seemed the only times he saw his father were when Leah was busy. A fine son he was turning out to be.

He built a fire in the fireplace and closed the doors so the warmth wouldn't escape, then sat down on the sofa.

"Good morning," Frank greeted him. He used the remote control to lower the volume, then turned toward his son. "I was beginning to think I'd have to start tagging along after Leah to see anything of you."

"I'm sorry, Dad. I…" He cleared his throat. "I know I haven't been paying much attention to anything else…."

Frank waved off his concern. "I plan to be around here a long, long time. Go ahead and take care of her. After you're married, you'll have plenty of time for the rest of the world."

"Married?" Bryce repeated. Was it that obvious that he wanted to marry Leah? After his marriage to Kay had failed so miserably, he had thought he would never marry again, would never run the risk of failing that way again. Yet whenever he'd let himself think about marrying Leah, he'd never once thought about failure.

"Of course you'll marry her. You can't keep sneaking around behind the kids' backs—you're far too old for that. And Leah deserves more. *You* deserve more."

"I don't know, Dad," he said slowly. "I've been divorced a long time. Getting married is a big change."

"You've been *alone* a long time," Frank disagreed. "Just because it didn't work out with Kay is no reason to refuse to take a chance with Leah."

"You're a fine one to talk," Bryce pointed out, his voice full of love. "You've been alone almost forty years, and you've never given any thought to marrying again, have you?"

Frank's eyes grew misty. "Your mother was the one love

of my life. From the moment I first laid eyes on her, I knew she was the only woman for me. If I couldn't have her…I didn't want anyone." He stared into the distance, seeing faded memories that Bryce could only guess at, and smiling gently.

Then he looked at his son again, and the smile faded. "Kay wasn't the right woman for you—never was and never could have been. I know you loved her," he added quickly when Bryce started to protest, "but you were too different. You both wanted different things from life. Kay wanted a successful husband, standing in the community, prestige and money, and you wanted…"

"Children," Bryce said quietly. "Someone who would give as much as she took. Someone who could share." He had never said those things out loud. Until last night he had never blamed Kay for her part in their troubles; he had taken all the blame himself.

Frank nodded. "Someone who loved *you* more than the things you could give her. Well, Leah's just about the most loving, giving woman I've ever met. Even though she is a bit prim, I couldn't ask for a better daughter-in-law."

A bit prim? Bryce thought of last night, and again this morning, in his bed—of her passion, her heat, those soft little cries she'd made when he had filled her with himself. He was torn in two—amused by the description of her as prim, and hungry to love her like that again.

"Let's go for a walk, son," Frank suddenly suggested.

"All right. Anyplace in particular?"

"Walk over to your uncle's house with me."

"Didn't Peter go to church this morning with Martha and the kids?"

"God would strike him down, the old thief, if he set one foot inside His church," Frank grumbled.

Peter was just as grumbly and cross when he found them standing on his porch, but it was clear that it was to hide his pleasure at his brother's visit. He invited Frank inside, but fixed a cold stare on Bryce. "Are you planning to come in, too?"

Bryce had told his uncle he could hate him until the day he died for refusing to let Peter talk to Frank when Terence had died. It seemed as if Peter was going to do just that. But that was all right. He had better things to do with his morning. Like loving Leah. "No," he said calmly. "I'm going back to the house. To see Leah."

He added the last part with just a hint of malice, well aware that it annoyed Peter no end to see his daughter-in-law with the nephew he despised.

"If she had any sense, she'd throw you right out," Peter mumbled as he closed the door on Bryce.

He returned to the inn and found Leah still in the dining room. The tables wore their Christmas cloths and held Christmassy centerpieces—music boxes, or poinsettias, or pine boughs encircling red and green candles. She was putting the finishing touch on the mantel decoration, a small village of ceramic houses, complete with miniature animals and people and tiny decorated trees.

He scooped her off her feet and kissed her, swallowing her cry of surprise in his mouth. He continued kissing her as he made his way carefully out of the room and through the halls to her bedroom. Delicately balancing her, he got the door open, carried her inside, shut the door with his foot and fell to the bed with her, covering her body with his.

She freed her mouth, laughing helplessly. "Bryce! What are you doing?"

"Make love to me," he demanded. "Now." He was kissing her again, her jaw, her throat, her ear.

"You must be crazy."

He shifted to press his hips against hers, so she could feel his hardness. "If wanting you is crazy, I must be insane," he whispered.

"But Frank..."

"Is at Peter's house. I just took him over there."

"My work…"

"Can be done later. I'll help you." He nuzzled the softness of her breast, wishing he could remove the shirt that stopped him from tasting her sweetness.

It was becoming more difficult to think of excuses when he touched her that way. Her nipple was budding from the heat of his mouth, swelling and aching for the warmth to enclose it. "The kids…" she whispered.

"Won't be back for at least an hour." She wanted him—he could hear it in the breathiness of her voice, could see it in the hazy blue ice in her eyes, could feel it in the moist heat from her body that cradled him—but she was reluctant. Dragging in a deep breath, he rolled off her onto his back, covered his eyes with one arm and said with mock resignation, "Go on, Leah, honey. Run while you can."

He felt the mattress move as she stood up, then waited for the sound of the door. He would just have to stay in here a while, he decided. He certainly couldn't walk around the house in this condition. As a matter of fact, he wasn't certain he could walk, period.

There was a quiet click—the unmistakable sound of the lock on the door. Uncovering his eyes, Bryce found Leah standing beside the bed, unbuttoning her blouse with slow, confident moves. She pulled it from her jeans, slid it off her shoulders and draped it over the closet doorknob. With one easy tug behind her back, the clasp of her bra came open, and it landed on the doorknob, too, dangling by one thin, peach-colored strap.

He stared, his eyes widened, his mouth dry, his throat too constricted to speak. She was beautiful…exquisite…gorgeous…stunning…lovely.

Leaning against the closet door, she removed her hightop sneakers but left her red socks on; then she unfastened the belt at her waist, but left it threaded through the denim loops. The fabric was old and worn, and the button easily popped loose. Keeping her eyes locked on Bryce's face, she slid down the zipper, then guided the jeans over her hips and to the floor, taking a pair of peach-tinted panties with them.

Stunned and weak, Bryce simply stared at her. She was thirty-five years old, the mother of four, and had the most perfectly formed body he'd ever seen. She was shy and innocent and hesitant, yet she had just made the job of undressing one of the most erotic acts he could imagine.

She moved onto the bed, climbing over him, rubbing against him, drawing an unwilling groan from him. "I've never undressed a man before," she said softly, with just a hint of a blush, as her fingers toyed with his collar. "I—I've never seduced a man before, either. What—" She cleared her throat, her embarrassment deepening. "What do you want me to do?"

He swallowed hard. Her breast was only inches from his hand—or his mouth. He wanted to feel it, to taste it, but he forced himself to lie still and do nothing. "What do you want to do?"

She cleared her throat again. "I—I want to touch you…to look at you…. But we haven't got much time, and most of all I want you inside me…like last night and this morning."

He rose from the bed and quickly removed his clothes, dropping them carelessly to the floor, then joined her once more, sinking into the softness of the mattress, against the softness of her. "Touch me, Leah," he invited, wrapping one strong arm around her shoulders and hugging her to him. "We have time, honey. Touch me."

She raised her hand, and it trembled. With fear or desire? he wondered; then he saw her eyes and knew the answer. She looked solemn, but not afraid. She knew she had nothing to fear with him, that she could stroke him, caress him, kiss him, and he wouldn't criticize or complain. He would find only pleasure in her touch.

The skin that stretched across his chest was soft, the bone and muscle beneath it hard. She touched his nipple and watched it harden, the same way hers responded to his touch. Leaning forward, she bathed it with her tongue, and he bit off a tiny little groan. When she slid her hand across his stomach, he sucked in his breath, and the muscles there flexed convulsively.

She took an innocent delight in his responses, marveling that she could give him such pleasure with no more than the touch of her hand. Then she moved her hand lower, taking the swollen length of his manhood in her palm, and all thought fled from her mind. He was taut, steely hard, yet sheathed in softness. He was heated and pulsing with the need that she had created, that she was increasing as she gently stroked him, up, down, then up again. She closed her palm around the tip, then rubbed her thumb in circles, feeling his moistness. Curious, she raised her thumb to her mouth, to taste him, and Bryce squeezed his eyes shut with a groan.

"Leah, I don't think I can wait...." His voice was unrecognizable, heavy with wanting.

"Now," she whispered, reaching for his shoulders. "Come into me now."

He lifted himself over her, his muscles tense with restraint. Last night had been easy and gentle, this morning violently hungry. This time... He groaned again when he felt her hand enclose him, guiding his way through the silken curls that nestled between her thighs, until the moist heat of her body replaced her hand. Today it would be... She moved tantalizingly beneath him, and he drove into her, filling her with his manhood, and an instant later filling her again, this time with the evidence of his release.

Brief, he completed the thought a moment later. This time it had been brief.

When the shudders racking his body finally subsided, he opened his eyes. Leah was looking at him, just a little bit awed. "I like to watch you," she said, raising one hand to his cheek. "You look so...intense."

He withdrew from her, then slowly began sliding back inside. "I do, huh? Let me see how *you* look when you—"

She chose that moment to arch against him, making him gasp as she took all of him, every inch. He remained motionless, supporting himself above her on one arm while his other hand on her hip urged her to move again, the same way. This time the gasp was hers as she repeated the action, sliding against the hard length of him, up, down, up again. Shivers rocketed through her, growing in strength until she was pleading, wordless cries rippling through her until they were followed by the most exquisite, most mindless pleasure she had ever known. Bryce was with her, accepting once more his own need and reveling once more in his own satisfaction.

He held her, their bodies still joined, his hands soothing her shivers. "Leah," he murmured thickly, pressing a kiss to her forehead. "Lovely, lovely Leah."

She lifted her head long enough to kiss his mouth. "Thank you," she whispered.

"For what?"

Her eyes met his. "For giving me more joy in the last few weeks than anyone has given me in the last thirty-five years. For showing me what it's like to feel…to want and need…and to receive. For being a patient, kind, gentle man and a patient, kind, gentle lover."

He would have told her then that he loved her, but his throat was tight, the lump there blocking his voice. Instead he gathered her even closer, shut his eyes and buried his face in the fragrant silk of her hair. In a heavy voice he said at last, "We need to talk, Leah."

He sounded so ominous that her body stiffened with dread. "About what?" she asked cautiously.

"Last night. This morning. And now. I—I wasn't exactly…prepared for this."

She looked at him without a hint of understanding. "Are you disappointed?"

There were times, Bryce thought, when the innocence he found so captivating could present something of a problem.

"No, not at all. That's not what I'm talking about, Leah. I mean…birth control. Contraceptives."

She blushed. "Oh."

That tiny response answered the question he had been about to ask: she hadn't been prepared, either. But he hadn't really expected her to be. He had known that she'd been celibate since Terence's death. Smiling reassuringly, he hugged her closer. "I'll take care of it, okay?"

She smiled, too, with gratitude and relief. "Okay."

Bryce stroked her back, running his hand lazily up and down her spine. "Leah, if you get pregnant…you know I'll be here, don't you?"

The last of the tension eased from her body, allowing her to mold herself against him. "Yes," she said huskily. "I know."

The most delicious laziness stole over her while they lay there in silence. She wanted to stay like this forever, just the two of them, naked and together. But she knew they didn't have forever. Not today, at least. "What time is it?"

He raised his wrist enough to see his watch. "Noon." With an exaggerated sigh he said, "I know, the kids will be home in about fifteen minutes." He rubbed her breast, gently pinching her nipple, then slowly released her. "Run away with me, Leah, to someplace where there aren't any distractions."

She slid from the bed and quickly retrieved a robe from the closet. Shy again, Bryce thought, a surge of protective love rushing through him. Then he saw the wary look in her eyes. Sitting naked on the edge of the bed, he caught her hands. "What's wrong?"

"My kids aren't distractions," she said uneasily. "They're…my life."

He stood up and put his arms around her. "Being a distraction isn't always negative. *You're* the loveliest distraction I've ever seen. I just meant that we don't get a whole lot of privacy here, you know? I want to have you to myself. I want to make love to you forever." He heard the front door slam and a familiar voice yell, "Mom?" and quickly released her.

He had just enough time to drag his clothes on. Snatching up his shoes, he gave Leah a kiss and quickly left her room. As the door closed behind him, Matthew came racing around the corner at the end of the hall. "Hey," the boy greeted him.

"Looking for your mom?"

"Nope. I was gonna ask her where you are. What are you doing?"

"I'm going to find a place I can sit down and put my shoes on."

"Why don't you come up to my room? You can sit there, and I have to change anyway." He tugged at the tie around his neck. "Mom says we have to dress nice for church, but I have to change as soon as I get home so I don't get dinner on my clothes."

Bryce followed him upstairs, taking a seat on the bed while Matthew disappeared into the closet. "How long are you going to stay here?" the boy called over his shoulder, tossing a long-sleeved sweatshirt onto the floor. A pair of sweatpants and bright orange sneakers followed.

"As long as I can," Bryce replied, tugging his own shoes on while he studied the orange ones lying near his feet. Kay would have had a fit before she would have allowed a pair of shoes that color inside her house.

Matthew reappeared and stripped to his underwear with the unconcern of a child. Dropping to the floor, he put on a pair of black padded soccer socks, his sweatpants and the shoes, meticulously tying the laces into bows that consisted of four loops and two knots each. Then he lay back, folded his arms under his head and stared up at Bryce. "You keep awful busy."

"I know. I've been spending some time with your mother."

"I haven't seen you much."

Bryce stood up and gathered the clothing Matthew had

dropped to the floor. First his father, now Matthew, he thought with dismay. Who would be the next one to prick his conscience? "Well, after lunch, why don't you and I do something together—just the two of us?" he suggested as he hung the child-sized suit on child-sized hangers in the closet.

"Can't. Today's the Christmas parade in town, and we always go to the Christmas parade. You'll come, too, won't you? And Uncle Frank?" Jumping up again, Matthew pulled his sweatshirt over his head while waiting for an answer. "Do you think Mom forgot? We always go, but she's been kind of busy lately, too—with you, I guess."

"I'm sure she didn't forget. If Dad feels like going, we can all go together, okay?"

When Matthew mentioned the parade over dinner, Leah pressed a kiss to his forehead. "Of course I didn't forget. We always go to the parade, don't we?"

"Yes," Martha agreed. "*Everyone* goes." She directed a stern look at her husband, then Frank.

"It's too cold to be standing out watching a Christmas parade," Frank grumbled. "Especially with *him* along." He jerked his head in Peter's direction, but when he saw the disappointment in Matthew's eyes, he relented. "But I suppose I could do it this one time."

The boy was clearly pleased. "What about you, Grandpa? You'll come, too, won't you?"

When Peter grudgingly said yes, Matthew leaped from his chair with a whoop. "Oh, boy, this is gonna be neat!" he exclaimed. "Just like a real family!"

A real family, Leah reflected as they drove in two cars to downtown Angel's Peak. Indeed, they were. But, as soon as they found parking spaces, the family split up, Douglas going off with his friends, Laurel and Megan with theirs. Martha offered to stay near the cars with the two older men, while Leah, Bryce and Matthew strolled along the crowded sidewalk.

When they passed a drugstore, Bryce grinned teasingly at Leah. "Wait here, will you? I need to get something."

"Can I come with you?" Matthew asked, unaware of his mother's blush.

"Not this time. You stay with your mother." He disappeared inside the store, returning less than five minutes later.

"What did you buy?" Matthew asked, reaching for Bryce's hand.

Bryce made sure the package was tucked deep inside his coat pocket before reaching for Leah with his free hand. "You're a nosy child, Matthew, just like your Uncle Frank. It looks like the entire town has turned out."

"They always do," Leah replied. "In a town as small as Angel's Peak, you do what you can for excitement—but you know that, don't you? I keep forgetting that you used to live here. Have you seen anyone you know?"

"The people I knew were kids the last time I saw them. I doubt if I would recognize any of them." Hearing the siren of Angel's Peak's one and only police car, the signal that the parade was about to begin, he slowed his steps. "We'd better head back."

Once they rejoined the others, they took up their places at the curb, Matthew sitting high on Bryce's shoulders. Bryce laid his arm over Leah's shoulders, pulled her close and nuzzled her ear, enjoying her soft fragrance. "Now that *that* little problem is taken care of, will you spend the night with me tonight?" he whispered.

Startled by the question, she turned a delicate pink, then looked around quickly to be sure no one else could hear. "I don't know," she whispered back. "Maybe part of it?"

His smile was resigned. "If that's the best you can offer..."

She knew he wasn't really annoyed, but she tried to explain, anyway. "Sometimes people come looking for me in the middle of the night—one of the kids or a guest or Martha. If I weren't there, they would worry."

"What if *I* come looking for you in the middle of the night? Will you let me stay?"

She looked up at him for a long, long moment. *Forever and ever.* "And if someone found you there?"

"Would that be so bad? Leah, these people—our family, your guests—they're not blind. They know what's going on. Do you think they'd be shocked to find us together?"

Leah couldn't believe they were having this conversation in hushed whispers with Matthew perched above them, Peter, Martha and Frank beside them, and a parade passing by in front of them. "We'll talk later, okay? During our walk tonight?"

Deliberately he bent to kiss her. "All right. Later."

"Later" came much more quickly than Leah would have liked. As soon as Matthew was tucked into his bed—by both Leah and Bryce, something new that the little boy liked very much—they got their coats and set off into the woods.

"Are you ashamed of our relationship?" Bryce demanded, breaking the silence around them.

"No, of course not."

"Then why do you want to pretend it's not happening?"

"I'm not pretending that, but just this morning, Bryce, you told me that what goes on between you and me is no one else's business, and now you're suggesting that we share a room, and the hell with whoever finds out." She said it in one long rush, then caught her breath and looked up at him, only to see him smiling.

"I've never heard you swear before," he teased. "Okay, Leah, we'll do it your way. Whenever you're in the mood to use my body, just let me know—"

She gave him a shove. "Would you stop it? Sometimes you make me want to scream!"

Catching her arms, he held her to him. "I thought you came pretty close to it this morning," he said in a confidential whisper.

She made a halfhearted effort to pull away from him,

then burst into laughter. Gently she brushed his hair from his forehead, tickling him with the fuzzy knit of her glove. "Oh, Bryce, you're good for me, you know that?"

Her sudden softening had a devastating effect on his body. He tried to ignore it by continuing with his teasing. "*I* know it, but I wasn't sure if you did. Are you sure you don't want to run away with me?"

Dreamily she considered the idea. "No responsibilities. No job, no guests, no paperwork, no children..." Clarity returned to her eyes. "Not that I mind the children—I love them very much—it's just that I've been with them twenty-four hours a day, seven days a week, ever since they were born. But they're not a burden, real—"

Bryce stopped her with a gentle touch. "I understand, Leah. You're the best mother a kid could possibly have—don't ever think otherwise. But everyone deserves a break now and then."

"Where would we go?" she asked, dislodging his hand, thinking longingly of a day or two in Asheville or Atlanta, or maybe even Charleston.

"Philadelphia."

She stared at him. "Philadelphia?"

"You sound disappointed."

"Well...it's not exactly my idea of a romantic get-away." But then, neither were Asheville or Atlanta. Charleston, maybe—the pictures she had seen of it were romantic enough.

"Philadelphia can be very romantic, if you see it with the right person." He paused briefly before continuing. "I need to go back. I have to put the house on the market, pack up my stuff, turn in my resignation—that sort of thing. It shouldn't take more than three or four days." There was another short hesitation. "I'd like you to go with me, Leah."

She walked away, brushed snow from a fallen tree trunk and sat down. "You're really going to do it, then." Give up his job, his house, his life.

Bryce crouched down in front of her, where he could see her face. "Yes," he agreed. "Of course, if it bothers you this much, maybe I shouldn't." Quickly he raised his hands in front of him. "Just teasing.... *Does* it bother you so much, Leah, that I want to live here?"

He was willing to give up so much for her, and what had she given him? Nothing but difficulty. "No," she replied softly. "I think it's wonderful. I think you're wonderful. And I can't imagine what in the world you see in me."

Bryce rested his hands on her thighs, balancing himself, and answered very gently. "I see a beautiful woman who is more giving, more sharing and more loving than anyone I've ever known. A woman I would like to spend the rest of my life with."

It wasn't "I love you," Leah considered, but it was enough. With a soft sigh, she opened her arms to him—her arms, her heart and her soul.

Over the next few days Bryce repeatedly broached the question of a trip to Philadelphia, but Leah repeatedly brushed it off. She couldn't spare the time away, she insisted. She had too much to do—planning the annual caroling party for the coming weekend and the open houses for Christmas week. She hadn't done her shopping yet, and Megan and Matthew needed costumes for the pageant at school. The monthly records for the inn were in a mess that had to be straightened soon, the inn was heavily booked for both weekdays and weekends until after New Year, and who would look after the children and Frank while she was gone?

"You're afraid to go, aren't you?" Bryce accused after yet another futile discussion in the workshop one morning. "Afraid of what the kids will think—afraid of what Peter and Martha will think. For God's sake, Leah, you're an adult! You don't need their permission to do something for yourself."

"No," she responded tiredly, "but I need their respect."

"And you think going to Philadelphia with me for four days—and, heaven forbid, four nights—will cost you their respect?" He tugged at his hair in frustration. "Leah, you've spent the better part of every night since Saturday in my room. Sharing a bed with me here is no different from sharing a bed with me six hundred miles from here, except there I'll be able to wake up with you."

He added that last part with a sullen frown, looking for all the world like Matthew in a pout. It made Leah smile, but the smile faded quickly. She put down her paintbrush and folded her hands together tightly. "Is that what this trip is about, Bryce? Having sex whenever you want? Spending an entire night together instead of only part of one? Not having the distractions of the kids or my job?"

She looked disappointed, and he had sworn long ago that he would never disappoint her. He couldn't help himself this time, though. "Yes, that's part of it," he admitted defensively. "Is it so wrong that I want some time alone with you, not just a few hours here or there, but completely alone?"

She felt honored that he wanted to be with her, and she said so softly. Then she admitted, "You're right, I *am* afraid. If I walk into that house and tell our families that I'm going to Philadelphia for a few days with you, they'll know that I'll be sharing your bed. They'll *know*. The kids will be upset. And as much as Peter and Martha love me, they're still Terence's parents, and Peter still doesn't like you. I don't want to do anything to hurt them."

"But it's okay to hurt me." He knew he sounded like a spoiled child, but he *was* hurt. She had just admitted that she didn't want her in-laws and her children to know that they were lovers. He understood her reasons for wanting to keep him a secret part of her life, but it still hurt.

"Bryce—" She reached across the table to take his hands, but he pulled back.

"No, that's okay." It was an obvious lie—there was

nothing okay about the situation—but he pretended anyway and gave her a taut smile. "I was planning to wait until next Monday, to see if I could change your mind. But since you don't want to go, I think I'll see if I can get reservations for this afternoon."

She had never seen him angry, but there was no mistaking the emotion in his face as he shrugged into his coat, and, for the first time in ages, she became angry, too. "That's not fair! You won't even try to understand my position."

"What position? You haven't taken one, Leah. All you're doing is hiding behind the excuse of the kids. They protect you from everything, don't they? And now you're using them to protect yourself from me."

"I wasn't aware that I needed protection from you," she said coldly, "but maybe I was wrong. If I've used the kids as an excuse, it's only because you refuse to accept my answer. *I don't want to go to Philadelphia with you.* Is that clear enough?"

He stared at her for a long time before answering with a single, ice-cold word. "Absolutely." When he walked out, the door slammed behind him.

Leah stood motionless for a moment, then very calmly picked up the paintbrush and turned back to the ceramic stocking-holder angel she'd been working on. The angel was a gift for Bryce, so that the stocking Laurel and Megan were making for him could hang with the rest of the family's. But she was too upset to work, and, her hand trembling, she put the brush down again and rested her fingers on the cool, haloed brown head.

She had lied to him. She *did* want to go away with him—to Philadelphia or anyplace else. It just wasn't that easy. She couldn't leave her kids or the inn during the holiday season simply because she wanted time alone with Bryce. She couldn't so easily admit to her family that her relationship with him was intimate. She couldn't shirk her responsibilities.

But didn't she deserve a holiday? Since Douglas had been born almost eighteen years ago, she had never spent a night away from the kids, except when each of the last three was born. She had never taken a vacation just for herself, not even a weekend trip to Asheville. In three years she had never taken a day off from the inn, not as long as there was a single guest in residence. Wasn't it time now?

Working hastily, she put away her paints, cleaned her brushes and set the workshop in order; then she left for the inn, pulling her coat on as she walked. She went first to Bryce's room, but he wasn't there. With forced calm she searched the house for him, stopping at last at the front desk. "Vicky, have you seen Bryce?"

Sensing trouble, the clerk met Leah's gaze slowly. "He…he left."

"Left?"

Vicky shrugged. "He got the airline numbers from the book, made a couple of calls from the phone room and left just a few minutes ago. With a suitcase." Reading the surprise and hurt in her boss's eyes, she hesitantly asked, "Didn't you know he was going?"

"Yeah. I just didn't think…" She sighed heavily. She just hadn't thought, period. "I—I'll be in my office, okay?"

"Leah? Is anything wrong?" Vicky asked sympathetically.

"No. No, everything's fine." But her smile wasn't fine; neither was the sheen of tears in her eyes, nor the way she bit her lip.

In her office she closed the door on the rest of the inn and immersed herself in the receipts, lists, schedules and inventories that littered her desk. For a while she managed to forget that Bryce wasn't down the hall with his father, or making one of a dozen minor repairs around the house, or waiting for Matthew to come home from school. She forgot that he'd been angry the last time she saw him—

angry and hurt. She even managed for a while to forget that he'd left the inn without saying goodbye to her.

He would be back in a few days. He would take care of his business and come home, where he belonged. He would probably even call tonight, and he would tell her that he missed her, and she could tell him that she was sorry.

She told herself all those things through the afternoon and evening, right up to the time she fell asleep. The next day she found it harder to believe them, and by Friday she was starting to worry. Even the children, who had been satisfied with her vague excuse about "business," were beginning to show concern. Just how long would his business take? they asked. And why hadn't he said good-bye? Why hadn't he called? Had he changed his mind about returning to Angel's Peak? Had he decided that he liked the city better after all? She couldn't answer their questions, or ease her own fears.

"You know the nice thing about airplanes, Leah?"

She was supposed to be working but had spent the last half hour staring out the window at the snow. Now she turned slowly to face Frank. "What's that?"

"They fly on schedules. The plane that took Bryce back to Philadelphia—it'll be making that same flight this afternoon, and tomorrow afternoon, and the next day.... Why don't you make sure you're on it next time?"

"I can't do that, Frank."

He settled into the straight-backed chair, crossing his legs and folding his arms stubbornly over his chest. "Why not?"

"I've got too many things to do."

"Like what?"

"Well, there's the party tomorrow night."

"You think we can't go out and sing a few Christmas carols without you?"

"But the buffet afterward—"

His brown eyes were sharp and chiding. "Miss Colleen does the cooking in this house, not you."

She acknowledged that with a sigh. "I have responsibilities, Frank. There's the inn."

"Good Lord, girl, you've got a staff that's efficient as hell. They can get along just fine without you. We can *all* get along just fine without you...except Bryce."

She clutched at that thought, wanting to believe it with all her heart. But if he needed her, why hadn't he called? Why hadn't he given her just one more chance? "What am I supposed to do with the kids, or have you forgotten about them?" she asked, using her final reason.

Now he looked insulted. "Have *you* forgotten about *me*? I'm perfectly capable of keeping an eye on four kids, and, if I need any help, there's Martha and Peter right across the yard." He hesitated, then looked at her with a kindness she had often seen in Bryce's eyes. "What's the real problem, Leah? Those are just excuses—you know it, and I know it. Why don't you just get on that plane and go to Philadelphia?"

He was right. She'd been through the excuses too many times with Bryce not to recognize them for what they were. They really didn't matter. Only the truth mattered. "He was angry with me when he left, and he...he hasn't called. He didn't even say goodbye." She rushed on, not wanting to give Frank time to respond. "He has friends there, Frank, and a job and a house—it's his home, more than Angel's Peak ever was. Now that he's there, what if he's decided that he doesn't want to come back here? What if he's decided that he doesn't really want me?" Her voice grew weak and sad. "I don't have any experience with this kind of thing. If I went six hundred miles without an invitation, and he wasn't glad to see me..." She shrugged, unable to continue.

"You had an invitation," he reminded her. "Numerous ones. Leah, we're not talking about some stranger here—this is Bryce. If you love him enough to commit yourself to him, then you've got to love him enough to trust him. You've got to know he wouldn't do anything to hurt you. And you've got to know that if you showed up on his doorstep, he would welcome you.''

She wanted to believe that, but she was still afraid. ''I've never been on a plane before.''

''It's fun. You'll enjoy it.'

''I've never been in a city before, either. Philadelphia is a whole lot bigger than Asheville.''

''You'll enjoy that, too. It'll make you appreciate Angel's Peak when you get back.'' He was gruffer now, more his usual self. ''You call the airline and get yourself a reservation on the first flight out tomorrow. That will give you this evening with the kids.''

Leah was reaching for the phone when he started toward the door. Pausing, she smiled her first smile in two days and said, ''Thank you, Frank.''

''You just have a good time.''

A good time? Leah felt as if she didn't know the meaning of the words when she climbed into the cab Saturday afternoon. She wanted more than anything to run back inside the terminal and catch the next flight back to Asheville. She had been foolish to come here, to let Frank convince her that Bryce would be glad to see her just because that was what she wanted so badly to believe.

Well, she would find out soon enough. If he didn't want her there, he would say so, and she would go back home and fall apart. But if he did want her... That would make all her jitters worthwhile.

''This is the address,'' the cabdriver said, glancing over his shoulder at her.

She stared at the house. It was beautiful, of brick, two-storied, with stately white columns that reached to the roof.

''Want me to wait?''

She started to say no, then realized that Bryce might not be home. If he wasn't, she would have to go somewhere;

it was too cold to wait outside for him. "Yes, please." She got out and walked up the broad pathway to the door.

The bell echoed through the house, its tones faint through the heavy door. Leah twined her fingers together and waited, and after a moment the door opened.

Bryce's chocolate-dark eyes widened slightly in surprise; then he smiled. "Hello."

Her own smile was weaker. "Hi."

He leaned one shoulder against the door frame, looking unconcerned and relaxed and incredibly handsome. "What are you doing here?"

Leah dragged in a shaky breath. "I'm not sure. Most likely making a fool of myself."

His smile deepened, but was still cool and a little bit guarded. "Somehow I can't imagine the very cool and proper Leah Cameron ever making a fool of herself."

"It happens to the best of us." Why didn't he do something—invite her in, take her in his arms, or tell her to go to hell? she wondered fretfully. She untwisted her hands and shoved them into her coat pockets, then shifted her weight from one foot to the other.

"Why are you here, Leah?" He folded his arms over his chest, unmindful of the cold. He wanted to greet her the way a man should greet his lover, with an embrace and a long, hungry kiss, but he remained where he was, waiting for her answer. In his heart he knew why she had come, but he wanted to hear her say it. He wanted to hear the words out loud, so he could treasure them.

He was asking a lot of her, but she knew she owed him a lot. If he would just give some sign that he was glad to see her, it would be so much easier, but he was simply watching and waiting, patient as always. She took a deep breath, wet her lips with the tip of her tongue and plunged in. "I'm here because I've missed you. I—I lied to you that day in the workshop. I *did* want to come here with you, but...you were right—I was afraid. I've spent half my life alone, and I've lived the other half for my family. Everything I did, I did for them. They were the most important part of my life.'' She dropped her gaze, away from the solemnity in his, then looked at him again. "This is new to me, Bryce. I've never had a lover, never had anyone to care about, anyone to give to. I don't want to hurt you. I don't want to lose you. You've given me so much, and I've given you nothing in return, but...I'm trying.''

If he had waited one instant longer to respond, her heart would have shattered into a million pieces, but he didn't wait. He stepped forward, his arms open, welcoming her into his embrace. Into his heart. Into his love.

They shared a kiss that left her weak and him hard. He wanted to make love to her right there on the floor, to remove her clothes and suckle her breasts, to stroke her until she cried, to fill her body with his again and again. He wanted to hide away inside her, to make up for the loneliness of the last three days, to chase away the bleakness that had come from living without her. His need was sharp, hard, unrelenting, but he forced it back. Raising his head, he smiled lazily and said, "You've given me everything, Leah.'' Including a hunger that couldn't be filled. "Would you be disappointed if I said that I really need to make love to you now?''

It sounded like a wonderful idea to her. She had been wanting and needing him for most of her life. "I would be disappointed if you didn't. My bags are in the taxi. Let me pay him—''.

"I'll do it.'' But for a moment he made no move to release her. For just a moment he needed to hold her. Then, quickly, he let her go and went out to the cab.

Leah looked around curiously while she unzipped her jacket. To the left were wide doors leading into a very formal living room, and to the right was a broad, curving staircase. The entry where she stood was sparsely furnished with only a Queen Anne table, an oriental vase and a painting, but the overall impression was one of elegance.

A rush of cold air brought her attention back to the door

as Bryce came in. He set her suitcase and shoulder bag on the floor, took her coat and hung it up, then wrapped his arms around her again. "How long can you stay?"

"How long are *you* staying?"

"I was planning to go home Wednesday. Is that all right?"

She wondered if he realized that he had called Angel's Peak home, or if he knew the rush of happiness that gave her. Rising onto her toes, she pressed a hard, excited kiss to his mouth. "That's perfect," she murmured. "Absolutely perfect."

She expected him to take her straight to bed, but instead he gave her a tour of the house, delaying the inevitable. Prolonging the anticipation. When they went upstairs he carried her bags, showing her the two guest rooms before they reached the master bedroom. In the doorway he paused, his eyes questioning.

The choice was hers, Leah realized. Did she want the respectability of a guest room or the comfort, the security, the sensual pleasure, of sharing Bryce's room? It was no contest. Taking her shoulder bag from him, she carried it to the center of the room, set it on the floor and turned in a slow circle.

There was an air of elegance in this room, too. It was large, dominated by a queen-size, four-poster bed of rich, gleaming cherry. There were matching pieces—a dresser, chest, nightstands—and a heavily upholstered sofa, chair and chaise. The rose print cushions were coordinated with the bed linens and the soft rose wallpaper. It was a woman's room—not frilly enough to make a man uncomfortable, but definitely decorated by a woman. By Kay.

Bryce watched her from the doorway, judging her response to the room. When she completed her slow, assessing circle, she faced him, her expression serious. "You have a lovely house."

Why didn't that feel like a compliment? he wondered. "Thank you."

"It's very elegant. Very rich." She slipped her shoes off, and her stockinged feet sank into the thick silver carpet.

He responded with a simple nod.

Grasping the hem of her sweater, she pulled it over her head and let it fall across the chaise. "Kay decorated it, didn't she?"

"Yes." He watched as she tugged her shirt from her slacks and unfastened each button. His throat was dry, his chest tight.

The plaid blouse joined the sweater, a vivid splash of turquoise against the subdued rose. "She's been gone six years, hasn't she? And you haven't changed a thing." She dropped her bra and undid the button on her slacks. Finally she stopped and looked at him. His chest rose rapidly under his gray-striped sweater, and beneath the soft charcoal fabric of his trousers, she could see the evidence of his arousal.

Raising her eyes to his face again, she asked solemnly, "Am I the only one taking part in this?"

The suitcase that Bryce still held hit the floor with a thud. He closed the door behind him and walked across the room to her. He replaced her hands with his own, pulling the zipper to its end, sliding her slacks and panties to the floor, then hastily discarding his own clothes.

Secure in the circle of his arms, she gently cradled his hardness, caressing the heated length. "Did you miss me?" she asked, nipping at his lower lip.

"Only once," he insisted, backing toward the chaise and pulling her with him.

"When was that?"

"It started the moment I left you—" he sat down, his legs stretched out, and lifted her on top of him "—and lasted until I opened the door and saw you there." He helped her settle across his hips, then reached down to cup his hand over the satiny curls between her thighs. With one finger he stroked through the curls, touching the budded, aching part of her, sliding gently inside her. She was ready for him, moist and heated, but he didn't take her, not yet.

He kissed her mouth and her throat, traveling a familiar path to her breast. Holding her nipple between his teeth, he suckled it, torturing her with his tongue while, much lower, he tortured her with his hand, stroking gently over her heat.

Desire simmered through her veins, growing more intense, more desperate, until she cried out, helplessly pleading, unable to bear his torment any longer. Shuddering with the force of her release, she sank against him, struggling to breathe, to relax, to regain control of herself.

But Bryce didn't give her that chance. Using his greater strength, he lifted her onto him, arching into her, surrounding his aroused flesh with her warmth. He guided her with the gentle pressure of his hands, aroused her with the soft taste of his kisses, encouraged her with the erotic whisper of his words, and this time, when the end came, it claimed them together.

Chapter 8

"It didn't matter."

Leah opened her eyes slowly. The sun that had been so bright in the sky when she'd arrived at Bryce's house was gone now, and twilight was settling over the room. "What didn't matter?" she asked after a delicately hidden yawn.

"The house. I never changed anything after Kay left because it didn't matter." He yawned, too, then settled Leah more comfortably at his side. "It wasn't a home. It was just a place to sleep at night." He looked around in the dim light, then hid his face in her hair. "It's pretty awful, isn't it?"

"No, it's beautiful."

"Just like in a magazine. The kind of place that you can't believe anyone actually lives in."

Leah stifled a giggle, because that was precisely what she had thought. The house was elegant and beautiful, but unreal. A setting for his elegant ex-wife. "Do you see her often?"

"Kay? Once in a while. We have some of the same

friends.'' He glanced at the luminous numbers on the clock beside the bed and groaned. ''Damn, I forgot—''

Leah was unceremoniously dumped from his arms as he left the bed. Rising onto one arm, she warily watched him. ''Am I in the way here?''

He grinned at her from the open closet, where he was going through the pockets of a classically tailored gray suit. ''Don't be ridiculous. I turned in my resignation at work Thursday, and my boss wanted to give a little party for me. I knew it was tonight, but seeing you erased it from my mind.'' He found the scrap of paper in the trousers. ''Eight o'clock. There's still time.''

It was six-thirty, Leah noticed. The caroling party at home would be starting about now, and she was missing it. Instead she was going to spend the evening alone in Bryce's house while he went to a party of his own.

''Did you bring a pretty dress?''

Her eyes jerked to his face. ''What?''

He repeated the question. ''Marv's wife Tara likes to show off her new clothes, so their parties are always pretty dressy.''

She was still staring at him, her expression blank. ''You want me to go with you?''

''Of course I do. Come on, Leah, you don't think I'd leave you here and go alone, do you?''

''But they're your friends. I won't know anybody. I won't fit in.''

He walked to the bed and leaned over her. ''You'll know me. And you fit perfectly with me.'' His lips brushed hers in a gentle kiss. ''If you don't want to go, honey, we don't have to.''

She didn't—the idea of meeting his friends made her nervous—but she couldn't let him skip a party in his honor. ''The only dressy outfit I brought is that white sweater and skirt.'' She stretched sinuously, her arms high above her head, then left the bed. Her suitcase with her robe was across the room, but the sweater Bryce had worn was at the foot of the bed. Modestly she reached for it, pulling it over her head. It was warm, too big, and smelled of him. She lifted her suitcase to the dresser, opened it and pulled out the clothes. "Will this be okay?"

Bryce's smile was slow, sexy and lascivious. "I've had fantasies about you and that sweater since the first night I saw you in it. Maybe tonight I can fulfill some of them." Then he sobered. "That will be fine, honey. How quickly can you get ready?"

The party was being held at his boss's house, he told her as they drove across town. He had gone to work for Marvin Jordan right out of college, and over the years they had become close friends. Tara Jordan was about Leah's age and very nice, but he felt compelled to warn her that some of the other women who would be there were friends of Kay's and might not be very welcoming.

As he drove along a narrow lane that led to a house about twice the size of the inn, Leah gave him a tight smile. "Thank you. My confidence needed that."

He squeezed her hand, then laid it on his thigh. "Don't be nervous. Just act naturally, and you'll charm everyone there."

They were met at the door by several servants. One took their coats; another escorted them to the living room, where a third offered them drinks. They paused in the doorway, Bryce looking for their hosts while Leah simply looked. "Tell me that Mr. and Mrs. Jordan don't live here alone," she said, awed by the sheer size of the room.

"Marv and Tara," he corrected. "Yeah, they do."

"How many rooms are in this house?"

"Thirty or forty. I'm not sure." He glanced down at her and smiled. "Don't let it intimidate you, honey. They're normal people, just like you and me."

She scanned the room again, this time paying more attention to the guests, particularly the women. Her own simple outfit, while nowhere near as expensive as most of the women's dresses obviously were, wasn't out of place, but she felt naked without jewelry. She couldn't see a single woman without some sort of stone on her fingers, her ears or around her neck. "Are all these people your friends?"

He clasped her hand tightly. "Not really. You'll meet my friends, starting with Marv and Tara. They must be around here somewhere."

The party had spilled over into several other rooms, so it took them some time to find their hosts. Leah followed Bryce through the crowd, trying to ignore the speculative glances that were being sent her way, yet growing increasingly uncomfortable with them.

They found Marvin Jordan in the den, where a small group of men were gathered around a big-screen television set. He was tall and rail-thin, his brown hair giving way to gray. He greeted Bryce, then turned his warm gaze to Leah. "Basketball," he muttered, gesturing toward the screen. "I considered telling them that the TV was broken, but then they would have skipped the party—no offense to you, Bryce. So…you're the first date Bryce has brought to one of our parties in a long time. Are you new to Philadelphia?"

"I'm just visiting," Leah replied.

He smiled broadly. "Ahh, that explains it." But before he could comment further, they were joined by a slim, pretty redhead.

"So the guest of honor has finally arrived." Tara Jordan brushed a kiss across Bryce's cheek, then slipped her arm through her husband's. "How is your father? I heard that he'd been released from the hospital. Is he all right?"

"He's doing really well. He's back home in Angel's Peak and says he feels better than he has in years."

"Angel's Peak." There was a hint of derision in Tara's voice. "I couldn't believe it when Marv told me that you're leaving Philadelphia to live in some tiny little hillbilly town in North Carolina. What could you possibly find in Angel's Peak that you can't get here?''

Leah stiffened slightly at the other woman's characterization of her hometown. If this woman was what Bryce considered nice, then she herself was definitely out of place here, she thought uneasily. She wished she had stayed home.

"Honey, before you embarrass me any further, maybe we ought to let Bryce introduce his date," Marv said with a grin. "You haven't given her a chance to say a word, and she speaks with such a lovely *Southern* accent."

Tara looked at Leah, and her face turned as red as her hair. "You're from Angel's Peak," she guessed. "I'm sorry. I didn't mean... Marv and Bryce will both tell you that I'm completely tactless, but I don't mean any harm with the things I say."

"She's right," Marv teased, enjoying her discomfort. "She *is* tactless, isn't she, Bryce?"

"Completely," he agreed.

The other woman was blushing even more as she extended her hand. "I'm Tara Jordan."

"Leah Cameron."

She wasn't prepared for the shock on the other couple's faces. Tara released her hand and grasped Bryce's, demanding, "Did you get married behind our backs, without an invitation for your dearest friends? Bryce, how could—"

"We're not married," he interrupted, then added so softly that only Leah could hear, "yet."

"So you just happened to find a woman with the same last name?" Marv asked dryly.

"Leah was married to my cousin," he explained. "We met when I was visiting my aunt and uncle."

Leah could see the questions in the other woman's eyes. The first chance Tara Jordan got, she would ask every one of them. Was she prepared to answer?

It didn't take Tara long to find an excuse to get her away from the men. On hearing that Leah owned a two hundred-year-old house, the redhead insisted on giving her a tour. "So…you're divorced," she commented as they climbed a long, broad staircase to the second floor.

"No," Leah said softly. "My husband was killed in an accident a few years ago."

"Oh, I'm sorry. Do you have any children?"

"Four."

Tara raised one eyebrow in surprise. "A ready-made family," she commented. "Bryce likes children, but I guess you probably know that. How long have you known him?"

"About a month. Your home is lovely."

"Thank you. It's too big for just the two of us, but then, it would be too big for twenty of us. They did things in grand style back in the old days, didn't they?" Tara led her through a series of bedrooms, each lavishly decorated with antiques. "Bryce seems quite fond of you."

Leah stopped to admire a collection of candlesticks. Without looking at the other woman, she cautiously echoed her words, "I'm quite fond of him."

"Let's be honest, Leah—you don't mind if I call you that?"

She shook her head.

"Bryce has been friends with Marv for twenty years, and I've known him almost fifteen. I saw what Kay did to him—the hell she put him through. You're the first woman he's gotten serious about since she left him, and I don't want to see him hurt again."

Tara's concern for Bryce was so obvious that Leah forgave her meddling. She looked at the other woman, her eyes cool and steady and sincere. "I don't want to see him hurt, either."

"He's giving up a lot for you."

"I didn't ask him to do it. It was his decision. He didn't even mention it to me until he had already made it."

"His friends are here."

"His family is in Angel's Peak."

"His father could come back here. He would, if Bryce asked him to."

Leah began walking again. Tara had no choice but to follow. "But Bryce wouldn't ask him. He knows that Frank is happy in Angel's Peak." She sighed softly. "Why do you feel it's so important for him to stay here?"

"If you disappoint him—" Tara let her words trail off.

Leah understood. It would be better for him to be in a familiar place with familiar faces. "Do you think I will?"

She studied Leah for a long time, then replied, "No. I think you're in love with him, aren't you?"

She smiled but didn't answer the question. The first time she acknowledged her love out loud, it wasn't going to be to anyone other than Bryce himself.

"When you meet Kay—"

Forgetting her manners, Leah interrupted her. "I have no intention of meeting Kay."

Tara laughed, a husky, throaty sound. "Oh, but you will. A lot of those women downstairs are friends of her. Before this night is over, at least one of them will have told her that Bryce came back from a month in North Carolina with a beautiful woman with a Southern accent. She'll find some excuse to show up at his house, believe me."

"Are *you* a friend of hers?"

She laughed again. "Are you kidding? I couldn't tolerate her even when she was married to Bryce. Kay comes from old money, and it shows. She's very elegant, very refined and cultured—and snooty. I, on the other hand, come from your average, run-of-the-mill, middle-class family. I married money, and that makes me less than acceptable in her eyes. Anyway, when you meet her, don't let her intimidate you."

Leah looked troubled by the warning. "Why should she

care if Bryce is seeing someone else? She left him a long time ago—she doesn't still care for him, does she?''

''No, she doesn't *care*. It's just her ego. As long as Bryce remained single and uninvolved, she could believe that he wasn't over her, that she was the great love of his life, that losing her was more than he could handle. It's petty and selfish, but some people are like that. They don't want something for themselves, but they don't want anyone else to have it, either.''

''I hope you're wrong.'' Leah didn't want to meet Bryce's ex-wife, to come face to face with the woman he had once loved.

''About Kay wanting to check you out?'' Tara shook her head. ''I *know* her. Just be prepared, and don't let her get to you. Come on, we'd better head back downstairs, or Bryce will come looking for you.''

Indeed, he was waiting for them at the bottom of the stairs. With a teasing remark for Tara, he reclaimed Leah and guided her into the living room, seeking out the people he considered friends for introductions.

Most of the people she met were nice, Leah reflected with some surprise. So they had money and were sophisticated and highly successful. Like Bryce, like Marv and Tara, they were basically nice people, extending the warmth and affection they offered Bryce to her, too. Of course, there were others who weren't so nice, who watched her with a mixture of curiosity and suspicion, who pumped her for information when Bryce wasn't nearby. Kay's friends, she guessed. When the evening was over, she was both relieved and sorry—relieved because she was tired, and now she could be alone once more with Bryce—and sorry because she would probably never see these people again.

''Was that so bad?'' he asked as they walked through the cold, starry night to his car.

''No, I had a nice time.''

"You sound surprised," he said with a chuckle.

"I am. Maybe I'm something of a snob, but I didn't expect people who live like this to be nice, especially to an outsider. Of course, they weren't being nice to *me*, but to your date."

He opened the door and waited until she'd settled herself in the front seat before closing the door again. Life would certainly be easier for both of them if she had more confidence, he thought as he circled the car. She could find so much more pleasure in living if she didn't have so much self-doubt, and he could give her more pleasure if it didn't require so much energy to convince her that he was sincere. But he had no right to complain. He had fallen in love with her, knowing that she was shy, innocent and insecure.

At home he led her through the house to the kitchen. It was the one room that she really liked, Leah decided as she watched him build a fire. Filling the entire rear half of the house, the room was divided into three separate but shared areas—the kitchen, dining room and family room. It had lots of warm brick, plenty of windows, good lighting and the big brick fireplace that filled an entire wall.

"Tonight was the caroling party," he remarked as he slipped out of his suit coat and dropping it onto a chair.

Leah nodded.

"This is the first time you've missed it, isn't it?" He tossed his tie on top of the jacket.

She nodded again. Slipping off her heels, she propped her feet on the low table and leaned back. The sofa was oversize, cushiony and as comfortable as her bed at home.

"Why didn't you wait until tomorrow to come? That way you still could have gone to the party."

Leah waited until he was settled next to her, his arm a comforting weight around her shoulders. "There are always plenty of parties. I wanted to be with you."

He liked the way she said it—simply, honestly, sincerely. "I'm very glad you came." He pressed a kiss to her forehead, then raised one hand to the V-neck of her sweater. "Does the family know that you're here with me?"

"Yes."

"And do they mind?"

She dropped her gaze to watch his fingers, long and narrow, as they toyed with the first button of her sweater. "No," she replied, her voice breathy. "Matthew was a little upset because he couldn't come, too, and Peter wasn't too thrilled, but…"

He slid the button free, and she lost her train of thought. His hand was a shadow against the winter white of her sweater, a soft, tantalizing, arousing, teasing shadow. There were eight buttons on her sweater, and now he had another one undone. He folded back the fabric, revealing the soft curves of her bare breasts.

"Remember the night you wore this outfit?" he asked hoarsely. "At the party before Thanksgiving?"

All Leah could do was nod. Her throat was dry, her heart pounding erratically.

"You said, 'Don't make me want you, because I couldn't say no.'"

She nodded again.

"Do you want me tonight, Leah?" A third button came undone at the gentle tugging of his fingers, followed swiftly by the fourth.

"Yes," she whispered.

"I want you, too. Sometimes I want you so badly that it scares me. No matter how much you give me, I still want more." The next button slipped loose. "I'll need you until the day I die."

The last three buttons gave way, and he pushed the two sides apart, revealing a broad strip of flesh. For a moment he simply looked at her; then he lowered her onto the sofa. He took one taut, swollen nipple into his mouth, bathing it with his tongue, and felt his own body swell in response until he thought he would explode with unrelenting need.

Together they removed their clothes, and Leah opened herself to him. Feeling her warm, moist welcome, he squeezed his eyes tightly shut and breathed her name in an agonized groan. "Oh, Leah..."

Leah lay back on the sofa, propped her shoeless feet on the coffee table and listened intently, but beyond the cleaning sounds Bryce was making across the room, she heard nothing. "There's no noise here—have you noticed?"

He thought of all the nights he had come home to the empty house and grinned wryly. "Yeah, I've noticed." It made him appreciate the bustle of the inn, the warm friendly voices, the sounds of the kids running in and out, or listening to the stereo, or even arguing. "How are the kids?"

She glanced at the phone. The first thing she had done as soon as they finished dinner was call home. Although she was having a wonderful time, after three days she was beginning to miss her family. "They're fine. Are you sure I can't help you clean up? I feel so lazy lying here while you work."

"You cooked. I can clean."

She finished her wine, set the glass on the table and uttered a satisfied sigh. Bryce was pampering her, spoiling her rotten, and she was loving every minute of it. For the first time in her life there was nothing for her to do. No children to get ready for school in the morning or bed at night, no mail or phone calls to answer, no reservations to handle, no million and one problems to solve. He had promised her a good time, and he was keeping that promise. He had taken her to his favorite restaurants, gone shopping with her, given her tours of his adopted home city, but most of all, best of all, he had made love to her. He had shown her things she'd never even dreamed about, made her feel things she'd never known existed. His lovemaking was sometimes lazy, sometimes fierce, sometimes easy and sometimes savage, but it was always tender and always absolute heaven.

When the doorbell rang, she started slightly. The inn didn't have a doorbell, since the door was always unlocked and guests were invited to walk right in. It was an intrusion she didn't want to grow accustomed to. "Want me to get that?"

His hands immersed in soapy water, he nodded. She walked down the hall, her socks slipping on the waxed floor, and reached the door just as the bell rang again.

The woman standing on the porch smiled coolly when she saw Leah. "Hello," she said in a perfectly modulated voice. "I'm Kay Cameron Wilson. And you must be Leah."

There was a brief moment of surprise, but it faded quickly. Tara Jordan had insisted that Kay would come, and somewhere in the back of her mind Leah must have expected it. She leaned against the doorjamb and answered almost pleasantly, "Yes, I guess I must."

The other woman studied Leah openly, curiously, causing her to shift uncomfortably before she returned the assessing gaze. She didn't like what she saw. Kay Wilson was a beautiful woman, her blond hair sleek and stylish, her makeup flawless, her voice cultured; in short, she had an aura of wealth and elegance. She wore a full-length fur coat, with diamonds and emeralds sparkling in her ears, at her throat and on her fingers. "Kay comes from old money, and it shows," Tara had said. Lord, did it ever! Leah thought with a hint of envy.

Her appraisal complete, Kay smiled. There was no mistaking the condescension in it. "Is Bryce here?"

"Yes, he is." Leah made no effort to step back and offered no invitation to enter. "Did you want to see him... or me?"

"He warned you about me, didn't he?" Kay asked with a smugly satisfied smile.

Leah's answering smile was polite but cool. "No. He's never mentioned you at all." It wasn't exactly the truth, but was close enough to count.

Some of Kay's satisfaction faded. "You're from North Carolina."

"Yes."

"And he's moving to North Carolina."

Leah nodded. "Why are you here?"

Her bluntness drew the other woman's approval. "Curiosity. It took him a long time to replace me, and I wanted to see who he had chosen."

"After so many years, does it matter?"

"Yes, in a way, it does."

Leah took a step back. "You may as well come in. It's too cold to stand in the door." She waited until Kay passed her, then shut the door firmly.

"Who was it, Leah?" Bryce called just before he appeared at the end of the hall. He was far more surprised by his ex-wife's visit than Leah had been. "What are you doing here?"

She smiled at Leah again. "I even have an excuse." Then, to Bryce, "I heard you're putting the house on the market. There are a couple of pieces of furniture I'd like to take off your hands—for a fair price, of course."

He looked from her to Leah. With her dismal lack of self-confidence, he expected her to be dismayed and upset, comparing herself to Kay and coming up short. But she was leaning against the wall, her long legs crossed at the ankle, her hands pushed into the pockets of her trousers, looking vaguely interested but unaffected. Turning back to Kay, he said, "You'll have to talk to the real estate agent about that. He's going to dispose of everything for me."

"Who's handling it for you?"

He got his briefcase from the shelf in the closet behind Kay, removed a business card and handed it to her. "Is that all you want?"

"More than enough." She smiled once more, then left, leaving the door standing open behind her.

Bryce closed the door, twisting the lock until it clicked. Then he looked at Leah, waiting for her to respond in some way to Kay's unexpected visit.

She moved away from the wall and walked back to the kitchen. "Did you finish the dishes?"

He ignored the question. "Don't you want to say anything?"

Sitting down on the sofa, she turned sideways to face the fire. "She's a beautiful woman."

He sat down behind her, automatically putting his arms around her. "Yes, she is." After a brief pause, he added, "So are you."

An afterthought, she guessed, as if it had taken him a moment to realize that he shouldn't compliment his ex-wife without offering a similar compliment to his current lover. What had he thought, seeing Kay and herself side by side? Beautiful, elegant Kay in her designer dress and fur coat and diamonds, and Leah in her jade-green sweater, navy trousers and socks. Next to Kay, Leah looked and felt like the original country bumpkin. Had Bryce noticed that? she fretted, then answered herself with another question. How could he have overlooked it?

"I'm sorry, Leah. I don't know why she was here."

"She came to see me."

He tilted his head to one side to look at her. The firelight touched her face with a golden glow, brought out the coppery shades in her hair, warmed the ice blue of her eyes. A moment ago he had called both her and Kay beautiful. It was a cool, unemotional word that suited his ex-wife perfectly, but it didn't begin to do justice to Leah.

She knew he was watching her, and she allowed herself a small smile. "Tara told me she would come, that she would want to see who you were involved with. And she did. She admitted it."

"Does that bother you?"

"She was curious. So was I. I'd wondered about the woman you loved for so many years, about the kind of woman who attracted you."

"Are you satisfied, now that you've met her?" he asked cautiously.

She smiled again, but this time there was a hint of sadness in it. "No. We're as different as day and night. Fire and ice. Ordinary and extraordinary."

He pulled her back against his chest, and she let him. "You got the first two right, but the last one's backward. You're the day, the sunlight, and Kay's the night. You're the fire, and she's the ice. But *you're* extraordinary, Leah, not her. You give love and happiness and comfort."

"But you gave *her* your love. For fourteen years."

He sighed softly. "Do you want to know about Kay and me?"

Did she? One part of her did, but another part was afraid—afraid of what he would say, afraid that she would hear love and longing in his voice as he spoke. At last she shook her head to indicate no, but her mouth formed the word yes.

Bryce settled her more comfortably against him. In the last six years he had rarely discussed the details of his marriage or his divorce—because they were too painful, he had thought. But he discovered now, as he began, that there wasn't any pain; there were only dull-edged memories that no longer held joy or hurt, happiness or sorrow. "We got married when I graduated from college. I was going to work and be the provider, and she was going to be the perfect wife. So I worked, and I bought her this house and her fancy clothes and expensive cars and jewels, but it was never enough. She always wanted more. I worked harder, usually twelve to fourteen hours a day, and I made lots of money, and Kay made a beautiful home for us and got us invited to all the right parties, to join the right clubs. We had everything a young couple could want…except a family, so one day I suggested to Kay that she cut back on her social activities so we could have a baby." He laughed softly. "You would have thought I'd asked her to cut off her arm. She had no intention of having a baby, she told me. Not ever. It might have ruined her figure, and it definitely would have interfered with her life-style." His hand slid over the soft curve of Leah's breast to her flat stomach. Four babies certainly hadn't hurt her figure.

"So…I worked even longer hours, and the rare times I was home, Kay wasn't. She had to attend this social function or that one, and, more often than not, she attended them without me, because I was working, or because I was too tired from working. Then, one day shortly after our fourteenth anniversary, she told me that she'd met a man at one of those parties. He was handsome, charming, wealthy and ten years younger than me. She had been having an affair with him for the last year."

He remembered the ugliness of the scene, but was still untouched by the bitter pain. "I was going to be noble and generous. I was going to forgive her for the affair. After all, she was my wife, and I loved her. I had been neglecting her for my work. I was going to forgive her, shape up and be a better husband. But you know what? She didn't want my forgiveness, and she didn't want me for a husband, either. Derek had offered to marry her once she'd gotten rid of me. The confession about her affair had been a prelude to telling me she wanted a divorce."

Leah raised her hand to his, sliding it into his bigger palm. She couldn't judge by the emotionless tone of his voice if the memories were painful for him, but she offered him support all the same.

"I fought her on the divorce. We had promised to stay together forever, and I just couldn't let it end that way. *Then* she got nasty."

In that low, blank voice he related the insults, every one

of them, sparing himself nothing. Selfish, unsatisfying, boring. The list went on. Then he took a deep breath, smelling Leah's fragrance. It was sweet...innocent. "Finally I let her go. I couldn't fight anymore. There was nothing left to fight for."

Leah broke the heavy silence that fell when he finished. Twisting in his arms, she faced him, her expression sympathetic but filled with dismay. "And you *believed* her?"

He lifted his shoulders in a shrug. "In the last years of our marriage, sex with Kay was...just sex. It wasn't exciting or particularly satisfying. She blamed me, and I accepted the blame."

She shifted positions again, carefully maneuvering until she was straddling his thighs. "You don't still believe...?" she asked, wrapping her arms around his neck.

Bryce laughed—an honest, healthy sound—and the somber mood was broken. "Good Lord, no. One night with you erased all my doubts. Kay and I were judging sex as lovemaking and were disappointed because it didn't measure up. But you can't make love to someone you don't love. It just doesn't work that way. It wasn't her fault, or mine. Between her social life and her refusal to start a family, and the hours I spent at my job, the love just got lost, and we couldn't get it back again."

You can't make love to someone you don't love. The simple sentence set Leah's heart soaring. What they did together in bed absolutely had to qualify as making love—nothing less could be so good. He *had* to love her. Even if he couldn't say it—and after hearing the story of his marriage and meeting Kay for herself, she could understand why he might find it difficult—he had to love her to make love to her.

She leaned back, thrusting their bodies into intimate contact. "Take me to bed, Bryce."

"You're a greedy little thing, aren't you?" he asked with a willing grin.

"Mmm. I want to make love to you. I want to show you…" She moved against him, finishing the thought silently. …*how much I love you.*

He lifted her to one side, then stood up and pulled her along behind him. "You can show me anything you want, honey," he promised. "Anything at all."

Leah rolled over, fitting herself snugly into the curves of Bryce's body. She was almost asleep when she remembered the question she had forgotten to ask. "Did I show you?"

"Show me what?"

Her voice was fainter, more distant. "How much I love you…"

Suddenly wide awake, Bryce carefully rolled over to face her, but she was asleep. The moonlight touched her face, illuminating the peaceful, innocent smile she wore. He touched her cheek gently with one finger, then brushed his mouth over hers. "I love you, too," he whispered. "Oh, Leah, I *do* love you."

He lay on his back, holding her close. Tomorrow would be their last day in Philadelphia. Wednesday morning they had to return to Angel's Peak. He wanted to make it a special day for Leah, and he could think of one way to make it *very* special: he could ask her to marry him. He wanted to take her home with a ring on her finger and the wedding date set.

What was the proper way to propose marriage these days? he wondered idly. Kay was the only other woman he had ever asked to marry him, and that had been so long ago that he couldn't even remember when or how he'd done it.

But it didn't really matter how he asked, as long as he *did* ask. As long as she said yes. As long as she agreed to spend the rest of her life, forever and ever, as his wife.

Tuesday morning they finished packing the items that Bryce wanted to take to Angel's Peak with him. Leah was surprised at how much he was leaving behind. The boxes stacked in the hallway, ready to be shipped, were filled with clothes, books and a few personal items. Everything else was to be left behind.

"Don't you want to take any of this?" she asked, opening her arms wide to include the furnishings around them. "Isn't there a single piece of furniture in this house that means something to you?"

Bryce looked around, then grinned. "I've got some fond memories of the bed and the chaise upstairs, but I don't need to take them with me, not when I'm taking *you*. Kay can have all of this if she wants it."

Leah sat down, a popular mystery novel in her hands. "You don't resent her at all, do you? Even after what she did to you." There was a curious mix of puzzlement, disbelief and pride in her voice.

He took the book from her and added it to the box that stood between them. "I resented what she did—her refusal to have children, the affair with Derek, the things she said—but not *her*. She was a part of my life for a very long time, Leah. She helped make me what I am today. I can't resent her for that."

"I try to feel that way about Terence, but it's hard. Sometimes I look at you, and I wonder why he couldn't have been more like you—more patient, more giving."

Bryce leaned back against the sofa and watched her while she looked through the stack of books he'd decided to keep. So far, she hadn't made any reference to last night's declaration of love. Did she even remember saying it? He wanted to ask her, to ask if she had meant it, but he forced himself to show some of that patience she had just credited to him. She would say it again, in her own time.

He forced his wandering mind back to the conversation. "Did Terence mistreat you?" He sounded normal and curious on the surface, but there was a thread of steel behind the words.

She heard it and hastened to reassure him. "He wasn't abusive, not at all. He never hurt the kids or me, at least not in that way. He was just very reserved, very untouchable. He couldn't give any part of himself to anyone else. He was…"

"Cold. Selfish."

Leah started to protest, then nodded. "At times. Most of the time. I finally accepted that he would never love me, but I couldn't accept that he didn't seem to love the kids, either. I was always so surprised that he didn't love his own children." She gave a little laugh. "That's silly, isn't it? Of all the people in the world, *I* should have been prepared for that. After all, my own father…" She slipped a few more books into the box, then held the flaps together while Bryce taped them.

"Honey, you don't know why your father and mother left you at the home," he said quietly. "Maybe they couldn't take care of you. Maybe they thought you would be better off with someone who *could* care for you, could feed and clothe you."

She shrugged, reaching for an empty box as Bryce moved the full one aside. "Their reasons don't really matter now, do they?"

Only, he suspected, because she didn't allow them to. She preferred to forget the parents who had abandoned her and to concentrate on the family who loved her.

Leah returned to the original subject. "If Terence had been different, if my parents had been different, then *I* would be different, too. And I'm glad I'm not. I like myself the way I am now. I wouldn't mind being prettier, or more sophisticated, or more confident, but I *like* me."

He pushed the box out of the way and tugged on her hand until she was lying on top of him, her breasts against his chest, her hips pressed intimately to his. "I like you,

too," he said with a broad grin. "I like you a whole lot....
Marry me, Leah."

So much for the romantic proposal he had intended. The
words had just popped out, without thought. But he
wouldn't call them back for anything in the world.

The startled expression on her face was comical. She
stared at him for a long time, then moved back until she
was kneeling between his legs. "Are you serious?"

"Absolutely." Reaching out, he laced his fingers through
hers, but didn't try to force her closer. "I want to spend
the rest of my life with you, Leah. I want to know that,
whatever happens, you'll be there. You'll be mine. I want
to live with you and the children. I want to help you take
care of them, to raise them and love them. I want you to
be my wife, Leah. Forever."

There was more he should say, more he needed to say.
I love you. But he couldn't quite form the words. Except
for the brief, secret whisper last night, Kay was the only
woman he had ever said those words to, and it had brought
him so much heartache. Leah was nothing like his ex-wife,
but that last protective barrier was firmly in place. It would
take time, security and a lot of love to remove it.

She was quiet, giving serious consideration to his proposal. The sentiments he had expressed were lovely and
touched the deepest part of her, but one thing was lacking.
In his entire beautiful little speech, he had used the word
love only once, and then in reference to her children. Did
he love *her*?

She wished she had the courage to ask, but she couldn't
face the risk of hearing him say no. She simply had to
believe. He had shown her love in everything he did, in
every part of their lives. She was insecure, but surely she
could recognize love when she saw it, when she felt it,
couldn't she?

She wanted to marry him with all her heart, with every
ounce of feeling she possessed. He would be a good hus-

band and father, one who would share himself with his family. He would make her life complete. There would be no more longing, no more loneliness, no more aching need to know a man's love.

Bryce didn't push her for an answer but simply waited. She was considering the idea of marriage from every angle, looking for any problems. He couldn't do that himself. The complexities of the issue meant nothing to him. All he knew was that he loved her, loved her family, and wanted to marry her. He counted on the strength of their shared love to solve any problems that cropped up.

"It wouldn't bother you to raise Terence's children?" she asked tentatively.

He shook his head.

"Would you want children of your own?"

"I don't know. It would be nice, but...you're almost thirty-six, and you've gone through that four times. I wouldn't ask you to do it again just for me. Your kids are great. I'm happy with them."

"Would you work at the inn, or would you want an outside job?"

"I could do all that paperwork you despise, but if I get in your way, I could get a job in Asheville."

"You know, Angel's Peak is a big change from Philadelphia. It's been all right for you so far, but you've only been there a few weeks. What about in a few months, or a few years? Will you still be happy there?"

He pressed a kiss to the back of her left hand. "I like Angel's Peak, Leah, and everyone I care about lives there—my father, Matthew, the other kids, and you. Especially you. I'll be happy wherever you are."

She still had difficulty accepting that. Traditionally, when conflicts arose between a man and a woman, the woman was expected to give in, to make the sacrifices, to please her man. Yet Bryce was willingly reversing the situation, sacrificing everything to be with her.

"Do you need time to think about it?" He had hoped that they could spend the afternoon picking out their rings and celebrating, but he couldn't pressure her to give an answer now. Marriage was a big step for her. She was cautious by nature, and he knew she would want to be certain that her answer was the right one.

"No." She smiled shyly. "I think in some ways I've been thinking about it ever since I met you. I love you, Bryce." Her smile grew brighter when she saw his surprise. "You thought I'd forgotten about saying that, didn't you? I wasn't *that* sleepy." Then she wet her lips nervously. "I love you, and I would like very much to be your wife."

He tried to speak the simple vow again, but fear held the words in his throat. Soon, he silently promised. He would tell her soon, but for now he would have to be satisfied with showing her. He pulled her to him and sealed her acceptance with a long, tender kiss.

Leaving the packing unfinished, he took her shopping. He bought her an engagement ring, a beautiful brilliant-cut diamond, that to Leah, unused to rings of any kind, seemed to weigh down her hand. They also chose simple matching gold bands for the wedding.

"Can we tell the family when we get home tomorrow?" Bryce asked as they dressed for dinner that evening.

Leah looked down at her left hand. Light reflected and sparkled from the multi-faceted gem. "Do you really think we could keep it from them?"

"You could take the ring off," he quietly offered. "You don't have to wear it yet."

She smiled slowly. "I wasn't talking about the ring. I've never been so excited or so happy in my life. I couldn't hide it from them, and I wouldn't want to try. We'll tell them as soon as we get there, all right?"

They rented a car in Asheville and drove to Angel's Peak, savoring their last hour of privacy. As soon as they arrived at the inn, Leah called the family together in the small private living room.

Their announcement met with little surprise but a great deal of happiness. Leah received kisses and hugs from the children, and they welcomed Bryce into the family. Martha embraced both of them, murmuring in Leah's ear, "Be happy with him, honey."

Frank hugged his son, kissed his future daughter-in-law and proudly said, "I told you so."

Matthew was the happiest of all. "Now I don't have to find something else to call you," he told Bryce, who held the boy in his arms. "As soon as you and Mom are married, I can call you Dad."

Bryce held him tighter. "I'd like that," he said in a husky voice. "I'd like that a lot."

Only Peter offered no congratulations. He stood in a corner, scowling darkly, and said nothing until Matthew called Bryce "Dad." His expression thunderous, he left the room, pushing past them without a word of excuse.

There was a moment's silence; then Martha spoke. "I'm sorry, Leah—"

She raised one hand. "It's all right, Martha. I'll talk to him." After gently touching Bryce's arm, she left to find her father-in-law.

He was in the small sitting room. Appropriate, Leah thought, since their first argument about Bryce had taken place in this room. He was standing at the tall, narrow window, looking out but seeing nothing. Closing the door quietly behind her, she went to stand near him.

He glanced at her, but said nothing. After a moment he looked out again. "Remember when you first came here?"

She nodded. "I was seventeen, pregnant, newly married and scared half out of my mind."

"You were a paradox—so timid and shy and afraid, yet determined to be a good mother to your unborn baby and a good wife to your new husband." He smiled at her, but it was sad. "You were, too. You were a better wife than Terence had a right to expect."

She said nothing.

"Terence was my son. My only child. I know he had flaws, but I loved him, Leah. He wasn't a very good husband, but he *was* the father of your children."

"Matthew never knew Terence," she said softly. "Douglas and the girls never knew him, either, because he never let them get close. He fathered them, but he wasn't their father. He never loved them, never made them feel wanted, never gave them anything—respect, time, affection, attention." She dabbed at the corners of her eyes. "Matthew needs a father, and Bryce wants a son. He's good to Matthew, Peter—doesn't that mean anything to you? He's good to all of us—good *for* us."

"He's using you." He made the accusation flatly, his voice empty of emotion but full of certainty.

"No."

He turned to look at her again. "Don't you find it odd that he stayed single for six years after his divorce, and now, in less than a month, he's fallen madly in love with you and can't wait to be married?"

The tears spilled over, rolling down her cheeks. "Do you find it so hard to believe that he could love me? Am I so worthless that no man could possibly want me?"

He pulled her into his arms. "Of course not. But Leah, I *know* him. I know what he's like. I know he can't be trusted. I love you, Leah, and I don't want to see you hurt, but I just can't see anything *but* hurt coming from him. He's a selfish man. He uses people when it's convenient and discards them when he's finished."

"I don't believe you." She pulled away from him and got a tissue from a corner table. "I know you blame him for part of your problems with Frank, but you're wrong about him. I love him, Peter, and he loves me. Can't you be happy for me?"

Looking at her with disappointment and dismay, he touched her hair lightly. "You really do love him, don't you?" His voice was heavy with acceptance. "Let's go back."

With his arm around her shoulders, they rejoined the family. Peter stopped in front of Bryce and, after a moment, extended his hand. When his nephew took it, he said, "I hope you two live a long and happy and loving life together. Take care of her."

Bryce knew how much Peter's blessing meant to Leah. Knowing that his uncle didn't approve of him, he was doubly grateful to receive it. "I will. Thank you, Peter."

They all sat together at dinner, where wine was served to toast Leah and Bryce's engagement. The guests and staff joined in, turning the meal into a gay celebration that lasted past the children's bedtimes.

When the impromptu party finally ended, the guests of honor sat alone in the living room, snuggled together on the sofa. The room was dark, with only the glow from the fireplace and the many-hued bulbs on the Christmas tree to light it.

"Considering the circumstances, I'd say the news of our impending marriage was well received," Bryce said, placing a kiss on top of Leah's head. "I know Peter wasn't happy, but…the kids took it well. Matthew's happy…and I am…."

"Me, too." She laid her head on his chest, where she could feel the steady beat of his heart. "Peter will come around. I think he's just concerned about you taking Terence's place in the kids' lives." It was a tactful lie, one that Bryce didn't believe for a moment.

"Maybe that's part of it, but the other reason is that he hates me." He raised her hand so he could see her ring. It pleased him to see it on her finger, a tangible symbol of their love. When it was joined by the slender gold wedding band, his life would be perfect.

"Why?" she asked softly. Long ago she had promised herself that if Bryce wouldn't offer an explanation about the past, she wouldn't ask. Now she needed to know, needed to break that promise. "Why does he dislike you so much?"

He gazed at the tree, admiring its beauty, pretending that the question she had asked didn't fill him with dread, but he couldn't stop the stiffness that spread through him. He had hoped that she would never have to know the details of the family feud and his own role in it, but he couldn't ignore her.

For a moment he looked at her, his eyes probing and a little sad. Would knowing change the way she felt about him, the way she looked at him, her blue eyes all soft and dewy with love?

"Bryce?"

He sighed deeply and turned back to the tree. "After my father and I left Angel's Peak, we didn't have any contact with Peter and Martha for twenty years—no letters, no phone calls, no secondhand gossip. It was as if they had never been a part of our lives. Then one evening, out of the blue, Peter called me. I don't know how he found out where I lived, and at the time I didn't care." At the time he hadn't cared about much of anything, he added silently. His life had been a living hell, and his uncle's problems had been the least of his concerns. "I was still holding a grudge about what had happened, but I was also curious about what he wanted after so many years, so I talked to him."

Leah shifted against him, and he lifted his arm away until she was comfortably settled; then he hugged her close again. He needed that contact with her while he talked. "He wanted to talk to Dad, but he didn't know how to find him. I refused to tell him. He was pretty upset, grieving. He told me that Terence had been killed in an accident. It had made him realize that nobody lived forever, and that when you were dead, that was it. There wouldn't be any second chances. So he wanted to talk to Dad, to settle things before it was too late. He needed him.''

''But you didn't think your father needed Peter,'' Leah said softly.

He shook his head. ''You don't know how it hurt my dad to have to leave here. The pain that Peter caused him... I couldn't forgive him, Leah. It had been twenty years, and I couldn't forget what he had done to my dad. I told him that I didn't give a damn about Terence's death, that he had probably deserved whatever had happened. I was pretty cold. He had lost his only son, and all he wanted was to talk to his only brother, and I wouldn't let him. I never even told Dad that he had called until last month.''

They sat in silence. A log in the fireplace crackled and fell, sending a shower of sparks into the air. The tension dancing through him was also crackling, awaiting a response from Leah.

''That was around the time when Kay left you, wasn't it?''

She had made the connection that he'd deliberately left out. He hadn't wanted to make any excuses for his behavior. In his eyes there were none. ''Yes.''

''You were dealing with your own grief then, Bryce. Don't punish yourself for it now.''

He looked down at her, holding her head with his hands in her hair. ''Losing a wife to divorce doesn't quite compare to losing a son to death.''

''In a sense it does. You and Peter had both lost someone you loved very much. You made a mistake, but it doesn't matter anymore. Peter and Frank are together; they're talking, although not too amicably, but they're working it out. Don't blame yourself for what you did then.''

He laid his head back and closed his eyes. ''At some time in your life, you have to accept the blame for the bad things you've done.''

"And the credit for the good," she reminded him. "I know that the good you've done far outweighs the bad. And in this case, Bryce, there's plenty of blame to go around. You don't need to take it all. Good heavens, you were only a boy when all this started."

"But I was a man when I did my part to prolong it."

Smiling fondly, she got up from the sofa and tugged at his hand. "Come on."

Opening his eyes, he resisted her. "Where?"

"To bed."

"Where?"

"In my room."

He studied her critically. There was no change—no dismay or disgust, no contempt. He had just told her the single worst thing he had ever done in his life, and she didn't care. She loved him anyway. He stood up and hugged her close for just a minute. "Have I told you that you are the most remarkable woman I've ever known?" he murmured before kissing her.

She teased him with her tongue. "No," she replied, also in a murmur. "But why don't you come to my room and show me there?"

Chapter 9

They called Christmas the season of miracles. Leah was beginning to believe it. As if the gift of Bryce's love wasn't enough to give her faith, the day after their return from Philadelphia, Peter and Frank announced that they had resolved their feud, once and for all. Although Leah couldn't find much difference in their behavior toward each other—they still liked to fuss and grumble—she was grateful to have their mysterious past settled.

"I could use a few more miracles, God," she said softly, raising her eyes heavenward. Christmas was only ten days away, and she had a million things left to do to get ready. Planning a wedding on top of that was simply beyond her capacity, but Bryce had generously agreed to wait on that—but only until January, he warned her. If she wasn't ready by the middle of the month, he was taking her to the nearest judge.

Briefly she thought that might be best. She was only nine days from her thirty-sixth birthday, and this was the second marriage for both of them. Maybe they should simply go to the courthouse and get it over with.

But every romantic, feminine part of her rejected that idea. That was the kind of wedding she and Terence had had, with Martha and Peter the only ones present. It had been solemn, brief and the most unromantic occasion she had ever experienced. Now she dreamed wistfully of a real wedding, with a white lace gown for herself and a tuxedo for Bryce, with candles, flowers, attendants, champagne and dancing. She knew it was unrealistic—she wasn't a young, innocent, virginal bride getting married for the first time. But she was certain she could find some middle ground, something not too formal, but romantic enough to give her a lifetime of memories. If only she had time!

That was the miracle she needed—time. Twenty-six hours in a day would do nicely, for a start. But barring that, less daydreaming and more working would have to suffice. Firmly she put the wedding out of her mind and turned to the papers in front of her.

Following tradition, she was hosting a reception at the inn on Christmas Eve. Engraved invitations had gone out weeks earlier, and the acceptances had begun to come in almost immediately. She had worked out every last detail with Martha, Colleen and Vicky, but she was going over the plans again. If anything could possibly go wrong, she wanted to find it and fix it first.

She fingered one of the extra invitations. Something similar would be nice for the wedding, she mused, but less formal. Just their names, the date and time…

Groaning aloud, she covered her face with her hands. How could she get any work done when all she could think about was Bryce and the wedding?

The knock at the door provided a welcome distraction. She called an invitation, and Peter stepped inside. "Martha said you have a box ready to go to Asheville. I'm going down this afternoon, so I can take it to the shop, if you'd like.''

She smiled wearily at her father-in-law. "I would appreciate that."

"Why don't you walk out to the workshop with me to get it? You look like you could use some fresh air, and I—there's something I'd like to say to you."

She agreed, even though she was certain he wanted to discuss Bryce. Maybe he would surprise her by not being critical of her fiancé.

He did surprise her when he finally began talking. "I owe you an apology, Leah," he said awkwardly. "When I first heard that Bryce had returned to Angel's Peak, I said some pretty nasty things to you for letting him stay here. I'm sorry about that."

"It's all right, Peter. You were angry. I don't even remember what you said." It was a lie, but her intentions were good. This time, that made it all right.

"I can't say that I would have chosen him as a husband for you, but I do hope you'll be happy together." He smiled faintly. "You know, you light up whenever he's around. It's like seeing the sun on a cold, snowy day."

"Like Martha," she said softly, "when she sees you."

The old man turned red. After more than forty years of marriage, she marveled, he could still blush.

"I'm glad you and Frank have worked things out."

"Well, if his son is going to marry my daughter-in-law, we've got to get along—for your sake, as well as the kids'. If that old goat is going to play step-grandfather to *my* grandchildren, I'm going to have to teach him how."

"So everything from the past is settled."

He looked down at her. "Not everything, but...we've done the best we could. I can't make it right, Leah—that's not in my power. All I can do is tell him how sorry I am that it ever happened, and he's accepted that. He understands about you and the kids...." His voice trailed off, as if he had said too much, and he quickly looked away.

She looked puzzled. They were near the guest house when she stopped walking and turned to study her father-in-law's face. "What about me and the kids? What do we have to do with the feud? We weren't around then."

"No, of course not." He looked at everything but her, scratched his head, frowned, shifted his weight from foot to foot, then uttered a frustrated curse. "I know I ought to tell you everything, to clear my conscience, but Lord, I hate to. I don't want you to hold this against me. I don't want to lose your respect, Leah. I've loved you like a daughter for eighteen years. You've been more like my own child to me than Terence ever was."

She laid a hand on his arm. "Peter, there is absolutely nothing you could do to make me stop loving and respecting you. You and Martha will always be two of the most important people in my life." More gently she added, "I *would* like to know how the children and I figure in the past problems between you and Frank, but you don't have to tell me unless you want to."

He looked around them once more, then gestured to the rockers on the porch of the guest house. "Let's sit down," he said wearily. "This might take a while."

Leah didn't suggest that they go inside out of the cold, but chose a rocker and seated herself.

"My father died when I was about Matthew's age," he began, staring off into the distant past. "Mama raised Frank and me alone, and I liked to think that she'd done a pretty good job of it. But I was wrong."

He fell silent. Leah rocked back and forth, waiting patiently, letting him proceed at his own rate.

"Frank had a job with a company down the mountain in Asheville—a sales position. When Katherine was still alive, they lived there, but after she died, he moved back here with Bryce, so Mama could help take care of him. They lived in this house here. Martha and I were living in the same house we're in now.''

He paused again, then continued in that halting fashion. He told of his love for the house and the land, of his pride in his family, in their history. He also talked of the frequent trips Frank's job required. His older brother was gone from Angel's Peak for days at a time, leaving Bryce in Anna's care, leaving all the work around the estate to Peter.

''After one of Frank's longer trips, he and Mama argued. She was old, her health was failing, and she wanted him to settle down, to quit traveling. Caring for Bryce was more than she could handle—not that he was a bad kid, just that she was a sick old lady. She wanted Frank to stay home, to take care of his son, to learn to take care of the estate, since it would be his one day. Well, Frank told her that he liked traveling, and he didn't need to learn to manage the estate because I was here, and I could do it for him. Whether he learned or not, he said, it would still be his when she died. It was family tradition, you see, for the eldest son to inherit.

''That made Mama mad. When he went out of town again against her wishes, she called the family lawyer and had a new will drawn up, leaving the estate to me.'' He looked away, but not before Leah saw the deep shame in his eyes. ''It was my idea. I was trying to turn her against Frank. Leah, I loved this place more than I loved my life. It was my home, and I had put everything I had into it. I just couldn't bear the thought of Frank inheriting it, when to him it was just a piece of land, just a house. He would have let it decay and fall down around our heads, or sold it out from under us.''

So he and the attorney, a good friend, had persuaded Anna to disinherit Frank. On his brother's return, Peter had spitefully informed him of the new will. Frank, predictably, had been furious. He and Anna had argued, then had refused to speak to each other for months.

After a while, Anna had had a change of heart. It wasn't right, she'd told Peter, to break a hundred and seventy-five years of family tradition because Frank wouldn't do what she wanted. After all, he was a grown man; he had to do what he thought was best for Bryce and himself. Peter had argued, pleaded and begged, but Anna had been adamant. With two servants as witnesses, she had drawn up a new will, once again leaving the property to Frank, with the stipulation that it had to remain in the family. If for any reason he no longer wanted it, ownership would pass to Peter.

She had told Frank about the second will, and he had naturally boasted of it to his younger brother. Then, during Frank's next business trip, Anna had died.

Leah sat unmoving in her chair. "But...how did you get the estate? Why didn't Frank inherit it?"

"As I said, he was out of town when she died. I found her. I had been trying every day to convince her to destroy the second will, to let the other one stand. I had gone to her room for yet another argument, and I found her. She had died in bed the night before. And I found the will." His voice was so low and heavy with humiliation that Leah could barely understand him.

"You found the new will. The one giving the house to Frank." Understanding came slowly, along with shock, but she tried to hide it.

Covering his face with his hands, he nodded. "And I burned it in the fireplace."

"Didn't the lawyer have a copy?"

"No. Because he was my friend, Mama decided she couldn't trust him with it. That was the only one, and I destroyed it."

"So that made the first will, naming you as heir, valid." She was having trouble keeping the dismay and disappointment from her voice. It wasn't her place to judge him, she reminded herself sternly. She wasn't going to betray him that way.

Leaving her chair, she knelt in front of his and put her arms around his shoulders. "Oh, Peter," she said, sighing. "And you've lived with this ever since. I'm so sorry."

"So you see what I meant when I said I can't make things right for Frank. All I can do is apologize."

She did see. She saw too clearly. The only way to make things right would be to return ownership of the estate to his brother, and he couldn't do that, because he no longer owned it. She did.

She drew back and got to her feet, cold, numb, stiff. Her land, her house, her business—they weren't hers at all. They belonged rightfully to Frank, and eventually they would have passed on to Bryce. They were his birthright, but because of Peter's deception, they were hers. An unpleasant shiver passed through her.

Peter stood up and laid his hands on her shoulders. "Can you forgive me, Leah? Can you understand why I did it and forgive an old man for a stupid mistake?"

She hugged him. "I told you, Peter: there is *nothing* you could do to make me stop loving you. I understand." And she did. What he had done was shocking and wrong, but loving the land and the house the way she did, she could almost understand his motives. Almost.

After a moment he released her and took a step back, embarrassed by the show of emotion. "If you'll get that box for me..."

Inside the workshop she added the last few items to the box and sealed it, then handed it over to her father-in-law. "Be careful," she said absently.

"I will. Are you going back to the house now?"

"Not yet. I'll be up in a little while."

He hesitated, shifting the box in his grasp. "Want me to build a fire for you?"

"No, I won't be here that long. You go on now." She

closed the door behind him, then walked to the fireplace, taking a seat on the stone hearth. It was no warmer inside than out, but she didn't notice. Cold had never bothered her much, especially when all her senses were frozen with shock.

The estate rightfully belonged to Frank. All her work, all her dedication, all her love, and the house and land belonged to Frank. She didn't think she could have been more stunned if someone had told her that one of her children belonged to someone else.

How could Peter have done it? He had practically destroyed his own family, all for a piece of land. Then he had kept his secret, had passed on the property to Terence and seen Leah take ownership of it, had watched her build her dreams, her hopes and her future on it, and had never told her that it belonged to someone else.

How it must have galled Frank, and Bryce, too, to have to ask permission to stay in the house that should have been theirs. At least the property had remained in the Cameron family. Once she and Bryce were married, Frank's ties to the estate would be strengthened even more.

Once she and Bryce were married... It was an ugly thought, as cold as the hearth where she sat, and it slithered its way into her mind. Once they were married, they would share everything jointly—the children, the love, the responsibilities...the estate?

No. She wouldn't think that. She *couldn't*. Bryce was a good man, an honest one, and she loved him. She trusted and believed in him. He wouldn't do that to her.

Sighing heavily, she stood up. Like Peter, she couldn't "make it right," but she had done the best she could in giving them both rooms at the inn for as long as they wanted them. That would have to be enough.

Feeling older, wearier and sadder, she left the cottage and returned to her office, turning her mind once more to work.

* * *

"What do you want for your birthday?"

Leah pretended to carefully consider Megan's question before answering, "To be young and beautiful."

Her daughter made a face at her. "You're already beautiful, Mom."

Leah laughed softly, contentedly. "But not young?"

"Well, you're not *old*. Seriously, what do you want?"

"Anybody who has a birthday on Christmas Eve doesn't deserve birthday presents," Douglas teased, leaning back against Leah's chair.

"Anyone who has a birthday three days after Christmas doesn't deserve presents, either," Megan shot back.

Leah snipped a thread from the jacket she was mending for Peter, an oversize red velvet coat that was part of his Santa suit. "I'll be happy with whatever you want to give me."

"Mom..." Megan turned with a sigh to Bryce, who was lying on the sofa with Matthew stretched out in front of him. "What about you? What do you want for Christmas?"

Bryce was absorbing the warmth of the homey scene around him: Leah, his love and his lover, soon to be his wife, and her children. His children. His family. It took him a moment to realize that Megan was speaking to him.

He could have said that he had everything he wanted right here in this room, but that answer would have displeased Megan as much as Leah's had. So he told her honestly the only thing he wished for. "I want January to get here." He was impatient for the holidays to pass and their wedding date to arrive. For all practical purposes they were already as good as married—he spent his days working with Leah in the office, his evenings with her and the children, and his nights in her bed—but it wasn't official yet. Until his ring was on her finger and she had traded Terence's name for his own, he wouldn't let himself fully relax.

"You guys are no fun," Megan said, a pout darkening

her face. Buying or making gifts for her brothers and Laurel was easier, because they had each made up a detailed wish list.

"You know what *I* want for Christmas?" Matthew raised his head from the pillow of Bryce's arm and looked at his older sister. "I want a new baby brother."

"Hey, that would be neat," Laurel said, turning from the television set for the first time all evening. "Are you guys going to have a baby?"

Before Leah could answer, Douglas spoke up. "Don't you think you're a little old to be getting pregnant again, Mom?"

She smiled gently at her son. "Don't you mean that *you're* a little old to be getting a baby brother?"

A flush colored his cheeks. "Well, it would be kind of odd, you know? I'd be old enough to be his father."

"So *are* you, Mom?" Laurel demanded. "Are you going to have another baby?"

Bryce was waiting for her answer, too, she realized, as curious as the children. She looked at each one of them, Douglas, Laurel, Megan, Matthew. For most people four kids would be enough, but there was always plenty of room for another one, especially for one whose father would love him as much as Bryce would. "I don't know," she said, meeting his eyes, her own soft with love. "We might."

He questioned her about it later, when they took their evening walk. "Would you really be willing to have another baby?"

She linked her arm through his, then directed a mock-haughty look his way. "Do you share Douglas's opinion that I'm too old?"

"No, not at all. But...are you serious?"

Because she knew how much it meant to him, she didn't tease. "Yes, I'm very serious. I realize that I'm almost thirty-six, but I'm in good health, and all four of my pregnancies were normal and easy. I don't see any reason why

I couldn't manage one more, if the doctor says it's okay.'' She leaned against him, squeezing him hard around the waist. "I love you, Bryce. Why wouldn't I want to have your baby?''

"Kay always said my desire for children was nothing more than male ego.''

"She was wrong. You have a lot of love to give. It's natural to want to give some of it to your own children.'' She slid her hand into his coat pocket, linking her fingers with his. "Bryce? Peter told me today about what happened between him and your father. I'm sorry.''

"What did he tell you?'' After twenty-six years of hostility, he couldn't help wondering what version Peter had given her—his own, or the truth.

"That he had convinced your grandmother to leave the estate to him instead of Frank. That when she changed her will to reinstate Frank as heir, he destroyed it, so that he would inherit.''

Shaking his head, he chuckled softly. "I'll be damned. The old bastard actually admitted it to you?''

She nodded. "Why didn't Frank take him to court? The servants who witnessed the last will could have testified in his behalf.''

"He *did* take it to court. It was the scandal of the century. The whole town took sides. You were only a little girl then. I don't guess you would have heard anything about it.''

They stopped at the fallen tree trunk, where Bryce sat down and pulled Leah snugly between his legs. "The two servants were the only ones who had actually seen the new will. The day Gran died, Peter sent them away. I always suspected that he paid them off—he inherited a large sum of money along with the property. And they might have known there would be a bitter fight over the will and simply not wanted to be caught in the middle. Whatever, Dad's lawyers never found them, so it was his word against the will Gran's former lawyer had drawn up.''

"If Peter hadn't destroyed the will, your father would have inherited the property. Eventually it would have belonged to you, but instead *I* own it. Does that bother you?"

He smiled faintly. "It doesn't matter anymore."

"Why not?"

He shrugged carelessly. "As soon as you and I are married, what difference will it make whether you own it or I do? It's all in the family."

She felt a chill creep through her bones. It was a simple, logical conclusion—one that she had reached herself only a few hours earlier. Why, then, did it bother her so much coming from him?

Leah lay awake most of the night, listening to Bryce's slow, even breathing and to the soft, settling sounds of the old house. His response to her question had left her too troubled to sleep. Why hadn't he left it at "It doesn't matter"? Why had she pressed him for reasons? And why was she letting it bother her? She believed that he loved her, didn't she? She trusted him, trusted his love, so she had to accept his response at face value. She had to believe that it didn't matter to him that she owned his father's land.

But if it did matter, it would explain a few other questions that had plagued her. Such as what a handsome, successful, sophisticated man like Bryce saw in an average, ordinary woman like her. Such as why he was willing to give up his life in Philadelphia to move to tiny Angel's Peak. Why, after six years alone, six years with very little involvement with women, he had suddenly fallen in love with her. Why, after the pain and heartache of his first marriage, he was willing to marry again. Why he was willing, even eager, to take on the burden of raising another man's children. And why he had never said the three simplest and most important words a man could say: "I love you."

He had assured her that he cared. He had shown her a

tenderness that she had only dreamed about. He had treated her as if she were the most important person in his life. But he had never told her that he loved her.

She stared dry-eyed at the ceiling in the moonlit room. Did he love her but simply have trouble putting it into words, as she had convinced herself, or did she want his love so badly that she had fooled herself into believing that she had it?

She couldn't find the answer in the night stillness. Only the man sleeping beside her could give her that answer, but she could never ask the question. Asking him for the words would negate the meaning behind them. Anyone could say the words. She needed to know if he felt them.

And she needed to know soon.

Saturday morning Leah remained in the dining room long after the others had left. Colleen had brought her a fresh pot of coffee, and she was on her third cup when Bryce returned to sit across from her.

"What's wrong?" he asked after a moment.

Slowly she raised her eyes to his face. She didn't know when he had joined her, whether he'd been there ten seconds or ten minutes. She didn't even know how long *she* had been sitting there until she looked at her watch. Breakfast had ended nearly an hour earlier, she realized, and she hadn't stirred from her seat. "Wrong?" she echoed dully.

"You didn't sleep much last night, did you? There are dark circles under your eyes." He reached across the table to touch her cheek, then pretended that he wasn't hurt when she moved back to avoid his hand. "You hardly spoke to the kids this morning, and you didn't even notice that the rest of us were here. What's bothering you, honey?"

When he reached for her hand this time, she accepted the contact, but couldn't stop herself from questioning it—his touch, his concern, even his endearment. Was this what it would be like from now on? she wondered unhappily. Always questioning his motives when he touched her, spoke to her, or made love to her?

He rubbed his thumb over her engagement ring. Her silence concerned him. Something was obviously troubling her, but he couldn't think of anything that could have upset her so much. She had been completely normal last night. They hadn't made love when they had gone to bed, but she had done nothing to indicate that that had bothered her. "Leah, I can't read your mind," he said softly. "The only way I can help you is if you talk to me. Tell me what's wrong. Please."

She pulled back her hand and picked up her coffee cup. "Nothing," she said, but her smile, meant to be reassuring, was pathetic. She made no effort to sustain it. "You're right. I didn't sleep well last night. I'm just tired."

He didn't believe her, but he didn't have the heart to call her a liar. Instead he rose from his chair and bent to kiss the top of her head. "I'm taking Matthew shopping this morning. I thought we'd have lunch in town. Is that all right?"

She nodded silently.

He walked toward the door, then turned back and hugged her tightly. "Whatever's wrong, we'll work it out, okay? We'll make it right, Leah, I promise."

When she was certain that he had left the house, she got her coat and went to her workshop. Half a dozen projects were scattered across the table—dated ornaments that she made for each of the children every year and small keepsakes for the guests who spent Christmas at the inn—but she ignored them, lighted a fire and sat on the hearth instead.

Bryce had often accused her of complicating matters, so maybe she could look at this simply, unemotionally—only the facts. He had returned to Angel's Peak to make arrangements for his father's return. He loved his father very much; there was nothing that he wouldn't do for Frank. He had a good job, a beautiful home and wonderful friends in Philadelphia. He had never said that he loved her.

There was more, but fear and self-doubt got in the way, preventing her from continuing. When he had asked her to marry him, she had believed that he *must* love her; after all, there was no other reason to marry her. But now there was—the land. The land that Peter had betrayed his brother and his mother for. The land that Terence had married Leah for. Now it seemed that Bryce was willing to marry her for it, too.

Could she bear that? Could she stand knowing, for the rest of her life, that marriage to her was the price he had paid to regain the estate that was rightfully Frank's? She had married Terence under similar circumstances and had nearly withered away from the lack of love. Could she endure it with Bryce?

He came to the cottage when he returned from town with Matthew, and the moment he walked in the door, she knew the answer was no. She had accepted the circumstances of her marriage to Terence because she hadn't really loved him. She had called it love, but she had been a lonely, affection-starved teenager who had known nothing about love except that she wanted it—wanted to give and to receive it. Now she knew the difference, and she couldn't live with less.

He didn't offer a greeting as he removed his coat and gloves. In spite of the fire, it was chilly in the room, so he put another log onto the grate before sitting down at the opposite end of the hearth.

Whatever had been bothering her earlier was tearing her apart now. He could see it in the bleakness in her eyes, in the taut line of her mouth, the tense clenching of her hands. He was torn between the desire to yell at her for refusing to confide in him and the need to hold her and offer his silent, unfailing support. In the end he did nothing.

"Why did you ask me to marry you?"

His smile was somber, with none of its usual joy. "Because I want to spend the rest of my life with you."

She gave him a long, unblinking look. Dissatisfied with his answer, she restated the question. "Why do you want to marry me?"

"Why do you find it so hard to believe that I want you?" he asked with an uneasy smile, trying to tease, to ease the tension between them, to ignore the sharp twist of dread forming in his stomach.

"No one else has ever wanted me." She said it plainly, unemotionally. A simple statement of fact that revealed none of the heartache and anguish behind it. "Terence didn't. My own mother and father didn't. Why should you?"

He knew what she wanted to hear—three tiny little words that would mean the world to her. The three most difficult words in the language for him. Saying them would give her the power to destroy him, as Kay had very nearly done...but she already had that power, didn't she? Whether he said the words or not, she already had his love. "Leah..."

He had waited too long to speak. She interrupted him with another cold, blunt question. "Is it because of this place? Because I own the house and the land that should have gone to your father?"

Bryce stared at her, his mouth open. Surprise wiped the words of love from his mind and dissolved the painful knot in his stomach. "Is that what this is about? The estate?" He gave her a hug, then kissed her soundly, so relieved that he didn't realize that she was stiff and ungiving in his arms. "Lord, you scared me. I thought something was *really* wrong. Do you think I care one way or the other about this property? As long as it stays in the Cameron family, what does it matter whose name is on the deed?"

She pushed him away, her face cold and pale, then stood up to pace. To keep him at a distance. "It matters to me, and I think it matters to you, too—a lot. I've been trying to figure out why you were interested in me. You could have any woman you wanted. Why me?'' She didn't pause long enough for him to answer, but rushed on, needing to say it, to get it all out. "I knew part of it was the kids. You've made no secret of how you feel about them, especially Matthew. He's been the son you never had. But you don't marry someone for her kids. There had to be something else that you wanted.''

Bryce folded his arms over his chest, feeling the pounding of his heart, and leaned back against the fireplace stones. ''There was,'' he said quietly. ''You. Yourself. Your love.''

Sadly she shook her head. ''I don't think love had much to do with it. *I* was the only one who ever mentioned love between us. You told me that you loved your father, your home, even that you loved my children. But you never said anything about loving me.'' She sat down once again on the stones, drawing her knees to her chest and locking her hands together. The position effectively shut him out. ''Maybe you *did* want my love,'' she murmured, almost to herself. ''Maybe you were selfish enough to want it all. Or maybe it was just the price you would pay to get the rest of it—the house, the land, a son.''

''You don't believe that, Leah.'' His voice was hoarse, his throat dry from the fear. ''I wanted to tell you,'' he said quietly, ''but I needed time to be sure—sure that you loved me, that it was going to last, that you wouldn't change your mind and leave me and take away everything I needed to be happy.'' He looked at her then, his eyes dark and sad. ''You know, saying the words doesn't change how I feel about you. It doesn't guarantee that you'll love me in return. It doesn't mean that you'll stay with me. I used to tell Kay that I loved her practically every day, and look what it got me.'' He saw her stiffen at the mention of his ex-wife and swore under his breath. ''I've tried to show you,

Leah, in every way I know. You have to believe that I love you."

"That's what I kept telling myself all those times when you talked about wanting and needing and forever. All those times when I told you that I loved you, and you said nothing in return." Her voice grew softer until it was a whisper, faint and quavery with emotion. "I thought, because of the way you treated me, that you *must* love me. But you haven't given me special treatment. You've been nice and gentle, but that's the way you are with everyone else. I just wanted so badly to believe that I was special to you."

"You *are* special, Leah, and I *do* love you."

She smiled sadly. "How easily the words come now, when it's too late."

The fear expanded, filling every part of him. "It's not too late!" he said fiercely. "Damn it, Leah, listen to me. I don't care about this place! Marrying you isn't going to give it to me, anyway. If I only wanted the land, I would take you to court, not marry you!"

"Why drag the Cameron name through another trial when it would be so much easier to..." She couldn't say it aloud. She believed it, but she couldn't say it.

Bryce was staring at her, his eyes dark with derision. "To seduce you?" He had no trouble saying it. "You think I seduced you, asked you to *marry* me for this property?"

She dropped her head to her arms, hiding her face. If she was wrong, if somehow, for some reason, he *did* love her, she was insulting him outrageously. But those were very unlikely ifs.

He surged to his feet, unable to sit still another minute. He tugged his hand through his hair as he walked restlessly to the end of the room and back, then shoved his hands into his pockets. "Of course, you're right," he said sarcastically.

Leah's head flew up, her eyes seeking his. The shock and hurt in her eyes did nothing to soothe his own pain.

"After living in Philadelphia for twenty-six years," he went on, "I decided that I absolutely had to have my rightful inheritance, so I came here to disgrace my family by proving that my uncle was a thief. But when I got here, I discovered that my uncle no longer owned the house. My cousin's beautiful, innocent, insecure widow did. You're right—it was so much easier and so much more pleasant to seduce you for the land rather than fight for it. Of course, it meant that I would have to marry you, but, hell, I can make a few sacrifices, can't I? I can put up with you and your kids in exchange for the estate." He swore viciously. "For God's sake, Leah, be reasonable!"

There was a painful silence. He stared at her, and she gazed sightlessly at the floor. He wasn't reaching her. He could see it in the slump of her shoulders, in the emptiness of her expression. Nothing he said was getting through that solid wall of fear and doubt and insecurity. Because he hadn't told her that he loved her before she'd found out about the feud, he was going to lose her.

Slowly he knelt in front of her, hesitantly reaching for her hands, afraid that she would shrink back from his touch. "What kind of man do you think I am?" he whispered. "Do you really believe that I'm capable of doing what you said?"

She heard the pain in his voice and ached to know that she had caused it, that she was going to increase it with her answer. "It's easier to believe that you would do that than to believe that you love me."

Pulling away from her, he stood up. "If you can believe that, Leah, then you don't love me. You *can't* love me, because you know nothing about me." He didn't mean that. If there was one person in life who loved him, it was Leah. But he couldn't stop himself from saying it, because he was hurt. Disappointed. Frightened. He looked at her for a long time, waiting for her to say something, to tell him that he was wrong, that she did love him. Then he got his coat and left the cottage.

Only last night he had thought that his life was perfect. Except for the mere technicality of the wedding, he had everything he had ever wanted. How had he lost it all so quickly, so completely?

He walked through the woods, circling the perimeter of the estate time after time, unmindful of the cold or the snow that had begun falling.

Every problem had a solution. If he thought long enough and hard enough, he would find the solution for this. He would find a way to convince Leah that he loved her—her and not this damned land. It didn't help knowing that it was his own fault for not telling her sooner. He had known from the start that she was unsure, that her confidence was nonexistent. He should have realized that she, of all people, would need to hear the words, but he had been too concerned with protecting himself, too afraid of losing again. Refusing to admit his love hadn't protected him from anything; instead, it had hurt both of them. How could he make her believe him now?

He could offer her a prenuptial agreement, relinquishing all claim to the estate. But what would that accomplish? Married or not, he *had* no claims, and no desire for any. He could ask her to live someplace else with him, to sell the inn and remove it completely from their lives.... No, he couldn't, he acknowledged with a fresh ache. She loved this place—more than she loved him.

He looked up at the night-dark sky as heavy, wet flakes of snow fell onto his face. He had been walking for hours, and he was numb all the way through from the cold, yet he was no closer to a solution. He had made only one decision: he wasn't going to let her go this easily. He wasn't going to live without her.

* * *

When he returned to the house, it was dinnertime. Every seat at the family table was filled, except his and Leah's. "Do you know where she is?" Martha asked him worriedly.

"The last time I saw her, she was in the workshop." He had come to tell them that he wasn't hungry and to get a look at Leah, to see if she might listen to him. He had nothing new to say—just "I love you"—but if he said it often enough, maybe it would make a difference. He was afraid that he didn't have anything else to offer.

"The lights aren't on out there," Frank said. "I checked."

Douglas started to rise from his seat, but Bryce laid his hand on the boy's shoulder. "I'll see if she's still there."

He got his coat, still cold from the solitary walk, and crossed the backyard to the cottage. Just inside the door, he stopped to let his eyes adjust to the darkness. There was the glow of embers in the fireplace, but the room was as cold as it was outside. "Leah?"

She was sitting on the hearth, in the same place he'd left her hours ago. She made no response, and for a long time he couldn't think of anything else to say. He just stood there and looked at her, feeling her pain as sharply as his own, wishing he could soothe it, wanting only to heal her with a love that she didn't believe he could feel.

After a moment, he closed the door and went to her, crouching down in front of her and taking her hands in his. Even through his gloves he could feel how cold her fingers were. "My God, Leah, you're half-frozen," he murmured. He released her, put a log onto the fire and added chunks of kindling. As soon as it was burning, he added another log, then sat down beside her.

When the heat from the flames reached her, she shuddered violently, suddenly aware of how cold she was, and moved closer to the fire. Closer to Bryce.

His eyes were closed, but he could feel her, could hear

the chattering of her teeth, could smell her fragrance. He longed to hold her, but didn't try. "They're worried about you up at the house."

"Tell them I'm all right," she whispered.

He gave a short, bitter laugh. "You've destroyed *my* life, but *you're* all right. God, Leah, I trusted you. How could you do this to us?"

How could he make her the villain? she wondered numbly. *She* wasn't the one who had been willing to trade marriage and love for a piece of land.

"Maybe that's part of the problem," he continued. "I trusted you...and you don't even know what that means."

Slowly she turned her head to look at him. In the light of the fire she was a warm mix of gold and copper. For a long moment their eyes met, reflecting the same emotions. Pain, sadness, sorrow. Then she spoke quietly. "Go away."

She hadn't given it any thought, but as soon as she heard her own words, she knew that was what she wanted. He had to leave. She couldn't go on living in the same house with him, eating at the same table, sleeping down the hall. One of them had to go, and even though her claim to the inn was dubious, her name was still on the deed. That meant Bryce had to move out.

"I'm not going to leave you like this, Leah. Listen to me. Trust me—"

She shook her head. Trust had gotten her into this predicament, but it couldn't get her out. It couldn't heal her heart. "I want you to leave the inn."

He was stunned. In the short time he had been there, the inn had become home to him. Leaving it now would be harder than it had been twenty-six years ago, because this time he would be leaving behind everyone he loved. "Are you kicking me out?"

Still looking into his eyes, she nodded. "I want you to go."

Maybe the damage between them was worse than he had

realized. If she was forcing him to leave the house against his will, maybe he had been right earlier. Maybe she didn't love him. What irony. He had never told her that he loved her, yet he did, and she had said it often, but apparently she didn't. "Are you forbidding me to visit here?"

She couldn't go that far. It was still his home—more his than hers—and his father was here. Reluctantly she shook her head. "You can still see Frank."

"And Matthew? And the other kids?"

"I think—I think it would be best if you stayed away from them." All she knew for sure was that he had to stay away from *her*. She couldn't bear seeing him and knowing that she had lost him—worse, that he had never loved her.

"I see. So we're all to be punished because of your fragile little ego." He gave the words an ugly twist, flavored with anger grown out of pain. "Damn you, Leah."

He was halfway across the room when she spoke his name. In spite of his anger and frustration, hope leaped inside him, hope that she would relent, that she would let him stay and give him a chance to convince her of his love. But when he turned back, that last bit of hope died, leaving him cold and empty inside. She was holding out her hand, and firelight glinted off the diamond that was cradled there.

Although he didn't want the ring, he accepted it. Maybe someday she would take it back. If she never did, he thought, it would serve as a bitter reminder never to trust a woman again.

Chapter 10

Three days had passed since the scene in the cottage—the worst three days of Leah's life. She pretended that everything was all right, that Bryce's leaving made no difference to her, that her heart wasn't broken solidly in two. The family pretended to believe her act, but she knew she wasn't fooling anyone. Bryce was gone, she had made him leave, and she was dying without him.

If anyone knew where he had gone, they weren't talking. She knew he hadn't returned to the inn to see his father, and Frank hadn't made any trips into town, although he had received several phone calls. She assumed that Bryce was at a motel in Angel's Peak, or possibly Asheville—either place too far away, yet far too close.

She had put off discussing his absence with the kids until she was certain she could handle it without falling apart. Tonight she had asked them to meet privately with her following dinner.

The living room was brightly lit, every lamp on, the small tree lighted, candles burning on the tables and the mantel. Like the rest of the house, the room was decorated for Christmas, with greenery, pine cones, mistletoe, a miniature Christmas village, a Santa music box and stockings. Crowded together on the mantel were nine angels holding nine stockings, including one next to Leah's, painstakingly embroidered with Bryce's name. After Christmas, she thought sadly, she would take it down and give it to Frank to give to Bryce.

Laurel and Megan were the first to arrive, followed by Douglas. Matthew came late, avoiding his mother to sit next to his brother.

Leah sighed. She loved her children very much, and there was no doubt that Bryce had loved them, too. Was she being selfish in depriving them of a father, simply because he hadn't loved *her*? He had respected her, had treated her well. Why hadn't that been enough for her?

Because she needed love. She had lived a lifetime without a man's love, and she needed it—needed it from Bryce. If he couldn't give that, none of the rest mattered.

She took a deep breath, then let her gaze rest for a moment on each child. Douglas, only a week and a half from his eighteenth birthday, looked more like his father—and more like Bryce—every day. In the last few days he had voluntarily taken on the task of spending more time with Matthew, trying to make up to his younger brother for Bryce's absence.

Laurel was sitting in the armchair opposite Leah's. She was growing up, too, losing her girlish roundness and slowly growing into a body that had become awkward in the last few years. Sprawled on her stomach on the floor was Megan, a younger, less formed version of Laurel. Neither girl had commented on Bryce's leaving, but Leah knew they both missed him. The bond they had formed with him was less demonstrative, less adoring than Matthew's, but strong all the same.

And Matthew. He sat on the sofa next to Douglas, clutching a bright green Tyrannosaurus. He had asked Leah a half dozen times a day when Bryce was coming back, where he had gone, why he had left without saying good-bye. He was the one who would be the most disappointed, who would hurt the most. It was his reaction that she dreaded the most.

She looked down at her left hand, where she had worn the beautiful diamond for less than a week. The older kids had noticed that it was gone and knew what that meant. Matthew didn't.

"I wanted to talk to you guys about Bryce." She twisted her hands together in her lap, wishing for the easiest and least painful way of saying this.

"When's he coming home?" Matthew asked, rubbing his nose with one small hand.

"We aren't going to get married."

She was only confirming what the older three had already guessed. They, along with Leah, turned their attention to Matthew. "But when is he coming home?" the little boy repeated.

"He's not." Leah felt tears stinging her eyes for the first time. "He's not going to live here anymore, honey."

His first reaction was confusion, then anger. "But why not?" he demanded. "He liked it here—he liked living with us! Why isn't he coming back?"

"Honey—"

"What did you do to him? It's all your fault! You made him leave, didn't you?" he accused, tears pooling in his dark eyes.

"Yes," she whispered, unable to see through her own tears. "But, Matthew—"

"I hate you!" he cried, jumping to his feet. "I hate you, and I don't want to live with you anymore!" He raced from the room, leaving his family in silence.

Finally Laurel got to her feet. "I'll check on him," she said awkwardly.

"I'll go with you." Douglas hesitated, then looked at his mother. "He didn't mean it, you know. It's just…he really liked Bryce a lot."

"We all did," Megan added as she, too, stood up. She received an elbow in the ribs from her sister. She glared at Laurel, but finished what she wanted to say. "We wanted him to be our father. I sure wish you hadn't sent him away, Mom."

They left her alone then in the brightly decorated room, and the tears came at last, scalding, heartbreaking tears of sorrow. Of loss. Of love.

Five days after leaving Angel's Peak, Bryce was back in Philadelphia and no closer to a solution than he'd been when he had left North Carolina. He just couldn't see any way to convince Leah that he loved her—especially from six hundred miles away.

Maybe he should return to Angel's Peak. He couldn't force his way back into residence at the inn, but at least he would be nearby, in town. At least he could see her. But he couldn't touch her. He couldn't hold her, or make love to her, or be a part of her life. That would be intolerable.

The worst part, he decided, was that he wasn't the one she was fighting. Deep down inside, she had to know that he loved her. What she doubted was herself, her own judgment. She doubted that she had anything to offer a man, that any man could want her, but she didn't doubt *him*. If only he could make her see that!

He called Frank every afternoon, keeping tabs not only on his father, but on Matthew and the others. On Leah. Frank had told him yesterday that the children knew the marriage was off, and that Matthew hadn't taken the news well. The old man had suggested that Bryce talk to the boy the next time he called, but Bryce had refused. Leah had made it clear that she didn't want him in contact with her son.

He propped his feet on the coffee table and sipped his coffee. He had to make plans. If he was going to stay in Philadelphia, he needed to take the house off the market, unpack the boxes that had never been shipped, find a job. But most of all he needed to accept that he was no longer going to be a part of Leah's life, that he wasn't going to be her husband, her lover or her children's father, that he wasn't going to have any children of his own.

And if he couldn't accept those things, he had to go back to Angel's Peak. He had to make her accept him. There were no other options.

"What are you doing here? I thought you were in South Carolina."

The honey-rich, cultured voice cut into his thoughts like an unwelcome, icy wind. He slowly lifted his gaze to see his ex-wife. "North Carolina," he corrected.

Kay removed the mink jacket that had been his thirteenth anniversary gift to her and let it drop onto the sofa. "Whatever," she said with an indifferent shrug. "Why are you here?"

"It *is* my house," he reminded her. "Why are *you* here?"

"I came over to decide which pieces of furniture I want."

"The agent gave you a key?" he asked sourly.

"I've always had one. You never asked for it when I moved out. Where is Leah?"

"Not here."

She sat down and crossed her silk-stockinged legs. "I can see that. Is there trouble in paradise?"

He sent her a warning glare. "I'm not in the mood for this, Kay. Leave me alone."

"There *is* trouble." She was sincere when she added, "I'm sorry. She seemed ideal for you."

His expression mocking, he tried to determine if that was an insult or a compliment. With another shrug she explained. "She's the kind of woman you should have married instead of me."

He acknowledged her accuracy with a nod.

"What happened?"

He couldn't believe that he was having this conversation with his ex-wife, of all people, but answered anyway. "You should enjoy this, Kay. She decided that she didn't want me, didn't trust me, didn't need me. She didn't do it with your finesse, but she got her own hits in."

For the first time he could ever remember, Kay looked embarrassed. "I've always regretted the way things ended between us," she admitted. "You were being so damned nice about the whole mess, and I just wanted out. I said a lot of things in anger—things that weren't true. I've never mentioned it since then, because I knew you were too intelligent to believe any of them, but...I am sorry, Bryce."

"I *did* believe them," he confessed quietly. "For a long time, Kay. You almost destroyed me with your anger."

"Does that have anything to do with why you're not fighting for Leah?"

His admission came haltingly, painfully. "I don't have any ammunition. How can I make her believe that I love her when she's convinced that I only want her land?"

Kay clamped her hand over her mouth to hold back a startled laugh, but didn't quite succeed. "I'm sorry, Bryce," she apologized quickly, seeing that he was offended, "but that's so ridiculous. You're the least materialistic man I've ever known. You never cared about property or houses or cars or clothes. All you ever wanted was a family." Understanding lighted her eyes. "She has one, doesn't she?"

"Two sons, two daughters."

"And you love her."

He nodded.

"And the kids."

He nodded again.

"Then what are you doing here? Go back to North Carolina. *Make* her believe you. Do such a good job of loving her that she can't help but believe you."

"It's not that easy," he protested.

"No," she agreed with a smile. "But it will be worth it."

He was still considering the conversation with Kay when the phone rang several hours later. Only Frank knew that he was here at the house; for an instant he worried whether something had gone wrong at the inn, but his father sounded the same as usual.

"Matthew is sitting here beside me," the old man said without wasting time on greetings. "I think you should talk to him."

Bryce rubbed his eyes in dismay. "Dad, I told you, Leah doesn't want me to have anything to do with the kids."

"Please."

After a moment, his answer came with a sigh. "All right."

Frank shifted the phone; then Bryce heard a tiny little "Hey." The boy sounded a million miles away, as lonely and depressed as Bryce felt.

"Hey, Matthew, what's up?"

There was a long silence; then Matthew answered, "I want to come live with you."

He should have refused the call. He wasn't prepared for this. Nothing could have prepared him for this. "Matthew, I miss you," he said cautiously. "I miss you a lot, but you can't come here. You have to stay there in Angel's Peak with your mom."

"I don't want to stay with her. She's mean, and I don't love her anymore. Please, I want to come and live with you. I'll be good. I won't cause you any trouble, I promise."

"Don't ever say that about your mom again," Bryce

warned, coming instantly to Leah's defense. "You have the best mother any boy could want, and I don't ever want to hear you say anything like that again."

"But she made you go away. I wanted you to be my dad, and she made you leave."

Matthew was crying, and Bryce felt close to it. "It's not your mother's fault, Matthew. I had to leave. Listen, little guy, I need you to stay there, to take care of your mom for me. I want you to make sure that she's all right."

"She cried," the boy admitted. "I never seen her cry before, but she did the other night. She never cried when you were here. We sure wish you would come back."

Did Leah also wish he would come back? Not likely, he admonished himself. If she wanted him, all she had to do was tell Frank. She knew he would come running.

"Will you be here for Christmas?"

"No," Bryce answered regretfully. He would be spending the holiday alone this year. "But my presents for you and the others are under the tree."

"We don't get the baby, do we?" That had been Matthew's Christmas wish. A new baby brother. It had been Bryce's, too.

"No," Bryce whispered. "I don't guess we do."

When the phone rang again Friday morning, Bryce was reluctant to answer it. He knew it wasn't going to be Leah, and she was the only person he wanted to talk to right now.

It rang again, echoing in the stillness. Tomorrow was Christmas Eve. Leah's birthday. She would be hosting a reception in the early evening, and after dinner the family was having a private party for her. He had been looking forward to sharing both events with her. Instead he would be alone in his empty house. What a way to spend Christmas.

The third ring seemed louder. He wondered how long

the caller would wait before giving up. If it was his father, he would let it ring forever.

He picked it up in the middle of the fourth ring. It *was* his father.

"You've got to come home," Frank said, interrupting his son's hello. "You're not going to believe what that woman has gone and done. When can you get here?"

"Come home for what? What's happened? What has Leah done?"

"Isn't there a flight that leaves around noon? If you can be on it—"

"Dad, tomorrow is Christmas Eve. The only way I'm going to fly out of here on such short notice at Christmas is to sprout wings. Now calm down and tell me what's wrong." His fingers ached from clenching the phone so tightly, but he couldn't force them to relax. Would he always worry this way whenever he heard Leah's name? Would there ever come a time when what she did didn't matter anymore? The answers were depressingly simple. He would always worry, and she would always matter. Always.

"I *am* calm!" Frank insisted, not caring that he didn't sound it. "I don't want to discuss this over the phone. I'll just tell you that Leah no longer owns the estate." He knew that would catch his son's attention. "Now, when can you get here?"

Bryce leaned back against the cushions numbly. She had sold the estate? She had let it pass from the Cameron family without even giving them a chance to take it off her hands? "Why did she do it?" he asked in dismay. "Where is she going? What is she going to do?"

"She hasn't decided yet," Frank answered in an imitation of her prim tone. "You make your reservations. When you get here, come to Peter's house. We'll talk there."

Bryce was able to get a flight to Asheville. Because of the holidays, he had to take a circuitous route that included hour-long stopovers in four different cities, but by ten o'clock that night he was once again back in Angel's Peak.

He parked his rental car next to the little cottage where Peter and Martha lived, then stood for a moment in the snow, looking up at the inn. The Christmas lights he had hung with the boys were on, round and bright in the clear night air. Lights burned in the sitting room, where through the open draperies he could see guests gathered in small groups. He couldn't tell if Leah was entertaining them tonight, or if that task had fallen to someone else.

The porch light came on behind him, and he heard his father's voice. "Bryce? Come on in here, son."

With one last wistful look at the inn, he turned toward the cottage.

Martha was at the house with the guests, his father informed him as he ushered him into the kitchen. Peter sat at the table, a pot of coffee and three cups in front of him. He filled the cups and set one in front of each man.

"All right," Bryce said with a grim sigh. "What's going on? What has Leah done to make you send for me?"

"Take off your coat and sit down," Frank urged. While Bryce obeyed, he pulled a folded document from the envelope in front of him. "I got these papers today. The lawyer was going to call you, too, but I told him that I would take care of it."

Papers? Lawyer? Bryce sat down in the closest chair and held out his hand. Frank laid the papers in it.

He skimmed over the document, but it made no sense. Reading it again, he forced himself to concentrate, to put the words together into sentences, and at last he understood what they were saying. His hand trembling, he put the papers down, then looked from his father to Peter. "She can't do this." His voice was a stunned whisper, weak and unsubstantial in the quiet room.

"She most certainly can," Peter disagreed. "The property belongs to her. She can do whatever she wants with it.'' He hesitantly reached out to his nephew but didn't touch him. ''Leah is a good woman—honest and loyal and just. She's trying to make amends for what *I* did so long ago in the only way she knows.''

''Make amends?'' Bryce echoed. He picked up the transfer deed, then threw it onto the table again. ''She took everything I love away from me, and *this* is supposed to make up for it?'' He shook his head in disgust. ''What is she going to do now? Where is she going to go? What about the kids? How is she going to support them? For God's sake, what's wrong with her?''

When neither man offered an answer, Bryce once again picked up the legal document and looked at it. One half of the estate had been transferred to Frank, one half to Bryce. She was giving up any claim to the property and the business, and she and the children would vacate the house before January 1.

And go where? he wondered. Angel's Peak was the only place she'd ever known, the estate the only real home she'd ever had.

He never should have gone back to Philadelphia. If he had stayed here, he might not have convinced her that he loved her, but maybe he could have stopped her from signing those papers. Through some misguided sense of justice, she had given up everything. Now she had nothing for herself, for her children...or for him.

Dropping the papers once again, Bryce walked to the window and stared at the inn. For the past week he had been searching for a solution to this problem with Leah, and she had handed it to him, neatly gift-wrapped in the deed transfer. It was so simple, so beautifully simple, that he knew she, with her knack for complication, hadn't even realized what she had done.

''Well?'' Frank asked testily. ''What are you going to do about this?'' He was tapping one long, bony finger on the papers, waiting impatiently for his son's answer.

Bryce was smiling as he turned to face the two older men. "First I'm going to thank Leah for the gift. Then I'm going to ask her to marry me."

"She's sent you packing once already," Peter pointed out. "What makes you think this time will be any different?"

"That." He nodded toward the papers. "Is her birthday party still scheduled for tomorrow night?"

Frank nodded.

Bryce addressed his next question to his uncle. "Can I stay here until then?"

After exchanging curious glances with Frank, Peter also nodded.

"Thanks. I'll get my bags." Outside at his car, he turned once more toward the inn. Leah had given him two precious gifts: his home, and her love. Tomorrow night he was going to give her a gift in return. Her doubts and fears would be put to rest forever, because tomorrow night she would know how much he loved her.

Leah stared into the open closet, her gaze skimming over the clothes hanging there, looking without touching for something suitable for tonight's party. She had never felt less like going to a party in her life, but she had made it through this evening's open house, and she would make it through the birthday party, too, for the children's sake.

It seemed as if, all her life, she had done everything for the children's sake. Yet yesterday, for the first time ever, she had made a decision that wasn't in the children's best interest. They didn't even know about it yet, but she would find the courage to tell them. Not until after Christmas—they deserved one more Christmas in the house that had been home to them all their lives—but soon she would tell them that they were moving. She didn't know where, she didn't know if she could even explain why, but she could tell them when.

She stared at the clothes, her eyes dark with fear. What was she going to do? She had always prided herself on her strength. After all, when you had no one else to rely on, you had to rely on yourself. But she was tired of being strong. She was tired of depending on herself, and of everyone else depending on her, too. Most of all, she was tired of being alone.

If she called Bryce, would he come back? she asked herself in a weak moment. Not if he had any brains. Only a fool kept coming back for more pain, and Bryce Cameron was definitely no fool. He had probably returned to Philadelphia, where he had a lovely home and wonderful friends and a boss who wouldn't hesitate to rehire the best executive he'd ever had. Why should he even consider returning to her?

At last she chose a light green dress. It was simple—plain, like herself, she thought disparagingly. She tugged it over her head and let the skirt fall softly around her calves. Fastening a darker green belt around her waist, she stepped into shoes of the same color, then went to the mirror above the dresser to brush her hair once more.

Staring at her reflection, she tried a smile. It wasn't very convincing, but considering the state of her life, it was acceptable. The kids wouldn't question it, and the adults would understand.

Everyone was waiting in the private living room when she entered. They sang "Happy Birthday," and she received hugs and kisses all around. Before she was allowed to cut the cake Colleen had baked, the children dragged her to the sofa to open her gifts.

Douglas handed her the final present. It was a small box, wrapped in elegant gold paper with a tiny silver bow. She held it flat in her palm, looking at it curiously. She had already opened gifts from each of the children, Peter and Martha, and Frank. Who was this one from?

She removed the bow and the thin strip of ribbon that

encircled the box and pulled the paper loose. It was a green velvet jeweler's box. The same kind her engagement ring had come in. Her hands shook when she opened it to find the familiar, beautiful, precious ring inside, and tears filled her eyes. She looked up hopefully and saw Bryce leaning against the wall, just inside the door. His pose was casual, but the intensity of his gaze as he watched her made her shiver.

The rest of the family moved back, leaving a clear path between them. They had known that he was here, she realized, every one of them. Not even Matthew was surprised by his appearance.

She finally brought her gaze back from him to the ring. Removing it from the box, she held it in her palm. She had worn the ring for only a few days, but her hand felt bare without it. Just as her life felt bare without Bryce. "I…" She stopped to clear her throat. "I can't accept this."

He struggled to remain composed, hiding the fear that her refusal aroused. His throat was constricted, and his palms were sweating. Last night his theory had seemed so reasonable and logical, but tonight, face-to-face with her, nothing seemed reasonable or logical. His future depended on tonight. If he was wrong…

Slowly he straightened, pushed his hands into his pockets and walked toward her. He looked at the ring in her hand, wishing it were on her finger instead. He picked it up, the gold warm from her flesh, then closed his fingers around it.

The brief contact of his fingertips made her hand burn, the heat spreading through her. Was that it? Was he going to take his ring and leave, without saying one word to her?

Even as she thought it, he spoke. "You have nothing to give me."

She flinched at hearing it stated so bluntly, but it was true. She didn't own anything but her clothes. The furniture, the dishes, all the household goods had come with the house. The house that now legally belonged to Bryce and Frank.

"No car, no land, no house, no dishes to eat off, no bed to sleep in. You have nothing, Leah, but your children and yourself."

There were nine people in the small room, and except for Bryce, all of them were absolutely silent. But it wouldn't have mattered if they'd all been shouting. He wasn't even aware of them. All he could see, all he could think of was Leah.

Avoiding his gaze, she bit her lip to stave off the tears that were burning her eyes. Not on her birthday, she vowed. Not on Christmas Eve.

"But that's all I've ever wanted," he continued in a quiet, firm, unemotional voice. "I never cared about the property, or the house, or anything else you had, Leah. I loved *you*. You accused me of wanting you only for the land, but now the land is mine—mine and my father's. And I still want you. I still love you." Kneeling in front of her, he gently took her hands in his. "I still want to marry you."

Leah sat very still, the urge to cry gone. What he said made a crazy sort of sense. If he wanted to marry her now, when she could give him nothing but herself, then he had to love her, didn't he? Only love could make a man take on an insecure, vulnerable and sometimes foolish woman like herself. Only love could make him want to marry her.

He watched her for a moment, his fears slowly easing. She was considering his statement, looking at each word for flaws, for truth. In her own complicated way she would analyze everything he had said; then she would reach a conclusion. This time he knew it would be the right one.

She looked down at their hands. The ring was still in his palm, the stone pressing into the soft flesh of her fingers. Christmas was the season of miracles, and she had just been given one—a second chance with the only man she had ever loved. He was everything she wanted and everything she needed. He was strong and dependable, gentle and tender, and he would never leave her alone. On top of that, he loved her and loved her children. All she had to do was accept him, and the miracle would be complete.

When she raised her eyes to him, she was smiling that sunlight smile that transformed her into the loveliest woman he had ever seen. Her eyes were blue and soft with happiness and joy. With love. She held his hands tighter and asked in a husky, drawling whisper, "Forever?"

Bryce smiled, too, gently, peacefully. He turned her hand over and slipped the diamond ring onto her finger, sliding it into place, then raising her hand to his mouth for a kiss. "Forever," he agreed. "I'll love you forever."

There were excited murmurs of approval from the family; then the party resumed, but neither Leah nor Bryce noticed. He kissed her, a short touch of his mouth that only hinted at the hunger inside him, then drew back to look at her. "Happy birthday," he whispered, tenderly brushing a hand across her cheek.

She admired her ring for a minute, then hugged him close and whispered in return, "Merry Christmas."

And it was, he thought with satisfaction. The merriest Christmas of his life.

* * * * *

Ring in the New Year with

New Year's Resolution:
FAMILY

**This heartwarming collection of three
contemporary stories rings in the
New Year with babies, families and
the best of holiday romance.**

Add a dash of romance to your holiday celebrations
with this exciting new collection, featuring bestselling
authors **Barbara Bretton, Anne McAllister** and
Leandra Logan.

Available in December,
wherever Harlequin books are sold.

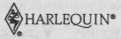
HARLEQUIN®

Look us up on-line at: http://www.romance.net

PHNY332

Every month there's another title from one
of your favorite authors!

October 1997
Romeo in the Rain by Kasey Michaels
When Courtney Blackmun's daughter brought home Mr. Tall,
Dark and Handsome, Courtney wanted to send the young
matchmaker to her room! Of course, that meant the single
New Jersey mom would be left alone with the irresistibly
attractive Adam Richardson....

November 1997
Intrusive Man by Lass Small
Indiana's Hannah Calhoun had enough on her hands taking
care of her young son, and the last thing she needed was a
man complicating things—especially Max Simmons, the
gorgeous cop who had eased himself right into her little boy's
heart…and was making his way into hers.

December 1997
Crazy Like a Fox by Anne Stuart
Moving in with her deceased husband's—*eccentric*—family
in Louisiana meant a whole new life for Margaret Jaffrey and
her nine-year-old daughter. But the beautiful young widow
soon finds herself seduced by the slower pace and the much-
too-attractive cousin-in-law, Peter Andrew Jaffrey....

**BORN IN THE USA: Love, marriage—
and the pursuit of family!**

Available at your favorite retail outlet!

Look us up on-line at: http://www.romance.net   BUSA3

162

**From the bestselling author
of *Jury Duty***

Laura Van Wormer

It's New York City's most sought-after address—a prestigious boulevard resplendent with majestic mansions and impressive apartments. But hidden behind the beauty and perfection of this neighborhood, with its wealthy and famous residents, are the often destructive forces of lies and secrets, envy and undeniable temptations.

Step on to...

RIVERSIDE DRIVE

**Available in January 1998–
where books are sold.**

DEBBIE MACOMBER

invites you to the

HEART OF TEXAS

Join Debbie Macomber as she brings you the lives
and loves of the folks in the ranching community
of Promise, Texas.

If you loved Midnight Sons—don't miss
Heart of Texas! A brand-new six-book series
from Debbie Macomber.

Available in February 1998
at your favorite retail store.

Heart of Texas by Debbie Macomber

Lonesome Cowboy	February '98
Texas Two-Step	March '98
Caroline's Child	April '98
Dr. Texas	May '98
Nell's Cowboy	June '98
Lone Star Baby	July '98

HARLEQUIN®

WELCOME TO *Love Inspired* ™

A brand-new series of contemporary inspirational love stories.

Join men and women as they learn valuable lessons about facing the challenges of today's world and about life, love and faith.

Look for:

Christmas Rose
by Lacey Springer

A Matter of Trust
by Cheryl Wolverton

The Wedding Quilt
by Lenora Worth

Available in retail outlets
in November 1997.

LIFT YOUR SPIRITS AND GLADDEN YOUR HEART with *Love Inspired* ™!

Steeple
Hill™

LI1297